THE
SCHOLARS

THE SCHOLARS
WU CHING-TZU

Translated by
Yang Hsien-yi and Gladys Yang
with a Foreword by
C. T. Hsia,
Professor of Chinese, Columbia University

Illustrations by Cheng Shih-fa

THE UNIVERSAL LIBRARY

GROSSET AND DUNLAP
A National General Company
New York

ISBN : 0-448-00263-9
Universal Library Edition 1972
Published simultaneously in Canada

Printed in the United States of America

CONTENTS

FOREWORD

The Scholars (Ju-lin wai-shih), completed around 1750 and first published two or three decades later, is one of the greatest novels in the Chinese tradition. It ranks with *Dream of the Red Chamber (Hung-lou meng),* a slightly later work of the Ch'ing dynasty (1644-1911), and four earlier works of the Ming dynasty (1368-1644) —*The Romance of the Three Kingdoms (San-kuo-chih yen-i), The Water Margin (Shui-hu chuan), Journey to the West (Hsi-yu chi),* and *Chin P'ing Mei*—as one of the six landmarks in the development of the traditional Chinese novel.* They are available in English in either partial or complete translations, and of the latter, Yang Hsien-yi and Gladys Yang's of *The Scholars,* first published by the Foreign Languages Press of Peking in 1957, is generally regarded as the best. It is a smooth and accurate translation which does adequate justice to the satiric realism and colloquial flavor of the original. It is a pleasure, therefore, to recommend its first American paperback edition, which should make this Chinese classic far more accessible to the Western reader.

The Chinese novel stemmed from the traditions of historiography and the oral storytellers. Professional reciters of history and legend had flourished as early as the Sung dynasty (960-1279), and the earliest specimens of longer fiction now extant are all crude compilations which had drawn heavily upon the oral tradition as transmitted by generations of these storytellers. The first full-length novels, such as *The Romance of the Three Kingdoms* and *The Water Margin,* are all historical romances written in competition with or in furtherance of the oral tradition. *Chin P'ing Mai,* a publication of the early seventeenth century, was the first novel to depict men and women in their actual bourgeois settings, but even in that work the rhetoric of the storytellers is oppressively present in its liberal inclusion of songs and descriptive passages in verse. Because of their ties with the historiographical and storytelling traditions, nearly all Ming novels are impersonal narratives in the sense that the novelist is content to narrate events without consciously stamping them with his own sensibility or philosophy. He appears, of course, very often in the guise of a didacticist, but the didactic portions of his work are detachable from

---

*These six form the focus of my study, *The Classic Chinese Novel* (Columbia University Press, paperback edition 1972).

the narrative proper and merely affirm the conventional wisdom of popular Confucianism, Buddhism, and Taoism, with which his readers are in ready sympathy. Both novelist and reader appear to take particular delight in the doctrine of retribution, a cardinal tenet of popular Buddhism. According to this belief, the virtuous will always be rewarded and the wicked punished: even if the latter prosper in their present round of existence, they will surely suffer in Hell and in their subsequent incarnations on earth.

The Scholars is in form a series of tenuously linked stories rather than a novel proper, but in all other respects, it is a truly revolutionary work in the history of Chinese fiction. Except for the prologue which gives an idealized biography of a historic painter, it is the first novel of its scope which borrows no characters from history or legend and maintains its identity as a work of sheer invention. More important, it departs from the impersonal tradition of Chinese fiction inasmuch as its author, Wu Ching-tzu (1701-54), makes significant use of autobiographical experience and models many of its scholarly characters upon his friends and acquaintances. In style, while he retains a minimal number of storytellers' formulas, he makes no use of songs or the stock poetic vocabulary. For the first time in a major vernacular novel, descriptive passages are completely integrated with the narrative text because they are now recorded in colloquial prose. In his avoidance of poetic clichés, Wu Ching-tzu has actually used his own eyes to observe people as well as places. Nanking, Hangchow, and several other cities of the Kiangsu and Chekiang provinces are vividly recalled with their teeming life and their famous scenic attractions still recognizable today.

Ideologically, *The Scholars* was the first work of satiric realism to achieve an almost complete dissociation from the religious beliefs of the people. Wu Ching-tzu has consciously adopted the viewpoint of an enlightened Confucian scholar and no longer feels the need to pretend to be a popular moralist. In his world, therefore, a good man does not necessarily get his just deserts while a bad man may prosper precisely because he is morally unscrupulous. The latter may be ridiculed, but he is no longer punished in conformity with a simplistic moral scheme. With all its surface objectivity as satire, therefore, *The Scholars* is a personal novel in yet another sense: it has incorporated an individual moral vision. Not all the episodes, of course, fall within the compass of that vision, but up to Chapter 37 (for more than two-thirds of the 55-chapter novel) the author is in clear command of his narrative as he examines one after another of his characters against the implicit ideal of moral integrity and sound learning.

Wu Ching-tzu was the scion of a scholarly family in Anhwei Province which had distinguished itself in government service in late Ming and early Ch'ing times. But Wu himself seems to have inherited from his father and grandfather a weak strain which ill prepared him for a competitive official life. He acquired the preliminary academic degree of *hsiu-ts'ai* at the age of twenty-two but had apparently no further luck in civil service examinations. When, at thirty-three, he decided to move his family from his native town to Nanking, he was already quite poor, having squandered his patrimony by his reckless generosity and careless management of his affairs. Nevertheless, he declined to advance himself when, three years later (1736), he was given the opportunity to participate in a special examination for scholars without advanced degrees. On the surface, therefore, he lived in Nanking the life of an idle scholar who composed poetry and prose to amuse himself and his friends. But two deeds distinguished him from the common lot of such scholars: once he gave what remained of his fortune to the renovation of a temple in honor of former sages, and in his later years he devoted himself to the writing of his novel to formulate his own impressions of the society around him and vindicate himself as a proud recluse of Confucian rectitude. The central character in the novel—Tu Shao-ch'ing—is a self-portrait.

The Scholars has a discernible structure of three parts flanked by a prologue (chap. 1) and an epilogue (chap. 55). Part I (chaps. 2-30) contains all the beloved stories of various types of individuals, including pseudo-scholars, exposed to satire and ridicule. Part II (chaps. 31-37) constitutes the moral backbone of the book and tells of Tu Shao-ch'ing and his good friends in Nanking, all scholars of sound character. Part III (chaps. 37-54) comprises a miscellaneous group of stories without apparent design. While several of these revert to the satiric and didactic modes of Parts I and II, several others are conventional romances in praise of military commanders and of men and women of extraordinary Confucian conduct. On the whole, this part leaves the impression of great unevenness.

The prologue and epilogue give idealized portraits of recluse-heroes against whom the counterfeit scholars in the main body of the novel are to be measured. Wang Mien, the artist-recluse of the prologue, is unlike his historic counterpart in being without a trace of worldly ambition. A filial son and bachelor, he flees the world of bureaucracy like a contagion and lives altogether a most solitary life. The prologue may thus give Western readers knowledgeable about Taoism the impression that the author is a Taoist in his preference for unsullied retirement. But in Confucianism, too, there is a strong tradition of eremitism which sanctions a scholar's decision to retire when the times are bad rather than serve the government and suffer the danger of contamination. In the epilogue the social usefulness of this kind of retirement is emphasized in the author's celebration of four plebeian heroes who would never dream of entering bureaucratic service but maintain nevertheless their moral and artistic integrity by being true to themselves in their chosen forms of self-expression, such as calligraphy, painting, and music. If the prologue is pessimistic in positing an ideal of unapproachable purity, then the epilogue is optimistic in its implication that, even if the scholar-officials are corrupt, men in humbler circumstances can nevertheless manifest a true culture in their everyday existence. To Wu Ching-tzu these men are the salt of the earth.

Part I of the novel begins with comic accounts of two old students, one over sixty and one fifty-four, who are able to wipe out their long years of poverty and humiliation by unaccountably passing their civil service examinations with flying colors. During the Ming and Ch'ing periods, the Chinese government had adopted a simplified examination system which prescribed a narrow course of studies and tested the degree candidates mainly with reference to their ability to write an extremely artificial type of essay*. It took a student years of sterile preparation to master this form of essay writing without actually enlarging his mind or making him better fit for government service. As a scholar who had repeatedly failed in this type of examination, Wu Ching-tzu was understandably disgusted with the system, and after exposing its absurd stupidity through the careers of the two old students in Chapters 2-3, he keeps harping on the topic throughout the novel. But it is not true, as has been generally believed, that *The Scholars* is in the main a satire on the examination system. Its satiric targets actually include many other types of individuals in search of fame, rank, and wealth. Thus the scholars who shun the bureaucratic path to cultivate fame in a social and literary context, such as the Lou brothers, Ch'u Kung-sun, and Tu Shen-ch'ing in Chapters 8-13, 29-30, are as much the objects of the author's ridicule as their examination-obsessed brethren.

Wu Ching-tzu loves to poke fun at the sheer ignorance of his pseudo-scholars, but basically, he is more concerned with morality than with learning. Thus despite his ignorance and provinciality, Ma Ch'un-shang, an anthologist of examination essays who first appears in Chapter 13, endears us to his comic ways because he is a kind man with high moral principles. Although grossly deficient in culture, he is infinitely to be preferred to the type of young opportunist who, despite his early display of filial piety and scholarly promise, readily compromises his moral integrity in his eagerness to seize every chance of personal advancement. K'uang Ch'ao-jen, the prominent example of this type (chaps. 15-20), is given the most ironic portrayal of all the characters in the novel.

---

*The *paku*, often contemptuously cited by Mao Tse-tung. A type of essay specially designed for the civil service examinations. The form, number of words, and language were strictly prescribed, and isolated quotations from the Confucian classics were chosen as subjects. It was given the name *paku* (eight paragraphs) because each essay must have no more and no less than eight paragraphs. *Publisher's note.*

The episodes about opportunist youths seem to imply that it would be far better for all concerned if most such would-be scholars could stay content as simple farmers, tradesmen, and artisans rather than expose themselves to the forces of corruption. They simply don't have enough pride in their human worth to withstand temptation. In the autobiographical hero Tu Shao-ch'ing, therefore, Wu Ching-tzu presents in deliberate contrast a man of aristocratic temper who would never stoop to gain an advantage for himself. Tu's career parallels the author's in every important way. The scion of a distinguished family, he, too, squanders his fortune and then moves with his wife to Nanking to live among his more congenial friends. His story up to his departure for Nanking is one of militant generosity: a number of people beg for financial assistance and, in granting them all their wishes, he systematically reduces himself to poverty. Most of these petitioners have no claim whatever on his bounty and they plainly impose upon him to advance their own selfish schemes. Yet Tu helps them with as much alacrity as he would those for whom he feels genuine sympathy. It would seem that he cannot disappoint a petitioner even though he has nothing but the greatest contempt for him. The same kind of pride dictates his refusal to take examinations after he has acquired a scholar's standing with his preliminary degree. Like the author himself, he declines to seize the opportunity for government service even when he is recommended for a special examination open only to eminent scholars without advanced degrees. And yet with all his proud nonconformity, there is not much that he can do or attempts to do, and his career peters out in Nanking amid intellectual conversations and mild hedonistic enjoyment of wine and nature. To the Western reader who would normally prefer a life of action to one of idleness even though that idleness serves as a camouflage for one's moral integrity, Tu's character should prove fascinating as well as puzzling.

Tu Shao-ch'ing is not entirely unmindful of service to society, of course. Again like the author, he and his friends in Nanking devote a good deal of their time and money to the construction of a temple in honor of an ancient sage. They seriously believe that regular worship at the temple to the accompaniment of Confucian ritual and music should, in the words of one of their spokesmen, "help to produce some genuine scholars who will be able to serve the government well." The account of the initial worhip at the newly erected temple in Chapter 37 is rather dull, but it constitutes an episode of climactic importance in a novel largely about counterfeit scholars and venal officials. The times are not yet ready for serious Confucian endeavors, the author seems to be saying, but in the meanwhile let's revive ancient ritual and music and purify men's hearts. It is characteristic of Wu Ching-tzu's satiric stance and perhaps even symptomatic of his incapacity for action that he assigns his chief hero and his friends a positive act of symbolic importance only.

The Scholars is famous not only for its portrayal of scholars and pseudo-scholars but for its gallery of ordinary men and women in their everyday plebeian, bourgeois, and official surroundings. With all its importance as an intellectual novel, it should prove more appealing today as a comedy of manners for its amazing representation of the bustling world of the author's time. We meet there rich salt merchants and small shopkeepers, bailiffs and yamen runners, actors and prostitutes, matchmakers and pimps, and impostors and confidence men of every description. Whereas the author tends to be schematic and therefore predictable in his portrayal of scholars and would-be scholars, he sketches the latter types with greater comic zest precisely because in relation to them he is less preoccupied with moral problems. Duly appreciative of its status as a classic novel of revolutionary technical innovations and serious moral and intellectual subject-matter, the Western reader nevertheless has every right to enjoy *The Scholars* primarily as a comic satire of panoramic scope which has captured for all ages the vanished manners of eighteenth-century China. In that sense Wu Ching-tzu is truly a worthy contemporary of Fielding and Smollett, who have similarly preserved for us the exuberant manners of eighteenth-century England.

C. T. HSIA
Professor of Chinese,
Columbia University
July, 1972

LIST OF PRINCIPAL CHARACTERS

CHANG CHIN-CHAI, *landlord in Fan Chin's district*

CHANG CHUN-MIN (Iron-armed Chang), *swordsman and charlatan*

CHAO HSUEH-CHAI, *physician and poet*

CHEN MU-NAN (Fourth Mr. Chen), *relative of Duke Hsu's family*

CHI WEI-HSIAO, *student, works in the customs*

CHIH HENG-SHAN, *teacher, Tu Shao-ching's friend*

CHING LAN-CHIANG, *pseudo-scholar, hat-shop manager*

CHOU CHIN, *poor teacher, later commissioner of education and chief examiner*

CHU CHIN-YU, *son of the prefect of Nanchang, Fan Chin's secretary*

CHU HSIEN-FU, *Chu Chin-yu's son*

CHU-KO TIEN-SHEN, *scholar*

CHUAN WU-YUNG, *pedant, protégé of the Lou brothers*

CHUANG SHAO-KUANG, *well-known Nanking scholar*

CONCUBINE CHAO, *Yen Ta-yu's concubine*

FAN CHIN, *poor scholar, later examiner*

FENG MING-CHI (Fourth Brother Feng), *champion of the unfortunate*

HSIANG TING, *magistrate of Antung, later intendant of Tingchang Circuit*

HSIAO CHIN-HSUAN, *scholar*

HSIAO HAO-HSUAN, *crossbow adept from Szechuan*

HSIAO YUN-HSIEN, *his son, military officer*

HSUN MEI, *Chou Chin's pupil, later palace graduate and inspector of the Salt Gabelle*

HUAN-CHENG, *servant in the Lou family*

HUNG KAN-HSIEN, *swindler*

KO LAI-KUAN, *actor of women's roles*

KUANG CHAO-JEN, *poor scholar, later senior licentiate*

KUO TIEH-PI, *seal-cutter* ,

KUO TIEH-SHAN (Filial Kuo), *son of Wang Hui*

LAI HSIA-SHIH, *Taoist priest*

LOU CHAN, *fourth son of Minister Lou, student of the Imperial College*

LOU FENG, *third son of Minister Lou, provincial graduate*

MA CHUN-SHANG, *licentiate, editor of* paku *essays*

MEI CHIU, *licentiate*

MISS LU, *daughter of Compiler Lu, wife of Chu Hsien-fu*

MRS. WANG, *Pao Ting-hsi's wife*

MU NAI, *highwayman, later soldier and sergeant*

NIU PU-LANG, *pedlar, later passes himself off as Niu Pu-yi*

NIU PU-YI, *Fan Chin's secretary, poet*

NIU YU-FU, *salt merchant's protégé*

PAN NUMBER THREE, *corrupt functionary in Hangchow*

PAO TING-HSI, *adopted son of Pao Wen-ching, son of Ni Shuang-feng*

PAO WEN-CHING, *actor*

PIN-NIANG, *courtesan*

SHEN BIG FOOT, *go-between, wife of Shen Tien-fu*

SHEN CHIUNG-CHIH, *a scholar's daughter who refuses to be a salt merchant's concubine*

SHUANG-HUNG, *Miss Lu's maid*

TANG CHOU, *brigade general*

TANG SHIH, *his son, licentiate*

TANG YU, *his brother, licentiate*

TSANG LIAO-CHAI, *licentiate*

TU SHAO-CHING, *brilliant scholar who squanders his fortune*

TU SHEN-CHING, *his cousin*

WAN, *secretary of the Imperial Patent Office*

WAN HSUEH-CHAI, *salt merchant*

WANG HUI, *Hsun Mei's classmate, later prefect of Nanchang, rebel*

WANG JEN, *Yen Ta-yu's brother-in-law*

WANG TEH, *licentiate, Wang Jen's brother*

WANG YI-AN, *pander*

WANG YU-HUEI, *licentiate*

WEI SSU-HSUAN (Fourth Mr. Wei), *Tu Shao-ching's friend*

WHISKERS WANG, *Tu Shao-ching's steward*

WU SHU, *student of the Imperial College, Nanking*

YANG CHIH-CHUNG, *senior licentiate, protégé of the Lou brothers*

YEN CHIH-CHUNG, *senior licentiate, local bully*

YEN TA-YU, *college scholar, Yen Chih-chung's brother*

YOO HUA-HSUAN, *Yu Yu-ta's cousin, scholar of Wuho County*

YU YU-CHUNG, *licentiate, brother of Yu Yu-ta*

YU YU-TA, *senior licentiate, tutor of Hueichi Prefectural College*

YU YU-TEH, *doctor of the Imperial College, Nanking*

THE
SCHOLARS

CHAPTER 1

In which an introductory story of a good scholar points the moral of the book

Men in their lives
Go on different ways;
Generals, statesmen,
Saints and even immortals
Begin as ordinary people.
Dynasties rise and fall,
Mornings change to evenings;
Winds from the river
Bring down old trees
From a former reign;
And fame, riches, rank
May vanish without a trace.
Then aspire not for these,
Wasting your days;
But drink and be merry,
For who knows
Where the waters carry the blossom
Cast over them?

The idea expressed in this poem is the commonplace one that in human life riches, rank, success and fame are external things. Men will risk their lives in the search for them; yet once they have them within their grasp, the taste is no better

3

than chewed tallow. But from ancient times till now, how many have accepted this?

However, at the end of the Yuan Dynasty[1] a really remarkable man was born. His name was Wang Mien, and he lived in a village in Chuchi County in Chekiang. When he was seven his father died, but his mother took in sewing so that he could study at the village school. Soon three years had passed and Wang Mien was ten. His mother called him to her and said, "Son, it's not that I want to stand in your way. But since your father died and left me a widow, I have had nothing coming in. Times are hard, and fuel and rice are expensive. Our old clothes and our few sticks of furniture have been pawned or sold. We have nothing to live on but what I make by my sewing. How can I pay for your schooling? There's nothing for it but to set you to work looking after our neighbour's buffalo. You'll be making a little money every month, and you'll get your meals there too. You start tomorrow."

"Yes, mother," said Wang Mien. "I find sitting in school boring anyway. I'd rather look after buffaloes. If I want to study, I can take a few books along to read." So that very night the matter was decided.

The next morning his mother took him to the Chin family next door. Old Chin gave them some breakfast, and when they had finished he led out a water buffalo and made it over to Wang Mien.

"Two bow shots from my gate is the lake," he said, pointing outside. "And by the lake is a belt of green where all the buffaloes of the village browse. There are a few dozen big willows there too, so that it is quiet, shady and cool; and if the buffalo is thirsty it can drink at the water's edge. You can play there, son; but don't wander off. I shall see that you get rice and vegetables twice a day; and each morning I shall give you a few coppers to buy a snack to eat while you're out. Only you must work well. I hope you'll find this satisfactory."

---

[1] 1279-1368.

4

Wang Mien's mother thanked Old Chin and turned to go home. Her son saw her to the gate, and there she straightened his clothes for him.

"Mind now, don't give them any reason to find fault with you," she charged him. "Go out early and come back at dusk. I don't want to have to worry about you."

Wang Mien nodded assent. Then, with tears in her eyes, she left him.

From this time onwards, Wang Mien looked after Old Chin's buffalo; and every evening he went home to sleep. Whenever the Chin family gave him salted fish or meat, he would wrap it up in a lotus leaf and take it to his mother. He also saved the coppers he was given each day to buy a snack with, and every month or so would seize an opportunity to go to the village school to buy some old books from the book-vendor making his rounds. Every day, when he had tethered the buffalo, he would sit down beneath the willows and read.

So three or four years quickly passed. Wang Mien studied and began to see things clearly. One sultry day in early summer, tired after leading the buffalo to graze, he sat down on the grass. Suddenly dense clouds gathered, and there was a heavy shower of rain. Then the black storm clouds fringed with fleecy white drifted apart, and the sun shone through, bathing the whole lake in crimson light. The hills by the lake were blue, violet and emerald. The trees, freshly washed by the rain, were a lovelier green than ever. Crystal drops were dripping from a dozen lotus buds in the lake, while beads of water rolled about the leaves.

As Wang Mien watched, he thought, "The ancients said, 'In a beautiful scene a man feels he is part of a picture.' How true! What a pity there is no painter here to paint these sprays of lotus. That would be good." Then he reflected, "There's nothing a man can't learn. Why shouldn't I paint them myself?"

Just then, he saw in the distance a fellow carrying two hampers over his shoulder and a bottle of wine in his hand. Hanging from one hamper was a rug. The man spread the rug under the willows, and opened the hampers. Behind him came three men in scholars' square caps, all some forty to fifty years old. Two were dressed in dark grey, and the third in a blue linen gown. Fanning themselves with white paper fans, they advanced slowly. The one in blue was fat. When he reached the willows he asked one of the men in grey, one with a long beard, to take the seat of honour, and another, a thin one, to sit on the rug opposite. He himself was evidently the host, for he sat in the lowest place and poured the wine.

They began eating. After a while, the fat man said, "Mr. Wei has come back. His new house is even bigger than the one in Bell Tower Street in the capital. The price was two thousand taels of silver, but, because the purchaser was so distinguished, the owner allowed him several dozen taels discount for the sake of the credit he would get from this transaction. On the tenth of last month Mr. Wei moved in. The prefect and the county magistrate called to congratulate him, and stayed there feasting until nearly midnight. There is nobody who does not respect him."

"The magistrate used to be Mr. Wei's pupil,"[1] said the thin man. "It was only right for him to pay his respects."

"My son-in-law's father is an old pupil of Mr. Wei's, too," said the fat man. "He has a post as magistrate now in Honan Province. The day before yesterday my son-in-law came to visit me, bringing two catties of dried venison—that's it on this dish. When he goes back, he's going to ask his father to write a letter of introduction so that I can call on Mr. Wei. Then, if Mr. Wei condescends to come to the village to return the visit, the villagers won't dare to turn their donkeys and pigs loose to eat the grain in our fields any more."

"Mr. Wei is a real scholar," said the thin man.

"Recently, when he left the capital," said the man with the beard, "I heard the emperor himself escorted him out of the city, taking his hand and walking nearly twenty steps with him. It was only after Mr. Wei had repeatedly bowed and entreated him to go no further that the emperor got into his sedan-chair and returned to the city. Judging by this, Mr. Wei will probably soon become a great official."

---

[1] A candidate who passed a civil service examination considered himself the "pupil" of the examiner who had passed him, and called the examiner his "patron."

6

The three men talked on and on; but Wang Mien saw that it was growing late, and led the buffalo back.

After that, Wang Mien no longer spent his savings on books, but asked someone to buy paints for him in the city, and learnt to paint lotus flowers. At first he did not do too well, but after three months he succeeded in capturing the very essence and shades of colour of the lotus. Though he painted on paper, his flowers seemed to be growing in the water, or as if freshly plucked from the lake and placed on a scroll. When the villagers saw how well he painted, some even bought his pictures. And when Wang Mien had money he bought good things for his mother. One person told another, until the whole of Chuchi County knew that he was a famous flower painter, and people vied with each other in their eagerness to buy. By the time he was eighteen he had stopped working for Old Chin, and spent every day doing some painting or reading old poems and essays. By degrees he no longer had to worry about his livelihood, and his mother was happy.

Wang Mien had genius. While still in his teens, he mastered the whole field of astronomy, geography, the classics and history. He was, however, eccentric. He did not look for an official post, and did not even have any friends. All day he studied behind closed doors; and when he saw in an edition of the poems of Chu Yuan[1] a picture of the poet's costume, he made himself a very high hat and a loose flowing gown. In the fresh and flowering spring he would take his mother out in a buffalo cart, and, dressed in his high hat and loose gown, flourishing the whip and singing songs, would drive all over the countryside and around the lake. Small groups of village children would tag after him, laughing; but he did not mind them. Only his neighbour, Old Chin, realized how remarkable he was; for Old Chin was an intelligent man, though a peasant, and he had seen Wang Mien grow up. He respected and loved Wang Mien, and often asked him to his thatched cottage to talk with him.

One day Wang Mien was sitting in Old Chin's cottage when a man wearing a bailiff's cap and blue cloth gown came in.

---

[1] China's earliest great poet (B.C. 340-278).

Old Chin welcomed him, and after an exchange of courtesies they sat down. This newcomer's name was Chai. He was a county runner and also a bailiff, but since Old Chin's son was his godchild he often came to the village to visit their family. Old Chin hastily called his son to make tea, kill a chicken and cook some meat to entertain the bailiff, and asked Wang Mien to accompany them.

When Bailiff Chai heard Wang Mien's name, he asked, "Is this Mr. Wang the flower painter?"

"Yes," said Old Chin. "How did you get to know of him?"

"Is there anyone in the county who doesn't know him?" retorted the bailiff. "The other day the county magistrate commissioned me to get twenty-four paintings of flowers to send to a superior. Knowing Mr. Wang's great reputation, I've come straight here; and now I'm lucky enough to meet Mr. Wang himself." Then he turned to Wang Mien and said: "I must trouble you to do some paintings. In two weeks I shall come to fetch them, bringing the payment from Magistrate Shih."

Old Chin pressed Wang Mien to consent and, to please the old man, he agreed.

He went home and took infinite pains to paint twenty-four pictures of flowers, each with a poem appended. Bailiff Chai reported his meeting with Wang Mien to the magistrate, who gave him twenty-four taels of silver. Of this sum Chai appropriated half, giving twelve taels only to Wang Mien. He took the flower album away with him, and then the magistrate sent it with some other presents to Mr. Wei.

When Mr. Wei accepted the gifts, the album alone attracted his attention. He looked at the paintings again and again, liking them so much that he could scarcely take his eyes off them. The next day he invited Magistrate Shih to a feast to thank him. They exchanged greetings, and drank several cups of wine.

"Yesterday I received your gift of a flower album," said Mr. Wei. "Is it the work of an old master or of a contemporary?"

Not daring to conceal the truth, the magistrate told him, "It was painted by a peasant in one of the villages in my county. His name is Wang Mien, and he is quite young. I believe he has just learnt to paint; but his work is unworthy of your distinguished notice."

Mr. Wei sighed and said, "I left home so long ago that, though my native place has produced so great a man, I did not know it. I am ashamed. He shows not only remarkable skill but exceptional insight, and in future his fame and rank will at least equal ours. I wonder if you would invite him to pay me a visit?"

"What could be simpler?" replied Magistrate Shih. "When I leave I shall send a man to invite him. He will be only too pleased to come."

When Magistrate Shih had taken his leave of Mr. Wei, he returned to his yamen and ordered Bailiff Chai to take an invitation card couched in most respectful terms to Wang Mien. Chai hurried down to the village to Old Chin's house, and sent for Wang Mien to step over. Then he told him what his business was.

Wang Mien smiled and said, "I must trouble you to inform the magistrate that Wang Mien is only a peasant and dare not accept such an invitation."

The bailiff's face fell. "When the magistrate invites, who dare refuse?" he demanded. "Especially as it was I who did you this favour! If I hadn't recommended you, how would His Honour know you could paint? You ought by rights to be rewarding me! Instead, after coming all this way, I don't see so much as a cup of tea, and you fob me off with excuses. And why won't you go, pray? Do you mean to say a county magistrate can't summon a common man? What am I to say to the magistrate when I get back?"

"It's not that, sir," said Wang Mien. "If I receive a summons from the magistrate, how dare I refuse? But you have brought an invitation, which means I am under no compulsion. I don't want to go. His Honour must excuse me."

"That doesn't make sense!" exclaimed the bailiff. "Served with a summons, you go. Asked by invitation, you don't. You simply don't know what's good for you!"

"Mr. Wang," put in Old Chin, "if the magistrate sends an invitation, he must mean well. So why not go? The proverb says, 'Magistrates can ruin families.' Why ask for trouble?"

"The bailiff doesn't understand, uncle," said Wang Mien, "but haven't you heard me tell the stories of the two ancient sages who refused to see their rulers? No, I'm not going."

"You are making it very difficult for me," said the bailiff. "What can I say to the magistrate when I go back?"

"In fact, it is difficult for you both," said Old Chin. "Mr. Wang doesn't want to go. But if he doesn't go, that'll be very embarrassing for Bailiff Chai. Now I have a plan. When you go back to the yamen, bailiff, don't say that Mr. Wang refuses the invitation, but just that he is ill and can't go. He will go in a few days when he is better."

"If he were ill," objected the bailiff, "I should have to get a signed statement to that effect from the neighbours."

They argued for some time. Then Old Chin prepared supper for the bailiff, and while he was eating told Wang Mien secretly to ask his mother for a little silver as messenger's fee. Only then did Chai consent to go back.

When Magistrate Shih heard the bailiff's report, he thought, "How can the fellow be ill? It's all the fault of this rascal Chai. He goes down to the villages like a donkey in a lion's hide, and he must have scared this painter fellow out of his wits. Wang Mien has never seen an official before in his life. He's afraid to come. But my patron charged me personally to get this man, and if I fail to produce him, Mr. Wei will think me incompetent. I had better go to the village myself to call on him. When he sees what an honour I'm doing him, he'll realize nobody wants to make trouble for him and won't be afraid to see me. Then I'll take him to call on my patron, and my patron will appreciate the smart way I've handled it."

Then, however, it occurred to him that his subordinates might laugh at the idea of a county magistrate calling on a mere peasant. Yet Mr. Wei had spoken of Wang Mien with the greatest respect. "If Mr. Wei respects him, I should respect him ten times as much," Magistrate Shih reflected. "And if I stoop in order to show respect to talent, future compilers of the local chronicles will certainly devote a chapter

10

to my praise. Then my name will be remembered for hundreds of years. Why shouldn't I do it?" So he decided to go.

The next morning the magistrate called for his chairbearers. Taking only eight runners in red and black caps, and with Bailiff Chai in attendance, he went straight down to the village. When the villagers heard the gongs, young and old flocked round to see the chair. Then the procession reached a cluster of huts. Wang Mien's door, of unvarnished wood, was firmly fastened. Bailiff Chai hurried forward to knock at the door, and after some time an old woman came out, leaning on a stick.

"He is not at home," she said in reply to Chai's inquiry. "Early this morning he took the buffalo out to water it, and he has not come back."

"The magistrate himself is here to speak with your son," said the bailiff. "How can you be so offhand? Tell me quickly where he is, so that I can fetch him back."

"He is really not at home," answered the old woman. "I don't know where he is." This said, she went in, closing the door behind her.

During this conversation the magistrate's chair had come up. Bailiff Chai knelt before the chair and said, "I asked for Wang Mien and found he is not at home. Won't Your Honour go to the local office to rest for a little, while I make further inquiries?" Then he escorted the chair past the back of Wang Mien's cottage.

Behind the cottage were a few strips of arable land and a big lake, its banks thickly grown with elms and mulberry trees. Then more fields could be seen, stretching to the horizon. There was a hill too, covered with fresh green trees, only a few hundred yards away. If you shouted, your voice would carry there. And round the foot of this hill, as the magistrate's chair advanced, came a little cowherd riding back to front on a water buffalo.

Hurrying over, Bailiff Chai called, "Little Chin! Did you see where Old Wang from next door went to water his buffalo?"

The small boy replied, "Uncle Wang has gone to Wang Market, seven miles away. He went to a feast with a relative there. This is his buffalo that I'm bringing home for him."

When Magistrate Shih heard this, he flushed angrily and said, "In that case, I need not go to the local office. Let us go back to the yamen." Thoroughly annoyed, his first impulse was to tell his attendants to arrest Wang Mien and punish him. Afraid, however, that Mr. Wei would call him hotheaded, he decided to swallow his anger and go back to explain to his patron that Wang Mien did not deserve to be honoured. He could punish the fellow later. Having reached this decision, he left.

Wang Mien had not really gone far. He came back presently and was reproached by Old Chin, who said, "You are too obstinate. He is the head of a county; how can you show such disrespect?"

"Please sit down, uncle," said Wang Mien, "and I will explain. This magistrate relies on Mr. Wei's authority to tyrannize over the common people here, and do all kinds of bad things. Why should I have anything to do with such a man? But now that he has gone back, he will certainly tell Mr. Wei; and if Mr. Wei becomes angry he may want to make trouble for me. So now I shall pack up my things, leave my mother, and go into hiding for a time. The only thing that worries me is leaving my mother here by herself."

His mother said, "Son, all these years, thanks to the poems and paintings you have sold, I have saved nearly fifty taels of silver. I don't have to worry about fuel and rice; and, old as I am, I'm hale and hearty. There's no reason why you shouldn't leave home and lie low for a time. You haven't committed any crime. The officers can't arrest your mother."

"She's right," agreed Old Chin. "Besides, if you bury yourself in this village, who will recognize your talents? Go to some big place, and who knows but what you may meet with recognition. I'll keep an eye on everything here for you, and see that your mother is all right."

Wang Mien bowed his thanks to Old Chin, who went home to fetch food and wine for his friend. They feasted late into the night. The next day Wang Mien got up before dawn, packed his belongings, and had breakfast; and then Old Chin arrived. Wang Mien bowed to his mother and to Old Chin; then, in tears, son and mother bade each other farewell. Wang Mien was wearing hempen sandals and carrying his possessions on his back. Old Chin, holding a small white lantern in his hand, saw him to the end of the village and, shedding tears, bade him goodbye. Then he stood, lantern in hand, gazing after Wang Mien until he could see him no more.

Braving the wind and dew, Wang Mien travelled day after day past large posting stations and small, till he came to the city of Tsinan. Although Shantung is a northern province, its chief city was rich and populous, packed with buildings. By the time Wang Mien arrived here, his money was spent, and he had to rent a small front room in a temple and tell fortunes there. He also painted pictures of flowers, and posted up a couple to sell to passers-by. Every day he told fortunes and sold paintings, and customers flocked to him. In this way six months flew by.

Now there were some rich men in Tsinan who took a fancy to Wang Mien's paintings and became regular customers. They did not come to buy themselves, but would send rough servants who shouted and wrangled and gave Wang Mien no peace. Finally, in exasperation, he painted a picture of a big ox and pasted it up in his shop, appending some satirical verses. After that he knew he could expect trouble, and planned to move to another town. One morning, as he was sitting in his room, his attention was attracted by a number of men and women, many of them in tears, passing down the street. Some were carrying pans, others had children in baskets suspended from a pole over their shoulders. Group after group passed, haggard, half-starved, their clothes in rags. They filled the streets, and some of them sat on the ground to beg. When Wang Mien asked where they were from, he found that they came from the villages by the Yellow River. Their fields and homes had been flooded, so now they were refugees; and since the government would do nothing for them, they were reduced to beggary.

Distressed by this sight, Wang Mien sighed and said, "Now the river has left its course again. This has invariably been a prelude to a period of great confusion. Why should I stay here?" Putting together his money and belongings, he started for home. When he reached Chekiang Province, he heard that Mr. Wei had gone back to the capital and Magistrate Shih had been promoted to another post. He could, therefore, feel easy in his mind about going home.

He bowed before his mother, and was happy to see that she was as healthy as ever. She told him that Old Chin had been very good to her, whereupon Wang Mien hastily unpacked a whole bolt of silk and a package of dried persimmons which he gave to Old Chin to express his thanks. And Old Chin prepared a feast for his home-coming. After that Wang Mien lived as before, chanting poetry, painting pictures and taking care of his mother like a good son.

Six years later, his mother, weak from old age, took to her bed. Every means was tried to cure her, but in vain. One day she called him to her and said, "I am near the end. The last few years everybody has been telling me that as you are so learned, I should advise you to go out and become an official. Of course, being an official would reflect credit on your forefathers. But the officials I have seen have all come to a bad end. And you are so proud that if you got into trouble it would be serious. Listen, son, to my dying wish: Marry, have children and care for my grave; but don't become an official. Promise me this and I shall die in peace."

In tears, Wang Mien assented. Then his mother breathed her last. Wang Mien mourned and wept so bitterly that all the neighbours shed tears. Old Chin helped him prepare the burial clothes and coffin, while he himself carried earth to make the grave. For three years he mourned.

A year after the period of mourning was over, the whole empire was plunged into confusion. Fang Kuo-chen occupied Chekiang, Chang Shih-cheng occupied Soochow, and Chen Yiu-liang occupied Hukuang. They were mere rebels. But at the same time, Chu Yuan-chang, who later became the first emperor of the Ming Dynasty,[1] raised soldiers in Chuyang, took Nanking, and established himself as Prince of Wu. His was a kingly army. He led his troops to defeat Fang Kuo-chen,

[1] 1368-1644.

and ruled over the whole province of Chekiang, so that villages and towns were at peace once more.

One day at noon, just as Wang Mien was returning from his mother's grave, he saw a dozen horsemen entering the village. The leader of the band wore a military cap and flowered silk costume. He had a clear complexion, his beard was fine, and he looked every inch a king. When this man reached Wang Mien's door, he alighted from his horse, saluted and said, "May I ask where Mr. Wang Mien lives?"

"I am he," replied Wang Mien, "and this is my humble house."

"I am in luck then," said the stranger, "for I have come specially to pay my respects." He ordered his followers to dismount and wait outside, and they tethered their horses beneath the willows by the lake.

The stranger took Wang Mien's hand and went into the house with him. They sat down in the positions of guest and host, and Wang Mien asked, "May I know your honourable name and what has brought you to this village?"

"My name is Chu. I raised troops in Chiangnan and was known as the Prince of Chuyang; but now, because I hold Nanking, I am called the Prince of Wu. The campaign against Fang Kuo-chen brought me here, and now I have come to pay my respects to you."

"I am an ignorant villager," said Wang Mien, "and did not recognize Your Highness. This is indeed an overwhelming honour for a simple peasant like myself."

"I am a rough and ready fellow," answered the Prince of Wu, "but at the sight of your scholarly bearing, my thirst for fame and wealth has vanished. When I was still in Chiangnan your fame reached my ears, and now I have come to consult you. The people of Chekiang have rebelled many times. What can I do to win their love?"

"Your Highness is far-sighted," said Wang Mien. "There is no need for a humble person like myself to say much. If you use goodness and justice to win the people, you will win them all — not only those in Chekiang. But if you try to conquer by force, weak as the people of Chekiang are, I am afraid they will not submit. Look at the case of Fang Kuo-chen whom you defeated."

The prince nodded and expressed approval; and sitting face to face they talked till evening. The prince's followers had brought rations, and Wang Mien went to the kitchen to make bread and fry leeks for the prince, sharing the meal with him. The prince then thanked him for his advice, mounted his horse and rode away.

That day Old Chin had gone to the county-seat. On his return he asked Wang Mien who his visitors had been; but instead of telling him that it was the Prince of Wu, Wang Mien simply said, "It was an army officer I knew when I was in Shantung."

In a few years the Prince of Wu pacified the country and established his capital at Nanking, so that once more the empire was united. His dynasty was called Ming, and his reign Hung Wu.[1] Once more the villagers could live at peace, enjoying the fruits of their labour. During the fourth year of the reign Old Chin went to the county-seat again, and on his return told Wang Mien, "Mr. Wei is in disgrace and has been sentenced to exile in Hochow. I have brought a bulletin to show you."

Wang Mien read it, and discovered that, since his surrender, Mr. Wei had continued to indulge in foolish display, calling himself his sovereign's old and trusted servant, until the emperor in anger had banished him to Hochow to look after the grave of Yu Chueh.[2] This decree was followed by the rules of the Board of Ceremonies for the civil service examinations. Candidates would be tested every three years, and required only to write *paku* essays[3] on the Confucian classics.

Pointing this out to Old Chin, Wang Mien said, "These rules are not good. Future candidates, knowing that there

---

[1] Chu Yuan-chang, the first emperor of the Ming Dynasty, is also sometimes called Emperor Hung Wu.

[2] A general who defended Hochow for the last emperor of the Yuan Dynasty, and was killed in battle by Chu Yuan-chang's troops. Since Wei Shu, a minister of the Yuan Dynasty, had surrendered to the first emperor of Ming, this punishment was a reminder to him that he had proved disloyal to his former master.

[3] See page 6 of the foreword.

16

ship and correct behaviour."

By now dusk had fallen. It was early summer and the weather was turning warm. Old Chin set a table on the threshing floor, and they drank wine. Soon the moon came up from the east, and shone so brightly that everything seemed made of glass. The water-birds had gone to their nests, and all was quiet. Holding his cup in his left hand, Wang Mien pointed to the stars with his right, and said, "Look! The Chains have invaded the Scholars.[1] That shows that scholars of this generation have hard times ahead."

As he spoke, a strange wind sprang up. It soughed through the trees, and made the waterfowl take wing, crying in alarm, while Wang Mien and Old Chin hid their faces in their sleeves for fear. Soon the wind dropped, and when they looked again they saw about a hundred small stars in the sky, all falling towards the south-east horizon.

"Heaven has taken pity on the scholars," said Wang Mien. "These stars have been sent down to maintain the literary tradition. But we shan't live to see it." Then they cleared away the things and went to bed

Later on, many rumours were heard to the effect that the government had ordered the Chekiang authorities to offer Wang Mien an official appointment. At first he ignored these rumours; but when more and more people began to talk of it he secretly packed his belongings and, without telling Old Chin, slipped away by night to Kuaichi Mountain. After another six months an envoy with an imperial decree, followed by retainers carrying silk and brocade, did actually come to Old Chin's door. They saw an old man of more than eighty, with a white beard and white hair, leaning on a stick. The envoy greeted him, and Old Chin invited him into his cottage to take a seat.

"Does Mr. Wang Mien live in this village?" asked the envoy. "His Majesty has appointed him Commissioner of Records. I have brought the imperial decree."

---

[1] Chinese names for certain constellations. The movements of the stars were believed to reflect human affairs.

"He belongs to this village," replied Old Chin, "but he disappeared long ago."

After Old Chin had served tea, he led the envoy to Wang Mien's house, and pushed open the door. The rooms were filled with cobwebs and the yard with weeds, so they knew it was true that Wang Mien had been gone for a long time. The envoy expressed regret, and went back to report to the emperor.

Wang Mien lived as a hermit in Kuaichi Mountain, and never disclosed his real name. When later he fell ill and died, his neighbours there collected some money and buried him at the foot of the mountain. During the same year, Old Chin died of old age in his home. Curiously enough, writers and scholars nowadays refer to Wang Mien as the Commissioner of Records, though actually he never served as an official for a single day, as I have tried to make clear. The foregoing is only the introduction to the story which I shall now begin.

CHAPTER 2

Provincial Graduate Wang meets a fellow candidate
in a village school. Chou Chin passes the examination
in his old age

In Hsueh Market, a village of Wenshang County, Shantung, there lived over a hundred families, all of whom worked
on the land. At the entrance to the village was a Kuanyin
Temple with three halls and a dozen empty rooms. Its back
door overlooked the river. Peasants from all around contributed to the upkeep of this temple, and only one monk lived
there. Here the villagers would come to discuss public business.

It was the last year of the Cheng Hua period[1] of the
Ming Dynasty, when the country was prosperous. One year,
on the eighth of the first month, just after New Year, some
of the villagers met in the temple to discuss the dragon lantern
dance which is held on the fifteenth. At breakfast time the
man who usually took the lead, Shen Hsiang-fu, walked in,
followed by seven or eight others. In the main hall they bowed
to Buddha, and the monk came to wish them a happy New Year.
As soon as they had returned his greeting, Shen reproved him.

"Monk! At New Year you should burn more incense before Buddha! Gracious Heaven! You've been pocketing
money from all sides, and you ought to spend a little of it.
Come here, all of you, and take a look at this lamp: it's only

--- --- ---
[1] 1487.

19

half filled with oil." Then, pointing to an old man who was better dressed than most: "Not to mention others, Mr. Hsun alone sent you fifty catties of oil on New Year's Eve. But you are using it all for your cooking, instead of for the glory of Buddha."

The monk apologized profusely when Shen had finished. Then he fetched a pewter kettle, put in a handful of tea leaves, filled the kettle with water, boiled it over the fire and poured out tea for them. Old Mr. Hsun was the first to speak.

"How much do we each have to pay for the lantern dance in the temple this year?" he asked.

"Wait till my relative comes," said Shen. "We'll discuss it together."

As they were speaking, a man walked in. He had red-rimmed eyes, a swarthy face, and sparse, dingy whiskers. His cap was cocked to one side, his blue cloth gown was greasy as an oil-vat, and he carried a donkey switch in one hand. Making a casual gesture of greeting to the company, he plumped himself down in the seat of honour. This was Hsia, the new village head for Hsueh Market.

Sitting there in the seat of honour, he shouted: "Monk! Take my donkey to the manger in the back yard, unsaddle it and give it plenty of hay. After my business here I have to go to a feast with Bailiff Huang of the county yamen." Having given these orders, he hoisted one foot on to the bench, and started massaging the small of his back with his fists, saying, "I envy you farmers these days. This New Year I've got invitations from everybody in the magistrate's yamen, literally everybody! And I have to go to wish them all the season's greetings. I trot about on this donkey to the county-seat and back until my head reels. And this damned beast stumbled on the road and threw me, so that my backside is still sore."

"On the third I prepared a small dinner for you," said Shen. "I suppose it was because you were so busy that you didn't come."

"You don't have to remind me," said Village Head Hsia. "Since New Year, for the last seven or eight days, what free time have I had? Even if I had two mouths, I couldn't get through all the eating. Take Bailiff Huang, who's invited me today. He's a man who can talk face to face with the magistrate. And since he honours me like this, wouldn't he be offended if I didn't go?"

"I heard that Bailiff Huang had been sent out on some business for the magistrate since the beginning of the year," said Shen. "He has no brothers or sons, so who will act as host?"

"You don't understand," said Hsia. "Today's feast is given by Constable Li. His own rooms are small, so he is using Bailiff Huang's house."

Eventually they started discussing the dragon lanterns. "I'm tired of managing it for you," said Village Head Hsia. "I took the lead every year in the past, and everyone wrote down what contribution he would make, and then failed to pay up. Heaven knows how much I had to pay to make good the deficit. Besides, all the officials in the yamen are preparing lanterns this year, and I shall have too much to watch. What time do I have to look at the lanterns in the village? Still, since you've mentioned it, I shall make a contribution. Choose someone to be responsible. A man like Mr. Hsun, who has broad lands and plenty of grain, should be asked to give more. Let each family pay its share, and you'll get the thing going." Nobody dared disagree. They immediately came down on Mr. Hsun for half the money, and made up the rest between them. In this way they raised two or three taels of silver, a record of the contributors being made.

The monk then brought out tea, sugar wafers, dates, melon seeds, dried beancurd, chestnuts and assorted sweets. He spread two tables, and invited Village Head Hsia to sit at the head. Then he poured out tea for them.

"The children are growing up," said Shen, "and this year we must find them a teacher. This temple can be used as a school."

The others agreed.

"There are a lot of families who have sons who should be in school," said one of them. "For instance, Mr. Shen's son is Village Head Hsia's son-in-law. Hsia is always getting notices from the magistrate, so he needs someone who can read. But the best thing would be to find a teacher from the county-seat."

"A teacher?" said the village head. "I can think of one. You know who? He s in our yamen, and he used to teach in chief accountant Ku's house. His name is Chou Chin. He's over sixty. The former magistrate placed him first on the list of county candidates, but he's never yet been able to pass the prefectural examination. Mr. Ku employed him as tutor for his son for three years; and his son passed the examination last year, at the same time as Mei Chiu from our village. The day that young Ku was welcomed back from the school he wore a scholar's cap and a broad red silk sash, and rode a horse from the magistrate's stable, while all the gongs and trumpets sounded. When he reached the door of his house, I and the other yamen officials offered him wine in the street. Then Mr. Chou was asked over. Mr. Ku toasted his son's teacher three times and invited him to sit in the seat of honour. Mr. Chou chose as entertainment the opera about Liang Hao, who won the first place in the palace examination when he was eighty; and Mr. Ku was not at all pleased. But then the opera showed how Liang Hao's pupil won the same distinction at seventeen or eighteen, and Mr. Ku knew that it was a compliment to his son. That made him feel better. If you want a teacher, I'll invite Mr. Chou for you." All the villagers approved. When they had finished their tea the monk brought in some beef noodles, and after eating these they went home.

The next day, sure enough, Village Head Hsia spoke to Chou Chin. His salary would be twelve taels of silver a year, and it was arranged that he should eat with the monk, whom he would pay two cents a day. It was settled that he should come after the Lantern Festival, and begin teaching on the twentieth.

On the sixteenth the villagers sent in contributions to Shen Hsiang-fu, who prepared a feast for the new teacher to which he also invited Mei Chiu, the new scholar of the village. Mei Chiu arrived early, wearing his new square cap, but Chou Chin did not turn up till nearly noon. When dogs started barking outside, Shen Hsiang-fu went out to welcome the guest; and the villagers stared as Chou Chin came in. He was wearing an old felt cap, a tattered grey silk gown, the right sleeve and seat of which were in shreds, and a pair of shabby red silk slippers. He had a thin, dark face, and a white beard. Shen escorted him in, and only then did Mei Chiu rise slowly to greet him.

"Who is this gentleman?" asked Chou.

They told him, "He is Mr. Mei, our village scholar."

When Chou Chin heard this, he declared it would be presumptuous on his part to allow Mei to bow to him. And although Mei Chiu said, "Today is different," he still refused.

"You are older than he is," said the villagers. "You had better not insist."

But Mei Chiu rounded on them, "You people don't understand the rule of our school. Those who have passed the prefectural examination are considered senior to those who have not, regardless of age. But today happens to be exceptional, and Mr. Chou must still be honoured."

(Ming Dynasty scholars called all those who passed the prefectural examination "classmates," and those who only qualified for this examination "juniors." A young man in his teens who passed was considered senior to an unsuccessful candidate, even if the latter were eighty years old. It was like the case of a concubine. A woman is called "new wife" when she marries, and later "mistress"; but a concubine remains "new wife" even when her hair is white.)

Since Mei Chiu spoke like this, Chou Chin did not insist on being polite, but let Mei Chiu bow to him. When all the others had greeted him too, they sat down. Mei and Chou were the only two to have dates in their tea cups — all the others had plain green tea. After they had drunk their tea two tables were laid, and Chou Chin was invited to take the seat of honour, Mei Chiu the second place. Then the others sat down in order of seniority, and wine was poured. Chou Chin, cup in hand, thanked the villagers and drained his cup. On each table were eight or nine dishes — pig's head, chicken, carp, tripe, liver and other dishes. At the signal to begin, they fell to with their chopsticks, like a whirlwind scattering wisps of cloud. And half the food had gone before they noticed that Chou Chin had not eaten a bite.

"Why aren't you eating anything?" asked Shen. "Surely we haven't offended you the very first day?" He selected some choice morsels and put them on the teacher's plate.

But Chou Chin stopped him and said, "I must explain — I am having a long fast."

"How thoughtless we have been!" exclaimed his hosts. "May we ask why you are fasting?"

"On account of a vow I made before the shrine of Buddha when my mother was ill," said Chou Chin. "I have been abstaining from meat now for more than ten years."

"Your fasting reminds me of a joke I heard the other day from Mr. Ku in the county town," said Mei Chiu. "It is a one character to seven character verse about a teacher." The villagers put down their chopsticks to listen, while he recited:

A
Foolish scholar
Fasted so long,
Whiskers covered his cheeks;
Neglecting to study the classics,
He left pen and paper aside.
He'll come without being invited next year.

After this recitation he said, "A learned man like Mr. Chou here is certainly not foolish." Then, putting his hand over his mouth to hide a smile, he added, "But he should become a scholar soon, and the description of the fasting and the whiskers is true to life." He gave a loud guffaw, and everybody laughed with him, while Chou Chin did not know which way to look.

Shen Hsiang-fu hastily filled a cup with wine and said, "Mr. Mei should drink a cup of wine. Mr. Chou was the teacher in Mr. Ku's house."

"I didn't know that," said Mei Chiu. "I should certainly drink a cup to apologize. But this joke was not against Mr. Chou. It was about a scholar. However, this fasting is a good thing. I have an uncle who never ate meat either. But after he passed the prefectural examination his patron sent him some sacrificial meat, and my grandmother said, 'If you don't eat this, Confucius will be angry, and some terrible calamity may happen. At the very least, he will make you fall sick.' So my uncle stopped fasting. Now, Mr. Chou, you are bound to pass the examination this autumn. Then you will be offered sacrificial meat, and I'm sure you will stop fasting."

They all said this was a lucky omen, and drank a toast to congratulate Chou Chin in advance, until the poor man's face turned a mottled red and white, and he could barely stammer out his thanks as he took the wine cup. Soup was carried in from the kitchen with a big dish of dumplings and a plate of fried cakes. They assured Chou Chin that there was no animal fat in the cakes, and pressed him to eat some. But he was afraid the soup was unclean, and asked for tea instead.

While they were eating the dessert, someone asked Shen, "Where is the village head today? Why hasn't he come to welcome Mr. Chou?"

"He has gone to a feast with Constable Li," said Shen.

"These last few years, under the new magistrate, Mr. Li has done very well," said someone else. "In one year he must make about a thousand taels of silver. But he is too fond of gambling. It's a pity he's not like Bailiff Huang. Bailiff Huang used to play too, but later he turned over a new leaf and was able to build a house just like a palace — it is very grand."

"Since your relative became the village head," said Mr. Hsun to Shen Hsiang-fu, "he's been in luck. Another year or two, and I suppose he will be like Bailiff Huang."

"He's not doing badly," said Shen. "But it'll be several years before his dream of catching up with Bailiff Huang comes true."

With his mouth full of cake, Mr. Mei put in: "There *is* something in dreams." And turning to Chou Chin he asked: "Mr. Chou, these past years, during the examinations, what dreams have you had?"

"None at all," replied Chou Chin.

"I was fortunate," said Mei Chiu. "Last year on New Year's Day, I dreamed that I was on a very high mountain.

The sun in the sky was directly above me, but suddenly it fell down on my head! Sweating with fright, I woke up and rubbed my head, and it still seemed hot. I didn't understand then what the dream meant, but later it came true!"

By this time all the cakes were finished, and they had another round of drinks. By then it was time to light the lamps, and Mei Chiu and all the others went home, while Shen Hsiang-fu produced blue bedding and escorted Mr Chou to the temple to sleep, where he settled with the monk that the two empty rooms at the back should be used for the school.

When the day came to start school, Shen Hsiang-fu and the other villagers took their sons, large and small, to pay their respects to the teacher; and Chou Chin taught them. That evening, when he opened the envelopes containing their school fees, he found there was one-tenth of a tael of silver from the Hsun family with an extra eight cents for tea, while the others had given only three or four cents or a dozen coppers apiece; so altogether he had not enough for one month's food. He gave what he had to the monk, however, promising to settle his account later.

The children were a wild lot. The moment Chou Chin took his eyes off them, they would slip outside to play hopscotch or kick balls. They were up to mischief every day, yet he had to sit there patiently and teach them.

Soon more than two months had passed and it began to grow warm. One day after lunch, Chou Chin opened the back gate and went out to stroll on the river bank. It was a small country place, with some peach trees and willows beside the stream, their pink and green beautifully intermingled. Chou Chin enjoyed the scenery until it began to drizzle. Then he went back to his doorway to watch the rain falling on the river and mist shrouding the distant trees, making them look even lovelier. The rain was beginning to fall more heavily when a boat came downstream — a small craft with a matting roof which could not keep out the wet. As it approached the bank, he saw a man sitting in the middle of the boat and two servants in the stern, while in the bow were two hampers. They reached the bank and the man ordered the boatman to moor the boat, then stepped ashore followed by his servants.

He was wearing a scholar's cap, a sapphire-blue gown and black slippers with white soles. His beard was combed into three tufts, and he looked a little over thirty. Coming to the temple gate he nodded to Chou Chin, then entered saying to himself, "This seems to be a school."

"Yes," said Chou Chin, accompanying him in and greeting him.

"And you, I suppose, are the teacher?"

"That is correct."

"How is it we don't see the monk?" the stranger asked his servants.

But just then the monk hurried in, saying, "Please take a seat, Mr. Wang, and I'll make tea for you." Then he told Chou Chin, "This is Mr. Wang Hui, a new provincial scholar. Please sit down and keep him company while I go to make tea."

The newcomer showed no false modesty. When the servants drew up benches he promptly sat himself down in the place of honour of it, leaving the teacher to take a lower seat.

"What is your name?" he demanded.

Knowing that this man was a provincial scholar, Chou Chin replied, "Your pupil is called Chou."

"Where did you teach before?"

"In the family of Mr. Ku of the county yamen."

"Aren't you the man who came first in that test which my patron, Mr. Pai, supervised? He said that you were teaching in Mr. Ku's family. That's right. That's right."

"Do you know my former employer, Mr. Ku, sir?"

"Mr. Ku is one of the secretaries in our office. He is one of my sworn brothers too."

Presently the monk brought in tea, and when they had drunk it Chou Chin said, "I read your examination essay over and over again, sir. The last two paragraphs were particularly fine."

"Those two paragraphs were not by me."

"You are too modest, sir. Who else could have written them?"

"Although not by me, they were not by anybody else either," said the scholar. "It was the first day of the examination, on the ninth, getting on for dusk; but I had still not finished the first essay, and I said to myself, 'Usually I write very quickly. What makes me so slow today?' As I was racking my brains, I dozed off on the desk. Then I saw five green-faced men leaping into the cell. One of them made a mark on my head with a big brush which he had in his hand, then darted away. Then a man in a gauze cap, red robe and golden belt came in, who shook me and said, 'Mr. Wang, please get up!' I woke up, trembling, bathed in icy sweat, and taking the pen into my hand began to write without knowing what I was doing. From this one can see that there *are* spirits in the examination school. When I made this statement to the chief examiner, he said that I ought to pass the very highest examination."

He was speaking with great gusto, when a small boy came in with a written exercise. Chou Chin told him to put it down, but Wang Hui said, "You go ahead and correct it. I have other things to see to." Then the teacher went to his desk while Wang Hui said to his servants, "Since it is dark and the rain has not stopped, bring the hampers here and tell the monk to cook a peck of rice. Order the boatman to wait. I shall leave tomorrow morning." He told Chou Chin, "I have just come back from visiting the graves of my ancestors, and did not expect to run into rain. I shall spend the night here."

While he was speaking, he caught sight of the name Hsun Mei on the little boy's exercise, and gave an involuntary start. He pursed his lips and his face was a study, but Chou Chin could not very well question him. When Chou Chin had finished correcting the exercise and sat down again as before, Wang Hui asked, "How old is that boy?"

"Seven."

"Did he start school this year? Did you choose that name for him?"

"I didn't choose the name. At the beginning of the term his father asked the new village scholar, Mei Chiu, to choose a name for him. And Mr. Mei said, 'My own name seems to be an auspicious one, so I will give it to him and hope that he will turn out like me.'"

"This is certainly a joke," said Wang Hui with a short laugh. "On the first day of this year I dreamed that I was looking at the list of metropolitan examination results. My name was on it — that goes without saying. But the third name was that of another man from Wenshang County called Hsun Mei, and I wondered at this, since there was no provincial scholar from my county called Hsun. Fancy it's turning out to be this little student's name! As if I could be on the same list as he!" He burst out laughing, then went on, "It's obvious that dreams are unreliable. Fame and achievement depend upon study, not upon any supernatural forces."

"Some dreams do come true, though," said Chou Chin. "The day that I arrived here, Mr. Mei told me that one New Year's Day he dreamed that a great red sun fell on his head, and that year, sure enough, he passed the prefectural examination."

"That doesn't prove anything," retorted Wang Hui. "Suppose he does pass the prefectural examination and have a sun falling on his head — what about me? I have passed the provincial examination. Shouldn't the whole sky fall on my head?"

As they were chatting, lights were brought in, and the servants spread the desk with wine, rice, chicken, fish, duck and pork. Wang Hui fell to, without inviting Chou Chin to join him; and when Wang Hui had finished, the monk sent up the teacher's rice with one dish of cabbage and a jug of hot water. When Chou Chin had eaten, they both went to bed. The next day the weather cleared. Wang Hui got up, washed and dressed, bade Chou Chin a casual goodbye and went away in his boat, leaving the schoolroom floor so littered with chicken, duck and fish bones, and melon-seed shells, that it took Chou Chin a whole morning to clear them all away, and the sweeping made him dizzy.

When the villagers heard about Wang Hui's dream that Mr. Hsun's son would pass the metropolitan examination in the same year as himself, most of them thought it a great joke, and Hsun Mei's classmates took to calling him Dr. Hsun. But their fathers and elder brothers were annoyed. Out of spite, they went to congratulate Mr. Hsun on being the father of a metropolitan graduate, until he was so angry he could hardly speak.

Shen Hsiang-fu told the villagers secretly, "Mr. Wang could never have said such a thing. It's all made up by that fellow Chou. He saw that the Hsun family was the only one in the village with money, so he spun this yarn to flatter them, in the hope that they would send him more food during festivals. Only the other day I heard that the Hsuns sent some dried beancurd to the temple; and they have often sent him dumplings and cakes too. Depend on it, this is the reason."

Everyone was indignant, and Chou Chin's position became precarious. But since he had been introduced by the village head, they could not dismiss him; and he went on teaching as best he could for a year. At the end of that time, however, Village Head Hsia also became convinced that the teacher was a fool, because Chou Chin did not come often enough to flatter him. So Hsia allowed the villagers to dismiss him.

Having lost his job, Chou Chin went home. He was extremely hard up. One day his brother-in-law, Chin Yin-yu, came to see him and said, "Don't take offence at what I say, brother. But all this study doesn't seem to be getting you anywhere, and a bad job is better than none. How long can you go on like this—neither fish, flesh nor fowl? I am going to the provincial capital with some other merchants to buy goods, and we need someone to keep accounts. Why don't you come with us? You are all on your own, and in our group you won't want for food or clothes."

"Even if a paralytic falls into a well, he can be no worse off than before," thought Chou Chin. "It can't hurt me to go." So he consented.

Chin chose an auspicious day, and they set off with a party of merchants to the provincial capital, where they stayed in a merchants' guild. Since Chou Chin had nothing to do, he strolled through the streets until he saw a group of workmen who said that they were going to repair the examination school. He followed them to the gate of the school and wanted to go in, but the gateman cracked his whip and drove him away.

That evening he told his brother-in-law how much he wanted to look over the examination school, and Chin had to tip the gateman to get him in. Some of the other merchants decided to go too, and asked the guild head to act as their guide. This

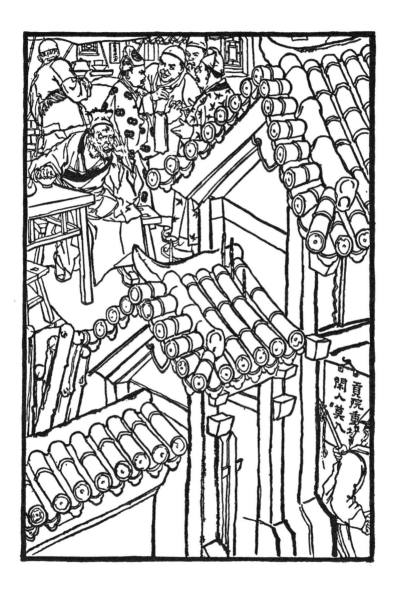

time they simply sailed through the gate of the school, because the gateman, whose palm had been greased, made no attempt to stop them. When they reached the Dragon Gate, the guild head pointed to it, and said, "This is the gate for scholars." They went into a corridor with examination cells on both sides, and the guild head told them, "This is Number One. You can go in and have a look." Chou Chin went in, and when he saw the desk set there so neatly, tears started to his eyes. He gave a long sigh, knocked his head against the desk, and slipped to the ground unconscious.

But to know whether Chou Chin recovered or not, you must read the next chapter.

CHAPTER *3*

Examiner Chou picks out true talent. Butcher Hu
cuts up rough after good news

When Chou Chin fell senseless to the ground, his friends
were greatly taken aback, thinking he must be ill.

"I suppose this place has been shut up so long that the air
is bad," said the guild head. "That must be why he has collapsed."

"I'll hold him up," said Chin to the guild head, "while you
go and get some hot water from the workmen over there to
bring him to."

When the guild head brought back the water, three or four
of the others raised Chou Chin up and poured water down his
throat till he gave a gurgle and spat out some phlegm. "That's
better," they said, and helped him to his feet. But when Chou
Chin saw the desk he beat his head against it again. Only,
instead of falling unconscious, this time he burst into loud sobbing. Not all their entreaties could stop him.

"Are you out of your mind?" demanded Chin. "We came
to the examination school to enjoy a bit of sightseeing. Nobody has died in your family. Why take on like this?" But
Chou Chin paid no attention. He just leaned his head against
the desk and went on crying. After crying in the first room,
he rushed over to cry in the second and then the third, rolling
over and over on the floor till all his friends felt sorry for
him. Seeing the state he was in, Chin and the guild head tried

32

to lift him up, one on each side; but he refused to budge. He cried and cried, until he spat blood. Then all the others lent a hand to carry him out and set him down in a tea-house in front of the examination school. They urged him to drink a bowl of tea. But he just went on sniffing and blinking away his tears, looking quite broken-hearted.

"What's your trouble, Mr. Chou?" asked one of them. "What made you cry so bitterly in there?"

"I don't think you realize, gentlemen," said Chin, "that my brother-in-law is not really a merchant. He has studied hard for scores of years, but never even passed the prefectural examination. That's why the sight of the provincial examination school today upset him."

Touched on the raw like this, Chou Chin let himself go and sobbed even more noisily.

"It seems to me you're the one to blame, Old Chin," said another merchant. "If Mr. Chou is a scholar, why did you bring him on such business?"

"Because he was so hard up," said Chin. "He had lost his job as a teacher; there was no other way out for him."

"Judging by your brother-in-law's appearance," said another, "he must be a very learned man. It's because nobody recognizes his worth that he feels so wronged."

"He's learned all right," said Chin, "but he's been unlucky."

"Anybody who buys the rank of scholar of the Imperial College can go in for the examination," said the man who had just spoken. "Since Mr. Chou is so learned, why not buy him a rank so that he can take the examination? If he passes, that will make up for his unhappiness today."

"I agree with you," rejoined Chin. "But where's the money to come from?"

By now Chou Chin had stopped crying.

"That's not difficult," said the same merchant. "We're all friends here. Let's raise some money between us and lend it to Mr. Chou, so that he can go in for the examination. If he passes and becomes an official, a few taels of silver will mean nothing to him — he can easily repay us. Even if he doesn't pay us back, we merchants always fritter away a few taels one way or another, and this is in a good cause. What do you all say?"

The others responded heartily:

"A friend in need is a friend indeed!"

"A man who knows what is the right thing to do, but doesn't do it, is a coward!"

"Of course we'll help. We only wonder if Mr. Chou will condescend to accept."

"If you do this," cried Chou Chin, "I shall look on you as my foster-parents. Even if I become a mule or a horse in my next life,[1] I shall repay your kindness." Then he knelt down and kowtowed to them all, and they bowed to him in return. Chin thanked them too. They drank a few more bowls of tea, and Chou Chin no longer cried, but talked and laughed with the others until it was time to return to the guild.

The next day, sure enough, the four merchants raised two hundred taels of silver between them. This they gave to Chin, who promised to be responsible for any expenses over and above that sum. Chou Chin thanked them again; and the guild head prepared a feast for the merchants on Chou Chin's behalf. Meantime Chin had taken the silver to the provincial treasury. As luck would have it, it was just the time for the preliminary test for the provincial examination. Chou Chin took the test and came first of all the candidates from the Imperial College. On the eighth of the eighth month he went to the examination school for the provincial examination, and the sight of the place where he had cried made him unexpectedly happy. As the proverb says, "Joy puts heart into a man." Thus he wrote seven excellent examination papers, then went back to the guild, for Chin and the others had not yet completed their purchases. When the results were published, Chou Chin had passed with distinction, and all the merchants were delighted.

They went back together to Wenshang County, where Chou Chin paid his respects to the magistrate and the local examiner, and officials sent in their cards and called to con-

---

1 This refers to the Buddhist belief in transmigration, and men's fear that in their next life they might not be human beings.

gratulate him. Local people who were no relations of his claimed relationship, and perfect strangers claimed acquaintanceship. This kept him busy for over a month. When Shen Hsiang-fu heard the news, he got the villagers in Hsueh Market to contribute to buy four chickens, fifty eggs and some rice balls, then went to the county-seat to congratulate Chou Chin, who kept him to a feast. Mr. Hsun, it goes without saying, came to pay his respects too.

Soon it was time to go to the examination in the capital. Chou Chin's travelling expenses and clothes were provided by Chin. He passed the metropolitan examination too; and after the palace examination he was given an official post. In three years he rose to the rank of censor and was appointed commissioner of education for Kwangtung Province.

Now though Chou Chin engaged several secretaries, he thought, "I had bad luck myself so long; now that I'm in office I mean to read all the papers carefully. I mustn't leave everything to my secretaries, and suppress real talent." Having come to this decision, he went to Canton to take up his post. The day after his arrival he burnt incense, posted up placards, and held two examinations.

The third examination was for candidates from Nanhai and Panyu Counties. Commissioner Chou sat in the hall and watched the candidates crowding in. There were young and old, handsome and homely, smart and shabby men among them. The last candidate to enter was thin and sallow, had a grizzled beard and was wearing an old felt hat. Kwangtung has a warm climate; still, this was the twelfth month, and yet this candidate had on a linen gown only, so he was shivering with cold as he took his paper and went to his cell. Chou Chin made a mental note of this before sealing up their doors. During the first interval, from his seat at the head of the hall he watched this candidate in the linen gown come up to hand in his paper. The man's clothes were so threadbare that a few more holes had appeared since he went into the cell. Commissioner Chou looked at his own garments—his magnificent crimson robe and gilt belt—then he referred to the register of names, and asked, "You are Fan Chin, aren't you?"

Kneeling, Fan Chin answered, "Yes, Your Excellency."

"How old are you this year?"

"I gave my age as thirty. Actually, I am fifty-four."

"How many times have you taken the examination?"

"I first went in for it when I was twenty, and I have taken it over twenty times since then."

"How is it you have never passed?"

"My essays are too poor," replied Fan Chin, "so none of the honourable examiners will pass me."

"That may not be the only reason," said Commissioner Chou. "Leave your paper here, and I will read it through carefully."

Fan Chin kowtowed and left.

It was still early, and no other candidates were coming to hand in their papers, so Commissioner Chou picked up Fan Chin's essay and read it through. But he was disappointed. "Whatever is the fellow driving at in this essay?" he wondered. "I see now why he never passed." He put it aside. However, when no other candidates appeared, he thought, "I might as well have another look at Fan Chin's paper. If he shows the least talent, I'll pass him to reward his perseverance." He read it through again, and this time felt there was something in it. He was just going to read it through once more, when another candidate came up to hand in his paper.

This man knelt down, and said, "Sir, I beg for an oral test."

"I have your paper here," said Commissioner Chou kindly. "What need is there for an oral test?"

"I can compose poems in all the ancient styles. I beg you to set a subject to test me."

The commissioner frowned and said, "Since the emperor attaches importance to essays, why should you bring up the poems of the Han and Tang Dynasties? A candidate like you should devote all his energy to writing compositions, instead of wasting time on heterodox studies. I have come here at the imperial command to examine essays, not to discuss miscellaneous literary forms with you. This devotion to superficial things means that your real work must be neglected. No doubt your essay is nothing but flashy talk, not worth the reading. Attendants! Drive him out!" At the word of command, attendants ran in from both sides to seize the candidate and push him outside the gate.

But although Commissioner Chou had had this man driven out, he still read his paper. This candidate was called Wei Hao-ku, and he wrote in a tolerably clear and straightforward style. "I will pass him lowest on the list," Chou Chin decided. And, taking up his brush, he made a mark at the end of the paper as a reminder.

Then he read Fan Chin's paper again. This time he gave a gasp of amazement. "Even I failed to understand this paper the first two times I read it!" he exclaimed. "But, after reading it for the third time, I realize it is the most wonderful essay in the world—every word a pearl. This shows how often bad examiners must have suppressed real genius." Hastily taking up his brush, he carefully drew three circles on Fan Chin's paper, marking it as first. He then picked up Wei Hao-ku's paper again, and marked it as twentieth. After this he collected all the other essays and took them away with him.

Soon the results were published, and Fan Chin's name was first on the list. When he went in to see the commissioner, Chou Chin commended him warmly. And when the last successful candidate—Wei Hao-ku—went in, Commissioner Chou gave him some encouragement and advised him to work hard and stop studying miscellaneous works. Then, to the sound of drums and trumpets, the successful candidates left.

The next day, Commissioner Chou set off for the capital. Fan Chin alone escorted him for ten miles of the way, doing reverence before his chair. Then the commissioner called him to his side. "First-class honours go to the mature," he said. "Your essay showed real maturity, and you are certain to do well in the provincial examination too. After I have made my report to the authorities, I will wait for you in the capital."

Fan Chin kowtowed again in thanks, then stood to one side of the road as the examiner's chair was carried swiftly off. Only when the banners had passed out of sight behind the next hill did he turn back to his lodgings to settle his bill. His home was about fifteen miles from the city, and he had to travel all night to reach it. He bowed to his mother, who lived with him in a thatched cottage with a thatched shed outside, his mother occupying the front room and his wife the back one. His wife was the daughter of Butcher Hu of the market.

Fan Chin's mother and wife were delighted by his success. They were preparing a meal when his father-in-law arrived, bringing pork sausages and a bottle of wine. Fan Chin greeted him, and they sat down together.

"Since I had the bad luck to marry my daughter to a scarecrow like you," said Butcher Hu, "Heaven knows how much you have cost me. Now I must have done some good deed to make you pass the examination. I've brought this wine to celebrate."

Fan Chin assented meekly, and called his wife to cook the sausages and warm the wine. He and his father-in-law sat in the thatched shed, while his mother and wife prepared food in the kitchen.

"Now that you have become a gentleman," went on Butcher Hu, "you must do things in proper style. Of course, men in my profession are decent, high-class people; and I am your elder too—you mustn't put on any airs before me. But these peasants round here, dung-carriers and the like, are low people. If you greet them and treat them as equals, that will be a breach of etiquette and will make me lose face too. You're such an easy-going, good-for-nothing fellow, I'm telling you this for your own good, so that you won't make a laughing-stock of yourself."

"Your advice is quite right, father," replied Fan Chin.

"Let your mother eat with us too," went on Butcher Hu. "She has only vegetables usually—it's a shame! Let my daughter join us too. She can't have tasted lard more than two or three times since she married you a dozen years ago, poor thing!"

So Fan Chin's mother and wife sat down to share the meal with them. They ate until sunset, by which time Butcher Hu was tipsy. Mother and son thanked him profusely; then, throwing his jacket over his shoulders, the butcher staggered home bloated. The next day Fan Chin had to call on relatives and friends.

Wei Hao-ku invited him to meet some other fellow candidates, and since it was the year for the provincial examination they held a number of literary meetings. Soon it was the end of the sixth month. Fan Chin's fellow candidates asked him to go with them to the provincial capital for the examination, but he had no money for the journey. He went to ask his father-in-law to help.

Butcher Hu spat in his face, and poured out a torrent of abuse. "Don't be a fool!" he roared. "Just passing one examination has turned your head completely—you're like a toad trying to swallow a swan! And I hear that you scraped through not because of your essay, but because the examiner pitied you for being so old. Now, like a fool, you want to pass the higher examination and become an official. But do you know who those officials are? They are all stars in heaven! Look at the Chang family in the city. All those officials have pots of money, dignified faces and big ears. But your mouth sticks out and you've a chin like an ape's. You should piss on the ground and look at your face in the puddle! You look like a monkey, yet you want to become an official. Come off it! Next year I shall find a teaching job for you with one of my friends so that you can make a few taels of silver to support that old, never-dying mother of yours and your wife—and it's high time you did! Yet you ask me for travelling expenses! I kill just one pig a day, and only make ten cents per pig. If I give you all my silver to play ducks and drakes with, my family will have to live on air." The butcher went on cursing at full blast, till Fan Chin's head spun.

When he got home again, he thought to himself, "Commissioner Chou said that I showed maturity. And, from ancient times till now, who ever passed the first examination without going in for the second? I shan't rest easy till I've taken it." So he asked his fellow candidates to help him, and went to the city, without telling his father-in-law, to take the examination. When the examination was over he returned home, only to find that his family had had no food for two days. And Butcher Hu cursed him again.

The day the results came out there was nothing to eat in the house, and Fan Chin's mother told him, "Take that hen of mine to the market and sell it; then buy a few measures of rice to make gruel. I'm faint with hunger."

Fan Chin tucked the hen under his arm and hurried out.

He had only been gone an hour or so, when gongs sounded and three horsemen galloped up. They alighted, tethered their horses to the shed, and called out: "Where is the honourable Mr. Fan? We have come to congratulate him on passing the provincial examination."

Not knowing what had happened, Fan Chin's mother had hidden herself in the house for fear. But when she heard that he had passed, she plucked up courage to poke her head out and say, "Please come in and sit down. My son has gone out."

"So this is the old lady," said the heralds. And they pressed forward to demand a tip.

In the midst of this excitement two more batches of horsemen arrived. Some squeezed inside while the others packed themselves into the shed, where they had to sit on the ground. Neighbours gathered round, too, to watch; and the flustered old lady asked one of them to go to look for her son. The neighbour ran to the market-place, but Fan Chin was nowhere to be seen. Only when he reached the east end of the market did he discover the scholar, clutching the hen tightly against his chest and holding a sales sign in one hand. Fan Chin was pacing slowly along, looking right and left for a customer.

"Go home quickly, Mr. Fan!" cried the neighbour. "Congratulations! You have passed the provincial examination. Your house is full of heralds."

Thinking this fellow was making fun of him, Fan Chin pretended not to hear, and walked forward with lowered head. Seeing that he paid no attention, the neighbour went up to him and tried to grab the hen.

"Why are you taking my hen?" protested Fan Chin. "You don't want to buy it."

"You have passed," insisted the neighbour. "They want you to go home to send off the heralds."

"Good neighbour," said Fan Chin, "we have no rice left at home, so I have to sell this hen. It's a matter of life and death. This is no time for jokes! Do go away, so as not to spoil my chance of a sale."

When the neighbour saw that Fan Chin did not believe him, he seized the hen, threw it to the ground, and dragged the scholar back by main force to his home.

The heralds cried, "Good! The newly honoured one is back." They pressed forward to congratulate him. But Fan Chin brushed past them into the house to look at the official announcement, already hung up, which read: "This is to announce that the master of your honourable mansion, Fan Chin, has passed the provincial examination in Kwangtung, coming seventh in the list. May better news follow in rapid succession!"

Fan Chin feasted his eyes on this announcement, and, after reading it through once to himself, read it once more aloud. Clapping his hands, he laughed and exclaimed, "Ha! Good! I have passed." Then, stepping back, he fell down in a dead faint. His mother hastily poured some boiled water between his lips, whereupon he recovered consciousness and struggled to his feet. Clapping his hands again, he let out a peal of laughter and shouted, "Aha! I've passed! I've passed!" Laughing wildly he ran outside, giving the heralds and the neighbours the fright of their lives. Not far from the front door he slipped and fell into a pond. When he clambered out, his hair was dishevelled, his hands muddied and his whole body dripping with slime. But nobody could stop him. Still clapping his hands and laughing, he headed straight for the market.

They all looked at each other in consternation, and said, "The new honour has sent him off his head!"

His mother wailed, "Aren't we out of luck! Why should passing an examination do this to him? Now he's mad, goodness knows when he'll get better."

"He was all right this morning when he went out," said his wife. "What could have brought on this attack? What *shall* we do?"

The neighbours consoled them. "Don't be upset," they said. "We will send a couple of men to keep an eye on Mr. Fan. And we'll all bring wine and eggs and rice for these heralds. Then we can discuss what's to be done."

The neighbours brought eggs or wine, lugged along sacks of rice or carried over chickens. Fan Chin's wife wailed as she prepared the food in the kitchen. Then she took it to the shed, neighbours brought tables and stools, and they asked the heralds to sit down to a meal while they discussed what to do.

"I have an idea," said one of the heralds. "But I don't know whether it will work or not."

"What idea?" they asked.

"There must be someone the honourable Mr. Fan usually stands in awe of," said the herald. "He's only been thrown off his balance because sudden joy made him choke on his phlegm. If you can get someone he's afraid of to slap him in the face and say, 'It's all a joke. You haven't passed any examination!'—then the fright will make him cough up his phlegm, and he'll come to his senses again."

They all clapped their hands and said, "That's a fine idea. Mr. Fan is more afraid of Butcher Hu than of anyone else. Let's hurry up and fetch him. He's probably still in the market, and hasn't yet heard the news."

"If he were selling meat in the market, he would have heard the news by now," said a neighbour. "He went out at dawn to the east market to fetch pigs, and he can't have come back yet. Someone had better go quickly to find him."

One of the neighbours hurried off in search of the butcher, and presently met him on the road, followed by an assistant who was carrying seven or eight catties of meat and four or five strings of cash. Butcher Hu was coming to offer his congratulations. Fan Chin's mother, crying bitterly, told him what had happened.

"How could he be so unlucky!" exclaimed the butcher. They were calling for him outside, so he gave the meat and the money to his daughter, and went out. The heralds put their plan before him, but Butcher Hu demurred.

"He may be my son-in-law," he said, "but he's an official[1] now—one of the stars in heaven. How can you hit one of

---

[1] A scholar who passed the provincial examination was sometimes eligible for such posts as that of a county magistrate.

the stars in heaven? I've heard that whoever hits the stars in heaven will be carried away by the King of Hell, given a hundred strokes with an iron rod, and shut up in the eighteenth hell, never to become a human being again. I daren't do a thing like that."

"Mr. Hu!" cried a sarcastic neighbour. "You make your living by killing pigs. Every day the blade goes in white and comes out red. After all the blood you've shed, the King of Hell must have marked you down for several thousand strokes by iron rods, so what does it matter if he adds a hundred more? Quite likely he will have used up all his iron rods before getting round to beating you for this, anyway. Or maybe, if you cure your son-in-law, the King of Hell may consider that as a good deed, and promote you from the eighteenth hell to the seventeenth."

"This is no time for joking," protested one of the heralds. "This is the only way to handle it, Mr. Hu. There's nothing else for it, so please don't make difficulties."

Butcher Hu had to give in. Two bowls of wine bolstered up his courage, making him lose his scruples and start his usual rampaging. Rolling up his greasy sleeves, he strode off toward the market, followed by small groups of neighbours.

Fan Chin's mother ran out and called after him, "Just frighten him a little! Mind you don't hurt him!"

"Of course," the neighbours reassured her. "That goes without saying."

When they reached the market, they found Fan Chin standing in the doorway of a temple. His hair was tousled, his face streaked with mud, and one of his shoes had come off. But he was still clapping his hands and crowing, "Aha! I've passed! I've passed!"

Butcher Hu bore down on him like an avenging fury, roaring, "You blasted idiot! What have you passed?" and fetched him a blow. The bystanders and neighbours could hardly suppress their laughter. But although Butcher Hu had screwed up his courage to strike once, he was still afraid at heart, and his hand was trembling too much to strike a second time. The one blow, however, had been enough to knock Fan Chin out.

The neighbours pressed round to rub Fan Chin's chest and massage his back, until presently he gave a sigh and came to. His eyes were clear and his madness had passed! They helped him up and borrowed a bench from Apothecary Chen, a hunchback who lived hard by the temple, so that Fan Chin might sit down.

Butcher Hu, who was standing a little way off, felt his hand begin to ache; when he raised his palm, he found to his dismay that he could not bend it. "It's true, then, that you mustn't strike the stars in heaven," he thought. "Now Buddha is punishing me!" The more he thought about it, the worse his hand hurt, and he asked the apothecary to give him some ointment for it.

Meanwhile Fan Chin was looking round and asking, "How do I come to be sitting here? My mind has been in a whirl, as if in a dream."

The neighbours said, "Congratulations, sir, on having passed the examination! A short time ago, in your happiness, you brought up some phlegm; but just now you spat out several mouthfuls and recovered. Please go home quickly to send away the heralds."

"That's right," said Fan Chin. "And I seem to remember coming seventh in the list." As he was speaking, he fastened up his hair and asked the apothecary for a basin of water to wash his face, while one of the neighbours found his shoe and helped him put it on.

The sight of his father-in-law made Fan Chin afraid that he was in for another cursing. But Butcher Hu stepped forward and said, "Worthy son-in-law, I would never have presumed to slap you just now if not for your mother. She sent me to help you."

"That was what I call a friendly slap," said one of the neighbours. "Wait till Mr. Fan finishes washing his face. I bet he can easily wash off half a basin of lard!"

"Mr. Hu!" said another. "This hand of yours will be too good to kill pigs any more."

"No indeed," replied the butcher. "Why should I go on killing pigs? My worthy son-in-law will be able to support me in style for the rest of my life. I always said that this worthy son-in-law of mine was very learned and handsome, and that not one of those Chang and Chou family officials in the city looked so much the fine gentleman. I have always been a good judge of character, I don't mind telling you. My daughter stayed at home till she was more than thirty, although many rich families wanted to marry her to their sons; but I saw signs of good fortune in her face, and knew that she would end up by marrying an official. You see today how right I was." He gave a great guffaw, and they all started to laugh.

When Fan Chin had washed and drunk the tea brought him by the apothecary, they all started back, Fan Chin in front, Butcher Hu and the neighbours behind. The butcher, noticing that the seat of his son-in-law's gown was crumpled, kept bending forward all the way home to tug out the creases for him.

When they reached Fan Chin's house, Butcher Hu shouted: "The master is back!" The old lady came out to greet them, and was overjoyed to find her son no longer mad. The heralds, she told them, had already been sent off with the money that Butcher Hu had brought. Fan Chin bowed to his mother and thanked his father-in-law, making Butcher Hu so embarrassed that he muttered, "That bit of money was nothing."

After thanking the neighbours too, Fan Chin was just going to sit down when a smart-looking retainer hurried in, holding a big red card, and announced, "Mr. Chang has come to pay his respects to the newly successful Mr. Fan."

By this time the sedan-chair was already at the door. Butcher Hu dived into his daughter's room and dared not come out, while the neighbours scattered in all directions. Fan Chin went out to welcome the visitor, who was one of the local gentry, and Mr. Chang alighted from the chair and came in. He was wearing an official's gauze cap, sunflower-coloured gown, gilt belt and black shoes. He was a provincial graduate, and had served as a magistrate in his time. His name was Chang Chin-chai. He and Fan Chin made way for each other ceremoniously, and once inside the house bowed to each other as equals and sat down in the places of guest and host. Mr. Chang began the conversation.

"Sir," he said, "although we live in the same district, I have never been able to call on you."

"I have long respected you," replied Fan Chin, "but have never had the chance to pay you a visit."

"Just now I saw the list of successful candidates. Your patron, Mr. Tang, was a pupil of my grandfather; so I feel very close to you."

"I did not deserve to pass, I am afraid," said Fan Chin. "But I am delighted to be the pupil of one of your family."

After a glance round the room, Mr. Chang remarked, "Sir, you are certainly frugal." He took from his servant a packet of silver, and stated, "I have brought nothing to show my respect except these fifty taels of silver, which I beg you to accept. Your honourable home is not good enough for you, and it will not be very convenient when you have many callers. I have an empty house on the main street by the east gate, which has three courtyards with three rooms in each. Although it is not big, it is quite clean. Allow me to present it to you. When you move there, I can profit by your instruction more easily."

Fan Chin declined many times, but Mr. Chang pressed him. "With all we have in common, we should be like brothers," he said. "But if you refuse, you are treating me like a stranger." Then Fan Chin accepted the silver and expressed his thanks. After some more conversation they bowed and parted. Not until the visitor was in his chair did Butcher Hu dare to emerge.

Fan Chin gave the silver to his wife. When she opened it, and they saw the white ingots with their fine markings, he asked Butcher Hu to come in and gave him two ingots, saying, "Just now I troubled you for five thousand coppers. Please accept these six taels of silver."

Butcher Hu gripped the silver tight, but thrust out his clenched fist, saying, "You keep this. I gave you that money to congratulate you, so how can I take it back?"

"I have some more silver here," said Fan Chin. "When it is spent, I will ask you for more."

Butcher Hu immediately drew back his fist, stuffed the silver into his pocket and said, "All right. Now that you are on good terms with that Mr. Chang, you needn't be afraid of going short. His family has more silver than the emperor, and they are my best customers. Every year, even if they have no particular occasions to celebrate, they still buy four or five thousand catties of meat. Silver is nothing to him."

Then he turned to his daughter and said, "Your rascally brother didn't want me to bring that money this morning. I told him, 'Now my honourable son-in-law is not the man he was. There will be lots of people sending him presents of money. I am only afraid he may refuse my gift.' Wasn't I right? Now I shall take this silver home and curse that dirty scoundrel." After a thousand thanks he made off, his head thrust forward and a broad grin on his face.

True enough, many people came to Fan Chin after that and made him presents of land and shops; while some poor couples came to serve him in return for his protection. In two or three months he had menservants and maidservants, to say nothing of money and rice. When Mr. Chang came again to urge him, he moved into the new house; and for three days he entertained guests with feasts and operas. On the morning of the fourth day, after Fan Chin's mother had got up and had breakfast, she went to the rooms in the back courtyard. There she found Fan Chin's wife with a silver pin in her hair. Although this was the middle of the tenth month, it was still warm and she was wearing a sky-blue silk tunic and a green silk skirt. She was supervising the maids as they washed bowls, cups, plates and chopsticks.

"You must be very careful," the old lady warned them. "These things don't belong to us, so don't break them."

"How can you say they don't belong to you, madam?" they asked. "They are all yours."

"No, no, these aren't ours," she protested with a smile.

"Oh yes, they are," the maids cried. "Not only these things, but all of us servants and this house belong to you."

When the old lady heard this, she picked up the fine porcelain and the cups and chopsticks inlaid with silver, and examined them carefully one by one. Then she went into a fit of laughter. "All mine!" she crowed. Screaming with laughter she fell backwards, choked, and lost consciousness.

But to know what became of the old lady, you must read the next chapter.

CHAPTER 4

In which a monk invited to say
masses is involved in a lawsuit, and a country gentleman
out to raise money runs into trouble

When Fan Chin's mother realized that everything in the house was hers, overcome with joy she fell senseless to the ground. The maids and her daughter-in-law, thrown into confusion, hastily summoned their master. Fan Chin hurried in, calling his mother, but she did not answer. At once he had her laid on the bed and sent for a doctor.

"The old lady's vital organs have been affected," said the doctor. "She is beyond saving."

Fan Chin called in several more physicians, but their diagnosis was the same, and he was in despair. As he and his wife watched by the bedside, weeping, he gave orders for the funeral; and when evening came the old lady breathed her last, so that the whole household was in a ferment all night.

The next day they called in a diviner, and found that the seventh was the old lady's unlucky number. On the third seventh day (the twenty-first), therefore, they must invite monks to say masses. Balls of white[1] cloth were hung over the front gate, and the new scrolls in the halls were pasted over with white paper. All the local gentry came to offer their condolences, and Fan Chin asked his fellow candidate

---

[1] White used to be the colour used in mourning in China.

Wei Hao-ku, in scholar's dress, to receive guests in the front hall. Butcher Hu was not up to appearing in public, but he bustled about between the kitchen and his daughter's room, helping to measure the white cloth or weigh meat.

When the second seventh day[1] had passed, Fan Chin gave his father-in-law a few taels of silver and told him to go to the temple in the market to ask a monk there whom he knew to invite other monks from the big monastery to recite the Buddhist scriptures, chant intercessions and say masses so that Mrs. Fan's soul might go to heaven.

Butcher Hu took the silver and went straight to the temple in the market where Monk Teng lived. There he found Abbot Huei Min from the monastery, too; for the abbot, who owned land nearby, often dropped in at the temple.

Monk Teng invited Butcher Hu to sit down, and said, "Mr. Fan was taken ill in front of my temple just after he passed the examination, but I was out that day and could not do anything for him. Luckily Mr. Chen the apothecary was on hand. He made some tea for him and acted as host in my place."

"That's right," said the butcher. "I also had some of his ointment, and was very grateful for it too. He's not here today, is he?"

"He hasn't come today," said the monk. "Mr. Fan soon got over his disorder; but the old lady's seizure was very unexpected. You must have been busy at home recently, Mr. Hu. We haven't seen you doing any business in the market."

"Yes. Since the sad death of Mr. Fan's mother, all the local gentry have called; and my former customers, the honourable Mr. Chang and Mr. Chou, have been in charge of the ceremonies. They sit there the whole day long with nothing to do, just making conversation with me, the three of us eating and drinking together. Whenever a guest comes, I have to bow and greet him—I'm sick and tired of it all. I'm an easygoing man, and I've no patience with all that. I'd like to keep out of the way. My son-in-law wouldn't mind, but those

---

[1] Chinese Buddhists believe that not till seven, twice seven or as many as seven times seven days after death does a spirit transmigrate to another body. Thus masses for a dead man are said within forty-nine days of his death.

gentlemen would probably think it strange. 'What use is a relative like this?' they might say."

Then he told the monk that Mr. Fan wanted to invite him to say masses. The moment the monk heard this, he was beside himself with excitement and bustled officiously off to make tea and prepare noodles for Butcher Hu. And then, in the butcher's presence, he asked the abbot to notify the other monks and to prepare incense, candles, paper horses and all that was necessary.

When Butcher Hu had finished his noodles and left, the abbot took the silver and set off for the city. Before he had gone half a mile, however, he heard someone calling: "Abbot Huei Min! Why don't you come to our village?" Turning his head, he saw that it was his tenant farmer, Ho Mei-chih.

"You seem to be very busy nowadays," said Ho. "Why don't you ever drop in to see us?"

"I would like to come," said the abbot. "But Mr. Chang in the city wants that field behind my house, and won't pay a fair price for it. I have had to refuse him several times. If I go to your village, his tenants there will start making no end of trouble, while if he sends men to the monastery to look for me, I can simply say that I am out."

"Never mind that," said Ho. "He may want the land, but he can't force you to sell. You're not busy today. Come to the village for a chat. That half leg of ham we cooked the other day is hanging in the kitchen waiting to be eaten, and the wine we brewed is ready too. We might as well finish them up. You can sleep in the village tonight. What are you afraid of?"

The abbot's mouth watered at these words, and his legs carried him along of their own volition. When they reached the village, Ho told his wife to cook a chicken, slice the ham and heat the wine. The abbot was warm after his walk, and sitting down in the yard pulled open his clothes to cool his chest and belly. His greasy face was glistening. Soon the food was ready. Ho Mei-chih carried out the dishes and his wife the wine. The abbot sat at the head of the table, Mrs. Ho at the foot and Ho at the side to pour out wine. As they ate, the abbot told them how in a few days' time he was going to Mr. Fan's house to say masses for the old lady's soul.

"I knew Mr. Fan's mother when I was a child," said Mrs. Ho. "She was an old dear. But his wife—the daughter of Butcher Hu of the south end of this village—with her dingy hair and red-rimmed eyes was a regular slattern. She never wore proper shoes, just shuffled about in straw sandals all summer. Yet now she will wear furs and be a fine lady. Fancy that!"

They were enjoying their meal when they heard a violent knocking on the gate.

"Who is it?" called Ho Mei-chih.

"Go and have a look, Mei-chih," said the abbot.

But no sooner had Ho opened the gate when seven or eight men rushed in. At the sight of the woman and the abbot drinking together at one table, they shouted, "Having a good time, aren't you? A monk carrying on with a woman in broad daylight! A fine abbot you are—knowing the law but breaking it."

"Stow that nonsense!" cried Ho Mei-chih. "This is my landlord."

Then they all swore at him. "Your landlord, eh? Does he have the run of your wife as well as your land?"

Without listening to the others' protests, they took a hempen rope and tied up the abbot, half-naked as he was, with the woman. Then they haled them off, together with Ho Mei-chih, to Nanhai County Court. There, the abbot and the woman, still tied together, were pushed up to a stage in front of a temple to wait for the magistrate, while Ho was thrown out. The abbot, however, had asked him in a whisper to go to Mr. Fan's house to report what had happened.

Because the abbot was to say masses for his mother, Fan Chin was impatient of any delay. He immediately wrote a letter to the magistrate, who sent a runner to release the abbot, let Ho Mei-chih take his wife home, and order the men who had accused them to appear in court the next day. These men took fright, and asked Mr. Chang to put in a word for them with the magistrate. Accordingly, the next morning when their case came up, the magistrate simply gave them a brief warning and drove them out. The upshot of the whole matter was that both the abbot and Mr. Chang's tenants had to bribe the yamen officials with several dozen taels of silver.

The abbot went to Fan Chin's house to thank him, and the next day took all the other monks there. They prepared an altar, on it set an image of Buddha, and on each side ranged the Kings of Hell. After eating noodles they clashed cymbals and chanted a chapter of the sutra. Then they sat down to their midday meal. The monks and Wei Hao-ku, who was master of ceremonies, were sitting at two tables eating when a servant announced that guests had arrived. When Wei put down his bowl and went out to welcome them, he found that they were Mr. Chang and Mr. Chou, wearing gauze caps, light-coloured gowns and black shoes with white soles. Wei Hao-ku took them to bow before the shrine, after which they went inside.

One of the monks said to the abbot, "That was Mr. Chang who went in just now. You and he own land next to each other, so you ought to have greeted him."

"Not I," said the abbot. "It's better not to cross Mr. Chang's path. My trouble the other day wasn't the work of any gang, but of his tenants. Mr. Chang had put them up to it. It was all a plot to squeeze so much silver out of me that I'd have to sell the land behind my house. But Mr. Chang, for all his tricks, only injured himself in the end; because when the magistrate wanted to beat his tenants, he lost his head and went, shamefaced, with his visiting card to beg them off. The magistrate was not at all pleased."

"Mr. Chang has done many unprincipled things," the abbot went on. "For instance, the daughter of Mr. Chou, who used to be magistrate of Chao County, is Mr. Chang's niece. The Chou family asked me to arrange a match for her, and I spoke to the Feng family in the next village—a very wealthy family. But then Mr. Chang insisted on giving the girl to this penniless young Mr. Wei, just because he had passed the prefectural examination and is supposed to be able to write poems. But a few days ago he wrote an intercession for the departed for Mr. Fan, and when I showed it to people they said he had written three characters wrongly; it was disgraceful. Soon the second

52

daughter is to be married. Heaven knows what kind of husband they will get her."

Just then the monks, hearing footsteps, winked to the abbot to stop talking. The two gentlemen came out, nodded in farewell, and were seen out by Wei Hao-ku. Then the monks finished eating, washed their faces, and all together blew trumpets, clashed cymbals, bowed before Buddha, burnt incense, lit tapers, spread rice, scattered flowers and performed their other rites. They kept this up for three days and three nights. After that the forty-nine days of mourning passed very quickly, and Fan Chin came out to thank those who had taken part.

One day Mr. Chang called, and asked to speak to Mr. Fan. He was invited into a small library in front of the shrine. Presently Mr. Fan came out in his mourning clothes, and began by thanking him for all his assistance during the mourning.

"Closely connected as we are, it was my duty to attend to your mother's funeral," said Mr. Chang. "Since your mother had a long life, she must have gone happily to heaven. Only this has delayed you in taking the final examination. No doubt you will have her buried by your ancestral tombs. Have you fixed on a date?"

"This year is not propitious," said Fan Chin. "We shall have to wait for next autumn. But I haven't got enough money."

Mr. Chang reckoned on his fingers. On the funeral banner they could use Commissioner Chou's name.[1] Wei Hao-ku could write the epitaph—but whose name should they use for it? Then there would be the cost of the funeral. Feasts, musicians and all the rest, with the food, payment to the gravediggers and geomancer,[2] would mount up to over three hundred taels of silver. While he was still counting, tea was served.

[1] It was the custom to ask an eminent citizen to inscribe the long banner used during a funeral with the dead person's titles and achievements.

[2] In the choice of a burial ground, great attention was paid to the lie of the land, the position of hills and water in the vicinity, and so forth; for these factors were believed to affect the fate of the descendants.

Presently Mr. Chang brought the subject up again. "Of course, the proper thing is to remain in retirement for three years," he said. "But on account of the funeral expenses, I think you would be justified in trying to raise some money. There is no need to be too scrupulous. Since your great success, you have not yet been to see your honourable patron; and Kaoyao County is extremely rich—we may be able to borrow some money there. I want to visit him too, so why don't we go together? I'll be responsible for all the expenses on the road and see that you're not troubled with them."

"This is exceedingly kind of you," said Fan Chin. "But I am not sure whether it is the correct procedure."

"The correct procedure varies according to circumstances," replied Mr. Chang. "I see no reason why you shouldn't go." Then Fan Chin thanked Mr. Chang again, and they settled a date for the journey.

They hired horses and, accompanied by attendants, set off for Kaoyao County. On the road they decided to make use of this visit to their patron to borrow his name for the epitaph. In a few days they reached the city of Kaoyao; but since the magistrate happened to have gone into the country to make an investigation, they were unable to enter the yamen and had to sit down in a temple to wait. The central hall of that temple was under repair, and the county foreman was there supervising the work. When he heard that friends of the magistrate had come, he hastily invited them into the guest room. Nine plates of refreshments were served, and the foreman poured tea for them. Presently a man came in wearing a scholar's cap, wide gown and black shoes with white soles. He had bulging eyes, a prominent nose and a beard.

As soon as this man came in he ordered the attendants to clear away the tea things. Then, after greeting Fan Chin and Mr. Chang, he sat down and asked them their names. When they had introduced themselves, the stranger said, "My name is Yen, and I live nearby. Last year, when my patron came to supervise the examination, I was lucky enough to be chosen senior licentiate. I am a good friend of Magistrate Tang's. No doubt you are both old friends of his?"

Fan Chin and Mr. Chang mentioned their relation to Magistrate Tang, and Senior Licentiate Yen appeared quite overwhelmed. The foreman excused himself and left, while one of Yen's servants brought in a hamper and a bottle of wine which he placed on the table. In the hamper were nine varieties of chicken, duck, salted fish and ham.

Senior Licentiate Yen invited them to take the seats of honour and, offering them wine, said, "I should have invited you to my poor home, but I felt it was unworthy of you; and, since you have to go to the yamen presently, I wanted to avoid unnecessary delay. So I have just provided a simple meal, in order that we may enjoy some conversation here. I hope you won't take this amiss."

Taking the wine cups from him, the two scholars said, "We have never called on you, yet we are accepting your hospitality." Senior Licentiate Yen protested politely and remained standing until they had drunk, but Fan Chin and Mr. Chang did not dare drink much for fear their faces would turn red. They put down their cups half full.

"Magistrate Tang is kind and benevolent," said Yen. "He is a great blessing to the county."

"Yes, he seems to have accomplished much here," said Mr. Chang.

"Gentlemen," said Yen, "human life is ordained by fate, and cannot be changed. When Magistrate Tang first came here, all the gentlemen of the county erected a pavilion three miles from the city to welcome him. I was standing at the pavilion door. Group after group with gongs, banners, canopies, fans, trumpets and many attendants passed by, then the magistrate's sedan-chair approached; and as soon as I saw His Honour's arched eyebrows, big nose, square face and large ears, I knew he must be a true gentleman. The remarkable thing, however, was that though there were dozens of people there to welcome him, he had eyes only for me. A scholar who was standing by looked from the magistrate to me and whispered, 'Did you know His Honour before?' I answered truthfully that I did not. Then he was fool enough to think that it was at him the magistrate was looking, and hastily stepped forward hoping to be spoken to. But when Magistrate Tang got down from the chair, greeted us all and looked past him, he realized that he had been mistaken and was most mortified. The next day I called at the yamen, and although His Honour had just returned from the county school and had a great deal of business to attend to, he immediately set it all aside and invited me in. He offered me tea twice, as if we had known each other for years."

"It must be because of your integrity that my uncle respects you so much," said Mr. Chang. "Recently, no doubt, he has frequently asked your advice."

"As a matter of fact, I haven't been to his office much lately," said Yen. "Frankly, I'm a straightforward fellow. Because I don't know how to cheat the villagers of an inch of silk or a grain of rice, all the magistrates have liked me. So though Magistrate Tang doesn't care for visitors as a general rule, there is a good understanding between him and me. For example, in the county examination the other month, when my son was placed tenth, His Honour called him in, questioned him carefully as to who his tutor was and whether he was engaged to be married or not, and took a great interest in him."

"My patron is an excellent judge of compositions," put in Fan Chin. "If he praised your son's composition, the young man must have real talent. I congratulate you."

"Not at all," said the senior licentiate. "Kaoyao is one of the most famous counties in Kwangtung," he continued. "In one year the taxes on grain, flowers, cloth, buffaloes, donkeys, fishing-boats, land, houses and so on come to more than ten thousand taels." Then, tracing figures on the table with his finger, he added in a low voice, "It seems that Magistrate Tang's methods only produce eight thousand taels, whereas Magistrate Pan who was here before him made ten thousand taels. There are still some ways in which he could make use of some of us leading citizens."

Fearing someone might be listening, he turned to the door. Just then a tousled, barefoot servant-boy walked in and said, "Master, they want you to go home."

"What for?" asked the senior licentiate.

"That man has come to ask for the pig we shut in this morning. He's wrangling with everyone in the house."

"If he wants the pig, let him pay for it."

"He says it's his."

"All right," snapped the senior licentiate. "You go first, and I'll come presently."

But the boy was unwilling to go back without him, and Mr. Chang and Mr. Fan said, "Since you have business at home, don't let us detain you."

"You gentlemen may not realize it," said Yen, "but that pig is really mine."

At that moment they heard the sound of gongs and stood up, exclaiming, "His Honour has come back!"

The two scholars adjusted their clothes and caps, called their attendants to take their cards, thanked Yen again, and went straight to the yamen. Magistrate Tang received their cards, on one of which was written "Your nephew Chang Chin-chai" and on the other "Your student Fan Chin."

"Chang has come time and again to get money: he is a confounded nuisance," he thought. "Still, since he has come with my newly successful student today, I had better not send him away." He ordered them to be invited in.

First Mr. Chang paid his respects, then Fan Chin saluted his patron. Magistrate Tang politely declined their homage, then invited them to sit down and drink tea. After exchanging some remarks with Mr. Chang, he praised Fan Chin's essay and asked, "Why did you not sit for the higher examination?"

"My mother has died," Fan Chin explained, "and I am in mourning."[1]

Magistrate Tang gave a start, and hastily called for a plain gown to change into, then bowed them into an inner room. Wine was brought and the table spread with birds'-nests, chicken, duck and two dishes of local fish and vegetables cooked in the Cantonese manner. They took their places at the table; but the cups and chopsticks were inlaid with silver, and Fan Chin hesitated to use them. The magistrate was puzzled, until Mr. Chang told him with a laugh, "On account of his

---

[1] For three years after the death of either parent a man had to observe mourning. During this period an official must retire from office, and a scholar could not take examinations.

mourning, Mr. Fan thinks he should not use these cups and chopsticks." The magistrate at once ordered them to be changed for a porcelain cup and ivory chopsticks; but still Fan Chin would not eat.

"He does not use these chopsticks either," said Mr. Chang.

Finally plain bamboo chopsticks were produced, and all was well.

Seeing how strictly Fan Chin observed the rules of mourning, Magistrate Tang was afraid he would not eat meat, and there was nothing else prepared. But to his relief, the magistrate saw Fan Chin pop a large shrimp ball from the dish of birds'-nests into his mouth.

"I have been very remiss," said Magistrate Tang. "We Moslems have no good dishes, only this simple fare. The only meat our religion allows us to eat is beef and mutton, but we dare not offer these to guests for fear they may not like them. Now we have received an imperial decree forbidding the slaughter of cows, and our superiors have ordered us to see that this rule is strictly enforced. So even in the yamen there is no beef." Candles were brought, and they read the orders on the subject.

Just then an attendant whispered something into the magistrate's ear, at which he got up and excused himself, saying he would be back presently. In a few minutes they heard him give the order, "Put it there!" Then he came in and sat down again at the table, apologizing for his absence.

"Mr. Chang, you have held official posts," said Magistrate Tang. "I would like your opinion on this. It's in connection with the prohibition of the sale of beef. Just now several Moslems got an old man to bring me fifty catties of beef and to plead with me saying that if I stop the sale of beef they will be forced out of business; and begging me to be more lenient. They want me, in fact, to shut my eyes to an illegal transaction. And they have sent this beef here. Should I accept it or not?"

"I should say certainly not, sir," replied Chang. "We officials owe allegiance only to the emperor, not to friends of the same faith. This reminds me of Mr. Liu in the reign of Hung Wu."

"Which Mr. Liu?" asked the magistrate.

"Liu Chi.[1] He passed the palace examination in the third year of the reign, coming fifth on the list."

"I thought he came third," put in Fan Chin.

"No," Chang contradicted him. "Fifth. I read his essay. Later he entered the Han Lin Academy. One day Emperor Hung Wu went to his house in disguise, just like the emperor in the old story who called on his friend one snowy night.[2] But that same day Prince Chang of Chiangnan sent Liu a pitcher of pickled vegetables, and Liu opened it in the emperor's presence only to find that it was full of gold. The emperor was very angry and said, 'He seems to think that scholars can control the state.' The next day he degraded Liu Chi to the post of magistrate of Chingtien, and had him poisoned. No, no, you can't accept the beef!"

When the magistrate heard Chang talk so glibly about one of the memorable events of that dynasty, giving all manner of circumstantial details, he could not but believe him. "How would you deal with the situation then?" he asked.

"In my humble opinion, this may enable you to win fame," said Chang. "Keep the old man here tonight. Tomorrow morning bring his case before the court, and give him several dozen strokes; then have him pilloried and pile the beef on him, posting up a notice by his side making his guilt clear. When your superiors see how incorruptible you are, your promotion will be assured."

The magistrate nodded. "Quite right," he said. Then the feast came to an end, and he lodged them in the library.

The next morning in court the first culprit called was a hen thief.

"You wretch!" said Magistrate Tang. "You have been found guilty several times, yet you are a hardened offender,

---

[1] Liu passed the examination during the Yuan Dynasty, and became an official during the Ming Dynasty. He was a native of Chingtien, but never served as magistrate there. It was not Liu, but someone else, who received gold in a jar of pickles.

[2] The first emperor of the Sung Dynasty, Chao Kuang-yin (960-975), called on his prime minister, Chao Pu, at night to discuss state affairs with him.

not afraid of being beaten. What shall I do with you today?"
With vermilion ink he wrote on the man's face, "Hen Stealer."
Then he pilloried him, tied a hen back to front on his head,
and threw him out. The man had just got outside the yamen
gate when the hen's droppings fell onto his forehead and
dripped down over his nose and moustache onto the pillory,
sending all who saw it into fits of laughter.

The next to be called was the old Moslem. Magistrate
Tang stormed at him for his wicked presumption, and gave him
thirty strokes. After that he put him in a large pillory, pack-
ing the fifty catties of beef so tightly around the man's neck
and face that only his eyes could be seen. He was pilloried in
front of the court as a public example.

The weather was hot. By the next day the meat was
crawling with maggots, and the day after that the old man
died. Several hundred Moslems were up in arms immediately.

Sounding gongs and stopping the market, they went clamouring to the yamen to protest.

"Even if it was wrong to send the beef, he shouldn't have
received a death penalty!" they cried. "This is all the fault
of that scoundrel Chang from Nanhai County. Let's break
into the yamen, drag him out and beat him to death! One of
us will be willing to pay for it with his own life."

But to know to what lengths the Moslems went, you must
read the next chapter.

CHAPTER 5

The Wang brothers deliberate
how to make a concubine the mistress of the house.
Yen Ta-yu dies

The Moslems were out for blood. They besieged the yamen gate so closely that not a drop of water could have trickled through, and threatened to drag Mr. Chang out and beat him to death. The magistrate was thoroughly frightened. After a careful investigation he discovered that one of his subordinates had told the Moslems of Mr. Chang's part in the business. "After all, I am head of the county and they dare not touch me," he told Mr. Chang and Fan Chin. "But if they break in and find Mr. Chang here, there's no knowing what may happen. I must think of a way to get you out of here. Once you have left, all will be well."

He immediately summoned his most reliable men to discuss the question. Luckily, the back of the yamen was hard by the north gate of the city, and after several men had slipped outside the city wall, Mr. Chang and Fan Chin were lowered to them by ropes. Then Chang and Fan changed into blue cloth gowns, straw hats and sandals, and, stealthily as stray dogs, swiftly as fish escaping from the net, fled back to the provincial capital.

Meantime examiners and officials had gone to the yamen gate to pacify the people and speak them fair, until gradually the Moslems dispersed. Magistrate Tang sent a detailed report of the whole business to the provincial commissioner of justice, who summoned him to the provincial capital. On entering the presence of the commissioner, Magistrate Tang took off his gauze cap and kowtowed again and again.

"To tell the truth, you acted a little too hastily," said the commissioner. "To pillory the culprit would have been punishment enough. Why pile the beef on the pillory? What sort of penalty is that? However, this insubordination must be nipped in the bud. I shall have to punish the ringleaders. Go back to your yamen, and take care not to act so rashly in future."

Magistrate Tang kowtowed again. "I bungled this affair," he confessed. "Since you have overlooked my fault, I owe you the same gratitude that I do to heaven and earth or to my parents. In future I promise to do better. But when your decision is made, Your Excellency, I hope you will allow me to punish the ringleaders in my own county, to recover some of the face I have lost." When his superior gave his consent, Magistrate Tang thanked him and left.

Some time later, five of the Moslem leaders in Kaoyao were found guilty of insubordination and sentenced to be pilloried in their own county. When Magistrate Tang received this order he issued a notice summoning his officers, and the very next morning swaggered into the court and punished the offenders.

He was just about to leave, when two men came in to appeal to him, and he ordered them to approach for questioning. The first was called Wang Erh, and he lived next door to Senior Licentiate Yen. In the third month of the previous year the Yen family's sucking pig had strayed into the Wangs' yard, but the Wangs had returned it immediately. Yen said, "To take a pig back like this means very bad luck." He forced the Wangs to buy it for eighty cents of silver. They had fattened it up till it weighed over a hundred catties, when it wandered into the Yens' yard by mistake. The Yen family shut it up, and when Wang's elder brother went to ask for it, Senior Licentiate Yen said, "It's my pig, and if you want it you must pay me the market price for it." Wang was a poor man—how could he find the money? But when he started to argue, Yen's sons took the bolt of the door and a rolling-pin and beat him within an inch of his life. He was lying at home now with a broken leg, so his younger brother had come to lodge a complaint.

The magistrate turned to the other plaintiff, who was between fifty and sixty years old, and asked, "What is your name?"

"Huang Meng-tung," was the answer. "I live in the country. In the ninth month last year I came to the city to pay my taxes. But I didn't have enough money, so I asked a go-between to borrow twenty taels of silver for me from Senior Licentiate Yen at three per cent monthly interest. I signed a contract with Senior Licentiate Yen, but I didn't take the money, for here in town I met a relative from the country who said he could lend me part of the amount and I should borrow the rest from friends in the country. He advised me not to borrow from Senior Licentiate Yen. After paying my taxes, I went back with this relative. That was more than six months ago. Just lately I remembered the agreement I had signed, and came back to town to ask Senior Licentiate Yen to give it back to me. But he demanded that I pay the interest for all these months. 'I didn't borrow the money, so why should I pay interest?' I asked. Senior Licentiate Yen said if I had taken the agreement back at once, he could have lent the money to someone else. As it was, I had prevented his using those twenty taels, and made him lose half a year's interest. Now I must pay it. I realized I was in the wrong, and asked the go-between to speak for me, promising to take Senior Licentiate Yen presents of pork and wine if he would give me back the contract. But he still insisted on having the money. Now he has seized my donkey and grain sacks as a fine, yet he still hasn't returned that contract. I ask you, sir, to judge such underhand dealings!"

"A man who is a senior licentiate ranks among the scholars," declared Magistrate Tang, "yet instead of doing good deeds, he cheats poor people like this. Disgraceful!" He approved both plaintiffs' petitions, and told them to wait outside.

Now somebody had already reported this to Yen. He was panic-stricken, and thought, "Both complaints are true, and if I have to appear in court I shall lose face. Better make myself scarce." He bundled some things together and fled to the provincial capital.

The magistrate signed a warrant and sent runners to Yen's house to arrest him, but he had flown. Then they went to his younger brother Yen Ta-yu. These two brothers did not live together. Yen Ta-yu had bought himself the rank of a scholar of the Imperial College and had more than one hundred thousand taels of silver. But, rich as he was, he was timid. When the runners showed him the warrant and he learned that his brother was not at home, he dared not offend them. He entertained them to a meal, gave them two thousand coins and sent them off. Then he hurriedly ordered a servant to ask his two brothers-in-law over to discuss the matter.

One of the brothers-in-law was called Wang Teh and the other Wang Jen. They were scholars, one of whom drew a subsidy from the prefectural school and the other from the county school. Both of them made a very good thing out of teaching, and were famous as tutors. When they received Yen Ta-yu's message, they came at once.

Yen Ta-yu told them all that had happened. "There's even a warrant out for his arrest. What's to be done?" he asked.

Wang Jen laughed and said, "Your brother is always saying how friendly he is with Magistrate Tang. How could he be frightened away by a little thing like this?"

"Never mind that," said Yen Ta-yu. "The fact is that my brother has gone, while runners from the yamen have been to my house looking for someone to arrest. I can't drop my own business to go and look for him. And he wouldn't come back anyway."

"His private affairs have nothing to do with you," said Wang Jen.

"That's where you're wrong," protested Wang Teh. "Because our brother-in-law is rich, the runners will consider him as lawful prey. If nothing is done, they can make things hot for him. I suggest that we go to the root of the matter by sending mediators to satisfy the plaintiffs. Then we can address an appeal to the magistrate and avoid further trouble."

64

"If mediators are needed," said Wang Jen, "we two can call on Wang Erh and Huang Meng-tung, and talk them round. We'll return the pig to the Wang family along with some silver to compensate for the elder brother's broken leg. And we'll look for Huang's contract and return it to him. Then we shouldn't have any more trouble."

"Yes," said Yen Ta-yu. "But my sister-in-law is a silly woman and my nephews are like young wolves—they never listen to reason. They'll refuse to return the pig and the contract."

"This is a serious matter," said Wang Teh. "If your sister-in-law and nephews are stubborn, that will be your bad luck. Because then *you* will have to pay the Wangs for the pig. As for the contract, in our capacity as mediators we will draw up a statement for Huang Meng-tung to the effect that the old contract is null and void. That's the only thing to do. Then you'll hear no more about it." They decided at once that this was the only solution, and handled the whole business very competently. And when Yen Ta-yu had spent over ten taels of silver on the plaintiffs and yamen officials, the case was closed.

A few days later, Yen Ta-yu invited the two Wang brothers to a feast to express his gratitude. When they made excuses and would not come, he ordered his servant to tell them that their sister was unwell and wanted to see them too. On hearing this, the two scholars came. Yen Ta-yu invited them into the front hall and offered them tea, then told a servant to inform his wife that they had arrived. Presently a maid invited them to Mrs. Yen's room, and they went in. Their sister had grown very pale and thin. She looked too frail to walk, yet she was preparing melon seeds, chestnuts and other sweetmeats for them. When she saw her brothers, she left her work and stepped forward to welcome them; and the nurse brought in the concubine's three-year-old son, in a silver necklet and red suit, to see his uncles.

While they were sipping tea, another maid announced, "The new wife asks permission to pay her respects."

"We won't disturb her," the Wang brothers responded politely. Then they sat down for a chat and asked after their sister's illness, urging her, since she was so weak, to take more cordials.

While they were talking, a feast was laid in the front hall and they were invited to the table.

In the course of conversation Senior Licentiate Yen's name came up. Wang Jen said to Wang Teh with a laugh, "I can't understand, brother, how anyone who writes so badly ever passed the examination and became a stipendiary."

"That was thirty years ago," Wang Teh answered. "In those days the examiners were all censors—what did they know about compositions?"

"He's been growing more and more peculiar," said Wang Jen. "Since we are related, we invite him to several feasts each year, but he never offers us so much as a cup of wine. It was only the year before last, when he became a senior licentiate and put up a flagstaff,[1] that he invited me to a feast."

"I did not go," said Wang Teh with a frown. "He made that senior licentiate rank a pretext to extract presents from everybody. County runners—even village heads—all had to fork out. He pocketed more than two hundred strings of cash altogether. But he never paid his cook, nor the butcher—even now he still owes them money. Every month or so they make a scene in his house. It's shocking."

"I am really ashamed of him," said Yen Ta-yu. "Though I have a little land, I don't mind telling you, our family of four usually feel it would be extravagant to buy pork. When my son is hungry, we just buy four cash worth of cooked meat for him. But although my brother has no land and so many mouths to feed, every other day he buys about five catties of pork and insists on having it cooked to a turn. Then they finish it all in one meal, and in the evening he gets fish on credit again. We inherited the same amount of land, but he has just eaten up his property; and now he sneaks out the family's ebony chairs through the back door to exchange for pork dumplings. What can I do about it?"

The Wang brothers burst out laughing, then said, "We've been so busy talking about that fool, we've forgotten to drink. Let's have the dice. Whoever wins first place among the palace

---

[1] When a man passed an examination he could set up a flagstaff before his ancestral temple; thus the whole clan shared his glory.

scholars shall drink a cup." Wang Teh and Wang Jen became palace scholars in turn, and drank a dozen cups apiece. Strangely enough, the dice seemed to know human affairs; because Yen Ta-yu did not become a palace scholar even once. Wang Jen and Wang Teh clapped their hands and roared with laughter, drinking until after midnight when they were carried home.

Mrs. Yen's illness went from bad to worse. Every day four or five doctors came to prescribe expensive cordials for her, but in vain. Soon she was completely bed-ridden, and Concubine Chao, the mother of the little boy, stayed by her bedside, giving her draughts of medicine and waiting on her hand and foot. After it became clear that the mistress was not going to recover, the concubine brought her child to the foot of the bed every evening and sat there weeping. And one night she said:

"All I pray for now is that Buddha will take me away in your place and let you get well."

"That's a silly way to talk," said Mrs. Yen. "Everyone's span of life is fixed. How can you change with someone else?"

"Don't say that," begged the concubine. "What does my death matter? But if anything happened to you, ma'am, the master would certainly marry again. He is over forty but has only one son; and if he marries again, the new wife will care only for her own children. A stepmother is always cruel. Then my son wouldn't live to grow up, and that would be the death of me. I'd rather die now, instead of you, to save this child's life."

Mrs. Yen said nothing.

Every day, with tears in her eyes, Concubine Chao nursed the sick woman and would not leave her. One evening, however, she left the room and did not come back for some time.

"Where is the new wife?" asked Mrs. Yen.

A maid told her, "Every evening the new wife burns incense in the courtyard and cries, praying to heaven and earth to let her die in your place, ma'am. This evening she thought you seemed worse, so she went out earlier to pray."

Still Mrs. Yen looked rather sceptical.

The next evening, however, when the concubine cried as she poured out all her fears again, the wife said, "Very well.

We can suggest to the master that when I die he should make you his wife."

At once Concubine Chao called Yen Ta-yu in, and told him what the mistress had said.

"In that case," said Yen, who had been hoping for this, "I must invite my brothers-in-law tomorrow morning to settle the matter, in order that we may have witnesses."

"Do as you think best," said his wife, with a weary wave of her hand.

Accordingly, Yen Ta-yu sent to invite the Wang brothers to come early the next day.

When they had seen the doctor's prescriptions and discussed what other famous physicians could be called, Yen took the brothers into his wife's room and told them their sister's wish, saying:

"Ask her yourselves."

They went up to the bed. Mrs. Yen was too weak to speak, but she pointed at the child and nodded her head. The two brothers pulled long faces and said nothing. Presently they were invited into the library to eat, but still they made no reference to the matter.

After they had eaten, Yen Ta-yu took them into a private room; and after speaking about his wife's illness, he said with tears, "Since your sister married me twenty years ago, she has been a true helpmate. But now that she is dying, what am I to do? The other day she mentioned that your parents' tombs needed repairing, and that she had a little gift to leave you as a memento." Having sent the servants out of the room, he opened a chest and took out two packets of silver, each containing a hundred taels. These he gave to Wang Teh and Wang Jen, saying, "Please don't take me amiss."

The Wang brothers took hold of the silver with both hands.

"Please don't have any scruples," Mr. Yen went on. "When you need money for sacrifices I'll be responsible for all expenses. Tomorrow I will send sedan-chairs to fetch your wives. Your sister has some trinkets to give them as souvenirs."

They had just gone back to the outer room when some guests arrived, and Mr. Yen went out to entertain them. By the time he came back, the Wang brothers' eyes were red with weeping, and Wang Jen said, "I was telling my brother that our sister is truly a woman in a million and does credit to our family. For I doubt if even you, sir, ever conceived such a noble scheme. If you still hesitate, then you are no true man."

"Do you realize," asked Wang Teh solemnly, "that the perpetuation of your line depends on making Concubine Chao your wife? For if our sister dies and you marry another, the new wife may torture our nephew to death. Then not only will your parents in heaven be ill at ease, but our ancestors also."

Striking his fist on the table, Wang Jen declared, "The great thing about us scholars is our adherence to principles. If we were writing a composition to speak for Confucius, we should take exactly the line that we are taking now. If you refuse to listen to us, we will never visit you again."

"I am afraid my relatives may object," said Mr. Yen.

"You can count on us," the brothers assured him. "But this thing must be done in a big way. Give us a few more taels of silver, and tomorrow we shall act as hosts and invite over a hundred of your relatives to a feast. While our sister's eyes can still see, you and Concubine Chao shall worship heaven and earth and the ancestors together, showing that she is your lawful wife. Then your relatives will have to hold their tongues."

Yen Ta-yu gave another fifty taels of silver to the Wang brothers, who then left, exuding righteousness from every pore.

The next day, accordingly, Wang Jen and Wang Teh came to Mr. Yen's house and wrote scores of invitations to relatives from the various branches of the family. And all of them came, with the exception of Senior Licentiate Yen's five sons from next door. When the guests had breakfasted, they went to Mrs. Yen's bedside to witness her will, which her brothers drew up and signed. Meantime Mr. Yen put on a scholar's cap, a blue gown and red silk sash, while Concubine Chao dressed herself in crimson and put a gold chaplet on her head. As they worshipped heaven and earth and the ancestors, Wang Jen drew on his vast erudition to write a most moving announcement of this marriage to the Yen ancestors. And having informed the ancestors, they left the shrine.

Then Wang Jen and Wang Teh sent for their wives, and kowtowed together to the new husband and wife. All the relatives congratulated them in order of seniority, after which the stewards, menservants and maidservants did reverence to their master and mistress. The new wife went in alone to bow before the dying mistress, calling her "Elder Sister." But Mrs. Yen had already lost consciousness.

These ceremonies at an end, the guests crowded into the great hall, second hall, library and inner chambers to sit down to more than twenty tables. They feasted till midnight.

Mr. Yen was acting as host in the great hall when his son's wet-nurse burst in breathlessly, and cried, "The mistress has passed away!"

Weeping, Mr. Yen went to the bedroom and found his new wife beating her head against the bed. At his entry, she gave a cry and fainted. They helped her up, prized open her teeth and poured hot water down her throat. Then she came to herself and rolled on the floor, tearing her hair and sobbing as if her heart would break. Not even her husband could calm her. While the servants were in the hall and the guests in the other rooms, the two sisters-in-law took advantage of the confusion to whisk away the clothes, gold, and pearls. One of them even picked up the gold chaplet that the new wife had let fall, and concealed it in her clothes.

Mr. Yen told the nurse to bring in his son, and threw a coarse linen cloth over the child's shoulders as a sign of mourning, the coffin had been ready for some time. They placed the corpse in the coffin, which had been set in the central hall. It was now dawn. All the guests filed in, bowed before the coffin and went home.

The next day, white mourning was sent to all the relatives— two lengths of cloth for each house. The new wife insisted that she should wear heavy mourning, but on this point the Wang brothers were adamant. In unison they quoted one of the sayings of Confucius, and warned her, "You must conform to etiquette. Now you stand in the relationship of a sister to the dead woman, and a younger sister mourning for her elder sister should only wear mourning for one year—fine linen and a white cloth head-dress."

The ceremony to be used was agreed upon, and the date of the funeral announced. They fasted, held the funeral, and spent four or five thousand taels of silver, observing the rites for half a year. We need not dwell on the details.

The new Mrs. Yen felt very much indebted to the Wang brothers. After the harvest she sent them two piculs of rice apiece, two piculs of pickled vegetables and four hams, to say nothing of chickens, ducks and other delicacies.

Soon New Year's Eve came round. Mr. Yen worshipped heaven and earth and the ancestors, then sat down to a feast with his new wife opposite him and the nurse and child sitting at one side of the table.

After drinking several cups of wine, tears rolled down Mr. Yen's cheeks as he pointed to a chest and said, "Yesterday the pawnshop sent three hundred taels of interest over. That was my first wife's private property. It used to come every year just before New Year's Eve, and I always gave it to her and let her do what she liked with it. Now they have sent it again, but there is no one to take it."

"You can't say there is no use for her money," said the new wife. "I remember how she used to spend it. In the old days, at every festival the nuns would send her presents and the flower-girls would give her little trinkets, while those blind girls who often came to play the three-stringed lyre wouldn't budge from the door. She gave them all money, she was so kind. And when she saw poor relations she would feed them even if she had nothing to eat herself, and give them clothes even if it meant going without herself. The money was all too little for her. Even if it had been more, she would have used it all. Her two brothers were the only ones who did not take a cent from her. To my mind it would be better to keep the money to spend it on charity after New Year in her name. And what's left won't be much; it could be given to your two brothers-in-law for their travelling expenses when they go to take the examination next year. This would be only right and proper."

As she was speaking, a cat under the table crawled up Mr. Yen's leg, and he gave it a kick. The frightened cat shot into the bedroom and jumped onto the canopy of the bed.

Then they heard a great crash. Something had fallen from the top of the bed and smashed the wine vat on the floor. Taking a candle they hurried in to look, and found that the silly cat had knocked off a piece of the bedstead, bringing down a big wicker basket full of dates which had fallen in the wine. Now the dates were scattered on the ground, the basket lying on its side; and it took the two of them to right it. Then, under the dates, they discovered paper packages containing five hundred taels of silver.

"I knew she couldn't have spent all that silver," said Mr. Yen with a sigh. "This must be what she saved over the years. She wanted to keep it in readiness for whenever I might need money in a hurry. But where is she now?"

He shed tears again, and called servants to sweep the floor while he and his new wife put a plateful of the dates on the table before the shrine and, kneeling there, wept again. Because of this, Mr. Yen did not go out to pay New Year visits, but stayed at home weeping from time to time, feeling out of sorts and in low spirits.

After the Lantern Festival, he felt stabs of pain in his heart. At first he just put up with them, doing his accounts as usual every night until midnight; but gradually he lost his appetite and wasted away till he was nothing but skin and bones. Yet he grudged the money to buy ginseng.

His wife begged him, "Don't trouble about all your business—you aren't well."

But he retorted, "My son is still small. Who else is there to see to things? As long as I live I must manage my affairs."

As spring wore on, however, he had a liver complaint and had to take to his bed, able only to drink a little gruel every day. When the weather became warmer, he forced himself to eat and made the effort to get up and walk about. But by autumn he was worse again and had to keep to his bed. When it was time to reap the early rice, he sent his stewards and menservants down to his estates; but he could not rest easy in his mind. One morning he had just taken his medicine when he heard the rustle of falling leaves against the window, and felt a fearful premonition. He heaved a long sigh, and turned his face to the wall.

The new wife brought the Wang brothers in to see how he was before they left for the provincial examination. Ordering a maid to help him, Mr. Yen struggled to a sitting position.

"We have not seen you for many days, and now you are thinner than ever," said the brothers. "It's good, though, that you still look so cheerful."

Mr. Yen asked them to be seated, wished them success in their coming examination, and offered them refreshments. He told them what had happened on New Year's Eve, and asked his wife to bring in some silver. "This was her idea," he told them. "She suggested that this small sum of money that my wife left should be given to you for your trip. I am very ill, and don't know if I shall see you again. After my death, I beg you to watch over your nephew as he grows up. Help him to study and pass the prefectural examination, so that he need not be bullied as I have been all my life by my brother."

Wang Teh and Wang Jen accepted the silver, each taking two packets. They thanked Mr. Yen profusely, said all they could to comfort him, then took their leave. From that time onward Mr. Yen sank daily. All his relatives came to ask how he was, his five nephews taking it in turn to help the doctors administer cordials. But after the Mid-Autumn Festival the doctors stopped prescribing medicine, and all the stewards and servants were summoned back from the estates.

For three days Mr. Yen hovered between life and death, too weak to speak. On the evening of the third day an oil lamp was lit on his table, and the room was crowded with relatives. They could hear the beginning of the death-rattle in his throat; but he refused to die. He took his hand from beneath the quilt and stretched out two fingers.

The eldest nephew stepped up to the bed and asked, "Do you mean that there are two relatives who haven't come, uncle?"

Yen shook his head.

The second nephew stepped forward and asked, "Do you mean there are still two lots of silver you haven't told us about, uncle?"

Yen stared hard at him, shook his head even more vehemently, and held out his fingers more earnestly than ever.

The wet-nurse, who was carrying his son, put in, "The master must be thinking of the two uncles who aren't here."

But when he heard this, he closed his eyes and shook his head. Only his fingers did not move.

Then the new wife hastily stepped forward, dabbing at her eyes. "They're all wide of the mark," she said. "I'm the only one who knows what you mean."

But to know what it was, you must read the chapter which follows.

CHAPTER 6

A gentleman's illness confounds his boatmen.
An injured widow accuses her brother-in-law

Lying there at the point of death, Yen Ta-yu stretched out two fingers and refused to breathe his last; and when his nephews and servants made various wild guesses whether he meant two people, two events or two places, he simply shook his head.

But now his wife had stepped forward to say: "I'm the only one who understands you. You're worried because there are two wicks in the lamp—that's a waste of oil. If I take out one wick, it will be all right."

Suiting her actions to her words, she removed one wick. All eyes were fixed on Mr. Yen, who nodded his head, let fall his hand, and breathed his last. Then all the family, great and small, began to wail and prepare for the funeral, placing the coffin in the central hall of the third courtyard.

The next morning servants went through the town announcing the funeral. Yen Chen-hsien, the leader of the clan, came with the other relatives to mourn, and they were kept to a meal and given white linen for mourning. The widow had a brother who worked in a rice shop and a nephew who worked the bellows for a silversmith, and they brought mourning gifts too. Buddhists and Taoists hung up long banners, chanted their scriptures and performed the funeral rites; while the widow and her little son wailed morning and evening before the coffin. All the stewards, menservants and maidservants were in mourning, and the house and gate were draped in white.

Soon the first seven days passed, and Wang Teh and Wang Jen returned from the provincial examination and came to mourn. They stayed for one day. After another three or four days, Senior Licentiate Yen came back too from the provincial capital. All his sons were mourning in their uncle's hall, so Senior Licentiate Yen was sitting alone with his wife after his luggage had been unpacked. He was just going to have a wash, when the wet-nurse from his brother's house came in with a servant carrying a case and a package.

"The widow sends you her greetings on your return, sir," she said. "Since she is in deep mourning, she can't come over to see you. It was our master's last wish that these two changes of clothing and this silver should be given you to remember him by. Please come over soon."

In the case Senior Licentiate Yen found two brand-new sets of silk clothes, and in the package two hundred taels of silver. Very pleased, he immediately asked his wife for eighty cents, which he gave to the nurse, saying: "Convey my thanks to your mistress. I will come over at once."

Then the nurse and the servant left. As he put the clothes and silver away, Senior Licentiate Yen questioned his wife carefully as to what she and their sons had received. When he had made sure that they had all got something, and that this gift was for himself alone, he changed into a mourning cap and white cloth belt and went across to the other house. He called his brother's name before the coffin, wailed a few times without shedding tears and bowed twice. The widow came out in deep mourning to thank him, and called her son to kowtow to his uncle.

"Fate has been cruel to us and cut off his father in the prime of life," she said, shedding tears. "We have no one but you to guide us."

"All men have their allotted span of life, ma'am," replied Yen. "My brother has gone to heaven, but you have a fine son. If you bring him up carefully, what have you to worry about?"

The widow thanked him, and invited him into the library for a meal, sending for the Wang brothers to keep him company. They greeted each other and sat down.

"Your younger brother seemed quite strong," said Wang Teh. "How was it that he died suddenly after one illness? Although we are such near relatives we were unable to see him before he died. We feel most upset about it."

"Even I, his elder brother," retorted Yen, "was unable to see him before his death. But as the proverb says, 'Public business comes before private affairs. The state comes before the family.' Our examinations are a great affair of state, and since we were busy on state business, even if we had to neglect our own relatives we need feel no compunction."

"You were in the provincial capital for more than half a year, weren't you?" asked Wang Teh.

"I was," replied Senior Licentiate Yen. "Commissioner Chou, the last examiner, recommended me for the rank of senior licentiate. He has a relative in this province who used to be magistrate of Chao County, so I went to the provincial capital to pay my respects. We took to each other immediately, and he pressed me to stay for several months. In fact, he insisted on marrying his second daughter to my second son."

"Did you stay in his house in the provincial capital?"

"No, I stayed with Chang Chin-chai. He had been a county magistrate too, and is Magistrate Tang's nephew. I got to know him at a feast in Magistrate Tang's yamen. He arranged the match with the Chou family."

"Didn't he come that year with a certain scholar named Fan Chin?" asked Wang Jen.

"That's the man," said Senior Licentiate Yen.

Wang Jen shot a glance at his brother, and said, "You remember, that was when they had trouble with the Moslems."

Wang Teh gave a sarcastic laugh.

Just then the feast was spread. While eating they began to talk again.

"Magistrate Tang has not been appointed examiner this year," said Wang Teh.

"Don't you realize, brother," said Wang Jen, "it's because last year he passed candidates who wrote essays in an outmoded style? All the examiners this year are young palace graduates, who go in for brilliant compositions."

"I don't know about that," objected Yen. "Even if a man has brilliance, he must still abide by the rules. If he pays no attention to the subject, and simply writes something showy, that can scarcely be called brilliant. My patron Commissioner Chou, for instance, who is most discriminating, always gives candidates who understand the tradition a first class. This year the same sort of men will still come first."

Yen said this because the two brothers had been ranked in the second class by Commissioner Chou. They took the hint, and dropped the subject of the examinations.

When the feast was nearly over, the brothers brought up the question of the lawsuit. "Magistrate Tang was really angry. It was lucky that your brother instead of pressing the issue took steps to settle the matter."

"He made a mistake," said Yen. "If I had been at home, one word from me to Magistrate Tang, and we could have broken the legs of those wretches Wang and Huang. How dare those common people take such liberties with gentlemen?"

"It is always better to be generous," murmured Wang Jen.

Yen's face turned red.

When they had drunk a few more cups together, the nurse came in carrying the boy and said, "The mistress asks Senior Licentiate Yen when the burial should take place. She doesn't know if this is a propitious year. And should our late master be buried among the ancestors or should another site be chosen? She hopes you will discuss it, sir, with these two gentlemen."

"Tell your mistress that I shall not be at home long," replied the senior licentiate. "I have to go back to the provincial capital for my second son's marriage at Mr. Chou's house. All questions connected with the funeral can be decided by these gentlemen. My brother can't be buried among the ancestors, though. You will have to look for another site. But wait till I come back to decide that." This said, he got up, bid them a curt goodbye and went home. The Wang brothers also left.

78

A few days later, Senior Licentiate Yen went with his second son to the provincial capital, and the widow was left in charge of the household. With plenty of money, rice, servants and cattle, she lived in great comfort, little guessing the cruel fate Heaven had in store for her. Very soon her son caught small-pox and ran a fever. The doctor said this was a dangerous disease, and used potent drugs to cure it, but the rash did not come out properly. And though the distracted mother offered prayers at many temples, it was all to no purpose—after one week the plump, white little fellow died. This time she wept more bitterly than at the death of the former wife, more bitterly, too, than at the death of her husband. For three whole days and nights she cried, crying until she had no more tears to shed. And then she buried her son.

She wanted to adopt Senior Licentiate Yen's fifth son, and invited the Wang brothers over to discuss the question. But they hummed and hawed. "We can't make any decision," they said. "Senior Licentiate Yen is not at home. And since it is his son, you should consult his wishes. How can we decide it for him?"

"My late husband had a little property," said the widow. "Now his son is dead, the servants have no master. The question of adopting an heir can't wait; but I don't know how long it will be before Senior Licentiate Yen comes back. The fifth son is not twelve yet, and if I adopt him they can trust me to love him and bring him up properly. When his mother knows what I want, I'm sure she will be glad to give him to me. And even Senior Licentiate Yen when he comes back will have nothing to say. Why can't you gentlemen take charge?"

"Well," said Wang Teh, "we can go over and speak to her."

"How can you suggest such a thing, brother?" protested Wang Jen. "The adoption of a son is an important matter—it can only be settled by the Yen family. However, since Mrs. Yen feels it's so urgent, the best thing we can do is to write a letter which she can get a servant to take post-haste to the provincial capital, urging Senior Licentiate Yen to come back and talk it over."

"That's a good idea," said Wang Teh. "But I don't imagine he will raise any objections when he does get back."

"That remains to be seen, brother." Wang Jen shook his head with a smile. "But that's the only thing for us to do."

The widow was mystified by his manner. However, they wrote a letter putting forward her proposal, and charged one of the family servants, Lai-fu, not to rest day or night on his way to the provincial capital.

Lai-fu travelled post-haste to the capital, and learned that Senior Licentiate Yen was staying in High Base Street. But when he reached the house and saw four attendants in red and black caps in the doorway holding whips, he was too frightened to go in. Presently, however, Yen's servant Ssu Tou came out, and he took Lai-fu in. In the hall there was a decorated sedan-chair, and beside it a canopy inscribed with Senior Licentiate Yen's official rank. Ssu Tou went in and brought back his master, who was wearing a gauze cap, official dress and black shoes with white soles. Lai-fu stepped forward, kowtowed and delivered the letter.

When Yen had read it he said, "I understand. But my second son is getting married today. You can help to wait on the guests."

Lai-fu went down to the kitchen where cooks were preparing the feast. The bridal room on the first floor was decked out in scarlet and green, and he would have liked to see it but he dared not go up.

Right up to sunset, not a single musician had arrived. In his new square cap and red sash, garlanded with flowers, the bridegroom was pacing anxiously up and down, demanding to know what had happened to them.

Yen shouted to Ssu Tou from the hall, "Hurry up and get those trumpeters!"

"Today's an auspicious day," said Ssu Tou. "Lots of people are getting married. Even if you gave the musicians eighty cents of silver they wouldn't come. But you only gave them twenty-four cents, then deducted another two cents, expecting the Chang family to force them to come. The musicians are very busy in other families—how can I get them here?"

"You dog!" roared Senior Licentiate Yen. "Hurry up and fetch them here! If they're late, you'll get a box on the ears."

Ssu Tou scowled and slunk off, grumbling. "He hasn't given us a single bowl of rice since morning, yet he throws his damned weight about."

Dusk fell and lamps had to be lit, but Ssu Tou did not reappear; and the sedan-chair bearers and attendants in red and black caps were impatient to be off.

"We had better not wait for the musicians," said the guests. "The auspicious hour has come. Let's go and fetch the bride."

The four attendants in red and black caps led the way with the canopy, while Lai-fu followed the chairs to the Chou house. The Chou family lived in a great mansion, and although several candles had been lit it was still dark in the courtyard. In the absence of musicians, the four attendants called out to announce their arrival in the dark courtyard. They went on shouting until Lai-fu felt quite embarrassed, and asked them to be quiet.

Someone from the Chou household gave them the order, "Please tell Senior Licentiate Yen that the bride will leave when the musicians come, not before."

There was bawling and brawling until Ssu Tou came back with two musicians—one flute player and one drummer. They struck up feebly in the hall, but were unable to play in harmony, and the bystanders could not stop laughing. The Chou family raised some objections; but there was nothing they could do, and the bride had to be sent off in her chair.

When several days had passed, Senior Licentiate Yen ordered Lai-fu and Ssu Tou to hire two boats manned by boatmen from Kaoyao County to take them home, promising the boatmen twelve taels of silver to be paid on arrival. One boat was for the bride and bridegroom, the other for the senior licentiate. They chose an auspicious day and took leave of their relatives. One pair of golden and another pair of white placards and four spears, all emblems of the yamen, had been borrowed from the former Chao County magistrate and placed on deck, and musicians were hired to pipe them to the boat. The overawed boatmen did their best to please these important passengers, and the journey passed without incident.

The last day of the trip, when they were less than ten miles from Kaoyao, Senior Licentiate Yen suddenly had a spell of faintness. He retched and vomited, while Lai-fu and Ssu Tou took his arms to prevent him from falling.

"I feel ill, I feel ill," he groaned. "Put me down, Ssu Tou, and boil some water."

He flopped down groaning and whimpering, while Ssu Tou and the boatmen hastily boiled water and took it to his cabin. Then the senior licentiate unlocked a case, took out a dozen small walnut wafers, ate a few of them, rubbed his stomach, and immediately felt better. He left a few wafers by the tiller, as if he had no further use for them. The steersman, who happened to have a sweet tooth, went on steering with his left hand while with his right he carried wafer after wafer to his mouth. Yen, however, pretended not to see what he was doing.

Presently their boats moored at Kaoyao wharf. Senior Licentiate Yen told Lai-fu to hire sedan-chairs and escort the young couple home first, while he called dockers to put all their luggage ashore. When the boatmen and dockers came to ask for tips, Yen went back to his cabin and made a show of looking round for something.

"Where has my medicine gone?" he asked Ssu Tou.

"What medicine?"

"That medicine I was eating just now. I put it by the tiller."

"Do you mean those walnut wafers you left by the tiller?" asked the steersman. "I thought you didn't want them, so I finished them up."

"Walnut wafers, indeed!" exclaimed Yen. "Do you know what those wafers were made of?"

"Just melon seeds, walnuts, sugar and flour, I suppose."

"You dog!" roared Yen. "Because I have these fits of dizziness, I spent several hundred taels of silver to buy this medicine. Mr. Chang of the provincial capital bought the ginseng in it for me when he was an official in Shangtang, and Mr. Chou bought the gentian when he was magistrate in Szechuan. You had no business touching it, you scoundrel!

Walnut wafers, indeed! Nearly a hundred taels' worth of medicine have disappeared down your throat! And what am I to take next time I have an attack? You've played me a dirty trick, you dog!"

He ordered Ssu Tou to open his portfolio, so that he could write a note to send this scoundrel to Magistrate Tang's yamen for a good beating.

With a scared, conciliatory smile the steersman said, "It tasted very sweet. I didn't know it was medicine. I thought it was walnut wafers."

"You still call it walnut wafers!" the senior licentiate bellowed. "Call it walnut wafers again· and I'll box your ears!" He had already written the note and now handed it to Ssu Tou who started to hurry ashore. The dockers helped the boatmen to stop him. Both lots of boatmen were scared stiff.

"He was wrong, Your Honour," they said. "He shouldn't have eaten your medicine. But he's a poor man. Even if he sells everything he has, he won't be able to pay you anything like a hundred taels of silver. And if he's sent to court he'll be ruined. Please be generous, sir, and overlook it."

But Senior Licentiate Yen only flew into a worse rage.

Some of the dockers came aboard and said to the boatmen, "You brought this on yourselves. If you hadn't asked the gentleman for tips, he would have gone to his sedan-chair. But once you stopped him, he found out about his medicine. Since you know you're in the wrong, why don't you kowtow and ask Senior Licentiate Yen's pardon? Do you expect him to pay you if you don't make good his loss?"

Then they all forced the steersman to kowtow.

Yen softened a little, and said, "Very well. Since you've all pleaded for him, and I am busy with my son's wedding, I shall deal with this scoundrel later. He needn't think he can get away." After more curses he swaggered to his sedan-chair, followed by the servants and luggage. He left the boatmen gaping—for he had gone off without paying for the trip.

Once home, Yen ordered his son and daughter-in-law to worship the ancestors, and called his wife out so that they might bow to her. His wife was causing a fine commotion, moving furniture.

"What are you doing?" Yen asked.

"You seem to have forgotten how small this house is," she retorted. "There's only one decent room in it. Since the new daughter-in-law comes from a good family, we must give her the best room."

"Rubbish!" said her husband. "I've got it all worked out. There's no need to turn things upside-down like this. My brother's house is big enough—they can stay there."

"It may be big, but what makes you think your son can move in?"

"Since that woman has no son living, one of our sons should inherit my brother's property."

"Yes, but it's our fifth son she wants."

"What right has she to decide?" demanded Yen. "Who does she think she is? I'm appointing an heir to my brother. It has nothing to do with her."

While his wife was still wondering what he meant, one of the widow's servants came to say, "Our mistress has heard that you are back, and invites you to go over for a discussion. The two Wang gentlemen are also there."

Senior Licentiate Yen accordingly walked over. After exchanging polite platitudes with Wang Teh and Wang Jen, he summoned the servants and ordered them to clean out the main suite, because the next day his second son would be moving in with his bride. When the widow heard that, she thought that he wanted her to adopt the second son.

She called in the Wang brothers and asked, "What did he say? When the daughter-in-law comes, she should stay in the back rooms while I stay in the front ones. In that way I can look after them better. Why should I move to the back? It's unheard of that a daughter-in-law should live in the best rooms, while her mother-in-law lives in the back."

"Don't get upset," said Wang Jen. "Let him say what he likes. Of course you have to be consulted."

They rejoined Yen, and after a little more conversation and a cup of tea, their servant came in to tell them that classmates were waiting for them to go to a literary meeting. Then they took their leave.

When Senior Licentiate Yen had seen them off, he sat down, summoned the dozen or so stewards and proceeded to issue orders. "My second son is coming here tomorrow as your former master's heir," he told them. "He will be your new master, and you must serve him well. Since Concubine Chao has no children, he will treat her as his father's concubine, and she has no right to stay in the front rooms. So tell the maidservants to sweep out the back rooms and move her things over, and clear the front rooms for your new master. Concubine Chao must keep her place. The new master will call her 'new wife,' and she should call him 'master' and his wife 'mistress.' In a day or so, when my daughter-in-law comes, Concubine Chao should pay her respects first, and then my son will greet her. We upper-class families have to observe such etiquette scrupulously. As for your accounts for the fields, houses and money in your care, you must bring them up to date at once, and I will check them before passing them on to my son. You'll find things very different from what they were under your old master, who left everything to his concubine and let you get away with anything. Anyone who tries to deceive me will get thirty strokes and be sent to Magistrate Tang's yamen and forced to pay up."

Promising to obey him, the stewards withdrew; and Yen went back to his own house.

Acting on Senior Licentiate Yen's orders, the stewards went to the widow's rooms to move out her belongings. She cursed them so roundly that they dared not touch a thing. But because they had all along resented the airs she gave herself, they now banded together to say, "How dare we disobey the master's orders? For, after all, he is the rightful master. If he becomes angry, what shall we do?"

Calling upon Heaven, the widow wept and stormed. She made a scene that lasted all night.

The next morning she took a sedan-chair to the yamen. Magistrate Tang was holding court, and she laid her case before him. After asking her for a written statement, the magistrate decreed that the matter should be decided by the clan.

Then the widow invited Yen Chen-hsien, the clan leader, and all the other relatives to a feast. But of all the local gentry,

Yen Chen-hsien feared Senior Licentiate Yen most, and all he would say was, "I may be clan leader, but this matter concerns the close relatives only, not the whole clan. That's all I can say to the magistrate."

As for Wang Teh and Wang Jen, they sat there like wooden figures, and would not express any opinion.

The widow's brother, the rice-merchant, and the nephew who worked for a silversmith had never been in such high society before. Each time they opened their mouths to speak, Yen glared at them so ferociously that they dared not utter a word. Besides, they were telling themselves, "She always thought so highly of those Wang brothers, and treated us like dirt. Why should we offend Senior Licentiate Yen for her sake? Only fools catch flies on a tiger's head. Much better say nothing and offend nobody."

All this made the widow behind the screen as frantic as an ant on a hot furnace. And when she saw that nobody was going to speak up for her, she started to reproach Yen from behind the screen, bringing up old grievances, crying, abusing him, stamping her feet, beating her breast, and raising a great uproar.

Yen lost his temper. "It's obvious that this shrew comes from a low family," he growled. "What upper-class person would behave like this? If she provokes me any more, I'm going to seize her by the hair, give her a good beating, and then ask a go-between to take her away and marry her off."

The widow's storming and sobbing could have been heard half way up the sky. She wanted to rush out to scratch and claw at Yen, and it took several maidservants to restrain her. When the others saw the ugly turn things were taking, they hurried the senior licentiate home.

The next day, the clan head and the others met to discuss what reply they should send to the county magistrate. Wang Teh and Wang Jen declared that as scholars they could take no part in any lawsuit, and the clan head wrote a non-committal statement to the effect that although the widow had indeed been a concubine, she had been made the second wife. However, it was also true that Senior Licentiate Yen felt it would be wrong for his son to acknowledge her as stepmother. In any event, it was up to the magistrate to make a decision.

Now Magistrate Tang happened to be the son of a concubine, and when he read the statement he thought, "Laws are one thing, but the human factor has to be taken into account too. And this Senior Licentiate Yen is a nuisance." He decreed, "Since the widow was made a wife, she should not be considered as a concubine. If Senior Licentiate Yen does not wish his son to be adopted, she may choose somebody else to adopt."

When Yen read this decree, he nearly went up in smoke. He straightway sent a petition to the prefectural government. But the prefect had concubines too, and he felt that the senior licentiate was causing unnecessary trouble. Having asked the Kaoyao yamen for details of the case, he issued a decree endorsing Magistrate Tang's decision.

Yen was furious. He appealed to the provincial commissioner of justice. But the provincial commissioner of justice ruled, "This is a trivial matter which should be settled by the prefect and the county magistrate."

Balked at every turn, Yen did not know how to save his face. Then it occurred to him, "Commissioner Chou belongs to the same clan as my daughter-in-law." He decided to go to the capital and beg Commissioner Chou to file a petition there, in order that he might have his rights.

But to know whether Senior Licentiate Yen was successful or not, you must read the next chapter.

CHAPTER 7

Examiner Fan examines the list of candidates
to repay his patron's kindness. Secretary Wang in the
Ministry of Works shows kindness to a friend

When Senior Licentiate Yen lost his case in the county and prefectural courts and the provincial commissioner of justice ignored his petition, he travelled post-haste to the capital, deciding to claim relationship with Commissioner Chou, in the hope that the latter would plead his case for him. Arrived at the capital, Yen found that Commissioner Chou had been promoted to the post of vice-president of the Imperial College; but he boldly sent in his card, claiming kinship.

When the card was presented, Vice-President Chou was puzzled, for he was unable to remember any such relative. While he was considering the question, his attendant brought in another card with the name Fan Chin on it, unadorned by any title. Chou Chin remembered that this was the student he had examined in Kwangtung, who had now passed the provincial examination and come to the capital for the final test.

"Show him in!" he ordered.

Pouring out respectful greetings as he entered, Fan Chin kowtowed again and again. The vice-president raised him up and asked him to be seated. His first question was:

"Do you know a Senior Licentiate Yen in your county? Just now he sent in a card, professing to be my relative. He told my man that he was a Cantonese, but I have no such relative."

"I saw him just now," said Fan Chin. "He is from Kaoyao County, and is related to a Mr. Chou there. I don't know whether Your Excellency belongs to the same Chou family."

"Although we have the same surname, we are not related; so this senior licentiate can be no relative of mine," declared Chou Chin. He called in his servant and ordered: "Tell Senior Licentiate Yen that I am busy with public affairs, and it is not convenient to see him. Give him back his card."

When the servant had left, Vice-President Chou said, "I saw from the Kwangtung list that you had distinguished yourself in the provincial examination there; so I have been looking forward to your arrival at the capital. How is it you delayed so long?"

Fan Chin told him about the death of his mother.

Unable to suppress a sigh, Vice-President Chou said, "Your scholarship is profound. Even if you have been delayed for a few years, you will certainly pass the metropolitan examination now. Besides, I have recommended you frequently to influential officials, and they are all eager to have you as their pupil. Just stay quietly in your lodgings to review your books thoroughly. If you are short of money, I shall be glad to help you."

"I shall never forget your great kindness," said Fan Chin.

After they had talked for some time the vice-president entertained Fan Chin to dinner, and then he took his leave.

When the results of the metropolitan examination came out, Fan Chin had indeed passed. He was given an official post as censor, and a few years later was made commissioner of education for Shantung. On the day that this decree was issued, he went to see Vice-President Chou.

"Although Shantung is my native place, I have no commissions to trouble you with," said Chou Chin. "I remember, though, that when I was teaching in Hsueh Market there was a pupil there called Hsun Mei. He was just seven at that time, but after all these years he must have grown up. He comes of a farmer's family, and I don't know if he has completed his studies; but if he takes the examination, I hope you will read his paper carefully. And if he shows any talent at all, I should be very much obliged if you would let him pass."

Fan Chin bore this in mind when he went to Shantung. But he had been supervising examinations for six months or more before he went to Yenchow Prefecture, where three temporary buildings had been put up for the prefectural examination; and Vice-President Chou's request slipped his mind. He remembered it only the night before the results were to be published.

"What could have come over me?" he thought. "My patron asked me to look out for Hsun Mei in Wenshang County; but I have done nothing about it! This is dreadful!"

In a flurry, he looked through the list of scholars who had taken the preliminary test for the provincial examination; but Hsun Mei's name was not there. Then he asked his secretaries for the list of those who had failed in the prefectural examination, and carefully checked their names and cell numbers. Fan Chin looked through more than six hundred papers, but could not find one by Hsun Mei. He was very worried.

"Is it possible he didn't sit for the examination?" he wondered. "But if he did sit for it, how dare I face my patron in future? I must make another careful search, even if it means postponing the results."

At a feast with his secretaries, he was so worried that he infected them with his own uneasiness.

"Sir," said a young secretary called Chu Chin-yu, "this reminds me of a story. Several years ago, an old scholar was appointed commissioner for Szechuan. One day he was feasting with Mr. Ho Ching-ming, when Mr. Ho got drunk and shouted, 'In Szechuan, essays like Su Shih's[1] only deserve the sixth rank!' The old gentleman made a mental note of this; and three years later, when he left Szechuan and met Mr. Ho again, he told him, 'I have been in Szechuan for three years, and checked the papers extremely carefully, but I did not find one by Su Shih. He can't have entered.'" Laughing up his sleeve, the young man continued, "In what connection did the vice-president bring up Hsun Mei's name, sir?"

---

[1] Su Shih is the other name of the famous eleventh century poet Su Tung-po. A scholar should have known this name.

Commissioner Fan was too simple to realize that he was being made a fool of. With a worried frown, he said, "Since Su Shih's essays were no good, it did not matter if he was not found. But Vice-President Chou wants me to help this Hsun Mei; and if I can't find him it will be rather embarrassing."

At that, Niu Pu-yi, an old secretary, suggested, "If he is from Wenshang County, why not look through the records of the dozen or so who have already passed the prefectural examination? If he has talent, he may have passed some days ago."

"Quite right! Quite right!" said the commissioner. Hastily checking through the entries, he found that the first name on the list was Hsun Mei; and his face lit up in a smile as the anxiety he had felt all day vanished.

The next morning, having graded the scholars who took the preliminary test for the provincial examination, he issued the results and despatched the first, second and third ranks of candidates for the provincial examination. The first on the list of the fourth rank was Mei Chiu, who knelt down while the examiner read his essay.

"Literary composition is a scholar's chief duty," said Fan Chin angrily. "How could you write such rubbish? Obviously you must be a troublesome busybody, neglecting your proper vocation. I ought to place you last; but I will be lenient and simply punish you with the rod according to the rule."

"I was unwell that day, sir," said Mei Chiu. "That is why my writing was confused. I beg Your Excellency to overlook it!"

"This is the order of the Imperial Court, which I cannot change. Attendants! Drag him to the bench, and punish him according to the rule!"

As the examiner's attendants were dragging Mei Chiu away to be beaten, the desperate candidate pleaded, "Sir! Have pity for my patron's sake."

"Who was your patron?"

"The present Vice-President of the Imperial College, Chou Chin."

"So you were Vice-President Chou's student? In that case, I will let you off this once." And Fan Chin ordered his attendants to free Mei Chiu.

Then Mei Chiu knelt down, while the examiner admonished him: "Since you are Vice-President Chou's student, there is all the more reason you should study hard; for when you produce a composition like this, you certainly disgrace his reputation. In future, mend your ways. If I find you writing like this at the next examination, I shall not pardon you again." He then told the attendants to drive Mei Chiu away.

Now the examiner came to the new scholars, and the first name he called from Wenshang County was that of Hsun Mei. A handsome young man answered from the crowd, and when he came forward the examiner asked him:

"Are you related to Mei Chiu who was here just now?"

Hsun Mei did not understand, and made no reply.

"Were you Vice-President Chou's student?" asked the examiner.

"Yes, he was my teacher at primary school."

"I was also Vice-President Chou's student," said Examiner Fan, "and when I left the capital he asked me to look out for your paper. I did not expect that without any help you would come first on the list. You are young and brilliant, and my patron did not teach you in vain. Go on studying hard, and you have a fine future before you."

Hsun Mei knelt down and thanked him.

When he had disposed of the other papers and sent off the new scholars to the accompaniment of gongs and trumpets, Commissioner Fan closed the session and shut the doors.

As Hsun Mei was leaving the examination school, he saw Mei Chiu standing by the door and could not resist asking: "When did you study with Vice-President Chou, Mr. Mei?"

"How would a youngster like you know?" retorted Mei. "It was before you were born. In those days he used to teach in the city and was employed as a tutor in the family of various yamen officials; it was only later that he came to our village. But by the time you went to school, I had already passed the examination, so you did not know about our relationship. I was always a favourite with my patron, who said that my compositions showed genius although they were unconventional; and, since this is exactly the same criticism that Commissioner Fan made just now, it shows that discriminating examiners have exactly the same criterion. You know, Commissioner Fan might easily have put me in the third rank; but, in that case, he would have had no chance to speak to me. He deliberately ranked me lower, in order that he could talk to me and mention his relationship to my patron to show that he was doing me a special favour. It was for the same reason that he placed you first. We scholars should appreciate these niceties of behaviour." After talking for some time, they went back to their rooms.

The next day, having seen Commissioner Fan off and hired horses, they returned to Hsueh Market together. The young man bowed to his mother, who was alone at home now that his father had died. She was a happy woman that day.

"Since your father died, times have been hard and we have had to sell most of our land," she said. "But now that you have passed the examination and become a scholar, you will be able to support the family by teaching."

Shen Hsiang-fu was old now, and could not walk without a stick; but he, too, hobbled over to congratulate them and arranged with Mei Chiu to collect money from the villagers to celebrate Hsun Mei's success. They collected two dozen strings of cash and borrowed the Buddhist temple for the feast.

Mei Chiu and Hsun Mei arrived first at the temple on the morning of the feast, and were greeted by the monk. They bowed before Buddha and nodded to the monk, who said, "Congratulations, Mr. Hsun, on becoming a scholar! This is a reward for all the good deeds your worthy father did to the glory of Buddha. You were just a child, with your hair in tufts, when you studied here."

He pointed out to them the shrine which the villagers had set up for Vice-President Chou. There were incense-burners and candlesticks on the table, and above it a memorial tablet on which was written in letters of gold an account of the vice-president's career. This had been presented by the villagers and the monk. When they saw their patron's shrine, the two scholars bowed reverently before it several times. Then they went with the monk to the rooms behind, where Chou Chin had

93

taught. The double door was open, overlooking the river. Several feet of the opposite bank had been washed away, while this side had grown out a little. The three back rooms had been separated from the rest by matting, and were no longer used as a school. The room on the left was occupied by a man from Kiangsi, on whose door was written Chen Ho-fu, fortune-teller. Mr. Chen was out, however, and his door was locked.

On the central wall of the hall were still pasted two scrolls in Chou Chin's writing: "Purge yourself of error to await the right season," and "Watch yourself and practise strict discipline." But the red paper had faded.

Pointing to these scrolls, Mei Chiu told the monk, "Since this is the vice-president's calligraphy, you shouldn't leave it here. Sprinkle the scrolls with water, so that you can take them down and have them remounted. You must preserve them."

The monk immediately did as he was directed, soon after which Shen Hsiang-fu arrived with the villagers to feast for a whole day.

Mrs. Hsun used a few dozen of the strings of cash presented to them to redeem some articles she had pawned and to buy several piculs of rice. The remainder was kept for Hsun Mei's travelling expenses when he took the next examination.

Next year he came first in the preliminary test for the provincial examination—truly brilliance shows itself in youth! Then, having passed the provincial examination with distinction, he went to the office of the provincial commissioner of finance and took his share of caps, plates, canopies, banners, wooden placards and travelling expenses. After that, without further delay, he went to the examination at the capital, and in this examination he won the third place.

According to Ming Dynasty regulations, a special seat was set in the room of a successful candidate, who sat down while attendants bowed to him. While this ceremony was being performed, it was announced, "Mr. Wang Hui, a fellow graduate from Wenshang County, has come to greet Mr. Hsun."

Ordering the attendants to remove the seat, Hsun Mei went out to greet the guest.

A white-haired, white-bearded man came in, took Hsun Mei by the hand, and said, "Our friendship was ordained by Heaven. We are not ordinary classmates."

When they had bowed to each other and sat down, Wang Hui went on, "I had a dream about you long ago, which shows that our fortunes were determined by fate. In future, let us work together and help each other."

Hsun Mei dimly recollected hearing something about this dream when he was a child; thus, as soon as Wang Hui mentioned it, he understood.

"Young as I am, I am most fortunate to be on the same list as you, sir," he said. "Since we are from the same county, I shall always come to you for advice in future."

"Are these your lodgings?"

"Yes."

"They are small and far from the court; it cannot be very convenient for you to live here. I am quite comfortably off, and I have bought a house in the capital. Why not come and stay with me? It will be more convenient for the palace examination." After chatting a little longer, Wang Hui left.

The next day, accordingly, Wang Hui sent men to move Hsun Mei's luggage to his house in Sticky Rice Lane, and they stayed together. At the palace examination, Hsun Mei was placed in the second rank, and Wang Hui in the third. Both of them were made assistant secretaries of the Board of Works, and appointed second-class secretaries when they had served their turn.

One day the two friends were sitting chatting when the servant brought in a red folder on which was written: "Your servant Chen Ho-fu pays his respects." Inside the folder was another note: "Chen Ho-fu of Nanchang County in Kiangsi is adept in consulting oracles and in divination, having practised in Kuanyin Temple at Hsueh Market in Wenshang County."

"Do you know this man?" Wang asked Hsun Mei.

"I remember there was such a man, who was said to be very successful in consulting oracles. Why not have him in to ask about our future careers?" So he called out: "Come in!"

The man who walked in wore a tile-shaped cap, a raw silk gown and a silk girdle, had a grey beard and looked over fifty. Bowing to the two scholars, he said: "I beg you gentlemen to be seated so that I can pay my respects."

Wang and Hsun declined, however, and bowed to him, then made him sit in the seat of honour.

"When you stayed in Kuanyin Temple in my humble district," said Hsun Mei, "I did not have the good fortune to meet you."

"I knew that you had come to the temple, sir," rejoined Chen Ho-fu with a bow. "Three days before, the Taoist saint Lu Chun-yang had made known to me in a séance that after noon on that day a noble man would arrive. But since you had not then received news of your promotion and the will of Heaven must not be disclosed, I deliberately avoided meeting you."

"May I ask who taught you to call up spirits?" inquired Wang Hui. "Can you call up Lu Chun-yang only, or other saints as well?"

"I can call up all spirits," replied Chen Ho-fu. "Emperors, generals, ministers, sages or gallants all come at my call. Frankly, gentlemen, for many years now I have not been roaming the country but living in the mansions of princes and the yamens of high officials. In the thirteenth year of Hung Chih I conducted a séance for Mr. Liu, Minister of the Board of Works, who wanted to ask the oracle what would be the fate of Minister Li Meng-yang who had been imprisoned for impeaching Lord Chang. To our amazement it was the Duke of Chou who appeared and wrote: 'In seven days the cycle will be complete.' Sure enough, on the seventh day, Minister Li was released, his only punishment being the deduction of three months' salary. Later Minister Li asked me to hold another séance; but for a long time the brush did not move. Then suddenly it started swinging wildly to write a poem, the concluding couplet of which ran:

I dreamed that I went south to visit my ancestral temple;
But who was there from the former capital?

"The gentlemen who were looking on did not know what spirit this was: only Minister Li understood the poem. He hastily burnt incense and prostrated himself to ask what great emperor was addressing him. Then as quick as lightning the brush wrote: 'Emperor Chien Wen.' They all dropped fearfully to their knees to prostrate themselves. That is why I say I can call up emperors and sages alike."

"With your great skill," said Wang Hui, "I wonder if you can tell us the various posts we are going to hold for the rest of our lives?"

"Certainly," replied Chen. "Future riches, rank, trials and penury or the span of a man's life can all be discovered from the oracles, whose predictions invariably come true."

Since he spoke so confidently, the two scholars said: "We would like to ask what our subsequent appointments are likely to be."

"Then let me ask you to burn incense, gentlemen."

"Wait a little," they said. "We must eat first."

They entertained Chen Ho-fu to a meal, while they told a servant to go to his lodgings to fetch the sand tray and oracle's brush.

"You must pray silently, gentlemen," Chen instructed them, then set up the brush above the disk. When he had prostrated himself and burnt a magic formula to invoke the oracle, he asked Wang Hui and Hsun Mei to support the brush. He then uttered an incantation and burnt another magic formula to beg the spirit to draw near; and at that the brush began to sway slightly. Chen Ho-fu told the servant to pour a cup of tea, and knelt to present this with both hands to the spirit. At that the brush described several circles, then stopped moving. Chen Ho-fu burnt another magic formula and ordered them all to be absolutely quiet, sending the servant and relatives out of the room.

After the time it takes for a meal, the brush began to move again and wrote: "Let Mr. Wang mark our pronouncement."

Wang Hui promptly let go of the brush and plumped down to kowtow four times, after which he asked: "May I inquire the great spirit's honourable name?" He then returned to hold the brush again.

The brush moved rapidly to trace the words: "I am Lord Kuan Yu, Conqueror of the Devils."

Chen Ho-fu was so overawed that he kowtowed as fast as a pestle pounding onions.

"Because of your sincerity today, we have been able to call up this mighty spirit," he told the two scholars. "That is not easy! You two gentlemen are in luck! But you must show great respect, for if there is the least negligence I don't know how I shall answer for it!"

The two scholars were also so overwhelmed with awe that their hair was standing on end. They let go of the brush to prostrate themselves four times before resuming their posts.

"Wait a moment!" said Chen Ho-fu. "This sand tray is small, and a great spirit like this may have lengthy injunctions which won't fit on it. Give me a sheet of paper to make a note of all that is written." Paper and brush were brought to Chen Ho-fu, while the other two went on supporting the brush, which wrote in a flash:

> *You are to be congratulated on achieving Hsia Dynasty rank and plucking red blossoms on high.*
>
> *There are misty waves on the river during your two days at the office.*
>
> *The horses leading the way turn out to be ministers of the celestial court.*
>
> *Meeting lutes and lyres, your heart aches at one cup of wine!*

After this, another sentence was added: "Set to the tune of 'Moonlight on the Western River.'" The three men could not make head or tail of this.

"The first sentence is the only one I understand," said Wang. "The Hsia Dynasty students took the examinations at the age of fifty, and I have just passed at fifty too.[1] That is right. As for what follows, I don't understand a word of it."

"The oracle never lies," said Chen Ho-fu. "If you keep this, its truth will be proved miraculously later. That line about ministers of the celestial court must mean that you will be promoted to the rank of prime minister."

Only too eager to believe this, Wang Hui felt overjoyed. Then Hsun Mei prostrated himself to ask for a message from

---

[1] Wang has made a blunder. The allusion to the Hsia Dynasty, taken from Mencius, referred to something quite different.

the oracle. For a long time the brush did not budge, and when they pleaded urgently for an answer it wrote: "Stop." Chen Ho-fu smoothed the sand on the tray to receive another message, but again the word "Stop" was written. He smoothed the sand three times, only to receive the same answer each time; after which the brush ceased moving altogether.

"The spirit must have returned to heaven," said Chen Ho-fu. "We must not trouble it any more." He then burnt another magic formula in farewell, packed up the brush, the incense-burner and the sand tray, and sat down with them again. And when the two scholars had presented him with half a tael of silver and a letter of introduction to the newly appointed Commissioner Fan, Chen Ho-fu thanked them and left.

That evening an attendant announced: "Someone has come from Mr. Hsun's family."

A Hsun family servant in mourning rushed in and kowtowed. "The old lady passed away on the twenty-first of last month," he reported, kneeling.

When Hsun Mei heard this he uttered a cry and fell to the ground, and Wang Hui had the greatest difficulty in reviving him.

Hsun Mei was about to send in a petition asking to go home for the period of mourning, when Wang said: "Think it over. It will soon be time for the appointment of officers, and we both stand a good chance; but if you announce your mourning you will have to go home and wait for another three years. Wouldn't that be a pity? Better hush this up until after the appointment."

"You are a real friend," said Hsun. "But I don't see how this can be hidden."

"Quickly order the man from your home to take off his mourning, and forbid him to let outsiders know of this. Tomorrow morning I will see what I can do."

Early the next morning they invited Chin Tung-yeh, the clerk who kept the records in the Board of Civil Office to come over and discuss the matter with them.

"Officials must not try to conceal their mourning," Chin told them. "Only if you are a key man in an important office can you suspend your mourning and remain at your post. But even then you have to be recommended by high-ranking officials—*we* are in no position to do anything. Of course, if such a recommendation comes, I shall do what I can for you. That goes without saying."

When they had begged Chin to do all he could, he left.

That evening Hsun Mei changed into a blue gown and a small cap, and went secretly to beg his two teachers, Vice-President Chou and Examiner Fan, to recommend him; and they both thought this might be arranged. After two or three days, however, their replies came: "Your official rank is too low for this. Permission to suspend mourning and remain at one's post is ordinarily granted only to a prime minister or some other very high officials. An officer holding an important frontier post may also be considered. But the post of second secretary of the Board of Works is a sinecure which makes any such recommendation difficult."

So there was nothing for it but for Hsun Mei to send in a petition to go home for the period of mourning.

"This funeral is going to cost money," said Wang, "and you are only a poor scholar. How will you manage it? Besides, I can see that you don't like dealing with such troublesome affairs. The best thing would be for me to take a holiday too, and go back with you. I will find the few hundred taels you need for the funeral."

"In my case it can't be helped; but why should I delay you too?"

"The appointments won't be made until next year," said Wang. "But since you must wait until you are out of mourning, you will have to miss your chance. In my case I can ask for leave for three or at the most six months, and still get back in time."

Hsun Mei could not refuse. Together they went home and arranged Mrs. Hsun's funeral. For seven days all the district and provincial officials came to offer their condolences, and the whole place was in a hubbub: men and women came from miles around to see the funeral. Shen Hsiang-fu was dead, but his son Shen Wen-chin had become village head in place of his father-in-law, Village Head Hsia; and he now offered his services to Hsun Mei. The funeral lasted two hectic months, after which Wang Hui, having lent Hsun Mei more than a thousand taels of silver, said goodbye and set out for the capital. Thanking him again and again, Hsun Mei saw him off to the boundary of the county.

Wang Hui reached the capital without adventure, and reported his return. Soon a servant came in with a messenger carrying a congratulatory announcement.

But to know what good news Wang Hui received, you must read the following chapter.

CHAPTER 8

In which Wang Hui meets a friend in need,
and the Lou brothers come upon a poor acquaintance

.Wang Hui had just come back to the capital and reported
his return when his servant brought in the messenger with the
congratulatory announcement.

"What good news is this?" asked Wang.

The messenger kowtowed and presented the announcement,
on which was written: "The provincial governor of Kiangsi
reports that an officer is needed for the prefecture of Nanchang.
This is an important post for which an able man is required;
and Wang Hui, junior secretary of the Board of Works, is
hereby appointed prefect of Nanchang."

When Wang Hui had rewarded the messenger with food and
drink and bowed before the announcement to express his
gratitude to the emperor, he packed his baggage and set out for
Kiangsi to take up his post. After some days he reached Nanchang, the provincial capital of Kiangsi, where old Prefect
Chu from Chiahsing in Chekiang had handed in his resignation
on the grounds of old age and ill health and moved out of the
yamen, leaving all business in the hands of the assistant sub-
prefect.

˙When Wang Hui arrived, all the subordinate officials paid
their respects, after which Prefect Chu called on him and Wang
returned his call. Because there were a few points in connection with the transfer on which they had not reached full

agreement, Prefect Wang would not take over at once. One day, however, Prefect Chu sent a servant to say:

"Besides being old and infirm, our master is rather deaf. He ought to come in person to receive your instructions as to the transfer; but, as it is, he will send his son here tomorrow in his place. He hopes you will help him in all the arrangements, sir."

Wang Hui agreed to this and prepared a feast in the yamen for Prefect Chu's son. Just after breakfast the next day a small sedan-chair arrived and a red card was handed in with the name Chu Chin-yu on it. Opening his door to invite him in, Wang Hui saw that his visitor was handsome, distinguished and well-bred. They exchanged greetings and sat down.

"It gave me great pleasure to meet your illustrious father," said Wang. "I am sorry to hear today that he is not well."

"My father is old and consumptive, so that he cannot stand any strain; and his hearing is impaired. I appreciate your concern, sir."

"Not at all. May I ask your honourable age?"

"I am thirty-seven."

"And have you always remained with your father?"

"When my father was a district magistrate I was still young. I studied in Shantung with the examiner, Mr. Fan, whom I helped to look through the examination papers; but for some years now—ever since my father was promoted to Nanchang and needed someone to help him—I have been with him here."

"Your father is still in his prime: why should he be so eager to retire?"

"My father maintains that officialdom is a stormy sea, which it is hard to endure for long. Moreover, at the time he passed the first examination he already had a small estate which will provide us with a frugal living, while the humble home of our ancestors suffices to keep out wind and rain; and for diversions he has music and gardening, as well as a few favourite haunts where he can while away the time. So in the press of public affairs he has always longed for a life of seclusion; and now he can realize his wish."

"The proverb says: Don't consult your son on the question of retirement. However, now that I see how high-minded you are, I don't wonder that your father can retire without regret. Soon," added Wang with a laugh, "when you pass the higher examinations, your father will enjoy his retirement even more."

"Human worth does not depend upon official position, sir," replied Chu Chin-yu. "My only wish is for my father to return home as soon as possible, so that I can study to please him. For I count this the greatest happiness a man can have."

"Admirable, indeed!" exclaimed Wang Hui.

Tea had been served three times and they now took off their outer gowns and sat down to discuss the transfer. Chu saw that Prefect Wang appeared to hesitate.

"You need have no misgivings, sir," he said. "During his period of office here my father has dressed plainly and eaten frugally like an ordinary scholar, so that he has saved about two thousand taels of silver. If you find an insufficiency of grain, horses or other supplies, please use this sum to make good the shortage. For my father knows that after serving for several years in the capital you cannot be wealthy; and he does not want to put you to any inconvenience."

Wang Hui was delighted to find him so generous and agreeable.

Presently the feast was served and they took their seats at the table. Then Prefect Wang asked slowly: "What are the special features of this district? What can one make out of the lawsuits here?"

"The people of Nanchang are a rough lot, quite lacking in finesse. As for the local lawsuits, my father paid little attention to them but let the district magistrates settle all disputes which did not involve important ethical issues, such as marriage and property; for he wanted the people to enjoy peace and quiet. Since my father never looked for profit, I cannot tell you whether there is any or not. Asking me about it is like asking the way from a blind man."

With a laugh, Prefect Wang rejoined: "It shows that the old saying 'Three years of good government—one hundred thousand taels of silver' is not always true."

Chu Chin-yu had drunk a few cups of wine and now, seeing how mercenary the new prefect was, he said: "There was little to commend during my father's term of office; but while he was prefect there were few lawsuits and fewer sentences passed; thus his secretaries could do pretty well as they pleased. I remember the former judicial commissioner telling my father that in his yamen three sounds only could be heard."

"What three sounds?"

"The reciting of poetry, the moving of chess-pieces, and the singing of operas."

"Very interesting, upon my word!"

Wang Hui let out a bellow of laughter.

"No doubt, sir, when you start to carry out reforms, three different sounds will be heard."

"What three sounds?"

"The clang of a balance, the rattle of an abacus, and the thud of bamboo rods."

Wang Hui answered solemnly, not realizing that the other was being sarcastic:

"Yes, as servants of the emperor, I suppose we should take our responsibilities seriously."

Chu Chin-yu was a good drinker and so was Prefect Wang. They drank toast after toast to each other, feasting until sunset. Then, when all questions in connection with the transfer had been settled and Prefect Wang had promised to take over, Chu Chin-yu took his leave.

A few days later, sure enough, Prefect Chu sent a sum of money to Prefect Wang, who drew up a statement of transfer for him. Then Prefect Chu with his son and family set out on a boat half filled with books and paintings for Chiahsing.

Prefect Wang had escorted them outside the city. On his return he did as Chu Chin-yu had foreseen and procured an outsize balance. Then he called in all his subordinates to examine them about possible spoils, not allowing them to conceal anything, so that all squeeze should come to him; and he checked on them every few days. The big bamboos were now in constant use. Wang Hui had these bamboos taken to his own quarters to be weighed and, when he found that one was considerably lighter than the other, he put secret marks on them. Thereafter, when he presided in court and ordered a culprit to be beaten with the big bamboo, if the lighter one was taken he knew that his men had been bribed and had the offenders beaten with the heavy one. Court runners and common people alike were beaten within an inch of their lives, until everyone in the city knew that this new prefect was a holy terror and feared him even in their dreams! And of course, when his superiors knew this, they declared that Wang Hui was the ablest officer in Kiangsi. In little more than two years he was praised on all sides.

Just at this time, Prince Ning revolted in Kiangsi, martial law was proclaimed, and the government promoted Wang Hui to the post of intendant of the Nankan Circuit, in charge of military supplies. As soon as he received this urgent appointment, he proceeded post-haste to Nankan.

Soon after his arrival, he set out in a high carriage drawn by four horses on a tour of inspection of the various stations, travelling by day and resting by night. One evening he put up in the public hostel, an old mansion which had belonged to a rich family. When he went in he saw a placard hanging in the hall, pasted with a strip of red paper on which was written, "The horses lead the way." At sight of this, he gave a start; but he took his seat in the hall while his subordinates and runners paid their respects to him, then he had the gate closed and took a meal. Suddenly a wind sprang up and the red paper was blown to the ground, revealing the words underneath on the placard. There, written in gold on a green background, were the characters "Ministers in the celestial court." Amazed, Wang realized that the oracle was true and that the two "days" in the sentence "Two days at the office," made the character *chang* in Nanchang. It was clear that everything was predestined. After he had despatched his business, he returned to his yamen.

The next year, when Prince Ning defeated the imperial troops at Nankan, the common people opened the city gates and fled for their lives. Powerless to resist, Intendant Wang hired a small boat and made off at dead of night; but in the middle of the Yangtse he was confronted by a hundred of Prince Ning's war vessels, packed with soldiers in shining armour. Millions of torches in this fleet lit up Wang's little boat and an order was issued for its capture. Then scores of soldiers leapt aboard, discovered Wang Hui in the cabin, tied his hands behind his back and bundled him aboard their flagship. Some of his attendants and boatmen were cut down; while the rest, to escape being put to the sword, jumped overboard and were drowned.

When Wang Hui, trembling with fear, saw Prince Ning sitting above him in the glare of many torches, he dared not raise his head; but Prince Ning hastily stepped down and with his own hands untied Wang's bonds, then ordered clothes to be brought for him.

"Acting on secret orders from the emperor's mother," said the prince, "I have raised troops to kill the traitors by the emperor's side. Since you are one of the ablest officers in Kiangsi, if you surrender I will have you promoted."

Still trembling, Wang Hui kowtowed and said: "I surrender gladly."

"In that case," said the prince, "let me offer you a cup of wine."

By this time Wang had a pain in his chest as a result of being bound. He received the wine kneeling, drained it at one gulp, then felt better and kowtowed again in thanks. Prince Ning appointed him judicial commissioner of Kiangsi; hence he had to accompany the rebel army.

When Wang Hui heard some of the rebels say that Prince Ning was the eighth son in the royal family, he realized that the musical instruments mentioned in the oracle referred to the eighth prince. So now all the lines had come true!

At the end of two years, the prince was defeated and captured by Count Wang Shou-jen, and his puppet officials were either killed or fled. Wang Hui in his yamen had no time to pack any valuables, but simply snatched up a casket containing a few old books and several taels of silver. Then, changing into blue clothes and a small cloth cap, he fled by night, not knowing in his panic where he was going. For several days he fled on foot and by boat, scared almost out of his wits.

Finally he reached Wuchen, a market-town in Chekiang, where his boat stopped to let the passengers go ashore for a meal. Taking several coins with him, Wang Hui followed the others ashore. Every table in the tavern he entered was full, except for one at which a young man was sitting. He looked familiar, though Wang could not place him,

"Here, sir," said the tavern-keeper. "Please sit with this gentleman."

Wang went to his table, and the young man stood up, and then sat down again with him. Wang could not resist asking where he was from.

"From Chiahsing," was the reply.

"May I know your honourable name?"

"My name is Chu Hsien-fu."

"There used to be a Prefect Chu at Nanchang. Is he any relation of yours?"

"He is my grandfather! But how did you guess?"

"So you are Prefect Chu's grandson! I am delighted to meet you."

"May I know your honourable name and district, sir?"

"This is no place for talking. Where is your boat?"

"At the bank."

As soon as they had settled their bills, they boarded Chu Hsien-fu's boat together and sat down.

"I met Prefect Chu's son, Chin-yu, at Nanchang," said Wang. "Is he your uncle?"

"He was my father."

"Your father! No wonder that I was struck by the resemblance! But why do you say 'was'? Can you mean that he has passed away?"

"The year after my grandfather retired from his post at Nanchang, we had the misfortune to lose my father."

When Wang heard this, he shed tears. "Your father showed himself a true friend to me that year in Nanchang," he said. "I never guessed that he was no more. How old are you now?"

"I am seventeen. But I have not yet asked your honourable name and native place."

"Are any of your servants or boatmen about?"

"No, they have all gone ashore."

Then Wang whispered into his ear: "I am Wang Hui, who succeeded your grandfather as prefect at Nanchang."

Young Chu gave a start. "I heard that you had been promoted to Nankan," he said. "Why are you travelling alone and in disguise like this?"

"When Prince Ning revolted, I fled from my post. But since the city was besieged, I was unable to bring away any money."

"Where are you bound for now?"

"Where can I go, poor wanderer that I am?"

Wang Hui omitted to mention that he had surrendered to Prince Ning.

"Since your circuit was lost, you can hardly return to the court," said Chu Hsien-fu. "But the world is wide, and what can you do without money? I have been on a journey at my grandfather's order to collect some money owed us by relatives in Hangchow; so I have some silver which I will present to you, sir, for your travels. Then you can find a quiet place, and settle down peacefully."

He produced four packages of silver, worth two hundred taels, and gave them to Wang Hui, who thanked him heartily.

"The boats on both sides should be starting now," said Wang. "We mustn't hold them up; so I will say goodbye. I am under such an obligation to you that, if I am spared, I am determined to repay you in full."

He knelt down on both knees.

Young Chu hastily knelt down too and they bowed several times to each other.

"Apart from my clothes and bedding I have nothing but a casket with a few old books in it," said Wang Hui. "However, now that I am travelling incognito I am afraid even this may give me away, so I shall leave it with you. Travelling light, I shall be better able to escape."

When Chu Hsien-fu agreed, Wang went straight to his boat to fetch the casket. Then shedding tears they took their leave of each other.

"Please give my respects to your grandfather," said Wang. "If I cannot see him again in this life, in my next life I shall repay his kindness by serving as his horse or dog."

After they had parted, Wang Hui took another boat to Taihu where he changed his name, shaved his head and became a monk.

Back in Chiahsing, Chu Hsien-fu told his grandfather how he had met Prefect Wang. Prefect Chu was startled.

"He surrendered to Prince Ning!" he exclaimed.

"He didn't tell me that. He just mentioned that he had escaped without bringing away any money."

"Although he is a rebel, he is an old acquaintance of mine. Why didn't you give him the money you had with you?"

"I did, sir."

"How much?"

"I had only two hundred taels. I gave it all to him."

Delighted, Prefect Chu declared: "You are a true son of your father." Then he told him the story of the transfer.

After this talk with his grandfather the lad went in to see his mother, who asked him about his journey and made much of him. Then he went to his own room to rest.

The next day he told his grandfather: "There were some books in Prefect Wang's casket." And he took them out to show him.

Prefect Chu saw that they were manuscripts of little interest, with the exception of one volume: *Random Notes on Poetry* by Kao Chi:[1] This consisted of over a hundred pages, exquisitely written, in the poet's own hand.

"This book used to be in the imperial library," said Prefect Chu, "and for years now scholars have longed for a chance to read it. This is the only copy in existence, which good fortune has thrown into your hands. You had better put it away safely and be careful whom you show it to."

When his grandson heard that there was not another copy of this book in the world, he thought: "Why shouldn't I print some copies in my own name? That would win me fame."

He set to work at once to have blocks made, setting his own name as editor under the name of Kao Chi. And when the blocks were ready, he printed several hundred copies which

---

[1] A scholar of the early Ming Dynasty, who was executed because he offended the emperor.

he presented to relatives, friends and acquaintances. All who saw this book were so delighted with it that they could hardly bear to put it down; and henceforward Prefect Chu's grandson was known throughout western Chekiang as a brilliant young scholar. Prefect Chu knew of this too late to prevent it, therefore he said nothing. But after that he gave his grandson lessons in versification and encouraged him to write occasional poems with other scholars.

One day the gate-keeper came in to announce: "Two gentlemen from the Lou family have arrived."

"Your uncles are here," Prefect Chu told his grandson. "Go quickly to welcome them."

Young Chu hurried out to greet them.

These two men were sons of Minister Lou, a native of Huchow who had served at court for more than twenty years and had sacrifices and posthumous titles decreed for him after his death. His eldest son was now the commissioner of transmission. These two brothers were his third and fourth sons, Lou Feng and Lou Chan, the one a provincial graduate and the other a student of the Imperial College. They were Prefect Chu's nephews.

Chu Hsien-fu followed his uncles into the courtyard, and Prefect Chu was so pleased that he left the hall to greet them on the steps in person. As the Lou brothers came in, they bowed to him. Prefect Chu raised them up and ordered his grandson to pay his respects to his uncles, after which he invited them to be seated, and tea was served.

"It is twelve years since last we saw you," said the Lou brothers. "When we heard in the capital that you had retired, there was not one of us but admired your wisdom. And we see today that your hair and beard have turned white. This shows how arduous the life of an official is!"

"I was never suited for official life," replied Prefect Chu. "After serving for many years at Nanchang without achieving anything, simply wasting government funds, I thought it best to retire. But when one year later my son died, I was stricken to the heart; for it seemed to me that this must be my punishment for becoming an official."

"Our cousin was so brilliantly gifted, who could imagine that he would die young?" said Lou Feng. "Fortunately, your grandson is old enough now to wait on you. He must be a comfort to you."

"When we heard of our cousin's death," said Lou Chan, "our grief at losing the best friend of our childhood without even being able to say goodbye to him made us nearly distracted. Our elder brother wept without ceasing for a whole day."

"Is your elder brother happy in his present post?"

"His office is not a lucrative one," they answered. "He is just whiling away time, with little business to attend to. It was because we found nothing to do in the capital that we decided to come back to the country."

After they had rested for a while, they changed their clothes and Chu Hsien-fu took them in to see his mother. Then he conducted them into the library, in front of which was a small garden furnished with a lyre, goblets, a stove and some stands. Here he invited them to sit to enjoy the quiet beauty of the bamboos and boulders, the birds and the fish-pond; and presently Prefect Chu, who had changed into country dress, came out leaning on a stick to accompany them. A meal was served outside, after which they brewed tea and chatted. When the conversation turned to Prince Ning's revolt, someone declared that his defeat was due to the genius of Count Wang Shou-jen, who had achieved great deeds and averted a calamity.

"To disclaim all achievement as he has done is most rare," said Lou Feng.

"I see very little difference between Prince Ning's rebellion and that of Emperor Yung Lo,"[1] put in Lou Chan. "But luck was with the emperor, so now he is called sagacious and divine; whereas Prince Ning had no luck, so now he is considered a rebel and bandit. That is hardly fair."

"Of course, it is foolish to judge men by their success or failure," said Prefect Chu. "But servants of the throne like ourselves should be careful how we discuss affairs of state."

This silenced Lou Chan.

---

[1] The fourth son of the first emperor, he seized the throne from his nephew in 1403. Yung Lo is the name of his reign.

The fact was that because these two brothers had failed in the metropolitan examination and were unable to enter the Han Lin Academy, they had a perpetual grudge against society. They were always declaring that since Yung Lo had usurped his nephew's throne, the Ming Dynasty had gone to the dogs; and whenever they had anything to drink, they would hold forth to this effect. This was why their elder brother, irritated by such talk and afraid that they might get into trouble, had persuaded them to return to the country.

After discussing a number of topics, the brothers asked: "What progress is our nephew making in his studies? Has a match been arranged for him yet?"

"I will be frank with you," said Prefect Chu. "This is my only grandson and I have spoiled him since he was a child. The truth is that all the tutors I have seen appear to be ignorant charlatans who beat or swear at their pupils on the least pretext. In fact, parents only engage them for their strictness. So, out of fondness for my grandson, I have never sent him to a tutor. When your cousin was alive he taught the boy himself; and after his death, feeling sorrier for the lad than ever, I bought him the rank of student of the Imperial College. He has not been preparing very hard for the examinations, but recently in my spare time I have taught him to write verses as a pastime; for, whatever fate may have in store for him, I want him to know how to rest content. He studies to please me."

"This is very wise of you, uncle," said the brothers. "As the saying goes: Better a virtuous scholar than an unprincipled official."

Prefect Chu told his grandson to show some of his verses to his uncles, and the Lou brothers could not praise them enough. After a stay of four or five days, they announced that they must leave; and during the farewell feast the question of Chu Hsien-fu's marriage came up again.

"Some of the big families here have sent to discuss it," Prefect Chu told them. "But I am a poor official and I was afraid they might demand exorbitant marriage gifts; so I delayed matters. If you have any relatives in Huchow, please look out for me. The family need not be rich."

The two brothers promised to do so, and soon the feast ended.

The next day the Lou brothers hired a boat and had their luggage carried aboard. Prefect Chu bade his grandson see his uncles off, and came to the hall himself to say goodbye.

"Since you are close relatives, we have been treating you just like members of the family," he said. "I hope you don't take this amiss. When you reach home and visit your ancestors' graves, please mention my name and explain that I am too advanced in years to pay my respects in person any more."

The two brothers listened with grave respect, then bowed to him; and the old man took their hands to escort them outside the front gate. Young Chu, who was waiting at the boat, bowed to his uncles when they arrived, and remained on the bank until the boat left.

Sitting in the small boat with their simple luggage, the two brothers looked at the mulberry trees which grew so thickly along either bank and the wild fowl which were crying as they flew. They had gone three or four hundred yards only when they came to a small creek and saw boats gliding out selling water chestnuts and lotus-roots.

"During the years spent in the dust of the capital, we never saw such peaceful loveliness!" they exclaimed. "The Sung poet was right who said: 'To retire is best!'"

That evening they reached a small village whose lights twinkled through the mulberry trees on the river.

"Tell the boatmen to moor the boat!" they ordered the servant. "There are houses here where we can get wine to pass a pleasant evening. We will spend the night here."

When the boatmen had done as they were told, the Lou brothers drank their fill, leaning against the gunwale and discoursing at random of things past and present.

The next morning while the boatmen were cooking, the brothers went ashore for a stroll. A man rounded the corner of a house, and bowed low when he saw them.

"Do you gentlemen remember me?" he asked.

But to know who this man was, you must read the next chapter.

CHAPTER 9

The Lou brothers redeem a friend. Second Captain Liu
assumes a false name to intimidate boatmen

The two Lou brothers were strolling towards the village
when a man rounded the corner of a house and kowtowed to
them. They hastily raised him up.

"Who are you?" they asked. "We don't recollect knowing
you."

"Don't you gentlemen remember your humble servant?"

"Your face is familiar, but your name has slipped our
memory."

"I am Chou San. My father Chou Chi-fu used to look after
your ancestral graves."

"In that case, what are you doing here?" they asked in
surprise.

"After all you gentlemen left for the capital," he told
them, "my father looked after the graves and did so well that
he was able to buy some nearby fields. Then because our
house was too small we bought another in the east end of the
village, leaving the old house to my uncle. Later some of my
brothers married, and that new house in the east quarter was
big enough for my two older brothers and their wives only.
But a sister of mine who married a fellow in New Market is
a widow now. She invited my father and mother here. and I
came with them."

"So that's it. Have there been people trampling on our family grave mounds?"

"Who would dare? Whenever magistrates and prefects pass by, they go in to pay their respects. Not a blade of grass has been touched."

"Where are your parents now?"

"They live at the end of the market in my sister's house, only a few steps from here. My father often speaks of your goodness to him and wishes he could see you gentlemen again."

"We've frequently wondered what became of old Chou Chi-fu," said Lou Feng to his younger brother. "If it's not far, why not go to see him?"

"Very well," agreed Lou Chan.

They took Chou San back with them to the bank, and told their attendant to order the boatmen to wait. Then, with Chou San leading the way, they went straight to the end of the market to a seven or eight-roomed house with its double wicker gate ajar.

"Dad!" shouted Chou San. "The young masters are here."

"Who's that?" called Chou Chi-fu.

He hobbled out leaning on a stick. At the sight of the two brothers he was overjoyed and, following them inside, put down his stick so that he could kneel to them. The two brothers hastily stopped him.

"An old man like you need not stand upon ceremony," they said.

They made him sit down with them.

Chou San brought in tea, which the old man offered to them himself.

"We meant to visit our ancestors' graves to sweep their tombs as soon as we reached home," said Lou Feng as they were drinking. "We expected to see you then. But since we made a detour to Chiahsing to visit Prefect Chu, we happened to pass this way; and how surprised we were to run into your son and learn that you were here! So we meet again after more than ten years! You are looking fitter than ever; and we hear that two of your sons are married and you now have several grandchildren. Is your wife here too?"

Even as he spoke, an old woman with white hair and white eyebrows came out to greet them. The two brothers returned her greeting.

"Go in quickly," Chou Chi-fu told her, "and bid your daughter prepare a meal for the two gentlemen." When the old woman had gone, he went on: "My wife and I shall never forget your father's kindness and yours. My old woman burns a stick of incense every day under the eaves, to pray that you gentlemen will become ministers too. Your elder brother is already a high official, isn't he, with a big sedan-chair?"

"We have both been away from home so long that we have done nothing for you," said Lou Chan. "Yet you talk like this, making us feel quite embarrassed."

"You have been looking after our family graves for many years," put in Lou Feng. "It is we who should be grateful. Why do you speak like this?"

"Prefect Chu has retired," said Chou. "What a pity that his son died! Has his grandson grown up yet?"

"He is seventeen this year," replied Lou Feng, "and very intelligent."

Chou San brought in the food· chicken, fish, duck and pork, neatly served up with several kinds of vegetables. When he had spread the table he invited the brothers to eat. But they had to drag Chou Chi-fu to the table by main force before they could prevail on him to sit down with them.

"You gentlemen can't be used to this weak country wine," said the old man as he was filling their cups.

"Why, this wine has body all right," said Lou Chan.

"I don't know what the world's coming to," Chou went on. "Things aren't what they used to be: even rice wine is poor stuff nowadays. My father used to say that in the good old days of Emperor Hung Wu from two pecks of rice you could brew twenty pints of wine; but later, when Emperor Yung Lo usurped the throne, everything changed, and two pecks would yield only fifteen or sixteen pints. Take this wine. I added as little water as I could, but it's still weak and tasteless."

"We are not heavy drinkers," replied Lou Feng. "This is good enough."

"The truth is, gentlemen, I am growing old and useless," said Chou, now in his cups. "But if Heaven takes pity on me and lets my children live to see times like those under Emperor Hung Wu, I shall die content."

Lou Chan looked at his elder brother and laughed.

"I've heard say," went on the old man, "that our dynasty would have been as perfect as the Chou Dynasty during Confucius' time, if Emperor Yung Lo hadn't seized the throne and ruined everything. Is this true?"

Lou Feng laughed.

"Where did a good old countryman like you hear this?" he asked. "Who told you?"

"I didn't know this before, to be sure; but the manager of the salt shop here used to come to our threshing floor in his spare time or sit with me under the shade of the willows. It was he who told me this."

The Lou brothers were surprised.

"What is the name of this gentleman?" they asked.

"He's Mr. Yang, a decent sort and a great reader. He always kept a book up his sleeve, and whenever he sat down would start reading. He used to stroll over here a good deal after meals; but we shan't be seeing him any more now."

"Where has he gone?"

"I don't know what the world's coming to. Although Mr. Yang was born a tradesman, he had no head for figures. When he wasn't strolling about outside, he would sit reading behind a screen in the shop, leaving all the business to his assistant. Everyone called him Mr. Loony. The shop-owner made him manager because of his honesty; but when he heard what a fool the man was, he came to the shop to look into the accounts and found seven hundred taels of silver missing. Mr. Yang had no idea where the money had gone, but refused to admit he was in the wrong, just spouting phrases out of some book to the proprietor and waving his arms indignantly. The shop-owner was angry and took the case to the Tehching district yamen. And when the district magistrate saw that this had to do with the salt trade, he immediately complied with the request and ordered Mr. Yang to be thrown in gaol until he could make good the deficit. And in gaol he has now been for pretty well a year and a half."

"Has he no property to pay up with?" asked Lou Feng.

"If he had, it would be all right," answered Chou. "But his family lives more than a mile out of this village and his two sons are idiots. They've neither learned a trade nor studied; they just live on the old man. How can he pay?"

"Brother!" exclaimed Lou Chan. "To think that this poor, out-of-the-way place should produce such a scholar, yet he should be victimized by a miser! Isn't it enough to make your blood boil? Can't we find a way to help him?"

"He hasn't broken the law: he has only run into debt," said Lou Feng. "All we need do is find out the details of the case in the city and clear his debt for him. There shouldn't be any difficulty."

"Excellent!" approved Lou Chan. "As soon as we get home tomorrow we'll see to it."

"Amida Buddha!" exclaimed Chou. "How eager you two gentlemen are to do good! Heaven only knows how many poor people you have helped in the past; and if you get Mr. Yang out of gaol, every single villager here will be moved."

"Don't talk about this in the village yet, Chi-fu," said Lou Feng. "Wait till we see what can be done."

"That's right," agreed Lou Chan. "If you say something before we are sure of success, it won't be good."

By now they had drunk enough wine, and rice was served. When the meal was at an end, it was time for the Lou brothers to go back to the boat. Chou Chi-fu, leaning on a stick, escorted them to the bank.

"I wish you a good journey," he said. "I will come to the city later to pay my respects."

He told his son, who was carrying a bottle of wine and some dishes and food, to put them on board for the gentlemen's supper. Only when the boat cast off did he turn back.

Once home, the two brothers had to see to some business and entertain guests for several days. This done, they sent for one of their stewards, Tsin Chueh, and ordered him to go to the district yamen to find out the name of the man arrested in New Market salt shop, how much money he owed, and whether he were a scholar or not. Tsin did as he was told. One of the yamen secretaries was a sworn brother of his; and when Tsin approached him with these questions, the secretary immediately copied out the required information from the files. Tsin took this report back to the two brothers, who read: "The owner of Kung Yu Chi Salt Shop in New Market charged the manager, Yang Chih-chung, with neglecting his work for many years and devoting his time to pleasure. He claimed that Yang's appropriation of more than seven hundred taels of silver was tantamount to embezzling tax money. The plaintiff has requested that Yang be compelled to pay up; but since he is a salaried licentiate we cannot proceed, and he must be deprived of his rank before he can be condemned. He is now in gaol pending a decision on his case from the provincial governor."

"How ridiculous!" exclaimed Lou Chan. "A salaried licentiate is a scholar, and all he has done is to use some money belonging to a salt merchant; yet they want to deprive him of his rank and penalize him. Did you ever hear of anything so unreasonable!"

"Did you find out if there was any other trouble?" asked Lou Feng.

"I made inquiries," said Tsin. "But there isn't any."

"In that case, take seven hundred and fifty taels from the sum that fellow from Huang Family Dyke paid the other day to redeem his fields, and pay them into the district treasury for Mr. Yang. After that, take our cards to the magistrate and tell him that this Licentiate Yang is a friend of your masters', so that the magistrate will release him. Use your name as a guarantor, and look sharp!"

"Don't lose any time, Tsin Chueh!" urged Lou Chan. "And when Licentiate Yang comes out of prison, don't say anything to him. He will come without any prompting to see us."

Tsin assented and made off. He took twenty taels of silver only, however, which he presented to the yamen secretary.

"Can't we think of some way to settle Licentiate Yang's case?" he asked.

"Since you have brought cards from the minister's house, what difficulty can there be?"

The secretary straightway sent the following memorandum to the magistrate: "This Licentiate Yang is connected with the Lou family, and two of the Lou gentlemen have sent in their cards and instructed their steward to act as guarantor. They want to know, too, on what grounds the scholar was arrested since this is not a case of embezzlement or corruption. Your Excellency is requested to give the matter your consideration."

This message from the Lou family threw the magistrate into a panic; but he could not give this as an answer to the salt merchant. Calling in the secretary, he bade him appropriate some of the salt tax to pay the merchant, accept Tsin Chueh's offer to act as guarantor, and release Licentiate Yang immediately — there was no need to bring in a verdict.

Tsin Chueh, who had pocketed over seven hundred taels of silver, reported that Licentiate Yang had been released; and the two Lou brothers naturally expected that he would come to express his gratitude. Yang, however, did not know the reason for his release. When he asked the runners outside the yamen, all they could tell him was: "A man by the name of Tsin Chueh acted as guarantor for you."

"I have never known anyone called Tsin," thought Yang.

After puzzling over the question for some time, he decided not to trouble about it any more. The important thing was that he was free, and could go home to his books.

He was welcomed home by his wife, who could scarcely believe their good fortune. His two idiot sons spent every day gambling in the market, and did not come home till midnight; so there was only a deaf, half-witted crone to make the fire, cook and look after the house. The next day Licentiate Yang walked round the village to look up his old acquaintances; but as Chou Chi-fu had gone to stay with his second son, whose wife had just been brought to bed of a son, Yang did not see him. How could he possibly guess that the Lou brothers had championed his cause?

When over a month had passed, the Lou brothers could not help feeling somewhat astonished. However, they called to mind the story of Yueh Shih-fu[1] and were convinced that Licentiate Yang must be a great scholar of the same type. In fact, this only increased their respect for him.

"Mr. Yang has still not appeared to thank us," remarked Lou Feng one day to Lou Chan. "He must be a remarkable man."

"If we admire him," said Lou Chan, "it stands to reason that we should call on him. Isn't it rather petty to wait for him to come and thank us?"

"I agree. But you know the old saying: When Your Grace does good, Your Grace should forget. If we call on him, won't it look as if we want to bring this business up?"

"We won't mention it. What could be more natural than to call on someone whose reputation has aroused in you a desire to make his acquaintance? Why should we let this stand in the way of getting to know him?"

"You are absolutely right," agreed Lou Feng. "We must set out by boat the day before, so that we can reach his house early and spend a whole day there."

They hired a small boat and set out that same afternoon without attendants, and had soon covered several dozen miles. It was late autumn, when days were short and nights long, and the river glimmered in the moonlight as their boatmen rowed along by the light of the moon. The river was crowded with vessels loaded with rice for different landlord families; but since their craft was small it could slip past the side of the larger boats. Toward midnight the two brothers were lying down to sleep when they heard shouts and blows. Their boat was carrying no lights and the cabin doors were closed; but looking through a crack Lou Chan saw a big vessel, brightly lit with two great lanterns, one of which bore the inscription "The Prime Minister's House", and the other "Commissioner of Transmission." On the deck of this large vessel stood several attendants looking as savage as tigers and wolves, who were lashing out with whips at all the boats in their way.

---

[1] A native of the state of Chi in the sixth century B.C. The minister Yen Ying rescued him from gaol; but Yueh Shih-fu did not thank the minister.

Lou Chan gave a start.

"Brother!" he whispered. "Take a look at this!"

Lou Feng did so, then exclaimed: "These men are none of ours!"

By this time the large vessel had overtaken them, and the men on it began to whip the boatmen of the brothers' small boat.

"It's a public waterway," protested one of the boatmen. "Nobody's stopping you. Why get tough and beat people?"

"Fool!" shouted the bullies. "Use your silly eyes to look at the names on the lanterns. See whose boat this is?"

"Your lantern says: 'The Prime Minister's House.' Which prime minister is that?"

"You perishing idiot! Are there two prime ministers in Huchow? It's Prime Minister Lou, of course."

"All right. But which of the Lou gentlemen does your boat belong to?"

"This is Mr. Lou Feng's boat, loaded with rice, as everybody knows. Any more of your lip, you dog, and we'll tie you up and ask Mr. Lou to send you to the district yamen tomorrow for a good beating."

"Mr. Lou is on *my* boat. Can you produce his double?"

The two brothers were chuckling to themselves, when the boatman opened the cabin door and asked Lou Feng to step on deck where the bullies could see him. He obligingly stepped to the prow. The moon had not yet set, so the light of the moon and the lanterns on the other boat illumined him clearly.

"To which branch of my family do you belong?" he asked.

The sight of Lou Feng threw the impostors into a panic, and they flung themselves on their knees.

"Our master doesn't actually belong to your family, sir," they said. "He is Mr. Liu, who used to be second captain. He collected this rice from his land and, thinking the river might be crowded, made bold to borrow your family's official insignia. Little did we think we should bump into your boat, sir. We have done very wrong."

"Although your master is no relative of mine, he is from the same district," said Lou. "I don't mind if he borrows my name and lanterns. But I cannot have you forcing your way along the river and beating people like this, because by claiming to belong to my house you are spoiling my reputation. You know very well that none of our household would dare do such a thing. Get up, all of you. When you go back to your master, you need not tell him how you met me; but see that this doesn't happen again. Don't be afraid. I am not going to hold this against you."

Promising to obey him and thanking him for his generosity, the captain's attendants scrambled to their feet, hastily extinguished the two big lanterns and moored by the side of the river.

On Lou Feng's return to the cabin, the two brothers had a good laugh. "You shouldn't have told them Mr. Lou was on board, or asked him to show himself," said Lou Chan to the boatman. "It was too bad of you to spoil their fun."

"If I hadn't told them," retorted the boatman, "they would have smashed up my boat, the savages! Now they've been shown up."

Then the two brothers undressed and went to sleep, while the boatmen rowed on through the night. By dawn they reached New Market. When the brothers had washed their faces, drunk some tea and eaten some pastries, they ordered the boatmen to wait for them and went ashore.

Walking to Chou Chi-fu's daughter's house at the end of the market, they knocked at the gate. But when they found that Old Chou and his wife had gone to visit their son, they would not sit down, though Chou's daughter asked them in to drink tea. Leaving the market, they walked down the main road for over a mile until they met a woodcutter carrying faggots.

"Where does Licentiate Yang live?" they asked.

"See that patch of red?" The woodcutter pointed into the distance. "That's just behind his house. This path will take you there."

Thanking him, they took the path he had pointed out through the thickets and brambles till they came to a hamlet with only four or five thatched cottages. Behind one of these cottages were two great maple trees whose leaves had turned red since the frost. Realizing that this must be Yang's house, they followed another path to his front gate. Before the house was a brook, and over it a tiny bridge. As the brothers crossed the bridge, they saw that the double gate was closed. At their arrival a dog began to bark. Lou F'eng knocked at the gate, and kept on knocking until an old crone came out, her clothes all tattered and torn. The brothers stepped forward.

"Is this Mr. Yang's house?" they asked.

They had to repeat the question before she nodded and answered: "Yes. Where are you from?"

"Our name is Lou, and we live in the city. We came to pay our respects to Mr. Yang."

The old woman was hard of hearing.

"Did you say Liu?" she asked.

"Not Liu, but Lou. Just tell your master that we're from the minister's house, and he will understand."

"Master isn't at home. He went yesterday to watch the fishing, and he isn't back yet. If you have something to say to him, come some other day."

Thereupon, not realizing that she ought to invite them in to have some tea, she went inside, closing the door behind her. The brothers stood there in dismay for some time. There was nothing for it, however, but to cross the bridge and go back to the city by the way they had come.

Yang Chih-chung did not get home till evening.

"This morning two men called Liu or something came from the city to see you," the old servant told him. "Said they live in some monastery."

"What did you say to them?"

"I told them, 'Master isn't at home. Come again another day.'"

"What Liu can this be?" wondered Yang. Then he remembered that the name of the runner who had arrested him when the salt merchant took the case to court was Liu. Now the fellow must be coming to demand money.

"You old, never-dying idiot!" he roared. "When people like that ask for me, just say I'm not at home. Why tell them to come back again? Good-for-nothing!"

The old woman answered back indignantly, whereupon Yang lost his temper, slapped her face and kicked her. After that, afraid that the runner would return he took to going out early every morning and wandering about till evening.

The Lou brothers, however, were not yet satisfied, and a few days later they hired another boat to take them to New Market. As before, they walked to Yang's door and knocked. But when the old crone opened the door and saw they were back again, she flew into a rage.

"Master is not at home!" she said angrily. "Why do you keep coming?"

"Did you tell him the other day that we were from Minister Lou's family?"

"Did I tell him! Because of you I got kicked and beaten. Why are you back again? Master isn't at home and he won't be back for some days. I've no time to waste talking: I've got to light the fire to cook dinner."

Without giving them a chance to speak, she slammed the gate and went back inside. And when they knocked again she paid no attention.

Completely at a loss, the brothers did not know whether to laugh or be angry. But after standing there for a little while, they decided it was no use creating a disturbance, and went back to the river. Their boat had gone several miles when they met another boat loaded with water chestnuts, manned by a small boy, who as he came up with them held on to their cabin window.

"Will you buy water chestnuts?" he called.

While the boatman made his boat fast to the boy's and was weighing out the water chestnuts, the brothers asked from the window: "Where do you live?"

"In New Market," said the lad.

"Do you know a Mr. Yang Chih-chung who lives there?" asked Lou Chan.

"Of course I do. He's a very kind old gentleman. The other day he took my boat to see the opera in the next village, and a piece of paper with writing on it dropped from his sleeve."

"Where is it?" asked Lou Feng.

"Here in the boat."

"May we have a look at it?"

The boy handed it to them. When the boatman had paid him for the water chestnuts, he rowed away.

The Lou brothers unfolded the white sheet of paper and read the following lines:

> *I dare not do anything wrong,*
> *Because I have studied old books.*
> *I have come through bitter frost and blazing heat,*
> *And now the spring breeze plays on my thatched hut.*

Yang's name was signed beneath.

They were most impressed.

"How sublime!" they exclaimed. "What an admirable character! But how unlucky we are in all our attempts to meet him!"

It was a bright day, although there was a nip in the air, and Lou Chan was sitting in the stern enjoying the view when a junk overtook them.

"Please heave to, Mr. Lou!" someone hailed him. "Our master is here."

When they had come alongside the junk, the stranger jumped aboard and kowtowed to Lou Chan. Then, catching a glimpse of the cabin, he said: "So the other master is here too."

But to know who the gentleman in the large boat was, you must read the chapter which follows.

127

CHAPTER 10

Compiler Lu chooses a brilliant son-in-law,
and Chu Hsien-fu marries into a rich family

The Lou brothers were on the river when a junk overtook them and a man called to them to stop, then came aboard to invite them to the other boat. They recognized him as the servant of Mr. Lu, a compiler of the Han Lin Academy who came from their district.

"When did your master return?" they asked.

"He has asked for leave and is on his way home."

"Where is he now?" asked Lou Feng.

"He is on that junk, and invites you both to come over."

The two brothers went aboard the junk, which was carrying the insignia of the Han Lin Academy; and Mr. Lu came out, in a square cap and private citizen's dress, to the door of the cabin. This compiler had been one of their uncle's pupils.

"Just now I saw Lou Chan from a distance, standing at the prow, and I was wondering how you came to be on this little boat," he said with a smile. "Now I find Lou Feng is here too. This is very interesting. Please come into my cabin."

They went in, exchanged courtesies and sat down.

"Since we took our leave of you at the capital," said Lou Feng, "half a year has passed. May we ask why you requested leave, sir, to return home?"

"All we poor academicians have to look forward to is a few commissions," said Mr. Lu. "Since all the lucrative jobs had been taken by others, I was sitting there in the capital with nothing to do, spending my own money. Moreover, though I am nearly fifty, I have no son but only one daughter whose marriage has not yet been arranged. I therefore felt my wisest course would be to ask for leave and return to see to some family affairs. But what were you two doing on that little boat without a single attendant? Where were you going?"

"We have nothing to do," said Lou Chan, "and since it was a fine, warm day my brother and I decided to come out for a little excursion. That was all."

"I called on an old friend this morning in a village over there," said Mr. Lu. "He invited me to lunch; but since I was eager to be home, I declined. He sent a feast to my boat, however, and I am very lucky to have met you both, for we can recall old times over the wine." He turned to an attendant to ask: "Has the second boat caught up yet?"

A boatman answered: "No, it's still a long way behind."

"Never mind," said Mr. Lu. "Bring the gentlemen's luggage aboard here, and send their boat back."

Then he ordered the feast to be spread and wine poured out, and as they drank they chatted about different yamens in the capital.

Presently Mr. Lu asked about the crops that year and whether their native place had recently produced any famous men. Given this opening, Lou Feng mentioned Yang Chih-chung and declared that he could be considered an extremely lofty character. Then, producing the poem, he showed it to the compiler. When Mr. Lu had read it, he looked at them quizzically.

"You two gentlemen are a match for all the patrons who ever existed," he said. "Even the Lord of Hsinling and the Lord of Chunsheng[1] could do no more. But few of these men who appear so brilliant are genuine scholars. In fact, to put it bluntly, if this fellow is really learned why hasn't he passed the examinations? What use is this poem? With your condescension and respect for genius, you must be the best patrons

[1] Nobles of the Kingdoms of Wei and Chi in the third century B.C., they both had over three thousand protégés.

this Mr. Yang has ever encountered in his life; yet he has twice avoided you, as if he were afraid of meeting you. Isn't the reason obvious? If I were you, I would not become too friendly with such people."

To this the two brothers made no answer. The feast continued for a long time, during which they touched on a multitude of topics, and when they reached the city Mr. Lu insisted on escorting the Lou brothers back before going home himself.

As soon as the brothers stepped across their threshold, the gate-keeper told them: "Master Chu is here. He is sitting with the third mistress."

Entering the inner hall, they found Chu Hsien-fu there, being entertained by Lou Feng's wife. As soon as the young man saw his uncles he knelt down; but they stopped him and invited him into the library, where he presented a letter and gifts from his grandfather, besides two copies of the *Random Notes on Poetry* by Kao Chi which he had published.

"You are a young genius, nephew!" declared his uncles after turning a few pages. "We are none of us up to you."

"I am nothing but an ignoramus," replied Chu Hsien-fu. "I hope my uncles will point out my mistakes."

The two brothers were delighted. That evening they spread a feast to welcome him, and lodged him in the library.

The next morning, after a chat with Chu Hsien-fu, the brothers changed into official dress, ordered a servant to take their cards, and went by sedan-chairs to call on Mr. Lu. After paying their respects they returned home, instructed their cook to prepare a feast for the next day, and sent an invitation to the compiler saying that they wished to celebrate his home-coming. Then they went to the library.

"We have invited a guest for tomorrow," they told their nephew with a smile. "We hope you will help us to entertain him."

Chu Hsien-fu asked who it was.

"He is Compiler Lu of this district," Lou Feng told him. "He passed the examination when our uncle was chief examiner."

"He is the most vulgar person you can imagine," put in Lou Chan. "But since we are connected and he invited us to

130

a feast the other day on his boat, tomorrow we are asking him here."

As they were speaking, the gate-keeper came in.

"Mr. Niu Pu-yi of Shaohsing is waiting outside to see you, gentlemen," he announced.

"Show him into the hall at once," ordered Lou Feng.

"Is this the Mr. Niu Pu-yi who used to be a secretary under Examiner Fan in Shantung?" asked Chu.

"Yes," answered Lou Feng. "How did you know?"

"He was formerly my father's colleague: that is how I know him."

"True," said Lou Chan. "We forgot that your father was there too."

Then the brothers went out to see Niu Pu-yi and, after talking to him for some time, brought him to the library where Chu Hsien-fu paid his respects.

"Just now," said Niu, "when I learned from your uncles that your father was no longer with us, I felt very sad. But now that I see how brilliantly you are following in his steps, I feel happy again. Is your grandfather well?"

"He is well, thank you, sir. He often thinks of you too."

"I remember how, when Examiner Fan was looking for some candidate's paper, your father told the story of Ho Ching-ming—that was an excellent joke."

He described what had happened and the Lou brothers and Chu laughed heartily.

"Mr. Niu," said Lou Feng, "we have been close friends for many years, so we need not stand on ceremony, and luckily our nephew is here to profit by your instruction. Won't you spend the day with us?"

Then a feast was spread and the four of them discussed literature over their wine until evening, when Niu Pu-yi took his leave and the two brothers saw him out, having ascertained his address.

The next morning a servant was sent to invite Mr. Lu; but only at midday did the compiler arrive, wearing his gauze cap and embroidered official gown. Upon entering the hall, he wanted to pay his respects before the shrine of his former tutor; but the two brothers declined again and again. Then

131

they took off their official robes and sat down, while tea was served. When the tea had been drunk, Chu Hsien-fu came in to pay his respects.

"This is our nephew," said Lou Feng. "He is the grandson of our uncle who was Prefect of Nanchang."

"I have long wished to make your acquaintance," said Mr. Lu.

Each deferring to the other, they sat down; and after the usual courtesies had been exchanged, two feasts were laid.

"You shouldn't have done this," said Mr. Lu. "Good friends like ourselves needn't stand on ceremony. In fact, I think this hall is too big and would prefer to have a single feast in your library; so that the four of us can talk comfortably at the same table."

Falling in with his wishes, the two brothers ushered him forthwith into the library, where he was charmed with the good taste with which the flowers and stands were arranged. When they had taken their seats, Lou Feng ordered incense to be burnt. At the word of command, a small boy with long hair took an ancient bronze incense-burner in both hands and carried it out, while two servants let down curtains round the room. An hour or two later, when they had drunk three cups apiece and the two servants returned to draw back the curtains, and the guests saw incense smoke wreathing the panels of the wall, filling the room with a delicious scent. Mr. Lu felt that he was in paradise.

"Incense must be burnt this way," Lou Feng told the compiler, "if you don't want to be troubled by the smoke."

Mr. Lu expressed his admiration. Then he started talking to Chu Hsien-fu about affairs in Kiangsi.

"Wasn't your grandfather's successor in Nanchang Wang Hui?" he asked.

"It was."

"Intendant Wang is in great trouble now. The government has set a price on his head."

"He surrendered to Prince Ning," said Lou Feng.

"He was cited as the ablest officer in Kiangsi," went on Mr. Lu. "Yet he was the first to surrender."

"He did wrong in surrendering," put in Lou Chan.

"According to the proverb," said Mr. Lu, "no troops, no food, why not surrender? But while many officers surrendered to Prince Ning and are now in hiding, he was the only one to surrender with several districts. So the government regards him as by far the worst offender and has offered a reward for his arrest."

When Chu heard this, he dared not breathe a word of what had happened.

Mr. Lu went on to tell the story, which neither of the brothers had heard, of how Wang Hui had consulted the oracle. He then quoted the poem set to the tune "Moonlight on the Western River," and explained how each line had come true.

"That oracle was a strange one," he declared. "It foretold only that he would surrender, but not what would happen after. Apparently, it was still uncertain whether he would have good fortune or bad."

"Coming events cast their shadows before," said Lou Chan. "And a fortune-teller is sensitive to these almost imperceptible signs. It is nonsense to talk of ghosts or fairies."

After the feast the two brothers showed Mr. Lu some of Master Chu's poems as well as the *Random Notes on Poetry* he had published, describing him as a young genius. Mr. Lu expressed his admiration.

"How old is your nephew?" he asked Lou Feng.

"He is seventeen."

"And when was he born?"

Lou Feng asked Chu Hsien-fu, who said: "On the sixteenth of the third month."

Mr. Lu nodded and made a mental note of the date. When evening came the party broke up and, after the two brothers had seen their guest off, they all turned in for the night.

Some days later, Chu announced that he must go back to Chiahsing. His uncles prevailed on him to stay for another day, and that day Lou Feng was in his library writing a letter to Prefect Chu when his serving-lad came in.

"The gate-keeper has something to report," he announced.

"Send him in."

The gate-keeper stepped in and told him: "There is a gentleman outside asking to see you."

"Tell him we are not at home and ask him to leave his card."

"He has no card. And when I asked him his name he wouldn't give it—just said that he wanted to speak to both masters."

"What does he look like?"

"He is between fifty and sixty, wearing a square cap and a silk gown. He looks like a scholar."

"It must be Yang Chih-chung!" thought Lou Feng.

Hastily putting away his letter, he called in his brother and told him that someone who might well be Yang Chih-chung had arrived.

"Invite him into the hall," he ordered the gate-keeper. "We shall see him at once."

The gate-keeper ushered the stranger into the hall, after which the two brothers came out to greet him and invited him to sit down.

"Your fame, which resounds like thunder, has long since reached my ears," said the stranger. "But hitherto I have had no opportunity of making your acquaintance."

"May we ask your honourable name?" said Lou Feng.

"Chen Ho-fu, at your service. I reside in the capital, but recently I accompanied Mr. Lu to your honourable district, so at last I am fortunate enough to meet you. I observe that Mr. Lou Feng's ears are whiter than his face—a sure sign that his fame will spread throughout the world; while the refulgence of Mr. Lou Chan's nose indicates that he will shortly receive news of official promotion."

The two brothers realized that this was not Mr. Yang.

"You are no doubt an adept at fortune-telling, sir," they said.

"I have a smattering of knowledge concerning the hexagrams, astrology, fortune-telling, medicine, surgery, yoga and chemistry, besides knowing how to consult the oracles," said Chen Ho-fu. "When I resided in the capital I was constantly invited by the ministers of all the great ministries and by the gentlemen of the literary yamens. And whenever I foretold promotion, it invariably came to pass. To tell you the truth, gentlemen, I always speak straight out, never keeping anything back or indulging in flattery. That is why great personages have always favoured me. As I told Mr. Lu the other day: 'In the twenty-odd years between my departure from Kiangsi and my arrival in your honourable province, I have travelled through nine provinces.'" When he had said this, he laughed heartily.

Then attendants served tea which they drank.

"Did you say that you came on the same boat as Mr. Lu?" asked Lou Chan. "We met Mr. Lu on the river and spent a day on his boat, but we did not see you."

"That day I was on the second boat," explained Chen Ho-fu. "Only that evening did I learn that you gentlemen had been there. It was my misfortune to have to defer making your acquaintance for several days."

"Your conversation is most edifying," declared Lou Feng. "We regret that we did not meet earlier."

"Mr. Lu has asked me to convey a message to you," said Chen. "May we speak in private?"

"Certainly," replied the two brothers, and invited him into the library.

Chen Ho-fu looked about him and saw the spacious courtyard outside and the elegant lyres and books.

"It is true that 'In heaven there is the mansion of the gods, and on earth the house of the prime minister,'" he declared. Then, hitching his chair forward, he said: "Mr. Lu has a daughter, who has just reached marriageable age. Since I am staying with them I know the young lady, and she is virtuous, gentle and beautiful. Because Mr. and Mrs. Lu have no son, this girl is the apple of their eye; so although many families have sought her hand in marriage, her parents would never consent. The other day, however, when Mr. Lu met Prefect Chu's grandson in your honourable house, he was struck by his genius. He has asked me to come and find out whether the young gentleman is married or not."

"The young man is our nephew," said Lou Feng, "and he is not married. We are most grateful for this mark of Mr.

Lu's high regard; but we would like to ask the age of the young lady and whether their horoscopes correspond."

"You need have no anxiety on that score," replied Chen with a smile. "Mr. Lu ascertained the date of your nephew's birthday when you entertained him to a feast here; and on his return home I cast both their horoscopes to see whether they could marry or not. The young lady is one year younger than the young gentleman, being sixteen this year. They are born for each other: their horoscopes accord in every single respect. And they are destined to enjoy long life, good fortune and a numerous progeny, with nothing to mar their happiness."

"So that was why he asked the date of our nephew's birthday during the feast," said Lou Chan to Lou Feng. "I wondered at the time, and now it seems he had this in mind all along."

"Excellent," said Lou Feng. "Since our nephew has found favour with Mr. Lu and Mr. Chen has come as go-between, we shall write immediately to our uncle, then choose an auspicious day to send to Mr. Lu's house to ask for the young lady's hand."

"I shall take the liberty of calling again some other day," said Chen Ho-fu, rising to take his leave. "But I must say goodbye for the present and go back to report to Mr. Lu."

When the Lou brothers had seen Chen Ho-fu off, they told Chu Hsien-fu what had happened.

"Since this is the case, you had better not go back to Chiahsing yet," they advised him. "We shall send your servant with a letter to your grandfather, and you may as well wait for his reply before you make any move."

Chu did as they said, and remained with them.

The servant came back about ten days later with Prefect Chu's letter, and reported: "When Prefect Chu heard this, he was very pleased. He ordered me to tell you that, since he cannot come himself, he hopes you will make all arrangements for him and decide whether Master Chu should stay in his wife's family or return home. Here is his letter, sir, and here are five hundred taels of silver for the wedding gifts. The prefect also says that there is no need for Master Chu to go home until after his marriage. The prefect's health is good, so there is no need to worry about him."

Having received this reply and the silver, the two brothers chose an auspicious day, asked Chen Ho-fu to act as go-between, and requested Niu Pu-yi to act as a second go-between for the bridegroom's family. Chen and Niu came to the Lou family where they were entertained to a feast, after which they mounted sedan-chairs preceded by servants carrying their cards, and were borne to Mr. Lu's house. Mr. Lu, who had prepared a feast for them, gave them his written consent to the match as well as the card containing the horoscopes of the betrothed couple. On the third day the Lou family sent scores of bearers with gold, silver, pearls, emeralds, jewellery, silk, embroidery, sheep, wine and fruit as gifts for the bride's family. And after these presents had been despatched they gave each go-between twelve taels of silver for new clothes and four taels of silver for wine and fruit. So everybody was happy.

The two brothers next asked Chen Ho-fu to fix a date for the wedding, and he chose the eighth of the twelfth month, which was an auspicious day. When they proposed this date to Mr. Lu, he requested that, since he had only the one daughter and was loath to part with her, Master Chu should stay with the Lu family. To this the Lou brothers agreed.

On the eighth day of the twelfth month, the go-betweens were entertained to a feast in the Lou mansion, which was hung with lanterns and decorated with streamers. When evening came the musicians struck up. The Lou family had more than eighty lanterns inscribed with official titles, and these, supplemented with the lanterns of Prefect Chu's family, filled three or four streets to overflowing. There was the whole regular wedding procession too, with banners, canopies, wind and stringed instruments and eight pairs of gauze lanterns — because the rain had just stopped and there were still clouds in the sky, the lanterns were covered with green oil-cloth shades — and behind came a great sedan-chair carried by four bearers, in which sat Chu Hsien-fu. After him followed four other chairs carrying the two Lou brothers, Chen Ho-fu and Niu Pu-yi, who were accompanying the groom to the wedding.

At the gate of Mr. Lu's house they sent in largesse to the attendants; then the gates swung wide open and music struck up to welcome them. The Lou brothers and the go-betweens descended from their chairs first and went in. The two brothers were wearing official robes and the go-betweens auspicious dress. Mr. Lu, in gauze cap and embroidered gown, satin shoes and gold belt, came out to welcome them, bowing as he invited them to ascend the steps. Then the musicians and sixteen lantern-bearers ushered in Chu Hsien-fu. In gauze cap and official gown, he was wearing flowers and had red silk over his shoulders. He entered the hall with lowered head, first presented a swan and then bowed to Mr. Lu who invited him to sit at the front table, while the two brothers, two go-betweens and he sat at side tables. Tea was presented three times, after which the feast was spread: one feast for each person, making six feasts in all. Mr. Lu went first to the bridegroom's table to toast him and Chu returned his toast, while music was played at the lower end of the hall. While Mr. Lu was going to the tables of the other guests, Chu had a quick look round and saw that he was in the old, old hall of an ancient mansion. Scores of great candles had been lit, so that the place was very bright.

These ceremonies at an end, the music stopped and Chu Hsien-fu left his table to greet his father-in-law, his two uncles and the two go-betweens, after which he returned to his place and sat down again. Players came in next, kowtowed to the feasters, then clashed their cymbals and beat their drums as they danced the "Dance of Official Promotion." After that, they performed "The Fairy Brings a Boy," and "Golden Seal."

Now it had been raining heavily for two days and, although the rain had stopped, the ground was still wet; so the players in their new boots had to make a detour as they entered from the courtyard. After the first three items an actor with a list of plays from which to choose went up to Chu's table and knelt down. A servant, who had just brought in the first bowl of boiled birds'-nests, told the actor to stand up. He did so, but just as he was presenting the list of plays — bang! — something dropped from the ceiling straight into the bowl, knocking it over and splashing the scalding soup into his face and over the table. It was a rat which had slipped from the rafters! The hot soup gave it such a fright that it knocked over the bowl as it scuttled for safety, jumping on the bridegroom's knee and smearing his red silk official gown with grease. All present were aghast. They hastily removed the dish, wiped the table clean and brought the bridegroom another gown into which to change.

Chu Hsien-fu modestly declined to choose a play; but after much discussion they settled on "Three Generations' Glory." Then the actor took his list away.

When they had finished several cups of wine and two courses, it was time to serve soup. Now the cook was a countryman who was standing in hobnailed shoes in the courtyard enjoying the plays as he held the tray with six bowls of soup. The servant had taken four of his bowls away, and there were still two left. But at the sight of an actor singing and posturing as a singsong girl, the cook was so carried away that he forgot all else, thought all the soup had been served and let the tray down to pour off any slops. The two bowls were smashed, and all the soup spilt. Losing his head, the cook bent down to mop up the soup, but two dogs got there before him and started licking it up. Furious, the cook kicked with all his might at the dogs. In his haste, however, he missed the dogs and one of his hobnailed shoes flew off ten feet into the air.

Now Chen Ho-fu happened to be sitting at the first table on the left, where two plates of food had been served: one plate of pork dumplings, the other of dumplings stuffed with goose fat and sugar. These dumplings were steaming hot and there was another bowl of soup before him. He was just raising his chopsticks to his mouth when something black hurtled from behind the table to smash the two plates of sweetmeats. And as Chen Ho-fu jumped up in a fright, he caught the bowl of soup with his sleeve and overturned it, so that it slopped all over the table. Everybody present was taken aback.

Mr. Lu was extremely put out, knowing this was most inauspicious; but he could not very well say anything. Instead, he called his steward and cursed him under his breath.

"What do you all think you are doing?" he hissed. "Idiots, to tell a fool like that to carry in the dishes! When the wedding is over, I shall punish you properly."

In this confusion the opera came to an end. The servants took candles to light Chu Hsien-fu to his bridal chamber, while the other guests changed their seats to watch more operas until it was dawn.

The following day Chu Hsien-fu went to the hall to thank his father and mother-in-law and feasted with them. After this he returned to his chamber, where wine was served again and husband and wife feasted together. By this time Miss Lu had changed out of her ceremonial dress into an ordinary gown, and when Chu looked at her closely he saw that her beauty would put the flowers to shame. She had three or four slave girls and nurses to wait on her, as well as two maids called Tsai-ping and Shuang-hung, both of whom were exceedingly pretty too. Chu Hsien-fu felt as if he were in paradise.

But to know what followed, you must read the next chapter.

CHAPTER 11

Chu Hsien-fu's wife embarrasses him by asking him
for an essay, and Instructor Yang recommends a man of worth
to the prime minister's household

When Chu Hsien-fu married Mr. Lu's daughter, even before he realized how accomplished she was, he was almost
bowled over by her beauty. She was not one of the usual run
of accomplished young ladies, however; for her father, having
no son, had brought her up as if she were a boy. When she
was five or six he had engaged a tutor to teach her the *Four
Books* and the *Five Classics*,[1] so that by the time she was
twelve she could expound the classics and read essays, having
thoroughly mastered the works of Wang Shou-hsi. She had
also learned to write the *paku* essays with their divisions into
eight paragraphs: "broaching the theme," "advancing the
theme," "embarking on the subject," "the first strand," "the
central strand," and so forth. Her tutor was paid as highly
as if he were teaching a boy, and he supervised her studies just
as strictly. She was an intelligent girl with a good memory.
By this time she had read all the works of Wang Shou-hsi,
Tang Shun-chih, Chu Ching-chun, Hsueh Ying-chi and other

---

[1] The *Four Books* were *The Analects of Confucius, Mencius, The
Great Learning* and *The Doctrine of the Mean.* The *Five Classics*
were the *Book of Songs, Book of History, Book of Change, Book of
Rites,* and the *Spring and Autumn Annals.* All these were important
Confucian classics.

famous essayists as well as the examination compositions from the chief provincial examinations, and could recite over three thousand essays. Her own compositions were logical, concise, and elegant; and her father often declared with a sigh that, had she been a boy, she would have sailed through all the examinations.

Whenever the compiler had leisure, he would tell his daughter: "If you write *paku* essays well, then whatever literary form you use — and this applies even to lyrics or descriptive poems — you will express yourself forcefully and exactly. If, however, you cannot write *paku* essays well, then all your writing will be unorthodox and third-rate."

Miss Lu took her father's instructions to heart. Her dressing-table and embroidery-stand were stacked with essays, and every day she annotated and punctuated a few. As for the poems, odes, elegies and songs that were sent her, she did not even glance at them, giving the various anthologies of poetry in the house to her maids to read, and occasionally asking them to compose a few verses for fun.

Now Miss Lu and Master Chu appeared an ideal couple, perfectly matched as regards family status, appearance and accomplishments. She took it for granted that her husband had completed his studies and would soon pass the metropolitan and palace examinations; yet, even after they had been married for nearly two weeks, he still paid not the slightest attention to the essays which filled her room.

"Of course, he must know all these by heart," she thought. "And he is newly married; he wants to enjoy himself and thinks this is no time for study."

A few days later her husband, returning from a feast, took from his sleeve a volume of poems to declaim by the lamp, and invited his wife to sit beside him and read with him. Too shy at the time to remonstrate, she forced herself to look at the poems for an hour until it was time to sleep. The next day, however, she could bear it no longer; and, knowing that her husband was in the front library, she took a piece of red paper and wrote down an essay subject: "When a man purges himself of error, his family will be well governed."

Then she called Tsai-ping and said to her: "Take this to the young master and say that my father requests him to write an essay for our edification."

Chu Hsien-fu laughed when he received this message.

"This is hardly in my line," he said. "Besides, not having been a month yet in your honourable house, I would prefer to write something more cultured. I really have not the patience to write these common compositions."

He thought this would impress his brilliant young wife, not realizing that this was just the sort of talk she disliked most.

That evening, when the nurse went in to see her young mistress, she found her frowning, sighing and in tears.

"Why, miss!" exclaimed the nurse. "You have just had the luck to marry a good husband: whatever is the matter with you?"

The girl told her what had happened that day.

"I thought he had already completed his studies and would soon pass the metropolitan examinations," she concluded. "Who could have imagined this? My whole life is ruined!"

The nurse reasoned with her for a little, until Chu Hsien-fu came in, to be treated rather coldly by his wife. Knowing what had caused this aloofness, he felt a twinge of shame; but neither of them liked to say anything. After this, they were not on the best of terms and she was very unhappy. But if she raised the question of the examinations, her husband would not reply; and if she insisted, he criticized her as worldly. So she became more and more depressed, until a frown never left her face.

"Don't be such a foolish girl," urged her mother when she knew this. "I think your husband is already very accomplished; didn't your father like him because he was a brilliant young scholar?"

"Listen, mother, do *you* know of anyone, past or present, who is entitled to be called a brilliant young scholar without having passed the examinations?" As she spoke she began to grow angry again.

"You are a married woman now," said Mrs. Lu and the nurse. "So don't carry on like this. Besides, you both come from such well-to-do families that even if your husband doesn't become an official you will lack for nothing as long as you live."

"Good sons don't live on their inheritance; good daughters don't wear clothes from their own homes after they marry. I believe in a man making his own way. Only a good-for-nothing would let his grandfather support him."

"Well," said her mother, "even so, your only course is to win him round gradually. You can't hurry him."

"Even if the young master can't pass," said the nurse, "you will have a son who can learn from you from the beginning instead of following his father's example. With a good teacher like you right in the family he will surely turn out to be a Number One Palace Graduate. He will reflect such credit on you that you can be sure of receiving a title."

At this, both the nurse and the mother began to laugh; but the young wife sighed and said no more.

When knowledge of this came to Mr. Lu's ears, he also set two composition subjects for his son-in-law, and Chu had to make shift as best he could to write two essays. But when the compiler read them, he discovered that they were full of words and phrases pillaged from poems, a line here resembling Chu Yuan's *Lament* and a line there reminiscent of the early philosophers. They were not proper essays at all. This was a great disappointment to Mr. Lu too; but he could not very well say anything. Mrs. Lu, however, doted on her son-in-law as if he were her own flesh and blood.

Soon it was the end of the year, and after New Year Chu Hsien-fu went home to pay his respects to his grandfather and mother. On the twelfth of the first month, after his return, the Lou brothers invited him to dine with them. When the young man arrived, they took him into the library and inquired after Prefect Chu's health.

"There are no other guests today," they said. "But during the New Year festival we wanted to invite you to drink a few cups of wine with us."

They had barely sat down, however, when the gate-keeper came in.

"Chou Chi-fu the grave-keeper has come," he announced.

144

The two brothers had been busy for over a month arranging Chu Hsien-fu's wedding, and when that was over they had started making preparations for New Year, with the result that they had forgotten all about Yang Chih-chung. Now the arrival of Chou Chi-fu suddenly reminded them of him.

Old Chou was invited in, and the two brothers and Chu Hsien-fu went to the guest hall. They found the old man wearing a new felt cap, a padded gown of thick blue cloth, and warm shoes. His son was carrying a big cloth bag full of fried rice and dried beancurd. When they came in and put down the bag, the two brothers greeted them.

"We are glad to see you, Chi-fu," they said. "But there was no need to bring all these presents, which it is difficult for us to refuse."

"When you say that, young masters," said Chou Chi-fu, "I could die of shame. These are only country products for you to give your servants."

Attendants were ordered to take in the presents, and Chou Erh was invited to sit outside while Chou Chi-fu was asked into the library. Introduced to Master Chu, he asked after his grandfather.

"I met your grandfather that day twenty-seven years ago when our old master died here," he said. "Well, well, we all have to grow old! Is your grandfather's hair white too?"

"His hair has been white for three or four years."

Chou Chi-fu would not sit down above Chu until Lou Feng insisted. "He is our nephew and you are an old man," said Lou Feng. "You must take the place of honour."

First they had a meal and then, while fresh dishes were brought in and wine was poured, the brothers described their two attempts to call on Yang Chih-chung.

"Of course, he couldn't know this," said Chou Chi-fu. "I have been living in East Village for the last few months, so there was no one to tell Mr. Yang. But he is as honest a fellow as you could find: he would never put on airs and deliberately avoid anyone. He is one of the most friendly people I know, and if he realized that it was you two gentlemen who had called on him, he would travel all night to see you. Tomorrow I will go back to tell him, and bring him here to pay his respects."

"Wait till after the Lantern Festival," said Lou Chan. "On the fifteenth you can go out with our nephew to watch the lanterns, and on the seventeenth or eighteenth we will call a boat and go with you to Mr. Yang's house. It is more fitting for us to call on him first."

"That's even better," said Chou Chi-fu.

That night after the feast, they sent Chu Hsien-fu back to the Lu family and kept Chou Chi-fu in the library.

The next day was the date for trying out the lanterns, and in the main hall they hung two huge pearl lanterns from the palace, which had been presented to the Lou family by Emperor Cheng Hua. These lanterns were the work of extremely skilful court craftsmen, and Chou Chi-fu called his son to look at them as a treat. On the fourteenth he sent Chou Erh home.

"After the Lantern Festival I shall come with the Lou gentlemen to New Market, and we shall call at your sister's house," he told him. "I shall not be home till after the twentieth. You go home first."

Chou Erh did as he was told.

On the evening of the Lantern Festival Chu Hsien-fu was dining at home with his mother-in-law and wife when a message came from the Lou brothers asking him over to drink with them before going out to see the lanterns. In front of the prefect's yamen was an enormous lantern in the form of a sea monster bearing a mountain on its back, and celebrations were taking place in all the temples and shrines to the accompaniment of cymbals and drums. Men and women alike had come out to enjoy the lanterns and the moon, and the authorities allowed the revelries to last till late into the night.

The next morning Chou Chi-fu told the Lou brothers: "I will go on ahead to my daughter's house in New Market and meet you there on the eighteenth, to go with you to see Mr. Yang."

The two brothers agreed, and saw him out.

Chou Chi-fu boarded a boat bound for New Market. There his daughter welcomed him, kowtowing because it was just after New Year, and gave him a feast. On the eighteenth, Chou Chi-fu decided to go to Yang Chih-chung's house to wait for the Lou brothers, saying to himself: "Mr. Yang is very hard up: how can he entertain our young gentlemen?" So he asked his daughter for a chicken, and went to the market to buy three catties of meat, a bottle of wine and various vegetables. Then, borrowing a small boat from a neighbour, the old man had all his purchases put aboard and rowed to where Yang Chih-chung lived. He moored the boat by the bank, and walked up to Yang's door to knock. Presently the door was opened and Yang Chih-chung came out holding a bronze urn which he was rubbing vigorously with a handkerchief. When he saw that it was Chou Chi-fu, he put down the urn and they greeted each other. Then Chou Chi-fu carried over the provisions from his boat.

"Why have you brought all this wine and meat here, Mr. Chou?" demanded Yang in surprise. "I presumed too much on your generosity in the past; yet you are still so good to me."

"Take it, sir," said Chou Chi-fu. "This is only poor stuff, and it's not for you but to entertain two honourable guests here. Give this chicken and meat to your wife and tell her to cook them well; then I'll tell you who your visitors are."

Putting his hands in his sleeves, Yang Chih-chung said with a laugh: "I don't have to tell *you*, Mr. Chou. Since I came out of gaol last year we've had nothing in the house, and many's the day we've eaten only a bowl of gruel. But on New Year's Eve that fellow Wang who keeps a pawnshop in the village remembered this favourite little urn of mine and offered me twenty-four taels of silver for it, wanting to take advantage of the fact that we had no rice or fuel for the festival. I told him: 'If you want this urn of mine, you must pay three hundred taels of silver for it, not a cent less. I should want a hundred taels just to pawn it to you for half a year. The few taels you have offered are not even enough to buy charcoal for this urn.' Then he took the money back— the dog—and that night we had to go without rice and fuel after all. So my old woman and I lighted a candle and I fondled this urn all night: that's how we passed New Year. Look at the colour of that patina! Today, since there was

147

no rice again for lunch, I was amusing myself with this urn to while away the time, never expecting to see you. Now we have wine and meat, but there is no rice."

"That can be remedied," said Chou Chi-fu. And taking out his purse he gave Yang twenty cents of silver.

"Quickly ask someone to go and buy several measures of rice," he said. "Then we can sit down and talk."

Yang Chih-chung accepted the silver and ordered the old servant to take a container to the market as quickly as possible for rice. When she had bought it she went to the kitchen to prepare the meal. Then Yang closed the door and sat down.

"Who are the honourable guests you said were coming today?" he asked.

"Sir, after your trouble in the salt shop, how did you get out of the district gaol?"

"As a matter of fact, I don't know. When the magistrate suddenly released me, I asked at the yamen gate and was told a certain Mr. Tsin had acted as my guarantor. I thought hard, but I didn't know anyone called Tsin. Do you have any inkling what it is all about?"

"It wasn't anyone called Tsin! That man Tsin is a steward under Mr. Lou Feng, the third of the Lou brothers of the prime minister's house. The two Lou gentlemen heard of your great reputation when they visited me, and when they went back to the city sent seven hundred taels of silver to the district treasury and told Tsin to act as guarantor. After you returned they came twice to call on you—didn't you know?"

Yang Chih-chung suddenly realized what had happened.

"Yes! Yes!" he cried. "That old maid of ours mixed things up. The first time, when I came back from watching people fishing, she said: 'Some man called Liu came from the city to see you.' I thought it must be that runner Liu, so I didn't want to meet him. And the next time, when I came back another evening, she said: 'That man Liu was here again today, but I sent him about his business.' And that was the last I heard of him. Of course, it wasn't Liu but Lou! But how could I guess it was the Lou family? I thought it was the runner from the yamen."

"A man who has been bitten by a poisonous snake will be frightened if he dreams of a rope three years after!" said Chou Chi-fu. "Because your lawsuit dragged on for a year, you imagined it must be the runner. I went on the twelfth of this month to pay my respects to the Lou gentlemen, and the two masters mentioned you and asked me to come with them to your house today. But I didn't want you to be caught unprepared, so I brought a few things along to act as host for you. Is that all right?"

"Since the two gentlemen have done me such a favour, I ought to go to the city to call on them. Why did you trouble them to come out here again?"

"Since they have decided to come, there is no need for you to call on them first. Just wait for them here."

After they had talked for some time, Yang Chih-chung made tea; and as they were drinking they heard knocking at the door.

"The young gentlemen have arrived," said Chou Chi-fu. "Hurry up and open the door."

As soon as the door opened, however, a man burst in roaring drunk, who fell down, staggered to his feet, rubbed his head and rushed inside. Yang saw that it was his second son. After gambling and losing in the market, he had got drunk and decided to come home and ask his mother for more money so that he might go out and gamble again. He had charged straight in.

"You drunken beast!" cried Yang Chih-chung. "Where are you going? Come and greet Mr. Chou."

Reeling tipsily, the young man made his bow, then disappeared into the kitchen. The chicken and pork simmering in one pan set his mouth watering; and he saw a pan of good rice, too, and a bottle of wine. Not troubling to ask where this feast had come from, he lifted the lid of the pan to get at the meat. His mother slammed the lid on again.

"Greedy pig!" cried Yang Chih-chung. "This food was brought by somebody else, and we're keeping it for guests."

Do you think his son would listen? Dodging tipsily about, he kept trying to grab something to eat. And when his father swore at him, he glared and answered back. Losing his temper, Yang snatched up a poker to drive him out, while Chou Chi-fu tried to restrain the young man by saying: "This wine and food are being kept for the gentlemen of the Lou family."

Dolt as he was, and drunk into the bargain, when Yang's son heard the name Lou, he dared not misbehave. And his mother, seeing that he was sobering up, smuggled him a leg of chicken and a big bowlful of rice and soup. When he had finished this, he flung himself on his bed and slept.

Only at sunset did the Lou brothers arrive, accompanied by Chu Hsien-fu. Old Chou and Yang Chih-chung went out to welcome them and ushered them in to the small room which had three rickety bamboo chairs on each side and a desk in the middle. On the wall hung a scroll inscribed with Chu Pai-lu's maxims on regulating the household, flanked with two strips of paper on which were written: "Three tumbledown rooms, one simple fellow." Above these was pasted an official announcement: "This is to inform you that the master of your house, Yang Chih-chung, has been appointed instructor for Chuyang County, Huaian Prefecture." But before they had time to read it through, Yang Chih-chung stepped forward to ask them to be seated. He himself went into the kitchen to fetch the tea tray which he offered to each of his guests.

When they had drunk the tea and exchanged the usual compliments, Lou Feng pointed to the announcement.

"May I ask if this is recent news?" he inquired.

"It dates from three years ago," said Yang, "before ill luck overtook me. I happened to become a salaried licentiate; but although I took the next examination sixteen or seventeen times, I failed to pass it. I was offered the post of instructor when I was growing old; but since it involved making reports to the superintendent and humbling myself to him I felt it would be too much for my self-respect, and excused myself on grounds of ill health. Then I had a great deal of trouble trying to get a medical certificate from the magistrate; and I had not resigned long when I was falsely accused by a money-grubber! So it seemed to me I should have done better to have accepted that post and gone to Chuyang, for then I should not have been imprisoned. If you two gentlemen had not gone out of your way to help me, I should probably have died in prison. How can I ever repay my debt of gratitude?"

"Why mention such a trifle?" asked Lou Feng. "When I hear how you resigned your post, sir, I am even more impressed by your lofty character and firm virtue."

"Friends should put their property at each other's disposal," said Lou Chan. "What we did is not worth mentioning. We are only sorry that we heard of this so late, and were not able to come to your assistance earlier."

When Yang heard how they spoke, he felt even greater admiration for them and exchanged some courtesies with Chu Hsien-fu.

Then Chou Chi-fu said: "Young masters, you have come a long way and must be hungry."

"A humble meal is already prepared," said Yang. "Please take seats in the back room." He invited them into a thatched hut which he had built as a diminutive library. It overlooked a tiny courtyard planted with several plum trees, a few twigs of which were already in blossom, since the last three or four days had been warm. The walls were covered with poems and pictures, a couplet in the middle reading:

At ease I inhale the sweet plum blossom by my window.
Let others pluck laurel in the moon and dance.

The two brothers could not repress a sigh of admiration, feeling as if they had wandered into fairyland.

When Yang had brought in the chicken, pork, wine and rice, they drank several cups of wine, then ate the rice. After that the table was cleared, tea was brewed and they began to talk freely. Mention of the deaf old crone's jumbled account of the Lou brothers' two calls set them all laughing heartily. The two brothers wanted to invite Yang Chih-chung to their house for a few days; but he declined.

"There are some mundane matters to attend to during New Year," he said. "However, in three or four days I shall count it a great honour to drink wine in your distinguished house."

They talked until the evening, when moonlight flooded the window and the sprays of plum blossom seemed to be painted on the window paper. The two brothers could hardly tear themselves away.

"I should invite you gentlemen to stay in my humble cottage," said Yang Chih-chung, "but I fear my poor accommodation might inconvenience you."

Then, taking their hands, he escorted the Lou brothers and Chu through the moonlight to their boat, after which he and Chou Chi-fu went back.

As soon as the two brothers and Chu Hsien-fu arrived home, the gate-keeper told them: "Mr. Lu has important business and asks Master Chu to go back. He has sent three messengers."

Chu Hsien-fu hurried home, where his mother-in-law told him that his refusal to study for the examinations had made her husband so angry that he had talked of taking a concubine so that he might have a son who would study and continue the family tradition. When she told Mr. Lu that he was too old and tried to dissuade him, he had become very angry. The previous evening he had fallen down and had a stroke, and now he was half paralysed, his mouth and eyes crooked. Tears were welling from his daughter's eyes as she sat beside him, sighing.

There was nothing the young man could do but hurry to the library to wait on his father-in-law. He found Chen Ho-fu there feeling the patient's pulse.

"Your pulse is rather feeble, sir," Chen Ho-fu told Mr. Lu. "The lungs control the breath, and the weakness here shows that you have a little phlegm. This is due to the fact that, though you have retired, like the good, loyal official you are, you still long to go back to court; and constant worry and depression have brought about this illness. The best way to cure it is by regulating your breath to get rid of the phlegm. I have observed that physicians nowadays often consider pinellia rather hot; thus when they treat cases of phlegm they use hermodactyl. Actually, hermodactyl is not efficacious in cases of phlegm. What you need is a tonic decoction composed of ginseng, atractylis ovata, pachyma cocos, dried liquorice root, ginger and dates. That will ease your kidneys so that the fiery humour does not rise easily; and then the illness will be cured."

152

Chen Ho-fu made out a prescription and, after taking four or five doses, Mr. Lu's mouth regained its normal shape although his tongue remained swollen. When Chen Ho-fu examined his patient again, he changed his treatment, prescribing certain pills and drugs efficacious against paralysis, until gradually Mr. Lu recovered. Chu Hsien-fu tended his father-in-law for more than ten days, during which time he had no proper rest.

One day when Mr. Lu was having an afternoon nap, Chu went to the Lou family where, hearing Yang Chih-chung's booming voice in the library, he knew that his uncles' guest had arrived. He went in to greet Mr. Yang and they sat down together.

"I was just saying," resumed Yang Chih-chung, "that since you two gentlemen admire true merit so much, although I am not worthy of your notice, I have a friend living in the hills in Hsiaoshan County who is a remarkable genius and a wonderful scholar. One might truly say of him: In retirement he would be a great scholar; and in office he could be the councillor of kings. Would you like to meet him?"

Marvelling, the two brothers asked: "Who is this remarkable man?"

Then, crossing his fingers, Yang told them his friend's name. But to know who this man was, you must read the next chapter.

CHAPTER 12

In which famous scholars feast at Oriole-Throat Lake, and a swordsman calls with a human head

"A man with my humble capacities is not good enough for gentlemen like you, who admire worth so much," Yang Chih-chung told the Lou brothers. "But I have a friend called Chuan Wu-yung from Hsiaoshan County who lives in the hills. If you invite him here to talk with you, you will see that he has the wisdom of ancient statesmen and the learning of scholars of old, which make him unrivalled among contemporaries."

"If he is such a remarkable man," said Lou Feng, much impressed, "why don't we go to pay our respects to him?"

"Suppose we hire a boat to go tomorrow, and ask Mr. Yang to accompany us?" suggested Lou Chan.

Just then the gate-keeper hurried in with a red visiting card.

"The newly appointed roadway officer, Mr. Wei, has arrived and sends you his respects," he announced. "He has brought a letter from the first master at the capital, and says he would like to speak to you."

"Nephew," said Lou Feng to Chu Hsien-fu, "will you entertain Mr. Yang while we see this visitor? We shall not be long."

They went to change their clothes before going to the reception hall.

Mr. Wei entered in full official dress, and after greeting each other they sat down in the places of guest and hosts.

"When did you leave the capital, sir?" asked the brothers. "We have not yet congratulated you on your distinguished appointment, but you are already honouring us with your presence."

"On the third of last month I received my appointment in the capital," replied Mr. Wei. "And that same day I had the privilege of meeting your brother who gave me this letter for you; hence I have presumed to come to pay my respects."

He presented the letter with both hands.

The elder brother opened the letter and read it, then handed it to his younger brother.

"It concerns the work of surveying," he told Mr. Wei. "Do you mean to set to work, sir, so soon after your appointment?"

"Yes," replied Mr. Wei. "This morning I received an order from my superior instructing me to lose no time, so today I have come to trouble you to inform me of the full extent of your honourable uncle's graveyard. For when I go there to pay my respects, I shall summon the local runners to examine the boundaries carefully, to see that those ignorant peasants do not cut firewood nearby or trespass on your property. I shall issue a warning to them."

"Will you then be leaving at once, sir?" asked Lou Chan.

"In three or four days, after reporting to my superior, I shall set out on a surveying trip."

"In that case," said Lou Feng, "we beg you to dine with us tomorrow in our humble house. And when you visit our poor mountainous graveyard, we shall naturally accompany you."

During this conversation the tea had been changed three times; and now the roadway officer bowed and took a ceremonious leave of the brothers.

When they had seen him off, they removed their official robes and returned to the library, very much upset.

"Something like this *would* happen!" they sighed. "Just as we were about to set off to see Mr. Chuan, this roadway officer comes to start measuring our estates. Tomorrow we have to entertain him to a meal, and we shall have to accompany him when he goes to measure our uncle's graveyard. That means we must postpone going to Hsiaoshan. What's to be done?"

"How you two gentlemen thirst after talent!" exclaimed Yang Chih-chung. "But if you are so eager to meet Mr. Chuan, there is no need to go yourselves. You can write a letter to which I will add a note, and we will ask one of your honourable servants to deliver it to Mr. Chuan in the hills, inviting him to pay you a visit. He will be only too glad to accept."

"I am afraid Mr. Chuan may wonder at our presumption," said Lou Chan.

"Official business has a way of piling up," said Yang. "If you don't do this, you will always be longing to meet him without ever being able to do so."

"That is right," agreed Chu. "My uncles may never find a free day to visit Mr. Chuan. But if you write an invitation and send a reliable man to deliver it with Mr. Yang's letter, I don't think Mr. Chuan will be offended."

Then and there the matter was settled. They prepared various presents, then ordered Tsin Chueh's son, Huan-cheng, to take the gifts and the letter to Hsiaoshan. Acting on his masters' instructions, Huan-cheng boarded a boat to Hangchow; and when the boatmen saw that his baggage was neat and his appearance good, they invited him into the inner cabin. There were already two men there in scholars' caps, whom Huan-cheng greeted. Then he sat down. After the evening meal, each unrolled his bedding and slept.

The next day, since there was nothing to do on board, they started to talk; and Huan-cheng heard the scholars discussing Hsiaoshan County. Travellers who meet on a boat always address each other as "passenger," so now he asked: "May I inquire your honourable district, passengers?"

"We are from Hsiaoshan," replied the scholar with a beard.

"Do you know a certain Mr. Chuan there?"

"There is no one of that name in Hsiaoshan," replied the younger of the two.

"I believe his name is Chuan Wu-yung."

"Chuan Wu-yung?" repeated the young passenger. "We have no scholar there by that name."

"Can it be *that* fellow?" said the bearded man. "That would be a joke." Then turning to the youth, he asked: "Don't you know about him? Let me tell you, then. He lives in the mountain and all his ancestors were peasants; but his father made enough money to send him to a country school to study. He studied until he was seventeen or eighteen, when a heartless village teacher did him a bad turn by insisting that he should go in for the examinations. Later on his father died, but this fellow was good-for-nothing: he could neither till the land nor trade. He just sat at home eating until he had eaten up all his property. He took the examinations for more than thirty years but never even passed the lowest, because he can't talk sense. He used to live in a tutelary temple where he took a few pupils, and every year he prepared for the examinations. In that way he was just able to make ends meet. But then he was unlucky again, for the other year he met the accountant of a Huchow salt shop in New Market— an old man called Yang—who came to collect bills. This Mr. Yang, who put up in the temple, was a complete lunatic, gabbling all the time about astronomy, geography and the arts of government. When Chuan heard him, he became possessed by a devil and lost his senses completely — he stopped taking the examinations and became a hermit! But once he became a hermit students stopped going to him; so now he has nothing to live on except what he cheats out of the country people. 'We are such good friends, there should be no difference between us,' he tells them. 'What's yours is mine, and all that's mine is yours.' This is his formula."

"He surely can't deceive many people that way," said the young man.

"Everything he possesses he has tricked out of people," retorted the man with the beard. "Still, since we belong to the same village, I won't say any more." Then he asked Huan-cheng: "Why did you inquire about this man?"

"For no particular reason," replied Huan-cheng. "I was just asking." But he was thinking: "Our third and fourth masters are a queer couple. So many high officials and magistrates come to pay their respects, yet they still feel they haven't enough friends and send me all this way, for no reason, to find such a swindler!"

Just then he saw a boat pass with two girls in it who looked very like the two maids in the Lu family. He gave a start and hastily leaned out to stare at them, only to find he was mistaken. After that the two other passengers did not talk to him any more.

A few days later Huan-cheng changed boats and reached Hsiaoshan where, after half a day's search, he found in a valley a miserable thatched hovel with white paper pasted on the door. He knocked and went in. Chuan Wu-yung was in mourning, with a big white cloth cap on his head. When he found out why Huan-cheng had come he put him up in his back room on a straw pallet, entertaining him that evening to beef and alcohol. The next day, he wrote a reply.

"I am most grateful for your masters' regard," he told Huan-cheng. "But I am in mourning now and cannot leave my home. Go back and convey my respects to your masters and to Mr. Yang, and tell them that I accept their magnificent presents. In another twenty days, when a hundred days have passed since my mother's death, I shall come to call on your masters. I have put you to a lot of trouble. Please take these two cents of silver to buy some wine."

He handed a small paper package to Huan-cheng, who accepted it.

"Thank you, Mr. Chuan," he said. "I hope you will come to the city on the day you have promised, so that my masters will not wait for you in vain."

"Of course," replied Chuan Wu-yung, and escorted him outside.

Huan-cheng boarded another boat and took Chuan Wu-yung's letter back to his masters in Huchow. They could not help feeling disappointed; but they changed the name of a large and most luxurious pavilion behind the library, calling it after Mr. Chuan, to show that they were waiting for him to come and stay there. They lodged Yang Chih-chung in a room behind this pavilion. Yang was old and asthmatic and needed someone to attend to him during the night; so he sent for his second son. And this dolt, it goes without saying, was drunk every evening.

About a month later Yang sent another letter to Chuan, urging him to come at once; and on the receipt of this Chuan put together a few things and took a boat to Huchow. He came ashore outside the city still in mourning clothes, some bedding on his left shoulder and the big cloth sleeve on his right arm flapping as he pushed his way clumsily down the road. When he crossed the drawbridge into the city, the road was packed; but he did not know that in order not to hold up traffic pedestrians going out of the city must keep to the left and those going in to the right. He charged forward, knocking into everything in his way.

Now a woodcutter who had just sold his firewood was walking out of the city with a pointed pole over his shoulder when Chuan Wu-yung barged into him, and Chuan's tall mourning cap was impaled on this pole. Pacing with lowered head, the woodcutter continued—oblivious—on his way. As for Chuan, he gave a start and rubbed his head, then discovered that his mourning cap had vanished. Catching sight of it on the pole, he waved frantically.

"That's *my* hat!" he shouted.

The woodcutter, however, was walking quickly and did not hear. Chuan was not used to walking in cities, and the fact that he was flustered made him blunder along more awkwardly than ever, without looking where he was going.

He had covered about one bow's shot, when he collided so violently with a sedan-chair that he nearly knocked the officer seated in it right out. The officer demanded furiously who he was, and ordered the two runners in front to tie him up. Yet instead of admitting that he was in the wrong, Chuan went on shouting and gesticulating. Then the officer alighted from his chair to question him, and the runners shouted to him to kneel down. But he simply glared at the officer and refused to kneel.

By this time sixty or seventy people had gathered round to watch; and out of this crowd stepped a man with big eyes and a few brown hairs on his chin, wearing a military cap and black silk jacket. He walked up to the officer.

"Please don't take offence, Your Excellency," he said. "This man is an honoured guest of the Lou family. Although he has knocked into you, I am afraid if you punish him the Lou gentlemen may hear of it, and that would not look good."

The occupant of the sedan-chair was Mr. Wei, the newly appointed roadway officer. So when he heard this he simply uttered a warning, to save his own face, then mounted his chair and rode away. Chuan Wu-yung saw that his champion was an old friend, a man skilled in the military arts and known as Iron-armed Chang.

Iron-armed Chang made Chuan sit down in a tea-house to recover his breath, and they drank some tea.

"The other day when I went to your house to offer my condolences, your servant told me you had received an invitation from the Lou gentlemen," said Chang. "Why do I find you knocking about by yourself outside the city gate?"

"The Lou family invited me a long time ago," replied Chuan, "but I am only just on my way there. I didn't expect to bump into an official who would make so much trouble for me. Thank you for helping me out. Why don't you come with me to the Lou family?"

The two of them proceeded together to the Lou house. The gate-keeper was taken aback by the sight of a man in mourning, minus his white cap, followed by such a martial-looking fellow. This strange couple clamoured to see his masters, but would not give their names.

"Your masters have been expecting us for a long time!" they insisted.

When he refused to announce them, they started bawling and shouting at the gate.

"Ask Mr. Yang to come out!" they roared. The gate-keeper had to obey them.

Yang was shocked to see the state Chuan was in.

"Haven't you even got a hat?" he asked with a frown.

He made them sit down on a bench in the gate-house while he hurried in to fetch an old scholar's cap for Chuan.

"Who is this stalwart?" he inquired next.

"This is the famous Iron-armed Chang of whom I was always telling you."

"I have long hoped to meet you," said Yang.

The three of them went in together, and they told him of the trouble they had just had at the city gate.

"You had better not mention it to the Lou gentlemen," he advised them.

That day the Lou brothers happened to be out, so the visitors followed Yang into the library where they washed their faces, had a meal and were well looked after by the servants.

When the two brothers returned from a feast that evening and found them in the library, they expressed regret at having been unable to meet earlier and pointed to the pavilion to show how they had looked forward to Chuan Wu-yung's arrival. The fact that Chuan had brought a swordsman with him convinced them that he was an exceptional man, and they ordered another feast to be spread. Chuan sat in the seat of honour with Yang and Iron-armed Chang opposite, while the brothers acted as hosts. During the feast they asked Iron-armed Chang how he came by his name.

"When I was young and strong," Iron-armed Chang told them, "my friends, for a wager, asked me to lie in the middle of the road and stretch out my arm for a cart to pass over it. An ox-cart came rumbling along, weighing at least four or five thousand catties. Its wheels passed right over my arm, but I simply flexed my muscles. There was a clatter and the cart was thrown several yards off. When they looked at my arm, it wasn't even bruised. So they gave me this nickname."

The elder Lou clapped his hands.

"After hearing of such a feat, we should consume a whole gallon of wine!" he declared. "Let us all change to big cups."

Chuan Wu-yung refused, however.

"A mourner cannot drink wine," he said.

Yang Chih-chung protested.

"The old and the sick need not observe the conventions," he quoted. "I noticed you eating quite heartily just now: so if you drink a cup or two it won't matter."

"Your remark is ill-founded, sir," retorted Chuan. "When the ancients speak of fasting they mean abstinence from such things as garlic, leeks and coriander, which, of course, I do not eat. In the same way, wine is absolutely forbidden."

"Naturally we shall not press you," said Lou Chan, hastily calling for tea.

"I know most of the military arts," announced Iron-armed Chang. "I can fight with eighteen different weapons on foot and eighteen different weapons on horse-back. I can use the whip, the mace, the axe, the hammer, the sword, the spear, the sabre and the halberd. In fact, I may be said to have mastered all these. But I am unlucky in my temperament, for whenever I see injustice done I must draw my sword to avenge the injured. I cannot resist fighting with the strongest in the empire; and whenever I have money, I give it to the poor. Thus I have ended up without a home, and that is how I come to be in your honourable district."

"This is exactly what one would expect of a hero!" exclaimed Lou Chan.

"Since our friend Chang has mentioned the military arts," said Chuan, "I might add he is seen at his best in a sword dance. Why don't you gentlemen ask him to give a performance?"

Delighted, the Lou brothers ordered servants to bring Iron-armed Chang a fine old sword which gleamed brightly when he unsheathed it beneath the lamp. He took off his jerkin, tightened his belt, picked up the sword and stepped out into the courtyard. The others followed him. The brothers bade him wait until lamps were lit; and at the word of command a dozen young servants came out, each with a candlestick, and candles were lit on each side of the courtyard.

Iron-armed Chang's sword whirled up and down, right and left, moving faster and faster through many figures till nothing but a brilliant glitter could be seen, with no man inside, and silvery serpents seemed to be darting in all directions. At the same time an icy wind made the onlookers shiver. Chuan took a copper basin from a stand and told a servant to fill it with water and spatter it over Iron-armed Chang; but not a drop reached him. Presently, however, he uttered a great cry, the brilliant glitter vanished, and there he stood with the sword in his hand, not in the least flushed or winded. Everyone applauded. Then they drank till nearly dawn and put the guests up in the library; for now Chuan Wu-yung and Iron-armed Chang were honoured guests in the prime minister's house.

One day Lou Feng told them: "Soon we must organize a big party and invite our honourable guests to the lake."

The weather was growing warm and Chuan Wu-yung's thick white gown was becoming too hot, so he decided to pawn it in order to buy some blue cloth to make a gown for the party. He did this without consulting the Lou brothers, entrusting the business to Iron-armed Chang, who pawned the gown for five hundred coins which Chuan put beside his pillow. He spent the day in the pavilion named after him, and that evening, when he went back to his room to sleep, he looked for his five hundred coins but could not find a single one. Knowing that no one else had been in the room except Yang Chih-chung's foolish son, who liked to loiter there, Chuan went straight to the gate-house. He found the young man sitting there talking nonsense.

"I want a word with you!" called Chuan.

"What do you want, uncle?" The young man was already drunk.

"Did you see the five hundred coins by my pillow?"

"Yes."

"Where have they gone?"

"I took them to gamble with this afternoon, and lost. I still have about a dozen coins left, which I mean to use to buy alcohol."

"What extraordinary behaviour! How could you take my money to gamble with?"

"Why, uncle, aren't you and I really one? What's yours is mine, and all that's mine is yours. What difference is there?"

Then turning on his heel the youth rushed out. Chuan glared furiously after him, but dared not say a word. He had to put up with the affront. And after this Chuan and Yang were not on good terms; for Chuan said Yang was a fool, and Yang said Chuan was a lunatic. But when Lou Feng saw that Chuan had nothing to wear, he made him a present of a light blue silk gown.

The brothers invited guests and hired two big boats; the cooks prepared a feast; and they filled another boat with attendants, and yet another with musicians and singers. This was the middle of the fourth month when the weather was clear and warm; so all the guests were wearing summer clothes and carrying fans. Although it could not be called a large party, they had collected quite a number of people. There were the third and fourth Lou brothers and Chu Hsien-fu, the scholar Niu Pu-yi, the instructor Yang Chih-chung, the scholar Chuan Wu-yung, the gallant Iron-armed Chang, and the diviner Chen Ho-fu. Mr. Lu had also been asked, but had declined the invitation. However, in addition to the eight guests there was also Yang Chih-chung's idiot son, making nine in all. Niu Pu-yi chanted poems, Iron-armed Chang performed his sword dance, Chen Ho-fu cracked jokes, the Lou brothers appeared extremely cultured and Chu Hsien-fu extremely elegant, while Yang Chih-chung looked venerable and Chuan Wu-yung eccentric: thus the party was unique. The cabin windows on both sides were opened so that they could hear music from the small boats as they drifted towards the lake. And presently a feast was spread and a dozen servants in wide gowns and tall caps poured wine and served the dishes. It goes without saying that the food was rare, the wine and tea were fragrant, and they drank till the moon was up. Then fifty or sixty lanterns were lit on the small boats and were reflected with the moonlight in the water, making it as bright as day. The music sounded even more clearly in the stillness, its strains echoing for miles around, so that watchers on shore stared at the revellers as if they were immortals, and none but envied them. Thus they boated all night.

When Chu Hsien-fu went in to see his father-in-law the next morning, Mr. Lu said: "Your uncles should spend their time quietly at home, studying to increase the reputation of their family instead of mixing with people like this. Such lordly ostentation is hardly proper."

Chu repeated this to his uncles the following day, and Lou Feng gave a loud laugh.

"How can your father-in-law be so vulgar?" he asked.

While he was speaking, the gate-keeper came in.

"Mr. Lu has been promoted to the post of reader," he announced. "The imperial decree has been issued and the bulletin has just arrived. You are requested to go and offer congratulations."

Upon hearing this, Chu Hsien-fu hurried home to congratulate his father-in-law.

That evening, however, Chu sent a servant flying to his uncles with bad news. When Mr. Lu received the imperial decree the whole family was delighted and he ordered a feast to celebrate; but suddenly his phlegm overwhelmed him and he lost consciousness. The Lou brothers were begged to go over at once.

Without waiting for their sedan-chairs, the brothers hurried across. But when they reached Mr. Lu's gate they heard loud sobbing and knew that he was dead. All the relatives had arrived and were discussing whom to appoint from the clan as his heir. Then the funeral began. And pale and haggard with sorrow, Chu Hsien-fu performed his duties like a good son-in-law.

Several days later, a letter arrived from the eldest Lou brother in the capital, and the third and fourth brothers discussed their reply together. It was towards the end of the month and the moon had not yet risen. The two brothers sat up talking by candlelight until nearly midnight, when they heard a thud on the roof and a blood-stained man dropped down from the eaves carrying a leather bag. By the light of the candle they recognized Iron-armed Chang.

The two brothers were very startled.

"What brings you, friend, to our inner chamber in the middle of the night?" they asked. "And what have you in that leather bag?"

"Please be seated, gentlemen," said Iron-armed Chang, "and let me explain. During my life I have had one benefactor and one enemy. I have hated my enemy for ten years without having an opportunity to kill him; but today my chance came and I have his head here. Inside this bag is a bloody human head! But my benefactor is some distance away, and I need five hundred taels to repay him for his kindness. Once this debt of honour is paid, my heart will be at rest and I can devote the rest of my life to you who have treated me so well. Believing that only you two gentlemen could help me—for no others are so understanding—I made bold to call on you tonight. But if you are unwilling to help, then I must go far away and never see you again."

Taking up the leather bag he started off.

"Don't do anything rash, friend!" cried the brothers, now thoroughly frightened. "Five hundred taels is a trifle — but what about this bag?"

"That's easy," replied Iron-armed Chang with a laugh. "I can remove all traces by means of certain arts that I know. But that will have to wait for the moment. If you will give me the five hundred taels, I shall come back in four hours, take out the object in the leather bag and apply a magic powder to it, so that it changes instantly to water and not a hair remains. You gentlemen might prepare a feast and invite guests to watch me."

Tremendously impressed, the two brothers hurried inside to fetch him five hundred taels. Then Iron-armed Chang put the bag down on the steps, stowed the silver about his person, thanked them and vaulted on the eaves. All they heard was a clatter on the tiles, as he vanished like lightning. The night was very still and the moon had just risen to shed its rays on the leather bag on the steps with its bloody human head.

But to know what happened to the head, you must read the chapter which follows.

CHAPTER 13

Chu Hsien-fu consults a worthy man about the examinations.
Ma Chun-shang puts his money at the service of a friend

The Lou brothers had given five hundred taels to Iron-armed Chang so that he might repay his benefactor, and he had left a leather bag containing a human head in their house. Although as members of the prime minister's house they could never get into serious trouble, the presence of a head dripping with blood on the steps of their inner chamber caused them a little uneasiness.

"A gallant like Iron-armed Chang can be counted on not to fail us," said Lou Chan to his brother. "So we must on no account act like the common herd. Let us prepare a feast and invite all our closest friends to wait for him to come and open this bag. It's not every day that you can see a head changed to water. Why not give a Human Head Party?"

Lou Feng agreed with him. As soon as it was light he gave orders for a feast to be prepared to which they invited Niu Pu-yi, Chen Ho-fu and Chu Hsien-fu, in addition, of course, to the three guests staying in their house. They described the occasion as a small drinking party, without disclosing the real reason for the feast, intending to take all their guests by surprise when Iron-armed Chang arrived and gave his display.

All the guests assembled and talked of this and that for six or seven hours; but Iron-armed Chang did not come. By midday there was still no sign of him.

"This is beginning to look odd," whispered Lou Feng to Lou Chan.

"Something must have held him up," replied Lou Chan. "As long as his leather bag is here, he is sure to come."

They waited till late afternoon, but still he had not come. And since the feast was ready, they had to invite their guests to table. It was a hot day and the brothers began to be worried.

"If he doesn't show up, what shall we do with the head?" they wondered.

By evening the leather bag was stinking. When the brothers' wives smelled it, they were uneasy and sent servants to ask the two masters to have a look. Then the Lou brothers had to pluck up courage to open the bag, only to find in it not a human head but a pig's head weighing six or seven catties!

The brothers gazed at each other in silent dismay, then ordered the pig's head to be taken to the kitchen for the servants to eat. Deciding after a whispered consultation to say nothing of this, they went back to accompany their guests; and there they were, feeling rather downcast, when the gate-keeper came in.

"A runner is here from Wucheng County with a card from the magistrate," he announced. "He has brought two runners from Hsiaoshan County and begs to be allowed to speak to you, sir."

"Most peculiar," commented Lou Feng. "What can their business be?"

Leaving his younger brother to entertain the guests, he went to the hall and ordered the runner to be admitted. The man came in and kowtowed.

"His Excellency, our magistrate, greets you," he said.

He then presented a warrant and a writ. Calling for candles, Lou Feng read this document, which ran as follows:

Magistrate Wu of Hsiaoshan County reports on a local case of kidnapping. According to the abbess Hui Yuan of Lan Jo Temple, her pupil, the nun Hsin Yuan, was seduced and kidnapped by a local vagabond named Chuan Wu-yung. This felon, before his crime was discovered, ran away to your county; hence we transmit this case to you and request your honourable county to deal with the matter and to send runners to assist our officers to find this culprit, who should then be arrested and brought back to our county for trial. This is urgent!

When Lou Feng had read this, the runner announced: "Our superior wishes to inform you, sir, that he has heard that you have harboured this felon, not knowing what manner of man he is. He requests you to hand him over to me. Runners from his own county are waiting outside, and I shall give him to them to take away. If he gets wind of this and escapes, it will be difficult to send an answer to Hsiaoshan County."

"I see," said Lou Feng. "Wait outside, will you?"

The runner withdrew to sit in the gate-house.

Thoroughly mortified, Lou Feng sent for his brother and Mr. Yang and showed them the writ and warrant for Chuan Wu-yung's arrest. Lou Chan was embarrassed too, but not so Yang Chih-chung.

"Mr. Lou Feng, Mr. Lou Chan, remember the proverb!" he urged them, "if a wasp gets next to your skin, remove your coat to shake it off. Since he has landed himself in this trouble, you gentlemen cannot protect him even if you want to. I will go and break it to him, then hand him over to the runners. He'll have to talk his own way out of this."

There was nothing the Lou brothers could do but let Yang go back to the library and explain briefly to the feasters what had happened. Chuan Wu-yung flushed crimson.

"Truth is truth; lies are lies!" he protested. "I'll go with him. I'm not afraid!"

Then the two brothers went in, not changing their manner to him, and expressed their indignation on his behalf. After drinking two parting cups of wine with him and presenting him with two packages of silver for his journey, they saw him out of the gate, ordered one of their servants to carry his luggage for him, and bowed in farewell. As soon as the two runners saw that the felon was out of the prime minister's house and the Lou brothers had gone in, they seized Chuan Wu-yung and loaded him with chains.

These two incidents left the Lou brothers rather discouraged. They ordered the gate-keeper, if strangers called, to say that they had returned to the capital. And henceforward they remained behind closed doors, devoting themselves to household affairs.

Soon after this, Chu Hsien-fu came to take his leave of them, explaining that his grandfather was ill and that he must go back to Chiahsing to nurse him. When the brothers heard this, they accompanied their nephew; but by the time they reached Chiahsing, Prefect Chu's illness had become very serious and seemed likely to prove mortal. Then the young man, at his grandfather's request, asked his uncles to arrange for his wife to be brought.

The Lou brothers wrote a letter home and sent a maid to explain the situation. Mrs. Lu was unwilling to part with her daughter, but the young lady understood the duties of a wife and said that she must go to nurse her husband's grandfather. By this time, Tsai-ping had married and Shuang-hung was the only maid left to accompany the bride. They hired two big boats, had her dowry put aboard and set off for Chiahsing; but when they arrived Prefect Chu was dead and Master Chu was head of the family. His young wife looked after her mother-in-law and managed household affairs so well that all the relatives praised her. The Lou brothers stayed there until after the funeral, when they returned to Huchow.

Chu Hsien-fu remained in mourning for three years. Having witnessed his two uncles' final disillusionment after so many gallant attempts to detect talent, his own ambition had left him and he printed no more copies of Kao Chi's *Random Notes on Poetry* to give to his friends.

By the time the period of mourning was completed, Chu Hsien-fu's eldest son was four; and every day his wife taught the child to read the *Four Books* and *paku* essays, while the young man stood by giving advice. He longed now to discuss the examinations with friends who had done well in them; but unfortunately all his acquaintances in Chiahsing thought of him as a poet and kept at a distance, with the result that he felt rather out of things. One day, however, as he was walking along the street he saw a red paper announcement in a new bookshop: "Our management has invited Mr. Ma Chun-shang of Chuchow to compile a collection of essays. Any gentlemen wishing to honour us with their essays should send them to Literary Ocean Bookshop, in the main street of Chiahsing."

"Here is a famous editor," thought Chu Hsien-fu. "Why not call on him?"

He hurried home to change his clothes and write a visiting card, then returned to the bookshop.

"Is Mr. Ma in?" he asked.

"He is upstairs," said the clerk, and called: "Mr. Ma! Here is a visitor for you."

"Coming!" responded a voice from upstairs, and Ma Chun-shang came down. Over six feet tall and powerfully built, he was wearing a scholar's cap, blue gown and black shoes with white soles. His face was swarthy and his beard sparse.

When they had greeted each other and sat down, Ma Chun-shang looked at Chu Hsien-fu's card.

"I have seen your honourable name appended to many poems, and have long wished to meet you," he said.

"Now that you have come to edit essays here, you will command the respect of all scholars. I have always wanted to make your acquaintance, and regret that we could not meet earlier."

Tea was brought to them from the shop, and they drank it.

"Did you pass your examination in Chuchow, sir?" asked Chu Hsien-fu. "You must undoubtedly have distinguished yourself."

"I have been a licentiate for twenty-four years; but although I have been favoured by the examiners and come first six or seven times in the preliminary tests, I am ashamed to say I have not done very well in the provincial examinations."

"It is a matter of luck. I am sure next time you will come first."

After they had talked for some time, Chu Hsien-fu rose to leave; and Ma Chun-shang asked where he lived so that he might return the visit the following day.

171

Then Chu Hsien-fu went home and told his wife: "To-morrow Mr. Ma Chun-shang, an expert on the examination essays, is coming to call on me. We must ask him to dinner."

Very pleased, she immediately set about making preparations.

The next day Ma Chun-shang changed into a loose gown, wrote a visiting card and called at Chu Hsien-fu's home. Chu ushered him in.

"We are not like ordinary friends, but have long been acquainted in spirit," said Chu. "Now that you have honoured me with a visit I hope you will favour us with your company while we prepare a simple meal. You must excuse our lack of ceremony."

Ma Chun-shang was delighted.

Then Chu Hsien-fu asked: "What is the chief criterion you employ in selecting essays?"

"The reasoning," replied Ma Chun-shang. "No matter how styles change, the reasoning remains the same. During the reigns of Hung Wu and Yung Lo we find one style, and during the reigns of Cheng Hua and Hung Chih another; but careful investigation shows that the reasoning remains the same. Generally speaking, it is bad enough to write essays which read like commentaries, but worse to imitate the style of odes and elegies. For essays which read like commentaries will simply lack the literary flavour, whereas those which sound poetic will not resemble the words of ancient sages. Of the two, therefore, the poetic type is worse."

"You have been speaking of *writing* essays. May I ask how one should *comment* upon essays?"

"The same principle applies: you must not look for what is poetical. I often read the old masters' annotations, and when they are in flowery language they remind us of odes or elegies, and the content is likely to have a bad influence on later scholars. How right the ancients were when they said: 'In writing an essay the mind should remain as clear as the human eye.' It must hold no dust, not even of jade or gold. So when I comment upon essays I try to use the language of Chu Hsi, often sitting up half the night to write one note. And because I write nothing carelessly, students who have read one of my commentaries may think out the principles for a dozen essays. When my selection is ready I will send it to you for your criticism."

As they were speaking a simple meal was carried in: boiled duck, boiled chicken, fish and a big bowl of tender, braised pork. Mr. Ma's appetite was enormous.

"You and I are like old friends now," he said as he raised his chopsticks, "so I won't stand on ceremony. I propose that we leave this fish and concentrate on the pork."

Falling to, he ate four bowls of rice and finished the whole bowl of meat. When the mistress knew this, she sent out another bowl; but he finished this too, soup and all. Then the table was carried out, tea was brought in and they began talking.

"Gifted as you are and coming from an illustrious family," said Ma Chun-shang, "you should have passed the examinations long ago. How is it that you are still in retirement?"

"Since my father died early I was brought up by my grandfather and occupied with family business: I had no time to study for the civil service."

"That was a mistake. Right from ancient times all the best men have gone in for the civil service. Confucius, for instance, lived during the Spring and Autumn Period[1] when men were selected as officials on the strength of their activities and sayings. That is why Confucius said: 'Make few false statements and do little you may regret, then all will be well.' That was the civil service of Confucius' time.

"By the time of the Warring States,[2] the art of rhetoric had become the road to officialdom: that is why Mencius travelled through Chi and Liang delivering orations to the princes. That was the civil service of Mencius' time.

"By the Han Dynasty,[3] the examination system was designed to select men for their ability, goodness and justice; and thus men like Kung-sun Hung and Tung Chung-shu were appointed to office. That was the civil service of the Han Dynasty.

---

[1] B.C. 770-403.
[2] B.C. 403-221.
[3] B.C. 206—A.D. 220.

"By the Tang Dynasty,[1] scholars were chosen for their ability to write poetry. Even if a man could talk like Confucius or Mencius, that would not get him a post; so all the Tang scholars learned to write poems. That was the civil service of the Tang Dynasty.

"By the Sung Dynasty,[2] it was even better: all the officials had to be philosophers. That was why the Cheng brothers and Chu Hsi propagated neo-Confucianism. That was the civil service of the Sung Dynasty.

"Nowadays, however, we use essays to select scholars, and this is the best criterion of all. Even Confucius, if he were alive today, would be studying essays and preparing for the examinations instead of saying, 'Make few false statements and do little you may regret.' Why? Because that kind of talk would get him nowhere: nobody would give him an official position. No, the old sage would find it impossible to realize his ideal."

This conversation made Chu Hsien-fu feel as if he were coming out of darkness into the bright light of day. He kept Mr. Ma to dinner too and they became sworn brothers; then the scholar said goodbye and went away. After this, they met nearly every day.

One day, in the bookshop, Chu Hsien-fu noticed on the table the proof of the frontispiece of Ma Chun-shang's *Selected Essays of Various Examinations*; and below the title was inscribed "Selected and annotated by Ma Chun-shang of Chuchow."

"I wonder if I might add my name to your distinguished work, in order to share a little of your fame?" suggested Chu with a smile.

"There are reasons against it," replied Mr. Ma gravely. "To get one's name on the frontispiece is not easy. In fact, it is only because I have done well in recent years in the preliminary tests and made a slight reputation for myself that my services are in request. Of course, your illustrious name is more than worthy of a place on the cover; but one of us

[1] 618-907.
[2] 960-1279.

174

only can have his name there, and that for a very good reason."

"For what reason, may I ask?"

"It is a question of profit and reputation. I don't want to spoil my reputation by giving the impression that I am out for profit; yet if I put your name down after mine, people will think that you finance the publication and that I am working for money. On the other hand, if I put your name before mine, that will mean that the little reputation I have enjoyed all these years will seem false. If you imagine our positions reversed, you'll see that you would feel the same way."

As they were speaking, a simple meal of one bowl of cabbage and two small dishes of vegetables was brought up from the shop.

"I can hardly invite you to share this simple fare," said Ma Chun-shang. "What shall we do?"

"What does it matter?" said Chu Hsien-fu. "But I know you're not used to a vegetable diet, so I brought some silver with me."

With that, he took out a piece of silver and asked the shopkeeper's second son to buy them a bowl of cooked pork. When they had eaten, he took his leave.

At home, Chu Hsien-fu and his wife gave their son lessons every evening till midnight; and if the boy did not know his lesson properly, his mother would keep him at it till morning, sending her husband to bed first in the library where her maid Shuang-hung brought him tea and water and waited on him. Shuang-hung could read poems and often brought verses for him to explain to her; and because Chu liked her, he gave her as a work-box the old casket presented to him by Prefect Wang, and inadvertently told her how he had met this rebel.

Now Huan-cheng, son of the steward in the Lou household, was a rascal who had reached an understanding with Shuang-hung when they were young; and one day he had the impudence to run away to Chiahsing and carry her off. Very angry, Chu Hsien-fu informed the county magistrate, who issued a writ and had them arrested and kept in custody in a runner's house. Huan-cheng asked a friend to plead with Shuang-hung's master and say that he was willing to pay a few dozen taels of silver for her if he could have her as his wife; but Chu Hsien-fu would not consent. If the runner had haled Huan-cheng before the magistrate again, the youth would not have escaped a beating and the girl would have been sent back to the Chu family. So Huan-cheng had to bribe the runner until his money was finished and all his clothes had been pawned.

One evening in the runner's house, Huan-cheng and Shuang-hung were discussing how they might pawn the old casket for a few dozen coins to buy food. Shuang-hung as a slave girl knew very little about politics.

"This casket used to belong to a high official," she told Huan-cheng. "So I think it must be worth a lot of silver. It would be a pity to sell it for a few coins."

"Did it belong to Mr. Chu or Mr. Lu?"

"To neither. It belonged to a much more important official than even Prefect Chu. I heard the master say that there was a certain Prefect Wang, who came after Prefect Chu at Nanchang and later became ever such a high official and made friends with Prince Ning. Prince Ning was trying all the time to kill the emperor; but the emperor killed him first, and he wanted to kill Prefect Wang too, but Prefect Wang ran away to Chekiang. For some reason or other the emperor wanted this casket as well, so Prefect Wang didn't dare keep it himself for fear he was discovered, and he gave it to our master. Our master kept it at home and gave it to me to keep needles and thread in, not knowing that I would bring it away. I think anything the emperor wants must be worth a lot of money, don't you? If you look inside the casket, you can still see the words that Prefect Wang wrote there."

"The emperor would hardly want this casket," said Huan-cheng. "You must have got it wrong. This can't be worth much."

At this point the runner, who had been listening outside, kicked open the door and came in.

"You silly fool!" he shouted. "Why let yourself be cooped up here when you can cash in on this treasure you've got?"

"What treasure have I got?"

"Idiot! If I tell you, it will be too good for you! Not only will you get a wife for nothing, but you should make a few hundred taels of silver into the bargain. If you treat me

to a big meal, though, and promise to divide the money fifty·
fifty with me, I'll tell you."

"As long as I have money I will give you half," said Huan-
cheng. "But I can't treat you, sir, unless I sell this casket
tomorrow."

"Sell the casket? If you do that, it will be the end of everything! I'll lend you money· The feast this evening is on
me. And what's more, if you need anything from tomorrow
onwards, you have only to ask me. You must repay me double,
though. I shall deduct it anyway," he added. "You won't
be able to get away with anything."

Thereupon the runner produced two hundred coins with
which he bought wine and meat. And he shared this meal
with the two young people, saying that he would charge this
to Huan-cheng's account.

As they were eating, Huan-cheng asked: "What is it you
said I should cash in on, sir?"

"Today we're feasting," said the runner. "Let's talk about
it tomorrow." That evening they played the finger-game and
drank till midnight, when all the two hundred coins were
spent.

The miserable Huan-cheng was so drunk that he slept till
noon the next day. The runner, however, got up at dawn to go
and consult another experienced runner.

"Which would be more profitable for us all?" he asked,
having explained the situation. "To inform on him or to try
a little blackmail?"

The old runner spat in disgust.

"Inform in a case like this?" he sneered. "What would you
get out of that? Take your time and negotiate with the other
side, and you can be sure of getting some money out of him.
To think you've been all· these years in this business, but you're
still so green that in a case like this you want to inform! Inform your mother's head!"

Ashamed yet pleased, the runner hurried home to find
Huan-cheng still in bed.

"Having a good time, aren't you," he cried, "still cuddling
that bitch at this time of day! Hurry up and get up. I want
to talk to you."

Huan-cheng got up at once, and as soon as he left his room the runner said: "Come on outside to talk."

The two of them went out hand in hand to a quiet tea-shop in that street.

"You're a fool, my lad," said the runner. "All you understand is eating, drinking and whoring. You've a prize in your hands, yet you don't know how to use it! Isn't that like going to a treasure-trove and coming away empty-handed?"

"Please tell me, sir, how to go about this."

"I don't mind advising you; but you mustn't forget to thank me."

Just then a man passed the door, called out a greeting and moved on. The runner noticed that this fellow looked thoughtful; so he told Huan-cheng to wait while he tiptoed after the other.

"He's beaten me up, but there are no wounds," he heard him mutter. "So I can't take the case to court. And if I wound myself the magistrate will easily find it out."

Then the runner quietly picked up a brick, charged forward like an avenging fury and hit the other man's head with the brick so that the blood gushed out.

The man stumbled.

"Hey! What are you doing?" he demanded.

"You were complaining that you had no wound. Isn't this a wound? And you couldn't have made it yourself either. I don't think the magistrate will be able to tell how it was done. Go ahead and lodge your complaint!"

The man thanked the runner from the bottom of his heart, then smeared his face with blood and went to lay his suit before the magistrate. To Huan-cheng, standing in the doorway of the tea-shop, this was another object lesson in finesse.

The runner came back and sat down.

"Yesterday evening I heard your wife say that that casket belonged to Prefect Wang," he said. "Now Prefect Wang went over to Prince Ning and then escaped; therefore he is a great traitor, and this casket is a most important piece of evidence. Since Mr. Chu is his friend and has hidden his belongings, if we inform on him he can be executed or sent into exile. What can he do to you?"

When Huan-cheng heard this, he felt as if he were waking from a dream.

"Why, sir!" he cried. "I will go and lodge a charge at once."

"If you report him, you silly boy, his whole family may be executed, but what good will that do you? You won't get a cent. And it's not as if you were sworn enemies. No, what you want to do is to send someone to frighten him into giving you several hundred taels and letting you have the girl for your wife without payment. That's what you must do."

"You are too good to me, sir! I shall do everything you say."

"Don't be hasty," said the runner. Then, paying for the tea, he walked out with the young man, adding: "When you get home, don't breathe a word of this to your wife."

Huan-cheng agreed. After this the runner lent him money to eat and drink to his heart's content, and he was very happy.

When Chu Hsien-fu pressed to have Huan-cheng haled before the magistrate again, the runner simply put him off, procrastinating from day to day, until Chu was so angry that he threatened to bring a charge against him.

"The time is ripe now," the runner told Huan-cheng. "What friends has Mr. Chu?"

"I don't know," replied Huan-cheng.

He asked Shuang-hung.

"In Huchow he has a great many friends, but here I haven't seen any," she said. "I did hear, though, that a certain Mr. Ma from some bookshop had called several times."

When Huan-cheng told the runner this, the latter said: "That's simple then."

He found a clerk to write an indictment for use against a rebel and then, taking this with him, made inquiries in different bookshops along the main road until he came to Literary Ocean. There he asked for Mr. Ma.

When Ma Chun-shang saw that he came from the yamen, although he did not know what the runner's business could be, he had to invite him to come upstairs and sit down.

"Sir," said the runner, "do you know a Mr. Chu of the family of Prefect Chu from Nanchang?"

"He is my best friend. Why do you ask?"

The runner looked round.

"Can we be overheard here?" he asked.

"No."

Then the runner hitched forward his chair and produced the indictment for Mr. Ma to read.

"When something like this happens," he said, "we servants of the public do what we can to soften the blow. I want to break this news to him so that he may be prepared."

When Ma Chun-shang read the indictment his face turned white and he asked for further details.

"This must at no costs be allowed to go forward," he said. "I must ask you to be kind enough, sir, to keep this indictment until Mr. Chu comes home—he has just gone to repair his grandfather's grave. We can discuss this when he comes back."

"That fellow wants to send it in today," said the runner. "This is a criminal offence. Who dares hold up the course of the law?"

"What is to be done then?" demanded Ma Chun-shang in dismay.

"Is it possible a learned man like you doesn't know? Fire cooks pork and money works wonders. All you need is some silver to buy the casket; then there won't be any more trouble."

Ma Chun-shang clapped his hands.

"An excellent idea!" he cried.

He locked his door and went with the runner to a tavern. Mr. Ma stood host. He ordered a good meal and they discussed the matter as they ate.

But to know how much money the runner demanded for the casket, you must read the next chapter.

CHAPTER 14

In which Chu Hsien-fu sees a friend off from the bookshop, and Ma Chun-shang meets an immortal in a mountain cave

Ma Chun-shang consulted the runner in the tavern on how to redeem the casket for Chu Hsien-fu.

"That fellow is clutching the indictment like a pawn ticket he's picked up," said the runner. "Do you think that for a few taels he will give up this rebel's property Mr. Chu has concealed? He will want two or three hundred taels at the very least. And even then I shall have to frighten him by saying: 'Informing on Mr. Chu is not going to do *you* any good; and if you impeach a man, you have to take the case from one yamen to another till you reach the very highest courts. Figure it out for yourself: can you afford to get involved in a lawsuit like that?' That's the way to scare him. Then when he sees the money and is itching to get it, he'll be willing to settle. I've come, out of the kindness of my heart, to let you know about this; because I'm just as anxious as you are to avoid trouble, and I don't like seeing any man ruined. But you've got to act quickly in this, sir. So I hope you'll consider what I've said."

"Two or three hundred taels are out of the question. As you know, Mr. Chu is away from home just now; so I shall have to try to settle this for him. But even if he were here, he couldn't raise such a sum at a moment's notice. It's true

181

that his grandfather held some official posts, but their family has come down in the world."

"Well, if there is no money and Mr. Chu won't appear in person, we had better not delay any longer. I'll return the indictment to Huan-cheng, and he can do what he likes with it."

"Don't say that!" protested Ma Chun-shang. "You hardly know Mr. Chu, but I am one of his best friends; and if I don't help him out, I shall be letting down a friend. I can only do what's within my power though."

"There you go again! If you want it to be within your power, so do I!"

"Let us go into this a little more carefully, officer. The fact is, the manager here has engaged me for several months to select essays, and I have a few taels of silver as salary; but I have to keep part of this for my own expenses. To settle this unfortunate business I'll try to squeeze out twenty or thirty taels—which Huan-cheng can consider as money for nothing."

"This is just like the proverb: The price is as high as the sky and the offer as low as the earth," said the runner angrily. "When I say two or three hundred taels, you say twenty or thirty! It's like kissing in straw helmets—the lips are far apart! No wonder they say you bookworms are hard to deal with: one might just as well try to squeeze water out of a stone. Well, I should have minded my own business instead of coming here to let myself in for this old wives' gabble."

He stood up, apologized to Mr. Ma for troubling him, said goodbye and started out.

Ma Chun-shang pulled him back.

"Let's sit down and talk this over," he said. "Don't be in such a hurry. Did you think I was lying to you just now? It's a fact that Mr. Chu is not at home. It's not as if I had got wind of this and hidden him so that I could bargain with you. Besides, as a man who lives in this district, you ought to know him, and Mr. Chu is not very open-handed. How can I be sure that he will pay me back? Still, if I let this matter take its course, I shall be sorry later. In a word, both you and I are outsiders. I count it my bad luck that I'm involved; but you must do your best to help as well. If I supply the money and you supply the labour, we can consider we've done a very good deed between us. It's no use if the two of us start wrangling."

"Now, Mr. Ma," said the runner, "I don't mind whether you pay the money or he pays it. Being in the same line, you're as close as sock and boot. But you've got to make it within my power to help. Let's be frank and put all our cards on the table: a few dozen taels are not going to settle anything. I tell you straight out: if you haven't got three hundred you must have at least two hundred before we can talk. It's not that I want to make things difficult for you; but what use are five or ten taels?"

When Ma Chun-shang saw that the runner meant business, he was very much alarmed.

"My salary is only a hundred taels, officer, and that's the truth," he said. "I've already spent a few taels, and must keep a few more for my journey to Hangchow. Though I turn my pockets inside out, the very most I can raise is ninety-two taels. If you don't believe me, come to my lodgings and see for yourself. You can search my luggage and cases, and if you find a single cent, I'm not a man! That's the truth of the matter, and it's up to you to help us. If you really can't, then there's nothing more I can do and Mr. Chu will just have to curse his fate."

"Sir," said the runner, "I see you are a loyal friend, and we servants of the law have hearts as well. If even mountains and rivers meet at last, it is only right for men to help each other. The trouble is that scurvy slave has set such a high price on the casket, I don't know if I can talk him round."

The runner paused for a moment as if to think. "I've another idea," he went on. "As the proverb says: Scholars express their friendship on paper. Now that Huan-cheng has kidnapped the slave girl and this other thing has cropped up, it doesn't look as if Mr. Chu will get her back. Why not write a marriage certificate stating that he has paid you a hundred taels as the price of the girl? With these ninety-odd taels of yours, that will make nearly two hundred; and though these two hundred don't actually exist, it will be enough to stop the scoundrel's mouth. What do you think of that?"

"It is all right as far as I am concerned, if you can play your part. There is no difficulty about the certificate: I'll see to that."

Thus the matter was decided; and after paying the bill at the tavern, Ma Chun-shang went back to his lodgings to wait.

Pretending to have gone to meet Huan-cheng, the runner took a long time to return to the bookshop, where Mr. Ma showed him upstairs.

"The trouble I've had over this!" declared the runner. "That slave kept demanding a thousand or eight hundred taels as if he had me at his mercy, claiming Mr. Chu should pay him as much as his family's worth. I lost my temper in the end and threatened to take him to the court. 'First we'll try you for kidnapping Shuang-hung,' I told him. 'We'll report the case to the magistrate and have you thrown into gaol. Then we'll see how you set about accusing people there!' That frightened him into listening to me. So I tricked him into giving me his casket which is downstairs now in the shop. If you will be good enough to write the certificate and count out the silver, I will send in a report to close his case and see that he clears off, so that this trouble doesn't crop up again."

"You have done very well. I've already written the certificate."

Ma Chun-shang handed the silver and the certificate to the runner, who, having counted the money and found that it came to ninety-two taels exactly, took the casket upstairs and gave it to Mr. Ma, then went away with the silver and the certificate.

The runner's first action on reaching home was to hide the certificate and make out a bill covering the money Huan-cheng had borrowed from him as well as his board and lodging and court expenses. This bill came to over seventy taels of silver, leaving Huan-cheng about a dozen taels only. He complained that this was too little.

"You kidnapped a maid," retorted the runner. "That's a criminal offence! And if I hadn't covered up for you, the magistrate would have broken your legs, you dog. I get you a wife and all this money for nothing; yet instead of thanking me you demand more silver. Come on! I'll take you to the magistrate to get a few dozen strokes for kidnapping, while Shuang-hung goes back to the Chu family. Let's see how you like that!"

This scolding shut the servant's mouth, and Huan-cheng hastily took the silver, thanked the runner profusely, and left with Shuang-hung for another province to look for a living there.

After Chu Hsien-fu's return from his ancestral tombs, he was just about to send a message to the runner to press him to have Huan-cheng tried when Mr. Ma arrived, and Chu invited him into the library. When Ma Chun-shang had asked after the tombs, he brought the conversation around to the casket. At first Chu's answers were evasive.

"Why try to hide this from me, friend?" said Ma. "Your casket is now in my room above the bookshop."

When Chu heard this, his face turned red.

Then Ma Chun-shang told him how the runner had reported the matter to him, how they had discussed it together and how he had had to pay ninety-two taels of silver to redeem the casket.

"Luckily, all is now well," he said. "As for the money, I spent it for friendship's sake and I naturally won't hear of your paying it back. But I had to tell you this so that you can send a man to my lodgings tomorrow to fetch the casket. Break it or burn it; but don't leave it about to cause more trouble."

Deeply moved, Chu Hsien-fu straightway placed a chair in the middle of the library and forced Mr. Ma to sit on it while he bowed to him four times. Then he asked him to wait while he told his wife what had happened.

"Mr. Ma has proved a true scholar and friend," he told her. "What character! What courage! How lucky I am to have such an honest man and true gentleman for a friend! My uncles befriended many people, but all of them showed up badly in the end. If they could have heard what Mr. Ma said just now, they would surely die of shame!"

With heartfelt gratitude his wife prepared a meal for Mr. Ma, then sent a servant back with him to fetch the casket and destroyed it.

The next day Ma came to say goodbye, since he was leaving for Hangchow.

"We have only just got together," said Chu. "Why must you leave so soon?"

"I worked as an editor in Hangchow before the bookshop here invited me to compile this work. And now that I have finished this task, there is nothing to keep me here."

"If your work is done, why not move into my humble house, so that I can listen to your instructions morning and evening?"

"This is not yet the time for you to entertain guests. Besides, all the Hangchow bookshops are waiting for me to select examination papers and I have other unfinished business there. It can't be helped: I must go. But whenever you have time, why not pay a visit to the West Lake? The fine scenery should add to your inspiration."

Unable to prevail on him to stay, Chu wanted to keep him to a farewell feast; but Mr. Ma declined.

"I must say goodbye to other friends too," he said.

He rose to go, and Chu saw him to the door. The next day Chu wrapped up two taels of silver and took these with some ham and other delicacies to Literary Ocean Bookshop to say goodbye, taking home two volumes of the newly published examination papers.

Ma Chun-shang travelled by boat to Broken Bay, where he asked his way to Literary Expanse Bookshop which was under the same management as Literary Ocean. He put up there. One day, after he had been there for some time without receiving any essays to edit, he put some money in his pocket and set out to visit the lake.

The West Lake has some of the finest scenery in the world. Everyone knows of the quiet seclusion of the Monastery of Ling Yin or the elegance of Tien Chu Monastery; but you have only to go out through Chientang Gate and pass Sheng Yin Monastery along Su Avenue to see Golden Sand Bay stretching before you and the Thunder Peak Pagoda; while as soon as you reach the Monastery of Pure Compassion, for several miles every five steps brings you to a pavilion and every ten steps to an arbour. Here are gilt galleries, and there thatched cottages and bamboo fences; here peach trees vie with willows;

there mulberry trees and flax overspread the plain. Dark trade-signs flutter above the wineshops, and red charcoal glows in the tea-house stoves, while men and women stream by, on pleasure bent, to throng the countless taverns and music halls.

Ma Chun-shang set off alone through Chientang Gate, a little money in his pocket. He drank a few bowls of tea in a tavern, then sat before the triumphal arch overlooking the lake to watch boat after boat of countrywomen on pilgrimages. Their hair was combed high and most of them wore blue or green, though the younger women favoured red silk skirts. The most comely had round white faces and high cheekbones; but quite a few had scars, pock-marks, ringworm and scabies. Five or six boats passed in the time for one meal; and the women were followed by their husbands, carrying umbrellas and a change of clothing. Once ashore, they made their way to the various monasteries.

Not finding much of interest here, Ma Chun-shang got up and walked nearly a mile further. The bank was lined with taverns hung with fat mutton, while the plates on the counters were heaped with steaming trotters, sea slugs, duck preserved in wine and fresh water fish. Meat dumplings boiled in the cauldrons and enormous rolls of steamed bread filled the steamers. But all these were beyond his means. His mouth watering, he walked into a noodle shop to have a bowl of noodles for sixteen coppers; then, still hungry, he went to the tea-shop next door and ordered a bowl of tea and two coppers' worth of dried bamboo shoots which he munched with relish.

After eating he came out and saw two boats moored under the willows by the shore. There were women pilgrims changing their clothes in the boats. One of them took off a black coat and put on a green cape; another changed a sky-blue jacket for an embroidered jade-coloured gown. Yet another, who was middle-aged, slipped out of a sapphire-blue silk tunic into a sky-blue silk gown embroidered with golden thread. There were about a dozen serving-women with them, who changed their dresses too. Then preceded by a maid carrying a round black gauze fan to shade her from the sun, each lady advanced slowly up the slope. The pearls on their heads sparkled brilliantly in the sun, and the jade pendents on their skirts tinkled prettily; but Ma Chun-shang strode past with lowered head, not casting so much as a glance at all these beauties.

After crossing the Six Bridges and rounding a bend, he found himself in fairly open country, where coffins coated with mud had been deposited to wait for an auspicious day for burial. Having walked over half a mile without coming to the end of all these coffins, Ma Chun-shang felt quite disgusted. He was thinking of turning back when he met a man.

"Is there anything worth seeing ahead?" he asked.

"The Monastery of Pure Compassion and Thunder Peak Pagoda are just round the corner," was the reply. "They're worth seeing, aren't they?"

Ma Chun-shang walked on for three hundred yards until he saw a pavilion in the middle of the lake connected by a wooden bridge with the shore. He crossed the bridge to a tea-house in front of the pavilion, where he drank a bowl of tea. The door to the pavilion was locked; but when he gave the caretaker a coin, he was admitted. The pavilion was divided into three rooms, and in the uppermost was an inscription by Emperor Jen Tsung. Ma Chun-shang gave a start when he saw this, and hastily straightened his cap, adjusted his sapphire-blue gown, and took from his boot a fan, which he carried as the tablet courtiers hold in the presence of the emperor. Then, very reverently he faced the wall, advanced in the manner prescribed by court etiquette, and bowed five times. This done, he rose to his feet, calmed himself and went back to sit in the tea-house. On one side there was a garden, but the waiter told him the finance commissioner was giving a party there, so no one could go in. The kitchen was outside, however; and the sight of bowl after bowl of birds'-nests and sea slugs being carried past, steaming hot, made his mouth water again.

When he left this place and passed Thunder Peak Pagoda, he could see many houses, some high, some low, in the distance. They were roofed with glazed tiles and set within winding red balustrades. Ma Chun-shang walked on till he came to a huge gate on which was written in letters of gold: "The Monastery of Pure Compassion, founded by imperial decree." Beside this large gate was a smaller one, through which he entered a great courtyard, paved with water-polished bricks; and passing through a second gate he found himself between two corridors leading to high flights of stone steps. Women from rich and noble families were strolling to and fro here, in small groups, dressed in silk and brocade. Whenever a breeze sprang up, you could smell the scent they used.

Ma Chun-shang was tall. He was wearing a high hat, and had a swarthy face and massive paunch. He barged about in his worn-out, thick-soled shoes, jostling his way through the crowd. But the women paid no attention to him, nor he to them.

After a hasty tour of this monastery, he went back to sit in the same tea-house again—its name, "The Southern Screen," was written in letters of gold — and here he drank a bowl of tea. On the counter there were plates of preserved oranges, sesame sweets, dumplings, cakes, dried bamboo shoots, dried dates and boiled chestnuts; and Ma Chun-shang bought a few coppers' worth of each to stay his hunger, without worrying about their taste. Then, tired out, he walked stiffly back through Clear Stream Gate to his lodgings, closed the door and went to bed. Because he had walked too much, he spent the next day in bed.

The day after, however, he got up to visit the Mountain of the Guardian Deity, Wu Mountain, which is inside the city. It was not far to the foot of the mount, where he found a broad flight of stone steps; and when he had climbed these and turned around, he saw several dozen more steps. He hurried up, not pausing for breath until he reached the top. In front of the big temple there tea was sold, and he drank a bowl before going in. This was the temple of Wu Tzu-hsu, councillor of the Kingdom of Wu. When Mr. Ma had bowed before the shrine, he examined all the inscriptions there carefully. There now seemed to be no way forward; but on the left he found a door inscribed with the name "Rocky Grotto," and through this there was a garden with a pavilion. Ma Chun-shang went in. The pavilion windows were closed; but when he looked through the door he saw an incense-burner on a table round which several men were standing. They appeared to be holding a séance.

"They must be asking some spirit whether or not they will pass the examinations," thought Ma Chun-shang. "I may as well go in myself and ask."

When he had stood there for some time, he saw a man kowtow, then rise.

"We have called up a poetess!" said his companions.

At this Ma Chun-shang smiled contemptuously.

"Is it Li Ching-chao?"[1] asked one.

"Is it Su Jo-lan?"[2] asked another.

"No!" cried a third, and clapped his hands. "It is Chu Shu-chen."[3]

"Whoever these spirits may be," thought Ma Chun-shang, "I doubt if they determine official careers. I had better be going."

He took two turnings and climbed some more steps which brought him to a wide flat road. To its left rose the mountain, dotted with temples, while to the right were buildings with inner and outer courtyards, whose wide open back windows gave a view in the distance of Chientang River. Some of these buildings were taverns or toyshops; others were dumpling, noodle or tea-shops; and in some you could have your fortune told. Tables for tea had been placed in front of the temples, and there were over thirty tea-houses alone on that road, which was a hive of activity.

A highly-painted woman in one of the tea-shops invited Ma Chun-shang in. But looking away he went to the shop next door, where he ordered a bowl of tea and twelve coppers' worth of savoury cakes which proved quite good.

Continuing up the road, he reached a large and magnificent temple built to the guardian deity, and into this he marched to have a look round. Then he took another turning which brought him to a small road containing taverns, noodle shops and a number of newly opened bookshops. In one shop he saw an advertisement pasted on the wall: "Famous selections of examination essays edited by Mr. Ma Chun-shang of Chuchow

---

1 A poetess of the twelfth century.
2 A poetess of the fourth century.
3 A poetess of the twelfth century.

are sold here." Ma Chun-shang was delighted. He went into the shop and sat down, picked up a copy of his book and looked at it, then asked the price and how the work was selling.

"Selected essays have a short vogue only," said the shopkeeper. "You can't compare them with the classics."

Then Ma Chun-shang got up and went out; and because he had rested his legs he walked on up the mountain.

There were no more houses now, for the road had become very steep; but Ma Chun-shang climbed a peak from which he could see Chientang River clearly beneath him to the left. There was no breeze that day, so the water was smooth as a mirror; and you could see the passing boats quite distinctly and even the sedan-chairs on the boats. He walked on until he saw the West Lake on his right and was able to make out Thunder Peak Pagoda and the Pavilion of the Lake's Heart, as well as the fishing boats which looked like tiny ducks floating on the water. Then, refreshed in spirit. he walked on.

He came to another big temple, with tables before it at which tea was served, and since his legs were tired, he sat down again. As he sipped his tea he gazed at the river on one side, the lake nestling among hills on the other, and on the far side of the river the blurred outline of distant mountains, some high and some low.

Ma Chun-shang drew a deep breath and quoted: "The earth, which carries mountains and feels them no burden and safely contains the waters of rivers and seas, supports the myriad forms of life!"

After two more bowls of tea he felt hungry and decided to start back, stopping for a meal on the way.

Just then a countryman came up carrying pancakes and a basket of boiled beef. This was a welcome sight and Ma Chun-shang bought several dozen coppers' worth of pancakes and beef, making a hearty meal of them at the table. His hunger satisfied, he decided to press on.

He had walked another bow-shot when he saw on his left a small path through thick weeds and brambles, and this took him through an infinite variety of curiously shaped rocks to a stone wall on which many famous men had written poems. He paid no attention, however, but forged ahead across a small stone bridge and up some narrow stone steps to another big temple.

Here was a narrow stone bridge, which looked difficult to cross; but holding the vine at one side, Ma Chun-shang walked over. In front of him stood a small temple to Saint Ting, and this he entered. The saint's image occupied the middle of the temple; on the left was a stork and on the right a stone slab inscribed with twenty characters. There were bamboo sticks there too for fortune-telling.

"Since I am stranded here," thought Ma Chun-shang, "I may as well see whether my fortune is good or bad."

He was about to bow before the saint, when he heard a voice behind him.

"If you want to be rich, Mr. Ma, why not ask my advice?"

Turning, Ma Chun-shang saw a man over six feet in height, in a square cap and silk gown, standing at the gate of the temple. His left hand was smoothing his silk belt and his right hand held a wand surmounted by a carved dragon's head, while the long white beard which flowed down to his waist gave him the unearthly appearance of a saint.

But to know who this man was, you must read the chapter which follows. •

CHAPTER 15

Ma Chun-shang attends the funeral of an immortal, and Kuang Chao-jen proves himself a filial son

Ma Chun-shang was just kneeling to learn his fortune when someone addressed him from behind, and he turned to see a man who looked like an immortal. Ma immediately bowed.

"I was not aware of your arrival, he said. "So I failed to greet you, sir. Since I have never had the honour of meeting you, may I ask how you knew that my name is Ma?"

"Is there anyone who does not know you? Now that you have met me, there is no need to ask your fortune. You had better come with me to my humble house."

"Where is your distinguished abode?"

"It is very near."

Taking Ma Chun-shang's hand, this stranger led him out of the temple to a wide flat road on which there was not a single stone, and in next to no time they had reached the temple of Wu Tzu-hsu.

Ma was surprised.

"This is a much shorter way!" he thought. "I must have taken the wrong road before. Unless, of course, he has some miraculous means of shortening the distance."

Soon they reached the gate of the temple.

"This is my humble home," said the stranger. "Please come in."

Behind the temple hall were spacious grounds and a garden, and in the garden stood a two-storeyed house with five large rooms and windows on all sides which overlooked the river and the lake. The old man invited Ma Chun-shang to his rooms upstairs, and after bowing to each other they sat down.

Four smart attendants in silk and brocade, each wearing new shoes, served tea punctiliously, and when their master bade them prepare a meal, they assented together before they left the room. Ma looked up and saw a scroll in the middle of the wall on which twenty-eight large characters were written. It was the following poem:

> *I came here when the capital moved south,*
> *But times have altered since those good old days.*
> *The lakes and hills are lovely as before,*
> *And chanting poems I wander through the world.*

Beneath was the poet's name: Hung Kan-hsien. Since Ma had read enough history to know that the capital had been moved south during the Sung Dynasty,[1] he was able to calculate that this man must be over three hundred years old. No doubt about it: he was an immortal!

"Is this fine composition yours, sir?" he inquired.

"Kan-hsien is my unworthy name. But this is simply something I dashed off not worth your consideration. If you enjoy poetry, I have a book of poems written by some provincial governors, commissioners and myself in praise of the West Lake. I would appreciate your criticism of them."

He produced a manuscript containing poems with seven characters to a line by different high officials. All the poems were about the lake, and there was a red, official chop under each. Ma Chun-shang praised the verses highly, then handed them back to Hung Kan-hsien, who put them away.

Presently dinner was served: a great dish of mutton cooked to a turn, a portion of duck preserved in wine, a large plate of ham and shrimp balls, and a bowl of clear soup. Consider-

---

[1] At the beginning of the twelfth century, Emperor Kao Tsung was driven south of the Yangtse River and set up his capital in Hang-chow.

ing it was not a feast, it was a very good spread; and, although Ma was not hungry, to express his appreciation of the kindness of this immortal he ate as much as he could.

"I have long known your great reputation," said Hung Kan-hsien when the table had been cleared. "All the bookshops must be eager to secure your help. How is it then that you had leisure today to go and ask your fortune in that temple?"

"I will tell you frankly, sir," replied Ma. "Though I edited a collection of essays in Chiahsing this year and received several dozen taels as remuneration, I spent the whole sum on behalf of a friend. And though I am now staying in a bookshop here, I have not yet received any essays. I have come to the end of my money and been feeling rather worried; so I came out for a stroll and thought I would ask my fortune in the temple to discover whether there is any likelihood of my making money or not. But now that I have met you, sir, and you have gone straight to the heart of my trouble, there is no need for me to ask my fortune."

"Making money is not difficult. You may have to wait a little, though, before amassing a real fortune. What would you say to making a little money as a start?"

"Provided I make money, I don't care whether it is much or little. I don't know, though, sir, what you have in mind?"

Hung Kan-hsien appeared to be pondering for a moment.

"Well, I will give you something to try out in your lodgings," he said. "If it proves satisfactory, come and ask me for more. And if this experiment fails, we can think of something else."

He went into his inner chamber, opened a package beside his bed and took out several pieces of charcoal which he gave to Ma, saying: "Take these to your lodgings and light a brazier; then heat these above the flames in some container and see what happens. Come and tell me the result."

Ma Chun-shang took the charcoal, said goodbye to Mr. Hung and returned to his lodgings. That evening he lit a brazier, placed some of the charcoal in a pot over it and, after the fire had crackled for some time, emptied the pot to find that the charcoal had turned into an ingot of silver! Overjoyed, he immediately heated six or seven pots more, obtaining from them six or seven more ingots. Then, uncertain whether this was real silver or not, he went to bed.

The next morning he went out early to have his ingots examined by the money-changers; and when they assured him that the silver was genuine he changed a part of it for several thousand coppers which he took back to his lodging. When he had put the money away, he hurried to Hung Kan-hsien's house to thank him.

Mr. Hung came out to meet him.

"How did it go last night?" he asked.

"It was miraculous!" exclaimed Ma.

He described what had happened and how much silver he had obtained.

"That's nothing," said Hung Kan-hsien. "I have some more here. You had better take it and try again." He produced another package which contained three or four times as much as the first, entertained Ma to another meal, then saw him off.

Ma Chun-shang's brazier was kept busy for the next six or seven days producing silver, until he had used up all the charcoal; and he found when he weighed the silver that he had eighty or ninety taels worth. Hardly able to contain himself for joy, he wrapped up the money and put it away.

One day Hung Kan-hsien sent a messenger to invite Ma to his house.

"You are from Chuchow and I am from Taichow," he said. "Coming from neighbouring districts, we can consider ourselves as fellow countrymen. I am expecting a guest today, and I would like to introduce you to him as my cousin; for that will give you the opportunity you want. This is a chance you must on no account miss."

"May I ask the name of your distinguished guest?"

"He is the third son of the former minister Hu, and his name is Hu Chen. The minister left a fortune to his sons, but this gentleman is so fond of money that he thinks he can never have enough and he wants to learn my method of producing silver. He is willing to spend thousands of taels for the equipment; but we need an intermediary. Now Mr. Hu has heard of your great name; and since you are selecting essays in Literary Expanse Bookshop and have a fixed address, he can trust you. In another seven weeks, after we meet today and settle this matter, I shall produce the philosopher's stone which can turn any metal to gold. That will be worth millions. But since I don't need so much money myself, I mean to bid farewell to this world and return to the mountain, leaving part of the philosopher's stone to you. Then you will want for nothing."

After the wonders he had seen Hung Kan-hsien perform, Ma had implicit faith in him. So they waited together for Mr. Hu.

Presently Mr. Hu arrived, greeted Mr. Hung, looked at Ma and asked: "May I know this gentleman's honourable name?"

"This is my cousin, Ma Chun-shang of Chuchow," said Hung Kan-hsien. "You see his name in all the bookshop advertisements for essays."

Mr. Hu greeted Ma with respect and they sat down together. When Mr. Hu cast his eyes round the room and noticed Mr. Hung's saintly appearance, the luxurious furniture and the four attendants presenting tea one after the other, and when he considered that Ma Chun-shang the editor was Mr. Hung's cousin, any misgivings he had had left him. He sat there in high good humour until it was time to leave.

The next day Hung Kan-hsien and Ma Chun-shang went by sedan-chair to return the visit. Ma presented Mr. Hu with a new selection of essays, after which Mr. Hu entertained them for some time; and soon after their return home a servant arrived from the Hu family with invitations for them both to a feast by the lake the following day.

"My master salutes you, gentlemen," said the servant. "The feast will be in the garden by Imperial Script Pavilion at the West Lake, and he hopes you will go there early tomorrow."

Mr. Hung accepted the invitations.

The next day they went by sedan-chair to the pavilion, found the gate of the garden wide open and Mr. Hu there to welcome them. Two tables had been spread and an opera was performed, and thus the day passed very pleasantly. Ma remembered how he had come here all alone and watched other people feasting, while today, by a happy coincidence, he was a

197

guest here himself. The wine, food and sweetmeats were of the best, and he made an excellent meal.

Mr. Hu arranged to invite them to his home again in a few days to sign a contract which Ma would witness. He also promised to have a laboratory prepared in his garden and declared that he would make an initial payment of ten thousand taels so that Mr. Hung could buy the necessary equipment and take up his quarters in the laboratory. This matter decided, in the evening the feast ended and Ma went back by sedan-chair to the bookshop.

When four days passed without any word from Hung Kan-hsien, Ma decided to call on him. But as soon as he went in, he found the four attendants in confusion and learned that Mr. Hung was seriously ill. In fact, the doctors declared that his pulse was so weak that further treatment was useless. Greatly shocked, Ma hurried upstairs to see the sick man; but he found him at his last gasp, unable to raise his head. Since Ma was a kind-hearted man, he stayed by his sick friend's side all night. Two days later, however, Hung Kan-hsien breathed his last.

The four attendants were at their wits' end; for when they searched the house for valuables, they found only four or five silk gowns which might be worth a few taels. There was nothing else: all the cases were empty. And now it appeared that these four men were not servants. One of them was Hung Kan-hsien's son, two were nephews, and one was his son-in-law. When Ma heard this he was appalled. But since there was no money to buy a coffin and he was a good man, he hurried to his lodgings to fetch ten taels of silver for the funeral expenses. Then while the son wailed beside the corpse and the nephews went out to buy a coffin, the son-in-law, who had nothing to do, took Ma to a neighbouring tea-house to chat.

"Your father-in-law was an immortal who had lived more than three hundred years," said Ma. "What made him die all of a sudden?"

"Three hundred years? Nonsense!" retorted the son-in-law. "The old man was only sixty-six this year. He was an old villain, a regular swindler. However much money he made, he always threw it away. That's why he's ended like this. To tell you the truth, sir, we were merchants before; but we gave up our business to help him bamboozle people. Now that he's gone, we shall have to beg our way home. All of us are in a bad way."

"By his bed the old gentleman had a number of packages of charcoal which would turn into silver if you heated them above a brazier."

"That wasn't charcoal! It was silver coated with charcoal! As soon as it was burnt, the silver reappeared. That was a trick to fool people; but when the silver was used up, that was the end of it."

"But there's another thing," persisted Ma. "If he wasn't a saint, how did he know that my name was Ma when he met me for the first time in Saint Ting's Temple?"

"He had you there again. When he came out of the Rocky Grotto that day after a séance, he saw you reading in the bookshop; and when the shopkeeper asked you your name, you told him you were the Mr. Ma who had edited that volume of essays. My father-in-law overheard you: that's how he knew. There aren't any saints in the world!"

Only then did Ma realize that the old man had made up to him in order to deceive Mr. Hu, and it was pure luck that Mr. Hu had not been swindled. Still, he thought: "What harm did he do me? I ought to be grateful to him."

They went back to prepare the body for the coffin, paid the rent for the temple rooms and hired men to carry the coffin outside Clear Stream Gate. Ma also prepared sacrificial meat and wine and paper coins, and saw that the coffin was properly bricked over. What was left of the ten taels he gave to the four men for their journey. After thanking him, they left.

When Ma had seen them off, he went back to the Mountain of the Guardian Deity to drink tea and noticed a new table outside the tea-house where a young fortune-teller was sitting. Although lean and undersized, this young man looked intelligent. But the curious thing about him was that although he had ink, brush and the characters for fortune-telling in front of him, he was reading a book. Out of curiosity, Ma went up to the young man, pretending that he wanted to have his fortune told, only to discover that the youth was reading his own new selection of essays.

When Ma sat on the stool beside his table, the young man put down his book.

"Do you want your fortune told, sir?" he asked.

"I have walked too far," said Ma. "I will just rest here if I may."

"Please do. I will fetch you some tea."

He brought a bowl of tea from the tea-house for Ma, then sat down with him.

Seeing how helpful he was, Ma asked: "May I know your name? And are you a native of this city?"

The young man knew from Ma's cap that he must be a scholar, so he answered: "Your pupil's name is Kuang. I am not of this city, but come from Yuehching District in Wenchow."

Ma saw that he was wearing a worn cap and thin, threadbare gown.

"Why have you come all this way to do work like this?" he asked. "You can hardly make enough to support yourself. How old are you, and have you parents or wife and children? Judging by your fondness for reading, you must be a student."

"I am twenty-two and not yet married. I have parents at home and have studied for a few years; but my family was too poor to let me complete my studies, so I came here last year with a firewood merchant to keep his accounts. Then that merchant lost his capital and could not go back, and I found myself stranded here. The other day a man came from my district and told me that my father was ill at home; and I am miserable because I don't know whether he is alive or dead." Tears as big as peas rained down his cheeks.

Ma felt very sorry for the youth.

"Don't take it so much to heart," he said. "What is your personal name?"

The young man stopped weeping to reply: "My name is Kuang Chao-jen. But I have not yet asked your honourable name and district."

"That you need not ask. I am the Ma Chun-shang whose name is on the cover of the book you were reading just now."

When Kuang Chao-jen heard this, he made haste to bow.

"Although I have eyes," he exclaimed, "I have failed to see Mount Tai!"

Ma bowed in return.

"Don't be so polite," he said. "Although we have met by chance, we are both scholars. It is growing late, so you won't have much business now. Why not stop work and come back to my rooms for a chat?"

"I should like to very much. Please remain seated, sir, while I clear up my things."

Kuang Chao-jen put his ink, pen and paper into a bundle which he slung over his back, and took this with his table and stool to the temple opposite. Then he accompanied Ma to Literary Expanse Bookshop and sat down in his room.

"Tell me, friend," said Ma, "do you want to go on studying or to go back to see your father?"

Kuang Chao-jen shed tears once more.

"I can't make enough to feed or clothe myself properly, sir," he replied. "What money do I have to continue my studies? No, no, that is out of the question. But to know that my father lies ill at home, yet not be able to go back to look after him, makes me feel worse than a beast! It upsets me so much that sometimes I've thought it would be better to kill myself."

"Come, come! That would never do," cried Ma. "Your filial piety should move heaven and earth. But sit down while I prepare a meal for you."

He entertained Kuang to supper.

"Now supposing you wanted to go home," he asked, "how much would you need for the journey?"

"I don't need much — just enough for the fare by boat for a few days. Once ashore again, I certainly wouldn't take a chair but carry my luggage on my back. Even if I skipped a few meals, that wouldn't matter. If I could just see my father again, I should die content."

"All right. Stay here tonight, and we'll think it over carefully."

Later in the evening, Ma asked: "How many years have you studied? Can you write compositions?"

Kuang replied that he could.

"In that case," said Ma with a smile, "I will make so bold as to set a subject and ask you to write a composition for me, to see how much chance you have if you study for the examinations. Have you any objection?"

"I was just wishing I could ask for your instruction. But I don't know how to write. I'm afraid you will laugh at me."

"Of course not! I will set a subject then, and you can write on it tomorrow."

This was no sooner said than done, after which Ma advised Kuang to go to bed.

When Ma got up the next day, the young man handed in his composition neatly copied out. Ma was pleased.

"You are diligent and quick," he said. "Very good! Very good!"

After reading the composition, he commented: "Your essay shows talent, but you are not sufficiently familiar with the method of reasoning."

Then, spreading the manuscript on the table and punctuating it with his brush, he explained the use of antithesis and analogy and other rules of *paku* composition.

Kuang bowed to express his thanks, then prepared to take his leave.

"Wait a minute," said Ma. "It's no good for you to stay too long in Hangchow. I'm going to give you your fare home."

"Since you are so good, I will just ask for one tael."

"No, no. When you get home you must have some money to support your parents, so that you have time to study. I am giving you ten taels. You can start a little business with it when you go back, and get a doctor to attend to your father."

Ma opened his case and took out ten taels, then found an old padded jacket and a pair of shoes which he gave to Kuang Chao-jen.

"Take this money home," he said. "I'm afraid it may be cold on the trip, and the shoes and jacket are for you to wear in the early morning and evening."

Kuang shed tears as he took these gifts.

"You are too good to me!" he exclaimed. "How can I ever repay your kindness? I would like to become your sworn brother in order to be able to ask for your advice in future. But you may think this too bold a request."

Ma was delighted, however, and allowed Kuang Chao-jen to bow to him. Then they bowed to each other and became sworn brothers. After this Ma prepared a simple farewell meal for the young man.

"If you take my advice," said Ma during the meal, "after you reach home you should consider passing the official examinations as the most important way of pleasing your parents. There is no other way for men to achieve fame. That fortune-telling is a low profession goes without saying; but even teaching and secretarial work are not proper careers. If, however, you are brilliant enough to pass the examinations, you immediately reflect credit upon your whole family. That 's why the *Book of Filial Piety* tells us that to reflect credit on your family and to spread your fame shows the greatest piety. At the same time, of course, you do very well for yourself. As the proverb says: There are golden mansions in study; there are bushels of rice and beautiful women. And what is study today if not our *paku* compositions? So when you go back to look after your parents, you must consider study for the examinations of prime importance. Even if your business does badly and you cannot give your father and mother all they want, that need not worry you. Writing compositions is the main thing. For when your father lies ill in bed with nothing to eat and hears you declaiming compositions, no doubt about it but his heart will rejoice, his sadness will disappear and his pain will pass away. This is what Tseng Tzu[1] meant when he spoke of pleasing the parents. And if you are not lucky enough to pass all the examinations, you will at least be able to become a stipendiary which will enable you to be a tutor and apply for titles for your parents. I am old and good-for-nothing, but you are young and brilliant. You must listen to me so that later, when you become an official, we may meet again."

Then Ma carefully selected a few volumes of essays from his bookcase and wrapped them up with the clothes.

---

[1] A disciple of Confucius, known for his filial piety.

"These are all good," he said. "Take them to read."

Reluctant as he was to leave, Kuang Chao-jen was eager to see his father again; so with tears in his eyes he said goodbye. Ma took his hand and went with him to his former lodging on the Mountain of the Guardian Deity to fetch his bedding, then saw him out of Clear Stream Gate and all the way to the boat. When the young man had gone on board, Ma went back to the city.

After crossing the Chientang River, Kuang looked for a boat to Wenchow. He hailed a passing vessel to ask whether they would take a passenger.

"This is Mr. Cheng's boat," replied the boatman, "and he is travelling on business for the governor. We can't pick anyone up."

Kuang was shouldering his luggage to turn away, when a white-bearded old man called from the cabin window: "It doesn't matter picking up one passenger, boatman. He will tip you for your trouble."

"Since the gentleman says so, you can come aboard," said the boatman.

He steered the boat to the bank and helped Kuang on deck.

Kuang put down his luggage and bowed to the old man. There were three men in the cabin: Mr. Cheng was sitting in the middle with his son on one side and a t veller from another district on the other. Mr. Cheng returned Kuang's greeting and told him to sit down.

Since Kuang Chao-jen was clever, did all he could to make himself useful, and addressed the old man respectfully, Mr. Cheng was so pleased with him that he invited him to share their meals. And after one meal, when they had nothing to do, Mr. Cheng remarked: "Nowadays human nature has deteriorated so much that even scholars show no filial piety. In Wenchow there are three brothers named Chang who have passed the first examination; but because the two elder brothers suspected that their father had left most of his property to their younger brother they were always making trouble at home. Their father was angry and reported them to the court; but these two brothers bribed the county and prefectural officials to forge a false statement and hush up the matter.

There was an old secretary in the prefectural court, however, who was a just man; and he reported the matter to the governor, who has ordered me to go to Wenchow to arrest the culprits."

"When you have arrested them and found out the truth," said the other traveller, "won't all the officials in the county and prefectural courts find themselves in trouble?"

"When the truth is discovered, they will all be punished."

When Kuang Chao-jen heard this, he sighed to himself as he thought: "So rich men are unfilial sons; but a poor man like myself who wants to be a good son can't. The unfairness of it!"

Two days later it was time for him to go ashore. Kuang Chao-jen thanked Mr. Cheng, and when the old man refused to accept payment for the meals, he thanked him again. He pressed forward, travelling by day and resting by night, till he reached his own village and came in sight of his home.

But to know what followed, you must read the next chapter.

CHAPTER 16

**A good son waits upon his father in Big Willow Village.
A good magistrate encourages a poor scholar
in Yuehching County**

When Kuang Chao-jen saw his home, covering two paces in one he hurried eagerly forward to knock at the door. At the sound of his voice, his mother came out to welcome him.

"Is it you, son?" she cried.

"I'm back, mother!"

He put down his luggage, straightened his clothes and bowed to her.

When his mother felt his clothes and found he was wearing a very thick padded jacket, a great weight was lifted from her mind.

"Since you left with that merchant over a year ago, I've been eating my heart out," she told him. "One night I woke up crying because I dreamed you had fallen into the water. One night I dreamed you had broken your leg. One night I dreamed that there was a big growth on your face; but when you showed it to me and I tried to take it off, I couldn't. One night I dreamed that you came home and stood before me in tears; and then I cried too until I woke myself up! One night I saw you in a gauze cap and heard you had become an official. I laughed and said: 'How can country folk like us become officials?'

"Then a man there told me: 'This official is not your son. Your son, however, has also become an official; but he will never come back to you any more.'

"That made me cry again and I said: 'If I shan't be able to see him again once he becomes an official, I'd rather he didn't become one.' I started sobbing so loudly that I woke up and woke your father too. He asked me what was the matter; and when I told him the dream from the beginning, he said I was crazy; but that same night he had a stroke which left him paralysed all down one side. He's sleeping now in the bedroom."

Old Kuang in the inner room knew by now that his son had come back; and this gave him a new lease of life. Kuang Chao-jen went in to him.

"Father!" he said. "Your son is back!"

Then he stepped forward and kowtowed. His father made him sit on the edge of the bed while he told him the whole story of his troubles.

"After you left, your third uncle took a fancy to our house. I was thinking of selling it to him, too, because I reckoned that even after renting rooms somewhere else we'd have a few taels left from the proceeds to set you up in a small business after you came home. People told me: 'Your house is right next to his, so if he wants it you should make him pay a few taels more.' But although he's so rich he likes to drive a hard bargain; and instead of paying more, he offered less than the market price. He knew quite well, you see, that we had no rice left at home; so he tried to cut the price. Well, that made me angry and I refused to sell; but then he played a dirty trick on me by asking the former owner to buy the house back at the original price. As you know, the former owner is one of my uncles; and he took advantage of his position as an elder to claim that his family property should never have been sold.

"I said: 'At any rate, you must pay me for the repairs I've done all these years.' But he wouldn't hear of it: he insisted on buying it back at the original price. We were wrangling that day in the ancestral temple, and he even struck me; yet all the rich relatives supported him because your third uncle had spoken to them beforehand. They accused me of having no family feeling! Your elder brother was no use either: what he said didn't cut any ice. And I was so angry that I fell ill as soon as I got home. After that, of course, things became even harder for us, until your elder brother let himself be talked into accepting the original price for the house and signed a receipt. They paid him the money in several lots, and it was soon spent. Then he saw that things looked bad and talked it over with his wife; and now they don't eat with us any more. I've nothing to give him and he's working on his own, so I had to let him have his own way. He takes his wares out every morning to one of the markets around; but he doesn't make enough to feed even the two of them. I lie here getting worse and worse, and your uncle keeps trying to turn us out because he wants to repair these rooms. What does he care whether I live or die? People come every few days to order us out, and we have to put up with their insults. We didn't know what had become of you either; and whenever your mother thought of you, she cried!"

"Don't worry any more, father," said Kuang Chao-jen. "You must rest quietly till you're better. In Hangchow I met a gentleman who gave me ten taels of silver, and tomorrow I shall start working to support you. If Third Uncle asks for the house again, you needn't be afraid. I'll answer him."

His mother came in to call him to a meal, and he followed her to the kitchen where he bowed to his sister-in-law who offered him tea. After drinking the tea and finishing his meal, he hurried to the market-place and spent what remained of his travelling money on a pig's trotter for his father to eat that evening. No sooner had he returned home than in came his elder brother, Kuang Ta, with his pedlar's kit. Kuang Chao-jen bowed and knelt down, but his brother raised him up and made him sit in the hall while he told him of the hard times they had had.

"Dad doesn't seem quite right in the head nowadays," said Kuang Ta with a frown. "He won't see reason. They want us to move out, but he won't give up the house; and so they take it out of me. You're his favourite; see if you can't talk him round."

This said, he carried his wares to his own room.

When the pig's trotter was cooked, Kuang Chao-jen took it with rice to his father and helped him sit up. His son's return had put the old man in good spirits, and since there was meat that evening he made a hearty meal. Then, taking what was left, Kuang Chao-jen asked his mother and brother in, and laid a table in front of his father's bed for their supper. The old man was pleased as he watched them eat, and Kuang Chao-jen sat with him till nearly ten, when he settled him comfortably for the night. Last of all, he brought his own bedding and lay down to sleep at his father's feet.

The next morning he got up early, took the silver to the market and bought about a bushel of beans and several pigs which he kept in a sty. He killed one pig, cleaned it, cut it up and sold it during the morning; and after that he made beancurd which he also sold. Then, having put his takings under his father's bed, he sat by the old man's side and, to cheer him up, described the scenery of the West Lake and the different sweetmeats sold there. He also repeated jokes he had heard in various places until his father was laughing.

In the evening Kuang Chao-jen helped his father sit up again for supper, then arranged him comfortably for the night, tucking his quilt around him. This done, he fetched a big iron lamp he had brought from Hangchow, filled it with oil and sat by his father's side to read essays. His father could not sleep well at night because he kept hawking or wanting to drink tea; so Kuang Chao-jen read till after midnight in order to be at hand whenever called. He went to bed very late each night and slept for two or three hours only, since he had to get up early to kill a pig and grind beans.

Four or five days later Kuang Ta came home early, bringing a pot of wine and a chicken which he ordered his wife to boil to welcome his brother home.

"Don't tell the old man," he said.

Kuang Chao-jen would not listen to him, however, but filled a bowl with chicken for his father and mother; and the two brothers were eating what was left in the hall when their third uncle came to demand that they move out. Kuang Chao-jen put down his wine and bowed.

"Well, well! So you're back, eh?" said his uncle. "Wearing such a thick padded jacket too! And while you were away you've learned to scrape and bow with the best of them!"

"I have been so busy these few days since I came back, uncle, that I haven't been able to call to pay my respects. Please sit down and have some wine."

Their uncle sat down, and after a few cups of wine brought up the subject of the house.

"Please have patience, uncle," said Kuang Chao-jen. "Since my brother and I are both at home, we don't intend to go on occupying your house for nothing; even if we can't afford to lease a house, we can at least rent a couple of rooms in order to leave this house to you. The thing is that our father is ill just now, and they say that when a sick man is moved it holds up his cure. We are anxiously inviting doctors to cure father; and if he recovers soon, we shall move at once. And if we hear that his illness can't be cured in a short time, we shall have no choice but to look for rooms and move away. For if we go on living in your house, uncle, not only will you be urging us all the time to move, but our own parents will feel uncomfortable about staying."

This frank yet polite way of talking left the uncle with nothing to say.

"We belong to one family and I don't want to hurry you," he replied. "It's just that all the repairs should be done together. If that's the way things are, you may stay here a little longer."

"Thank you, uncle!" replied Kuang Chao-jen. "I can promise you that we won't be too long."

"Won't you have another cup of wine?" asked Kuang Ta as their uncle rose to leave.

He declined, however, and went away.

Kuang Chao-jen was soon doing a brisk business in pork and beancurd, selling all his goods by midday, then taking his earnings home to keep his father company. Whenever he made a little extra, he would buy a chicken or duck or some fish from the market for his father, because the old man suffered from phlegm and could not eat much pork. As for kidney and tripe, Old Kuang had these constantly, to say nothing of cordials. Thus the old man lived in comfort, and by degrees his illness improved. When he spoke of moving house, though, Kuang Chao-jen said:

"You are only just beginning to recover, father. Wait until you are strong enough to walk with my help before you talk of moving."

And when the third uncle sent people to demand the house, Kuang Chao-jen managed to put them off.

Kuang Chao-jen had extraordinary energy: he plied his trade in the morning and sat up late at night looking after his father and studying. Nobody could have worked harder. And if he had time in the middle of the day, he went out to play chess with the neighbours. One day after the midday meal, when his father had eaten and he had nothing to do, Kuang Chao-jen went to the threshing floor with a distant relative who was a cowherd. They turned over a crate to serve as a table and settled down to a game of chess. Presently a white-bearded old man strolled over with his hands behind his back to watch the game. "Aha!" he exclaimed after watching for some time. "You've lost."

Kuang Chao-jen looked up and saw that it was the village headman, Pan. So he stood up, called him by his name and bowed.

"I was wondering who you were," said the headman. "Now I remember. You're Old Kuang's second son who left home the year before last. When did you get back? Is your father better yet?"

"I have been back for half a year, uncle; but I dared not disturb you by calling simply to pay my respects. My father is still bed-ridden, but he has taken a turn for the better. It was good of you to ask after him. Please come to our house for a cup of tea."

"No, no, I won't trouble you," said Pan.

He stepped up to Kuang Chao-jen, pushed back the young man's cap, then took his hand and examined the palm most carefully.

"I don't want to flatter you," he said, "but I know something about fortune-telling and you have noble features. When you reach twenty-seven or twenty-eight you are going to have good luck: a wife, children, wealth, and rank will all be yours. The centre of your brows is turning yellow — a sign that a high official will soon come into your life." Turning up the lobe of Kuang Chao-jen's ear, he added: "You will have an unpleasant surprise as well, but nothing serious. And after that you'll do better every year."

"Why, uncle, I ply my small trade and all I ask is not to lose my capital. If I make a few coins every day to support my parents, I thank heaven, earth and Buddha. How can *I* hope to become rich and noble?"

"No. You won't be a trader long," declared Pan. And after saying this, he left them.

The third uncle kept pressing the Kuang family to move out, becoming more and more insistent until Kuang Chao-jen could delay matters no longer and had to take a firm stand. Then his uncle grew angry, and threatened that unless they moved out within three days he would send men to tear down the house. Kuang Chao-jen was worried, but he kept this from his father. On the evening of the third day, he had put his father to sleep and lit his iron lamp to study, when he heard a great uproar outside. He first thought his third uncle must have sent men to tear down their house; but presently he heard hundreds of people shouting and the window paper was lit by a crimson glare. With a cry of dismay, he ran to the door and saw that the village was on fire. The women hurried out too.

"Mercy!" they cried. "We must move out quickly!"

Kuang Ta scrambled up in a daze, with no thought for anything but his shoulder pole and wares. His stock was an assortment of sesame sweets, dried beancurd, clay figurines, children's flutes and cymbals, and women's hairpins. Some of these he grabbed up, some he let fall and most of the clay figurines and sweets were smashed to pieces as, sweating with terror, he snatched up his load and hurtled out.

By now the fire was more than ten feet high and balls of flame were falling into their courtyard. Kuang Chao-jen's sister-in-law had caught up a bundle of bedding, clothing and shoes; but whimpering with fright, she was walking back inside instead of outside. His mother was too appalled to move a step. The fire shed a crimson light over the whole countryside, and the shrieking and sobbing were deafening; but Kuang Chao-jen had one thought only. Disregarding his mother for the time being, he seized a quilt, picked his father up from the bed and carried him carefully out on his back to the open ground outside the gate. This done, he rushed back, seized his sister-in-law and showed her the way out, then carried his mother out too. By this time the fire had reached their door, so that they could barely get through. But Kuang Chao-jen said: "All's well! Father and mother are safe!"

He made his father lie down on the ground, wrapping him up well in the quilt, and told his mother and sister-in-law to sit beside him. But when he looked for his brother there was no sign of him—Kuang Ta had fled in terror. The fire crackled, sputtered, roared and sparked, its crimson flames like a leaping golden dragon; and since country folk do not know how to put out a fire and the water supply was far away, it went on burning half the night. Even then, the threshing floor was a mass of smoke and ashes, and the air was fiery hot.

All the houses in the village were burnt to the ground, and Kuang Chao-jen was wondering what to do when his eye fell on the monastery on the main road south of the village; so there he carried his father, while his sister-in-law helped his mother to hobble painfully after them. A monk came out to greet them, but when he knew their errand he refused them admittance.

"After this fire all the villagers whose houses have been burnt are homeless," he said. "If all of them move to our monastery, even if we built two extra wings we couldn't hold them all. Besides, you have a sick man, which complicates matters."

Just then an old man walked out of the monastery, and when Kuang Chao-jen saw that it was the headman, Pan, he stepped forward to bow to him and described how their house had caught fire.

"So your house was burnt too last night!" exclaimed Mr. Pan. "That's too bad."

Then Kuang Chao-jen told him how he had hoped to put up in the monastery for the time being, but had been refused admittance by the monk.

"Monk," said the headman, "Old Kuang is one of the best men in our village, and his son has such fine features he is sure to make good in future. You monks have always held that in doing good to others lies the greatest good for yourselves. Why don't you lend them a room for a couple of days? They won't stay longer than they have to, and I shall give you some incense money."

When the monk heard the headman say this, he dared no longer refuse to admit the Kuang family but gave them a room. Then Kuang Chao-jen carried his father in and made him lie down; and Mr. Pan came to inquire after Old Kuang, who thanked him. After the monk had brewed a pot of tea for them, the headman went home; but presently he sent over rice and dishes for them. Only in the afternoon did Kuang Ta arrive, grumbling because his younger brother had not helped him to salvage his wares.

Kuang Chao-jen realized that they could not stay long there, so he asked the headman to rent them one room and a half near the monastery on the main road. It was lucky that he had not gone to bed on the evening of the fire and therefore still had his capital on him, for this meant he was able to go on earning his living by killing pigs and making beancurd; and in the evenings he read essays by lamplight as before.

The shock had made his father's illness worse; but, worried as he was, Kuang Chao-jen kept on with his studies. One night he had read till nearly midnight, and was declaiming an essay with great gusto when he heard gongs sound outside the window and saw a sedan-chair pass, surrounded by torches and followed by outriders He knew this must be the county magistrate, but he went on reading aloud while the party passed.

Now the magistrate decided to spend the night in the village office, for he marvelled to himself: "How remarkable to find a man studying so hard late at night in a little country place like this! I wonder whether he is a successful candidate or a student? Why not send for the headman to find out?"

214

He forthwith sent for Mr. Pan and asked him: "Who is it that studies at night in that house near the monastery, south of the village?"

The headman knew that this was where the Kuang family lived.

"Their house was burnt down," he explained, "so they rented a place there. The man studying is Old Kuang's second son, Kuang Chao-jen, who reads every night till well after midnight. He is not a scholar though, nor even a student, but simply a small tradesman."

The magistrate was impressed.

"Here is my card," he said. "Take it to Mr. Kuang tomorrow, and tell him I shall not ask to see him now; but the preliminary test is near and he should register for it. If he can write essays, I'll do what I can for him."

After receiving this order, the headman left.

Early the next morning, when Mr. Pan had seen the magistrate off to the city, he ran to where the Kuang family lived, knocked at the door and opened it, then cried: "Congratulations!"

"What is it?" asked Kuang Chao-jen.

The headman took from his cap the card bearing the magistrate's name, Li Pen-ying, and gave it to Kuang Chao-jen, who was greatly surprised.

"Who is this for, uncle?" he asked.

"As the magistrate was passing by, he heard you reading essays and had me in to ask about you. When I told him how poor you were and what a filial son, he gave me this card for you and asked me to tell you that the preliminary test is near and he wants you to register for it. He intends to pass you. Didn't I tell you the other day that there were signs of good fortune on your face, and a high official would soon come into your life?"

Kuang Chao-jen was overjoyed. And when he showed his father the card and told him what had happened, the old man was happy too. That evening, when Kuang Ta came back and saw the card, Kuang Chao-jen told him about it also; but his brother would not believe him.

A few days later a notice was posted in the district announcing the preliminary test; and Kuang Chao-jen bought examination paper and went in for this test. When the results were published, he had passed; and he bought more examination paper for the next test. When the magistrate took his seat in court, Kuang Chao-jen's name was the first to be called.

"How old are you?" asked Magistrate Li.

"I am twenty-two."

"You write quite well. If you work even harder to prepare for the next test, I shall see you through." Kuang Chao-jen bowed and thanked him, then took his paper and left.

When the results of the second preliminary test were published, he was first on the list. After this news reached his village, Kuang Chao-jen went to thank the magistrate, who invited him in and asked after his family, then gave him two taels of silver.

"This is only a small part of my salary," said he. "Take it for your parents. When you reach home you must work even harder; and if you come to see me before you go to the prefecture for the next examination, I shall help you with your travelling expenses."

Having expressed his thanks Kuang Chao-jen withdrew.

When he returned home he gave the silver to his father and told him what the magistrate had said. The old man was very grateful. Holding the silver in his hand, he kowtowed to Heaven from his pillow; and only then did Kuang Ta believe that his younger brother had passed. The villagers were impressed too when they heard that Kuang Chao-jen had come first on the list and that the magistrate had received him; so they banded together to send him congratulatory gifts. And, on his father's instructions, Kuang Chao-jen gave a feast in the neighbouring monastery.

This happened near the end of winter, and in spring, when the new term began, the imperial examiner went to Wenchow to preside over the prefectural examination there. Kuang Chao-jen called on Magistrate Li to take his leave, and was given another two taels with which he travelled to Wenchow. When he had taken the examination, Magistrate Li called on the examiner, bowed and said: "This Kuang Chao-jen, whom I passed first in the county examination, is a poor scholar and a good son." He proceeded to relate all his filial deeds.

"Moral character counts more than literary attainments in a scholar," said the examiner. "If a man shows high moral qualities, literary accomplishments are secondary. I have read Kuang Chao-jen's essays, and although his exposition is not always very clear, he shows talent. Rest assured that I shall remember your wishes."

But to know whether Kuang Chao-jen passed the prefectural examination or not, you must read the next chapter.

CHAPTER 17

Kuang Chao-jen revisits his old haunts.
Dr. Chao ranks high among the poets

After Kuang Chao-jen left to take the prefectural examination, his father missed him so much that twenty days' absence seemed to him like two years; and every day, with tears in his eyes, he watched for his son's return. One day he said to his wife: "Our second son has been gone all this time now, and we don't know whether he has been lucky enough to pass or not. I may die at any moment, and I shan't be able to see him on my death bed." At the thought of this he shed tears.

As his wife was comforting him they heard shouts and blows outside, and a fierce-looking fellow burst in accusing Old Kuang's elder son of taking over his pitch in the market. When Kuang Ta would not admit that he was in the wrong, but answered back furiously, the other man seized his pedlar's kit, spilled out the contents and kicked the baskets to pieces.

Kuang Ta threatened to drag him to court.

"The magistrate is a friend of my brother's!" he shouted. "Think I'm afraid of you? Let's go to the yamen!"

When Old Kuang heard this, he called his son in.

"Don't talk like that," he said, "we're a respectable family, who've never picked quarrels with people or gone to court. Besides, you were in the wrong to occupy his stand. You'd better ask someone to apologize to him for you, instead of brawling like this and upsetting my peace of mind."

His son would not listen to him, but stamped out in a rage to go on quarrelling, until all the neighbours gathered round to reason with him and try to drag the two belligerents apart. Then Pan the headman arrived on the scene, and persuaded the other man to quiet down.

"Pick up your things, Young Kuang," he urged, "take them inside."

So Kuang Ta gathered together his things, cursing as he did so.

Just then two men appeared, with a strip of red paper.

"Does a Mr. Kuang live here?" they asked.

The headman realized that these were messengers from the examination school.

"Good! Master Kuang has passed!" he said. "Young Kuang, take these two gentlemen in to your father."

Kuang Ta had just finished gathering together his wares. Picking up his shoulder pole he led the two messengers into the house, while the headman advised the other man to make off. The two messengers congratulated Old Kuang, who was lying in bed, and pasted up an announcement on which was written: "This is to inform you that Mr. Kuang Chao-jen of your honourable family has been classed first on the list by the imperial examiner."

The old man was very pleased. He told his wife to boil tea, fill two dishes with sweets and dried beancurd from his elder son's pack, and boil a dozen eggs for the messengers. The headman also came to offer his congratulations, bringing a dozen eggs with him. Then they boiled all the eggs together, and kept Mr. Pan and the messengers to a meal. After they had eaten, Old Kuang offered the messengers two hundred coins as a tip; but they said it was not enough.

"I'm a poor man, and our house was burnt down," he told them. "It was very good of you to come to announce my son's success, and this is just a trifle to spend on tea."

Mr. Pan reasoned with them as well and gave them another hundred coins, after which the messengers left.

Only four or five days later, after Kuang Chao-jen had seen the examiner off, did he come back in his scholar's cap and gown to pay his respects to his parents. His sister-in-law had gone home to live since the fire, so he had only his brother to greet; but Kuang Ta treated him more warmly now that he had become a licentiate. The headman collected money and chose a day on which to hold a feast to congratulate him in the monastery, collecting more than twenty strings of coins this time and killing two pigs as well as a number of chickens and ducks. The feasting went on for two whole days. The monk tried to make up to the new licentiate too.

After consulting his father, Kuang Chao-jen decided to give up his beancurd business, and handed over what was left of the money to his brother so that he could rent two more rooms and start a small grocery shop. This meant that his sister-in-law was able to come back and the family was united again, while the money made in the shop was enough to support them all.

A few days after this, Kuang Chao-jen went to the city to thank Magistrate Li, who now treated him as an equal, entertained him to a meal and offered to be his patron. After Kuang Chao-jen's return home, the two messengers from the examination school came to the house again, and he asked Mr. Pan to help entertain them.

"The county tutor wants Mr. Kuang to call on him," said the men. "He must prepare presents for the interview."

Kuang Chao-jen was annoyed.

"I recognize only my own patron," he said. "Why should I call on this tutor and give him presents?"

"You mustn't talk like that," Pan told him. "If our county magistrate is your patron, that is your private affair; but this tutor has been appointed by the government to supervise scholars here; so even if you pass all the examinations you will still be considered his pupil. How can you refuse to call on him? Since you are a poor scholar, not much will be expected of you. Just give the messengers twenty cents of silver each." When a date had been fixed for his visit, the messengers left; and on the day appointed Kuang Chao-jen took presents to his tutor. His father ordered him to offer sacrifice at the graves of their ancestors on his way back.

The day that Kuang Chao-jen came back from the family tombs, his father took a turn for the worse and began to sink rapidly. Cordials proved ineffective, the old man's appetite gradually failed, and although Kuang Chao-jen offered prayers and consulted oracles, the answer was always discouraging. Then he suggested to his brother that they should use his former capital for the funeral expenses while the shop carried on as usual. Thus they bought a coffin, prepared clothes and made a scholar's cap to fit the old man's head, so that all was ready. One day he would lose consciousness completely, but the next he would be slightly better.

When at last the old man knew that his end was near, he called his sons to his bedside.

"I'm not going to get over this," he told them. "I shall soon be in my grave. I've been a failure all my life, and I can't leave you a single piece of land—I even lost the house. Now, Chao-jen, you have been lucky enough to pass the examination, and may go further later. But fame and fortune are external things after all; it's goodness that really counts. You have been a good son and a loyal brother when it wasn't easy; and I don't want you to change and start thinking yourself high and mighty now that things are going more smoothly for you. After I'm dead and you've finished mourning, you must lose no time in finding a wife. But choose a girl from a poor family: don't try to better yourself by marrying into a family that's rich and noble. Your brother is no good; but you must go on showing him the same respect that you would me."

The two brothers wept as they listened. Then the old man closed his eyes and died, the whole family began to wail, and Kuang Chao-jen's lamentations would have moved heaven and earth as he made ready for the funeral.

Since they were cramped for space, the coffin was interred in the ancestral graveyard after the first seven days, and all the villagers attended the funeral. When the two brothers had called to thank the mourners, Kuang Ta opened shop again while Kuang Chao-jen went every seven days to sacrifice before his father's tomb.

He had just reached home one evening after offering sacrifice when Mr. Pan called.

"Do you know that the county magistrate is in trouble?" he said. "The sub-prefect from Wenchow has been sent to take away his seal. Since he is your patron, you had better go to the city to see him."

The next day, accordingly, Kuang Chao-jen changed out of mourning dress and set off to the city to see his patron. As he was approaching the city, however, he found that the citizens had made up their minds to keep Magistrate Li and, sounding gongs and stopping the market, had surrounded the sub-prefect sent to dismiss him and attempted to take the seal back by force. The city gates were closed in broad daylight and the whole place was in an uproar.

Unable to enter the city, Kuang Chao-jen went home to wait for news; and on the third day he heard that officers had been sent from the provincial capital to pacify the people and arrest the ringleaders. Three or four days later, he was coming back from his father's tomb when Mr. Pan accosted him again.

"Things look bad!" warned the headman. "There's going to be trouble!"

"What trouble?" asked Kuang Chao-jen.

"I'll tell you inside."

They went into Kuang Chao-jen's house and sat down.

"Yesterday a pacification commissioner arrived in the county town and the people scattered," said Pan. "The authorities have ordered this commissioner to find out who headed the riot, and he has arrested a few men. Now two bad runners in the yamen have informed against you, too, saying that since the magistrate treated you well, you must be one of the ringleaders. Of course, there's nothing in it; but the authorities will be looking into the question, and who knows what their decision will be? If they think there is something in the charge, they may send to arrest you. If I were you, I'd go to another province to lie low for a time. If no trouble comes of this, well and good. If it does, I'll do what I can for you."

Kuang Chao-jen was quite staggered.

"What bad luck!" he cried. "Thank you for telling me. But where can I go?"

"Just think: what place do you know best?"

"Hangchow is the only place I know well; but I have no friends there."

"If you go to Hangchow, I will give you a letter to a cousin of mine there. He is my third cousin, so he is called Pan Number Three, and he works in the finance commissioner's yamen. He lives on the hill in front of the yamen. If you call on him, he'll look after you, because he's a very open-handed fellow. You'll be all right."

"In that case, I'll thank you to write a letter, uncle. I had better leave tonight."

While Mr. Pan was writing the letter, Kuang Chao-jen asked his brother and sister-in-law to look after everything at home, then with tears in his eyes said goodbye to his mother, put his things together, pocketed the letter and left. The headman saw him to the highway.

With his pack on his back, Kuang Chao-jen tramped for several days until he reached Wenchow. There was no boat when he arrived, and therefore he had to put up at an inn, where he found a lamp lit and a traveller sitting at the table quietly reading a book. He had a lean, sallow face and sparse moustache and, because he was a short-sighted fellow and absorbed in his reading, he did not see Kuang Chao-jen come in; but when the latter came over and greeted him, he stood up and returned the greeting. He looked like a merchant, this man, in his black silk coat and tile-shaped cap.

When they had sat down, Kuang Chao-jen asked: "May I inquire your name and your native place?"

"My name is Ching Lan-chiang and my home is twenty miles from here. I have a shop in the provincial capital which I am on my way to visit; but since there is no boat today, I am staying here for the night." Seeing from Kuang Chao-jen's square cap that he was a scholar, Ching asked: "May I know your distinguished native place, sir, and your honourable name?"

"My name is Kuang Chao-jen and I come from Yuehching County. I too am waiting for a boat to Hangchow."

"Good," said Ching. "Tomorrow we can travel together."

Then the two of them went to sleep.

The next morning they boarded a boat and hired a cabin between them; and once they were aboard and had put down their luggage, Mr. Ching produced a book. Kuang Chao-jen did not like to ask what it was, but a glance at the colourful marginal notes told him that it was a volume of poetry. At lunch, Mr. Ching took up the book again; and when they sat sipping tea, Kuang Chao-jen said:

"Last night you told me, sir, that you had a shop in the provincial capital. May I ask what shop it is?"

"A hatter's."

"Since you have a shop, why do you read these books?"

Mr. Ching laughed.

"Did you think only successful candidates in square caps read books?" he asked. "There are many famous scholars in Hangchow who don't think much of the *paku* essays. I may tell you, sir, that my name—Ching Lan-chiang—has appeared in all the anthologies of poetry for the last twenty years. When officials visit Hangchow, they all come to write poems with us."

Thereupon he opened his case, which was in the cabin, took out several dozen sheets of paper and handed them to Kuang Chao-jen.

"These are my unworthy effusions," he said. "I would like to have your criticism."

Ashamed of his tactlessness Kuang Chao-jen took the poems and, although he could not understand them, pretended to read them through and praised them as best he could.

"Who was your examiner?" asked Ching Lan-chiang.

"The newly appointed one."

"This new examiner used to work with Mr. Lu of Huchow, who is a poet and friend of mine. Our poetizing parties were attended by Mr. Yang Chih-chung, Mr. Chuan Wu-yung, Chu Hsien-fu of Chiahsing, the grandson of Prefect Chu, and the two sons of Minister Lou—the third and fourth brothers. They are all good friends of mine. There was a Mr. Niu Pu-yi too, but unfortunately I only knew him by reputation: we never met."

When Kuang Chao-jen heard Ching speak of all these scholars, he asked: "I suppose you also know Mr. Ma Chun-shang who compiles essays for Literary Expanse Bookshop?"

224

"One of those *paku* essayists, isn't he? I know him, of course, but not well. To tell the truth, we Hangchow scholars don't set much store by men of that type. Ours is quite a large group, and when we reach Hangchow I shall introduce you to some of its members."

Hearing this, Kuang Chao-jen was filled with amazement.

They travelled together to Broken Bay where the boat moored; and, just as they were going to have their luggage carried ashore, Ching Lan-chiang, who was standing in the prow, saw a sedan-chair stop on the bank. From the chair alighted a man in a scholar's cap and sapphire-blue gown, who was holding a white paper fan, with a poem on it, from which hung a square ivory seal. Followed by a servant carrying a medicine chest, this man was about to enter a house, when Ching called to him: "Dr. Chao! I haven't seen you for a long time! Where are you going?"

The doctor turned.

"Aha!" he cried, "so it's you! When did you arrive?"

"Just this moment. My luggage hasn't been carried ashore yet." Then, turning back, Ching called into the cabin: "Please come out, Mr. Kuang. I want you to meet my best friend, Dr. Chao Hsueh-chai."

Kuang Chao-jen came out and they went ashore together. Then the three of them bowed to each other and entered the tea-house into which Ching had ordered the boatman to carry their luggage.

"May I ask this gentleman's name?" said Dr. Chao.

"This is Mr. Kuang of Yuehching County," Ching told him. "We came here in the same boat."

After an exchange of courtesies, they sat down and ordered three bowls of tea.

"What has kept you away so long?" asked Dr. Chao. "I have been missing you all this time."

"I had some vulgar business to attend to," replied Ching. "Have there been any poetry meetings?"

"Naturally. Last month when old Mr. Ku of the Imperial Patent Office came here on a pilgrimage to Tien Chu Monastery, he invited us there for the day to write poems. And when Commissioner Fan of the Office of Transmission asked leave to visit his ancestors' tombs, although his boat stopped here for one day only, he invited us aboard to compose poetry and entertained us for a whole day. After that, Censor Hsun came to borrow money from the governor; but instead of working on the governor he invited us to his rooms every day to write poems. They all asked after you. Now Mr. Hu is collecting funeral odes for Mr. Lu of Huchow, and has sent several dozen sheets of paper to me I can't dispose of them all, so it's very fortunate that you've come: you can relieve me of a couple of sheets." He paused to sip his tea, then asked: "I take it that Mr. Kuang is a scholar too. Under which examiner did he pass?"

"The present one," said Ching.

Dr. Chao smiled.

"In that case," he said, "he is a classmate of my eldest son."

After they had drunk some tea Dr. Chao left to see a patient, and Ching asked: "Where would you like your luggage taken, Mr. Kuang?"

"To Literary Expanse Bookshop for the time being."

"Very well," said Ching. "I will leave you then. I am going to my shop. It is on the main street facing the Guardian Angel's Monastery at Beancurd Bridge. I hope when you're free you'll drop in for a chat."

He called for a porter and left.

When Kuang Chao-jen took his luggage to the bookshop and inquired for Mr. Ma, he learned that Ma Chun-shang had gone back to Chuchow. The manager of the bookshop recognized him, however, and let him spend the night there. The next day Kuang Chao-jen took his letter of introduction to the finance commissioner's yamen to look for Pan Number Three; but when he found his house, the servant told him:

"Third Master is away. He left a few days ago on official business for the examiner's yamen at Taichow."

"When will he be back?"

"He has only just left. He will probably be away a month or more."

Kuang Chao-jen then made his way to the main street to look for the hatter's shop near Beancurd Bridge; but he drew a blank here too. When he questioned the neighbours, they said: "Mr. Ching? On a fine day like this he will be pretty sure to have gone to the Six Bridges to admire the spring scenery and look at the flowers and willows while he writes poems about the lake. When he can get such inspiration outside, he's not likely to stay in the shop!"

Kuang Chao-jen turned away; but after walking down two streets, he caught sight of Ching Lan-chiang in the distance with two men in scholars' caps. When Kuang Chao-jen came up with them, they greeted each other and Ching, pointing at one of his companions who was pock-marked, said: "This is Mr. Chih Chien-feng." Then, pointing to the other, who had a beard: "This is Mr. Pu Mo-ching. They are two of our leading poets."

"Who is this gentleman?" asked the poets.

Ching Lan-chiang introduced Kuang Chao-jen, who told him: "I called just now at your shop, but found you out. Where are you going?"

"Nowhere in particular: we are just strolling. But when good friends meet, they shouldn't separate. Why not go to the pavilion for a few cups of wine?"

"An excellent idea," said the other two.

They took Kuang Chao-jen with them to a tavern, chose seats and sat down. When the waiter asked what dishes they wanted, Ching ordered twelve cents' worth of assorted meat, one plate of pork crackling and one of bean sprouts.

After the wine was brought in, Chih Chien-feng asked: "Why didn't you call on Dr. Chao today?"

"He is entertaining an extraordinary guest," replied Pu Mo-ching.

"What's extraordinary about the guest?"

"I assure you, he's most extraordinary! If you'll each drink a cup of wine, I'll tell you about him."

Chih Chien-feng poured out wine and they drank.

"This guest is named Huang," said Pu Mo-ching. "He passed the palace examination in the third year of Cheng Te,[1] and is now magistrate of Ningpo. When he was in the capital he knew Mr. Yang Chih-chung; and since Yang Chih-chung is a friend

_____
1 1508.

of Dr. Chao and knew that Mr. Huang was coming to Chekiang, he gave him a letter of introduction to our doctor. It so happened, though, that Dr. Chao was not in when Mr. Huang called, and didn't see him."

"Many officials call on Dr. Chao," said Ching. "There is nothing extraordinary in Mr. Huang's not being able to see him."

"He was really out that day," said Pu. "But the next day he returned Mr. Huang's call, and when they met they started comparing notes. Don't you think it was strange?"

"What was strange?" they demanded.

"Mr. Huang was born in the same year and same month, on the same day and at the very same hour as Dr. Chao!"

"Yes, that *is* extraordinary!"

"But there's something more extraordinary to follow. Dr. Chao is fifty-nine this year and has two sons and four grandsons, while his wife has grown old with him; but he is still an ordinary citizen. Mr. Huang has passed the metropolitan examination and is a magistrate; but he lost his wife when he was thirty, and he has neither sons nor daughters."

"That is *really* extraordinary!" cried Chih Chien-feng. "They were born under the same stars, yet their fortunes have been totally different—they have nothing at all in common! This shows that astrology and horoscopy are unreliable."

They had been drinking a fair amount as they talked, and now Pu Mo-ching said: "Gentlemen, I have a problem for you. Here are Mr. Huang and Dr. Chao, who were born under the same stars: one has become an official but is alone in the world, while the other has a houseful of children and grandchildren but has not become an official. Which of the two is the luckier? Which would you rather be?"

As no one expressed any opinion, Pu Mo-ching said: "Let Mr. Kuang speak first. What do you think, Mr. Kuang?"

"If one can't have the good fortune of both," said Kuang Chao-jen, "in my humble opinion, it would be better to be Dr. Chao."

The others clapped their hands and cried: "Well said!"

"The fact remains," said Pu Mo-ching, "that officialdom is the goal of our study; and although Dr. Chao is fortunate in many respects, he has not yet passed the examinations. This isn't just our opinion: he himself regrets that he's never become an official. But of course, if you want to be an official and at the same time enjoy Dr. Chao's happiness, that's asking too much! There are such men in the world, true; but since we have raised this problem we can't admit the possibility, for then there ceases to be any problem. In my opinion, better to be an official than to have a happy family life. In other words, choose to be Mr. Huang rather than Dr. Chao. What do you think?"

"I don't agree," said Chih Chien-feng. "Although Dr. Chao is not an official, his eldest son has passed the provincial examination; and when the young man passes the metropolitan examination a title will be given his father. Won't the son's officialdom be enough for the father?"

"No!" cried Pu Mo-ching with a smile. "That's not the case. Once there was an old gentleman whose son had already reached high position, who still insisted on taking the examination himself. When his name was called, however, and the examiner would not accept him as a candidate, he threw down his paper and cursed: 'It's all the fault of my beast of a son that I can't wear a real official cap.' Judging by this, a son's rank can't satisfy the father."

"You're all wide of the mark," said Ching Lan-chiang. "Fill up and drink three cups each, then listen to me."

"And what if we disagree with you?" asked Chih Chien-feng.

"In that case I'll drink three cups more."

"That is fair," they agreed, then filled their cups and drank.

"Gentlemen," said Ching, "when you choose officialdom, is it for the sake of fame? Or for the sake of profit?"

"For fame," they answered

"Then you must realize that although Dr. Chao has not become an official his poems are printed in dozens of anthologies and read all over the empire. Who hasn't heard the name of Chao Hsueh-chai? In fact, he is probably much more famous than most scholars who have passed the metropolitan examination." Having said this, he roared with laughter.

"Very nicely reasoned, indeed!" said the others, and drained their wine.

This was the first time that Kuang Chao-jen had heard such views expressed.

"We have had a pleasant encounter today." said Ching Lan-chiang. "Let us choose *lou* as our rhyme and go back to write a poem apiece. We'll copy them out on one sheet of paper and send them to Mr. Kuang for his criticism." Then they left the tavern and went their different ways.

If you want to know what next befell Kuang Chao-jen, you must read the following chapter.

CHAPTER 18

Famous scholars invite Kuang Chao-jen
to a poetical meeting. Pan Number Three
calls on a friend in a bookshop

When Kuang Chao-jen returned from the feast that evening to his bookshop, he went straight to sleep. The next morning the manager came upstairs to his room and when he had sat down, said: "I have a proposal to make."

"What is it?"

"A friend of mine and I are putting up some capital to publish a selection of *paku* essays; and we want to trouble you to edit them for us. We want the job well done and quickly done. There are over three hundred essays altogether: how long do you think that would take you? We are pressed for time because we must have the book ready for the merchants to take to Shantung and Honan to sell. If it comes out after they've left, we'll have missed our chance. We shall print your name on the title page, and when the book comes out you will receive a few dozen copies as well as several taels of silver. Do you think you can manage this?"

"About how long can I take?"

"If you could finish it within a fortnight, that would leave us a margin of time. But we could allow you twenty days at the most."

Calculating that he should be able to do the job in a fortnight, Kuang Chao-jen accepted the offer. The manager im-

231

mediately carried a pile of examination essays upstairs, and at midday he prepared four special dishes for Kuang Chao-jen.

"When the proofs are out and when the book is published I will invite you again," he said. "On ordinary days you will just have simple meals; but on the second and sixteenth of every month you will have meat with us; and we shall supply you with tea and oil for your lamp."

Kuang Chao-jen was quite delighted. That evening, having lit his lamp, he worked away without stopping until he had annotated fifty essays, when the fourth watch sounded from the watch-tower on the city wall.

"At this rate," he said cheerfully, "I shan't need a fortnight."

Then he blew out his lamp and went to sleep.

The next morning he got up early to go on with his editing, and by working all day and late into the night he was able to finish seventy or eighty essays a day. On the fourth day he was at work in his room when someone called from below: "Is Mr. Kuang in?"

"Who is it?" asked Kuang Chao-jen, and hurried downstairs to find Ching Lan-chiang there with a scroll in his hand. Ching bowed to him and said: "I am sorry to have delayed so long before coming."

Kuang Chao-jen asked him upstairs where he unrolled the scroll on the table.

"These are the poems we agreed to write with the rhyme *lou* at our meeting the other day," said Ching. "We had all finished our poems when Chao Hsueh-chai saw them and didn't want to be left out, so he wrote another poem with the same rhyme; and as we wanted his poem to come first, we had to copy ours out again. That's why I have brought this only today for your criticism."

Kuang Chao-jen saw that the scroll was headed: "Small Gathering in the Tavern in Late Spring, with the Rhyme *lou*." Chao Hsueh-chai, Ching Lan-chiang, Chih Chien-feng and Pu Mo-ching had written a poem apiece, signing their names underneath: and the dazzling white paper and brilliant red of the seals made such a brave show that Kuang Chao-jen pasted the scroll on his wall before sitting down.

"That day I trespassed on your hospitality and had too much to drink," said Kuang Chao-jen. "I came back very late."

"You haven't been out recently, have you?" asked Ching.

"No. The manager here has asked me to select a few essays, and I have to hurry to get them ready for the printers. That's why I haven't been able to call on you."

"Selecting essays is a good thing, but today I'm going to take you to call on someone."

"Who is he?"

"Never you mind. Change your gown and let's go; then you'll find out."

Kuang Chao-jen changed his clothes, locked his door and walked downstairs with Ching.

"Well, where are we going?" he asked when they were in the street.

"We are going to see Mr. Hu, the third son of the former minister of the Board of Civil Office. It's his birthday today and all our friends will be there. And since I have to offer congratulations, I decided to take you along. You can meet a lot of people there, because all those whose names you saw on the scroll will be there."

"I have never met Mr. Hu. Shouldn't I take a card?"

"Yes, you should."

They went into a chandler's to buy a card and Kuang Chao-jen borrowed a brush at the counter to write his name, then put the card in his sleeve as they walked on.

"Mr. Hu is most hospitable," said Ching. "But he's extremely timid. When his father died he shut himself up and dared not see a soul; so he was always being cheated, but had no one to complain to. The last few years, though, since he made friends with us, we have helped him. And now his family is more respected, and nobody dares to cheat him any more."

"If he's a minister's son, how dare people cheat him?"

"A minister? That's past and done with. Right now he has no one at court and is only an ordinary scholar. 'A dead prefect is not as good as a live rat.' Who's afraid of Mr. Hu? Men nowadays fawn upon the rich and powerful! But our friend Dr. Chao is such a famous poet that all the high officials call on him; and when people see a sedan-chair with yellow umbrellas[1] at his gate one day and seven or eight runners in red and black caps they can't help standing in awe of him. And when they see Dr. Chao's chair going every other day to Mr. Hu's house, as it has been recently, they suspect that Mr. Hu must be quite powerful too. His nearby tenants pay their rent much more readily now; and Mr. Hu is grateful to us."

As Ching was speaking, they met two other men in loose gowns and square caps whom he accosted.

"Aren't you going to congratulate Mr. Hu on his birthday?" he asked. "Who else are you going to fetch that you're coming this way?"

"We were coming to fetch you; but since we have met, let's go on together. Who is this gentleman?"

Ching introduced them to Kuang Chao-jen, saying: "This is Mr. Chin Tung-yeh and this is Mr. Yen Chih-chung." Then, pointing at Kuang Chao-jen, he told the others: "This is Mr. Kuang Chao-jen."

They bowed to each other and walked to the huge gate of the former minister's house. There they gave their cards to the gate-keeper, who invited them into the hall; and when Kuang Chao-jen looked around he saw hanging in the middle of the hall a tablet bearing the words: "A Pillar of the Empire" in the emperor's calligraphy. On both sides of the hall were nanmu-wood chairs, on which the four men sat. Presently Mr. Hu appeared wearing a square cap, a dark purple silk gown and black shoes with white soles. He had a small beard and was about forty years old. He bowed modestly to them all and politely disclaimed their compliments, thanking them once more as he asked them to be seated. Chin Tung-yeh took the seat of honour, with Yen Chih-chung in the second place and Kuang Chao-jen in the third; while Ching Lan-chiang, as a local man, sat with Mr. Hu at the bottom of the table.

When Chin Tung-yeh had thanked their host for his hospitality a few days previously, Mr. Hu asked Yen Chih-chung: "When did you arrive here from the capital?"

---

[1] Umbrellas were part of an official's equipage, and their colour denoted his rank. Prefects used yellow umbrellas, magistrates blue.

"Only the other day," said Yen. "Since I stayed in the capital with Vice-Director Chou, who is a relative of mine, I saw a great deal of Commissioner Fan; and when Commissioner Fan asked for leave to repair his ancestral tombs and invited me to accompany him, I took this opportunity to visit my family."

"Where is Commissioner Fan staying?"

"He is on the boat and will not be coming into the city since he is leaving in a few days. It was because I met Dr. Chao Hsueh-chai the other day and he mentioned that today was your birthday that I came to offer my congratulations and talk with you about old times."

"When did you come here, Mr. Kuang?" asked Mr. Hu. "What is your honourable native place and where are you staying?"

"He is from Yuehching County," answered Ching, "and he hasn't been here long. He came on the same boat with me, and is now staying in Literary Expanse Bookshop selecting essays."

"Yes, yes," said Mr. Hu. "I have long heard of your fame."

As they were speaking, servants brought in tea; and after the tea Mr. Hu stood up and invited them into the library. There they found two white-bearded old men in square caps, who were standing very much on their dignity. When the newcomers entered these two rose slowly to their feet, and Senior Licentiate Yen, who knew them, stepped forward.

"So Mr. Wei and Mr. Sui are here. Let us pay our respects," he said.

Then they bowed to each other and sat down. Mr. Wei and Mr. Sui showed no false modesty, but went on sitting in the seats of honour.

Presently a servant came to announce that other guests had arrived, and Mr. Hu went out. Ching Lan-chiang asked what part of the country the two old gentlemen came from.

"This is Mr. Wei Ti-shan, a great scholar of Chienteh County," said Senior Licentiate Yen. "And this is Mr. Sui Chen-an of Shihmen County, a senior licentiate. These two gentlemen have been editing essays in Chekiang for twenty years, and their selections are read all over the empire."

Ching Lan-chiang bowed deeply to express his admiration; but the two old men did not trouble to ask their names.

Sui Chen-an, however, had met Chin Tung-yeh in the college at the capital.

"Since we left Peking, many years have passed," he said. "What brings you here now? I suppose you have completed your work and are waiting for promotion."

"No," said Chin Tung-yeh. "Recently all kinds of men have come for posts. But after Wang Hui who was sent out as an official surrendered to Prince Ning and the court arrested the eunuch Liu Ching and kept investigating the records in our department, I was afraid that if I stayed too long I might be involved in trouble. So I asked for leave and came away."

As they were speaking, noodles were served; and when they had eaten, Mr. Wei and Mr. Sui began to speak of the *paku* essays.

"Editing nowadays is going to the dogs," declared Mr. Wei.

"Very true," agreed Mr. Sui. "We ought to have edited a few essays from the last examination as models of criticism."

Mr. Wei cast a searching glance round.

"There were no essays in the last examination!" he stated.

"Excuse me, sir," Kuang Chao-jen could not help saying, "there are printed selections of the essays of the last examination everywhere. Why do you say there were no essays?"

"May I ask this gentleman's name?" said Mr. Wei.

"This is Mr. Kuang of Yuehching County," Ching told him.

"When I say that there were no essays," announced Mr. Wei, "I mean that none of them came up to standard."

"Surely," demurred Kuang Chao-jen, "if the candidates passed, their essays must have been up to standard. What other criterion is there?"

"My friend," said Mr. Wei, "you obviously do not understand. Essays express the teachings of the sages, and they must be written according to definite rules, unlike other frivolous forms of literature which you may write as you please. Thus from an essay you should be able to see not only the writer's rank and fortune, but also whether the empire is passing through a period of prosperity or decline. The Hung Wu and Yung Lo periods had one set of rules; the Cheng Hua and Hung Chih periods had another. Each reign has its particular rules which have been handed down from one group of scholars

236

to another, forming an orthodox tradition. Now some of the candidates who pass the examinations may have written according to the rules, while others pass thanks to luck; but only those essays selected and annotated by us are assured of immortality. If we find no essays worth selecting from a certain examination, we say that there were no essays."

"We are not afraid of not passing the examinations, friend," put in Mr. Sui. "Our one fear is lest our three essays should not stand up to criticism *after* we have passed; for that would prove that we merely passed by chance, which would be something to be ashamed of all our lives." He turned to ask Mr. Wei: "Have you seen the selection of essays made recently by that fellow Ma Chun-shang?"

"Precisely! That kind of man is ruining the editing business. He has been staying in Prefect Chu's home at Chiahsing, where they talk of nothing but heterodox studies; and although I understand he has a flair for frivolous writing, he has not the faintest conception of the rules of essays. The result is that he creates extraordinary confusion, and even good essays are spoilt by his abominable commentaries! Whenever I see students reading his selections, I tell them to delete his notes."

As they were speaking, Mr. Hu came back with Chih Chienfeng and Pu Mo-ching, and the table was laid for a meal. They had to wait till the evening, however, until Dr. Chao arrived, before they could start. At last, at about eight o'clock, his sedan-chair turned up, with two men running before and behind it carrying two torches each. Alighting from the chair, Dr. Chao bowed to all the guests and apologized for keeping them waiting so long. And since by this time many relatives had arrived, three tables were spread instead of two and all of them took their seats. After the feast was over the guests went home.

Kuang Chao-jen, on his return to his lodgings, annotated some more essays before going to bed. In six days he finished editing the three hundred-odd essays, then wrote a preface in which he elaborated the opinions he had heard in Mr. Hu's house. He also used some of his spare time to call on the various acquaintances he had made at Mr. Hu's dinner. When his work was finished, the manager of the bookshop took away the manuscript, coming back to say: "When Mr. Ma stayed in my brother's shop, he spent two months over three hundred essays; and when we pressed him, he lost his temper. We had no idea that you would be so quick! And the men I showed it to said you had done a very careful job, in addition to being so fast. This is excellent! If you stay here, sir, you will be in demand with all the bookshops: you will have plenty of business!"

Then he handed Kuang Chao-jen a packet containing two taels of silver. "When the book is published, sir," he said, "I shall let you have fifty copies."

He also prepared a feast for Kuang Chao-jen upstairs.

As they were feasting, a servant came in with a note written on fine Sungchiang paper folded in the manner of an invitation card. Kuang Chao-jen unfolded it and read, "On the fifteenth of this month we shall meet at the West Lake to write poems. The cost will be twenty cents of silver per head." Below were the names of those invited: Wei Ti-shan, Sui Chen-an, Chao Hsueh-chai, Yen Chih-chung, Pu Mo-ching, Chih Chien-feng, Kuang Chao-jen, Hu Mi-chih and Ching Lan-chiang — nine in all. A postscript read: "Your share can be sent to Mr. Hu." When Kuang Chao-jen saw that all the others had accepted, he accepted too, weighed out twenty cents from the silver he had just received, and gave this to the servant to take away with the invitation.

That evening he had nothing to do, and he thought: "The day after tomorrow at the West Lake they will be writing poems, and if I can't join in, it will look bad."

So he borrowed a book entitled "Versification Primer" from the bookshop, and sat down to study it by his lamp. Since he was a very intelligent young man, after studying for one night he grasped the principles of versification; and the next day, after reading the primer again from dawn till dusk, he took up his brush and wrote a poem which seemed to him actually superior to those pasted on the wall. He then read the book through once more, hoping to improve on his technique.

On the morning of the fifteenth, Kuang Chao-jen had put on his scholar's cap and gown and was just about to leave the house, when Ching Lan-chiang and Chih Chien-feng called for him. The three of them went out through Clear Stream Gate to where the others were waiting for them in a small boat. Once aboard, however, they discovered that neither Dr. Chao nor Senior Licentiate Yen had arrived.

"Where is Mr. Yen?" they asked Mr. Hu.

"Commissioner Fan wanted to leave yesterday," replied Mr. Hu. "Mr. Yen just paid his share, then left for Canton."

As the boat rowed across the lake, Pu Mo-ching remarked to Mr. Hu: "I heard there was some trouble in Mr. Yen's family about the adoption of an heir, which kept him running all over the place for help. What happened?"

"I asked him yesterday," said Mr. Hu. "It's all settled now. His second son has been made heir and the inheritance has been divided into two shares of three-tenths and seven-tenths, with his brother's concubine taking three-tenths. So that's all right."

Presently they reached Flower Bay, where they urged Mr. Hu to go ashore to borrow the garden for their feast. When Mr. Hu tried to do so, however, the door was shut in his face. And although he blustered, the caretaker paid no attention.

Ching took the man aside and asked him the reason.

"Everybody knows what a skinflint Mr. Hu is!" said the caretaker. "How many feasts does he give here each year that I should put myself out for him? Last year he borrowed this place for two tables of guests, but didn't give a single tip! And when he left he didn't get anyone to clean the place up; instead he insisted that there must be two pecks of rice left over and ordered his servant to carry them back. I'm not going to wait upon gentlemen like that!"

There was nothing for it but to borrow a monk's quarters at Yu Chien's Temple,[1] where the monk brewed tea for them. Mr. Hu, who had all their money, asked Ching Lan-chiang to go with him to do the shopping, and Kuang Chao-jen volunteered to accompany them. They went first to a shop selling ducks, where Mr. Hu stabbed the ducks' breasts with his ear-

---

[1] Yu Chien was a minister of war during the fifteenth century who was slandered and killed.

pick to see how fat they were, then asked Mr. Ching to bargain for the plumpest bird. Since theirs was a large party, they also bought several catties of meat, two chickens, a fish and some vegetables, which they ordered the servant who had come with them to carry back first.

Next they decided to buy some meat dumplings for a snack, and went into a shop where they found thirty dumplings. These dumplings were three coppers each, but Mr. Hu refused to give more than two coppers and started quarrelling with the shop people. Finally Ching Lan-chiang succeeded in making peace, and instead of dumplings they bought noodles which Ching carried. They went on to purchase dried bamboo shoots, salted eggs, fried chestnuts, melon seeds and other sundries to go with the wine; and these Kuang Chao-jen helped to carry.

When they had taken everything to the temple and given it to the monk to prepare, Chih Chien-feng asked: "Why didn't you get the cook to do this, Mr. Hu, instead of going to such trouble yourself?"

Mr. Hu looked surprised.

"That would have cost more," he said. He then weighed out a piece of silver and ordered his man to buy rice.

All this had kept them busy until the afternoon, and now Chao Hsueh-chai arrived in his sedan-chair, alighted and told the carrier to bring him his medicine chest, then took from it a packet containing twenty-four cents of silver which he gave to Mr. Hu. By this time the feast was ready and they sat down to eat.

After the meal, wine was served and Dr. Chao proposed: "We have a good gathering today: we must have some poems."

They drew lots for the rhymes, and when each man had picked a different rhyme, they drank a few more cups of wine before dispersing. Mr. Hu ordered his man to pack into a hamper all the sweetmeats and food left over; and, sure enough, he asked the monk how many pecks of rice remained, and had that packed up too. Then having given the monk five cents for incense, he made his servant carry all the left-overs back to the city.

Kuang Chao-jen, Chih Chien-feng, Pu Mo-ching and Ching Lan-chiang strolled back together; and since they were very merry, they talked and laughed and loitered on the way. By the time they reached the city dusk had fallen.

"It is dark now," said Ching Lan-chiang. "We had better hurry."

"What does that matter?" asked Chih, who was roaring drunk. "Everyone knows the famous scholars who write poetry at the West Lake! Didn't Li Pai[1] stroll about at night in his silk palace gown? Besides, it's only just dark. Don't worry! Nobody will dare to challenge us!"

He was gesticulating merrily when two tall lanterns and two smaller ones bearing the words "The Assistant Salt Gabelle Comptroller" loomed up in front of them. The comptroller recognized Chih and sent men to fetch him to his chair.

"Chih Chien-feng!" he said. "How do you — a merchant of our gabelle — come to be so drunk and disorderly in the street?"

Too drunk to stand upright, Chih staggered from side to side.

"I'm Li Pai," he retorted, "who walks at night in silk palace gown."

At this point the comptroller caught sight of his scholar's cap.

"There are no scholars among the salt merchants in our yamen!" he declared. "How dare you wear such a cap? Take it off, officers! Tie him up!"

Pu Mo-ching stepped forward to put in a word for his friend.

"If you are a scholar," cried the comptroller angrily, "how dare you get so disgustingly drunk at night? Arrest this man and take him to the college!"

Ching Lan-chiang saw that things looked bad, so he quietly tugged Kuang Chao-jen in the dark and skedaddled with him up a small alley; and once back at his lodgings, Kuang Chao-jen went upstairs to bed. The next morning he went out to see what had happened to Chih Chien-feng and Pu Mo-ching. They were not in serious trouble, he found, but were writing their poems as arranged.

---

[1] 701-762. A great poet of the Tang Dynasty.

Kuang Chao-jen wrote a poem too. And when he saw that the poems by Mr. Wei and Mr. Sui were full of terms used in the *paku* essays and phrases cribbed from old commentaries, he felt that his own effort was in no way inferior to theirs. They copied these poems on seven or eight sheets of paper, one of which Kuang Chao-jen pasted on his wall. A fortnight after this his selection of essays was published, and he was given a feast that evening at which he got very drunk. The next morning he was still in bed when someone downstairs shouted: "Mr. Kuang! Someone to see you!"

If you want to know who Kuang Chao-jen's visitor was, you must read the chapter which follows.

CHAPTER 19

**In which Kuang Chao-jen finds a good friend
and Pan Number Three comes to grief**

Kuang Chao-jen was in bed upstairs when he heard that a caller had arrived. He flung on his clothes and hurried downstairs to find a man in an officer's cap, black silk gown and thick-soled black shoes. This man had a dingy beard, high cheekbones, sallow complexion and piercing eyes.

"Are you Mr. Kuang?" he asked.

"My unworthy name is Kuang. May I ask your honourable name?"

"Pan, at your service. The other day I read my brother's letter telling me of your arrival here."

"So you are Mr. Pan!" Kuang Chao-jen made haste to bow, then invited his visitor upstairs.

"I was out that day," said Pan, "when you favoured me with a call. I arrived back the day before yesterday and read the letter in which my brother describes your genius and many good deeds. I feel the greatest respect for you."

"I came here specially to throw myself under your kind protection," said Kuang Chao-jen, "but you were away on public business. I am delighted to meet you today."

He went downstairs to fetch tea and asked one of the shop assistants to buy two plates of cakes, which he carried upstairs. Pan had been reading the poems on the wall.

"Oho!" he said at the sight of the cakes. "There was no need for that!"

As he took the tea he pointed to the wall.

"Why go around with that crowd, Mr. Kuang?" he asked.

"What do you mean, sir?"

"Why, they're a notorious pack of fools. This fellow Ching is a hatter, who started out with two thousand taels as capital; but he's squandered the lot on poetry. Whenever he brushes hats in his shop he recites lines about rain falling during the Spring Festival, until he's become a laughing-stock for all his customers and neighbours. And now that he has lost his capital he is using poetry as an excuse to sponge on everybody he meets. He's a public nuisance. Then that man Chih used to be a merchant for the Salt Gabelle; but since I came back I heard in the yamen that a few days ago the assistant comptroller had him arrested and dismissed from the service for chanting poems on the street when he was drunk. He'll soon be stony broke. While you're away from home, Mr. Kuang, you should turn your hand to something profitable. Why mix with men like that?"

Pan had eaten two cakes, but now he pushed the plate aside.

"What good are cakes?" he said. "Let's go out for a meal."

He told Kuang Chao-jen to lock his door, and they went out to a restaurant by the yamen where Pan ordered a whole duck, one portion of sea slugs with pork, and a large dish of pork. Seeing that it was Mr. Pan, the restaurant people nearly fell over backwards trying to please him, choosing their choicest and fattest pork and duck for him and cooking the sea slugs to a turn. Pan ordered two pots of wine to drink before they started on the rice, and what was left over he gave to the waiters. He did not ask for the bill on the way out either, but merely said: "This is on me."

Hastily bringing his hands together in a salute, the manager answered: "Yes, sir! Certainly, sir."

As they left the shop, Pan asked, "Where would you like to go now?"

"I was thinking of calling on you, Mr. Pan," said Kuang Chao-jen.

"Very well. Come on over."

They walked up a lane to a house with a double wooden gate in a blue wall, and through an inner gate to a hall where a group of men were gambling around a table.

"You dogs!" cried Pan. "Have you nothing better to do than waste time here?"

"We heard that you had just come back, sir," they answered. "We're collecting the proceeds of our gambling to welcome you home."

"I don't want any money or welcome from you," growled Pan. Then, thinking better of it, he added: "All right. I have a friend here: let's see you put up some money as a welcome for him."

Kuang Chao-jen wanted to bow to him, but Pan stopped him. "Don't trouble," he said. "We did our bowing just now. Take a seat."

He went inside to fetch two thousand coins, then told the gamblers: "This two thousand is Mr. Kuang's share which you can use. All the surplus winnings today will go to him." And to Kuang Chao-jen he said: "Just sit here and watch them. Whenever the kitty is full, you can pocket the cash and let them start again." He pulled over a chair and made Kuang Chao-jen sit down, while he sat beside him to watch.

Presently a man called to ask Pan's advice; and when he went out he saw that it was Wang Number Six, who kept a gambling house.

"I haven't seen you for a long time, Number Six," said Pan. "What do you want me for?"

"Would you mind stepping outside with me?" asked Wang.

Pan followed him to a quiet tea-house.

"There's a chance of making money, sir," Wang told him. "So I came straight to you."

"What is it?"

"Yesterday the police from Chientang County yamen caught some louts in Mao Family Fair raping a maid called Lotus, who has run away from a family in Yuehching County. The police caught this gang right in the act and reported them to the magistrate, who gave them each a few dozen strokes before letting them go; and he has sent this Lotus back to Yueh·

ching. Now there's a rich man here named Hu, who's taken a fancy to this girl and asked me if we can't find some way to get hold of her. He's willing to fork out a few hundred taels for her. Do you think it can be done?"

"Who was put in charge of her?"

"Huang Chiu."

"Has he gone himself?"

"No, he sent two of his men."

"When did they leave?"

"Yesterday."

"Does Huang Chiu know about this Mr. Hu?"

"Of course he does. He wants to make some money too; but he doesn't know how to."

"That is easy," said Pan. "Bring Huang Chiu here and we'll talk it over."

Wang Number Six assented and went off.

Pan Number Three was sitting there alone, sipping tea, when another man burst in.

"Mr. Pan!" he cried. "I've been looking for you everywhere! So you were here all the time drinking tea!"

"What do you want?"

"About ten miles outside the city lives a man called Shih Men-ching, who decided to sell his younger brother's widow to a man called Huang Chiang-fu. In fact, he pocketed the money; but his sister-in-law refused to marry again. He consulted a go-between and they decided to have her kidnapped; but the go-between said: 'I don't know your sister-in-law; you'll have to tell me how to recognize her.' 'She goes out every morning to collect firewood behind the house,' said Shih. 'If you lie in wait there tomorrow, you can carry her off.' Well, they went ahead with this plan; but the next morning Shih's wife went out instead of his sister-in-law, so they carried off the wrong woman! Huang lives more than ten miles away, and he has already slept with her. When Shih went to ask for his wife back, Huang wouldn't give her up; so he has appealed to the court and the suit has just started. The trouble is that they never drew up a marriage certificate, so there is no proof; and now Huang wants to have one made out, but those villagers don't know how to do it. That's why I came to you, sir. He hopes you can also handle the yamen side for him, and he will send you a few taels of silver as a present."

"Why get so excited over a little thing like this?" demanded Pan. "Sit down. I'm waiting for Huang the runner."

Soon Huang Chiu arrived with Wang Number Six.

"So Mr. Hao is here too," he said, when he saw the other man.

"That has nothing to do with you," said Pan. "He's here for something else."

Pan and the runner sat at one table, Wang and Hao at another.

"How do you plan to settle this business, sir?" asked Huang.

"How much is he willing to pay?"

"Mr. Hu says if he can get the girl, he'll pay two hundred taels—but that must cover all the costs."

"How much do *you* want to make out of it?"

"If you can pull this off, sir, I'll be satisfied with a few taels. You don't think I'm going to wrangle with you, do you?"

"That's all right then. There is a scholar from Yuehching County in our family who happens to be a friend of the county magistrate there. I shall ask him to get a report from the magistrate stating that this girl Lotus has been sent back to her own home. At the same time I shall find someone here to get authority from our magistrate to fetch her back; so thac we can hand her over to Mr. Hu. What do you say to that?"

"Excellent!" said Huang Chiu. "But there's not a moment to lose: you will have to get busy at once, sir."

"I shall get authority from the magistrate today. Tell Mr. Hu to bring the money at once." When the runner had consented and left with Wang, Pan took Hao back with him to his house.

The gamblers were still there. When their game was over Pan saw them out, but kept Kuang Chao-jen behind.

"Won't you stay for the night?" he asked. "I have something to discuss with you."

Taking him to a back room upstairs, he drafted a marriage certificate for Kuang Chao-jen to copy, then showed this to Hao telling him he could have this the next day when he brought the money. This done, he sent Hao away.

After supper, Pan lit the lamp and dictated a faked writ to Kuang Chao-jen, then chopped it with one of the many false seals made of dried beancurd which he had in the house. Next he produced a vermilion brush and asked Kuang Chao-jen to write out an order of recall. And when all their work was done, he brought out wine and they drank together. "These are what I call worthwhile jobs, which won't be wasting your time," said Pan. "Why play about with those fools?"

That night Pan kept Kuang Chao-jen there. And the next morning when the two lots of money arrived, he gave him twenty taels to take back with him. Kuang Chao-jen accepted the money gladly, and sent some home through a friend to increase his brother's capital. Various bookshops asked him to edit essays for them, and from now on he had a share in all Pan's profits; so he was gradually able to cut a better figure. He also took Pan's advice and kept away as much as possible from the scholar-poets.

One day about two years after this, Pan Number Three called on him.

"I've not seen you for a long time," he said. "Let's go and have a drink."

Kuang Chao-jen locked his door and accompanied Pan; but they had not walked many yards when a servant from Pan's house came up to them.

"There is a guest waiting for you, sir, at home," he said.

"You had better come with me," Pan told Kuang, then took him to his house and asked him to wait in an inner room while he talked to the caller in the hall.

"I haven't seen you for a long time, Li Number Four," said Pan. "Where have you been?"

"I have been at the examiner's yamen," replied Li. "I have something to talk over with you, and was afraid you might not be at home. Now that I've found you, I'm sure we shall be able to pull this off."

"What are you up to now?" demanded Pan. "I've never worked with anyone so close-fisted. You can't bear parting with a cent!"

"There's money in this."

"What is it?"

"Well, the imperial examiner will soon be coming to Shaohsing, and there is a man called Chin Tung-yeh who has been a clerk in the Board of Civil Office for a number of years and made some money, who wants his son to take the examination. But his son Chin Yao is an absolute idiot. So now, with the examination coming, his father wants to find a substitute. The trouble is that this examiner is very strict: we shall have to think out a new way. That's why I've come to talk it over with you."

"How much is he prepared to pay?"

"To pass the examination in Shaohsing is worth a cool thousand taels. If he takes this short cut, we can ask at least five hundred taels. The substitute will be difficult to find though; and there's the problem of how to disguise him, how much to pay him, how much to spend in the yamen, and how to divide what's left between ourselves."

"If it is only five hundred taels altogether and you want a share of it, I am not interested," declared Pan. "You can get a little money out of Mr. Chin for your trouble, but you can't touch this five hundred."

"All right. I'll do anything you say. But tell me how to manage it."

"You needn't trouble your head over it," said Pan. "I shall find a substitute and settle with the yamen. All you need do is tell Mr. Chin to give you the five hundred taels to deposit in a pawnshop, just paying me thirty taels first for minor expenses. I guarantee that his son will pass. If he doesn't, I won't touch the five hundred taels. Will that suit you?"

"There can be no objection to that," said Li.

So the matter was settled, and a date fixed for the payment. When Pan had seen Li out, he rejoined Kuang Chao-jen.

"I'm counting on you for this, my friend," he said.

"I heard what you said, and I'll do what I can for you. But will I have to write the essay outside and try to pass it in, or go in to take the examination for him? I must say I haven't the courage to pass myself off as someone else."

"Don't you worry. I'll look after you. You don't think I'd let you get into trouble, do you? When he brings the money, I'll go to Shaohsing with you."

Kuang Chao-jen then returned to his lodgings.

A few days later Pan called for him with his luggage, they crossed the Chientang River, travelled straight to Shaohsing and found quiet lodgings in an alley near the examiner's office. The next day Li brought the candidate to see them. When the examiner had announced the time of the examination, Pan took Kuang Chao-jen at midnight to the gate-house of the examination school, where he made him take off his scholar's costume and put on a tall black hat, a blue cloth gown and a red belt. Then he whispered some urgent instructions and left him, taking Kuang's clothes away with him.

At dawn three cannons were fired, the examiner entered the hall, and Kuang Chao-jen, holding an usher's stick, mingled with the other ushers who bustled noisily in to stand on guard by the second gate. When the examiner called the roll and reached the name of Chin Yao, Kuang winked at the young man—who was forewarned—and instead of going to his appointed cell he slipped into the shadow while Kuang stepped back to join him. Behind the backs of the others, Chin took off his cap and they exchanged caps and clothes. Then Chin picked up the stick and joined the ranks of the ushers, while Kuang Chao-jen took the paper to the cell and wrote an essay. He handed in his paper rather late, then returned to his lodging without anyone discovering the imposture. And when the results were published, Chin Yao had passed with distinction.

Pan Number Three accompanied Kuang Chao-jen back to Hangchow and gave him two hundred taels as his reward.

"Don't squander this windfall, friend," he advised him. "Put it to some good use."

"What do you mean by that?"

"Your term of mourning is over, and it's high time you married. I have a friend called Cheng—a very good sort—who works in the provincial government. His son is in the yamen as well. He asked me to find a husband for his third daughter, and I've had you in mind all along because you're the right age for each other and would make a handsome couple. But as long as you had no money I couldn't propose you seriously. Now, if you're interested, I have only to say the word. You can live with them, and I'll help you pay for the wedding."

"You are far too good to me, Mr. Pan, and I'm only too willing. But now that I have some money, why should I ask you to spend any more on me?"

"You don't understand. Your future father-in-law's house is small. Even if you stay with him for a time, you will have to rent a house yourself eventually; because there will be two of you, and you will have children as well. You won't be like a visitor here any more. Since we are closer than brothers, why shouldn't I spend some more on you? In future, when you rise high, you'll have plenty of chances to pay me back."

Kuang Chao-jen was overwhelmed with gratitude. True to his word, Pan proposed the match to Mr. Cheng, compared the young couple's horoscopes and only asked Kuang for twelve taels to buy trinkets and four costumes for the bride. The wedding was to take place on the fifteenth of the tenth month, and when that date arrived Pan prepared a good meal and invited Kuang Chao-jen over in the morning.

"I am your go-between," said Pan as they were eating. "I'll escort you there today. And this meal can be considered your feast to thank the go-between."

At that they both laughed.

After the meal Pan made the young man take a bath and change into a completely new outfit which he had prepared for him: a new square cap, new shoes and a new sapphire-blue silk gown. Then the auspicious hour arrived and they went in two sedan-chairs, preceded by lanterns, to the bride's home. Mr. Cheng lived in a three-roomed house in a small alley by the yamen. As Pan handed over two hundred coppers as largesse, the door which had been closed at the bridegroom's arrival was opened and old Mr. Cheng came out; and when he and his prospective son-in-law recognized each other as fellow passengers on the same boat some years before, they felt this marriage must have been predestined. Kuang Chao-jen bowed to his father-in-law, then went in to bow to his mother-in-law and greet his brother-in-law, after which a feast was served at the end of which Pan left. Then Kuang Chao-jen was invited into his bridal chamber, and the beauty of his bride threw him into raptures. They drank together, and became husband and wife. The next morning, Pan Number Three sent over a feast for Kuang Chao-jen to thank his father-in-law. Mr. Cheng invited Pan to accompany them, and they feasted for a whole day.

Soon a month had passed, and since Mr. Cheng's house was cramped for space it proved inconvenient for the young couple to stay there. For forty taels of silver Pan rented four rooms for Kuang Chao-jen near the bookshop; and when he had bought furniture and other household utensils, they moved in. By the time Kuang had entertained his neighbours and bought two bushels of rice, all his money was spent. But luckily he had Pan to help in all these transactions by buying things cheaply for him, and fortunately the bookshops asked him to edit two more volumes of essays, paying him a few taels of silver and giving him a number of copies which he could sell. So the young couple managed to make ends meet. Just over a year after a daughter was born to them, and husband and wife lived happily together.

One day Kuang Chao-jen was standing at his door when a man in a big cap and blue gown came along.

"Does Mr. Kuang of Yuehching County live here?" he asked.

"I am he," replied Kuang. "Where do you come from?"

"Censor Li has sent me to Chekiang to bring you a letter, sir."

Kuang Chao-jen asked the messenger to come in and sit down. When he read the letter, he found that the accusations against his patron had proved groundless and that a few months after being reinstated Mr. Li had been summoned to the capital to take up the post of supervisory censor there. He was now writing to invite his pupil to come to the capital, where he could help him. Kuang kept the messenger to a meal while he wrote a grateful reply stating that he would pack up and leave as soon as possible for the capital to receive his master's instructions. Then he sent the messenger off.

Almost immediately after this, he received a letter from his elder brother announcing that the imperial examiner was going to Wenchow District to supervise an examination and asking him to go back to take it. Kuang Chao-jen dared not miss this opportunity. He told his wife and invited her mother over to keep her company, then packed his things and went to take the examination. When the results were announced, the examiner singled him out for praise, placing him first in the first rank and recommending him for the Imperial College on the ground of his pious conduct. Exultantly, Kuang Chao-jen thanked the examiner, and when he had seen him off he went back to Hangchow to discuss with Pan how to return to Yuehching County to put up a wooden placard and erect a flagpole in his ancestral temple to honour the family. He also ordered three court costumes from an embroidery shop, one for himself, one for his mother and one for his wife; and when these costumes were ready he borrowed three taels from all the bookshop managers, who also sent him other gifts.

Kuang Chao-jen was about to choose an auspicious day for his return to Yuehching when Ching Lan-chiang called to see him and invited him out to a tavern. While they were drinking, Kuang told him all that had happened; but after expressing his admiration Ching steered the conversation round to Pan Number Three.

"Have you heard the news?" he asked.

"No. What has happened?"

"He was arrested last night and is now in gaol."

Kuang Chao-jen was aghast.

"Surely not!" he exclaimed. "I was with him at noon yesterday. Why should he be arrested?"

"It's quite true," declared Ching. "I wouldn't have known, but for the fact that I have a relative who is a police officer in the district yamen. It's his birthday today, and when I went to congratulate him everybody was talking about this. That's how I heard. It seems that the order came down from the provincial governor, so the county magistrate dared not delay but sent to arrest him at midnight, fearing he might escape. They surrounded the house and arrested him then and there. The magistrate didn't ask a single question, simply tossed the warrant to him to read. And when Pan saw it he didn't even attempt to defend himself, but kowtowed to the magistrate and let himself be taken away. He had walked to the door of the hall when the magistrate called the runners back and ordered them to put him in the inner prison with the bandits. He's in for trouble all right. If you don't believe me, I can take you to my relative's place to see the warrant."

"That would be best," said Kuang. "May I trouble you, sir, to take me there? I wonder what he was accused of?"

They paid the bill, left the tavern and went straight to the house of the police officer, whose name was Chiang. He was entertaining friends; but when he saw them he invited them into the library and asked the reason for their visit. Ching Lan-chiang told him: "My friend would like to see the warrant for that man Pan, who was arrested last night."

Chiang produced a notice pasted on a board, which read:

It appears that Pan Tze-yeh is a local criminal who has been making use of his official position and concealing his real character to practise legal chicanery, lending money at exorbitant rates of interest and injuring the people— there is no crime of which he is not guilty. Such a criminal should not be tolerated for a moment. See that your county magistrate loses no time in arresting this man and trying him, in order to bring him to justice. This is extremely urgent.

Then followed the accusations against Pan Number Three. First, he had embezzled large sums of money; secondly, he had hushed up several murders; thirdly, he had used the official seal of the county yamen and the vermilion brush for fraudulent purposes; fourthly, he had forged several official seals; fifthly, he had kidnapped women; sixthly, by usury he had driven people to suicide; seventhly, he had bribed the school officers and found substitutes for candidates for the examinations. . . . There were other accusations too. When Kuang Chao-jen read this, he nearly took leave of his senses.

But to know what followed, you must read the next chapter.

254

CHAPTER 20

Kuang Chao-jen meets good fortune in the capital.
Niu Pu-yi dies far from home at Wuhu

When Kuang Chao-jen saw the warrant, his face turned
pale. He felt as if his skull had been split open and icy water
poured in. For though he could not say so, he was thinking: "I was involved in two of these cases. If he's put to
trial and cross-examined, Heaven help me!"

He and Ching Lan-chiang said goodbye to the officer and
went out to the street, where Ching left him.

Kuang was too worried that night to sleep. But when his
wife asked what the trouble was, he did not tell her the truth.

"I have been recommended to the Imperial College and must
be going to the capital to become an official," he said. "You
can't stay here by yourself: I shall have to send you to my
home in Yuehching County to stay with my mother while I go
to Peking. If all goes well, I shall ask you to join me."

"Don't worry about leaving me," said his wife. "I shall
stay here and get my mother to come over and keep me company. But don't ask me to go to the country; I'm not used to
that kind of life. That wouldn't do at all."

"You don't understand," said Kuang. "While I am here, I
can make enough to live on; but once I'm gone how are you
going to manage? Your father can barely support himself: he
can't feed you as well. I can't send you there, in any case,
because they don't have enough room. Remember that now I'm

255

going to be an official you will be a great lady: if you lived there, that would look too undignified. No, you must go to my home. We can raise forty taels by renting these rooms, and when I've taken what I need for my journey to the capital, you can put the rest in my brother's shop and draw a little each day. Things are cheap in our part: you can eat chicken, fish, duck and meat every day. What's wrong with that?"

Still his wife would not hear of going to the country, and when he insisted she lost her temper and they had several angry, tearful scenes. In the end, not caring whether she consented or not, Kuang asked a man in the bookshop to sublet the house for him and came home one day with the money. When his wife still refused to leave, he asked her parents to talk her round. Mrs. Cheng sided with her daughter; but Mr. Cheng, influenced by the fact that his son-in-law would now be an official, scolded his daughter sharply and called her a silly girl. Realizing she could not have her own way, she finally gave in. A boat was hired and the household goods put on board. Kuang asked his brother-in-law to take his wife home with a letter to his brother explaining that she would invest some money in the shop and draw what she needed each day. Soon the day of departure came. His wife bade a tearful farewell to her parents, boarded the boat and left.

Kuang Chao-jen also packed and went to the capital. There his patron, Censor Li, was delighted to hear he had passed another test and been selected to enter the Imperial College.

"An examination is shortly to be held to select tutors," Li told him. "I shall be in charge of it, and I can guarantee you will pass. You had better bring your luggage here and stay with me for a few days."

A few days after Kuang had accepted this invitation his patron asked if he were married. Kuang feared such a high official might despise him if he said that his father-in-law was a runner in a provincial yamen.

"Not yet," he answered.

"It's high time you were," said his patron. "You've reached the age when a man should marry. I will find a wife for you."

The next evening Li sent an old steward to the library.

"The master sends you his respects, sir," he said to Kuang. "Yesterday you mentioned that you had not yet taken a wife. Our master's niece, who has been brought up by our mistress, is now nineteen and both beautiful and talented. She is here now, and our master would like to marry her to you, sir. He will defray all the wedding expenses, so as not to trouble you. He has sent me to ask your consent to this union."

This was a terrible shock to Kuang Chao-jen. He wanted to declare that he was married; but he had stated the contrary the previous day. He feared that to accept would be wrong, until it occurred to him: "There is an opera about Tsai the Number One Scholar who had two wives; and it was considered a great romance. I suppose it doesn't matter."

So he consented.

The censor was delighted. He went in to tell his wife the happy news, chose an auspicious date for the wedding and prepared lanterns, decorations and a dowry worth several hundred taels for his niece. When the day arrived, drums and cymbals struck up as Kuang Chao-jen, dressed in gauze cap, round collar, golden belt and black shoes, bowed to the censor and his wife. Then, to the accompaniment of stringed instruments, he was led to the bridal chamber. When the bride's red veil was removed, he saw that Miss Hsin the bride was lovely enough to outshine the moon and put the flowers to shame. And not only was she a ravishing beauty, but she had brought him a sizable dowry into the bargain! Kuang felt he was gazing at a goddess and his spirit had flown to heaven. So he lived in luxury with his young wife, enjoying several months of more than earthly happiness.

The time soon came, however, when Kuang Chao-jen passed the examination for tutors and had to return to his own province to get a testimonial from the local authorities. With tears in his eyes, he said goodbye to his wife and set out for Chekiang, and his first act on reaching Hangchow was to call on his other father-in-law, Mr. Cheng. Great was his consternation when he went in to find the old man's eyes red-rimmed with weeping, his brother sitting there in the seat of a guest, and his mother-in-law wailing in the inner room. In bewilderment Kuang bowed to his father-in-law.

"When did *you* arrive, brother?" he asked. "Why is everyone crying?"

"First bring your baggage in," said his brother. "When you've washed and had a cup of tea I'll tell you."

After washing, Kuang went in to greet his mother-in-law. But pounding the table and banging the bench she rounded on him tearfully.

"You're at the bottom of this!" she cried. "But for you my girl would still be alive!"

Only then did he realize that his first wife was dead. He hurried to the outer room to question his brother.

"After you left and your wife came home," said Kuang Ta, "she was so good that mother was very pleased with her. But coming from the city she wasn't used to our country ways. She couldn't do any of the work your sister-in-law does, but she didn't like to sit idle while her mother-in-law and sister-in-law waited on her. She worried so much that she started coughing blood. Mother's health is good, so she looked after your wife instead of the other way round; but that only made your wife feel worse. She went into a decline, and because there are no good doctors in the country, in less than a hundred days she died. I've only just arrived: that's why Mr. and Mrs. Cheng are crying."

Kuang could not help shedding tears.

"What of the funeral?" he asked.

"When your wife passed away," replied Kuang Ta, "there wasn't a cent in the house. I couldn't take money from the shop — even if I had, it wouldn't have been enough. There was nothing for it but to give her the funeral clothes and coffin prepared for mother."

"Quite right," said Kuang Chao-jen.

"After we laid her out," continued his brother, "there was no place in the house to keep the coffin. We've left it behind the temple until you go back for the burial. You're here just in time. You'd better pack up at once to come back with me."

258

"It's not yet time for the burial," said Kuang Chao-jen. "But I think I still have a few taels left. Take them back and add some more bricks to the wall round the coffin, till it's strong enough to last a few years. As her father just said, she's a lady now. When you return home engage a painter to make a portrait of her in her phoenix head-dress and embroidered costume; and during festivals sacrifice to her at home and tell her daughter to burn incense to gladden her spirit. Last time I went home I had an embroidered dress made for mother too. When relatives ask her out, she should wear it to look different from the common herd. Another thing: when you go back you must tell the villagers to address you as 'Sir.' We'll have to live in style and keep up appearances. When my post is decided, I shall ask you and your wife to come to share my splendour."

So dazzled by this speech that he nearly fainted, Kuang Ta promised to do as he was told. That evening the Chengs prepared a feast for Kuang Chao-jen, and he slept in their house. The next day he went out to make some purchases, and gave several dozen taels of silver to his brother to take back.

Three or four days later, Ching Lan-chiang came to look for him, accompanied by his relative Chiang who was a clerk in the district yamen. When they saw how cramped Mr. Cheng's house was, they suggested going to a tea-shop. This was no longer the same Kuang Chao-jen, however, whom they had known. While not refusing in so many words, he made it quite clear that he did not want to go to a tea-house.

Ching understood his reluctance and said: "Now that Mr. Kuang is coming here to get a testimonial from the local authorities before taking up an official position, it probably would not be quite the thing for him to sit in a tea-shop. I have been wanting to ask you to a feast anyway, so let us go to a restaurant. That will look more dignified."

Thereupon Ching invited them to a tavern.

"Sir," he asked when the wine had been poured, "is your present post as tutor one likely to lead to promotion?"

"It certainly is," replied Kuang. "Scholars like myself who reach officialdom through proper channels are imperial tutors whose pupils are the sons of nobles."

"Is it like ordinary teaching?"

"Indeed not! Our college is just like a yamen, with official seats, vermilion ink, brushes and inkstones set out in proper order. When I take my seat there in the morning, if a pupil sends in a composition I have only to mark it with my vermilion brush for him to retire. My lowest-ranking students are officers of the third rank by inheritance, and if they accept official posts, they become provincial governors or generals; but they will always have to kowtow to me. Take the libationer of the Imperial College, for instance, who is my tutor. He's the son of the present prime minister, so the prime minister counts as my grand-tutor too. The other day when the prime minister was ill, he refused to see all the court officials who went to inquire after his health, but asked me alone in to sit on his bed to talk to him for a while."

When Kuang had finished speaking, Chiang said slowly: "Our friend Pan Number Three is still in gaol. The other day he told me very eagerly that he had heard you had come back, sir, and that he would like to see you to talk over his troubles. I don't know how you feel about it."

"Pan Number Three is a stout fellow," said Kuang. "Before this trouble of his, when he invited us to taverns he would order at least two ducks, to say nothing of mutton, pork, chicken and fish. He wouldn't touch the kind of set meal this place serves. It's a pity he's in this fix! I would have gone to the gaol to see him, but my position has changed. As a servant of the throne I have to abide by the law; and to call on him in such a place would show no respect for the law."

"You are not a local official," countered Chiang, "and you would only be visiting a friend. What harm can there be in that?"

"Gentlemen," said Kuang, "I shouldn't say this, but to friends it doesn't matter. In view of what our friend Pan has done, if I had been in office here I would have had to arrest him. If I were to go to the prison to call on him, it would look as if I disapproved of the sentence. That is not the way of a loyal subject. Besides, all the yamens here know I have come back for my testimonial. If I were to go to the gaol and the story reached my superiors, my official reputation would be ruined. How can I do such a thing? I will trouble you, Mr. Chiang, to send my regards to Pan Number Three and tell him that I shall remember him. If I am lucky enough to be appointed to some profitable post on my return to the capital, I shall be glad to send him a few hundred taels in a year or so to help him."

The other two saw he was not to be persuaded. When the meal was over they parted, Chiang going to the gaol to tell Pan Number Three what had happened.

When Kuang Chao-jen received his testimonial, he packed up and boarded a boat on which he had booked a berth to Yangchow. He found two men sitting in the middle cabin: an old man dressed in a pale yellow silk gown with silk belt and red shoes, and a middle-aged man in a sapphire-blue gown and black shoes with white soles. Since both of them were wearing scholars' caps, Kuang greeted them, sat down and asked their names.

"My name is Niu Pu-yi," replied the old man.

"I have long wished to meet you," said Kuang, who had heard of Mr. Niu from Ching Lan-chiang.

He inquired the name of the other.

"This is Mr. Feng Cho-an," answered Niu Pu-yi. "He has passed the provincial examination and is going to the capital for the next test."

"Are you bound for the capital too, Mr. Niu?"

"No. I am going up the river to Wuhu County to call on a few friends. Since Mr. Feng and I are friends, we are travelling together; but I shall leave this boat at Yangchow to take the Nanking boat down the Yangtse. May I ask your honourable district, your name and your destination?"

Kuang Chao-jen told them his name.

"So you are the famous Chekiang editor," said Feng. "I have read much of your distinguished work."

"I have my share of literary fame," responded Kuang. "During the last five or six years since I went to Hangchow I have selected essays by students and scholars and written commentaries on the *Four Books*, the *Five Classics* and the *Anthology of Ancient Essays*. According to the record I have kept at home, I have produced ninety-five volumes in all.

Each time a book of mine is published, ten thousand copies are sold; and travellers from Shantung, Shansi, Honan, Shensi and Peichih fall over each other in their eagerness to buy, all dreading the possibility that it may have sold out. One of my works published the year before last has already been reprinted three times. To tell you the truth, gentlemen, scholars of the five northern provinces respect my name so highly that they often light incense and tapers to me on their desk, calling me 'Master Kuang of sacred memory.' "

"Sir!" Niu Pu-yi laughed. "That must be a slip of the tongue. Only the dead are described as 'of sacred memory.' Since you are still among us, how can they refer to you in that way?"

"No, no," insisted Kuang, flushing. "It is used as a sign of respect!"

Niu Pu-yi decided not to argue with him.

"A certain Ma Chun-shang selects essays too," said Feng. "What do you think of him?"

"He is a good friend of mine," answered Kuang Chao-jen, "but although he understands the rules, he lacks genius and therefore his books don't sell too well. And the circulation is most important, you know; for if a book doesn't sell, the bookshops lose money. My selections, however, are read even in foreign countries."

They talked for several days until they reached Yangchow, where Feng and Kuang took a Huaian boat to Wang Family Camp, then went ashore to proceed by land to the capital.

Niu Pu-yi went on alone by boat down the Yangtse, past Nanking to Wuhu, where he lodged in a small temple called Sweet Dew Temple at Floating Bridge. This temple had three rooms in front, that in the centre housing a shrine to Saint Vajrapani. The left-hand room where firewood and straw were stored was locked, while the right-hand room opened into a large courtyard which led to the three main halls and the two rooms behind them. One of these rooms was occupied by an old monk, and Niu Pu-yi now put up in the other. During the day he would go out to call on friends and in the evening he would light his lamp and chant poems. Noticing that he seemed lonely, the old monk often brewed tea and took it to his room to talk with him till midnight; and when there was moonlight they would sit in the courtyard to talk over past and present. They were on the best of terms.

Then Niu Pu-yi fell ill, and the doctor sent for prescribed many draughts of medicine to no purpose. One day Niu Pu-yi asked the monk to come in and sit on the edge of his bed.

"I am over three hundred miles from home, living here as a stranger, yet you have looked after me very well, father," he said. "I didn't expect to fall ill like this, but now it seems I'm done for. I have no children at home, only a wife under forty. And the friend who travelled part of the way here with me has gone to the capital for the examination; so there is no one closer to me than you. I have six taels in the casket by my bed, and if I die, I'll trouble you to buy a coffin. I have some coarse cloth garments too with which you might raise money to ask a few monks to say masses so that my soul can mount to heaven. Just put the coffin on any vacant plot of land you can find, writing on it: 'Niu Pu-yi, a scholar of the Ming Dynasty.' Don't burn my body. If relatives come from my home to take my body back, I shall be grateful to you in the nether regions."

The monk could not help shedding tears.

"Set your mind at rest," he answered. "To speak of bad luck usually brings good luck. But if anything should happen to you, I shall carry out all your wishes."

Niu Pu-yi then struggled to a sitting position to take from under the matting of his bed two books which he handed to the monk.

"These two volumes contain all the poems I have written," he said. "They don't amount to much; but all my friends are mentioned there, so I don't want them to be lost. I'll give them to you, too, father. If some future scholar should come across them and publish them for me, my ghost will rest content!"

The old monk received the poems with both hands. Then seeing Niu Pu-yi gasping for breath, he hurried anxiously into his own room to boil some nephelium and lotus-seed broth. He took this to Niu Pu-yi's bedside and helped him up in order tc feed him. But the sick man was too weak to eat; after two sips he sank back with his face to the wall. In the evening the death-rattle sounded in his throat, and with a last gasp for breath he gave up the ghost. The old monk wept bitterly for him.

This happened on the third day of the eighth month of the ninth year of the reign of Chia Ching,[1] when the weather was still hot. The old monk lost no time in taking the silver to buy a coffin, then laid the dead man out and asked a few neighbours to help him lift the corpse into the coffin. He also made time to don his priestly robe and take his clapper to chant a requiem beside the coffin.

"Where can I put it?" he wondered next. "I'd better clear the firewood out of that room and put the coffin there."

Telling the neighbours his plan, he took off his priestly gown and with their help stacked the firewood in the courtyard and put the coffin in the left-hand room. He also set a table there with incense-burners, candlesticks and pennons to call back the spirit.

These preparations completed, the old monk bowed to the shrine and wailed again. Then he invited all those present to sit in the courtyard while he brewed several pots of tea for them. He also prepared gruel and bought twenty catties of wine, some wheat gluten, dried beancurd and other vegetables which he asked one of the neighbours to cook. When everything was ready, he set the dishes before the coffin, poured a libation and bowed, then carried the dishes and wine to the guests in the courtyard.

"Mr. Niu was a stranger," said the monk, "but he entered into his last rest here, leaving nothing behind him; and I couldn't do all that had to be done alone. Amida Buddha! I've kept you all busy for a whole day, and being a monk I can't offer you a proper feast but merely some wine and a few vegetable dishes. I hope you will consider doing good as its own reward, and not take offence at my lack of courtesy."

"We are all near neighbours," they answered. "When anything like this happens, it is our duty to help. But we have

[1] 1530.

cost you a lot of money, father, and we feel very bad about it. Why should you talk like that?"

After finishing the wine, the dishes and the gruel, they all went home.

A few days later, true to his word, the old monk asked monks from Good Luck Monastery to chant Buddhist canons for one whole day for Niu Pu-yi's soul. As for himself, morning and evening when he chanted sutras or opened or closed the gate, he would go to the coffin to burn incense there and shed a few tears.

About eight o'clock one evening, the old monk had finished his evening devotions and was about to close the gate when he saw a young man of seventeen or eighteen, with a folded paper in his right hand and a book in his left, come in to sit down at the foot of the shrine and begin to read by the light there. Unwilling to disturb him, the old monk let him read on until nearly midnight, when he left. The following day the youth came in again, and when he had done so for four or five days the monk could restrain his curiosity no longer. The next time the young man came in, he went up to him.

"Where do you live, son?" he asked. "Why do you come here every evening to study?"

The young man bowed to him, addressed him as "Father" and folding his hands respectfully told him his name.

But to know who he was, you must read the following chapter.

CHAPTER 21

An ambitious youth takes a false name. An old man who misses his friend falls ill

When asked his name by the monk, the young man who was reading in Sweet Dew Temple stepped forward with a bow.

"My name is Niu, father," he answered, "and I live in the street in front. Because I was brought up in my grandmother's home in Pukow, they call me Pu-lang. I lost my parents when I was young and have only a grandfather of over seventy, who can just make ends meet by keeping a small chandler's shop. He sends me out every day with this list of debts to collect payment; and one day when I passed the school and heard them reading, it sounded so pleasant that I stole some money from the shop to buy a book. I'm sorry if I've disturbed you."

"Not long ago," declared the monk, "I was saying that though some people spend so much to engage tutors for their sons and younger brothers, the lads won't study. And here are you stealing money to buy a book to study—that's a good sign! But the ground is cold here and the light by the shrine is dim. I have a table in the hall and a hanging lamp: why don't you sit there to study? You would find it more comfortable."

Niu Pu-lang thanked the old monk and followed him into the hall which was very peaceful and contained a square table with a hanging oil lamp above it. From that day onwards

Niu Pu-lang would read on one side of the hall while the monk practised yoga on the other, and so they continued till midnight every night.

One day, when the old monk overheard what Niu was chanting, he walked over.

"Why, son!" he said. "I thought you wanted to pass the examinations in order to go up in the world, and that you had bought essays to study. Now I hear it's poems you're reading. What use are they?"

"Tradesmen like us can't dream of passing the examinations," said Niu Pu-lang. "All I want is to read a few poems to acquire a little refinement."

Hearing him speak in this lofty manner, the old monk asked: "Can you understand those poems you're reading?"

"Very few of them. But when I can understand one or two lines, that makes me happy."

"Well, if you like poetry, when you have read some more I'll show you two volumes of poems which I am sure will make you even happier."

"What poems are those, father? Why not let me see them now?"

"Don't be in such a hurry!" The monk laughed. "You'll have to wait a while."

Some time after this the monk went to the country to recite Buddhist sutras for a certain family and was away for several days. He had locked his room and asked Niu Pu-lang to keep an eye on the hall.

"What poems can the old monk have that he won't show me?" wondered the lad. "He's making my mouth water." Then he thought: "Asking is not as good as taking."

That evening he opened the old monk's room and slipped in. On the table were an incense-burner, an oil lamp, a rosary and some tattered old canons; but when Niu Pu-lang looked through these, he could not find any poems.

"Can the old man have been deceiving me?" he wondered. A search by the bed, however, revealed a casket with a copper lock, and when he unlocked it he found inside two well-wrapped volumes with silk covers bearing the title *The Poems of Niu Pu-yi*.

"This is it!" cried Niu Pu-lang.

Hastily taking the books, he refastened the casket and left the room, locking the door behind him. And when he studied the two volumes under the lamp he could have jumped for joy; for whereas he usually read Tang Dynasty poems which were too difficult for him, these were written by a contemporary and he could understand five or six out of every ten. He was in raptures. He also noticed such titles as "To Prime Minister So-and-so," "Thinking of Examiner Chou," "A Visit to the Lake with Mr. Lou, Also Dedicated to the Commissioner," "Saying Goodbye to Censor Lu," "To Intendant Wang." The remaining poems were dedicated to prefects, district magistrates, county magistrates or other high officials.

"These are all titles of present-day officials," thought Niu Pu-lang. "Apparently a man who can write poems doesn't have to pass the examinations in order to make friends with great officials. This is wonderful!"

Then it occurred to him: "This man's name is Niu and so is mine; and he has only written a pen-name Niu Pu-yi on these volumes without putting down his real name. Why shouldn't I add my name to his? I will have two seals made and stamp these books with them: then these poems will become mine and from now on I shall call myself Niu Pu-yi."

When he went home that night and thought about it, he could not sleep for joy.

The next day he filched some more money from his grandfather's till and went to the shop of a certain Kuo Tieh-pi who cut seals near Good Luck Monastery. Walking up to the counter he greeted Kuo Tieh-pi, then sat down.

"I would like you to cut two seals for me," he said.

"Please write down your names." Kuo handed him a paper.

Then, omitting the character *lang* from his name, he wrote: "One seal with Niu Pu in incised characters. One seal with Pu-yi in relief."

When Kuo Tieh-pi read this, he looked Niu Pu up and down.

"Are you Mr. Niu Pu-yi?" he asked.

"Pu-yi is my unworthy name."

Kuo Tieh-pi hastily ducked out from under the counter, bowed once more, and asked Niu Pu to be seated while he poured out tea.

"I have long heard of the Mr. Niu Pu-yi who lives at Sweet Dew Temple but does not see callers, and whose friends are all great scholars and officials," he said. "Excuse my lack of respect! I shall cut your distinguished seals free of charge, for I dare not ask for any fee. Some of my friends here admire your poetry, sir; and one day we shall make bold to call on you."

Niu feared Kuo might go to the temple and find out the truth.

"You are too polite," he said. "But at the moment some officials in the next district have asked me to go there to write poems. And I may be away for some time. I shall leave tomorrow, so you had better wait, sir, till my return when we can meet again. I shall call for the seals tomorrow morning."

Kuo Tieh-pi agreed to this. And the next morning Niu Pu collected the seals, stamped the two volumes and put them away in a safe place. Every evening he continued to read poems in the temple.

One afternoon his grandfather, old Mr. Niu, was sitting in the shop with no customers to serve when Old Pu who owned the rice shop next door dropped in for a chat. Mr. Niu kept medical wine in his shop and he now heated a pot of it and produced two pieces of beancurd cheese, some dried bamboo shoots and salted vegetables. He put these on the counter and they started drinking.

"You are doing well, friend," said Old Pu. "Business has not been bad during the last few years, and your grandson has grown up into a clever chap. Your luck will come now that you have such a descendant."

"That's not the way it is!" replied Mr. Niu. "I've been unlucky in my old age. Both my son and daughter-in-law have died, leaving me only this lout of a lad who is not yet married although he is already eighteen. I send him out every day to collect debts, and he often stays out till midnight. Believe it or not, that's happened more than once. I'm afraid the young fellow knows too much and is going to bad places. And if he ruins his health that way, who will bury my old bones when I die?"

Talking of this made him sad.

"That's not hard to settle," said Old Pu. "If you're worrying because he hasn't founded a family, why don't you find him a wife? Then you can live together as a regular household. He'll have to marry sooner or later."

"Ah, my friend," retorted Mr. Niu, "my business is so small, we can barely eke out a living as it is. Where could we find the silver to get him a wife?"

"There *is* a way," said Pu after a moment's thought, "but I don't know whether you'd agree to it or not. It wouldn't cost you a cent."

"What do you mean?"

"I had a daughter who married into the Chia family in the grain transport business. Unfortunately she died and my son-in-law left home to do business; but they had a little girl whom I have brought up. She's nineteen this year — one year older than your grandson. If you have no objection, I will give her to your boy. Since we want to be related, I wouldn't ask you for any presents and you needn't ask me for a dowry: all we need do is prepare a few simple clothes. And since we are living next door to each other, we have only to open a door and lead her over. We can save all the wedding expenses."

Old Mr. Niu beamed.

"This is very good of you," he said. "Tomorrow I will send a go-between to your house."

"No, no, there's no need for that. I'm not her paternal grandfather, so why should we stand upon such ceremony? I'll give her away, and I'll act as go-between. All you need to buy is two cards. Then I'll send her horoscope over, you get someone to choose an auspicious day, and the thing will be done."

Mr. Niu hastily poured out a cup of wine and presented it to his friend with a bow. So the matter was settled and Old Pu went home.

That evening when Niu Pu came back and learned from his grandfather of Old Pu's kind proposal, he dared not refuse. The next morning they wrote two red cards: one requesting

Old Pu to act as go-between, the other asking the Chia family for the girl's hand. When the bride's family received these, they sent over the horoscope; and Mr. Hsu the diviner, asked by Mr. Niu to choose an auspicious day, selected the twenty-seventh of the tenth month for the wedding. Old Niu sold the few bushels of rice he had left to make a green padded jacket, red padded skirt, blue overall and purple trousers, all four garments being of cotton. He sent these with four trinkets to the other family three days before the wedding.

On the morning of the twenty-seventh, Mr. Niu's first act was to move his bedding to the counter which would now be his bed; for he had only one room and a half, and the half room served as a shop while half of the other room was to be the bridal chamber and half a sitting room. Having given up his bed, Old Niu helped his grandson arrange the new curtains and bedding. They also cleared a small table and set it under the skylight where there would be light for the bride to comb her hair at the mirror. When the room was ready, they built a matting shed in the back courtyard to serve as kitchen. This kept them busy all morning, after which the old man gave Niu Pu money to do the shopping.

Old Pu had prepared a mirror, candlesticks, tea-pot, basin, chamber-pot and two pillows which were now carried over by his elder son, Pu Cheng, who bowed to Mr. Niu as soon as he had put them down. Very much embarrassed, Mr. Niu asked him to take a seat while he hurried behind the counter to fetch two pieces of candied orange and some crystallized fruit from a pot. He then poured out a bowl of tea and presented it with both hands.

"I don't like giving you so much trouble," he said.

"Don't say that, uncle," replied Pu Cheng. "This is our duty."

He sat down and drank tea.

Presently Niu Pu came in wearing a new tile-shaped cap, new blue cloth gown, new shoes and new socks. He was followed by a man carrying several large pieces of pork, two chickens, a big fish and some bamboo shoots and celery, while he himself had brought the oil, salt, pepper and other spices.

"Come quickly and pay your respects to your uncle," said Old Niu.

Niu Pu put down his things and bowed to Pu Cheng, then dismissed the porter with a tip and carried the food to the kitchen. At this point, Mr. Pu's second son, Pu Hsin, came in with a work-box containing the bride's needle, thread and the uppers of the shoes she was making. He had also brought a big tray holding ten tea cups with fruit in them for the ceremony the next morning. Mr. Niu prevailed on him to have some tea too, and Niu Pu bowed to him also. After sitting there for a while the two brothers took their leave, and Mr. Niu went to the kitchen to prepare for the feast, which kept him busy all day.

When evening came he lit two tall, red, flower-decorated candles from the shop in the bridal chamber and asked two old women of the neighbourhood to lead the bride over to bow before the candles while he prepared a feast for them in the bridal chamber. After that he set another table in the sitting room, lit candles, prepared bowls and chopsticks, and invited the Pu family over. First he poured a libation to heaven and earth; then, filling another cup, he offered it to Old Pu and asked him to sit in the seat of honour.

"I owe this match to you, my friend," he said. "And I am more grateful than I can say. But we are too poor to entertain you to a proper feast: we can only offer you a cup of watery wine. I'm afraid this will also make both uncles lose face. You must excuse us."

He made a deep bow and Old Pu bowed in return. Mr. Niu wanted to bow to Old Pu's sons as well, but they declined repeatedly, bowed to him and sat down.

"This can't be called a feast," went on Mr. Niu. "But now that we are one family I am sure you will not laugh at me. Of course, although we have nothing else, we do have tea and charcoal; so now I'm going to brew a pot of good tea for you and hope you will keep me company till dawn, when the bride and bridegroom will come out to kowtow. This is all I can do to express my thanks."

"My granddaughter is just a girl and doesn't know how to behave," said Old Pu. "Her father is away, too, so that she brings no dowry at all — I can hardly hold up my head for shame. But I'll be glad to stay here till dawn: I've been wanting to talk to you anyway, my friend."

So when the feast was over, Pu Cheng and Pu Hsin went home, while Old Pu sat there till the next morning when the bride and bridegroom dressed themselves and came out. They asked Mr. Niu to take the seat of honour and kowtowed first to him.

"Grandson," said Old Niu, "it hasn't been easy bringing you up; and now thanks entirely to your new grandfather you've been able to get married and have a family of your own. Starting today, I shall leave you in charge of the shop and all the business — you'll do the buying in, selling and giving credit. I'm old and the work's become too much for me. I shall just sit here to help keep an eye on things, and you can consider me as an old assistant. You've got a good wife: I hope you'll live together to be a hundred and have many sons and grandsons."

After kowtowing to Mr. Niu, they asked Old Pu to accept their respects and kowtowed to him.

"If my granddaughter does anything wrong," said Old Pu to Niu Pu, "point it out to her. You must respect your elders, my girl, and obey your husband. You're the only woman in the house: so see that you work hard and don't give Mr. Niu cause for anxiety."

When Old Pu had helped the young couple up, he declined Mr. Niu's invitation to breakfast and went home. After that, the three of them lived together.

Niu Pu did not go to the temple for some time after his marriage. One day, however, he happened to pass that way to collect a debt. As soon as he reached Floating Bridge he saw five or six horses loaded with baggage and attended by guards outside the temple; and when he went closer he saw three or four men in big felt hats and silk tunics sitting on the benches west of the main hall. Holding whips in their left hands and tugging at their beards with their right, they sat cross-legged so that you could see their pointed black shoes with white soles.

Niu Pu dared not go in, but the old monk caught sight of him.

"Why haven't you been here for so long, son?" he called. "Come on in — I want to talk to you."

Screwing up courage to enter, Niu Pu saw that the monk had packed his belongings and was about to leave.

"Why are you all packed up, father?" he asked in surprise. "Where are you going?"

"Those men out there have come from Mr. Chi, the general commandant of the capital," said the monk. "He used to be my disciple, and now that he has become a great official he has sent these men to invite me to become the abbot of Pao Kuo Monastery in the capital. I wouldn't have gone if the friend who died here recently had not told me that he had a friend who had gone to take the metropolitan examination. I shall make use of this trip to the capital to look for him and see if he will take the coffin back. If I succeed, I shall have discharged my duty toward my dead friend. The other day I told you, didn't I, that there were two volumes of poems that I wanted to show you? Well, those are the work of my friend who is dead. They are in the casket under my pillow. I've no time now to get them out, but you can open the casket and take them for yourself. There is some bedding too which I can't take with me, and some other odds and ends. You may take them all. Please look after this place for me until I come back."

Niu Pu was about to ask some more questions when the strangers came in.

"It is still early enough to cover a few dozen miles," they said. "Please mount quickly, father, so as not to hold us up."

They carried out the luggage, hustled the old monk into the saddle and mounted themselves. Niu Pu saw them out and had barely time to wish the old monk a safe journey before the horses galloped off with pounding hooves. As soon as they were lost to sight, Niu Pu went back inside to make an inventory of the things, then took the lock from the old monk's room, walked out, locked the temple gate and went home to sleep.

The next morning he went back to the temple, thinking: "Since the old monk has gone and there's nobody to expose me, why not pass myself off as Niu Pu-yi?" So he took a sheet of white paper and wrote on it: "The lodging of Niu Pu-yi." After that he took to going there every day.

About a month later Old Niu, who was sitting in the shop with nothing to do, decided to check the accounts. He found that they had very few debtors left and that only a few dozen coins were coming in every day — barely enough for rice and fuel. When he figured that seven-tenths of the capital was lost and the shop would soon have to close, he was so angry that he could only glare about him in silence. That evening on Niu Pu's return, the old man demanded an explanation; but Niu Pu was unable to clear himself and simply mumbled some literary jargon with a great deal of other nonsense. His grandfather fell ill of rage, and since he was an old man of seventy with a lowered resistance and had no cordials to help him, in less than ten days he died.

Niu Pu and his wife started wailing at the top of their voices and Old Pu, hearing them, hurried over. When he saw the dead man he called out: "Old friend!" and his tears fell like rain.

"This is no time for you to cry," he said, seeing Niu Pu weeping too bitterly to speak. "Tell your wife to attend to your grandfather while we go to see about a coffin and mourning."

Niu Pu wiped his eyes, thanked Old Pu and went with him to a shop the old man knew, where they bought a coffin on credit. They also bought white cloth and asked a tailor to make mourning clothes as quickly as he could. That same evening the body was put in the coffin, and the next morning they hired eight carriers to bear the coffin to the ancestral graveyard. Old Pu also enlisted the services of Mr. Hsu the diviner, and rode on a donkey to choose a place for the grave. This done, he saw his friend buried and after weeping once more returned with the diviner to the city, leaving Niu Pu to watch by the grave for three days.

As soon as Old Pu reached home, all sorts of tradesmen came to demand payment, and he promised them they should have their money. When Niu Pu came back, however, he discovered that all the capital in the shop was only enough to pay the five taels owed to the coffin shop: there was nothing left for the draper, the tailor or the coffin-bearers. The only thing to do was to let the house to the sluice-keeper on the bridge for fifteen taels of silver; and after paying off debts Niu Pu was left with little more than four taels, which Old Pu told him to keep until the following Spring Festival when he should build a tomb for his grandfather. Since Niu Pu and his wife had nowhere to live, Old Pu cleared a room for them and told them to move in and leave their house to the sluice-keeper. When they moved over he prepared a meal to welcome them and sat with them for a while in their room; but the thought of his dead friend set him sobbing again.

Presently it was New Year's Eve and Old Pu's sons celebrated with wine, a good meal and a charcoal brazier. Old Pu gave Niu Pu a few catties of charcoal for his room too, and some wine and dishes, telling him to set up his grandfather's shrine and sacrifice before it.

On New Year's Day he told the young man to go to the grave to burn paper money.

"Go to your grandfather's grave," he said, "and tell him that I am growing old and the weather is too cold for me to come myself to wish him a happy New Year."

Then he cried again, while Niu Pu went to do as he was told.

Only on the third day after New Year did Old Pu go out to pay New Year greetings. After drinking a few cups of wine and eating a little in a friend's house, he was passing Floating Bridge when the festive air of the sluice-keeper's house with the red paper pasted outside made him feel a pang and start weeping bitterly. He was turning home when he met a nephew who insisted on taking him to their house. His niece, dressed in her best, came out to wish him a happy New Year and kept him to tea at which dumplings of glutinous rice were served; and though Old Pu did not want to eat more than two, his niece pressed him to take another two. On his way home the wind was against him and he felt rather unwell; and by evening he had a headache and high fever so that he had to go to bed. Physicians were sent for. But some said that owing to worry he was suffering from phlegm, some that he ought to perspire, others that a warm sedative was needed, and yet others that being old he required stimulants. They could not agree on their diagnosis. Pu Cheng and Pu Hsin were alarmed and stayed by his side all day, while Niu Pu came morning and evening to ask after the old man.

One evening Old Pu was lying in bed when he saw two men climb through the latticed window, approach his bed and hand him a paper to read. But when he asked the others, they said there was no one there. Old Pu took the paper and found that it was an official summons with a list of names on it marked with vermilion ink. There were thirty-four or thirty-five names in all, the first being that of his old friend Niu Hsiang and the last his own name Pu Tsung-li. Just as he was about to question the messengers, however, he blinked, and both men and summons disappeared.

But to know whether Old Pu recovered or not, you must read the chapter which follows.

CHAPTER 22

In which Niu Yu-fu adopts a grandnephew
and Wan Hsueh-chai entertains guests

Reading the summons from the nether world as he lay in
bed, Old Pu knew that his time had come. He immediately
called his two sons and their wives to his side to say a few last
words to them and describe what he had just seen.

"Dress me quickly in my funeral clothes!" he said. "I am
going to my last rest."

Pu Cheng and Pu Hsin wept as they hastily brought the
burial clothes and put them on him.

"I'm glad my old friend and I are on the same list," he
muttered. "He is the first and I am the last. He has stolen a
march on me, but I shall overtake him!"

Then a convulsion seized him. His two sons could not
prevent him from falling back on his pillow, and they saw that
he had breathed his last.

All was ready for the funeral. The customary fasts and
sacrifices were observed, the death announced and the funeral
rites carried out; and Niu Pu helped to entertain the guests.

Now Niu Pu knew a few scholars who kept taking advantage of the prevailing confusion to push their way in unin-
vited. To begin with the Pu family enjoyed the novelty of
their company, but they soon found it too much of a good thing
and, as tradesmen, lost patience with these bookworms with

their foolish, high-falutin talk. Pu Cheng and Pu Hsin complained more than once.

One day when Niu Pu went to the temple and unlocked the gate, he found a letter on the ground which had been pushed through a crack in the door. He picked it up and read: "My name is Tung Ying. When in the capital for the examination I read your remarkable works in the house of my friend Feng Cho-an, and I have been most eager to make your acquaintance. I called at your distinguished residence, but to my great regret found you out. Tomorrow morning I hope you will condescend to stay in for a short time, so that I may receive your instruction."

Niu Pu realized that this man was looking for Niu Pu-yi. But since it was clear from the letter that they had never met, he thought: "Why shouldn't I pass myself off as Niu Pu-yi and see this Mr. Tung? He says he has taken the examination in the capital, so he must be a high official. I'll get him to meet me in my uncles' home to impress them."

He promptly went inside and found a piece of paper.

"Niu Pu-yi is now staying with his relatives, the Pu family," he wrote. "Callers are requested to go to the Pu family rice shop in the street south of Floating Bridge."

Having locked the door and pasted this note on the gate, he went home.

"Tomorrow a Mr. Tung will be calling on me," he told the Pu brothers. "He is going to be an official, so we must treat him with respect. I shall have to trouble you, First Uncle, to clear up the sitting room tomorrow morning, and you, Second Uncle, to bring us in two cups of tea. His visit will reflect credit on us all, so I hope you won't mind helping me out."

Delighted to hear that an official would be calling at their house, his uncles consented readily.

The next day Pu Cheng got up early to sweep the sitting room floor and move the rice bins outside the window under the eaves. He set six chairs facing each other, and told his wife to light a charcoal brazier and boil a kettle of tea. Then he found a tray, two cups, two spoons and four nepheliums, two of which he put in each cup. Thus everything was ready.

About the time for the morning meal, a man in black appeared with a red card in his hand.

"Does a Mr. Niu live here?" he asked all down the street. "The honourable Mr. Tung is coming to see him."

"He is here," said Pu Cheng, then ran in quickly with the visiting card.

Niu Pu went out to welcome the visitor, and from the sedan-chair which stopped at the door descended the provincial graduate Mr. Tung. Wearing a gauze cap, a light blue silk gown with a round collar and black shoes with white soles, he had a slight beard and clear complexion and seemed to be in his thirties. When they had entered and bowed to each other, they sat down in the respective positions of guest and host. Mr. Tung was the first to speak.

"I have long heard of your great name and read your excellent poetry," he said. "And I have been most eager to meet you. I imagined you as a venerable old scholar and am amazed to find you so youthful: this increases my respect."

"I am a rustic fellow who scribbles at random," replied Niu Pu. "I blush to be honoured with such high praise from you and Feng Cho-an."

"No, *I* am the one to feel honoured."

Then Pu Hsin brought in two cups of tea. Approaching from the upper end of the room, he handed one cup to Mr. Tung and the other to Niu Pu, then planted himself bolt upright in the middle of the room.

"My servant is a country bumpkin with no manners." Niu Pu bowed to Mr. Tung. "I hope you will not despise us."

Mr. Tung laughed.

"A lofty character like yourself need not worry about such trifles," he replied.

Pu Hsin flushed right down his neck and scowled as he strode out with the tray.

"Where are you going now, sir?" asked Niu Pu.

"I am to serve as a magistrate and am on my way to Nanking to await my appointment. My luggage is still on board, but I was so eager to see you that I broke my journey to call on you twice. Now that I have had the honour of this interview, I shall go on by boat tonight to Soochow."

"You have conferred high distinction on me by your visit," said Niu Pu, "but I have not acted as host for even one day. Must you leave at once?"

"We are friends in literature," said the other. "Why should we worry about the usual etiquette? When my appointment is settled, I shall invite you to my yamen so that I can hear your instruction early and late."

Having said this he rose to go and Niu Pu could not detain him.

"I shall come to your boat to see you off," said Niu Pu.

"Please do not trouble," said Mr. Tung. "As soon as I board the boat it will start, and I shall not be able to entertain you."

So they bowed and said goodbye to each other, and Niu Pu saw him out to his chair.

When Niu Pu came back inside, he was met by an angry, red-faced Pu Hsin.

"Listen to me, nephew!" he growled. "Whatever mistakes I make, I'm still your uncle and senior. It didn't matter your asking me to take in the tea — you couldn't do anything else. But how could you talk like that to Mr. Tung? Why do you act like this?"

"When an official calls," said Niu Pu, "according to proper etiquette you should serve tea three times. You served it once only, then disappeared. Instead of being thankful that I don't complain, here you are complaining yourself. This is preposterous!"

"Now then, don't talk like that, nephew," said Pu Cheng. "Even if my brother did take the tea from the wrong side of the room, you shouldn't have drawn Mr. Tung's attention to it! You shouldn't have made Mr. Tung laugh at us!"

"Just the sight of you two yokels would be enough to make him laugh. He didn't have to wait for you to bring in the tea wrongly."

"Tradesmen like us don't want visits from gentlemen like him!" declared Pu Hsin. "We got nothing out of his visit: we were only laughed at!"

"I dare swear that but for the fact that I'm staying here, no gentleman would visit you even if you waited one or two hundred years!"

"Don't talk nonsense!" cried Pu Cheng. "You may know a gentleman, but you're no gentleman yourself!"

"Ask anyone you like which is better: to sit with gentlemen and bow as equals or to serve tea to gentlemen and blunder so that you get laughed at?"

"Don't speak like that to us!" shouted Pu Hsin. "We want no such gentlemen here!"

"Is that so? Tomorrow I'll tell Mr. Tung and have him send you with his card to the Wuhu County yamen to be beaten!"

"This is too much!" they roared. "A nephew wants to have his uncles beaten! We made a mistake feeding you all this year. Come on to the yamen and see who's the one to be beaten!"

"Do you think I'm afraid of you? Come on!"

His uncles dragged him to the yamen gate.

The magistrate had not yet entered the court, and as they were waiting outside the screen Kuo Tieh-pi the seal-cutter came along and asked what they were doing there.

"Mr. Kuo," said Pu Cheng, "you know the proverb: A pack of rice wins you a friend; a bushel wins you a foe. It was a mistake to feed him for so long."

Kuo Tieh-pi reproached Niu Pu too.

"It is a law of nature that young folk must obey their elders," he said. "You had no right to talk like that. But it doesn't look good either for relatives to go to court." He drew them into a tea-shop and told Niu Pu to pour out tea for his uncles.

"Listen, nephew!" said Pu Cheng. "Now our father is dead and we have too many mouths to feed — my brother and I can't manage. Let's take this chance, while Mr. Kuo is here, to talk things over. Of course we'll keep our niece; but you ought to find some work for yourself. You can't go on living on us."

"Is that all you wanted to say?" retorted Niu Pu. "That's easy. I'll move out my things today and live on my own, in order not to trouble you any more."

By the time the tea was drunk the dispute was settled. They thanked Kuo Tieh-pi and went their different ways.

Pu Hsin and Pu Cheng went home while Niu Pu sullenly fetched a quilt from their house and moved to the temple. There, having nothing to live on, he pawned the old monk's cymbals and drums. Then, since he was at a loose end, he called on Kuo Tieh-pi, only to find him out. On the shop counter, however, he saw a new gazette, and when he looked through it he discovered that Tung Ying of Jenho County, Chekiang, had been appointed magistrate of Antung County.

"The very thing!" he cried. "Why not call on him?"

He strode back to the temple, rolled up his bedding, pawned the monk's incense-burner and stone chime for over two taels of silver; and then, without calling at the Pu house to tell them, took a boat up the Yangtse. The wind was behind the boat, so in twenty-four hours they reached Swallow Cliff near Nanking where he had to change for Yangchow, and he went to an inn.

"All today's boats have gone," the inn-keeper told him. "You will have to spend the night here and take a boat tomorrow afternoon."

Niu Pu put down his luggage, stepped outside and saw a junk moored by the bank.

"Won't that junk be going?" he asked.

"You won't be able to afford it," said the inn-keeper with a laugh. "That junk is waiting for a gentleman."

When Niu Pu went in again, the waiter brought him a pair of chopsticks, two cold dishes, a plate of ham, another of dried beancurd and artemisia, a bowl of soup and a large bowl of rice.

"The rice is two coppers a bowl," said the waiter when asked the price. "The ham one cent and the vegetables half a cent."

Niu Pu made a hearty meal, then went out again.

He saw on the bank a sedan-chair carrying three loads of luggage and accompanied by four attendants. The man who alighted from the chair wore a scholar's cap, sandalwood-coloured silk gown and black shoes with white soles. He was carrying a white paper fan, had a grey beard and seemed about fifty, with eyes like a hedgehog and prominent cheekbones.

"I am going to Yangchow to the Salt Gabelle to see the salt commissioner," said this man to the boatmen. "If you behave well, I shall reward you at Yangchow; but if you are careless, I shall have you arrested and sent with my card to the magistrate to be severely punished."

The frightened boatmen promised to do their best. They helped him aboard and began to carry his luggage to the junk.

As they were bustling about with the luggage, the innkeeper said to Niu Pu: "Now's your chance! Look sharp!"

Niu Pu carried his luggage to the stern of the junk and one of the boatmen pulled him aboard, cautioning him with a wave of his hand not to make a noise as he stowed him in the hold.

When all the luggage had been brought aboard, Niu Pu saw the attendants go to the main cabin and take out official lanterns which they hung outside the cabin door. They then told the boatmen to bring out the stove and light a fire at the prow to boil water for tea which they took in to the passenger. It was dark by now, so lanterns were lit and the four attendants gathered at the stern to prepare dishes and heat wine; and when all was ready they took the food to the cabin and lit a red candle. Niu Pu, peeping through a crack, could see the passenger sitting in front of the candle at a table spread with four dishes. A wine cup in his left hand and a book under his right hand, he was nodding as he read. After he had read for a while, rice was brought in and he ate. Then he blew out the candle and went to bed, and Niu Pu also dropped quietly off to sleep.

That night a strong east wind sprang up, while at midnight rain began to patter down, and the matting roof of the hold leaked. Toss and turn as he might, Niu Pu could not sleep.

"What are we stopping for, boatmen?" asked the man in the cabin at dawn.

"There is a strong head wind," replied one boatman, "and Huangtien Bay is in front. It is very dangerous. Last night several dozen boats stopped here; and none of them dares go on."

As the day became bright, the boatmen heated water for the passenger, the attendants washed their faces in the back cabin, and when they had finished the boatmen filled a basin for Niu Pu. Then he saw two attendants go ashore carrying an umbrella, while another washed a fine Kinhua ham over the side of the boat. Presently the two other attendants came back with a fish, a roast duck, some pork, bamboo shoots and celery; and after the boatmen had cooked the rice they prepared the dishes. When all was ready, the food was served in four big dishes and carried with a pot of heated wine to the main cabin. After the passenger had finished, the four attendants sat on the deck to eat what was left over, then swabbed the deck clean. Only then did the boatman produce a plate of salted turnips and a bowl of rice from under the matting and offer them to Niu Pu.

Although the rain had almost stopped, the wind was still high. During the morning, the passenger removed a plank from the back of the cabin and caught sight of Niu Pu.

"Who is this man?" he asked.

"This is our extra fare," said one boatman smiling disarmingly.

"Why don't you come into the cabin, young man?"

This was what Niu Pu had been hoping for. He quickly entered the cabin and knelt down, but the other signed to him to rise.

"We are too cramped here for such ceremony," he said. "Sit down."

"May I presume to ask your distinguished name, sir?"

"My name is Niu Yao or Niu Yu-fu. I come from Hueichow. What's your name?"

"My name is also Niu. And my family originally came from the same district."

"Since your name is Niu," said Niu Yu-fu, "our family must have been the same five hundred years ago. You had better call me great-uncle."

Niu Pu was rather taken aback; but the other man looked so dignified that he dared not refuse.

"What official mission takes you to Yangchow, great-uncle?" he asked.

"The fact is," said Niu Yu-fu, "that I know a great number of officials, all of whom want me to stay in their yamens; but I am too lazy to go. I am on my way to stay with Wan Hsueh-chai. He is not very important, but he invites me because I know so many officials and have some prestige. Each year he asks me to stay with him and gives me a few hundred taels for secretarial work, the work being, naturally, purely nominal. Since I don't like to stay in his vulgar house, I put up in Tzewu Temple. Now that you've become my relative, I shall be able to use you." Then he called to the boatman: "Bring in his luggage. I shall pay his fare."

"After meeting a relative, sir," said the boatman, "you ought to increase your tip."

That evening Niu Yu-fu shared his meal with Niu Pu in the main cabin, and that night the wind dropped and the weather cleared. By daybreak they reached Yicheng and moored by Yellow Mud Bank, and when Niu Yu-fu had got up and washed he took Niu Pu ashore for a walk.

"It is rather troublesome preparing meals on board," said Niu Yu-fu. "Grand Spectacle Tavern here serves very good vegetarian food: let's have a meal there." Turning back to the boatman he charged him: "Prepare your own meal: we are going to the Grand Spectacle Tavern. We shall come back soon, so there is no need to follow us."

They walked to the restaurant and up the stairs.

A man sitting there in a scholar's cap looked startled when he saw Niu Yu-fu.

"So it's you!" he cried.

"Fancy meeting you here!" exclaimed Niu Yu-fu.

"Who is this?" asked the stranger when they had bowed to each other.

"This is my grandnephew." Niu Yu-fu turned to Niu Pu. "Come here quickly to meet a gentleman who has been my sworn brother for twenty years—Mr. Wang Yi-an. We used to be colleagues in the same yamen."

Niu Pu bowed to him, then they sat down. The waiter brought them rice, a bowl of fried wheat gluten and a bowl of beancurd, and the three of them started to eat.

"We haven't met since that year when we said goodbye in Mr. Chi's yamen," said Niu Yu-fu.

"Which Mr. Chi was that?"

"The general commandant of the capital."

"We certainly can't complain about the way Mr. Chi treated us."

As they were talking, two scholars in square caps walked up the stairs. The one in front was wearing a yellow silk gown, the front of which was stained with grease, and the one behind a black gown with tattered sleeves. "Isn't that Wang Yi-an," cried the scholar in yellow, "the pimp for that brothel in Feng Family Lane?"

"It is," agreed the scholar in black. "How dare he strut about here in a scholar's cap?"

He walked over, tore off Wang's cap and gave him a resounding slap on the face. Wang grovelled on the ground, kowtowing as fast as a pestle pounding onions; but that only made the two scholars more angry than ever. And when Niu Yu-fu spoke up for Wang they spat at him.

"A scholar to share a meal with a pander!" they said. "It might be excusable if you didn't know who he was; but to plead for him now that you know is unforgivable! Get out of here, before we make things hot for you!"

When Niu Yu-fu saw that nothing could be done he nudged Niu Pu, hurried downstairs to pay the bill and went quickly back to the junk.

The two scholars gave the pander a thorough beating. Even though the restaurant owner intervened and made Wang Yi-an apologize, they would not stop but threatened to take him to the yamen. Only when Wang in desperation produced three taels and seventy cents of silver and gave this to them did they let him go.

Niu Yu-fu and Niu Pu boarded the boat and sailed to Yangchow, stopping at Tzewu Temple, where the priest came out to welcome them. When they had settled their luggage they went to bed. The next morning Niu Yu-fu produced an old scholar's cap and a blue silk gown, and gave them to Niu Pu.

"Today we must call on our host, Wan Hsueh-chai," he said. "You had better wear this cap and gown."

They hired two sedan-chairs and ordered two servants to follow them, one of them with a bundle. By the river they came to a tall gate-house where seven or eight clerks were sitting talking to a wet-nurse. They alighted here and went in.

"So Mr. Niu is back," said the clerks, all of whom seemed to know Niu Yu-fu. "Please sit in the library, sir."

Passing through an arch with tigers carved on its base and a courtyard paved with polished bricks, they reached a hall in the middle of which hung a great placard with the inscription "Hall of Contemplation" written in gilt characters by the salt commissioner, Hsun Mei. This was flanked by a couplet in gilt calligraphy: "Study is good, farming is good: To want to make good is excellent. To build up an estate is hard, to maintain it is also hard; but if you know this they cease to be difficult." In the centre hung a painting by Ni Yun-ling, and on the desk stood a great block of unpolished jade. There were twelve rosewood chairs in the hall and on the left a huge mirror six feet high. They passed behind this mirror through a double door to a courtyard inlaid with pebbles, and walked along a corridor with vermilion railings skirting the lake to a hall with three rooms divided by bamboo curtains where there were two young servants on duty. When these boys saw the visitors, they lifted the curtain and invited them in. The furniture here was all of highly polished nanmu-wood, and on the white scroll in the middle of the hall was written in black characters: "Cultivate Flowers and Compose Poetry." Sitting down, they drank tea until their host Wan Hsueh-chai walked in dressed in a scholar's cap, a pale yellow silk gown and crimson shoes. In his hand was a gilt fan. Wan bowed to Niu Yu-fu who called Niu Pu over.

"This is my grandnephew," he said. "Come and pay your respects to this gentleman." Then they sat down, Niu Pu in the lowest seat.

"What detained you so long in Nanking, my friend?" asked Wan Hsueh-chai when fresh tea was served.

"The trouble is that I am too well-known," replied Niu Yu-fu. "As soon as I put up in the Temple of Imperial Favour in Nanking, the crowds started coming, with paper, fans and albums, all wanting some calligraphy or poems from me. And men who had been given subjects and allotted rhymes for poems came to ask for my advice too. I hadn't a moment to myself! Then, just as I had shaken them off, the second son of Duke Hsu learned somehow or other of my arrival and sent one batch of retainers after another to invite me over. Since his attendants all belonged to the fifth rank of officers of the imperial guards and they called several times, I had to go and stay with him for a few days. He wouldn't hear of my leaving either. It was only when I said that you required my presence urgently, sir, that I managed to get away. The duke's son is another admirer of your poems: he has annotated them himself." Saying this he took two volumes of poems from his sleeve and presented them to Wan Hsueh-chai.

"I have never met your grandnephew before," said Wan. "How old is he and what is his literary name?"

Since Niu Pu was too dazzled to speak, Niu Yu-fu answered for him: "He is only twenty and still too young for a literary name."

Wan Hsueh-chai was about to read the poems, when a servant darted in. "Dr. Sung has arrived," he announced.

Wan Hsueh-chai stood up.

"I ought to keep you company," he said, "but my seventh concubine is ill and I have asked Dr. Sung to have a look at her. I must go to discuss the case with him, so please excuse me for the time being. Make yourselves at home here, and after dinner please stay for the evening." Saying this he left them.

The servants brought in four cold dishes and two sets of bowls and chopsticks and moved a table out for the meal.

"They are only just setting the table now," said Niu Yu-fu. "It will be some time before the food is ready. Let us look around. There are some pleasant rooms over there that you should see."

He led Niu Pu across a bridge and along the lake. In the distance could be seen a multitude of pavilions, some high and some low. The willow-bordered path by the lake was so narrow that Niu Yu-fu had to turn his head as he walked to ask Niu Pu: "Why didn't you answer our host when he spoke to you just now?"

Staring at Niu Yu-fu's face, Niu Pu lost his footing and fell into the lake. Niu Yu-fu hurried to his rescue, and fortunately there was a willow there to hold on to, so he was able to drag him out. The young man's shoes and stockings were soaked, however, and half his gown was wet. Niu Yu-fu was most annoyed.

"You obviously don't know how to behave in public!" he said sternly. Then he called his servant to fetch a gown from his bundle for Niu Pu to change into, and sent him back first.

But to know what followed, you must read the next chapter.

CHAPTER 23

The poet who discloses a secret is beaten, and a widow looks for her husband

When Niu Pu fell into the lake and made such an exhibition of himself, Niu Yu-fu told a servant to have him sent back first in the sedan-chair. Niu Pu returned to the temple in a very bad temper, to sit there glowering. After some time he found some dry shoes and socks to change into; but when the priest came to ask whether he had eaten, he didn't like to admit that he hadn't; so he said he had, and went hungry the better half of a day. Niu Yu-fu did not come back till late from his feast in the Wan house; but when he went upstairs he gave Niu Pu another talking to, and the lad dared not answer back. Then they went to sleep.

The next day, nothing happened; but on the day after that Wan sent again to invite them over, and Niu Yu-fu ordered Niu Pu to look after their rooms while he went by himself in a sedan-chair.

Niu Pu had lunch with the priest.

"I'm going to Magnolia Monastery in the old city to visit another priest, Mr. Niu," said the Taoist. "You had better stay in."

"I have nothing to do here," replied Niu Pu. "I would rather go with you."

He locked his door and went with the priest to a tea-house in the old city. The waiter brought them a pot of tea, a plate of sweets and another of spiced beans.

"How close is your relationship to your great-uncle, Mr. Niu?" asked the priest. "We have never seen you here before."

"We met on the way and found out that we belonged to the same family," replied Niu Pu. "I used to be in Magistrate Tung's yamen in Antung County. He's a hospitable gentleman, I must say. I remember when I first went there, I no sooner presented my card than he sent two attendants out to help me from my sedan-chair. I wasn't in a chair, however, but riding on a donkey; and when I wanted to alight, the attendants wouldn't let me. The two of them led my donkey straight in to the pavilion, the donkey's hooves going cloppety-clop on the wooden floor. Then the magistrate opened the gate himself and came out to meet me, and we entered hand in hand. He kept me there for over twenty days and when I said goodbye, after giving me seventeen taels and forty-five cents of fine silver, he escorted me through the hall and saw me on to my donkey. 'If you do well elsewhere, so much the better,' he said. 'If not, come back again.' There are not many men like that! I am on my way back to him now."

"Gentlemen like that are certainly rare!" agreed the priest.

"What is the position of this Mr. Wan Hsueh-chai who is our host?" asked Niu Pu. "When will *he* become an official?"

"Wan?" said the priest with a little snort. "Only your great-uncle would respect the Wan family. As for officialdom, even if official caps were flying all over the sky and one fell on his head, he wouldn't be allowed to keep it."

"That's strange! He doesn't come from a low-class family like a prostitute's, an actor's, a runner's or a soldier's — why should anyone stop him becoming an official?"

"Don't you know how he started? Well, I'll tell you; but you mustn't tell anyone else. When he was a boy he was a bondservant in the household of Mr. Cheng who owned the Universal Salt Shop here. He served in the library and when he was eighteen or nineteen his master Cheng Ming-ching, who saw what a bright lad he was, made him a small steward."

"What do you mean by small steward?"

"If the salt merchants here ask a friend to negotiate for them in the Salt Gabelle or to see officials or customers, they pay him a few hundred taels each year and call him the great steward; and a servant who attends to minor affairs in the Salt Gabelle or runs errands is called the small steward. Wan did very well as a small steward: he was able to put by a few taels of silver every year. He started by carrying a little merchandise only, but later he sold licences and was able to trade on a big scale. His luck was good too. In those days the price of a salt licence was high, and when he had made forty to fifty thousand taels of silver he bought his freedom, purchased this house and set up in the salt business himself. He did so well that he became a millionaire. Meanwhile, Cheng Ming-ching went bankrupt and returned to Hueichow, so nobody brought up the fact that Wan had been a bondservant. Last year, though, by spending several thousand taels of silver Wan married his son to the daughter of a Hanlin scholar. On the wedding day there was a great fluting and drumming, and their lanterns filled half a street: it was a grand turn-out! On the third day the bride's family was coming to pay a visit and Wan had prepared feasts and operas as entertainment; but Cheng Ming-ching came early in the morning by sedan-chair and sat in his hall. Wan had to kneel down and bow to his former master and pay him ten thousand taels of silver to make him go away and not expose him."

While they were talking, two priests came out from Magnolia Monastery to invite Niu Pu's companion to a meal, so he said goodbye and left.

After drinking a few cups of tea Niu Pu went back to the temple. Niu Yu-fu had already returned and was sitting downstairs with several large parcels of silver on the table beside him, because the upstairs door was still locked. Niu Yu-fu told him to open the door upstairs at once and take the silver up.

"Didn't I tell you to keep an eye on things?" he complained. "Why did you wander off?"

"While I was standing at the gate," lied Niu Pu, "I saw the assistant magistrate from our county pass by. He got down from his chair when he saw me and insisted on taking me to his boat for a chat because we hadn't seen each other for so long. That's why I went out."

When Niu Yu-fu heard he had been with an official, he voiced no further disapproval, but asked: "What is his name?"

"His name is Li and he comes from Peichih. He has heard of you."

"If he moves in official circles, of course he has heard of me."

"He says he knows Mr. Wan too."

"Yes, Hsueh-chai has friends all over the world." Then, pointing to the silver, he said: "This comes from Wan Hsueh-chai. His seventh concubine is ill and the doctor says she has caught a chill and the prescription requires a hibernating toad. Although he has offered several hundred taels, he has not been able to buy one in Yangchow; and now, hearing that such toads are obtainable in Soochow, he has given me three hundred taels to get one for him there. I have no time, so I recommended you. And if you go, you can make a few taels commission."

Niu Pu dared not refuse, and that evening Niu Yu-fu bought a chicken and wine for a farewell dinner upstairs.

"I have something to tell you, great-uncle," said Niu Pu, "that I heard from our assistant magistrate, Mr. Li."

"What is it?"

"Though you and Mr. Wan are on very good terms, you are only literary friends: he doesn't trust you with money matters. The assistant magistrate says that Mr. Wan has one really intimate friend and that if you mention that you are on good terms with that man, he will have complete confidence in you and trust you with everything. Then not only will your fortune be made, great-uncle, but even I as your grandnephew will be able to feather my nest."

"Who is this good friend of his?"

"Mr. Cheng Ming-ching of Hueichow."

"He has been my sworn brother for twenty years!" Niu Yu-fu laughed. "Of course I know him! All right, I'll remember that."

After drinking they went to bed, and the next day Niu Pu took the silver, said goodbye to his great-uncle and boarded a boat for Soochow.

The following day Wan Hsueh-chai invited Niu Yu-fu to another meal, and he was carried there by sedan-chair. At Wan's house he found two salt merchants—Ku and Wang— and when they had bowed to each other, the merchants declared that since they were Wan's relatives they could not take precedence of Niu Yu-fu, making him sit in the seat of honour. They drank tea and talked about the salt trade, after which a feast was spread with two tables each laid for two. Wine was served and the first dish was "Winter-Insect Summer-Weed."[1] "Try this dish," Wan invited them. "It's not a local thing; yet we can find plenty of it in Yangchow city. But when it comes to a hibernating toad, there's none to be had for love or money!"

"Haven't you got one yet?" asked Mr. Ku.

"No, there aren't any in Yangchow," replied Wan. "Yesterday I asked Mr. Niu's grandnephew to go to look for one in Soochow."

"Such rarities may not be obtainable in Soochow either," said Mr. Wang. "He may have to search for it among some of the old families in Hueichow. You might find one there."

"True," said Wan. "All the best things come from Huei-chow."

"Not only the best things," added Mr. Ku, "but the most able men too."

This was a reminder to Niu Yu-fu.

"There is a Mr. Cheng Ming-ching in Hueichow, Hsueh-chai," he said. "Is he a friend of yours?"

Wan turned red as a beetroot but did not answer.

"He is my sworn brother," went on Niu Yu-fu. "He wrote to me only the other day saying that he would probably be coming to Yangchow soon and would be sure to call on you."

Wan was so angry that his hands turned icy cold and he could not utter a word.

"Since ancient times," interposed Mr. Ku, "it has been said that a man may have acquaintances all over the world,

---

[1] A fungus grown in southwest China, which could be used as medicine or as food.

but very few true friends. Let us drink today and forget about the past."

At last the feast ended and they scattered.

For several days Niu Yu-fu heard no more from Wan. But one afternoon when he woke up from his nap upstairs a servant brought in a letter.

"This came from Mr. Wan's house," said the man, "but the messenger left without waiting for an answer."

Niu Yu-fu opened the letter and read: "The mother of Wang Han-cheh, a relative of mine in Yicheng, will soon be celebrating her seventieth birthday, and he would like you to write an essay for the occasion in your distinguished calligraphy. I hope you will condescend to go there immediately."

When Niu Yu-fu had read this, he asked the servant to call a small, fast boat and set out that same evening for Yicheng. He went ashore the next morning at Choupa and asked the way in a rice shop to Mr. Wang's house.

"You mean the harbour-master's house?" said the shop-assistant. "It's the one with the new gate facing east in Buddhist Cloud Street."

Niu Yu-fu walked to the house and went straight in. There were three halls, and the chairs in the central hall were piled with congratulatory messages in gilt characters, while at a long table on the left by the window a scholar was writing with lowered head. When this man saw Niu Yu-fu he put down his brush and came over. And great was Niu Yu-fu's dismay to see that he was wearing a yellow gown with a big grease stain in front.

This scholar recognized Niu too.

"You are the fellow who sat down in Grand Spectacle Tavern to eat with that pander," he said. "What are you doing here?"

Niu was just beginning to abuse him, when Wang Han-cheh came out.

"Please sit down, sir," he said to the scholar. "This has nothing to do with you."

The scholar then sat down.

Wang Han-cheh clasped his hands in salute without bowing to Niu, and took a seat.

"Are you Niu Yu-fu?" he asked.

"I am."

"We are a branch of Mr. Wan's salt business. Mr. Wan wrote to me yesterday saying that you are an undesirable character who makes friends with bad people; and from now on we shall dispense with your services."

He produced one tael of silver and handed it to Niu.

"I shall not detain you," he said. "Please suit yourself when you leave."

"I don't want your tael of silver!" shouted Niu, beside himself with anger. "Wan Hsueh-chai shall hear about this!"

He threw the silver on a chair.

"If you don't want it, I can't force you to take it," said Wang. "But I wouldn't advise you to go to Mr. Wan's house, because you won't be admitted."

Snorting with rage, Niu stalked away.

"Excuse me if I don't see you out," said Wang, giving a casual salute as he went back inside.

Niu Yu-fu had to take his servants to a tavern at Choupa, where he kept growling: "You dirty swine, Wan Hsueh-chai!"

One of the waiters laughed as he went past.

"Mr. Wan Hsueh-chai is very easy to get on with," he said. "It's only if you mention the Cheng family that he becomes angry."

Niu immediately ordered a servant to question the waiter.

"Mr. Wan used to work for Cheng Ming-ching," he was told. "He can't stand hearing it mentioned. You must have said something about this, to make him so angry."

When the servant reported this, Niu suddenly saw light.

"So that young scoundrel cheated me!" he swore.

After spending the night there he hired a boat to Soochow to look for Niu Pu; but once aboard, realizing that he was short of money, he dismissed two of his servants and took only two rough fellows with him. In Soochow they found Niu Pu sitting in Huchiu Pharmacy. He greeted Niu Yu-fu and asked: "What brings you here, great-uncle?"

"Have you found a hibernating toad?" asked Niu Yu-fu.

"Not yet."

"They have discovered one in a family in Chenchiang. You must fetch the money at once and come with me to buy it. My boat is outside the city gate."

He went with Niu Pu to fetch the silver and board the boat, but said nothing of his purpose on the way. After breakfast one day, however, when they had travelled for several days and reached a deserted stretch of land called Dragon Robe Island, Niu Yu-fu glared at Niu Pu.

"Do you know that you're going to get a beating?" he roared.

Terrified, Niu Pu asked: "What have I done to offend you, great-uncle? Why do you want to beat me?"

"Curse you!" bellowed Niu Yu-fu. "You played a dirty trick on me!"

Without stopping for an explanation, he ordered his two men to strip Niu Pu of all his clothes, even his cap, shoes and socks. They trussed him up, beat him within an inch of his life, then carried him ashore, dumped him there, hoisted sail and left.

Niu Pu lay there in a daze. They had dumped him on the edge of a cesspool, so that the least move would roll him right into it. He had to lie perfectly still, suppressing his groans. Hours passed before another boat came by and stopped to let a passenger come ashore. Then Niu Pu called frantically for help.

"Who are you?" asked this traveller. "Who stripped off your clothes, then tied you up and left you lying here?"

"I am a scholar of Wuhu County," said Niu Pu. "Magistrate Tung of Antung asked me to go to his yamen to act as his secretary; but I met robbers on the way who took away all my clothes and luggage, leaving me only my life. Take pity on me, sir, and save me!"

"Are you going to the Antung yamen?" demanded the other in surprise. "I come from Antung myself. Let me undo these ropes for you." Niu Pu was stark naked and looked a terrible sight.

"Wait here while I fetch you some clothes," said the man who had saved him. "Then you can come aboard."

He brought him some cloth garments, a pair of shoes and a tile-shaped cap.

"This is not a scholar's cap," he said, "but you had better wear it until we come to a town where you can buy a square cap."

When Niu Pu had put on the clothes he knelt down to thank the other, but the traveller raised him up and helped him to the boat, where all were amazed at his story and asked his name.

"My name is Niu," he said. "May I know my benefactor's name?"

"My name is Huang" said the other, "and I am from Antung County too. I trade in theatrical costumes. The other day I went to Nanking to buy some additional costumes for a company and was on my way home when I chanced upon you and was able to save you. Since you are going to the magistrate's yamen, you had better travel with me to Antung and stay with me while you prepare clothes for your visit to the yamen "

Niu Pu thanked him and let Mr. Huang pay all his expenses.

It was very hot, and because Niu Pu had been trussed up naked for half a day and exposed to the sun and the stench of the cesspool, as soon as he was aboard he developed acute dysentery. After three or four days he was as thin as a ghost and aching in every limb from his beating.

"It looks as if his end has come," whispered the passengers in the cabin. "We had better put him ashore while he is still alive. It will be very awkward if he dies."

Mr. Huang, however, would not hear of this.

On the fifth day, Niu Pu suddenly smelt beans.

"I would like some bean broth," he said to the boatman.

Everybody on board tried to dissuade him.

"I want to eat," he insisted. "I shan't blame you if I die."

There was nothing they could do but send ashore for some beans. They boiled a bowl of broth for him and when he had drunk it, his belly gave a great rumble and he felt better. Crawling into the cabin he thanked all the passengers, then lay down to sleep; and in two more days he gradually recovered.

On reaching Antung, Niu Pu put up with Mr. Huang, who bought him a square cap, some clothes and a pair of shoes. He put these on to call on the magistrate. Magistrate Tung was pleased to see him and entertained him to a feast, then invited him to stay in the yamen. Niu Pu, however, declined.

"I have a relative in your honourable district," he said. "It will be better if I stay with him."

"Very well," replied the magistrate. "But even if you stay with your relative, I hope you will often visit me so that I may receive your instruction."

Then Niu Pu left.

When Mr Huang saw that Niu Pu was indeed a friend of the magistrate, he felt the greatest respect for him. Niu Pu went to the yamen every two or three days, and at the same time, on the strength of his reputation as a poet, accepted some bribes and influenced the magistrate on certain matters. Mr. Huang also gave him his fourth daughter in marriage; so he stayed on happily in Antung.

Then Magistrate Tung was promoted his successor being a certain Mr. Hsiang who was also a native of Chekiang Province. During the transfer, the new magistrate asked the old whether there was anything he could do for him.

"There is nothing really," replied Magistrate Tung. "But I have a friend named Niu Pu-yi, who is a poet, staying in your honourable county, and I should be most grateful if you would see that he is all right." When Magistrate Hsiang consented, Magistrate Tung set off for the capital, accompanied for thirty miles by Niu Pu, who came back only on the third day.

On his return his wife told him: "Yesterday a man called and said he was your uncle from Wuhu who happened to be passing this way. I kept him for a meal and then he left. He said he would come back in a few months' time."

"I have no such uncle," thought Niu Pu in surprise. "Who can it be? I shall have to wait for him to come back before I know what to do."

Magistrate Tung went straight to the capital, reported his arrival and went the next day to draw lots for his new appointment. Feng Cho-an, who had passed the metropolitan examination and whose name was now on the official list, was staying near the ministry, so Tung dropped in first to call on him. Assistant Secretary Feng invited him to sit down, and they talked on general topics.

"Your friend Niu Pu-yi was in Sweet Dew Temple in Wuhu . . ." said Magistrate Tung.

He had no time to say that he had called on Niu Pu-yi nor that he had met him again in Antung, for at that moment a servant came in.

"The time has come for distributing posts," he announced.

Magistrate Tung immediately asked to be excused and went to the office to draw lots. He received the position of Magistrate of Kueichow, and hastily packed up and went to his new post without calling on Secretary Feng again.

Some time after this, Secretary Feng ordered a servant to take a letter home. He also gave him ten taels of silver and asked: "Do you know Mr. Niu Pu-yi's house?"

"I do," said the man.

"Then take this ten taels of silver for Mrs. Niu. Tell her I wanted to send her word that her husband is staying in Sweet Dew Temple in Wuhu County. Don't forget. And say that this money is for her travelling expenses."

The servant went home as instructed. After seeing his mistress and dealing with various family affairs, he walked to a closed wicker-gate in a narrow alley. Just as he reached the gate, a boy came out carrying a basket to buy rice. When the servant told him that he had been sent by Secretary Feng in the capital, the lad showed him into the hall and then went inside, reappearing presently.

"Was there any message?" he asked.

"What relation are you to Mrs. Niu?" asked the servant.

"She is my aunt."

Then the servant handed him the ten taels of silver.

"My master told me to bring this silver to Mrs. Niu as travelling expenses, and to tell her that Mr. Niu is now in

Sweet Dew Temple at Wuhu," he said. "He has sent you this message so that you needn't worry."

The boy asked him to sit down while he took the money inside. Looking round, the servant saw that on the middle wall they had hung a single tattered old painting with poems pasted on either side, while six rickety bamboo chairs were all the furniture of the room. In the courtyard next to the wicker-gate was a raised flower-bed on which a wisteria vine was growing. He did not have long to wait before the boy came out with a cup of tea and a package containing two cents of silver which he gave to the man.

"My aunt thanks you for the trouble you have taken," he said. "This is for you to buy tea. When you go back, give her regards to your mistress; and when you return to the capital give her regards and thanks to your master and tell him that she received the message."

The servant thanked him and left.

This gift of silver made Mrs. Niu sad.

"He is growing old now," she thought, "yet he spends all his time away from home. And we have no children. I had better use these ten taels to go to Wuhu to fetch him back."

Her mind made up, she locked up her ramshackle cottage and asked the neighbours to keep an eye on it, after which she and her nephew took a boat to Wuhu and found their way to Sweet Dew Temple by Floating Bridge. The double gate was closed but she pushed it open and went in. There were neither incense-burners nor candlesticks before the shrine; and when she went further in, she found the latticed window of the main hall was falling to pieces. An old Taoist priest was sitting in the courtyard mending his clothes; but he could only gesticulate in answer to her questions, because he was deaf and dumb. When she asked whether Niu Pu-yi lived there, he pointed to a room in front.

Mrs. Niu went back with her nephew and saw that the room next to that with the shrine had not even a door. She entered and found a large coffin and a three-legged table listing to one side. The pennon above the coffin had disappeared, only its pole remaining. And because the roof had no tiles, the rain had seeped through to obliterate all the writing on the coffin except the two words "Ming Dynasty," while of the characters beneath only one line was left. Mrs. Niu could not repress a shudder.

She went back to ask the old priest: "Is Niu Pu-yi dead?"

The priest, however, simply waved his hands and pointed outside.

"He means that uncle isn't dead but has gone somewhere else," said her nephew.

Then Mrs. Niu left the temple, making inquiries all along the street, and everyone she questioned told her they had not heard of anyone dying in the temple. Finally she reached Kuo Tieh-pi's shop near Good Luck Temple.

"Niu Pu-yi?" said Kuo. "He has gone to Magistrate Tung's yamen in Antung County."

Now that she had reliable information, Mrs. Niu decided to go to Antung to look for her husband.

But to know whether she reached Antung or not, you must read the chapter which follows.

CHAPTER 24

Niu Pu is involved in a lawsuit, and Pao Wen-ching
goes back to his old trade

After Niu Pu married into the Huang family in Antung,
they gave him three or four front rooms and on his door he
posted a notice: "Niu Pu-yi, Poet and Essayist." He was
sitting at home one morning when there came a knock and
he opened the door to see an old neighbour from Wuhu County
called Shih, who was nicknamed The Rat. He was a notorious
old swindler. Niu Pu was rather taken aback, but he had to
bow to this fellow and ask him to sit down while he went in
to fetch tea.

"This is that uncle of yours who came last year and said
he would be back," said his wife, who had been watching from
behind the screen.

"He is no uncle of mine!" protested Niu.

He took tea out and offered it to The Rat.

"I hear you are in luck," said The Rat. "And I see you've
married again here!"

"I haven't seen you for many years. Where have you been?"
asked Niu.

"Oh, wandering about in Huaipei and Shantung. I was
passing this way, and it happens that all my money is spent;
so I've called on you to borrow a few taels. You must help
me out!"

"We may be old neighbours," said Niu, "but we never did business together. Besides, I am a stranger here, staying with my father-in-law. What money can I give you?"

"You ungrateful cub!" The Rat gave a sneering laugh. "Think how much you had from me when I was spending money like water! Yet now that I try to save your face—since I see you've married a second wife here and it wouldn't be quite the thing to expose you—you still talk to me like that!"

"What do you mean?" retorted Niu angrily. "When did I ever have money from you? I've never seen you spending money like water! An old man like you should be thinking of doing good deeds, instead of cheating people all the time."

"Niu Pu!" warned The Rat. "Be careful what you say! Think of all the crooked things you did in your early days! You may still be able to fool others, but you can't fool me. You're guilty of bigamy, you know. You've deserted your Pu family wife over there and deceived your new Huang family wife here. If you don't hand over a few taels quietly now, I'll report you to the Antung yamen!"

"Do you think I'm afraid of you!" Niu leapt to his feet. "Let's go to the yamen!"

They dragged each other out of the door and straight to the yamen gate where two runners who knew Niu Pu hastily stopped them to ask what was the matter. The Rat launched into a denunciation, accusing Niu of deceiving both the Pu family and the Huang family and of masquerading under a false name.

"He's a well-known crook from my county called The Rat," declared Niu. "And now he's old and shameless. Last year he came to our house when I was away, passing himself off as my uncle in order to get a free meal. Now he's turned up again to demand money. This is outrageous!"

"All right, Mr. Niu!" said the runners. "But he's an old man, and even if he's not your relative he's an old neighbour of yours. Probably he really has come to the end of his money. And as the proverb says: Poverty at home isn't poverty, but poverty on the road is killing. Still, even if you have money you won't want to give him any now; so suppose we raise a few hundred cash for you so that he can continue on his journey."

Still The Rat was not satisfied.

"It's no use causing trouble here!" the runners told him. "Mr. Niu is a very good friend of our magistrate's. An old man like you shouldn't behave so disgracefully, when it'll make things worse for you!"

This stopped The Rat's blustering. He took the money, thanked them all and left.

Niu Pu thanked the runners too, then started home. He had not gone far, when a neighbour accosted him.

"Mr. Niu!" he called. "Come over here a moment!" Having pulled him into a quiet alley, the neighbour went on: "Your wife is having a row with somebody!"

"With whom?"

"Just after you left a sedan-chair arrived with a load of luggage, and your wife let in a woman. That woman swears that she is your former wife and insists on seeing you. She and your wife are at it now hammer and tongs! Your wife wants you to go back at once."

At this Niu felt as if plunged into icy water.

"This must be the work of that damned old Rat," he thought. "He's sent my first wife along to stir up trouble!"

There was nothing for it, though, but to pluck up courage and go back. When he stood outside the door listening, however, it wasn't his first wife he heard carrying on inside, but somebody with a Chekiang accent. He knocked at the door and went in; and when he and the woman met, neither knew the other.

"Here is my husband!" cried Niu Pu's wife. "Do you still claim him as yours?"

"You're not Niu Pu-yi!" exclaimed Mrs. Niu.

"I certainly *am*," declared Niu Pu. "But I don't know you, ma'am."

"I am Niu Pu-yi's wife. You have taken my husband's name, you wretch, as an advertisement! You must have murdered my husband! Don't imagine you're going to escape,"

306

"There are plenty of people with the same name," retorted Niu Pu. "How does that prove that I murdered your husband? This is fantastic!"

"You must have killed him! I went all the way to Wuhu to the Sweet Dew Temple and was told that he was at Antung. Impostor! Give me back my husband!"

Weeping and wailing, she told her nephew to seize Niu Pu, then mounted her chair and raised a great outcry all the way to the yamen. The magistrate was just leaving when she made her complaint, and he told her to send in a written charge. When this was received, runners summoned all those concerned and a notice was posted up of the time of the trial, which was to take place three days later at noon.

There were three cases that day, the first involving the murder of a man's father, the plaintiff being a monk. This monk stated that he had been gathering firewood on the mountain when he noticed that one of the cows grazing there kept staring fixedly at him. Strangely moved, he went up to the cow, whereupon tears gushed from the beast's eyes; and when he knelt down before it, the cow licked his head, its tears falling faster and faster. The monk realized that this must be his father whose soul had entered the body of a cow. He pleaded tearfully with the owner of the cow to give him the beast in order that he might keep it in the temple. Then, however, a neighbour had taken the cow away and killed it. The monk had now come to court with the man who had given him the cow as his witness.

When Magistrate Hsiang had heard the monk's story, he questioned the neighbour.

"Three or four days ago this monk led the cow over and sold it to me," said the neighbour, "and I killed it. But yesterday the monk came back to claim that this cow was his father so I must pay him some more, because he had sold it too cheaply. When I wouldn't give any more money, he started abusing me. I've heard say that the cow wasn't his father at all. For years now this monk has shaved his head and put salt on it; and whenever he sees cattle grazing, he picks out the fattest cow and kneels before it, so that the cow licks his head. Any cow licking salt will shed tears. Then he declares that this cow is his father and goes crying to the owner to ask to have it given him; and when he gets it he sells it. He has done this many times. Now he is accusing me. I beg Your Honour to decide between us!"

The magistrate called the owner of the cow.

"Did you really give him the cow for nothing?" he asked.

"Yes. I didn't ask for a single cent."

"Transmigration has always been considered a mystery," declared Magistrate Hsiang. "But this is simply incredible. Besides, if he really believed that the cow was his father, he ought not to have sold it. This bald-pate is a scoundrel!"

Having sentenced the monk to twenty strokes, he dismissed the case.

The second case involved a poison charge. The plaintiff, Hu Lai, was the dead man's elder brother, and the defendant a Dr. Chen An. Magistrate Hsiang called the plaintiff.

"How did he poison your brother?" he asked.

"My brother was ill, so I called in Dr. Chen. But the day after the doctor gave him medicine, my brother had a fit and jumped into the water. He was drowned. Obviously he must have been poisoned!"

"Were you enemies?"

"No."

Magistrate Hsiang then called the doctor.

"What medicine did you prescribe for Hu Lai's brother?" he asked.

"He had caught a chill," replied Dr. Chen, "so I prescribed a medicine to make him sweat which included eight drachms of *asarum*. There was a relative there at the time—a squat, round-faced fellow — who said that three drachms of *asarum* would prove fatal. But that's certainly not what the *Pharmacopoeia* says. Three or four days after this, his elder brother jumped into the river and was drowned; but how can he blame me for that? You can analyse the properties of all the four hundred herbs that exist, Your Honour, without finding one which will make people jump into the river! This is ridiculous! I am a professional man, and this slander is bad for my practice! I beg Your Honour to judge between us!"

308

"I have never heard such nonsense!" agreed Magistrate Hsiang. "A doctor is a servant of humanity. And when you have a sick man in the house, Hu Lai, you ought to look after him. Why did you let him get out and jump into the river? How can you blame that on the doctor? The idea of bringing such a case to court!" Thereupon he dismissed the case.

Mrs. Niu was the plaintiff in the third case, and she accused Niu Pu of murdering her husband. When Magistrate Hsiang called on her, she told him how she had travelled from Chekiang to Wuhu and from Wuhu to Antung.

"Now he has taken my husband's name," she concluded. "If I don't ask him what has become of my husband, whom can I ask?"

"That doesn't follow," replied the magistrate. "Do you know this woman, Mr. Niu?"

"I know neither her nor her husband," protested Niu Pu. "Yet she suddenly came to my home demanding her husband. It was a bolt from the blue!"

"Apparently Mr. Niu here and your husband are both called Niu Pu-yi," said Hsiang to Mrs. Niu. "But there are many people in the world with the same name. Of course Mr. Niu doesn't know the whereabouts of your husband. You had better look for him elsewhere."

Mrs. Niu started sniffling and sobbing and insisted her husband must be avenged, until the magistrate lost patience with her.

"Very well," he said. "I will send two runners to escort you back to Shaohsing. You can appeal to your own magistrate! It's not my job to look into this unsubstantiated charge. You may leave too, Mr. Niu."

When the magistrate had dismissed the court, two runners accompanied Mrs. Niu to Shaohsing.

This affair was later reported to the higher authorities, and Magistrate Hsiang was accused of letting his friendship for poets interfere with his judgement of murder cases. An investigation was ordered, and the matter was reported to the judicial commissioner. This commissioner's name was Tsui and, as the nephew of a eunuch, he had started life with a hereditary title and later been promoted to his present position.

One evening he ordered his secretary to copy out the charge, and read it carefully under the lamp. The charge began: "This is to denounce an incompetent, irresponsible magistrate in order to purge the civil service. . . ." Then followed many charges against Hsiang Ting, Magistrate of Antung.

The judicial commissioner was studying this document carefully when he noticed a man kneeling in the shadow cast by the lamp, and saw that it was an actor named Pao Wen-ching who served in the yamen.

"What do you want?" he asked. "Get up to speak."

"I heard just now, sir," said Pao, "that charges are being brought against Magistrate Hsiang of Antung County. I don't know this gentleman personally; but ever since I studied drama under my tutor from the age of seven or eight, I have read his plays. He's a great scholar and a writer of genius, yet it has taken him more than twenty years to reach the rank of magistrate: it does seem a shame. And now it looks as if he'll be dismissed. Besides, he's in trouble only because he respected scholars. May I beg you, sir, not to condemn him?"

"Who could imagine that you would take such an interest in scholars!" exclaimed the commissioner. "Since even you want to help a scholar, of course I want to help him too. But if I let him off, he won't know that he has you to thank. I'll tell him what has happened and send you to his yamen so that he can give you a few hundred taels to show his gratitude, which you can use as capital when you go home."

Pao Wen-ching kowtowed in thanks, and the commissioner told his servant to inform the secretary that no further investigation was required in the case of the Magistrate of Antung.

A few days later, Commissioner Tsui sent a runner with a letter to accompany Pao Wen-ching to Antung. When Magistrate Hsiang opened the commissioner's letter he was amazed and hastily ordered his men to open the gate of his house and invite Mr. Pao in, going out himself to welcome him. Pao Wen-ching came in, in a black gown and small cap, and knelt to pay his respects. Magistrate Hsiang wanted to raise him up and to bow in return.

"Who am I to be greeted as an equal!" protested Pao.

"You come from my superior's yamen and you are my benefactor," replied Magistrate Hsiang. "You should let me pay my respects. Please get up so that I may bow to you to express my thanks."

Still Pao declined and, when the magistrate pulled him up, he refused to be seated.

In desperation, the magistrate said: "Judicial Commissioner Tsui sent you here, and if I treat you discourteously he will take it as a slight."

"Although you want to honour me, sir," said Pao, "this would run counter to court etiquette and I dare not consent to it."

He stood there with his hands at his sides to give brief answers to the magistrate's questions, then withdrew to the corridor. When Magistrate Hsiang asked relatives to entertain him, Pao Wen-ching still declined resolutely; but later, when one of the stewards was sent to keep him company, he looked pleased and sat in the steward's room laughing and talking.

The next day the magistrate prepared a feast in the library and poured out wine for Pao Wen-ching, but the latter knelt down to decline this honour; and, asked to be seated, once more declined. There was nothing the magistrate could do but send the feast to the servant's quarters and ask his stewards to eat with the actor. And for this Pao insisted on offering thanks. Magistrate Hsiang then wrote a letter to express his gratitude to the judicial commissioner and wrapped up five hundred taels of silver for the actor; but Pao would not take a cent.

"This is the stipend the court gives to gentlemen," he protested. "I am a common man—how dare I use His Imperial Majesty's silver? If I were to take this silver for my family, I should certainly die for my presumption. Have pity on me, Your Honour, and spare my unworthy life."

Since he spoke so emphatically, the magistrate could not insist. He therefore reported this in another letter to the judicial commissioner and then, after entertaining Pao for several days, had him escorted back to Nanking. When Commissioner Tsui heard what had happened, he considered Pao a fool; but there the matter rested. After some time the commissioner was promoted and took Pao with him to the capital.

As soon as he reached Peking, however, Commissioner Tsui fell ill and died. And since the actor had no friends in Peking and was a native of Nanking, he packed up and went home.

Nanking was the capital of the first Ming emperor and its inner wall has thirteen gates, its outer wall eighteen. More than ten miles across and forty miles in circumference, the city boasts several dozen large streets and several hundred small alleys which are thronged with people and filled with gilt and painted pavilions. The Chinhuai River which flows through Nanking measures over three miles from the east to the west ford; and, when its water is high, painted barges carrying flutists and drummers ply to and fro on it day and night. Within and without the city stand monasteries and temples with green tiles and crimson roofs. During the Six Dynasties[1] there were four hundred and eighty temples here, but now there must be at least four thousand eight hundred! The streets and lanes house six or seven hundred taverns, large and small, and over a thousand tea-shops. No matter what small alley you enter, you are bound to see at least one house where a lantern is hung to show that tea is sold; and inside the shop you will find fresh flowers and crystal-clear rain water on the boil. These tea-shops are always filled.

At dusk, bright horn lanterns hang from the taverns on both sides of the road, several thousand lanterns on each main street making the highways as bright as day, so that passers-by need not carry lanterns with them. Late at night, when the moon is up, boats playing soft music glide up and down the Chinhuai, enchanting all who hear them with their clear, tender strains. Girls in the houses on both banks roll up their curtains and lean over the railings to listen quietly, dressed in light gauze and with jasmine flowers in their hair. In fact, as soon as the drums sound in the lighted boats, screens are rolled up and windows opened on both sides of the river, and the scent of the ambergris and sandalwood burnt in the houses here floats out to mingle with the moonlight and mist on the

---

[1] The Six Dynasties lasted from the third to the end of the sixth century. All of them had their capital at Chienkang (present-day Nanking).

river, until you fancy yourself in paradise or fairyland. There are the government singsong girls from the courtesans' quarter too, in their bright, fashionable costumes, who welcome travellers from all parts. Thus every day seems like the Spring Festival and every night like New Year's Eve.

Pao Wen-ching lived at West Water Gate near Treasure Gate. If, in the old days, a hundred cows, a thousand pigs and ten thousand bushels of grain were said to pass through Treasure Gate every day, there must now have been a thousand cows, ten thousand pigs and more grain than could be counted! Going through West Water Gate, then, Pao went home and saw his wife. His family had been actors for several generations and were still in the theatre business. There were three guild centres for actors at Huaiching Bridge and one temple to the god of drama; and at West Water Gate was another guild centre and another temple. At these centres hung the names of the different companies, and to engage actors one had to write down on their board a few days in advance the date they would be required. Pao Wen-ching's name was up in the West Water Gate centre. The rules of the theatre were extremely strict, and if an actor did anything wrong, his whole guild had to go to the temple to burn incense, while on their return to the centre the case would be tried by all; and they could beat or punish the offender, who dared not complain. There were operatic companies here, with about a dozen men to each, dating from the days of the first Ming emperor, and each company still had a stone tablet in the temple with the names of the different actors inscribed on it. Moreover, the descendants of those players whose names were on the tablets, if they remained in the theatre, enjoyed certain hereditary privileges. Even when they were only a few years old they were called "Elders," and they had to be consulted on all the affairs of the company before any decision could be reached. The name of Pao's grandfather was on the first tablet.

When Pao reached home, after settling various domestic problems he took out his flutes, pipes, three-stringed guitars and lutes to examine them. Some of the strings were broken, some of the instruments cracked and all of them thick with

313

dust. Presently he put them aside and went to a tea-shop near the guild centre to meet fellow actors.

In the tea-shop he saw a man in a tall hat, sapphire-blue gown and black shoes with white soles, drinking tea alone. Going closer, Pao saw that it was Pock-marked Chien, who played old men's parts in his company.

"When did you come back?" asked Pock-marked Chien. "Sit down and have some tea."

"When I saw you at a distance," remarked Pao, "I thought it was a gentleman of the Han Lin Academy who had wandered in by mistake to drink tea; but it's only you after all, you old sinner!" He took a seat at the same table.

"You've just been to the capital, Wen-ching, and seen a few officials," said Pock-marked Chien, "so now you try to impress us with your Hanlins."

"That's not what I meant," countered Pao. "But it's not right in our profession to wear those clothes. If *you* wear clothes like that, what can the scholars wear?"

"That was true twenty years ago," retorted Chien. "But nowadays when folk celebrate birthdays or weddings in Nanking, even if we go there with one pair of candlesticks they have to ask us to sit down to a meal with them; and high officials sometimes have to take lower seats. As for those pedants who only pass the local examinations, I scorn to look at them."

"Friend!" protested Pao. "If you give yourself such airs, you deserve to remain an actor in your next life. In fact, if you become an ass or a horse, it will simply serve you right!"

As Pock-marked Chien dealt him a blow, laughing, the waiter brought them cakes.

While they were eating, an old man walked in leaning upon a dragon-head stick. He was wearing a hood, a dark purple silk gown and black shoes with white soles.

"Mr. Huang!" called Pock-marked Chien. "Come and have tea with us!"

"I was wondering who you were," replied the old man. "So it's you two! I couldn't recognize you until I came close, but you can't blame me for that. I'm eighty-two this year: my eyes should be a little dim. When did you come back, Pao Wen-ching?"

"I only arrived a few days ago and have not yet had time to call on you, uncle. How quickly time passes! It's fourteen years since we last met. I remember the year that I left here I saw you perform in 'The Waiter in the Tea-Shop' in Duke Hsu's house. Are you still with the company?"

Mr. Huang shook his head.

"I gave up acting long ago," he said.

When they had sat down again and ordered more cakes, the old man said to Chien: "The other day Mr. Chang, the provincial scholar outside the South Gate, invited us to play chess. Why didn't you go?"

"I had work that day," replied Chien. "Tomorrow Mr. Hsueh who lives beyond the Drum Tower is having a birthday; and he has asked some of my pupils to put on a show. We ought to go ourselves to congratulate him."

"Which Mr. Hsueh is that?" asked Pao.

"He used to be prefect of Tingchow," said Mr. Huang. "He is the same age as I — eighty-two this year. The court has made him a country elder."

"Seeing the leisurely and dignified way you pace along, leaning on your stick," said Pao, "I think you ought to be a country elder too, uncle. Look at this old gentleman, Mr. Chien! Why compare him to a retired prefect? Even ministers and vice-ministers couldn't look more grand!"

Not realizing that Pao was poking fun at him, the old man beamed with pleasure. Then they finished their tea and left. Although Pao Wen-ching did not approve of the ways of these players he said no more. He wanted to find some boys to start a small company of his own, so started searching all through the city for some who would be suitable. One day on the slope leading up to the Drum Tower he met a man.

But to know who it was that Pao Wen-ching met, you must read the next chapter.

315

CHAPTER 25

**Pao Wen-ching meets an old acquaintance in Nanking
and Ni Ting-hsi finds a bride in Anching**

Pao Wen-ching was looking in the north city for boys for
his opera company when, half way up the Drum Tower slope,
he met a man in an old felt hat, tattered black silk gown and
shabby red shoes. His grey beard flecked with white made him
look over sixty, and he was carrying a battered fiddle pasted
with a white paper on which was written: "Musical instruments mended."

Pao stepped forward and clasped his hands in salute.

"Can you mend instruments, uncle?" he asked.

"I can."

"May I trouble you then to step into that tea-shop with
me?"

They went to a tea-shop, sat down and ordered tea.

"May I ask your name, uncle?" inquired Pao.

"My name is Ni."

"Where do you live?"

"A long way from here — at the Three Arches."

"You say you mend musical instruments, Mr. Ni. Can you
mend the lute and three-stringed guitar?"

"Yes."

"My name is Pao. I live at West Water Gate and work in
the theatre. I have some instruments at home which are in
very bad condition and I would like you to repair them. I don't

know, though, whether I should trouble you to come to my house to mend them, or send them to your house."

"How many instruments are there?"

"Seven or eight, I should say."

"Seven or eight would be difficult to carry; I had better come to your house. It shouldn't take more than a couple of days to mend them, and I shall ask you only for the midday meal. I will go home in the evening."

"Very good," said Pao. "But I hope you won't take offence if we can't entertain you well. When can I trouble you to come?"

"Tomorrow I am busy. I will come the day after tomorrow."

Just as they agreed on this, a hawker passed the door with a load of pachyma cakes and Pao bought half a catty to share with Mr. Ni, after which he took his leave.

"I shall expect you then, uncle," he said, "the day after tomorrow in the morning."

Mr. Ni agreed, and each went his way. On his return home Pao told his wife to have all the instruments cleaned and carried into the sitting room.

The morning that Mr. Ni arrived he was offered tea and cakes and then started repairing the instruments. After some time, two boys who were staying in the house to study for the stage brought in a vegetarian meal which Pao shared with Mr. Ni. In the afternoon Pao went out.

On his return he said to the old man: "We have treated you very shabbily, uncle, giving you such a poor meal. It was most impolite. Let us go out to a restaurant now. You had better leave the other instruments for tomorrow."

"I shouldn't put you to so much trouble," said Mr. Ni.

They went to a tavern, found a clean, quiet table and sat down.

The waiter came over and asked whether there were more guests.

"No more," said Mr. Ni. "What do you have?"

Ticking off the items on his fingers, the waiter said: "Joint, duck, fish casserole, mandarin fish in wine, mixed grill, chicken,

317

tripe, fried pork, Peking-style fried pork, sliced pork, meat balls, mackerel, boiled fish head, and cold pork."

"You needn't treat me as a guest," said Mr. Ni to Pao. "Let us have a simple cold dish."

But Pao would not hear of this. He ordered first a portion of duck to go with the wine, then sliced fried pork and rice. The waiter disappeared with the order into the kitchen, to reappear shortly with one portion of duck and two pots of wine.

Pao stood up to pour a cup of wine for Mr. Ni, then sat down to drink.

"You look like a man who has studied, uncle," he said. "Why do you spend your time mending instruments?"

"Mine is a sad story," replied Mr. Ni with a sigh. "I passed the district examination at twenty — thirty-seven years ago. But unfortunately my book-learning spoiled me for any other work, so that I grew poorer every day; and because I had many mouths to feed, I had to turn my hand to this. There was nothing else I could do."

"So you are really a scholar!" exclaimed Pao. "I have been very remiss. May I ask how many sons you have, and whether your wife is in good health?"

"My wife is still alive. I had six sons, but I cannot bear to speak of them."

"What do you mean?"

At this juncture, Mr. Ni was in tears. Pao refilled his cup with wine.

"If you have any trouble, uncle," he said, "don't be afraid to tell me. I may be able to help you."

"I had better not. If I tell you, you will laugh at me."

"Who am I to dare laugh at you? You can speak freely, uncle."

"Well, the truth is that I had six sons, one of whom died; but now only the youngest is left at home. The other four —" At this point he broke down again

"What happened to the other four?"

"You're a good sort," said Mr. Ni when pressed like this. "I don't suppose you will laugh at me. The truth is that, because I had nothing to live on, I sold those four sons of mine to people living in distant provinces."

318

When Pao heard this, he could not help shedding tears.

"The pity of it!" he cried.

"That's not all, either!" continued the old man, still weeping. "I shan't be able to keep even this youngest son. I shall have to sell him too."

"How can you and the boy's mother bear to part with him, uncle?"

"We've nothing to eat at home. If we keep him, he will just have to starve with us. Better give him a chance to live."

Pao Wen-ching felt very sorry for the old man. "I've a proposal to make," he said after a pause. "But I don't know how to say it, uncle."

"If you have anything to say, just speak out."

Pao was about to tell him, but stopped again.

"Better not," he declared. "If I say it, I may offend you."

"Certainly not. Say what you like and I won't be offended."

"Then I'll make bold to offer a suggestion."

"Go on. Go on."

"If you must sell your youngest son, uncle, and sell him to someone in another province like the others, you will never see him again. Now I am more than forty years old, but I have only one daughter — I've never had a son. If you don't look down on my humble profession but let me adopt the lad, I shall present you with twenty taels of silver and bring him up as best I can. During festivals he can go back to see you, and if your luck changes he can return to you for good. How would that be?"

"If you will do that," cried Mr. Ni, "it must mean that my boy's lucky star is on the rise. Of course I agree. But if you adopt him and have the trouble of bringing him up, I shan't take any money from you."

"Oh, no," protested Pao. "I shall certainly send you twenty taels."

Then they finished their meal and paid the bill. It was nearly dark when they left the tavern, so Mr. Ni went home while Pao went back to tell his wife what he had arranged, and she was very pleased with the suggestion.

The next morning when Mr. Ni arrived to repair the instruments, he said to Pao: "When I went back and told my wife what we discussed yesterday, she was very grateful too. Now you have only to say the word and I will choose an auspicious day and bring my son over."

Pao was delighted, and from that time on they addressed each other as relatives.

A few days later, the Pao family invited Mr. Ni and his son to a feast to draw up the contract for the adoption to be witnessed by the left-hand neighbour Mr. Chang the draper, and the right-hand neighbour Mr. Wang the chandler. When they had all arrived, the contract was drawn up as follows:

> Ni Shuang-feng of his own free will and with the consent of his wife gives his sixth son, Ni Ting-hsi, now sixteen years old, to Pao Wen-ching as his adopted son, because Ni Shuang-feng cannot support him. The boy's name will be changed to Pao Ting-hsi. It will be Pao Wen-ching's duty to bring him up and find him a wife, and as a descendant of the Pao family he will take part in ancestral sacrifices. Both sides have agreed to this. Should the boy meet with any accident, both parties will bow to the will of Heaven. This contract has been drawn up as evidence, and must be kept for ever.
>
> The first day of the tenth month,
the sixteenth year of the period of Chia Ching.

When this document had been signed by Mr. Ni and the two witnesses, Pao Wen-ching produced twenty taels and gave them to Mr. Ni, then thanked them all. From that time onwards, there were constant visits between the two families.

This Ni Ting-hsi, now known as Pao Ting-hsi, was a very clever lad. And since he came from a good family, Pao would not train him for the stage but made him study for two years before taking him into the business. When the boy was eighteen, old Mr. Ni died. Pao Wen-ching contributed several dozen taels for the funeral and went several times to mourn beside the coffin, instructing his adopted son to put on heavy mourning and follow the coffin to the grave.

Gradually Ting-hsi proved himself very useful. His stepmother could not forget that he was an adopted son and did not love him as she did her own daughter and son-in-law; but Pao Wen-ching loved him more than if he had been his own son, because he came from a respectable family. He took the lad with him whenever he went out to tea-shops and taverns or on business trips; and he let him earn commissions so that he could buy new clothes, caps, shoes and socks. He was thinking, too, of finding a wife for him.

One morning he was just about to go out with Pao Ting-hsi when a man on a donkey rode up to their door, dismounted and came in. Pao Wen-ching saw that it was Shao a steward of Minister Tu of Tienchang County.

"When did you come over, Mr. Shao?" he asked.

"I crossed the river specially to see you, Mr. Pao!"

Pao bowed to him and told his son to bow too, then asked Shao to sit down and brought him water to wash and tea to drink.

"To the best of my recollection," said Pao while the steward was drinking, "the old lady in your family must be seventy this year. Have you come over to order operas? Is your master well?"

"You've guessed rightly!" Shao laughed. "My master told me to order twenty plays. Do you have a company of your own, Mr. Pao? If you do, we'll ask your company over."

"I have a small company, and we shall be very glad to do what we can. But when will you be wanting us?"

"At the end of the month." Having told the donkey-man to bring in the luggage and take the donkey back, Shao extracted a parcel of silver from his bedding and handed it to Pao.

"Here are fifty taels of silver, Mr. Pao, to be going on with," he said. "The rest will be paid when your company has arrived."

Pao Wen-ching accepted the money and that evening prepared a feast with large dishes and big bowls to entertain the steward till nearly midnight. The next day Shao went out shopping, and after he had shopped for four or five days he hired a boat and went back. Pao then packed up and took Pao Ting-hsi and his company to perform at Minister Tu's house in Tienchang County. They stayed there for over forty days and made nearly two hundred taels of silver. All the way back, father and son were expressing their gratitude to the Tu family, for the old lady had given each of the young actors — and there were over a dozen of them — a padded jacket and a pair of shoes and socks as an extra. When the boys' parents knew of it they were very grateful too and came to thank Pao Wen-ching, who was now giving performances as before in Nanking.

One day they went to Shangho to perform at night. The opera ended just before dawn and the players took back the properties, while Pao and his son visited a bath-house, had some tea and cakes and walked slowly back.

"There's no need to go in," said Pao when they reached their gate. "A man at Inner Bridge has ordered plays for to· morrow: we may as well go to collect payment now."

Pao Ting-hsi followed his father to Lane End where they saw a yellow umbrella, four red-and-black-capped guards, a canopy and a big sedan-chair coming towards them. Realizing that this must be a high official from another district passing that way, father and son stood back against the wall to watch and let the umbrella and guards go past. When the canopy passed them, they saw written on it: "Prefect of Anching." Pao Wen-ching was looking at the canopy when the sedan-chair came up. The official in the chair gave a start at the sight of him; and when Pao turned back to look at the official, he saw that it was no other than Mr. Hsiang, the former magistrate of Antung who had now been promoted. As soon as the chair had passed, the official spoke to one of his black-coated runners who rushed over to Pao Wen-ching. "His Excellency asks whether you are Mr. Pao?" said the runner.

"Yes, I am. Was your master promoted from Antung?"

"Yes. His Excellency is staying in the Chang family's riverside house by the examination school, and he asks you to call on him there."

This said, he darted off to catch up with the chair.

Pao took his son to a chandler's shop near the examination school where he bought a card on which he wrote: "Your servant Pao Wen-ching pays his respects." When they reached the Chang house by the river and heard that Mr. Hsiang had already come back, Pao handed his card to the gate-keeper.

"Please tell His Excellency," he said, "that Pao Wen-ching is waiting to see him."

The gate-keeper took the card and said: "Wait here."

Pao and his son had been sitting on the bench for some time, when a boy came out from the house.

"Gateman!" he called. "His Excellency asks whether a Mr. Pao Wen-ching has come or not?"

"Yes, I've got his card here," said the gate-keeper, and hurried in to present it.

Then they heard someone calling: "Show him in at once!"

Pao told his son to wait outside while he went in with the gate-keeper. When he reached the house, Mr. Hsiang came out, wearing civilian dress and a gauze cap.

"So my old friend is here!" he said with a smile. When Pao knelt to pay his respects, Mr. Hsiang raised him up with both hands.

"If you insist on being so polite all the time, my friend," he said, "you will make things very difficult for me."

He begged him to be seated. Then after kneeling once more, Pao sat down on the lowest stool and Mr. Hsiang sat down too.

"More than ten years have passed since we parted," said the official. "I am old now, and your beard is turning white."

Pao stood up. "I did not know of your promotion, Your Excellency," he said. "I have not yet congratulated you."

"Please sit down," said Mr. Hsiang, "and I will tell you about it. After two years in Antung I became first a sub-prefecture magistrate and then a sub-prefect in Szechuan, and only this year was I promoted to this office. What have you been doing at home since Mr. Tsui died?"

"I was an actor by profession, and when I came home I had nothing to do, so I have been making a living by training a small company."

"Who was the young man walking with you?"

"He is my son. I left him at the gate, not daring to bring him in."

"But why not?" asked Mr. Hsiang, and sent a man to invite Master Pao to come in. When a boy brought Ting-hsi in, his father told him to kowtow to Prefect Hsiang, and the prefect raised him up.

"How old are you?" he asked.

"I am seventeen, sir," replied Ting-hsi.

"He has all the air of a gentleman's son," said Mr. Hsiang, and told him to sit by his father. "Is your son following the same profession as you, Wen-ching?" he asked.

"No, I have not trained him for the stage. He has studied for two years and is now our accountant."

"That's good," said Mr. Hsiang. "Now I have to call on various superiors. Don't go away, but stay here to dinner. After I come back I shall have more to say to you."

He then changed his dress and was carried off in his chair.

Pao Wen-ching and his son went to the servants' quarters to see Old Wang, the steward who was in charge of the inner gate, whom Pao knew. They greeted each other, and Pao Wen-ching told his son to greet Wang too. Old Wang's son was already over thirty and had grown a moustache. The old man was so taken with Pao Ting-hsi that he gave him a red silk purse embroidered with gold thread which contained one tael of silver. And when Ting-hsi had thanked him, they sat down to talk until lunch.

Prefect Hsiang came back late in the afternoon. When he had taken off his official robes and sat down in the same room as before, he asked Pao Wen-ching and his son to come in.

"Tomorrow I have to go back to my yamen," he said. "So I shall not have time for a good talk with you."

He ordered the servant-boy to bring a package of silver from his room, and this he gave to Pao.

"Here are twenty taels of silver for you," he said. "After I have left, go home and get ready to leave your company in someone else's charge for the time being, so that you can come to my yamen with your son in a week or two. I have more to say to you."

Pao took the silver and thanked the prefect.

"I shall come with my son to pay our respects in less than a fortnight," he said. Then Prefect Hsiang kept him to a feast, after which Pao and his son went home to bed.

The next morning Pao went back to see Prefect Hsiang off, and on his return home he and his wife decided to leave the company in charge of his son-in-law Mr. Kuei and the tutor Mr. Chin. Pao then made ready all he needed for the trip, buying ribbons, soap and other Nanking specialities for the yamen servants.

A few days later he took a boat from West Water Gate. When they reached Chihkou, two new passengers came aboard and sat in the cabin with Pao and his son; and in the course of conversation Pao mentioned that he was going to Prefect Hsiang's yamen. Then the two men, who were clerks from Anching Prefecture, started making up to him, treating him and his son to wine and meat all the way.

One night when the other passengers were asleep, these clerks whispered to Pao: "If you can get Prefect Hsiang to approve a petition we have, we will give you two hundred taels. Then there's another case which is being sent up by the county yamen — if you can get the prefect to reject it, we'll give you another three hundred. Please put in a good word for us, Mr. Pao."

"I won't deceive you, gentlemen," said Pao. "I am an old actor — a low-class fellow. The prefect has condescended to send for me to go to his yamen; but who am I to mention such matters to him?"

"You think we're lying, Mr. Pao?" asked the clerks. "Just consent to plead for us, and we'll pay you the five hundred taels in advance, as soon as we land."

Pao Wen-ching laughed. "The prefect once offered me five hundred taels at Antung," he said. "If I were so fond of silver, I should not have declined it as I did. But I dared not accept it. I know that I'm destined to be poor and to live by the sweat of my brow. How can I take this money behind the prefect's back? Besides, if a man had right on his side, he would never try to bribe other people with several hundred taels; and if my request were heard it would be unfair to the other side — that would count against me when I settle my accounts in the next life. I don't dare do such a thing, and I hope you two gentlemen won't do anything of the kind either. The proverb says: The yamen is a good place to do good deeds. You are in the prefect's service and you mustn't spoil his reputation nor risk losing your own property and lives."

Such talk sent chills up the two clerks' spines, and they changed the subject to hide their discomfiture.

The next morning Pao and his son reached Anching and sent in their card at the gate of the prefect's house. Prefect Hsiang ordered their luggage to be put in the library where they were to stay. Every day Pao and his son ate at the same table as the prefect's relatives, and he presented them with several lengths of silk and cloth to make new inner and outer garments.

One day Prefect Hsiang sat down with Pao Wen-ching in the library.

"Is your son engaged?" he asked.

"I have not been able to afford it yet."

"I have a proposal, but I am afraid of offending you. If you agree, however, it will give me great pleasure."

"How dare I disobey your instructions, sir?"

"You know my chief steward, Wang. He has a daughter who is very clever and a great favourite with my wife, who keeps the girl with her and combs her hair and binds her feet herself. She is seventeen this year — the same age as your son. The Wangs have served my family for three generations and I have looked out his bond and given it back to him to show that I no longer consider him as a servant. I have also bought a clerk's post for his son, so that after five years he can become the district prison warden. If you have no objection, your son can marry into the Wang family; then he will have a brother-in-law who is in the official world. What do you say?"

"This is too kind of you, sir! I don't know how to express my gratitude! But my son is an ignorant boy: Mr. Wang may not want him as his son-in-law."

"I have spoken to him and he is very fond of the lad. The wedding won't cost you a cent: all you need do is write a card tomorrow and call on Wang. I shall be responsible for the bed-curtains, bedding, clothes, trinkets and feasts, and see that the young couple are properly married. All we ask of you is to be the father-in-law!"

Pao knelt down to thank him, but Prefect Hsiang raised him up with both hands.

"This is nothing," he said. "In future I must find a better way to repay your kindness."

The next day Pao Wen-ching took his card to call on Old Wang, and Old Wang returned the call.

At midnight an officer from the provincial government suddenly rode up, accompanied by the sub-prefect in a sedan-chair. Marching straight into the hall, they asked for Prefect Hsiang. The whole yamen was in a flurry.

"This looks bad!" they said. "He must have come to take away the prefect's seal!"

But to know whether Hsiang was demoted or not, you must read the following chapter.

CHAPTER 26

After receiving promotion, Prefect Hsiang
mourns for a friend. After his father's death,
Pao Ting-hsi marries a wife

When Prefect Hsiang heard that an official had arrived to take over his seals, he immediately summoned the secretaries in charge of punishments and finance.

"I want you gentlemen to check all the documents in your departments," he said. "Go through them very carefully. Be sure not to overlook anything."

Then he hurried out from his house to greet the sub-prefect. The latter showed him a document, whispered into his ear, then mounted his sedan-chair and went away, leaving his escort behind. When Prefect Hsiang went back inside, his relatives and Pao Wen-ching crowded round to question him.

"It is all right," said the prefect. "Nothing to do with me. The prefect of Ningkuo is in trouble, and I am to take over his seals."

Horses were prepared at once, and Prefect Hsiang set off with the escort that same night for Ningkuo

In the yamen they bought trinkets, prepared clothes, bed-curtains and bedding, re-papered the rooms and made all ready for the marriage of Old Wang's daughter. This kept them busy for several days, until Prefect Hsiang came back and chose the thirteenth of the tenth month for the wedding. On that day, drummers played outside the yamen as the two masters of ceremony ushered in the bridegroom. Pao Ting-hsi, a flower in his cap and a red sash over his shoulders, was wearing a satin gown and black shoes with white soles. When he had bowed to his father he walked over—to the accompaniment of music—to bow to his father-in-law and mother-in-law, while Young Wang came out in official robes to keep him company. And after tea had been served three times, he was taken into the bridal chamber for the wedding ceremony, which we need not describe in detail.

Early the next morning the young couple paid their respects to Prefect Hsiang and his wife, and Mrs. Hsiang presented them with eight more trinkets and two new costumes. The feasting lasted for three days, not a soul in the yamen being left out of the fun. When they had been married for a month, Young Wang had to leave for the capital to receive an appointment. Pao Wen-ching gave him a farewell feast, after which Pao Ting-hsi saw his brother-in-law to the boat and travelled with him for a whole day before returning. From now on, life in the yamen for Ting-hsi was perfect bliss.

Soon New Year passed, work was resumed, and candidates from the various counties came to take the prefectural examination.

"I have to go to the examination school to invigilate," Prefect Hsiang told Pao Wen-ching and his son. "If I take my servants as inspectors, there is bound to be cheating. But I trust you both completely—will you help out for a few days?"

Acting on the prefect's instructions, Pao Wen-ching and his son inspected the grounds of the examination school and searched each cell. There were three examinations at Anching. Some of the candidates had found substitutes, others slipped essays to each other. In fact, they were up to every conceivable trick: passing notes, throwing bricks, winking and making signs to one another. When soup dumplings were served, Ting-hsi was disgusted to see how they pushed and jostled for the food. One candidate, on the pretext that he must go to the latrine, slipped over to the mud wall which surrounded the school, knocked a hole in it, and put his arm through this hole to receive an essay from an accomplice. Ting-hsi, who caught him red-handed, wanted to hale him before Prefect Hsiang. But his father stopped him.

"My son is only an ignorant boy," he said to the student, "while you, sir, are a respectable scholar. Hurry back to your cell now to write your paper. If the prefect found you here, that would be awkward."

Having scooped up some soil to stop up the hole in the wall, he escorted the candidate back to his cell.

When the results of the examination were published, Chi Wei-hsiao of Huaining County was first on the list. His father, who had passed the military examination in the capital during the same year in which Prefect Hsiang passed the civil one, was now at home waiting to take up a post as a second captain. A few days after the results came out, Second Captain Chi called to express his thanks and Prefect Hsiang kept him to a feast in the library, asking Pao Wen-ching to accompany them. Chi took the seat of honour, Prefect Hsiang the place of host, and Pao Wen-ching a seat at the side.

"Everybody in the prefecture agrees, sir," said Chi, "that this examination was conducted most fairly and wisely."

"I have not corrected papers for a long time," replied Prefect Hsiang. "But thanks to my friend Pao's supervision in the examination school, there was no cheating this time."

This was the first time Chi had heard Pao's name mentioned, and as it emerged that Pao was an old actor the captain began to raise his eyebrows.

"The scholars of this generation are going from bad to worse," declared Prefect Hsiang. "If you talk to metropolitan graduates and academicians about studying the classics and continuing our best traditions, they will call you a pedantic visionary; while if you speak to them of understanding the new and gaining a wide knowledge of the old, they will accuse you of being a dilettante. They are loyal neither to their sovereign nor to their friends! In fact, they are inferior to my friend Pao here; for although his is a despised profession, he invariably conducts himself like a gentleman."

He described some of Pao Wen-ching's virtues, whereupon Second Captain Chi registered profound respect. When the feast ended, they parted.

330

Three or four days later the captain invited Pao Wen-ching to a meal at which Chi Wei-hsiao, who had come first in the examination, accompanied them. He was a handsome young man.

"May I ask the young gentleman's name?" said Pao Wen-ching.

"Wei-hsiao," replied the captain.

When Pao Wen-ching returned to the yamen he praised Chi Wei-hsiao's fine features to Prefect Hsiang, predicting that the young man had a great future before him.

Some months after this, Ting-hsi's young wife died in childbirth. Pao Wen-ching and his son wept as if their hearts would break.

"Don't grieve too bitterly," urged Prefect Hsiang. "She was destined to die. You mustn't take it so to heart. You're still young, Ting-hsi, and I promise to find another wife for you later. If you keep on weeping, you will upset my wife even more."

Then Pao Wen-ching also ordered his son to stop weeping; but he himself fell ill. He was troubled with phlegm, and fits of coughing often kept him awake half the night. He wanted to go home, but did not like to suggest this to Prefect Hsiang. As luck would have it, however, Prefect Hsiang was promoted to the post of intendant of Tingchang Circuit in Fukien.

"We must congratulate you on your new appointment, sir," said Pao Wen-ching. "I ought to accompany you to your new post, but I am growing old and my health is no longer good. I will respectfully bid you farewell, sir, and go back to Nanking, leaving my son to attend you."

"It is a long, difficult journey to Fukien, my friend," said the new intendant, "and you are old. I had no intention of asking you to go. But you must keep your son to look after you—why should I take him? I have to go to the capital for audience with the emperor, so I will see you off to Nanking first. Leave it to me."

The following day he sealed up a thousand taels of silver and had a servant carry this package to the library.

"You have been with me for more than a year now, Wen-ching," said Intendant Hsiang, "and not once have you asked the slightest favour. I feel very much upset too because the daughter-in-law I found for you died. I want you to take this thousand taels home to buy some property and find another wife for your son, so that you can spend your last years in comfort. If I pass Nanking again after my next appointment, I shall have a chance to see you once more."

But Pao Wen-ching refused the silver.

"Things have changed now," said Intendant Hsiang. "As head of a circuit I can easily spare a thousand taels. If you won't accept them, I shall feel very much offended."

Then Pao Wen-ching dared no longer refuse, but kowtowed to express his thanks. Intendant Hsiang ordered a large boat for him and entertained him to a farewell feast before seeing him off in person. Pao Wen-ching and his son knelt down with tears in their eyes to say goodbye. And Intendant Hsiang's cheeks were wet, too, at parting.

Father and son travelled back with their silver to Nanking; and when they told Mrs. Pao of the Intendant's kindness, the whole family was overwhelmed with gratitude. Then, sick as he was, Pao Wen-ching went out to buy a house and two sets of theatrical costumes which he hired out to two companies. What remained of the money was spent on household needs.

Some months later, Pao Wen-ching's illness grew worse and he had to take to his bed. When he knew that his end was near, he called his wife, son, daughter and son-in-law to his bedside.

"I want you to live in harmony as a happy family," he told them. "And don't wait until the mourning is over to find a wife for Ting-hsi—this is important."

Then he closed his eyes and died. The whole family started weeping bitterly as they prepared for the funeral. They set the coffin in the middle of the room and held a wake for several days, while the actors from the four guild centres came to mourn. Ting-hsi asked a diviner to find a suitable site for the grave and to choose a day for the burial; but there was no one to write an inscription for the pall. He was in a quandary when a man in black rushed in.

"Is this Mr. Pao's house?" he asked.

"Yes," said Ting-hsi. "Where are you from?"

"Intendant Hsiang of the Tingchang Circuit in Fukien is here," replied the other. "His sedan-chair is already at your gate."

Ting-hsi hastily changed from mourning to ordinary clothes, and knelt outside the gate to receive the intendant.

When Hsiang alighted from his chair and saw the gate draped in white, he asked: "Is your father dead?"

"Yes, sir," answered Ting-hsi, in tears.

"When did he pass away?"

"Four weeks ago tomorrow."

"On my return from court I happened to be passing this way, so I decided to call on your father, little thinking that he was already no more. Take me to his coffin."

Weeping as he knelt there, Pao Ting-hsi declined this honour. But Intendant Hsiang would not listen to him and went in to where the coffin stood.

"Wen-ching, my old friend!" he cried.

After weeping bitterly, he presented a stick of incense and bowed four times. Mrs. Pao also came out to thank him.

Back in the hall, Intendant Hsiang asked: "When is your father to be buried?"

"On the eighth of next month," replied Ting-hsi.

"Who has written the inscription?"

"I have consulted several people, but they all say the phrasing presents difficulties."

"What difficulties? Bring me paper and a brush."

Ting-hsi immediately fetched writing materials, and Intendant Hsiang picked up the brush and wrote:

> The coffin of Pao Wen-ching, a good citizen of the Ming Dynasty, aged fifty-nine. This inscription is respectfully inscribed by his old friend Hsiang Ting, metropolitan graduate of the second class, knight of the fourth rank and intendant of Tingchang Circuit in Fukien.

"Take this to the funeral shop to have it mounted," he said when he had finished writing. "My boat is leaving tomorrow morning, but I have a little contribution to make to the funeral which I will send over this evening."

After drinking a cup of tea, he mounted his sedan-chair and Ting-hsi followed him to the boat where he kowtowed before returning home. That evening Intendant Hsiang sent a steward with a hundred taels of silver to the Pao family. The steward would not even wait for tea, but hurried straight back to the boat.

On the eighth of the next month the pall with the inscription was ready. Music was played and paper emblems carried in procession as monks, Taoist priests and dirge-singers saw Pao Wen-ching to his last resting place outside the South Gate. All the actors in the city attended the funeral, the mourners filling several dozen tables in a restaurant outside the South Gate. And so Pao Wen-ching was buried.

One day, more than half a year later, Chin Tzu-fu called and asked to speak to Mrs. Pao. Ting-hsi invited him to take a seat in the hall while he went in to tell his mother. And presently Mrs. Pao appeared.

"We haven't seen you for a long time, Mr. Chin," she said. "What wind has blown you here today?"

"Yes," said Chin. "I haven't called on you for a long time, ma'am. You are doing pretty well. You rent your costumes to a different company now, don't you?"

"Those other companies only performed in town and didn't have many engagements," replied the old lady. "That's why we're renting our costumes now to Literary Fount Company. Half the players used to be our apprentices, and they tour the Hsuyi and Tienchang Districts where there are plenty of rich folk and country gentry. That's why they're not doing badly."

"In that case, your family must be making more money than ever."

Just then tea was served.

"I've come today to propose a match for Ting-hsi," went on Chin Tzu-fu after the tea had been drunk. "If this marriage takes place, you'll find yourselves even richer."

"What family does the girl belong to?"

"The Hu family at Inner Bridge. Her father used to work in the finance commissioner's yamen and he married her to Wang San-pang who kept the Peace and Prosperity Pawnshop, but in less than a year Wang San-pang died. The girl is only just twenty-one and very good-looking—as pretty as a picture! Because she's still young and has no children, her family want her to marry again. This Wang San-pang left her a houseful of stuff: one big bed, one summer bed, four chests and four cupboards. The chests are so crammed with clothes that you can't get your hand into them. And on top of all that she has two or three gold bracelets, two pure gold tiaras, and more pearls and jewels than you can count. There are two maids, as well, who'll go with her: Ho-hua and Tsai-lien. She and Ting-hsi are the right age for each other and would make a handsome couple. It would be a fine match."

Mrs. Pao was delighted.

"Thank you, Mr. Chin!" she said. "I'll ask my son-in-law to make inquiries. And if everything's as you've said, I'll trouble you to be the go-between."

"There's no need to make inquiries," protested Chin. "But do so if you want to. I'll come back later for your answer."

Pao Ting-hsi saw him out.

That evening when Mrs. Pao's son-in-law Kuei came back, she told him all she had heard, and asked him to make further inquiries. And Kuei asked her for a few dozen coins so that he could go to a tea-shop the following morning.

The next day Kuei called on a match-maker, Shen Tien-fu, whose wife—the well-known Big Foot Shen—was a go-between too. He took Shen Tien-fu out to a tea-house to sound him out about this match.

"What!" cried Shen Tien-fu. "Do you mean Spitfire Hu? That's a long story. Buy a few cakes first, and I'll tell you when I've eaten."

Kuei went next door to buy eight cakes which he divided with the match-maker. Then he asked:

"Well, what's her story?"

"Wait till I've finished eating," said Shen.

When he had finished the cakes, he demanded: "Why do you ask about her? Surely nobody is thinking of marrying her, is he? The woman is quite impossible. Any man who marries her will be taking a fury into his house."

"What do you mean?"

"She's the daughter of Slant-necked Hu, who worked for the finance commissioner. After her father died, she lived with her brother; but he was no good—he gambled and drank and sold his post in the finance commissioner's yamen. Because she wasn't bad-looking, he sold her when she was seventeen as a concubine to Mr. Lai of North Gate Bridge. She wasn't content to be a concubine, though. When people called her 'Concubine' she swore at them and insisted on being called 'Madam.' And when Mrs. Lai knew this, she slapped her face and drove her away. Later on she married Wang San-pang, who was waiting to be appointed to the post of assistant magistrate. She was a real wife this time, but she went too far. She cursed the stupid elder son and his wife three or four times a day, and kept beating the servants and slave girls every few hours. They all hated her like poison.

"Then, in less than a year, Wang San-pang died. Her stepson suspected that she'd helped herself to all his father's valuables, so he went into her room to search; and all the servants and maids joined in, hoping to get their own back. But, expecting something of the sort, she'd hidden a whole casket of gold, pearls and jewels in her chamber-pot; so they ransacked her room in vain. They searched her, too, but couldn't find any money on her. And she made that an excuse to go screaming and sobbing to Shangyuan County Court, where she brought a charge against her stepson.

"When the case was called, the magistrate gave her stepson a good dressing-down, then said to her: 'You've already married twice: why should you remain a widow? Since it doesn't look as if you and your stepson can live in the same house, you had better ask him to give you a share of the property and move out. It's up to you whether you marry again or not.' She moved into one of Wang's houses in Rouge Lane, and she has such a reputation that nobody dares cross her. All this happened seven or eight years ago, which means she must be twenty-five at the very least; but she claims to be twenty-one."

"Is it true that she has a thousand taels of silver?"

"She must have spent it during these years," replied Shen. "But her gold, pearls and jewels, with her silks and brocades, must be worth five or six hundred taels. That she has."

"If she has five or six hundred taels," thought Kuei, "my mother-in-law will be satisfied. And if she's a shrew, so much the worse for my precious brother-in-law!"

So he said: "It's my father-in-law's adopted son who wants to marry her, Mr. Shen. The match was proposed by Chin Tzu-fu, who used to teach the young actors for them. Never mind about her being a spitfire. If you can fix this up for us, of course she'll pay the go-between handsomely. Why not do it?"

"That's not difficult," said Shen. "I'll go home and tell my wife to call on her, and I guarantee we can bring it off. But your side will have to pay the go-between."

"Very well," replied Kuei. "I must be off now. I'll come back later for her answer."

He paid the bill, and they left the tea-shop to go their different ways.

When Shen Tien-fu went home and told his wife about this, Big Foot shook her head.

"Heavens!" she exclaimed. "That woman is hard to please! She wants a husband who's rich, handsome *and* an official; and there mustn't be any mother-in-law, father-in-law, brothers-in-law or sisters-in-law. She never gets up before noon or lifts a finger in the house. Every day she takes eight silver cents' worth of medicine, and she won't eat meat, but insists on duck one day, fish the next, and soup made of water-cress and fresh bamboo shoots on the third, while in between she must have orange comfits, dragons' eyes and lotus seeds to nibble at. She's a big drinker too. Every evening she drinks three catties of sweet wine with fried sparrows and sea-shrimps. When she goes to bed, those two maids of hers have to take it in turn to massage her legs till nearly midnight before she will sleep. You said just now that it was a man in the theatrical business who wants her; but can any theatre man support her in such style?"

"Spin her a yarn!" suggested Shen Tien-fu.

"Well," said Big Foot, "I can hide the fact that he's in the theatre, and I needn't tell her that they hire out costumes. I'll say that he's passed the provincial examinations and should become an official any day now, and that his family keeps a big shop and owns a good deal of land. How about that?"

"Very good!" agreed Shen. "Very good! That's the way to talk to her!"

When Big Foot had finished her meal, she went to Rouge Lane and knocked at Mrs. Wang's door. Ho-hua opened it.

"Where are you from?" she asked.

"Does Mrs. Wang live here?"

"Yes. What's your business?"

"I've come to propose a match to her."

"Please take a seat in the hall. Our mistress has only just got up, and hasn't finished dressing yet."

"Why should I sit in the hall? I'll go inside to see her." So saying, the go-between lifted the curtain and walked in.

Mrs. Wang was sitting on the edge of the bed binding her feet, while Tsai-lien held a box of alum for her. Knowing that Big Foot was a match-maker, Mrs. Wang asked her to sit down and ordered tea for her. She spent the time it would take for three meals to finish binding her feet, then combed her hair, washed her face and put on her clothes so slowly that the sun was nearly sinking before she was dressed.

"What is your name?" she asked, when at last she was ready. "What brings you here?"

"My name is Shen," answered Big Foot. "I've come to propose a match, so that I can drink at your wedding."

"What family?"

"The Pao family is on the main road by West Water Gate. Everyone calls it Provincial Graduate Pao's family. They have a large estate and keep a big shop. They must be worth millions of strings of cash. Mr. Pao is twenty-three, and has no parents, no brothers, no children. For some time now he's been asking me to find him a good wife, but I couldn't think of anyone suitable except yourself. That is why I've made bold to call on you, ma'am."

"What is this provincial graduate's position in the family?"

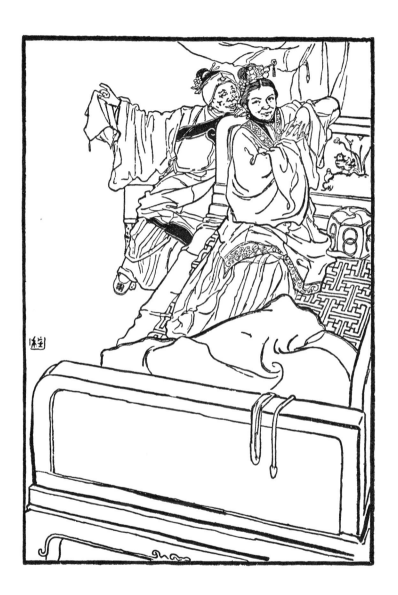

"He is the gentleman who wants to marry. There's only the one graduate in the family!"

"Did he pass the civil examination or the military one?"

"The military," replied Big Foot. "He can draw a bow weighing a hundred catties, and lift a three-hundred-catty weight. He's a very powerful man."

"You must know, my good woman," said Mrs. Wang, "that I've moved in the best circles. I'm not just anybody. A month after I married Mr. Wang, his elder daughter's wedding took place. She married a country gentleman named Sun, whose family had three large halls. They had lit a hundred candles and set out peck measures and fairies made of sugar, and they gave a magnificent feast and entertainment. The musicians played softly as I was welcomed in by old Mrs. Sun, who had on a phoenix head-dress and a gown of patterned brocade. They gave me the seat of honour at the highest table. I was wearing a veil of pearls as big as peas which covered my face completely, and I had one maid on each side of me who parted the pearls before I could sip their sweetened tea. The feast went on all night, with one opera after another. The next day when I went home, the four servants with me made a spot on the white silk skirt embroidered with gold that I was wearing, and I wanted to have them all put to death. Even when the four of them came to my room and knelt down to thump their heads on the ground, I wouldn't let them off. If you're not telling the whole truth about this match—if you've deceived me in the least little thing—you're going to be sorry for it!"

"Of course!" cried Big Foot. "I always stick strictly to the truth: I've not got the usual match-maker's mouth. If you find out that I've said one word that isn't true, I'll come and ask you to slap my cheeks."

"Are you sure?" demanded Mrs. Wang. "All right. You can tell the Pao family that I'm willing. I'll be waiting to hear from you."

She wrapped up several dozen coins, some dates and some cakes, and told Big Foot to take these home for her children.

But to know whether the marriage took place or not, you must read the next chapter.

CHAPTER 27

In which Mrs. Wang quarrels with her husband, and Ni Ting-chu finds his brother

Big Foot went home to report that Mrs. Wang was willing, and Shen Tien-fu announced this to Kuei when he arrived the next morning for news.

"My wife went over and had a long talk with her," said Shen. "The woman's more than willing. But we told her she'd have no father-in-law or mother-in-law, so don't let Mrs. Pao take the betrothal presents herself. If you bring four trinkets tomorrow, I'll send my wife across with them; then as soon as a day has been chosen, the bride can be carried over."

Kuei went back to his mother-in-law.

"It's a fact that the widow has several hundred taels of silver," he told her. "But she's something of a shrew, and may bully her husband. Still, that's their affair. It needn't worry us."

"It needn't worry us," agreed Mrs. Pao. "He's got so above himself that he needs a scold to keep him in his place."

Having decided in favour of the match, she sent for Pao Ting-hsi and told him to ask Shen Tien-fu and Chin Tzu-fu to be his go-betweens.

"People of modest means like ourselves should find a bride from a poor family," said Ting-hsi. "A woman like this is likely to make trouble."

"You poor, good-for-nothing fool!" jeered his foster-mother. "Anyone can see you were a pauper's brat, the way your mind runs on poverty! You'll die of poverty yet! All those chests and cases of hers will make a fine show when you've married her. What do *you* know, you fool?"

Ting-hsi dared say no more, but asked Kuei to go with him to call on the go-betweens.

"After all your kindness, mother, not a word of thanks do you get!" declared Kuei. "If he's going to be so difficult, I'm blowed if I'll help him!"

Mrs. Pao reasoned with him.

"Ting-hsi doesn't know any better," she concluded. "Don't let what he says annoy you."

Then Kuei agreed to go with him.

The next day they invited the go-betweens to a feast; but because Ting-hsi had to go out with his company, Kuei helped entertain the guests for him. Mrs. Pao produced four gold and four silver trinkets which had belonged to Ting-hsi's first wife, and gave them to Shen Tien-fu as betrothal presents. Shen pocketed half of them for himself, giving four to Big Foot to take to Mrs. Wang; and when the widow had accepted them, the wedding was fixed for the thirteenth of the tenth month. On the twelfth her four chests, four wardrobes and two double beds were carried over with her basins, buckets and pewter ware. Her two maids came over by sedan-chair with the furniture, and when they saw Mrs. Pao they wondered who she could be, but did not like to ask. After setting the room in order, they sat down to wait.

The next morning Kuei's wife arrived by sedan-chair, and Mrs. Pao asked Chin Tzu-fu's wife and Pock-marked Chien's wife to escort the bride to the house. Towards evening the bridal chair arrived, with four pairs of lanterns and torches. The bride and groom went to the marriage chamber, recited the usual phrases, bowed before the decorated candles, drank wine together, and all the rest of it.

At the fifth watch, when it was time for the bride to pay her respects to her husband's ancestors, she was furious to learn that she had a mother-in-law. She kowtowed sullenly a few times, without offering tea or shoes,[1] then went straight back to her room. Her maids kept coming out to demand rain water for their mistress's tea and charcoal for her incense, or to ask the cook to make dumplings or soup for her. They bustled in and out non-stop, and it was "Our mistress this," and "Our mistress that" all the time.

"*I'm* the mistress here!" declared Mrs. Pao. "She's not even the young mistress. Call her the young wife."

When the maids reported this, the bride nearly burst with rage.

The third day after the wedding the Pao family invited a number of actors' wives in. The custom in Nanking is for all brides to invite good luck by going to the kitchen on the third day and cooking a fish, which stands for fortune. Now the fish had been bought and the fire was ready, but when they asked the young wife to start cooking she refused to budge.

"This won't do!" cried Pock-marked Chien's wife, bustling in. "Now that you're the daughter-in-law here, you must do what's expected of you."

Then Ting-hsi's wife sulkily took off her brocade gown, put on an apron, and went to the kitchen. She scraped the fish three or four times with a knife, picked it up by the tail, and flung it into the boiling pan. Pock-marked Chien's wife, who was standing by the stove watching, had her face spattered with hot water and her gold-embroidered brocade jacket soaked.

"Look out!" she called angrily, jumping with fright, then hastily mopped her face with a handkerchief.

Ting-hsi's wife threw down her knife, and flounced scowling back to her room. And that evening, when the guests took their places for the feast, she refused to join them.

The following evening, Ting-hsi came into the bedroom to change his clothes before going out with his company. Because he had worn a tile-shaped cap instead of the gauze official hat all these days, his wife suspected that he was not a provincial scholar after all.

---

[1] It was the custom for a bride to present tea-leaves and shoes which she had made herself to her father and mother-in-law as her first gift to them.

"Where are you going so late?" she asked as he put his cap on.

"Out on business," replied Ting-hsi, and left.

"What business can that be?" wondered his wife. "Perhaps he has to go through the accounts at that shop of his."

He was not back till dawn.

"Why did you have to stay all night in your shop?" she asked.

"What shop?" demanded Ting-hsi. "I'm in charge of a theatre company. We've just come back after giving an all-night performance."

This was the last straw. His wife nearly choked with rage. Falling backward with a scream, she clenched her teeth and lost consciousness. Ting-hsi hastily ordered the maids to revive her with ginger water; but when she came to she sobbed and screamed, rolled on the ground and tore her hair. Then, wailing loudly, she tried to climb on the wooden roof of the bed, and began to sing snatches of opera. Rage and disappointment had made her mad! When Mrs. Pao and her daughter ran fearfully in, they did not know whether to laugh or to cry.

"This is the result of phlegm in her digestive tract," pronounced the doctor whom they called in. "Her constitution is weak. She must take ginseng and amber."

Each dose of medicine cost five silver cents, and she was ill for two years, by the end of which all her clothes and trinkets and even her two maids had been sold. Then Kuei and his wife made a proposal to Mrs. Pao.

"He's only an adopted son, who's never been any good," they said. "And he's leading us a fine life with this mad wife of his. If things go on like this, our house and capital won't be enough to buy her ginseng and amber! What shall we do then? We'd better turn him out now, and disown him. Once we're clear of him, we can live comfortably on our own."

When Mrs. Pao agreed and told Ting-hsi he and his wife must go, the young man was appalled and persuaded their neighbours, Wang Yu-chiu and Chang Kuo-chung, to speak for him.

343

"You can't do this, Mrs. Pao!" they said. "Your old man adopted him, and he's helped in the business all these years. How can you turn him out?"

Mrs. Pao immediately launched into a description of Ting-hsi's unfilial conduct and his wife's wicked ways.

"I can't abide him, and that's that," she declared. "If he stays, then we go!"

"If you must drive him out," said the two neighbours when they found they could not talk her round, "at least give him some money so that he can start a business. How are they to live if you send them away empty-handed?"

"He *came* here empty-handed, with nothing but a few mangy hairs on his head!" she retorted. "I've fed and clothed him all these years, and got him two wives. Goodness knows how much we spent on that wretched father of his too! I'm not asking him to pay me back, but he's not going to get any more out of me."

"Still, you can afford to be generous," said the neighbours. "You ought to do something for him, Mrs. Pao."

They kept on at her till she had to promise her foster-son twenty taels if he would move out. Ting-hsi shed tears as he took the money, and a few days later moved into a room Wang Yu-chiu had cleared for him behind his shop. Twenty taels was too little to form another company of players, and he did not know how to start any other business; so they gradually ate their way through their silver. When it was nearly gone, Ting-hsi's wife had to give up taking ginseng and amber; whereupon she grew well enough to sit at home snivelling and scolding. So things went on for some time.

One day when Ting-hsi came back from a stroll Wang Yu-chiu hailed him.

"Did you ever have a brother in Soochow?" he asked.

"I'm an only son," replied Ting-hsi. "I have no brothers."

"I'm not talking about the Pao family. I mean the Ni family at the Three Arches."

"Yes, I had several elder brothers; but I was told my father sold them all when they were young, and what became of them I don't know. I never heard of one in Soochow."

"Just now somebody was making inquiries all down the street. He told Mrs. Pao next door: 'Mr. Ni is looking for his sixth brother.' When Mrs. Pao didn't say anything, he came here. And I thought it might be you he was looking for. Were you the sixth in your family?"

"Yes, I was."

"When he couldn't find you, the fellow went further on. He's sure to come back this way. Why don't you wait for him in my shop?"

Very soon the stranger returned.

"This is Mr. Ni," Wang Yu-chiu told him. "What is your business with him?"

"Where are you from?" asked Ting-hsi. "Who is looking for me?"

The stranger produced a red card from his girdle and gave it to Ting-hsi, who read:

> The adopted son of Pao Wen-ching of West Water Gate. Pao Ting-hsi, who used to be called Ni Ting-hsi and was the sixth son of Ni Shuang-feng, is my brother. I am Ni Ting-chu. If my brother can be found, bring him to the government hostel to see me. This is urgent!

"That's right!" exclaimed Ting-hsi. "No mistake about it! Who are you?"

"My name is Ah-san. I work for your brother."

"Where is he now?"

"He's an official in the provincial governor's yamen at Soochow, with a salary of a thousand taels of silver a year. He's in the government hostel here now. If you are his sixth brother, sir, please come with me."

This was a stroke of luck! Ting-hsi went with Ah-san to the hostel at Huaiching Bridge.

"Would you mind waiting, sir, in the tea-shop on the bank," suggested Ah-san, "while I go to fetch my master?"

Ting-hsi sat there until Ah-san came back with another man wearing a square cap, dark brown silk gown, and black shoes with white soles. He had a short beard and looked about fifty. As he entered the tea-house, Ah-san pointed Ting-hsi out. and the latter made haste to greet him.

"So you are my sixth brother!" exclaimed the stranger, catching hold of him.

"Elder brother!" cried Ting-hsi.

They embraced and sobbed bitterly for a time, then sat down.

"Brother," said Ni Ting-chu, "I was in Peking when you were adopted by the Pao family, so I knew nothing whatever about it. After I was twenty I learned how to be a secretary, and I've worked in a number of yamens. Whichever province I was in, I looked for my brothers, but I never found them. Five years ago, on my way to Kwangtung with a magistrate, I learned from an old neighbour at the Three Arches that you had been adopted by the Pao family and that both our parents were dead!"

At this he broke down again.

"The Pao family..." began Ting-hsi.

"Wait till I've finished, brother!" Ni Ting-chu cut him short. "These last few years I've been lucky to be with Governor Chi, who treats me very well and pays me a thousand taels of silver a year. We were in Shantung for some time, and this year he was transferred to Soochow as provincial governor. Since this is my home province, I hurried here to look for you. I mean to use my savings to buy a house in Nanking, and move my wife down from Peking so that we can all live together. I take it you have married too?"

"Yes, brother," said Ting-hsi, and proceeded to describe how he had been adopted, how good Mr. Pao had been to him, how the wife he had married in Prefect Hsiang's yamen had died, how he had married again and been turned away by Mrs. Pao.

"Never mind," said Ni Ting-chu. "Where is your wife now?"

"We've borrowed a room from one of Mr. Pao's neighbours for the time being."

"I'll go back with you to see her before we make further plans."

Having paid for the tea, they went back together to Wang Yu-chiu's shop; and when Wang had greeted them Ting-hsi took his brother in to meet his wife, who was dressed like any housewife now all her fine clothes and jewels were gone. Ni

Ting-chu took from his purse four taels of silver, and gave them to her as his present on meeting. At the sight of such a respectable relative her spirits rose, and she brought in tea herself, which Ting-hsi handed to his brother.

"I must go back to the hostel for a while," said Ni Ting-chu after one cup of tea. "But I'll be back very soon to have a good talk with you. Don't go out."

When he had gone, Ting-hsi consulted with his wife.

"We must have a good meal ready for my brother when he comes back," he said. "Let's buy a duck, a few catties of meat and a fish, and ask Mr. Wang to prepare four dishes for us."

"Bah! You blockhead!" sneered his wife. "Do you think someone living in the provincial governor's yamen will be impressed by duck and pork? He'll come *after* his meal, of course. He's not interested in your food! No, hurry up and weigh out thirty-six cents of silver to buy sixteen dishes of sweetmeats and a few bottles of good, sweet wine. That's the way to do it!"

"You are right, my dear," agreed Ting-hsi.

He weighed out the silver, bought wine and dishes, and carried them home.

That evening a sedan-chair arrived, preceded by two lanterns bearing the inscription of the provincial governor's yamen and followed by Ah-san. His brother was back!

"I haven't much money with me here," said Ni Ting-chu, when he had alighted and come in. "I've only brought about seventy taels for you."

Ah-san carried this silver packet by packet from the sedan-chair, and gave it to Ting-hsi.

"Take it, brother," said Ni Ting-chu. "Tomorrow I have to go back to Soochow with Governor Chi. I want you to find me a house as fast as you can — anything from two to three hundred taels will do. And when you and your wife have moved in, pack up and come to Soochow. I'll ask Governor Chi to give you my whole salary for this year to bring back to Nanking as capital for a business or to buy some property which will bring in rents."

Ting-hsi accepted the silver, and offered his brother wine. While drinking they spoke of all the unhappiness they had known since their family broke up, and were moved to tears. Not till the second watch did Ni Ting-chu leave.

The next day Ting-hsi asked Wang Yu-chiu to call a house agent to find him a house. Then all the neighbours knew that Mr. Ni who worked in the provincial governor's yamen had come to see his brother; and they started calling Ting-hsi Mr. Ni instead of Mr. Pao, and addressing his wife too with respect. In half a month's time the agent found a suitable house in Shih Family Lane near Floating Bridge. It had three front rooms and four courtyards; and the owner, Censor Shih, being away from home, was willing to lease it for two hundred and twenty taels. Having agreed to this price, Ting-hsi paid twenty taels down, then chose a day to move in. On that day all the neighbours brought congratulatory gifts, even Kuei contributing his share, so anxious was he now to keep in with them. Ting-hsi invited guests for two days, and redeemed some of his wife's clothes and trinkets which had been pawned. As for her, she began to feel unwell again. Every few days she would send for the doctor and take eight cents' worth of medicine. So the seventy taels gradually melted away.

Then Ting-hsi packed up and took a boat to Soochow to join his brother; but the wind was against them, and the boat had to moor by the north shore. On the second day they reached Yicheng and stopped at Yellow Mud Bank, for the high wind made crossing the river out of the question. Going ashore for a snack, Ting-hsi met a young man in a square cap, jade-coloured gown and crimson shoes, who looked him over from head to foot.

"Aren't you my Uncle Pao?" asked this youth.

"My name is Pao," admitted Ting-hsi, much surprised. "May I ask your name? Why do you call me uncle?"

"Didn't you marry Mr. Wang's daughter in Prefect Hsiang's yamen at Anching?"

"Yes. How did you know?"

"I married Mr. Wang's granddaughter. Doesn't that make you my uncle?"

"I can't have you calling me uncle," replied Ting-hsi with a smile. "Come and drink some tea with me."

348

Entering a tea-house, they ordered tea and a plate of Yicheng dumplings.

"What is your name, sir?" asked Ting-hsi.

"My name is Chi. Don't you remember me, uncle? When I took the district examination, I saw you invigilating. That's how I knew you. Later your father came to dine with us. Have you forgotten?"

"So you are Captain Chi's son!" exclaimed Ting-hsi. "How did you come to marry Mr. Wang's granddaughter?"

"After Prefect Hsiang's promotion, Mr. Wang stayed behind in Anching," replied Chi Wei-hsiao. "And when my father-in-law was appointed a warden, all the local gentry took him up out of respect for his father. So my family arranged this marriage."

"Very good," said Ting-hsi. "Is your respected father well?"

"He died three years ago."

"What brings you here?"

"Inspector Hsun of the Salt Gabelle is a classmate of my father's, so I am going to call on him. Where are you off to, uncle?"

"I am on my way to Soochow to visit a relative."

"When will you come back?"

"In twenty days or thereabout, I expect."

"If you have nothing better to do when you return, do come to Yangchow, uncle. You'll find my address on the college list, and I'll be your host there."

"I will certainly come," promised Ting-hsi.

Then they parted, Ting-hsi taking the boat to Soochow. And no sooner did he go ashore at the West Gate than he bumped into his brother's man, Ah-san.

But to know what Ah-san said to him, you must read the next chapter.

CHAPTER 28

Chi Wei-hsiao takes a second wife in Yangchow.
Hsiao Chin-hsuan compiles a book in Nanking

At the West Gate Ting-hsi met his brother's servant, Ah-san, followed by a man carrying sacrificial offerings, silver paper coins and paper horses suspended from a pole over his shoulder.

"Is Mr. Ni in the yamen, Ah-san?" asked Ting-hsi. "Where are you taking these things to?"

"So you are here, sir!" exclaimed Ah-san. "When my master came back to the governor's yamen from Nanking, he sent someone to Peking to fetch the mistress. The man returned with the news that she had died the month before, and my master was so upset that he fell very ill, and in a few days he breathed his last. His coffin is outside the city, and I've put up at an inn for the time being. Today is the first seventh day since he left us, so I'm taking these things to sacrifice at his grave."

Ting-hsi's eyes nearly started from his head, and for a moment he was speechless.

"What!" he demanded at last. "Is your master dead?"

"Yes, sir. He has passed away."

Ting-hsi fell weeping to the ground, and Ah-san had to help him up. Instead of going into the city, he went to where his brother's coffin had been interred, placed the sacrificial food before it, poured a libation of wine, and burnt the paper money.

"Your spirit cannot have gone far, brother," he sobbed. "I came just too late to see you once more!"

He wept bitterly, till Ah-san prevailed on him to go back to his inn for the night.

The next day Ting-hsi bought more offerings and paper coins with his travelling money, and went back to his brother's grave. On his return he stayed for several days in the inn, until all his money was spent and Ah-san had moved elsewhere. Then for about a tael of silver he pawned the new silk gown he had made for his visit to the yamen, and decided to look up Chi Wei-hsiao before doing anything else. Having taken a boat to Yangchow and discovered from the college list that Chi was staying in the Temple of Religious Renewal, he made his way there immediately.

"Mr. Chi?" said the monk. "He's marrying into the Yiu family today, next door to the salt company in Five Cities Lane. You'll find him there."

Ting-hsi went straight to this house. The gate was hung with coloured streamers, and one of the three great halls was filled with guests. Between two red candles burning on the central desk hung a painting of a hundred children, flanked by a vermilion couplet:

May soft breeze and brilliant moon remain unchanged;
For a brilliant scholar is matched with a beautiful girl!

Chi Wei-hsiao, in a new square cap and scarlet gown, was entertaining guests. He stood up in surprise to greet Ting-hsi, and invited him to be seated.

"Have you just come back from Soochow, uncle?" he asked.

"Yes," said Ting-hsi. "And when I heard you were getting married, I came to drink at your wedding."

"What 's this gentleman's honourable name?" asked the guests.

"This is my wife's uncle, Mr. Pao," replied Chi.

"So he is your uncle! We are delighted to meet him."

"Will you introduce these gentlemen?" asked Ting-hsi.

"These are Mr. Hsin Tung-chih and Mr. Chin Yu-liu," said Chi, indicating the two men in the seats of honour. "They are well-known Yangchow scholars. There have never been any poets to equal them, and their calligraphy is quite unrivalled. It would be hard to find a third to match them in the whole world."

Just then dinner was served. The two poets sat in the places of honour, Ting-hsi next to them, and the other guests, who were relatives of the Yiu family, filled up the rest of the table. After dinner, while the relatives and Chi Wei-hsiao went into an inner room to prepare for the wedding, Ting-hsi chatted with the two scholars.

"These rich Yangchow salt merchants are a contemptible lot!" declared Mr. Hsin. "Take the case of that fellow Feng from down river, who has literally hundreds of thousands of taels. Since he asked me here from Hueichow, when I had been here half a year I said to him: 'If you want to show your appreciation, you might give me two or three thousand taels.' But not a cent would he part with! Later I told people: 'Mr. Feng really ought to give me that silver. He won't be able to take those hundreds of thousands of taels with him when he dies, and will be a poor ghost like any other. But when the King of Hell builds his palace and wants a tablet for it, he's bound to ask me to write the inscription, and he'll pay me ten thousand taels at the very least. Then there's no telling but what I may give a few thousand to Feng. Why should he be such a miser?'"

They all laughed.

"You are absolutely right!" agreed Mr. Chin. "Not long ago Mr. Fang from down river asked me to write a couplet for him — twenty-two characters altogether. When he sent a servant over with eighty taels to thank me, I called the fellow in. 'Go back and tell your master that a price was fixed for Mr. Chin's calligraphy in the prince's palace in Peking,' I said. 'Small characters cost a tael apiece, and big ones ten taels., At this standard rate, these twenty-two characters are worth two hundred and twenty taels. You can't have them for a cent less!'

"After the man delivered this message, that swine Fang, to show that he had money, called in his sedan-chair to pay me two hundred and twenty taels. But when I gave him the scrolls, he simply t-t-tore them up! I flew into such a rage, I broke open his packets of silver and threw the money in the street for salt-carriers and dung-carters to pick up! I ask you, gentlemen, aren't scoundrels like that beneath contempt?"

Just then Chi Wei-hsiao came back. Noodles were served, and the four of them sat down to table.

"I've heard that when rich officials from the Salt Gabelle go to a noodles shop," said Ting-hsi, "they simply sip a mouthful of soup from an eight-cent bowl of noodles, and give the rest to their chair-bearers. Is that true?"

"Quite true," said Mr. Hsin.

"It's a put up show," declared Mr. Chin. "They fill up at home on rice from the bottom of the pan before going to the noodles shop!"

They chatted and joked till evening, when music sounded and Chi Wei-hsiao was led to the bridal chamber. After feasting the guests left, Ting-hsi going to the inn by the customs house for the night. The next day he came to offer congratulations and see the bride, then sat down in the hall.

"Nothing has happened to your first wife to my knowledge," he whispered to Chi Wei-hsiao. "Why have you married again?"

Chi pointed to the couplet.

"A brilliant scholar and a beautiful girl!" he said. "To romantics like myself, as long as an ideal couple can meet, one wife more or less makes no difference!"

"I see," said Ting-hsi. "Where did you get the money for this?"

"As soon as I came to Yangchow, Inspector Hsun gave me a hundred and twenty taels, and put me in charge of the customs duties. I shall probably be here for some years, so I've taken another wife. When are you going back to Nanking, uncle?"

"Well, the fact is, nephew, I couldn't find the relative I went to Soochow to see. And now I haven't got the fare back to Nanking."

"That's easily settled," said Chi. "I can give you enough money for the journey. And I'd be grateful if you would take a letter to Nanking for me."

Just then Mr. Hsin and Mr. Chin came in with a Taoist priest and another man to visit the bridal chamber. Chi Wei-hsiao took them in, and after joking there for some time they came back and sat down.

"This Taoist friend is called Lai Hsia-shih," said Mr. Hsin to Chi. "He's another of our Yangchow poets. And this is Mr. Kuo Tieh-pi of Wuhu, a fine engraver of seals. They took advantage of this happy occasion to make your acquaintance."

Chi Wei-hsiao asked where they lived, and promised to return the call.

"The other day Mr. Pao mentioned that he came from Nanking; may we ask when he will be going back?" inquired Mr. Hsin and Mr. Chin.

"In a day or two," answered Chi.

"In that case we shan't have the pleasure of travelling together," they said. "But in this vulgar place true worth is not appreciated. We mean to go to Nanking too."

After talking for some time, the four of them left.

"Who is the friend to whom you want me to take a letter, nephew?" asked Ting-hsi.

"A man from Anching, whose name is also Chi — Chi Tien-yi. We're not related, though. He came out with me, and he's completely incompetent, so now that I shan't be going back I must write to tell him to go home."

"Have you written the letter yet?"

"Not yet. I'll write it this evening. If you come tomorrow, uncle, you can take the letter and the travelling money, and leave the day after tomorrow."

Having agreed to this, Ting-hsi left. And that evening Chi Wei-hsiao wrote the letter and wrapped up fifty cents of silver for his uncle to collect the next day.

The following morning a guest arrived by sedan-chair, and sent in a card on which was written: "Your classmate, Tsung Chi."

Going out to greet him, Chi saw that he was a dignified-looking man in a square cap and wide gown.

"May I ask what district you are from?" inquired Chi, when he had ushered his visitor inside.

"I come from Hukuang, but have spent most of my time in the capital, where Mr. Hsieh Mao-chin and I served as tutors in the Prince of Chao's family. Being on my way home now, and having heard of your great reputation, I made a point of coming to pay my respects. I have brought a small portrait, to ask you to inscribe a few words. When I go to Nanking, I shall ask the famous scholars there to favour me with some inscriptions too."

"Your great fame long since reached my ears like thunder," responded Chi. "I am ashamed to display my incompetence before a connoisseur like yourself."

By this time the tea had been drunk, and Chi bowed his visitor back to his chair. Then Ting-hsi arrived, took the letter and money, and expressed his thanks.

"When you reach Nanking, uncle," said Chi, "please don't forget to go to Number One Scholar's Square, and urge my friend Chi Tien-yi to go home. A man can easily starve to death in Nanking! He mustn't stay there at any cost!"

This said, he saw his uncle out.

With his silver, Ting-hsi bought a passage back to Nanking. When he reached home and told his wife the unhappy news, she abused him roundly, and because Censor Shih kept dunning them for payment and they had no money, they had to vacate the house and forfeit their twenty taels deposit. Having nowhere else to go, they were reduced to borrowing one room from some relatives of Ting-hsi's wife, named Hu, at Inner Bridge. A few days after his return, Ting-hsi took the letter to Number One Scholar's Square for Chi Tien-yi. After reading it, Chi Tien-yi offered him some tea

"Thank you very much, Mr. Pao," he said. "I understand now."

Then Ting-hsi took his leave.

Chi Tien-yi was too short of cash to find himself proper lodgings, and he could not afford more than eight coins a day to buy four cakes of unleavened bread, out of which he had to make two meals. He slept on the counter of a seal shop. When he received the letter and knew that Chi Wei-hsiao would not be coming, he began to feel desperate; but he had no money to go back to Anching, and after eating his bread each day could only sit brooding in the seal shop. One day when he could not buy even bread, a man in a square cap and black gown came in and greeted him. Chi Tien-yi asked him to sit down on the bench beside him.

"May I know your name, sir?" asked the stranger.

"My name is Chi."

"Can you tell me whether there are any well-known scholars here who compile essays?"

"Plenty of them! I know Wei Ti-shan, Sui Chin-an, Ma Chun-shang, Chu Hsien-fu, and Kuang Chao-jen, to say nothing of Chi Wei-hsiao, who was here with me not long ago. They're all famous scholars. Which would you like?"

"It doesn't matter which. I've two or three hundred taels of silver to spend on compiling a collection of essays. I'll trouble you to fetch one of your friends here, to collaborate with me."

"May I know your honourable name and place of origin, so that I can tell them who you are?"

"My name is Chu-ko, and I come from Hsuyi County. I dare say they have heard of me. Will you go and fetch one of them, then?"

Chi Tien-yi asked Chu-ko to wait there while he went out.

"Though these men often come to the shop, goodness knows where are they now," he thought "I haven't the faintest idea how to set about finding them. What a pity Chi Wei-hsiao isn't here! Never mind! All I need do is walk towards West Water Gate, keeping a good lookout, and grab the first of them I meet. I should be able to make a few meals out of him."

As he reached the gate, he saw a man with baggage enter the city, and was delighted to recognize Hsiao Chin-hsuan of Anching.

"Fine!" He hurried forward to clutch him. "When did you arrive, brother?"

"So it's you, Tien-yi!" exclaimed Hsiao. "Is Chi Wei-hsiao with you?"

"He went to Yangchow some time ago, I'm staying here. You've come just at the right time! I've got a good job for you — but you mustn't forget to thank me for it!"

"What good job?"

"Never mind that. Just come with me, and I guarantee you a good time."

Hsiao Chin-hsuan accompanied him to the seal shop, where Chu-ko was craning his neck to watch for Chi's return.

"Mr. Chu-ko!" shouted Chi Tien-yi. "I've brought you a famous scholar!"

Chu-ko ushered them into the shop, and when they had greeted each other they left Hsiao's baggage there while they went to a tea-house. After an exchange of courtesies, they sat down and introduced themselves.

"My name is Chu-ko Tien-shen."

"I am Hsiao Chin-hsuan."

Chi Tien-yi explained that Mr. Chu-ko had several hundred taels of silver to spend on compiling a book of essays.

"I have had some experience in editing myself," said Chu-ko. "But since I have come to this great metropolis, I want to ask a well-known scholar to take me under his wing. Now that I have met Mr. Hsiao, I feel like a stranded fish put back into water!"

"I am afraid my poor talents may prove unequal to the task," rejoined Hsiao.

"There is no need for you both to be so polite," said Chi. "You will soon be like old friends. Why don't you invite Mr. Hsiao to an informal meal, Mr. Chu-ko, so that we can discuss this business in detail?"

"A good idea," replied Chu-ko. "Since I am a stranger here, I shall have to ask you to a tavern."

They paid for the tea, and went to a big eating-house on Three Mountains Street. Hsiao sat in the seat of honour, Chi opposite him, and Chu-ko in the place of host. When the waiter came, Chi ordered pigs' trotters, duck, and fish preserved in wine — the two last to be served with the wine. The pork was to be eaten later with the rice and three cents' worth of soup. Presently the waiter brought the wine in, and they started drinking.

"The first thing we must do," said Chi, "is to find some roomy, quiet lodging. Then, when you have chosen your essays, you can have the engravers there and watch them cut the blocks."

"The quietest place I know is the Temple of Kindness Repaid outside the South Gate," said Hsiao. "There is no noise, the rooms are a good size, and the price is reasonable. Suppose we go there after this meal and have a look?"

By now they had finished several pots of wine, and the waiter brought them the trotters and rice. Chi Tien-yi stuffed himself till he could eat no more. Then, having settled the bill downstairs and gone back to the seal shop to ask the man there to keep an eye on Hsiao's baggage, they walked to the South Gate. That was such a lively quarter, with carriages like strings of dragons and unending streams of horses, that it took our three friends a long time to squeeze their way out. Presently they entered the grounds of the Temple of Kindness Repaid.

"Let's look for a place near the gate," suggested Chi.

"No, let's go further in," said Hsiao. "That'll be quieter."

They walked some distance, past the home for retired monks, till they came to a monastery and knocked at the gate, which was opened by an acolyte. When he heard that they were looking for rooms, he ushered them in; and the abbot came sleepily out, in a black brocade hat and robe of raw silk, carrying his beads. After greeting them he invited them to be seated, then asked their names and where they came from.

"I have plenty of rooms," he said, when he learned their business. "All the officials come to stay here. Please choose for yourselves, gentlemen."

They went inside and looked at three rooms, then came out and sat down again with the abbot to ask the price. He demanded three taels of silver a month, and would not knock off a cent however much they protested. Even when Chu-ko offered two taels forty cents, the abbot would not take it, but began to scold the acolyte.

"Hurry up and sweep the floor!" he ordered. "Tomorrow Censor Shih from Lower Floating Bridge is holding a feast here. We can't let him find the place in a state like this."

Hsiao lost patience.

"The rooms are good," he said to Chi. "But it's rather far to the market."

"Guests staying here can't manage with one servant only to cook and shop," remarked the abbot woodenly. "You need one cook, and one man to fetch and carry."

"When *we* stay here," said Hsiao with a laugh, "in addition to a cook and a manservant, we'll have a bald-headed ass[1] to drive to market. That will save time!"

The abbot glared furiously as the three men stood up to go.

"We will take our leave now," they said, "and let you know our decision later."

The abbot saw them out.

They walked another half mile or so, and knocked at the door of a priory. The prior came out to greet them, his face wreathed with smiles, offered them seats in his hall, brewed fresh tea for them, and spread the table with nine dishes of sweetmeats including the best cakes made with orange peel and honey, as well as walnut wafers.

When they mentioned that they wanted rooms, he said: "Certainly. Please choose whichever you fancy, and move straight in."

They asked the rent.

"That's a small matter," said the prior. "I shall count your visit an honour. Just make what contribution you please toward the incense, and I shall be more than satisfied."

Impressed by the superior way in which he spoke, Hsiao said: "I hope you won't be offended, father, if we offer you two taels a month for disturbing you here?"

To this the prior assented readily. Then Hsiao and Chu-ko waited in his room while Chi went back to town for the baggage. And having ordered a novice to sweep out their rooms and move in the necessary furniture, the prior brought in fresh tea and kept his guests company until the baggage arrived late that afternoon. Hsiao told Chu-ko to wrap up two silver taels, seal the packet, and send it to the prior, who came out again to thank them. Then the three men lit their lamps and began to think of supper. Chu-ko weighed out a little silver for wine and food, and Chi made yet another trip to the city, bringing back a waiter carrying four pots of wine and four dishes—salted sausages, sea shrimps, frogs'

---

[1] Chinese Buddhist monks have their heads completely shaved; so "bald-headed ass" is a term of abuse for monks.

legs and jelly-fish—with which the table was spread. Chu-ko was a country fellow, who had never seen sausages before.

"What are these?" he asked.

"Taste them and see," said Hsiao.

"It's bacon," said Chu-ko after a couple of mouthfuls.

"Go on! Does bacon have a skin like that round it? That casing's made of pigs' guts!"

Chu-ko had never eaten jelly-fish either.

"What's this crispy stuff?" he asked. "Tastes good. Let's have some more of this in future."

After finishing their wine they prepared for bed. Since Chi had no baggage, Hsiao lent him a quilt in which to wrap himself.

Early the next morning the prior came in.

"Will you three gentlemen condescend to share a simple meal with me to celebrate your arrival?" he asked. "After-wards, I can show you round the temple grounds."

"It's very good of you, father!" they answered.

The prior invited them into a room on the ground floor of another building, where four large dishes were served. After breakfasting they began to stroll outside.

"Let us go to see Tripitaka's Hermitage,"[1] said the prior, and led them to a lofty hall with a tablet inscribed in letters of gold: "Home of the First Holy One."

Passing through two more rooms, they came to winding steps with balustrades, and climbed up to another building. They did not suspect that there was anything behind this; but when the prior opened the double door at the back and invited them to walk through, they came out upon a great plot of level ground, as high as any house, which had an ex-cellent view on all sides. In the middle were huge trees nearly sweeping the sky and thousands of bamboos, their leaves rus-tling in the breeze. In the very centre was the pagoda where the relics of the monk Tripitaka of the Tang Dynasty had been buried. After enjoying themselves here for some time,

---

[1] Hsuan Chuang (Tripitaka, A.D. 596-664). He went to India to study Buddhism, translated seventy-five sutras from Sanskrit, and dictated the *Record of Western Regions.*

they went back with the prior, who entertained them that evening with nine dishes and wine.

"I have not invited guests since my appointment to this post," said the prior while they were drinking. "The day after tomorrow I am holding a feast and hiring actors. I hope you three gentlemen will come and watch the plays. Of course there will be no charge."

"We shall certainly come to congratulate you," they replied.

Presently the feast ended.

Two days after that nearly five dozen guests were due from the county and city yamens. The cooks and waiters had arrived in good time, and so had the actors, with their chest of costumes and stage properties. The prior was chatting with his three lodgers when a novice hurried in.

"That fellow is back, father!" he cried.

But to know what followed, you must read the next chapter.

CHAPTER 29

Chu-ko Tien-shen meets a friend in the priory, and Tu Shen-ching takes a concubine in Nanking

The prior was chatting with his three lodgers when in hurried a novice.

"That fellow is here again, father!" he reported.

The prior excused himself and went out.

"Is it that wretch Lung San?" he asked.

"Yes," said the novice. "And he's up to even stranger tricks this time. Go and see for yourself, father."

The prior went downstairs, past the tea attendant who was fanning his stove at the gate, and into the hall. There was a man sitting there—a swarthy man with brown eyes and a bushy moustache, who was wearing a paper chaplet, a woman's blue cotton tunic, white skirt and large embroidered slippers. Two chair-bearers standing in the courtyard were demanding their fare.

As soon as the stranger caught sight of the prior, he smiled broadly.

"I've come early, husband, to see to everything for you on this happy day," he announced. "Will you pay the chair-bearers for me?"

"What is it this time, Lung San?" demanded the prior with a frown. "What a spectacle you're making of yourself!"

He made haste to pay the bearers.

"Come on now, Lung San!" he urged. "Take off those clothes! Do you want to look a figure of fun?"

"How heartless you are, husband!" responded Lung San reproachfully. "You're an official now, yet you haven't given me the gold chaplet and fine scarlet costume an official's wife should wear, so I've made a paper chaplet for myself. *Let* people laugh if they like. I'm your wife, aren't I? Why should you tell me to take it off?"

"Lung San! This is no time for joking! Even if you were angry with me for not inviting you today, you should have come in a decent manner. Why dress yourself up like this?"

"How can you say such a thing, husband? Nothing can come between husband and wife. How could I be angry with you?"

"I'll admit I was in the wrong," said the prior. "You had a right to be annoyed when I didn't invite you today. But take off those clothes now and sit down to have a drink. People will think you crazy if they see that outfit."

"I'm the one in the wrong," said Lung San. "A wife should stay in the inner chambers preparing refreshments, peeling fruit, and supervising the preparations. Who ever heard of a woman sitting in the hall? What *will* people think?"

Thereupon he sailed into the bedroom.

"Lung San!" cried the prior, following him in helplessly. "You won't be able to get away with any of your tricks today! And if the yamen officials hear of this, it'll be a bad look-out for both of us!"

"Don't worry, husband! Don't you know the saying: Officials can't interfere in family disputes?"

While the prior stamped with rage, Lung San sat himself calmly down and called for the novice.

"Tell the tea attendant to bring the mistress tea!" he ordered.

The prior paced up and down in a fluster, and just as he reached his threshold who should arrive but Hsiao, Chu-ko and Chi! He could not keep them out either.

"Well!" exclaimed Chi Tien-yi. "Where did this lady come from?"

"Please be seated, gentlemen!" said Lung San, rising.

363

The prior was speechless with rage, while his three lodgers could not help laughing. And at this moment the novice burst in again.

"Mr. Yiu from the yamen has arrived!" he reported.

The prior went out to greet Mr. Yiu and Mr. Kuo, two clerks in the yamen. When they had bowed and sat down they heard voices in the next room, and walked over to investigate. Once again, the prior could not stop them.

"Whatever is this?" they asked when they saw Lung San.

Unable to conceal their amusement, all five guests burst out laughing together.

"Gentlemen!" said the prior desperately. "This man is a swindler, who keeps coming to cheat me."

"What is his name?" asked Yiu, chuckling.

"He's called Lung San."

"Lung San," said Kuo, "today we are celebrating the prior's new appointment. Why should you come here to make trouble? Hurry up and take off those clothes, and clear out!"

"This is our private affair, gentlemen," replied Lung San. "It's none of your business!"

"Nonsense!" exclaimed Yiu. "You're simply trying to black-mail him! If it's money you're after, this is no way to get it."

"Let's all contribute a little silver to get rid of this scoundrel," suggested Hsiao. "Otherwise it's going to look too bad."

But Lung San refused to leave.

While they were discussing what to do, the novice came in again.

"Mr. Tung from the ministry and a Mr. Chin are here!" he announced.

In walked Mr. Tung and Chin Tung-ya.

"Is that Lung San?" said Chin, who recognized him. "You dog! After stealing dozens of taels from me in the capital, how dare you show yourself here in this costume? You're obviously up to your old tricks again, you miserable swindler!"

"Take that chaplet and clothes off him!" he ordered his servant-boy. "Then throw him out!"

At that Lung San lost his head, and removed his chaplet and clothes himself.

"I'm just here to wait on you, sir," he said humbly.

"Who wants you waiting on him?" roared Chin. "You were trying to cheat the prior here! Later on I don't mind asking him to give you some money to start a business; but if you make any more trouble now, I'll have you sent straight to the yamen!"

When Lung San, all his bluster gone, had thanked Chin Tung-ya and slunk off, the prior took his guests downstairs, greeted them again, and begged them to be seated. He could not thank Chin enough!

"You spend most of your time at home, Mr. Chin," said Kuo, when the attendants had brought tea. "When did you come here?"

"I had to spend so much money in my last post that I decided to resign," said Chin. "By the time I reached home, my son had been lucky enough to pass the examination and enter college; but to our surprise that caused a lot of trouble. And although virtue is bound to triumph in the end, I lost quite a little silver in that lawsuit. Since there was nothing to do at home, I went to Yangchow to look up Inspector Hsun of the Salt Gabelle, who was my friend in the capital; and he was kind enough to recommend me to the Salt Guild, which paid me several hundred taels of silver."

"Do you know what has happened to Inspector Hsun, Mr. Chin?" asked Tung.

"No. What?"

"He was arrested a few days ago for embezzlement."

"Is that so!" exclaimed Chin. "Well, fortune is fickle!"

"Where are you living now, sir?" asked Kuo.

"Mr. Chin has bought himself a house on the river at Lucky Crossing Bridge," answered Tung.

"We shall call on you another day," said everyone.

Chin thereupon ascertained the names of the prior's three lodgers.

"You are all famous scholars," he declared. "I have written some commentaries on the classics myself. In future I shall ask for your instruction."

Soon several dozen guests had gathered, but the last to arrive were three men in square caps accompanied by a Taoist priest, whom nobody knew.

"Which is Mr. Chi Tien-yi?" asked one of the newcomers in the square caps.

"I am," replied Chi. "What is your business with me, sir?"

The stranger took a letter from his sleeve.

"Our friend Chi Wei-hsiao sends you his best regards," he said.

Upon opening the letter, which he read with Hsiao and Chu-ko, Chi Tien-yi learned that these four men were Hsin Tung-chih, Chin Yu-liu, Kuo Tieh-pi and Lai Hsia-shih.

"Please be seated," he said.

When the four men declined because there was company, the prior begged them to stay.

"You have come a long way, gentlemen, and we are honoured by your visit," he declared. "Please sit down."

Since he insisted, the four men took seats. Then Chin Tung-ya asked them whether the news about Inspector Hsun was true.

"He was arrested the day that we left Yangchow," said Kuo.

Plays were performed while they feasted. In the evening Mr. Hsin and Mr. Chin went back to the city, having taken rooms in East Garden Monastery. Gradually all the other guests left too, only Kuo Tieh-pi and Lai the Taoist priest staying behind to spend the night in Chu-ko's room. The next day Lai went to Divine Pleasure Temple to look for a fellow priest, and Kuo Tieh-pi rented a room outside the gate of the Temple of Kindness Repaid to open a seal shop there.

Chi Tien-yi and his friends opened an account at General Fortune Tavern outside the temple gate, where they could order meals on credit, and every day spent forty to fifty cents on food and wine. When the selection of essays had been made, they engaged seven or eight engravers, bought about a hundred reams of paper—also on credit—and prepared to start printing. Now that nearly five months had gone by very little was left of Chu-ko's two hundred odd taels of silver. But they continued to eat heartily every day without paying cash.

"Mr. Chu-ko's money is nearly finished," said Chi to Hsiao one day as they were strolling in the temple grounds, "and we've run up a good many debts. Suppose the book doesn't sell well, what shall we do?"

"He started this of his own free will," replied Hsiao. "Nobody forced him. When his silver runs out, he'll just have to go home for more. That's *his* lookout!"

Chu-ko's arrival put a stop to this conversation. After walking a little further, they were going home together when a sedan-chair and two bearers carrying baggage came towards them. Our three friends turned back and followed this procession towards the temple. The curtains of the chair were drawn, so that they could see the passenger—a young man in a square cap, who looked vaguely familiar to Chu-ko as the chair flashed past.

"I believe I know the man in the chair," he said.

He hurried forward to accost the traveller's servant.

"Where are you from?" he asked.

"Our master is the seventeenth Mr. Tu of Tienchang."

When Chu-ko came back, the three of them watched the chair and baggage draw up at the abbot's house next to the home for old monks.

"The man who just passed is the grandson of Minister Tu of Tienchang," said Chu-ko. "I have met him. He is a famous scholar in our district. I wonder what he is doing here? I must call on him tomorrow."

The next day, however, when Chu-ko went to pay a call, he was told Mr. Tu was out. Two days later Tu returned the call, and the three men went out to greet him. It was a balmy, late spring day, and Tu, who was wearing a lined orange gauze gown and silken slippers, had a fan inscribed with a poem in his hand. As he drew near, they were struck by the whiteness of his skin, the brightness of his black eyes, and the grace and distinction with which he carried himself. This man was both talented and handsome, and was one of the most brilliant scholars in the Yangtse Valley. After exchanging greetings they sat down, and Tu asked Hsiao and Chi their names and where they came from.

"My name is Tu Shen-ching," he volunteered. "I haven't seen you, Mr. Chu-ko, for half a year—not since the examination last year."

"Last year," Chu-ko told Hsiao and Chi, "Examiner Shen set a poetry test for students from twenty-seven counties in our prefecture. Mr. Tu came first on the list."

"I simply dashed off some doggerel," said Tu with a laugh. "It was nothing worth mentioning. In fact, I was taking medicine that day because I felt rather unwell, so I handed in my paper as quickly as I could."

"Your honourable family enjoys such a reputation in the Yangtse Valley that men from every province look up to it, sir," said Hsiao. "And you are the most gifted of all your brilliant kinsmen. Now that I have been fortunate enough to meet you, I shall seek your advice in all matters."

"You are all famous scholars," replied Tu. "It is *I* who must hope for *your* instruction."

After drinking a cup of tea in the hall, they adjourned to the inner room where the tables were piled with proof sheets marked in red, which made a colourful sight. Having glanced through these, Tu Shen-ching set them aside. Then he came upon a poem by Hsiao Chin-hsuan entitled "A Visit in Spring to Black Dragon Pool."

"These images are fresh," commented Tu. "Is this your masterpiece, Mr. Hsiao?"

"That is my poor work. Will you give me your opinion of it, sir?"

"With your permission, I have a superficial observation to make. *Shih*[1] should be written in a lofty style. But take these two lines in your verse:

Is it distress that has turned the peach blossom red?
The willow has suddenly grown a heart-rending green.

Aren't they rather too laboured? Yet if you add the one word 'Say' to 'Is it distress that has turned the peach blossom red?' you have a perfectly good line in the *tz'u* style. By changing the metre and adding a slightly awkward second line, however, I feel you have made it somewhat flat."

---

[1] The *shih* was the ancient, classical verse form. The *tz'u* was a later form.

This brief comment was enough to make Hsiao break into a cold sweat.

"Judging by your views on poetry, sir," said Chi to Tu, "you would get on capitally with my kinsman, Chi Wei-hsiao."

"Is he a relative of yours?" asked Tu. "I have seen some of his poems. He has a certain flair."

Presently he took his leave.

The next day he sent them the following note: "The peonies in my garden are in bloom, and I have prepared a few light refreshments. Will you favour me with a visit?"

The three men hastily changed their clothes and walked over. They found another man sitting with Tu, and after exchanging greetings they urged the stranger to take the seat of honour.

"My friend Pao is one of the family," interposed Tu. "He doesn't want to sit above you gentlemen."

Chi Tien-yi realized that this was the Mr. Pao who had brought him the letter from Yangchow.

"This gentleman is Chi Wei-hsiao's uncle," he told his friends. "What are you doing here, sir?"

"Don't you know, Mr. Chi?" asked Pao with a laugh. "My family has been dependent upon the Tu family for generations. My father and I owe more than I can say to Minister Tu. Hearing that the seventeenth master was here, I naturally came to pay my respects."

"Enough of that," said Tu. "Ask them to serve the wine."

Then Pao Ting-hsi and a servant-boy carried over a table.

"I decided to dispense with the usual dishes today, gentlemen," remarked Tu. "I have nothing to offer you but fish, cherries and bamboo shoots to go with your wine while we talk."

Sure enough, a few simple dishes only were served, while their cups were filled with the best orange wine from Eternal Quiet Store. Tu Shen-ching was an extremely heavy drinker who ate next to nothing. After raising his chopsticks to invite his guests to fall to, he took merely a few bamboo shoots and cherries himself. The moment their cups were empty, they were refilled; and at noon, when Tu called for dessert, the attendants brought in boiled meat dumplings, duck dumplings, cakes fried in goose fat, and spicy wafers. To round off, each had a bowl of the choicest Luan tea with rain water. Then the host, who had taken nothing but one wafer and one bowl of tea himself, ordered the table to be cleared and more wine brought.

"When good friends gather to enjoy celebrated flowers, they must write poetry," declared Hsiao. "Suppose we choose the rhymes now?"

"I know this has long been the practice in poetry societies, sir," said Tu with a smile. "But in my humble opinion it is such a vulgar way of showing refinement that we would do better just to chat."

He glanced at Pao Ting-hsi.

"Let me try to entertain you," offered Ting-hsi, laughing.

He fetched a flute from his room, removed the silk wrapper, and sat down at the table to play. As the shrill music rang out, a little lad who had come to stand beside him clapped his hands and sang one of the songs of Li Pai. His voice was piercingly sweet and the melody utterly delightful. The three guests set down their cups to listen, leaving Tu Shen-ching drinking alone. They sat there till the moon came out, lending the peonies an unearthly loveliness und transfiguring a great guelder-rose in the garden till it appeared one mass of dazzling snow. The three guests could hardly sit still for delight, and Tu was by now quietly drunk.

At this point the abbot paced slowly in with a silk-covered box from which he took a string of Chimen firecrackers.

"I have come to sober you up, gentlemen," he said.

As the fireworks went off with a series of bangs, Tu leant back in his chair and roared with laughter. Even after the monk left, yellow sulphurous smoke wreathed the table at which they were sitting. The three guests, who were also quite tipsy now, stood up unsteadily and took their leave.

"I am drunk," laughed Tu. "Excuse me if I don't see you out. Ting-hsi, show these three gentlemen out for me, then come back here for the night."

Taking a candlestick, Ting-hsi saw the guests out and barred the door after them. Hsiao and his friends reeled back to their lodgings as if in a dream. The next day their paper dealer asked for his money, and made a scene when none was forthcoming. Then the manager of General Fortune Tavern wanted his bill settled, and Chu-ko had to give him two handfuls of loose silver to be going on with. The three of them decided to return Tu Shen-ching's hospitality; but since they could not prepare a feast in their rooms they would have to ask him to the tavern.

A day or two later the weather was perfect, and after breakfast the three men called on Tu. In his courtyard they found a woman with big feet sitting on a bench talking to one of the servant-boys, who stood up at their approach.

"Who is she?" asked Chi Tien-yi.

"Big Foot Shen, the go-between," replied the boy.

"What is she doing here?"

"She has come on some business."

Realizing that Tu must be taking a concubine, the three men asked no more questions, but went in. Tu, who had been pacing up and down the verandah, invited them in, offered them seats, and told the boy to serve tea.

"It is such a fine day," said Chu-ko, "we want to ask you to come out with us."

Taking the boy with him, Tu went out with the three men, who insisted on taking him to the tavern. Knowing that he did not like pork, Chi Tien-yi ordered duck, fish, tripe, minced meat and wine. After two cups of wine, they urged Tu to eat, and he forced himself to swallow a mouthful of duck, but brought it up again immediately, to the great embarrassment of all. Because it was still early they did not drink much, but had the rice brought in. Tu steeped a bowl of rice in tea and made an effort to eat; but he could not finish it, and gave what was left to his boy. The meal at an end, they went downstairs and paid the bill.

"Shall we saunter up Rain Flower Mount, Shen-ching?" suggested Hsiao.

"That would be very pleasant," agreed Tu.

They walked to the hill, and in the temples there saw the stately shrines to Fang Hsiao-ju and Ching Ching.[1] Then they

---

[1] These two men supported Emperor Chien Wen against Yung Lo, who usurped the throne. They were both killed.

climbed to the hill top, and gazed at the smoke from the thousands of houses in the city, the Yangtse River like a white silk girdle, and the golden glitter of the glazed pagoda. There was a pavilion at the top of the hill, and here Tu strolled in the sun for a long time watching his shadow, while Chu-ko went to have a look at a small tablet in the distance, then came back and sat down.

"That tablet marks the place where the ten branches of the clan were killed," he told them.

"It is wrong, gentlemen, to speak of ten branches of the clan being killed," said Tu. "The severest punishment meted out under Han Dynasty law was to wipe out three clans: the father's, the mother's, the wife's. The nine branches of the clan executed with Fang Hsiao-ju were the families of the great-great-grandfather, great-grandfather, grandfather, father, sons, grandsons, great-grandsons and great-great-grandsons. In other words, they were all the father's clan. His mother's and wife's clans were not involved, much less his pupils'. Besides, Emperor Yung Lo could not have been as cruel as that. If Yung Lo had not stirred up this dynasty, but left the government in the hands of that weakling Chien Wen, the empire would now be as weak as in the time of the Six Dynasties."

"What is your opinion of Mr. Fang, sir?" asked Hsiao.

"Fang was an impractical pedant. When there were so many more important matters to discuss, why should he speak only of the rightful succession? To be publicly executed in his court robes was no more than he deserved!"

They sat there till the sun began to sink in the west, and two dung-carriers set down their empty pails on the hill to rest.

"Brother!" said one, clapping the other on the shoulder. "Now that we've finished business for today, why not go to drink a jugful of the water from Eternal Quiet Fountain, then come back here to watch the sunset?"

"It's true that in a place like Nanking even cooks and porters are cultured!" laughed Tu.

They walked down the hill and back to the temple.

"Won't you come to our rooms for a while?" asked Chu-ko.

"Thank you," said Tu.

Upon entering their lodgings, they found Chi Wei-hsiao sitting there.

"How did you get here, brother?" asked Chi Tien-yi, very pleased.

"I asked for you in the seal shop, and learned that you had moved here. Will you introduce me to these gentlemen?"

"This is Mr. Chu-ko Tien-shen of Hsuyi. And this is Mr. Hsiao Chin-hsuan from our district. You know him, don't you?"

"Do you live by the North Gate, sir?" asked Chi Wei-hsiao.

"That's right," said Hsiao.

"And this gentleman?" asked Chi Wei-hsiao.

"You will be even more delighted to make this gentleman's acquaintance," replied Chi Tien-yi. "He is Mr. Tu Shen-ching, seventeenth grandson of Minister Tu of Tienchang. You must have heard of him."

"Is this the Mr. Tu whose poems won him first place last year in the examination for twenty-seven counties in your prefecture?" Chi Wei-hsiao spoke with respect. "I have long wanted to make his acquaintance, but never had the opportunity!"

He prostrated himself. When Tu Shen-ching had kowtowed to him in return, the two of them got up, greetings were exchanged, and they all sat down. Just then someone came in, laughing boisterously.

"Will you spend the night drinking, gentlemen?" he cried. Chi Wei-hsiao saw that it was Pao Ting-hsi.

"How do you come to be here, uncle?" he asked.

"I am in the service of the Tu family, and this is the seventeenth master. Why shouldn't I be here? Do you know Mr. Tu too, nephew?"

"We are all good friends, not mere strangers who meet on the road," quoted Hsiao.

"Although I am young," said Chi Wei-hsiao, when they were all seated, "I have travelled a good deal and seen a good many people; but never in my life have I seen anyone so handsome and distinguished as you, Mr. Tu. You look like one of the immortals! Sitting opposite you, I feel I must be in heaven!"

"Our meeting reminds me of Mr. Cheng Lien's voyage on the ocean,"[1] responded Tu. "This is an inspiring occasion."

But to know what followed, you must read the next chapter.

---

[1]Cheng Lien lived in the Spring and Autumn Period (722-481 B.C.). His pupil Po Ya played the lyre well, and in order that he should have the best environment for mastering his art Cheng Lien took him to an island and left him there. Po Ya became a great musician; and later Chinese scholars used this allusion to Cheng Lien to express appreciation of a friend's literary or artistic attainments.

CHAPTER 30

In which a lover of handsome youths
seeks a friend at Divine Pleasure Temple, and a splendid
contest is held at Carefree Lake

Tu Shen-ching and Chi Wei-hsiao took to each other at once;
but because Chi had rooms in the Temple of Imperial Favour
he had to hurry back into town as soon as it grew dark, while
Pao Ting-hsi went back with Tu, who bought wine for him.

"What kind of man is Chi Wei-hsiao?" asked Tu.

Ting-hsi described how Chi had been placed first in the
prefectural examination by Prefect Hsiang, and had later married a grand-daughter of the prefect's steward, Wang, thus
becoming his own nephew; how this year Inspector Hsun of
the Salt Gabelle had given him several hundred taels, and how
he had married into the Yiu family at Yangchow. He told the
whole story in full, and Tu smiled as he drank it all in. He
kept Ting-hsi there for the night, was very moved when he
heard how good Prefect Hsiang had been to the Pao family,
and roared with laughter when Ting-hsi described his marriage
to Mrs. Wang and the life she had led him. Finally they went
to sleep.

The next morning Chi Wei-hsiao called with Tsung Chi,
who had served in the prince's palace. After the customary
greetings, Mr. Tsung declared that while with the Prince of
Chao he had written poems with the seven famous scholars of
the capital; whereupon Tu remarked that two of them were

his uncles. Then mention was made of a third scholar, Tsung Tzu-hsiang.

"Senior Secretary Tsung was my father's classmate," said Tu.

But when Mr. Tsung declared that he and Secretary Tsung were kinsmen of the same generation, Tu made no reply. Presently tea was served, after which Mr. Tsung left, while Chi remained behind to chat.

"Wei-hsiao," said Tu, "nobody irritates me more than these people who can talk about nothing except their official connections! Just now this fellow Tsung said he was the senior secretary's cousin! I'm afraid Secretary Tsung would disown such a miserable cousin!"

Lunch was served, and as they were at table the servant-boy came in.

"Big Foot Shen to see you, sir!" he announced. "She is waiting outside."

"Show her in," said Tu. "What does it matter?"

When the go-between came in, Tu had a stool placed for her.

"Who is this gentleman?" asked Big Foot.

"This is Mr. Chi of Anching. Well, have you done what I asked you yet?"

"That's why I'm here, sir. After you entrusted this matter to me I searched nearly the whole of Nanking for you, because you're such a handsome gentleman that I felt just any pretty girl wouldn't do for you. Now, thanks to all the inquiries I've been making, I've found a girl who lives at Flower Arch, whose family has a few looms. Their name is Wang. She's as pretty as a picture — prettier! And this lovely girl, who's seventeen this year, has a brother one year younger. If he were properly dressed and made up, not one of the female impersonators in the ten Huaiching Bridge companies could compare with him! He can sing and act a little too. This girl is perfect for you. Won't you have a look at her, sir?"

"Very well," said Tu. "Tell her to be ready for me tomorrow."

Assenting to this, Big Foot left.

"Congratulations!" said Chi.

"I am doing this simply to continue my family line, sir," replied Tu with a frown. "If not for the necessity of that, why should I take a concubine?"

"A brilliant scholar and a beautiful girl!" quoted Chi. "We should enjoy ourselves while we are young. I fail to understand your attitude, sir."

"You don't know me, Wei-hsiao," said Tu. "As our first emperor said: 'If not for the fact that I was born of a woman, I would kill all the women in the world!' Have you ever met a woman you could respect? I assure you, they affect me so painfully, I can smell a woman three rooms away!"

Before Chi could question him further, the boy brought in a visiting card.

"A Mr. Kuo from Wuhu has called!" he announced.

"I don't think I know any Kuo from Wuhu," said Tu.

Chi looked at the card.

"This is Kuo Tieh-pi, who has a seal shop at the temple gate," he said. "He's probably cut two seals for you. You'd better ask him in."

Tu told his servant to admit the visitor, and in came Kuo Tieh-pi. Having bowed, he embarked on a most fulsome speech.

"Your distinguished family can boast three sons who came first in the examinations," he declared. "You produce six ministers in four generations, and your pupils and former dependents are to be found everywhere. There are more of them serving as provincial governors, judges and other high officials than anyone can count. Even your stewards, when they leave you, become officers of the ninth rank! When I was a child I heard them say: 'Mrs. Tu's son is the greatest genius the world has ever known. In no time at all he will come first in the palace examination!'"

Taking a small, silk-lined box containing two square seals from his sleeve, he presented it with both hands to Tu, who accepted it, made conversation with Kuo for a time, then stood up to see him out.

"Why did he have to talk in that disgusting way?" exclaimed Tu on his return. "That fellow had all his facts right, though!"

"Your family history is common knowledge," said Chi.

Tu kept Chi for a meal, and when the wine was served they began to talk freely.

"Are you fond of climbing, or visiting rivers and lakes?" asked Chi.

"My health is not up to it," replied Tu. "I find climbing mountains or visiting lakes too strenuous."

"Are you a music-lover?"

"I like to listen to music occasionally; but if I hear it too often it jars on my ears."

A few more cups, and Tu was a little tipsy.

"Wei-hsiao!" he said, and heaved a long sigh. "Since ancient times men have been the slaves of love!"

"No love is greater than that between the sexes," replied Chi. "Yet you said just now you had no interest in women."

"And is love confined to that between men and women? No, the love of friends is stronger! Just look at the story of the Lord of Ngo[1] and his embroidered coverlet. And in all history I consider Emperor Ai of Han, who wanted to abdicate in favour of his friend, showed the truest understanding of love. Yao and Shun were no better than this, for all their polite deferring to others. But what a pity that no one understands this lofty love today!"

"True," rejoined Chi. "Have you never had a friend who really understood you?"

"If I could live and die with such a man, I would not be grieving and pining away like this! But I have not been lucky enough to find a true friend, and that is why I so often give way to melancholy!"

"You should look for a friend among the actors."

"That proposal is even more wide of the mark, Wei-hsiao! To seek a true friend among actors is like looking for a grand romance in the courtesans' quarter. Nothing could be more impossible. No, they alone deserve unqualified praise who require a spiritual affinity and a friendship transcending

---

1 The Lord of Ngo was devoted to a singer in the state of Yueh, and covered him with an embroidered coverlet. Later this incident was used as a classical allusion to describe love between men.

378

the flesh. Their friends must be some of the greatest men of the time!"

He struck his knee and sighed.

"But there's no such man in the world. No, Heaven has condemned gallant Tu Shen-ching to pine away alone!"

With this, he shed tears.

"Why, the man is possessed!" thought Chi. "Let me play a trick on him."

"You mustn't say there is no such man in the world, sir," he declared. "I know a young man who is neither an actor nor a scholar, but a Taoist priest. He is handsome and elegant, but not in any feminine way—his is true masculine beauty. It always irritates me to hear people praise a handsome man by declaring he looks like a woman. How ridiculous! Anyone who likes feminine beauty can look at women. But there is a masculine beauty too, which is seldom recognized."

"A truer word was never spoken!" cried Tu, clapping the table. "But tell me more about this man."

"He is so fastidious that, although many people have tried to make friends with him, he holds himself aloof. He loves genius, though. Because I am a few years older than he is, I don't feel good enough for him, so I have never ventured to make any advances. Would you care to meet him, brother?"

"When can you bring him here?"

"He wouldn't be the extraordinary man I said he was if I could bring him over just like that. You must call on him yourself."

"Where does he live?"

"In Divine Pleasure Temple."

"What is his name?"

"I can't tell you that now. If word of this came to his ears, he would keep out of your way and you would never see him. I'll write his name on a piece of paper and give it to you sealed, but you mustn't open it till you reach the gate of Divine Pleasure Temple. If you open it there, you'll have no difficulty in finding him."

"Very well," agreed Tu with a laugh.

Chi Wei-hsiao went inside, closed the door, wrote for some time, sealed up his paper carefully and inscribed a Taoist magic formula on it. He gave this to Tu.

"I will leave you now," he said. "After you have seen this marvellous man, I shall come back to congratulate you."

His host saw him out.

"You must take a message to Big Foot Shen tomorrow morning," Tu told his servant. "Tell her I have no time to go to see the girl at Flower Arch, but will go the day after tomorrow. And call the chair-bearers tomorrow morning. I am going to Divine Pleasure Temple to see a friend."

The next morning he washed with soap, changed into new clothes and scented himself lavishly; then, with Chi Wei-hsiao's paper in his sleeve, went by sedan-chair to Divine Pleasure Temple. He left the chair at the gate, and stepped over the threshold to open Chi's note.

"Go to Cassia Pavilion at the end of the north corridor," he read, "and ask for Lai Hsia-shih, who is newly arrived from Yangchow. He is your man."

Tu ordered his chair-bearers to wait, and took a winding path through the temple grounds. From a building in front he heard the sound of music, and through the open doors could see three rooms. In the central room sat a eunuch in charge of the imperial tombs, dressed in a dragon-embroidered gown. A dozen actors on the benches to his left and seven or eight young acolytes on the benches to his right were singing and playing musical instruments.

"Can Lai Hsia-shih be here?" wondered Tu.

He took a good look at the young Taoists in turn, but none of them was particularly handsome. Then he looked at the players, but they were quite commonplace too.

"Lai Hsia-shih has too much self-respect to mix with a group like this," he decided. "I must go to Cassia Pavilion to find him."

Arrived at Cassia Pavilion he knocked at the door, and a priest invited him in and gave him a chair.

"I have come to call on Mr. Lai, who recently arrived from Yangchow," said Tu.

"He is upstairs," replied the priest. "Please wait here, sir, while I fetch him."

He went away, and presently a fat priest came downstairs. He wore a Taoist's cap and brown robe, had a dark, greasy face, bushy eyebrows, a big nose and thick beard, and looked over fifty. He bowed to Tu and sat down.

"May I know your name and where you come from?" he asked.

"I come from Tienchang, and my name is Tu."

"Do you belong to the honourable Tu family of Tienchang which gave us such a handsome donation?"

"I do."

The Taoist's face broke into a smile.

"I did not know you were here, sir, or I would have called to pay my respects," he said obsequiously. "How dare I put you to the trouble of visiting me, sir?"

He immediately called for fresh tea and refreshments.

"This must be Lai Hsia-shih's master," thought Tu.

"Is Lai Hsia-shih your pupil?" he asked. "Or your pupil's son?"

"I am Lai Hsia-shih."

Tu gave a start.

"What! *You* are Lai Hsia-shih?"

He could not help himself. Hiding his face in his sleeve he shook with laughter. The mystified Taoist placed refreshments on the table and busied himself with the tea; then he produced a volume of poems from his sleeve and asked for Tu's criticism. The young man had to read the poems, but after two bowls of tea he rose to go. Lai insisted on walking hand in hand with him to the main entrance, where he asked:

"Do you live at the Temple of Kindness Repaid, sir? I will come tomorrow to spend a few days with you."

He saw Tu right out, and watched his chair leave before turning back himself.

As for Tu, he laughed all the way back.

"That dog, Chi Wei-hsiao!" he thought. "What a liar he is!"

As soon as he reached home his servant announced that visitors were waiting for him. Tu went in and found Hsiao

Chin-hsuan, Hsin Tung-chih, Chin Yu-liu and Chin Tung-ya. Mr. Hsin presented him with some calligraphy, Chin Yu-liu with a couplet, and Chin Tung-ya with a copy of his *Commentaries on the Four Books*, asking for his criticism. After they had sat down and explained the reason for their coming, tea was served, and they left. Tu snorted.

"A yamen clerk!" he said to the boy. "And he leaves his post to take up the interpretation of the classics! Is it for fellows like this to write commentaries on the works of the sages?"

As he was speaking a boy arrived with a letter from Mr. Tsung, asking Tu to append some characters to a portrait. Exasperated as he was, Tu had to consent, and he wrote a note for the lad to take back. The next day he went to see the girl, decided to take her as his concubine and gave the betrothal presents, arranging for her to be brought to his house within three days. Moving to a house by the river to receive her kept him busy.

The next day Chi Wei-hsiao called to offer his congratulations, and Tu went out to greet him.

"Excuse me for not coming yesterday to congratulate you on your marriage," said Chi.

"I did not prepare for guests yesterday," replied Tu.

"Did you find that marvellous man the day before?"

"You dog! You deserve a beating, but I'll let you off because your trick was not too vulgar!"

"Why do I deserve a beating? I told you he had masculine, not feminine, beauty. You can't deny that, can you?"

"I'm really going to beat you now!"

While they were laughing the Taoist arrived with Tinghsi to offer congratulations, and Tu and Chi were hard put to it not to laugh; but Tu signed to his friend to keep quiet. They all exchanged greetings, and Tu kept his guests to a meal. After the meal Tu mentioned the eunuch he had seen in Divine Pleasure Temple with actors on his left and acolytes on his right singing and playing to him.

"Why should a man like that have all the luck?" asked Chi. "It's too bad!"

"I want to consult you, Wei-hsiao," said Tu, "about a rather amusing scheme I have in mind."

"What is it?"

"How many opera companies are there, Ting-hsi, by West Water Gate and along the riverside?"

"Over a hundred and thirty."

"I want to choose a date and hire a big place for a contest, at which all the men who play girls' parts shall perform a scene each. Wei-hsiao and I will watch them and take notes of each; and a few days later we'll publish a list of their marks, ranking them according to their looks and acting. We'll post these results in some public place. We can't ask them to come for nothing, though. We'll give each actor fifty cents, two new pouches, and a fan inscribed with a poem. Wouldn't that be amusing?"

"Why didn't you tell me this wonderful idea earlier?" cried Chi, leaping up. "This is too marvellous for words!"

"Let me go and notify them," said Ting-hsi, smiling. "They'll get fifty cents each, and when you gentlemen have marked them and posted up the results, they'll be famous. I shouldn't be saying this, but the truth is, whoever comes out high on the list, even though he's had a powerful patron all along, will be able to make his patron cough up more. They'll be falling over each other in their eagerness to come!"

"Fine!" Lai Hsia-shih clapped his hands. "Even I shall be seeing life! Will you gentlemen allow me to be present on that day?"

"Of course!" replied Tu. "We shall be sending invitations to all our friends."

"Let's decide on the place first," suggested Chi.

"I live at West Water Gate, and know the district outside the gate very well," said Ting-hsi. "Let me hire the pavilion in Carefree Lake for you. It's large and cool."

"Uncle Pao will go and tell the actors, that goes without saying," said Chi. "But we'd better write a notice too. Which day is it to be?"

"It's the twentieth of the fourth month now," said Lai. "It will take Mr. Pao some time to notify everyone; so we must allow a couple of weeks for that. What about the third of next month?"

"Fetch a red card, Wei-hsiao," said Tu. "I'll dictate an announcement to you."

Chi fetched a card, and took up his brush.

"This is to announce that Chi Wei-hsiao of Anching and Tu Shen-ching of Tienchang are holding a contest in the pavilion of Carefree Lake on the third of the fifth month," said Tu. "Any actor in this province who wishes to take part should hand in his name and come to the lake at the time appointed, to act any scene of his choice. Each participant will receive fifty cents, two pouches, a fan inscribed with a poem, and a handkerchief. Those whose appearance and performance are outstanding will receive additional prizes. The contest will not be cancelled for rain or bad weather."

This notice was given to Pao Ting-hsi. And the boy was sent to buy over a hundred fans, which were inscribed by Chi, Tu and Lai. Then they decided on their guests. Chi spread a sheet of red paper on the table, and wrote: Mr. Tsung, Mr. Hsin, Mr. Chin Tung-ya, Mr. Chin Yu-liu, Mr. Hsiao Chinhsuan, Mr. Chu-ko, Mr. Chi, Kuo Tieh-pi, the prior, Mr. Lai Hsia-shih, Mr. Pao. With the two hosts, this made thirteen altogether. So eleven invitation cards were written in the names of Chi and Tu.

They had been busy with these preparations for some time, when in came the concubine's brother, Wang Liu-ko. With him was a porter carrying gifts for his sister: two ducks, two chickens, one goose, one piece of pork, eight varieties of cakes, and wine.

"You have come just at the right time!" exclaimed Tu.

As the lad greeted him, Tu took him by the arm and looked him over. Sure enough, he was a beautiful boy—better-looking even than Tu's concubine. Tu told him to come back after seeing his sister, and ordered the servants to dress the fowl he had brought.

Upon Wang Liu-ko's return, Tu told him their plan for a contest in the lake pavilion.

"How splendid!" cried Liu-ko. "I shall take part too."

"Won't you sing us something today as well?" suggested Chi.

Wang Liu-ko laughed. That evening when they had drunk some wine, Pao Ting-hsi played his flute and Lai Hsia-shih beat the clapper as Liu-ko sang "The Farewell at the Pavilion" from *The Western Chamber*. The air was a charming one, and he sang for the time it takes to eat three meals. The party did not break up till all were drunk.

On the day appointed, two property boxes were taken to Carefree Lake. Chi and Tu as hosts arrived first, then the guests assembled, and Pao Ting-hsi brought about six dozen actors playing women's parts who had put down their names for the contest to pay their respects to Mr. Tu. Tu bade them have a meal, then dress up and walk through the pavilion so that the judges could have a good look at them, and finally go up to the stage to perform. The players assented and left. The scholars, looking round the pavilion, saw that it had windows on all four sides and was surrounded by water. A soft wind had raised ripples on the lake. After putting on their costumes, the actors were to cross the bridge to the pavilion. Tu ordered the middle door to be closed, so that when the actors had crossed the bridge they should go round by the corridor to the latticed gate on the east, and then through the pavilion to leave by the gate on the west. In this way the spectators could see them clearly and judge of their charm and looks.

When the actors had finished their meal, they put on their costumes and make-up. They were all wearing brand-new head-dresses and jackets. One by one they crossed the bridge and walked across the pavilion while Tu and Chi, who had paper and brushes concealed in their hands, made notes. Soon the feast was served, and music sounded as the first actor ascended the stage. One acted "The Feast," another "The Drunken Singer," yet others "Borrowing Tea" or "Killing the Tiger." No two scenes were the same. Wang Liu-ko presented "The Nun Longs For Earthly Pleasures." When night fell hundreds of lamps were lit, high and low, making everything as bright as day. And the melodious singing lingered in the air. Rich yamen officials, merchants and shop-keepers in the city, hearing of the contest, hired fishing boats, fixed up awnings and hung up lanterns, then had themselves rowed to the middle of the lake to watch. When they were pleased, they applauded and cheered. This went on till dawn, by which time the city gates were open and they went home.

A day later, the results were posted up outside West Water Gate. First on the list was Cheng Kuei-kuan of the Fragrant Wood Company; second, Ko Lai-kuan of the Divine Harmony Company; third, Wang Liu-ko. The remaining sixty-odd actors were listed in order of merit. When Pao Ting-hsi took Cheng Kuei-kuan to call on Tu and thank him, Tu gave Pao two taels of gold to take to the silversmith and have them made into a gold cup with the inscription: "Brighter than Cherry Chen."[1] This cup was the actor's prize. All the others received pouches, silver, handkerchiefs and fans.

When the men who were friends with the first ten actors on the list saw the notice, they were delighted. Some of them invited their protégés home to celebrate, others gave parties in honour of the occasion in taverns. One feast followed another, the festivities continuing for three or four days. News of this travelled from West Water Gate to Huaiching Bridge, and the fame of the seventeenth Mr. Tu spread throughout the Yangtse Valley.

But to know what followed, you must read the next chapter.

---

[1] Girl favourite of Prince Shih Hu of the fourth century.

CHAPTER 31

Visitors call on a gallant
in Tienchang County. Good friends drink wine
in Tu Shao-ching's library

Pao Ting-hsi was amazed at the amount of money Tu Shen-ching had spent on the contest.

"Why don't I take advantage of his generosity to borrow a few hundred taels?" he thought. "Then I can start another opera company, and make enough to live on."

Having reached this decision, he made himself so useful every day in the house by the river that Tu began to feel under an obligation to him. And late one night, when none of the servants were in the room, they had a frank talk.

"What do you live on, Mr. Pao?" inquired Tu. "You ought to go into some kind of business, you know."

At this question, Ting-hsi plumped down on both knees. Quite taken aback, Tu helped him up.

"What is the meaning of this?" he asked.

"You are as kind as heaven and as generous as the earth to put that question to your humble servant, sir!" cried Ting-hsi. "But I used to manage an opera company, and that is the only trade I know. If you want to befriend me, sir, will you be good enough to lend me a few hundred taels, so that I can start another company? As soon as I have money, I will repay you."

"That should be easy," said Tu. "Sit down, and let's talk it over. A few hundred taels isn't enough to start an opera company—you'll need at least a thousand. Between ourselves, I don't mind telling you that although I have a few thousand taels of ready money, I don't want to spend it at the moment. Why not? In the next year or two I expect to pass the palace examination, and after that, of course, I'll need a lot of money; so for the time being I must hold on to what I have. Regarding this company of yours, I can tell you somebody who can help. It will be the same as if I helped you myself. But you mustn't let him know I put you up to this."

"Who else but you will help me, sir?" demanded Ting-hsi.

"Steady on. Listen to me. There are seven main branches to my family. The Minister of Ceremony belonged to the fifth branch. Two generations ago, the head of the seventh branch passed first in the palace examination, and his son was prefect of Kanchow in Kiangsi. He was my uncle, and his son is my twenty-fifth cousin, Shao-ching. He's two years younger than I am, and has passed the district examination too. My uncle was an honest officer, who didn't add anything to the family estate and left no more than ten thousand taels at his death. But, like a fool, Shao-ching acts as if he had hundreds of thousands. He doesn't know the difference between good silver and bad, yet he loves to act the patron. Anyone with a bad luck story can be sure of substantial help from him. Why don't you stay and help me out till autumn, when it's cooler? Then I'll give you your fare to Tienchang. I guarantee you'll get your thousand taels."

"I hope you will write a letter of introduction for me, sir, when the time comes."

"No, no. That would never do. He likes to be the one and only patron helping anybody—he doesn't like others to join in. If I were to write, he would think I'd already helped you, and wouldn't trouble to do anything for you. You must apply to someone else first."

"To whom?"

"My cousin used to have an old steward called Shao, whom you ought to know."

"He came one year when my father was alive," said Ting-hsi after thinking hard. "He arranged for us to give a performance for the old mistress's birthday! I saw the Prefect of Kanchow too."

"Excellent! Old Shao is dead now, and the present steward is a thoroughgoing scoundrel called Whiskers Wang, whom his master trusts implicitly. My cousin's weakness is this: anybody who claims to have known his father—even a dog—wins his respect. You must call on Whiskers Wang first. The rascal likes drinking and, if you treat him to wine and persuade him to tell his master that you were a favourite with the old prefect, then Shao-ching will shower you with silver. He doesn't like to be addressed as the master, so call him 'the young master.' Another of his peculiarities is that he can't stand talk about officials or rich men. Don't tell him, for instance, how good Prefect Hsiang was to you. Keep on harping on the fact that he is the only true patron in the world. And if he asks you whether you know me, tell him you don't."

This conversation left Pao Ting-hsi overjoyed. He made himself useful in Tu's household for another two months, until the end of the seventh month when the weather began to grow cooler. Then he borrowed a few taels from Tu Shen-ching, packed his luggage, and crossed the river to travel to Tienchang.

The day that he crossed the Yangtse, he put up for the night at Liuho. The next morning he rose early and travelled a dozen miles or more to a place called Fourth Mount, where he went into an inn and sat down. He was just going to ask for water to wash when a sedan-chair stopped at the gate. From it alighted an old man in a square cap, white gauze gown and red silk slippers, who had the red nose of a heavy drinker, and a long, silky, silvery beard. As this old man came in, the inn-keeper hastened to take his luggage.

"So it is the fourth Mr. Wei!" he cried. "Please take a seat inside, sir!"

As Mr. Wei entered the main room, Ting-hsi stood up and bowed. Mr. Wei returned his greeting. Ting-hsi urged him to take the seat of honour, and sat down himself in a lower place.

"I believe your name is Wei, sir," he said. "May I venture to ask your honourable district?"

"My name is Wei, and I come from Wuyi in Chuchow. What are your name and district, sir? And where are you bound for?"

"My name is Pao, and I am a native of Nanking. I am on my way to Tienchang, to visit the Mr. Tu whose grandfather was a Number One Scholar."

"Which Mr. Tu? Shen-ching or Shao-ching?"

"Shao-ching."

"There are sixty or seventy young men in the Tu family, but those are the only two who keep open house. The rest stay behind closed doors at home to prepare for the examination and look after their estates. That's why I asked straight away which of the two you meant. They are both well known all down the Yangtse Valley. Shen-ching is a most cultivated individual, but a little too effeminate for my taste. Shao-ching is a true gentleman of the old school. I'm on my way to see him too. We can travel together after we've eaten."

"Are you related to the Tu family, sir?"

"I was a classmate and sworn brother of Prefect Tu's. We were very close friends."

Upon hearing this, Ting-hsi's manner became even more respectful.

After their meal, Mr. Wei mounted his chair again. Ting-hsi hired a donkey, and trotted along beside the chair. When they reached Tienchang city gate, Mr. Wei dismounted.

"Let us walk to the house together, Mr. Pao," he said.

"Pray go on ahead in your chair, sir," replied Ting-hsi. "I want to see his steward first, before paying my respects to Mr. Tu."

"Very well," said Mr. Wei, and mounted his chair again.

When he reached Tu's house, his arrival was announced by the gate-keeper. Tu Shao-ching hastened out to meet him, and invited him into the hall, where they exchanged greetings.

"We have not seen each other for half a year, uncle," said Shao-ching. "I ought to have called to inquire after your health and that of your wife. Have you been well?"

"Quite well, thank you. There is nothing to do at home at the beginning of autumn, and I remembered your garden and reckoned the cassia must be in full blossom now. So I came to pay you a visit and drink with you."

"When tea has been served, I will invite you to have a rest in the library."

When a boy brought in tea, Tu Shao-ching gave him the order:

"Bring in Mr. Wei's baggage, and put it in the library. Then pay the chair-bearers and send them away."

Presently he led Mr. Wei by a passage from the back along a winding path to the garden. As you went in you saw three rooms with an eastern exposure. A two-storeyed building on the left was the library built by the Number One Scholar, overlooking a large courtyard with one bed of *moutan* peonies and another of tree peonies. There were two huge cassia trees as well, in full bloom. On the other side were three summer houses, with a three-roomed library behind them overlooking a great lotus pool. A bridge across this pool led you to three secluded chambers where Tu Shao-ching used to retire to study.

He invited Mr. Wei into the library with the southern exposure. The two cassia trees were just outside the window.

"Is old Lou still here?" asked Mr. Wei as he sat down.

"Mr. Lou's health has been very poor recently," replied Shao-ching, "so I have made him move into the inner library. He has just gone to sleep after taking his medicine. I'm afraid he won't be able to come out to greet you, uncle."

"If he is ill, why don't you send him home?"

"I have brought his sons and grandsons here to prepare his medicine. In this way I can inquire after his health morning and evening."

"After being with your family for thirty-odd years, hasn't the old man put by a substantial sum of money? Hasn't he bought any property?"

"After my father was appointed Prefect of Kanchow, he gave the books for the entire property to Mr. Lou. Mr. Lou was in complete charge of all financial transactions, and my father never questioned him. Apart from his salary of forty taels of silver a year, Mr. Lou didn't touch a cent. When the time came for collecting rent, he would go down to the

country to visit the tenants himself; and if they prepared two
dishes for him, he would send one away and eat one only.
Whenever his sons or grandsons came to see him, he would
pack them off after two days, and would never allow them to
take a cent beyond their travelling money. In fact, he used
to search them as they were leaving, to make sure none of
the stewards had given them any silver. But in collecting
rents or interest, if he discovered any of our friends or relatives were in difficulties, he would do his best to help them.
My father knew this, but didn't query it. Sometimes when
my father's debtors were unable to pay, Mr. Lou would burn
their notes of hand. Though he is an old man now with two
sons and four grandsons, he is still no richer than before. I
feel very bad about it!"

"A true gentleman of the old school!" exclaimed Mr. Wei
admiringly. "Is Shen-ching at home and well?"

"My cousin has gone to Nanking."

Just then Whiskers Wang took up his stand outside the
window with a red card in his hand, but did not presume to
enter.

"What is it, Wang?" asked Shao-ching, catching sight of
him. "What's that in your hand?"

The steward came in and handed the card to his master.

"A man called Pao is here from Nanking," he announced.
"He's a theatre manager, who has been away from home for
the last few years and has only just come back. Now he's
crossed the river to pay his respects to you, sir."

"If he's in the theatre, tell him I have guests and can't
see him. Keep his card, and ask him to leave."

"He says he was very kindly treated by our late master,
sir. He wants very much to see you to thank you."

"Did my father help him out?"

"Yes, sir. One year Mr. Shao fetched his company across
the river, and the prefect took a great fancy to this Pao
Ting-hsi. He promised to look after him."

"In that case, show him in."

"I met this fellow Pao from Nanking on the road," said
Mr. Wei.

Whiskers Wang went out to fetch Pao Ting-hsi, who advanced reverently. He looked round the spacious garden, and could see no end to it. Upon reaching the library door, he saw Tu Shao-ching sitting there with a guest. Tu was wearing a square cap, jade-coloured lined gauze gown, and pearl-decked shoes. He had a rather sallow complexion and eyebrows which rose obliquely, like a portrait of the God of War.

"That is our young master," said Whiskers Wang. "You can go in."

Pao Ting-hsi went in, knelt down and kowtowed.

"We are old friends," said Tu, helping him up. "Don't stand on ceremony."

Ting-hsi rose to his feet and exchanged greetings, first with Tu, then with Mr. Wei. Tu Shao-ching invited him to be seated on a lower seat.

"I owe your father such a debt of gratitude that even if my bones are ground to powder it will be hard to repay him," said Ting-hsi. "Because things have not gone well with me these last few years and I have been busy touring with my players, I did not come to pay my respects to the young master. Only today have I come to inquire after the young master's health. I hope you will forgive me, sir, for being so remiss."

"Just now," said Tu, "my steward Wang told me that my father took a great fancy to you, and meant to look after you. Since you are here, you must stay, and I will see what I can do for you."

"Dinner is ready, sir," announced Whiskers Wang. "Where would you like it served?"

"Why not here?" suggested Mr. Wei.

"We need a fourth," said Tu, and after a moment's hesitation called the library boy, Chia Chueh.

"Go out through the back gate and invite Dr. Chang over," he ordered.

Chia Chueh assented and left.

Presently the boy returned accompanied by a man with large eyes and a brownish moustache, who was wearing a tile-shaped cap and a wide cloth gown. Swaying as he walked in imitation of a scholar's gait, he came in, greeted them, sat down, and asked Mr. Wei's name.

"And what is your honourable name, sir?" inquired Mr. Wei, after giving his own.

"I am Chang Chun-min," was the reply, "and have served the Tu family for many years. I have a smattering of medical knowledge, and the young master does me the honour of calling me in every day to attend to Mr. Lou. How has the old gentleman been since he took his medicine today?"

Tu Shao-ching ordered Chia Chueh to go and find out.

"Mr. Lou had a nap after his medicine," reported the boy on his return. "He is awake now, and feels rather better."

"Who is *this* gentleman?" asked Chang, indicating Ting-hsi.

"This is my friend Pao from Nanking," replied Tu.

While they were speaking the table was spread, and they sat down: Mr. Wei in the seat of honour, Chang Chun-min opposite him, Tu Shao-ching in the place of host, and Pao Ting-hsi in the lowest seat. Their cups were filled, and they began to drink. The dishes to go with the wine had all been prepared at home, and were delicious. There was ham that had been hung for three years, and crabs weighing half a catty each, removed from their shells before cooking.

"I have no doubt you have attained great skill in your calling," said Mr. Wei to Chang Chun-min while they were eating.

"A thorough knowledge of Wang Shu-ho[1] is not as good as experience of many diseases," quoted the doctor. "I won't deceive you, sir. I have knocked about a good deal outside without reading many books, but seeing plenty of patients. Only recently, thanks to the young master's advice, have I learned the need for book knowledge. So I am not teaching my son medicine, but have engaged a tutor for him; and he is writing compositions which he brings to show Mr. Tu. The young master always comments on them for him, and I

---

[1] A physician of the Tsin Dynasty, whose books are medical classics.

also study these comments carefully at home, in this way learning something about literary composition. In another year or two I'll send my son in for the district examination, and he will get his share of dumplings as a candidate. Then, when he sets up in practice, he can call himself a scholarly physician!"

Mr. Wei laughed long and loud at this speech.

Then Whiskers Wang brought in another visiting card.

"Mr. Wang, the salt merchant at the North Gate, is celebrating his birthday tomorrow," he announced. "He has asked the magistrate as guest of honour, and invites you too, sir. He begs you to be sure to go."

"Tell him I have guests and cannot go," replied Tu. "How ridiculous the fellow is! If he wants a good party, why doesn't he invite those newly-rich scholars who have passed the provincial and metropolitan examinations? What time do I have to keep officials company for him?"

Whiskers Wang assented and left.

"You are a great drinker, uncle," said Tu to Mr. Wei. "You used to sit up half the night drinking with my father. We must have a good drinking session today too."

"Yes," replied Mr. Wei. "I hope you don't mind my saying this, friend; but though your food is first-rate, this wine bought in the market is too new. You have one jar of wine in your house which must be eight or nine years old by now. Assuming, that is, you still have it."

"I didn't know that," said Tu.

"You wouldn't know," rejoined Mr. Wei. "The year that your father went to take up his post in Kiangsi, I saw him to the boat, and he told me: 'I've buried a jar of wine in my house. When my term of office is up and I come home, we'll do some serious drinking together.' That's why I remember. Why don't you ask your household?"

"The young master couldn't have known this." Chang Chun-min smiled.

Tu Shao-ching went to the inner chambers.

"Though Mr. Tu is young, he is one of the most gallant gentlemen in these parts," declared Mr. Wei.

395

"The young master is so good to everyone too!" put in the doctor. "If anything, he's too open-handed. No matter who makes a request of him, he gives the fellow taels and taels of silver."

"I've never seen such a generous, noble gentleman in all my life!" chimed in Ting-hsi.

Tu Shao-ching went to the inner chambers to ask his wife if she knew anything about this wine, but she did not. He asked all the servants and maids, but none of them knew. Last of all he questioned his wet-nurse, Shao.

"There *was* such a jar," she recalled. "The year that our late master became prefect he brewed a jar of wine and buried it in a small room at the back of the seventh courtyard. He said it was to be kept for Mr. Wei. The wine was made of two pecks of glutinous rice and twenty catties of fermented rice. Twenty catties of alcohol went into it too, but not a drop of water. It was buried nine years and seven months ago, so it must be strong enough now to blow your head off. When it's dug up, don't drink it, sir!"

"Very good," said Tu.

He ordered the wet-nurse to unlock the door of the room where wine was stored, and went in with two servants. They dug up the wine jar, and carried it to the library.

"I've found your wine, uncle!" he cried.

Mr. Wei and the two guests stood up to look at it.

"That's it!" cried Mr. Wei.

The jar was opened, and they ladled out a cupful. It stood as thick as gruel in the cup, and had a rich bouquet.

"This is capital!" exclaimed Mr. Wei. "I'll tell you how we must drink this, friend. Send out for another ten catties of wine to mix with it. We can't drink it today, so just leave it there for the present. We'll drink all day tomorrow. These two gentlemen must join us."

"We will certainly keep you company," said Chang.

"Who am I," asked Ting-hsi, "to drink this fine wine the prefect has left? Tomorrow will be the happiest day of my life!"

Presently Chia Chueh was told to fetch a lantern and escort the doctor home. Ting-hsi slept in the library with

Mr. Wei, and Tu Shao-ching waited till the latter had gone to bed before retiring himself.

The next morning Pao Ting-hsi rose early and went to Whiskers Wang's room. Chia Chueh was sitting there with another servant.

"Is Mr. Wei up yet?" asked Whiskers Wang.

"He's up and washing his face," said Chia Chueh.

"Is the young master up?" the steward asked the other servant.

"He's been up a long time. He's in Mr. Lou's room, watching them prepare the medicine."

"Our master is an extraordinary man," declared Whiskers Wang. "Mr. Lou is only one of the prefect's employees! When he fell ill, our master should have given him a few taels of silver and sent him home—why keep him here and treat him as one of the family, waiting on him hand and foot?"

"How can you say that, Mr. Wang!" protested the servant. "When we prepare gruel or dishes for Mr. Lou, it's not enough for his sons and grandsons to inspect them—our master has to see them too before they can be given Mr. Lou! The ginseng pot is kept in the mistress's room, and of course she prepares the ginseng and other medicines herself. Every morning and evening, if our master can't take in the ginseng himself, it's the mistress who takes it in to the patient. If the master hears you talking like that, he'll give you a good dressing down!"

Just then the gate-keeper came in.

"Go in, Uncle Wang, and announce that the third Mr. Tsang is here," he said. "He's sitting in the hall, waiting to see the young master."

"Go and fetch the master from Mr. Lou's room," said Whiskers Wang to the servant. "I'm not going there to ask after Lou's health!"

"This just shows how good your master is," declared Ting-hsi.

Presently Tu Shao-ching came out to see Mr. Tsang, and after exchanging greetings they sat down.

"I haven't seen you for some days, Third Brother," remarked Tu. "What have you been doing in your literary groups?"

"Your gateman told me you had a guest from some distance," said Tsang. "Shen-ching seems to be enjoying himself so much in Nanking that he doesn't want to come back."

"Uncle Wei from Wuyi is here," said Tu. "I'm preparing a feast for him today, and you must stay to it too. Let's both go to the library now."

"Wait a little," said Tsang. "I have something to say to you. Magistrate Wang here is my patron, and he's told me many times how much he admires your talent. When are you coming with me to see him?"

"I must leave it to you, Third Brother, to call on magistrates and pay your respects as a student," replied Tu. "Why, in my father's time—to say nothing of my grandfather's and great-grandfather's — heaven knows how many magistrates came here! If he really respects me, why doesn't he call on me first? Why should I call on him? I'm sorry I passed the district examination, since it means I have to address the local magistrate as my patron! As for this Magistrate Wang, who crawled out of some dust-heap to pass the metropolitan examination —I wouldn't even want him as my student! Why should I meet him? So when the salt merchant who lives at the North Gate invited me to a feast today to meet the magistrate, I refused to go."

"That's why I'm here," said Tsang. "Magistrate Wang wouldn't have accepted the invitation if the salt merchant hadn't told him you would be there too; but he wants to meet you. If you don't go, he will be very disappointed. Besides, your guest is staying here, so you can keep him company tomorrow if you go out today. Or, if you like, I'll keep your friend company today while you go to the salt merchant's."

"Please don't insist, Third Brother," said Tu. "Your patron is no lover of worth or talent; he likes to accept students simply in order to collect presents from them. He wants me as his student, does he? He must be dreaming! In any case, I have guests today; and we've cooked a seven-catty duck, and unearthed some nine-year-old wine. The salt merchant will have nothing so good to offer me! I won't hear another word about going! Come with me now to the library."

He started marching Tsang off.

"Stop a minute!" cried Tsang. "What's the hurry? I've never met Mr. Wei. I must write a card."

"All right."

Tu ordered a servant to bring an inkstone and card, and Mr. Tsang wrote: "Your kinsman and fellow candidate, Tsang Tu."

He bade the servant take this to the library, then went in with Tu Shao-ching. Mr. Wei came to the door to greet them, and they took seats. Chang Chun-min and Pao Ting-hsi, who were also there, sat down too.

"May I inquire your second name?" Mr. Wei asked Tsang.

"Mr. Tsang's second name is Liao-chai," said Tu. "He was one of the best students of my year, and is a good friend of Shen-ching's as well."

"I am delighted to make your acquaintance," said Mr. Wei.

"I have long wanted to meet you, sir," rejoined Tsang.

Tsang knew the doctor, but looking at Pao Ting-hsi he asked:

"Who is *this* gentleman?"

"My name is Pao," replied Ting-hsi. "I have just arrived from Nanking."

"If you come from Nanking, do you know Mr. Tu Shen-ching?"

"I have met the seventeenth master."

When they had breakfasted, Mr. Wei brought out the wine and added ten catties of new wine to it, then ordered the servants to light plenty of charcoal and pile it when it was red by the cassia trees, setting the jar of wine on top. After the time it takes for a meal, the wine was hot. Chang Chun-min helped the servant take down the six window frames and move the table to under the eaves. They then took seats, and fresh dishes were served. Tu Shao-ching called for one gold and four jade cups, which he filled by dipping them into the wine. Mr. Wei had the gold cup, and after each drink exclaimed: "Marvellous!" They had feasted for some time when Whiskers Wang led in four servants carrying a chest. Tu asked what it was.

"This is a chestful of new autumn clothes for you, sir, and for the mistress and young gentleman. They have just been made, and I've brought them for you to check. I've already paid the tailor."

"Leave them there," said Tu. "I'll look at them when we've finished drinking."

No sooner had the chest been set down than the tailor came in.

"Tailor Yang is here," announced Whiskers Wang.

"What does he want?" asked Tu.

He stood up and saw the tailor walk into the courtyard, kneel down and kowtow, then burst out sobbing.

"What is the matter, Mr. Yang?" demanded Tu, much surprised.

"I've been working all this time in your house, sir," said the tailor. "This morning when I received my pay, I didn't know that my mother would suddenly be taken ill and die. I didn't foresee this when I went home, so I used all the money to pay my fuel and rice bills. And now I haven't got a coffin for my mother, or mourning. There's nothing I can do but come back and beg you to lend me a few taels of silver. I'll work off the debt gradually."

"How much do you want?"

"I'm a poor man. I dare not ask for a lot. Six taels, if that's not too much, sir. Otherwise four taels. I must be able to pay it back by tailoring."

"I don't want you to repay it," said Tu, much moved. "You may be in a small way of business, but you can't treat your mother's funeral casually, or you will regret it all your life. What good are a few taels? You must buy a sixteen-tael coffin at the very least; and with clothes and miscellaneous expenses you will need twenty taels altogether I haven't got a cent in the house at the moment—wait though! This chest of clothes can be pawned for twenty taels. Wang, you take this chest for Mr. Yang, and give him all the money you can raise on it. . . . I don't want this to prey on your mind, Mr. Yang. Just forget it. You aren't drinking or

400

gambling with my silver, but seeing to the most important event of your mother's funeral. We all have mothers, don't we? It's only right for me to help you."

The tailor carried out the chest with Whiskers Wang's help, crying as he did so. Tu Shao-ching came back to the table and sat down.

"That was a fine deed, friend!" said Mr. Wei.

Ting-hsi shot out his tongue

"Amida Buddha!" he exclaimed. "I didn't know such a good man existed!"

They feasted all day. Since Tsang was not a heavy drinker, by the afternoon he was sick and had to be helped home. Mr. Wei and the others drank till the third watch, and broke up only when the jar of wine was empty.

But to know what followed, you must read the next chapter.

CHAPTER 32

In which are described the gallant deeds of Tu Shao-ching, and the last words of Mr. Lou

After the party broke up, Mr Wei slept till late the next morning, then told Tu Shao-ching that he must be leaving.

"I mean to call on your uncle and cousin," he said. "I enjoyed myself enormously at the feast you so kindly prepared yesterday! I don't suppose I shall have such a good time anywhere else. Well, I must be going. I haven't even returned your friend Tsang's call, but please give him my best regards."

Shao-ching kept him for another day. The day after that he hired chair-bearers, then took a jade cup and two costumes which had belonged to the prefect of Kanchow to Mr. Wei's room.

"You are the only sworn brother my father had, uncle," he said. "I hope you will often come to see me, and I shall visit you more often to inquire after your health. I want you to take this jade cup to drink from And please accept these two costumes which belonged to my father, for when you wear them I shall feel I am seeing him again."

Mr. Wei accepted these gifts with pleasure. Pao Ting-hsi joined them over another pot of wine, after which rice was served. Then Tu and Ting-hsi saw Mr. Wei out of the city and bowed before his sedan-chair as he left. Upon their return, Tu went to Mr. Lou's room to see how he was. The old man affirmed that he was better, and that he would send his grandson home, keeping his son only to tend him.

Tu Shao-ching agreed to this. Then, remembering that he had no money, he sent for Whiskers Wang.

"I want you to sell my land within the dyke to that man," he told him.

"That fellow wants to get it cheap," objected Whiskers Wang. "You asked for one thousand five hundred taels, sir, but he's offered one thousand three hundred only. So I don't dare make a deal with him."

"One thousand three hundred will do."

"I just wanted to be clear on that before leaving, sir. Otherwise you might abuse me for selling it too cheaply."

"Who's going to abuse you? Hurry up and sell it. I need money right away."

"There's another thing I wanted to say, sir. When you've got the silver, I hope you'll put it to good use. It's a pity to sell your property, if you're only going to give hundreds and thousands of taels away for no reason."

"Have you seen me give silver away for no reason? You want to get something out of it, I know; but you can stow all that hypocritical talk. Be off with you now!"

"I was only making a suggestion," said Whiskers Wang.

Upon leaving the room, the steward whispered to Ting-hsi:

"Good! There's hope for you. I'm going to the dyke now to sell some land, and when I come back I'll think up a plan for you."

Whiskers Wang returned several days later having sold the land for one thousand and several hundred taels, which he brought home in a small bag.

"This is only ninety-five per cent pure silver, sir," he reported to his master. "It was weighed by the market balance, which gives thirteen and a half cents less to the tael than the official balance. And he deducted twenty-three taels forty cents for the middleman there, while the witnesses to the contract took another twenty to thirty taels. We had to foot both those bills. Here is the silver, sir. Let me fetch the scales so that you can weigh it."

"Who's got the patience to listen to your fiddling accounts! Since the silver's here, why weigh it? Take it inside and have done with it!"

"I simply wanted to make it clear," said the steward.

Now that Tu Shao-ching had this silver, he called Mr. Lou's grandson to the library.

"Are you leaving tomorrow?" he asked.

"Yes, sir. Grandfather told me to go."

"I have a hundred taels of silver here for you, but you mustn't let your grandfather know about it. You have a widowed mother to keep; so take this silver home and set up in some small business which can support you both. If your grandfather recovers and your second uncle is able to leave, I shall give him a hundred taels too."

Delighted, Mr. Lou's grandson took the silver and concealed it on his person, then thanked the young master. The next day, when he took his leave, Mr. Lou would not let him be given more than thirty cents of silver for the road. When Tu Shao-ching returned from seeing him off, he found a countryman standing in the hall who knelt down and kowtowed as soon as he saw the young master.

"Aren't you Huang Ta, who looks after our ancestral temple?" asked Tu. "What are you doing here?"

"I used to live in a cottage by the ancestral temple which your father bought me," replied Huang Ta. "After all these years the place needed repairing, and I made bold to take some dead trees from your graveyard to replace the beams and pillars. But some gentlemen of your family found out, and said I'd stolen the trees. They thrashed me within an inch of my life, and sent a dozen stewards to my cottage to take back the trees, who pulled down even those parts which were all right before Now I've nowhere to live; so I've come to beg you to speak to your clan, sir, and ask them to give me a little money for repairs from the communal fund, so that I can go on living there."

"My clan!" exclaimed Tu. "It's no use speaking to them. If my father bought you the cottage, it's obviously up to me to repair it. Since it's in ruins, how much will you need to build a new one?"

"A new one would cost a hundred taels. If I make do by repairing it, forty to fifty taels should be enough."

"Very well," said Tu. "I'm short of money at the moment, so just take fifty taels. When that's spent you can come back."

He fetched fifty taels for Huang Ta, who took the silver and left.

Then the gate-keeper came in with two cards.

"The third Mr. Tsang invites you to a feast tomorrow, sir," he announced. "This other card is to ask Mr. Pao to go along too."

"Tell the messenger to give my compliments to the third master," said Tu. "I will certainly go."

The next day he went with Pao Ting-hsi to Tsang's house. Tsang Liao-chai had prepared a good meal, and he invited Tu very respectfully to be seated and poured him wine, after which they chatted at random. Towards the end of the meal Tsang filled a cup with wine, raised it high in both hands and walked round the table to bow and present the cup to Tu. Then he knelt down.

"Brother!" he said. "I have a favour to ask."

With a start, Tu hastily set the wine on the table and knelt down to take Tsang's arm.

"Are you out of your mind, Third Brother?" he demanded. "What do you mean by this?"

"I won't get up till you've drunk that cup and promised to help me."

"I don't know what you're talking about. Get up and tell me."

Ting-hsi also tried to raise Tsang to his feet.

"Will you promise?" asked Tsang.

"Of course!" replied Tu.

"Then drink this cup of wine."

"I will drink it in a minute."

"I'm waiting for you to drain it."

Only then did Tsang stand up and resume his seat.

"Go ahead with whatever you have to say," prompted Tu.

"The examiner is at Luchow now, and it will be our turn next. The other day I tried to buy a licentiate's degree for someone, and paid the examiner's agent three hundred taels of silver. But later he told me: 'Our superiors are very strict, and I dare not sell this degree. Let me sell you a salaried scholar's rank instead, since you have already passed the preliminary test.' So I gave him my own name, and that is how I became a salaried scholar this year. But now the man who wanted to buy the licentiate's degree is demanding his money back; and if I don't return him three hundred taels, the whole business will be made public. This is a matter of life and death! You must help me, brother! If you will lend me three hundred taels of the money you got for your land to settle this business, I'll pay you back gradually. You promised just now to help."

"Pah!" exclaimed Tu. "I thought you were in real trouble when it was nothing but this all the time! You didn't have to put on such an act — kowtowing and pleading — for such a trifle! I'll give you the silver tomorrow."

"Well said!" cried Ting-hsi, clapping his hands. "Let's have large cups to drink to this!"

At once large cups were brought, and they drank until Tu was tipsy.

"Tell me, Third Brother," he said, "what made you so set on this salaried scholar's rank?"

"You wouldn't understand!" retorted Tsang. "A salaried scholar has a better chance of passing the next examination, and once you pass that you become an official. Even if you don't pass, after a dozen years you become a senior licentiate, and when you've taken the palace examination you'll be appointed a magistrate or a judge. Then I shall wear boots with knotted soles, hold court, pass sentence and have people beaten. And if gentlemen like you come to raise the wind, I'll have you locked up and fed on beancurd for a month, till you choke to death!"

"You ruffian!" cried Tu with a laugh. "You are utterly contemptible!"

"What a joke!" chuckled Ting-hsi. "You two gentlemen should each drain a cup after that."

Later that evening they parted.

The next morning Tu told Whiskers Wang to take a casket of silver over, and the steward received another six taels as his tip. On his way back he stopped at the fish shop for a bowl of noodles, and found Chang Chun-min there.

"Come over here, Mr. Whiskers, and sit with me!" called the doctor.

Whiskers Wang went over to his table, and when the noodles were brought started eating.

"I want you to do something for me," said Chang.

"What is it? Do you want a present because you've cured old Lou?"

"No, old Lou's disease is incurable."

"How much longer has he got?"

"Not more than a hundred days, probably. But you needn't tell him that. I want you to do something for me."

"Go on."

"The examiner will soon be here, and my son wants to take the examination; but I'm afraid the college authorities will say I'm an outsider. I'd like your young master to speak to them."

"That's no use." Whiskers Wang made a sign of dissent. "Our young master has never had anything to do with that lot. And he doesn't like to hear of people sitting for the examinations. If you ask him that, he'll advise you not to enter the boy!"

"What's to be done then?"

"There *is* a way. I'll tell Mr. Tu your son isn't allowed to sit; but the examination school in Fengyang was built by our young master's father, and if Mr. Tu wants to send in a candidate, who's to stop him? That'll goad him into doing something for you — he'll be willing even to spend money!"

"Handle it as you think best, Whiskers. If you pull it off, I'll not fail to thank you."

"As if I wanted thanks from you! Your son is my nephew. I'll be quite satisfied if he kowtows a few times to his old uncle when he's entered the college and is wearing a brand-new square cap and blue gown!"

This said, Chang Chun-min paid for the noodles and they left.

Whiskers Wang went home and asked the servants: "Where is the young master?"

"In the library," was the answer.

He went straight to the library, where he found Tu Shao-ching.

"I delivered the silver to the third Mr. Tsang," announced the steward. "He is very grateful to you, sir. He says you've saved him from serious trouble, and made it possible for him to become an official. Nobody else would be willing to do such a thing."

"A mere trifle," said Tu. "Why come here and gabble about it?"

"I've something else to report, sir," said the steward. "You've paid for Mr. Tsang's degree, and built a cottage for the caretaker of the ancestral temple. Very soon now the examinations are going to be held, and they'll be asking you to repair the examination school. Your father spent thousands of taels building that school, but other people have had all the advantage of it. If you were to send in a candidate, who would dare oppose him?"

"Candidates can enter themselves. Why should I send one?"

"If I had a son and you sent him in, would they dare say anything?"

"Of course not. Those college scholars are no better than slaves themselves."

"The son of Dr. Chang at the back gate has been studying. Why don't you tell him to sit for the examination?"

"Does he want to?"

"His father is an outsider — he dares not enter."

"Tell him to enter. If any scholar says anything, tell the fellow *I* sent him."

"Very good, sir."

With this, Whiskers Wang left.

Mr. Lou's illness was taking a turn for the worse, and Tu Shao-ching, who had invited a second physician to attend him, stayed at home in low spirits.

One day Tsang called.

"Have you heard the news?" he asked, without waiting to sit down. "Magistrate Wang is in trouble. Yesterday evening they took away his seal, and his successor is pressing him to move out of the yamen. But because everyone says he is a corrupt official, no one will put him up. He's at his wit's end!"

"What is he doing?"

"He just stayed in the yamen last night. But if he doesn't move out tomorrow, he'll be in for a big loss of face! Who's going to lend him rooms, though? He'll have to move into the Old Men's Home!"

"Really?"

Tu ordered the servant to fetch Whiskers Wang.

"I want you to go at once to the yamen," he said, "and ask the attendants to inform Magistrate Wang that if he has nowhere to stay, he is welcome to come here. He needs rooms badly — hurry up!"

The steward hastened off.

"You refused to meet him before," said Tsang. "What makes you offer him accommodation today? Just think, you may find yourself involved in his trouble; and if there's a riot the mob may destroy your garden!"

"Everybody knows the good my father did for this district," replied Tu. "Even if I hid bandits here, no one would break into my house. Don't worry about that, brother. As for this Mr. Wang, it's lucky for him he knew enough to respect me. To have called on him the other day would have been making up to the local magistrate; but now that he's been removed from office and has nowhere to live, it's my duty to help him. When he receives my message, he's sure to come. Wait till he arrives, and you can talk to him."

Just then the gate-keeper came in to announce: "Dr. Chang is here."

Chang Chun-min walked in, knelt down and kowtowed.

"What is it this time?" asked Tu.

"It's about this business of my son taking the examination, sir. I'm extremely grateful to you."

"I have already promised to help."

"When the scholars knew it was your wish, sir, they had no objections, but they insisted that I raise a hundred and twenty taels to help repair the college; and where can I get so much money? That's why I've come to beg your help, sir."

"Will a hundred and twenty be enough? You won't need more later?"

"I won't need any more."

"That's easy. I'll pay it for you. All you have to do is write an application to enter the college, promising to contribute towards the repairs, and bring it here. You take it to the college for him, Third Brother. You can get the silver here."

"I am busy today," said Tsang to the doctor. "I'll go with you tomorrow."

Having expressed his thanks, Chang Chun-min left. The next moment Whiskers Wang came flying in.

"Magistrate Wang has come to call!" he announced. "He's at the gate and has left his chair."

Tu and Tsang went out to meet him. The magistrate was wearing a gauze cap and the clothes of a private citizen. He came in and bowed.

"I have long wished to make your acquaintance, sir, but lacked the opportunity," he said. "It is exceedingly good of you to put me up in your distinguished residence during my present difficulties, and I feel ashamed to trespass on your hospitality; I have therefore come to express my thanks before profiting more fully by your instructions. It is lucky my friend Tsang is here too!"

"A trifle like this is beneath Your Honour's notice," replied Tu. "Since my poor house is empty, I hope you will move in at your earliest convenience."

"I came here to ask my friend to call with me on my patron," said Tsang. "I little thought my patron would honour us first with a visit."

"Don't mention it!" said the magistrate.

He bowed his way to his chair, then left.

Tu Shao-ching kept Tsang, and gave him a hundred and twenty taels to settle Dr. Chang's business the following day; and Tsang took the silver home with him. The next day Magistrate Wang moved in. And the day after that Chang Chun-min gave a feast in Tu's house, to which Tsang and Ting-hsi were also invited.

410

"It's time for you to speak up," said Whiskers Wang to Ting-hsi in private. "According to my calculations, he'll soon reach the end of that silver; and if anyone else comes to ask for money, there'll be none left for you. You must speak this evening."

By this time all the guests had arrived, and the feast was laid in the library by the hall. The four of them went to the table; but before taking his seat Chang Chun-min offered a cup of wine to Tu Shao-ching to express his gratitude, then filled another cup and bowed his thanks to Tsang. During the meal they chatted at random. Then Ting-hsi addressed Tu.

"I have been here for half a year, sir, and seen you spend money like water," he said. "Even the tailor carried handfuls of silver away. But in my seven or eight months here I've had nothing but a little meat and wine—not a copper have I seen. Why should I carry on with this thankless job, getting nothing for my pains? I'd better wipe my eyes and go somewhere else to weep. I will take my leave of you tomorrow."

"Why didn't you mention this earlier, Mr. Pao?" asked Tu. "How could I know you had this on your mind? You should have spoken out."

Ting-hsi hastily filled a cup and passed it to him.

"My father and I both made a living by managing an opera company," he said. "Unhappily my father died, and instead of proving a credit to the old man I lost my capital. I have an old mother, yet I can't support her. I am the most miserable of men, unless the young master will give me some capital to take home so that I can provide for my mother."

"How admirable that an actor should show such filial piety!" exclaimed Tu. "Of course I will help you!"

Ting-hsi stood up.

"Thank you, sir, for your goodness!" he said.

"Sit down," replied Tu. "How much money do you need?"

Ting-hsi glanced at Whiskers Wang, who was standing at the foot of the table, and the steward stepped forward.

"You'll need a good deal of silver, Mr. Pao," he said. "It'll cost you five to six hundred taels I should think to get together a company and buy costumes. The young master doesn't have so much here. All he can do is give you a few dozen taels to take back across the river, and you can make a start with that."

"A few dozen taels is not enough," said Tu. "I'll give you a hundred taels to start training a company. When that's finished, you can come back again."

Ting-hsi knelt down and thanked him.

"I would have done more for you before letting you go," said Tu, stopping him, "but Mr. Lou is seriously ill, and I have to be ready for any emergency."

Tsang and Chang praised Tu's generosity, and soon the party broke up.

Mr. Lou's illness was becoming daily more serious.

"My friend," he said one day, when Tu was sitting at his bedside, "I hoped I might recover, but now it doesn't look as if I shall, and I want you to send me home."

"I have not been able to do all I should for you, uncle," said Tu. "How can you speak of going home?"

"Don't be foolish! I have sons and grandsons; and though I've spent my life away from home, it's natural now to want to go home to die. No one's going to accuse you of turning me out."

"In that case I won't keep you," said Tu with tears in his eyes. "I've prepared your coffin, uncle; but now you won't be needing it, and it's not easy to take. So I'll give you a few dozen taels instead with which to buy another. The clothes and bedding are all ready, and you can take them with you."

"I will take the coffin and clothes, but don't give any more silver to my sons and grandsons. I want to leave within the next three days, and since I can't sit up I'll have to be carried in a litter. Tomorrow go to your father's shrine and inform his spirit that Mr. Lou wishes to take his leave and go home. I have been with your family for thirty years, as one of your worthy father's closest friends; and since his death your treatment of me has left nothing to be desired. Your conduct and learning are unparalleled; and your son in particular is a boy of extraordinary promise—you must bring him up to be an honest man. You are not a good manager, however, and don't make the right friends; so you will soon come to the end of your property! I like to see you acting in a just and generous manner, but you must consider with whom you are dealing. The way you are going on, all your money is being tricked out of you by people who will never repay your kindness; and while we say charity expects no reward, you should distinguish between those who deserve help and those who don't. The third Mr. Tsang and Chang Chunmin, of whom you see so much, are unscrupulous characters. And recently this Pao Ting-hsi has joined them. There are no good men among players, yet you want to be his patron. As for your steward, Whiskers Wang, he's even worse! Money is of small account, and after I'm dead you and your son must imitate your noble father in everything. If you have virtue, it doesn't matter even if you go hungry. Your closest friend is your cousin Shen-ching; but though Shen-ching is brilliant you can't trust him too far. Imitate your worthy father, and you won't go wrong. Since you set no store by officials or by your own family, this is no place for you. Nanking is a great metropolis, and there you may find friends to appreciate your talent and be able to achieve something. What's left of your property won't last long! If you take my advice, I shall die happy!"

"I shall remember all your excellent advice, uncle," replied Tu with tears in his eyes.

He went out immediately and ordered his men to hire four bearers to carry Mr. Lou to Taohung by way of Nanking, then gave Mr. Lou's son over a hundred taels to take home for his father's funeral. On the third day, he saw Mr. Lou off on his journey.

But to know what followed, you must read the next chapter.

CHAPTER 33

Wherein Tu Shao-ching and his wife take a pleasure trip,
and Chih Heng-shan discusses ceremony with his friends

After Mr. Lou went home and Tu Shao-ching had no one
to reason with him, he spent money more and more recklessly.
As soon as the first lot of silver was finished, he made
Whiskers Wang sell another piece of land for over two thousand taels, which he proceeded to squander. He also gave
Pao Ting-hsi a hundred taels to take home with him across
the Yangtse. When Magistrate Wang's business was settled,
he vacated his rooms and left. Then Tu spent another half
year or so at home, until his silver was nearly finished and
he decided to make over his house to the clan and move to
Nanking. His wife when consulted agreed to this, and though
others tried to dissuade him he would not listen. After a
busy half year the house was finally made over, and by the
time all the debts were settled and everything in pawn had
been redeemed, he had over a thousand taels left.

"I'm going to pay a visit to my nephew Lu in Nanking,"
he told his wife. "When I've found a house, I'll come back
for you."

Thereupon he packed his baggage to cross the Yangtse
with Whiskers Wang and the servant-boy Chia Chueh.
Whiskers Wang, who saw that matters were in a bad way,
helped himself to twenty taels of silver during the journey
and made off. Tu simply laughed, however, and went on alone

with Chia Chueh. When he reached the house of his mother's relatives, the Lu family, at Granary Lane, his nephew Lu Hua-shih invited him in and they exchanged greetings in the hall. Tu then went upstairs to bow before the tablets of his grandfather and grandmother, after which he paid his respects to Hua-shih's mother, and ordered his boy to unpack the ham, tea and other local produce he had brought for her. Lu Hua-shih took him into the library for a meal, inviting the tutor he had engaged this year, to accompany them. When the tutor had greeted him, Tu urged him to take the seat of honour and asked his name.

"I am Chih Heng-shan. May I inquire your honourable name?"

"This is my Uncle Tu from Tienchang," replied Hua-shih.

"Is it Mr. Tu Shao-ching? You are known throughout the country, sir, for your noble deeds. I had heard your fame but never seen your face, and little thought to meet so distinguished a guest today!"

He stood up to bow once more.

The tutor was thin, with eyebrows that nearly met in the middle, long fingers and brilliant eyes. Realizing that he was no ordinary man, Tu treated him warmly from the start. When, after the meal, Tu mentioned that he wanted to find a house, Chih Heng-shan was delighted.

"Why don't you find yourself a riverside house, sir?" he suggested.

"The very thing!" replied Tu. "Suppose we search for a house now and look at the River Chinhuai at the same time?"

Bidding Hua-shih remain at home, Mr. Chih walked out with Shao-ching. At Number One Scholar Square they saw some new book covers pasted up in a bookshop. One of the titles read: "Commentaries on Examination Essays by Ma Chun-shang of Chuchow and Chu Hsien-fu of Chiahsing."

"This Chu Hsien-fu is the grandson of Prefect Chu of Nanchang," said Tu. "We are relatives. So since he is here I had better call on him."

He went in with Mr. Chih. Chu Hsien-fu came in to greet them, and they exchanged the usual compliments Then Ma Chun-shang came in, bowed and inquired their names.

"This is Mr. Tu Shao-ching of the family of the Number One Scholar in Tienchang," said Chu. "This is Mr. Chih Heng-shan of Chujung. They are two of our leading scholars, and my one regret is that we did not meet earlier."

"Shao-ching wants to look for rooms," said Mr. Chih when tea had been served. "We mustn't stay longer today."

On their way out they saw a man leaning over the counter reading a poem.

"This is *my* work!" he declared, pointing at the book.

The four others walked up to him, and saw that lying beside him was a white fan inscribed with poems. Chu Hsien-fu opened it and read: "Mr. Lan-chiang."

"It's Ching Lan-chiang!" he cried with a laugh.

Ching Lan-chiang looked up. When he saw the two strangers he bowed and inquired their names.

"We had better go to look for rooms," said Tu, taking Chih's arm. "We can call on these gentlemen later."

They walked past Huaiching Bridge and Chih Heng-shan, who knew the way, found a house agent to show them several houses by the river, but not until they reached East Water Gate did they find anything satisfactory. Since this was the year for the county examinations, these rooms were exceedingly dear. The rent of this house was eight taels a month.

"Very well," said Tu. "We'll rent it first, and see about buying it later."

The custom in Nanking is to demand a deposit and the first month's rent in advance. The house agent and the landlord went straight to Lu's house at Granary Lane to draw up the contract, and Tu paid them sixteen taels. Since his relatives prepared wine to entertain him and Mr. Chih, and they chatted till it was late, the tutor spent the night there.

They had barely washed their faces the next morning when someone called from outside the door: "Where is Mr. Tu Shao-ching?"

Before Tu could go out to see who it was, a stranger had entered.

"Don't tell me your names," he said. "Let me guess."

After looking at them steadily, he stepped forward and laid one hand on Tu.

416

"You are Tu Shao-ching!" he declared.

"I am Tu Shao-ching," agreed Tu with a smile. "This is Mr. Chih Heng-shan, and this is my nephew. What is your honourable name?"

"You are a legendary figure, sir," said the visitor. "And your commanding presence—so unlike Mr. Chih's mature dignity—struck awe into my heart. That is how I knew you. I am Chi Wei-hsiao, at your service."

"Are you the Mr. Chi who judged the operatic contest?" asked Chih. "I have been looking forward to meeting you."

Chi Wei-hsiao sat down.

"Your good cousin has already left for the north," he told Tu.

"When did he leave?" asked Tu in surprise.

"Only three or four days ago. I saw him to Dragon River Station. He is a senior licentiate now, and has gone to the capital to take the examination. I understand you scatter gold about like dirt, sir. In that case, why have you been hiding at home for so long, instead of bringing your money here to give us all a good time?"

"I am here now," replied Tu. "I have taken a riverside house, and mean to send for my family."

"Wonderful!" Chi Wei-hsiao clapped his hands. "I must find myself a couple of rooms next to yours, and bring my wife here to keep Mrs. Tu company. Will you pay for our house too?"

"Certainly," replied Tu.

Presently a meal was served, and they prevailed on Chi Wei-hsiao to stay. While at table his description of how he had tricked Tu Shen-ching into calling on the Taoist priest made them laugh so violently that they nearly choked. The moment the meal was over, Ma Chun-shang, Chu Hsien-fu and Ching Lan-chiang called. After chatting for a time, they saw these guests out; but no sooner had they come back than Hsiao Chin-hsuan, Chu-ko Tien-shen and Chi Tien-yi called. Chi Wei-hsiao joined them, and after a little conversation left with the three other guests. Then Tu Shao-ching wrote a letter home, and sent a man to Tienchang to fetch his household.

Early the next morning, when he was about to return the calls of Chi Wei-hsiao and the others, Kuo Tieh-pi and Lai the Taoist priest arrived. Tu ushered them in, and at the sight of the priest and the memory of the previous day's conversation he could not repress a smile. After a little polite conversation the priest produced a book of poems, and Kuo Tieh-pi presented Tu with two seals. He accepted their gifts, and having drunk tea they left. Tu then went out to call on the others. He spent seven or eight days with the Lus, and in the course of discussing ceremony and music with Chih Heng-shan, he became very friendly with the tutor. When at last his household arrived in four boats, which moored by the riverside house, Tu took leave of the Lu family and moved to his new quarters.

The next day everyone came to offer congratulations. This was early in the third month, when the houses by the river were beginning to be filled and music could often be heard. Tu Shao-ching prepared a feast, and invited four tables of guests, including Chi Wei-hsiao, Ma Chun-shang, Chu Hsien-fu, Chi Tien-yi, Chih Heng-shan, Lu Hua-shih, Ching Lan-chiang, Chu-ko Tien-shen, Hsiao Chin-hsuan, Kuo Tieh-pi and Lai Hsia-shih. Chin Tung-ya, who lived in a neighbouring riverside house and had called, was invited too. The tea attendants and cooks were the first to arrive; then Pao Ting-hsi brought the boys he was training for his Three Founts Company to kowtow to Mr. and Mrs. Tu, who regaled them with fruit. Next the landlord of the house introduced a flower-seller named Yao, and Mrs. Tu asked her to stay. By midday all the guests had arrived, and every window was opened. The visitors sat where they pleased or leaned over the balcony to watch the water, sipping tea as they chatted, leafing through the books on the tables, or sitting at ease enjoying themselves—each did exactly as he liked. Then a sedan-chair arrived accompanied by Pao Ting-hsi, who had brought his wife to pay her respects to the young mistress. When she alighted and entered the house, Mrs. Yao burst out laughing.

"Everybody in Nanking knows this woman," she told Mrs. Tu. "What made her take it into *her* head to call?"

In Mrs. Tu's presence, however, Mrs. Pao was on her best behaviour; and Mrs. Tu invited her to stay too. When Tu went to his wife's room, Mrs. Yao and Mrs. Pao paid him their respects. The presence of so many guests inspired Pao Ting-hsi to make all manner of quips and jokes, and the time passed merrily till the feast was ready. Then Tu invited his guests to take their seats, and not till late that night did the party break up. Ting-hsi, carrying a lantern to escort his wife's chair, left too.

A few days later, because it was Mrs. Tu's first visit to Nanking, she expressed a wish to see some of the sights.

"That can easily be arranged," said her husband.

He ordered several sedan-chairs, and invited Mrs. Yao to join their party. Two or three maids accompanied them by chair, and the cook carried food and wine for them to Yao Garden on Mount Chingliang, which they had hired for the occasion. Yao Garden was a large park which you entered by a wicker gate. The path inside the gate was paved with white pebbles and bordered by scarlet balustrades, shown off to advantage by green willows on either side. Passing a three-roomed building they came to a place where wine was usually sold, but today all the tables had been removed. Beyond this was a path up the mountain. At the summit was an octagonal pavilion, and here the meal was spread while Mrs. Tu, Mrs. Yao and the others looked at the scenery from the pavilion. On one side was Mount Chingliang with bamboo groves dotted up and down its slopes, on the other a charming view of Lingyin Temple its red walls embedded in greenery. They had not been sitting there long when Tu Shao-ching arrived by chair with his golden goblet, which he placed on the table and filled with wine. Then, revelling in the spring warmth and balmy breeze, he carried the goblet to the balustrade and started to do some heavy drinking. Very drunk at last, he took his wife's hand and walked out of the garden, holding the golden goblet and roaring with laughter. So they strolled several hundred yards down the hillside while the other women followed them, laughing merrily. All who saw were shocked and amazed. When Tu and his wife had mounted their chairs and left, Mrs. Yao and the maids plucked branches of peach blossom and loaded their chairs with these, then were carried home.

It was late by the time Tu reached the riverside house, but he found Lu Hua-shih waiting there.

"Uncle Chuang from North Gate Bridge has heard of your arrival, uncle," said Lu, "and wants very much to see you. He hopes you will wait in tomorrow, so that he can pay his respects."

"I have always treated Mr. Chuang as my teacher," replied Tu. "I didn't invite him the other day, because he cannot bear to mix with those poets; but I was about to call on him. How can I trouble him to come here? Please go back as fast as you can, nephew, and send a messenger to convey my regards and say I shall call on him tomorrow."

Hua-shih assented and left.

Tu Shao-ching had barely closed the gate after seeing him off, when knocking was heard. The servant-boy opened the gate and let someone in.

"Master Lou is here, sir," he announced.

Tu Shao-ching saw that it was Mr. Lou's grandson, dressed in mourning, who prostrated himself weeping.

"My grandfather has died," he announced. "I came specially to tell you, sir."

"When did he pass away?"

"On the twenty-sixth of last month."

Tu Shao-ching wept, then prepared sacrificial offerings that same night. Early the next morning he mounted a sedan-chair and set out for Taohung. Chi Wei-hsiao came over early that day, having heard of the outing to Yao Garden; but learning that Tu had gone to Taohung, he had to leave regretfully.

Upon reaching Taohung, Tu Shao-ching wept bitterly several times before Mr. Lou's coffin, then hired Buddhist monks to perform several days' masses for the dead man's spirit. Many of the Lou family relatives were invited. Tu stayed there for four or five days, weeping again and again, till all the people of Taohung marvelled.

"How good the Tienchang Tu family is!" said some.

"The old man must have been a fine character, or Mr. Tu would not be showing such respect," said others. "We should acquit ourselves like this old man."

When Tu Shao-ching gave an additional several dozen taels of silver to Mr. Lou's family to buy a burial ground, the whole Lou clan, men and women, came to thank him. Then after crying bitterly once more before the coffin he left.

When he reached home his wife told him: "The day after you left, a courier from the provincial government and a messenger from Tienchang County yamen arrived with a despatch for you. I told them you were away, and they put up at an inn, but they've been back every day since. I don't know what their business is."

"Strange!" said Tu.

While he was wondering what this might mean, the servant-boy announced: "The courier and messenger to see you, sir."

Tu Shao-ching went out, greeted the courier, and sat down. The courier congratulated him, and the messenger presented a despatch, which had already been opened.

Tu read:

A despatch from Governor Li regarding the recommendation of men of talent. By order of the emperor, an investigation is being made of scholars from all parts of the country. Our office has ascertained that Tu Shao-ching, a scholar of Tienchang, is a man of fine character and outstanding literary attainments. We therefore request the college instructors of his district to invite him to proceed forthwith to the provincial capital for a test, in order that we may report to the government and that he may be summoned for an audience with the emperor and be given an appointment. This matter is urgent!

"Governor Li was my grandfather's student," reflected Tu after reading this. "He counts as my uncle, which must be why he has recommended me. I can't possibly accept. But since he has been so good, I must prepare to leave at once, and go to his yamen to thank him."

He kept the courier to a meal, presented him with several taels for the road and the messenger with another two taels, then dismissed them. Having no money for the journey, he pawned his gold goblet for thirty taels, then set sail with his servant-boy for Anching. Upon his arrival he found that Governor Li had left on public business. When he came back several days later, Tu Shao-ching presented his card, and the attendant opened the gate and invited him into the library. The governor came in, and Tu bowed to him and inquired after his health. Governor Li offered him a seat.

"After my patron died, I often wondered what had become of you and your cousins," said the governor. "I had long heard of your outstanding talents and virtue, and so when the government adopted the ancient practice of offering posts to scholars living in retirement I made so bold as to name you. You must not think of declining."

"My talents and learning are of the poorest," replied Tu. "You overrate me, sir, and I am afraid I should let you down."

"Don't be unduly modest. Let me arrange it with your county government."

"I am extremely grateful for this undeserved honour. But mine is a rustic nature, and I have grown accustomed to country ways. My health has also been poor recently. I must beg Your Excellency to find someone else."

"How can sons of official families refuse to take up office? My information was not at fault, and I insist on recommending you."

Tu Shao-ching dared say no more. Governor Li kept him there that night, and asked his opinion of a number of poems and essays which he had written.

The following morning Tu took his leave. He had not brought much money with him, and as a result of staying a few days extra and having to tip the attendants at the provincial government, by the time he hired a boat for Nanking he had not the three taels for the fare. The wind was also against them, so that it took four or five days to reach Wuhu. There the boat was unable to make headway, and the boatman asked for money to buy rice. But when Tu bade his boy make a search, it appeared they had only five coppers left. He decided he would have to pawn some clothes, and walked gloomily ashore to the Temple of Good Luck, where he sat down at a table, drank some tea and ate three cakes because he was hungry. The bill came to six coppers—which meant that he could not leave the tea-shop! He noticed a Taoist priest passing, but did not take a good look at him. The Taoist, however, turned back to stare at Tu, then hurried over.

"What brings you here, sir?" he asked.

"So it is Lai Hsia-shih! Sit down and have some tea," laughed Tu.

"Why are you alone here?" inquired Lai.

"When did *you* come?" asked Tu.

"After trespassing on your hospitality that day, I received a letter from Magistrate Chang of Wuhu County, inviting me here to write poems. That's why I came. I am living at Boat Watchers Pavilion, where I have a wonderful view across the river. Won't you come to my lodgings?"

"I went to Anching to see a friend, and on my way back the wind held us up here. I should like to accompany you to your quarters."

Lai Hsia-shih paid for the tea, and they walked together to Boat Watchers Pavilion. The Taoist in the temple came out to ask who this honourable guest was.

"It's Mr. Tu of the family of the Number One Scholar in Tienchang," Lai told him.

The Taoist evinced great respect, and begged Mr. Tu to be seated while he made tea. Presently he noticed, pasted on the wall, a poem about Boat Watchers Pavilion dedicated to Lai Hsia-shih and signed by Wei Ssu-hsuan.

"This poem is by the fourth Mr. Wei of Wuyi," said Tu. "When was he here?"

"Mr. Wei is upstairs now," replied the Taoist.

"Why, then, let us go up and see him!"

They went upstairs together.

"Mr. Wei!" called the Taoist. "Mr. Tu of Tienchang is here!"

"What's that?" asked Mr. Wei, walking out.

"Uncle!" cried Tu Shao-ching. "Your nephew is here."

Mr. Wei smoothed his beard with both hands.

"I was wondering who it could be," he said, chuckling. "So it's you, Shao-ching! What brings you to these wild parts? Sit down while I brew some tea for you, and tell me all you've been doing. Where have you come from?"

Tu told him briefly about Governor Li's offer.

"I didn't bring enough money with me," he concluded, "and I've only five coppers left. It was Mr. Lai who paid for my tea just now. I've no money to pay the boatmen or buy food."

"Capital!" Mr. Wei laughed heartily. "So this is the end of the great patron! But a fine fellow like you needn't worry about such trifles. Stay and have a meal with me. A former student of mine who lives in Wuhu passed the examination the other day, and when I went to congratulate him he gave me twenty-four taels of silver. When we've finished our meal and the wind has shifted, I'll give you ten taels."

Tu sat down to drink with Mr. Wei and Lai Hsia-shih. They remained at table till the afternoon, watching the boats on the river from the pavilion window; and gradually the little banners on the junks, which showed the direction of the wind, veered.

"Good!" cried Mr. Wei. "The wind has changed."

They leaned over the window sill to gaze at the river, as the setting sun bathed the upper half of thousands of masts in a rosy light.

"The weather has cleared and the north-east wind has dropped," said Tu. "I will say goodbye to you, uncle, and go back to my boat."

After giving Tu ten taels of silver, Mr. Wei and Lai saw him to his junk. The Taoist asked to be remembered to all his friends in Nanking, then they made their farewells and Lai and Mr. Wei turned back.

Tu Shao-ching spent that night on the boat. At the fifth watch a gentle south-west wind sprang up, and the boatmen hoisted sail. With a following wind it took only half a day to reach White River Harbour, where Tu paid for his passage, had his baggage carried ashore, and took a sedan-chair home.

His wife, who was waiting for him, laughed merrily when he told her how he had run out of money on the trip.

The next day he went to North Gate Bridge to call on Mr. Chuang Shao-kuang.

"Governor Hsu of Chekiang Province invited our master to visit the West Lake with him," he was told. "He won't be back for several days."

Tu then went to the Lu house at Granary Lane to see Chih Heng-shan. The Lus kept him to a meal, and he and Mr. Chih started chatting.

"Scholars nowadays think only of the examinations," complained Mr. Chih. "To write a couple of lines of poetry is considered the height of accomplishment, while the sciences of ceremony, music, military affairs and agriculture are completely ignored! When the first emperor of our dynasty pacified the country, his achievements were comparable to those of Tang and Wu;[1] but he set up no system of ceremony or music. Now that you have been recommended, Shaoching, you must do some good work for the government, to justify this generation of scholars."

"I have already declined to accept any appointment," replied Tu. "I'm afraid I could achieve nothing, and would only make discriminating people laugh at me. Hence I think it better not to take office."

Chih Heng-shan fetched a roll of paper from his room.

"I want your advice on something," he said.

"What is it?"

"The worthiest man Nanking has produced, past or present, is Tai Po,[2] who founded the Kingdom of Wu. Yet there is not a single temple dedicated to him, though you find temples to the God of Literature and the God of War everywhere. I want to persuade some friends to contribute enough to build

---

1 King Tang overthrew the house of Hsia in the seventeenth century B.C. and founded the Shang Dynasty. King Wu overthrew the house of Shang in the twelfth century B.C. and founded the Chou Dynasty.

2 The eldest son of King Tai Wang of Western Chou, who lived during the twelfth century B.C. Because he gave up his throne to his younger brother, he was considered a great sage.

a temple to Tai Po. Then in mid-spring and mid-autumn we can sacrifice with the ancient ceremonies and music. In this way people will practise ceremony and music, and that should help to produce some genuine scholars who will be able to serve the government well. But it'll cost several thousand taels. I've prepared a scroll here, and anyone who would like to contribute can sign it. How much will you give, Shao-ching?"

"This is an admirable scheme!" cried Tu, delighted.

He took the scroll and unrolled it.

"Tu Shao-ching of Tienchang donates three hundred taels," he wrote.

"That's a handsome donation," said Chih. "I'm going to give the two hundred taels I've saved from my tutorial fees during the last few years."

He wrote this down.

"Hua-shih, you should be able to give fifty taels too," he urged.

This also was written on the scroll. Then Chih Heng-shan rolled it up again, and they went on talking. Presently one of Tu's servants arrived.

"A messenger from Tienchang County yamen wants to see you, sir," he announced. "Will you please come home?"

Tu left Chih Heng-shan and went back to his house.

But to know what followed, you must read the next chapter.

CHAPTER 34

Scholars meet to speak of music and ceremony.
The emperor summons a talented man

"What did the messenger say?" Tu Shao-ching asked his boy, after leaving Mr. Chih.

"He said your summons has arrived, sir; and Governor Li has ordered Magistrate Teng to ask you to go to the capital to become an official. Magistrate Teng is staying in the Temple of Imperial Favour. He sent to ask you to stay in, sir, so that he can deliver the summons in person."

"In that case, I won't go home by the front door," said Tu. "Hire a boat at once. I'll go in by the balcony over the river."

The boy hired a boat with an awning at Lower Floating Bridge. Once home, Tu put on an old gown and old cap, swathed his head in a handkerchief, and lay down on the bed.

"Tell the messenger that I have suddenly been taken ill," he ordered the boy. "And ask Magistrate Teng not to trouble to come. As soon as I am better, I shall call to thank him."

The boy sent the messenger off with this news.

"When you are invited to court to become an official, why refuse on the pretext of illness?" asked Mrs. Tu with a smile.

"Don't be absurd! What! leave an amusing place like Nanking? Don't you enjoy having me at home, to go out with you in the spring and autumn to look at the flowers and drink wine? Why do you want to pack me off to Peking? Suppose I take you along too? It's a cold place, the capital, and you're

427

so delicate that one gust of wind there would freeze you to death! That would never do. No, no, I'd better not go."

Just then the servant-boy came in.

"Magistrate Teng is here," he announced. "He's sitting in the front room, and insists on seeing you, sir."

Ordering two servants to support him, Tu tottered out looking desperately ill to greet the magistrate. He knelt down, then failed to get up again. The magistrate hastily helped him to his feet, and they sat down.

"The court has issued an important decree, and Governor Li asks for your help," said Magistrate Teng. "I had no idea you were so ill. How soon do you think you will be able to travel?"

"I'm afraid my illness may prove incurable, hence what you ask is impossible," replied Tu. "I must beg Your Honour to make my apologies for me."

He took a petition from his sleeve and gave it to the magistrate, who, in view of the circumstances, did not like to prolong his visit.

"I will take my leave, sir," said Magistrate Teng. "I fear I have tired you. All I can do is send in a report to my superiors, and await Governor Li's decision."

"Thank you, Your Honour. Forgive me if I do not see you out."

The magistrate bade Tu farewell, and left in his sedan-chair. He lost no time in reporting to Governor Li that Tu Shao-ching was seriously ill and could not undertake a journey. As it happened, Governor Li had just been transferred to Fukien as provincial governor there; thus the matter was allowed to drop. And when Tu heard of the governor's departure he was jubilant.

"Good!" he exclaimed. "This is the end of my career as a licentiate. I shall not sit for the provincial examination or the yearly tests again, but take life easy and attend to my own affairs."

Having told the magistrate that he was ill, Tu Shao-ching did not stir from his home for some time. One day he declined an invitation to a feast from Mr. Hsueh, one of the local gentry who lived in Drum Tower Street. Chih Heng-shan went,

428

however, and so did Ma Chun-shang, Chu Hsien-fu and Chi
Wei-hsiao. They were sitting there when two other guests
arrived: Hsiao Po-chuan of Yangchow and Yu Ho-sheng of
Tsaishih, two young scholars. Both of them had white skin
and red lips, carried themselves with an air, dressed in the
height of fashion and were lavishly scented. The nickname of
one was Lovely Yu and of the other Miss Hsiao. They greeted
the assembled company, and sat down.

"I invited my friend Chien from Huaiching Bridge to keep
you all company," said Mr. Hsueh. "But he is busy today, and
could not come to this modest repast."

"Do you mean Pock-marked Chien, the actor who plays
men's parts?" asked Chi Wei-hsiao.

"That is the man."

"When you invite scholars to a meal, sir," said Chih, "would
you let an actor sit at the same table?"

"That has been done for a long time now," replied Hsueh.
"Today I have invited old Mr. Kao, who likes nothing better
than talking with this actor. That's why I asked Chien to
come."

"Which Mr. Kao is that?" inquired Chih.

"He comes from Liuho, and is a reader now in the Han
Lin Academy," answered Chi Wei-hsiao.

As they were speaking, the gateman came in.

"Mr. Kao is here," he announced.

Mr. Hsueh went out to meet him. Mr. Kao wore a gauze
cap and a gown embroidered with serpents. Upon coming in
he greeted the others, then sat down in the place of honour.

"Friend Chi," he said—for he knew Chi Wei-hsiao—"I'm
sorry I was out the other day when you called. I haven't had
time yet to read the masterpiece you so kindly gave me. Who
are these young gentlemen?"

When Lovely Yu and Miss Hsiao had given their names,
he questioned Ma Chun-shang and Chu Hsien-fu.

"We are the compilers of the *Commentaries on Examination Compositions* you see in all the bookshops," replied Ma.

"Mr. Chu is the grandson of Prefect Chu of Nanchang,"
put in Lovely Yu. "My father served as an examiner in
Nanchang. So Mr. Chu and I are related."

429

Last of all, Mr. Kao ascertained Chih Heng-shan's name.

"Mr. Chih is an authority on ancient ceremony and music," said Chi Wei-hsiao. "He is one of the famous scholars of the south."

To this Mr. Kao said nothing.

When tea had been served three times, they took off their outer garments and were invited into the library. Though Mr. Kao was their senior, instead of standing on ceremony he was very merry, joking and chatting freely with the others.

"Why don't I see my friend Chien?" he asked, once in the library.

"He couldn't come today," replied Hsueh.

"Too bad! Too bad!" exclaimed Mr. Kao. "Now the whole feast will lack style!"

Mr. Hsueh had prepared two tables, and they took their seats. While feasting they discoursed upon Chekiang scholars and the beauty of the West Lake, then exchanged stories about all the protégés the Lou brothers had gathered.

"I can't take an interest in such things," declared Lovely Yu. "What interests me is that girl Shuang-hung in Mr. Chu's household. The mere mention of her name leaves a sweet taste in your mouth!"

"That's natural," said Chi. "You are so lovely yourself, you like lovely girls."

"All my life," remarked Hsiao, "I have admired compilers of the Han Lin Academy. I am sorry I never met Compiler Lu. Judging by what I've heard of him, he must have been a fine man; and had I known him I would certainly have asked for his instruction. What a pity that he died!"

"There'll be no more gallant deeds like those performed by my uncles in the Lou family," sighed Chu Hsien-fu.

"What do you mean?" demanded Chi Wei-hsiao. "I fancy the Tu cousins from Tienchang are even more open-handed than your uncles!"

"Shao-ching is the better of the two," asserted Chih.

"Gentlemen," said Mr. Kao, "are you referring to the son of the prefect of Kanchow?"

"Yes, sir," replied Chih. "Do you know him?"

"Tienchang is next to Liuho," said Mr. Kao. "Of course I know him. And, if you'll allow me to say so, this Shao-ching is the first complete wastrel his family has produced! His ancestors were physicians who for generations performed good deeds and acquired land and property. In his grandfather's time they rose in the world; but though his grandfather was an official for several dozen years, he didn't make any money. Shao-ching's father managed to pass the metropolitan examination yet only became a prefect—that was foolish enough. And while in office he showed no respect for his superiors but simply tried to please the people, talking nonsense about 'fostering filial piety and brotherly love, and encouraging agriculture.' Such phrases are mere figures of speech to be used in compositions, yet he took them seriously, with the result that his superiors disliked him and removed him from his post! This son of his is even more preposterous, frittering away his time and mixing with Buddhist monks, Taoist priests, artisans and beggars. Not a single respectable friend does he have! In less than ten years he ran through sixty to seventy thousand taels of silver. Then, with Tienchang too hot to hold him, he moved to Nanking, where he takes his wife to the taverns to drink every day, and parades with a copper bowl like a beggar! Who could have thought his family would produce such a ne'er-do-well! When I teach my sons and nephews at home, I hold him up as an awful example. Pasted on each boy's desk is the warning: "Don't imitate Tu Shao-ching of Tienchang!""

Chih Heng-shan turned red.

"He was recently summoned to court to take up an appointment," he said. "But he refused to go."

"What of it?" Mr. Kao gave a sarcastic laugh. "If he had any learning, he would pass the examinations, wouldn't he? Ha! What credit attaches to the other type of appointment?"

"You are right, sir!" cried Hsiao, then turned to the others. "We of the younger generation should take Mr. Kao's words as a maxim," he declared.

They drank and chatted for some time, and then the party broke up. Mr. Kao was carried off in his sedan-chair, while the rest walked home.

"Mr. Kao was obviously running Shao-ching down just now," said Chih Heng-shan. "Yet he actually showed our friend off to great advantage. From ancient times till now, gentlemen, there have been very few men as remarkable as Shao-ching."

"Still, there was some truth in what Mr. Kao said," remarked Ma Chun-shang.

"Never mind that," put in Chi Wei-hsiao. "That riverside house of his is a fascinating place. Let us all call on him tomorrow, and make him treat us to wine!"

"We two will pay our respects at the same time," said Yu Ho-sheng.

To this they all agreed.

The next morning, Tu Shao-ching had just got up and was sitting in his front room when his neighbour, Chin Tung-ya, brought over a volume of his *Commentaries on the Four Books* to ask for criticism. Tu put it on the table, and had read a dozen or so passages when Chih Heng-shan, Ma Chun-shang, Chu Hsien-fu, Hsiao Po-chuan, Chi Wei-hsiao and Yu Ho-sheng arrived. They bowed and sat down.

"I have not been out for a long time, and have therefore failed to profit from your instruction," said Tu. "Your visit today is an unexpected pleasure. Who are these two gentlemen?"

Yu and Hsiao introduced themselves.

"Why isn't Ching Lan-chiang with you?" asked Tu.

"He has opened another hat shop on Three Mountains Street, and is attending to his business," said Chu.

The servant brought tea in.

"This is no time for tea," declared Chi Wei-hsiao. "We came today for wine."

"Certainly," replied Tu. "We can have a good talk first."

"The other day," said Chih Heng-shan, "you gave me a copy of your *Commentary on the Book of Songs,*[1] which I admired immensely. Would you be so good as to tell us one or two of your general principles?"

---

[1] A collection of poems, most of them anonymous, dating from the twelfth to the sixth century B.C.

"Are you studying only the poems likely to be set for the examinations, sir?" asked Hsiao.

"I take it you base your notes on the *Yung Lo Reader for Candidates*," said Ma Chun-shang.

"Well, let us hear what Shao-ching has to say," suggested Mr. Chih.

"When Chu Hsi[1] annotated the classics," said Tu, "he set forward his own views, expecting posterity to compare them with the commentaries of other scholars. Nowadays, however, all the other commentators have been dropped, and Chu Hsi is the sole authority. But he can't be blamed for the narrow-mindedness of later generations. I have been reading some of the other old commentators, and there are a few points on which I would appreciate your advice. In 'The Gentle Wind from the South,' for instance, when the old commentators say the mother of seven sons wanted to marry again, I feel that can't be right. The women of those days married at twenty, thus if she had seven sons—all grown-up, mind you—the mother must have been over fifty. How could she think of marrying again? That phrase 'discontented with her home,' as I see it, means simply that she was not satisfied with her food and clothing; so she raised a rumpus and her seven sons admitted they were to blame. This is a new interpretation."

"It sounds logical!" Chih Heng-shan nodded.

"And what do you gentlemen think of 'The Lady Says: The Cock Has Crowed'?" asked Tu.

"That is one of the poems of the state of Cheng," said Ma Chun-shang. "Surely all it means is that she was chaste."

"Yes," said Chih. "Still, it is difficult to appreciate its full significance."

"I don't agree," said Tu. "The thing is that those scholars who hanker secretly after becoming officials want to cut a fine figure before their wives. Their wives again, who want to become great ladies but can't, find fault with everything and quarrel the whole time with their husbands. Look at this couple, though. They haven't the slightest desire for official rank. They play the lyre and drink, completely contented with their

---

[1] 1130-1200, a philosopher.

433

lot. This is how true gentlemen of the first three dynasties regulated themselves and their families. But no earlier commentators have pointed this out either."

"Well said!" approved Chu Hsien-fu.

"In my opinion," continued Tu, "the poem 'The Chen and Wei' is simply about a married couple who took a stroll together. I see no reference in it to illegitimate love."

"No wonder you and your wife enjoyed yourselves so much the other day in Yao Garden," said Chi Wei-hsiao. "You were keeping up the romantic old tradition of lyre-playing and drinking, and presenting each other with orchids and peonies!"

They all laughed heartily.

"Listening to Shao-ching's conversation is like drinking elixir," said Chih Heng-shan.

"*Here* comes the elixir!" cried Yu Ho-sheng.

Then, looking round, they saw the servant-boy bring in wine.

The table was laid with wine and dainties, and the eight of them sat down together. Soon Chi Wei-hsiao had drunk a few cups too many.

"Shao-ching!" he declared. "You are really the greatest romantic of all time! I'd feel bored in your place looking at flowers and drinking with a wife over thirty. With your talents and reputation, and living as you do in such a fine place as this, you ought to take a beautiful concubine who also possesses literary gifts. Then a brilliant scholar and a beautiful girl could enjoy themselves together."

"Remember what Yen Tze[1] wrote, Wei-hsiao," said Tu. " 'Though my wife is old and has lost her bloom, I remember when she was young and lovely.' I consider concubinage as absolutely counter to the will of Heaven. The population of the earth is limited; therefore if one man takes several wives, other men must go wifeless. I would like to make a law for the government allowing a man to take a concubine—not more than one—only if he has no son by the time he is forty. And if this concubine does not bear a son, she should be

---

1 A minister of the state of Chi in the sixth century B.C.

married to someone else. This would mean fewer men without wives, and would help to strengthen general morality."

"What a romantic principle of government, sir!" exclaimed Hsiao.

"If ministers of state took their duties equally seriously," sighed Chih, "the whole world would be at peace!"

Then, the drinking at an end, amid much laughter the guests took their leave.

A few days later, Chih Heng-shan walked over alone, and found Tu in.

"The plans for Tai Po's Temple are taking shape," said Chih. "I have brought a draft of the ceremony and music to be used, and would like your opinion of it."

Tu took the manuscript and read it.

"There's another man whose opinion we should ask," he said.

"Who is that?"

"Mr. Chuang Shao-kuang."

"He came back the day before yesterday from Chekiang."

"I was meaning to call on him," said Tu. "Let us go there together now."

They took a boat with an awning to North Gate Bridge, went ashore, and came to a house on the main street facing south.

"This is the place," said Chih.

They entered the great gate, were announced by the gateman and greeted by the master of the house. Chuang Shao-kuang, who came of a long line of scholars in Nanking, had written a poem of seven thousand characters when barely twelve, which had won him fame throughout the country. Nearly forty now, he had a great reputation, but he closeted himself at home to write and was very particular as to what friends he made. Hearing that these two callers had arrived, he came out to meet them. He wore a square cap and light gown of azure gauze, his beard was sparse and his complexion sallow. Bowing ceremoniously as he came out, he greeted Tu and Chih, and they sat down.

"I have not seen you for several years, Shao-ching," said Mr. Chuang. "I was glad to hear you are living by the

435

Chinhuai River, to add further charm to its beauty. You made short work of extricating yourself from that trouble the other day!"

"I meant to call on you then," replied Tu, "but had to leave on account of an old friend's death. By the time I returned you had already left for Chekiang."

"*You* are always at home, my friend," said Chuang to Chih. "Why don't you call more often?"

"I have been running to and fro in connection with Tai Po's Temple for some time," replied Chih. "Now the plan is materializing, and I have brought for your criticism an outline of the music and ceremony we propose to use."

He took a notebook from his sleeve, and handed it over. Chuang Shao-kuang read it carefully from beginning to end.

"I shall naturally give you all the help I can in an affair of such consequence," he promised. "But I have to leave home for a time on business. I shall be back in three months at the most, possibly in two. We can go into the question carefully then."

"Where are you going this time?" asked Chih.

"I have been recommended by Governor Hsu of Chekiang, who has now been promoted to the post of vice-minister of the Ministry of Ceremony. Since a decree has come ordering my attendance at court, I have no choice but to go."

"You will not be able to come back immediately," said Chih.

"Don't worry," replied Chuang. "I shall come straight back, in order not to miss the great sacrifice at Tai Po's Temple."

"We can't arrange the sacrifice without you, my friend," said Tu. "I hope you will be back soon."

Chih Heng-shan asked if he might see the official summons, and a servant-boy was sent to fetch it. Tu and Chih looked at it together.

"The recommendation of a talented scholar by Vice-Minister Hsu of the Ministry of Ceremony," they read. "By imperial decree, Chuang Shao-kuang must proceed to court for an audience."

"We will take our leave now," they said, "and come back to see you off when you leave for the capital."

"There is no need for that," replied Chuang. "We shall be seeing each other again soon."

He escorted them out, and Tu and Chih left.

That evening Chuang Shao-kuang had a farewell feast with his wife.

"You were never willing to become an official before," she said. "Why are you going this time as soon as you are ordered?"

"We are not hermits," replied her husband. "Since a decree has been issued summoning me to court, it is my duty as a subject to go. Don't worry, though. I shall come straight back. Lao Lai-tzu's wife will have no excuse to despise me."[1]

The next day, when the local officials of Nanking came to hasten his departure, they found Mr. Chuang already gone. He had quietly hired a small sedan-chair and, accompanied by one servant-boy and a porter to carry his luggage, gone by his back door to the West Gate. He travelled by water to the Yellow River, and after crossing it went on by carriage to Shantung. About twelve miles beyond Yenchow he stopped at a village called Hsin Family Station for tea. It was still early, and he could perhaps have persuaded the coachman to cover another dozen miles that day, but the inn-keeper dissuaded him.

"I tell you, sir, we've been plagued with bandits in these parts recently," said the inn-keeper. "Travellers passing this way have to set out late and break their journey early. Though you're not one of those rich merchants, you'd still better be careful."

When Mr. Chuang heard this, he bade the coachman stable their horses.

His servant chose a room, carried in the baggage, unpacked the bedding and spread it on the *kang*, then brought his master tea. Soon bells were heard outside, and a train of

---

[1] During the Spring and Autumn period (722-481 B.C.) the King of Chu invited Lao Lai-tzu to court, but his wife persuaded him that it would be undignified to accept an appointment.

over a hundred mules arrived, loaded with silver bullion in wooden sheaths. The escort looked like a military officer. He was accompanied by a man of over sixty, about six feet tall, who had a grizzled beard and wore a felt hat, archer's costume and brown ox-hide boots. At his belt was a catapult. These two men dismounted and walked into the inn carrying their whips.

"We are escorting tax silver from Szechuan to the capital," they told the inn-keeper. "It is growing late, so we will spend the night here and leave early tomorrow. We expect good service."

The inn-keeper assented with alacrity. The officer watched his porters carry the silver into the inn, and when the mules were stabled he hung up his whip and came inside with the old man. They bowed to Chuang Shao-kuang and sat down.

"I understand you are an official escort from Szechuan," said Chuang. "And I take it this gentleman is your friend. May I inquire your honourable names?"

"My name is Sun," replied the escort. "I hold the rank of a second captain. My friend is Hsiao Hao-hsuan, a native of Chengtu."

When they asked the reason for Mr. Chuang's journey to the capital, he told them his name and why he had been summoned to Peking.

"I have long known of Mr. Chuang Shao-kuang of Nanking as one of the best scholars of our time," said Hsiao. "Little did I think we would meet today like this."

He expressed profound admiration.

Seeing that Hsiao was such a dignified and remarkable old man, Chuang took a fancy to him.

"The country has been at peace for so long that local government has become a mere empty show," he said. "Although bandits are rife, the authorities take no steps to put an end to robbery. I hear that the stage in front is infested with brigands, so we shall have to be on our guard."

"Set your mind at rest, sir," replied Hsiao with a smile. "I have some slight skill in archery, and can hit anything I aim at within a hundred paces. If bandits attack us, I need only draw my crossbow and they will be done for. One after another they'll all drop dead!"

"If you doubt my friend's skill, sir," said Captain Sun, "let us ask him for a demonstration."

"Nothing would please me better," replied Chuang, "if it is not inconvenient."

"Not at all!" answered Hsiao. "I like to show my poor skill."

He picked up his catapult and strode into the courtyard, then drew two pellets from the silk bag at his belt. By this time Chuang and Sun had walked into the yard too. Hsiao raised his catapult, shot one pellet high into the sky, then sent a second winging after the first, so that they collided and burst in mid air. Mr. Chuang was loud in his praise and the inn-keeper, who had looked on, was amazed. Then Hsiao put away his catapult and they went inside to sit down. After some conversation they dined and went to bed.

The next day Captain Sun rose before it was light to bid his muleteers bestir themselves; and when the porters had carried out the silver, he paid the bill and left. Mr. Chuang got up too and washed his face, then ordered his boy to rope the baggage, paid his bill and left with the others. Dawn had not yet broken by the time they had covered three or four miles, and the morning star still hung in the sky. Suddenly in the black forest ahead they saw men stirring.

"Look out! There are bandits ahead!" shouted the muleteers, driving their hundred-odd mules to the foot of a slope at the side of the road.

In a flash Hsiao had his catapult in his hand, and Captain Sun on horseback had drawn his sword. A signal arrow whistled overhead, and the next moment a large body of horsemen galloped out of the wood. With a cry Hsiao stretched his catapult. But, crack! the catapult string snapped in two. As several scores of bandits came flying towards them, shouting together, the horrified captain turned his horse about and fled, while the muleteers and porters ducked to the ground to hide themselves. Then the brigands drove off the hundred mules loaded with silver by a small road.

Chuang Shao-kuang sat speechless in his carriage for a time. Indeed, he was not sure what exactly had happened. When the snapping of his string made it impossible for Hsiao to display his might, he spurred his horse back down the road they had come. Galloping up to a small inn, he hammered at the gate, and the inn-keeper realized at once that he had been robbed.

"Where did you put up last night, sir?" he asked.

Hsiao told him.

"That fellow is a spy for the brigand chief Chao Ta," said the inn-keeper. "He must have cut your catapult string last night."

It was useless to repent his folly, but in his desperation Hsiao hit on a plan. He pulled out a lock of his hair to repair the catapult string, then galloped back to join Captain Sun, who told him that the robbers had taken a path to the east. It was light now. Hsiao flew forward on his steed and soon came in sight of the bandits, who were urging the mules forward as fast as they could. He whipped his steed to overtake them, then raised his catapult—and the pellets rained down like hail on lotus leaves! At that, sheltering their heads and abandoning the silver, the bandits turned tail and fled for their lives. It did not take Hsiao and Captain Sun long to drive the mules back to the main road, where they met Chuang and told him all that had happened, at which he exclaimed in wonder. They journeyed on together for half a day, and then Chuang, who was travelling light, took his leave of the others and went on by carriage alone.

A few days later he reached Lukouchiao, and saw a man riding a mule towards him.

"Who is the gentleman in this chair?" asked this man, when he reached the sedan-chair.

"A Mr. Chuang," replied the carriers.

"Is it Mr. Chuang from Nanking?" asked the other, jumping down from his mule.

Mr. Chuang was about to alight, when the stranger knelt down and bowed to the ground.

But to know what followed, you must read the next chapter.

440

CHAPTER 35

The Son of Heaven consults a worthy man, but Chuang Shao-kuang declines all posts and goes home

As soon as the stranger leapt down from his mule to prostrate himself, Chuang alighted from his carriage and knelt to raise him up.

"Who are you, sir?" he asked. "We have never met."

The stranger rose to his feet.

"There is a village a mile in front, sir," he said. "If you will allow me to accompany your carriage there, we can talk in the inn."

"Very well," agreed Chuang.

He mounted his carriage, the other mounted his mule, and together they made their way to the inn, where after exchanging courtesies they sat down.

"In the capital I calculated the time it would take for the imperial summons to reach Nanking, sir, and reckoned that you should be arriving any day now," said the stranger. "So I rode out through Changyi Gate to accost all the mules, sedan-chairs and carriages on the road; and at last I have found you! It is a privilege to meet you."

"What is your honourable name and place of origin?" inquired Chuang.

"I am Lu Hsin-hou of Hukuang. As a young man I determined to collect the works of all the famous scholars of our dynasty; and in twenty years I have virtually accomplished my aim. But because Kao Ching-chiu—one of the four great men of letters at the beginning of our dynasty—was executed, none of the collectors keep his works. In fact, I found one collector only in the capital who had them. I came to Peking, purchased this book for a high price, and was on the point of returning home when I heard that the emperor had summoned you, sir, for an audience. Since I read the books of old writers who have turned to dust, I felt I must not let slip the chance of meeting you—one of the worthiest men of our generation. And so, after waiting for some time in the capital, I came out to make inquiries for you along the road."

"I was staying idly in Nanking with no desire for an official career," responded Chuang. "But when His Majesty deigned to send for me, I had no choice but to come. I am delighted by this unexpected encounter, and only sorry we must part so soon. Let us put up in this inn, and tonight we can have a good talk."

They proceeded to discuss the work of well-known writers.

"Your interest in old books shows your respect for learning, sir," said Chuang. "But it is better to have nothing to do with forbidden books. Although there is nothing treasonable in the writings of Kao Ching-chiu, since Emperor Hung Wu took a dislike to him and his works are now banned, I would advise you not to read them. My view of study is this: One should first read widely, and then specialize. The main thing is to think for oneself. If on your way home you will honour me with a visit, I have some writings on which I would appreciate your advice."

Lu Hsin-hou accepted this invitation. The next morning they parted, Lu setting off for Nanking to await Chuang's return.

Chuang entered Peking by Changyi Gate, and put up in the Protector's Temple. At once Vice-Minister Hsu sent a servant to wait on him, then came in person to pay his respects.

"Did you have a hard journey?" asked the vice-minister.

"I am a countrified fellow, unaccustomed to travel," replied Chuang. "And I felt like a willow withering at the approach of autumn. Because I was exhausted after the long journey

I neglected to call to pay my respects to you, yet you have honoured me with a visit instead."

"I hope you will make ready as quickly as possible," said Hsu. "In three or four days you will probably be sent for."

It was then the first of the tenth month of the thirty-fifth year of Chia Ching.[1] Three days later, Vice-Minister Hsu sent over the following imperial edict copied out by the Imperial Chancery:

On the second day of the tenth month, the Imperial Chancery received this order from the emperor: Since succeeding to our ancestors' great task, we have sought day and night for talented men to strengthen our government. We have heard that a good sovereign reveres his ministers as teachers. Indeed, this has been proved true since ancient times. To manifest this principle, therefore, we summon Chuang Shao-kuang, recommended by the vice-minister of the Ministry of Ceremony, for an audience on the sixth.

At the fifth watch on the sixth day, the imperial guards ranged themselves outside Wu Men, the emperor's entire retinue took their places, and the ceremony of assembly was performed while all the officers waited in readiness. In the glare of a hundred torches the prime minister arrived, Wu Men, the main gate, was opened, and the officials entered through side gates. They proceeded through Fengtien Gate to Fengtien Palace, where heavenly music was being played and they could barely hear the herald bid them take their places. A whip cracked three times, eunuchs trooped out from the inner palace bearing golden censers of ambergris, and palace maids with long-handled fans escorted the emperor to his throne. Then the officials hailed the Son of Heaven and prostrated themselves in obeisance. And Chuang, in a court cap and official robes, followed suit. After that, as the music ceased and the court was dismissed, twenty-four elephants with magnificent vases on their backs moved off by themselves. It was indeed as the poet once described:

_____

1 1556.

443

Bright flowers smile on robes and swords of state,
As stars grow dim on high;
And willow leaves are brushed by silken flags
Before the dew is dry.

So the officials dispersed.

Chuang returned to his lodgings, removed his state robes, and was pacing up and down when Vice-Minister Hsu called. Chuang went out to meet him in civilian dress, and tea was served.

"His Majesty's entry into the palace today was a rare ceremony," said Hsu. "I advise you to stay in your rooms, sir, for no doubt you will soon be summoned again."

Three days later, indeed, the following imperial edict was received:

Let Chuang Shao-kuang appear at the inner court on the eleventh. And let him be provided with a horse from the palace stables.

On the eleventh, Vice-Minister Hsu saw Chuang to Wu Men, and waited in the waiting room while Chuang entered alone. Two eunuchs led forward a horse from the imperial stable and invited him to mount it, kneeling as he set foot to the stirrup. When he was in the saddle they took the bridle — even the reins were of the imperial yellow! — and conducted him slowly through Chienching Gate. Chuang dismounted outside Hsuan-cheng Palace, where he was announced by the two eunuchs and ordered to advance. He entered, holding his breath, and saw the Son of Heaven in civilian costume on his splendid throne. Chuang walked forward and prostrated himself.

"We have reigned for thirty-five years," said the emperor. "During that time, thanks to heaven, earth and our ancestors, the world has known peace and there have been no disturbances within our borders. But not all our subjects are warmly-clad and well-fed, while even gentlemen have been unable to act in accordance with the principles of ceremony and music. We have summoned you all this way, sir, to ask what is of first importance in educating the people. We hope you will do your best to outline a plan for us. Do not hesitate to speak freely."

444

Just as Chuang was about to reply, he felt a stab of pain on the top of his head. In agony, he bowed.

"I thank Your Majesty for this mark of favour," he replied. "But I cannot give a detailed reply at once. Pray allow me to reflect carefully before submitting a memorial."

"Very well," said the emperor. "You must draw up a plan for us. But we hope it will be something practicable, according to the spirit of the ancients while conforming with the customs of the present day."

This said, he rose and withdrew. Chuang went out through Chincheng Palace, where eunuchs waiting with the same steed escorted him outside Wu Men. There Vice-Minister Hsu met him, accompanied him out of the Forbidden City, then left him.

The moment he was back in his lodgings, Chuang took off his cap. In it he discovered a scorpion!

"So this was my Chang Tsang!"[1] he laughed. "It does not seem as if our Confucian ways will avail in this age!"

The next day, upon rising, he burnt incense and washed his hands, then consulted the hexagrams. The answer received was: "A hermit in the mountain."

"Quite right," said Chuang.

Then he drew up in detail ten policies for educating the people, and wrote a request to be allowed to return home. He sent these documents to the Office of Transmission.

After this, all the officials of the nine ministries and six boards came to pay their respects; and though Chuang had little patience with such formalities, he had to return their calls. Then the prime minister approached Vice-Minister Hsu.

"His Majesty means to show great favour to this Mr. Chuang from Nanking," he said. "Why don't you bring him to see me, sir? I should like to have him as my pupil."

The vice-minister could not broach this directly to Chuang; he proposed it, however, in a roundabout fashion.

"Since there is no Confucius in our age," said Chuang, "I have no desire to be any man's pupil. Besides, the prime minister has served so many times as chief examiner that he

---

[1] In the Warring States period, Duke Ping of Lu wanted to meet Mencius, but Chang Tsang dissuaded him.

has innumerable members of the Han Lin Academy as his pupils. Why should he choose a rustic like myself? I dare not accept this honour."

When Hsu reported this, the prime minister was angry.

A few days later, in the palace, the emperor consulted the prime minister.

"We have studied Chuang Shao-kuang's ten policies carefully," he said. "His learning is profound. Can he be made a chief minister?"

"Chuang Shao-kuang certainly possesses remarkable abilities," replied the prime minister. "The whole court and country rejoiced when Your Majesty singled him out for special favour. There is, however, no precedent in our dynasty for appointing as minister a man who has not passed the metropolitan examination; and such an appointment might give rise to the belief that promotion depends upon chance. But let it be as Your Majesty pleases."

The emperor sighed, then ordered the prime minister to decree:

Permission is hereby granted Chuang Shao-kuang to return home. Let him be given five hundred taels from the Imperial Treasury, and let Lotus Lake in Nanking be presented to him, that he may continue writing to glorify this great age.

After this decree was issued, Chuang went once more to Wu Men to express his gratitude, then bade farewell to Vice-Minister Hsu, and prepared to go home. All the officials came to see him off, and having taken his leave of them he once more hired a carriage and drove out of Changyi Gate.

Because it was a cold day, they covered a greater distance than usual and were unable to find an inn. They therefore drove up a small lane to a thatched cottage to ask for a lodging. It was a single-roomed cottage in which an oil lamp was burning, and an old man of sixty or seventy was standing at the gate. Chuang walked up to greet him.

"I am a traveller, grandad, and have overshot the inn," he said. "If you will take me in for the night, I will pay for my lodging tomorrow."

446

"What traveller carries his house with him, stranger?" responded the old man. "I would willingly put you up, but I have only the one room where my wife and I — both of us over seventy — lived. And unhappily my old woman died this morning, and I have no money for a coffin, so her body is still in the house. Where could you sleep, stranger? You have a carriage, too, which couldn't be taken inside."

"That does not matter," replied Chuang. "All I need is space for one, so that I have somewhere to sleep tonight. The carriage can stay at the gate."

"In that case, you may share my bed," said the old man.

"Very well," replied Chuang.

Going inside, he saw the old woman's corpse lying stiff and stark on the ground beside the earthen *kang*. He spread out his bedding, bade his servant and coachman sleep in the carriage, and urged the old man to take the inner half of the *kang*. But having laid himself down on the outer half, Chuang tossed and turned, unable to sleep. At midnight the corpse began to stir. Chuang gave a start, gazed at it fixedly, and saw it spread its hands as if about to sit up.

"She's *alive*!" he exclaimed.

He hastily shook the old man, but could not wake him.

"How can an old fellow sleep so soundly?" he wondered.

When he sat up to look, however, he discovered that the old man's breathing had stopped and he was dead! Turning round, he perceived that the old woman had risen stiffly to her feet, and was showing the whites of her eyes. She was not alive, but a walking corpse!

In terror, Chuang rushed out, woke the coachman, and made him ram the carriage against the door to prevent her coming out. He then paced up and down outside alone.

"All sorts of mishaps arise from activity," reflected Chuang ruefully. "Had I stayed quietly at home instead of travelling to the capital, I should have been spared this shock! Still, death comes to all. I must be lacking in my understanding of truth to be so easily alarmed."

Calming himself, he sat down in the carriage till the day was bright, by which time the walking corpse had fallen to the ground, making two corpses lying stretched out in the cottage.

"The poor old couple!" said Chuang. "Though I simply spent the night here, if I don't bury them, who will?"

He ordered the servant and coachman to find a village, bought two coffins for several dozen taels, and hired villagers to carry them to the cottage and lay out the corpses. Then he purchased a suitable plot of ground from a neighbour and supervised the old couple's burial. Finally he bought offerings and paper money, wrote a funeral address, shed tears and sacrificed. All the villagers came and bowed to the ground to thank him.

Leaving Taierhchuang, Chuang hired a fast boat, on which he was able to read to his heart's content. In a few days he reached Yangchow and spent one day at the customs house waiting for a junk to take him down the Yangtse to Nanking. He had no sooner boarded this vessel the next morning than two dozen smart sedan-chairs drew up on the bank, and the salt merchants employed by the government in the Huai River area sent in their cards. Since the junk was small, Chuang invited ten of them aboard first. Some, who were his relatives, addressed him as uncle, great-uncle or cousin. After exchanging greetings they all sat down. The man in the second seat was Hsiao Po-chuan.

"Though His Majesty wished to make you a minister, you declined all official rank," said the merchants. "What nobility of mind this shows!"

"I understand Mr. Chuang's scruples," said Hsiao Po-chuan. "With his rare gifts, he wishes to enter upon an official career the orthodox way, and looks down upon appointment by recommendation. He has come back now to wait for the next examination. Since the emperor knows him, he is sure to come first on the list."

"How can you speak of looking down on such an important institution as appointment by recommendation?" demanded Chuang with a smile. "As for the next examination, I am sure it is you who will come first, my friend. I shall be waiting in retirement to hear the good news."

"Will you be meeting the salt commissioners while you are here?" asked Hsiao.

"I am anxious to reach home," replied Chuang. "My boat will be leaving soon."

Then these ten men took their leave and went ashore, and Chuang received the rest of his callers in two groups. He was beginning to be intensely irritated when the salt commissioners arrived, and after them the local salt gabelle officials, the prefect of Yangchow and the magistrate of Chiangtu County. Fuming inwardly, he saw the last of his callers ashore, then ordered the junk to cast off at once. That evening, when the salt merchants brought six hundred taels which they had raised between them for his expenses on the river, his junk had already gone so far they could not overtake it. They had to carry their silver back.

With a following wind, Chuang soon reached Swallow Cliff.

"Today I shall see the beauties of the Yangtse again!" he cried in delight.

He hired a boat with an awning, had his luggage carried aboard, and was rowed to the West Gate where he engaged a porter. Then he walked home, bowed before his ancestors' shrines, and greeted his wife.

"I promised to be back in three months at the most, possibly two," he told her with a smile. "What have you to say now? Was I telling the truth, or not?"

His wife laughed. That evening they drank to celebrate his return.

The next morning he had barely washed his face when the servant came in.

"Reader Kao of Liuho is here," he said.

Chuang went out to receive him. He had no sooner seen Reader Kao off than the provincial commissioner of finance called, the mayor called, the postmaster called, the magistrates of Shangyuan and Chiangning counties called, and the local gentry called. He was kept hard at it changing into his thick-soled boots and changing out again, until at last he lost patience completely.

"This is too much!" he declared to his wife. "Since the court has presented me with Lotus Lake, why should I stay

449

here where all these people give me no peace? Let us move to the lake as quickly as possible, to enjoy ourselves in peace."

No sooner said than done. They moved that same night to Lotus Lake.

This was a huge lake, almost as large as the West Lake in Hangchow. From the wall on its left you could see Cockcrow Temple. Thousands of bushels of water chestnuts, lotus roots, lotus seeds and caltrops were produced here every year; and there were seventy-two fishing boats which every morning supplied the whole city with fish. Four of the five big islands in the lake were fitted with libraries; and that in the middle, with its immense garden and house containing dozens of rooms, became Chuang's home. In the garden were old trees, their trunks thicker than a man could encircle with his arms; and with plum, peach, pear, plantain, cassia and chrysanthemums there were flowers at every season. There was also a grove of tens of thousands of bamboos. Chuang's house had large windows on every side from which he could enjoy the lakeside scenery, as enchanting as fairyland. A boat was moored at his gate, and to visit any of the other islands he had simply to ferry across; but without this boat, not a soul could reach him. In this garden, then, Chuang lived.

"How lovely the lake and mountains look!" he said one day with a smile to his wife, as they leaned over the balcony to watch the water. "And all this is ours! We can enjoy ourselves here every day, unlike Tu Shao-ching, who has to take his wife to Chingliang Mountain to see the blossom!"

When at leisure, he would prepare wine and make his wife sit beside him to read Tu Shao-ching's *Commentaries on the Book of Songs* aloud. And at the best passages he would drain a large cup, and they would both laugh heartily. So he lived there without a care.

One day, someone on the far bank hailed the boatman, who rowed across. Going out to receive this guest, Chuang saw that it was Lu Hsin-hou.

"I have been looking forward to meeting you ever since we parted on the road," said Chuang, delighted. "How did you find your way here?"

"I went to your honourable house yesterday," replied Lu, "and came on here today. You are living like an immortal — how I envy you!"

"We are completely cut off from the world here," said Chuang. "Although this is not Peach Blossom Stream,[1] it comes very close to it. I hope you will pay us a long visit, for next time you may not be able to find the way."

Wine was served and they drank together till nearly midnight, when a servant came in.

"Hundreds of troops are here from the Prince of Chungshan's residence!" he announced breathlessly. "They've over a thousand torches! They've seized all seventy-two fishing boats, and ferried troops across to surround our garden completely!"

Chuang was greatly taken aback.

Another servant came in.

"There is a brigade general in the hall," he announced.

Chuang went out, and the general greeted him.

"May I ask what my family has done?" inquired Chuang.

"Your honourable household is in no way involved," replied the other. Then he whispered: "Someone reported that Lu Hsin-hou has the works of Kao Ching-chiu — which are banned — hidden in his house. We heard from the capital that this man has studied the military arts, so troops were sent out to arrest him. We traced him today to you, sir, and I am here to ask for him. I hope you will not let him know, for then he may attempt to escape."

"Leave this to me, general," said Chuang. "Tomorrow I will ask him to give himself up, and be responsible for seeing that he does so."

"If you say so, sir, that will be all right," replied the brigade general. "I will take my leave now."

Chuang saw him out. The brigade general issued an order, and all the troops rowed back to the other side of the lake. Lu Hsin-hou had heard the reason for their coming.

---

[1] This was a fairyland described by the poet Tao Yuan-ming. A fisherman came here by accident; but though he marked the path by which he left, neither he nor others could find the way back again.

"I am no coward," he said. "I wouldn't dream of running away and involving you. I'll give myself up tomorrow!"

"You will have to spend a few days only in gaol," said Chuang with a smile. "In less than a month I guarantee you will be at liberty to enjoy yourself again."

When Lu Hsin-hou had given himself up, Chuang sent over a dozen letters to various high officials at court. Then an order came down for Lu Hsin-hou's release and the informer was punished instead. When Lu went to thank Chuang, the latter kept him as a guest.

A couple of days later, two more visitors hailed the boat to ferry them to the island. Going out to welcome them, Chuang found they were Chih Heng-shan and Tu Shao-ching.

"Capital!" cried Chuang and quoted: "'While I am longing to talk with you, you arrive!'"

He asked them into a pavilion overlooking the lake, and Chih told him they hoped to settle the ceremony and music for Tai Po's Temple. Chuang feasted them for a whole day, and they drew up a detailed plan of the ceremony and music to be used, which Chih took back with him.

Soon New Year came and went. In the middle of the second month Chih Heng-shan invited Ma Chun-shang, Chu Hsien-fu, Chi Wei-hsiao, Hsiao Chin-hsuan and Chin Tung-ya to meet in Tu Shao-ching's riverside house to discuss the sacrifice at Tai Po's Temple.

"Whom shall we find as master of ceremonies?" they asked.

"We shall be sacrificing to a very great sage," replied Chih. "The master of ceremonies should be a sage himself, to be worthy of Tai Po. That is the kind of man we must find."

"Whom have you in mind?"

Raising his first and second fingers, Chih told them the man's name.

But to learn his name, you must turn to the next chapter.

CHAPTER 36

A true Confucian is born
in Changshu County. A worthy man becomes Master
of Ceremonies in the Temple of Tai Po

Now in Changshu County of Soochow Prefecture was a village called Unicorn Sash Village. Here lived over two hundred families of farmers. The only man who did not work on the land was a Mr. Yu, who studied and passed the prefectural examination during the Cheng Hua period,[1] and then remained a licentiate for thirty years, teaching in the village school. Unicorn Sash Village was five miles from Changshu; but, except to take the examinations, Mr. Yu never went to town. He lived to be over eighty. His son, who was also a teacher, failed to pass the examinations; and when he reached middle age without an heir, he and his wife went to a temple to beg the God of Literature for descendants. He dreamed that the god handed him a slip of paper bearing this sentence from *The Book of Change*:

The gentleman cultivates virtue by good conduct.

So when Yu's wife conceived and in due course gave birth to the future Dr. Yu, he went back to the temple to offer thanks, and named his infant son Yu-teh, which means Cultivating Virtue. At three, the child lost his mother, and his

---

[1] 1465-1487.

father took him to live in the household where he was teaching, starting his schooling when he was six. When the future doctor was ten, Mr. Chi of Unicorn Sash Village engaged Mr. Yu to teach his son, and employer and tutor hit it off famously together. After teaching there for four years, Mr. Yu fell mortally ill and on his deathbed entrusted his son — then fourteen — to Mr. Chi.

"Your lad is not like other children," said Mr. Chi. "When you are gone I shall make him my son's tutor."

He immediately wrote his name on a card and carried it to the library to pay his respects to the new teacher, taking his nine-year-old son with him. And after that Dr. Yu taught in Chi's household.

Changshu had more than its share of men of letters. There was a scholar at this time called Yun Ching-chuan, who excelled in writing poems and essays in the ancient style. When nearly eighteen, Dr. Yu began to study poetry with him.

"You are a poor scholar, Master Yu," said Mr. Chi. "And poetry alone will be of no use to you. You must learn some skill by which you can make a living. In my youth I studied geomancy, and learned how to tell fortunes and select sites. I will be glad to teach you all I know, for it may serve you in good stead some day."

Dr. Yu paid careful attention to his instructions.

"You should buy a few collections of *paku* essays to study too," advised Mr. Chi. "Then later, if you pass the examinations, you'll find better teaching jobs."

Acting on his advice, Dr. Yu bought some *paku* essays and studied them. At twenty-four he passed the prefectural examination. The following year Mr. Yang of Yang Family Village, six miles away, engaged him as a tutor at thirty taels a year. He proceeded to his new post in the first month, and returned to Mr. Chi in the twelfth month for the New Year holiday.

Two years passed.

"Your father arranged a match between you and the Huangs' daughter," said Mr. Chi. "It is time you married."

Yu had a dozen taels left from that year's pay, and by drawing another dozen in advance he had just enough for his marriage. Mr. Chi lent the young couple a room, and at the end of the honeymoon Yu went back to his post. Two years later he had saved nearly thirty taels, with which he was able to rent a four-roomed cottage near Mr. Chi and hire a servant-boy. After Yu's return to his post, this servant-boy walked a mile to the market every morning to buy the fuel, rice, oil, flour or vegetables needed, then returned to help his mistress. As a result of child-bearing, Mrs. Yu's health failed; but a tutor's pay was not enough to buy medicine. After a regimen of three meals of gruel a day, however, she gradually recovered.

The year that Dr. Yu was thirty-two, he found himself without a job.

"How are we to manage this year?" asked his wife.

"Don't worry," he replied. "Ever since I started teaching I've made an average of thirty taels a year. If my contract in the first month was for twenty-odd taels only, I'd feel anxious; but by the fourth or fifth month there'd always be one or two extra pupils, or some compositions to correct, to make up the thirty taels. On the other hand, if my contract happened to be for a few taels more, I'd be very pleased, thinking: 'Good! I'm doing better this year!' But then as sure as fate there'd be some emergency at home to use up those few extra taels. So you can see all that happens to us is predestined, and it's no use worrying."

Some time later, sure enough, Mr. Chi came over and told Yu that the Cheng family in a village at some distance wanted him to select a burial ground. Taking his geomancer's compass with him, Yu exerted himself to the best of his ability to find a suitable graveyard; and when the location had been fixed the Cheng family paid him twelve taels. He then hired a small boat to take him home. It was about the middle of the third month, and the banks on either side of the river were covered with peach blossom and willows, while a light wind helped the boat along. Yu was in the best of spirits. After a while they reached a quiet spot, where a man with a boat full of cormorants was fishing. But as Yu leant out from his cabin window to watch, he saw another man on the bank opposite throw himself into the river! Yu started in horror, then hastily bade his boatman save the fellow. They pulled him aboard, sopping wet, but fortunately it was a mild day. Yu made him take off his wet clothes, borrowed a dry suit for him from the boatman, then asked him into the cabin and inquired why he had tried to take his own life.

"I come from these parts and work on the land," was the answer. "I tilled a few fields for a landlord, but he tricked me out of all my harvest. Then my father fell ill and died, and I had no money for a coffin. I could see no reason to go on living — death seemed a better way out!"

"This proves your filial piety," declared Yu. "Still, you mustn't think of dying. I have twelve taels here, which have been given me. I cannot let you have them all, because I need money to live on during the next few months. But I'll give you four taels, and when you show it to your neighbours and relatives and tell them your trouble, I am sure they will help you. Then you will be able to bury your father."

He unpacked the silver, weighed out four taels, and handed them to the other, who accepted the silver and thanked him.

"May I ask who it is who has been so good to me?" said the stranger.

"My name is Yu, and I live in Unicorn Sash Village. But we mustn't waste time talking. Make haste to despatch your business."

After renewed thanks, the stranger left.

Dr. Yu proceeded home, and in the second half of that year found another teaching post. At the end of the winter a son was born to him; and because Mr. Chi had helped him in so many ways, he called the child Kan-chi (Thanking Chi). He taught for five or six more years until he was forty-one, when there was another provincial examination.

"I am sure you will pass high on the list this year," said Mr. Chi, when he came to see him off.

"Why do you say that?" asked Dr. Yu.

"You have done so many secret acts of kindness."

"What secret acts of kindness have I done, uncle?"

"Well, for one thing, you put your whole heart into finding that family a burial ground. And then I've heard how you saved that fellow whose father had died. These are all secret acts of kindness."

Dr. Yu smiled.

"Good deeds should be done so unobtrusively that none but the doer knows of them," he said. "Since you have heard of these things, uncle, they aren't secret acts of kindness any more."

"Yes, they are," insisted the old man. "This year you will pass."

On his way home from Nanking after taking the provincial examination, Dr. Yu caught cold and fell ill. The day that the results were published, heralds came to the village and Mr. Chi accompanied them to Yu's home.

"You've passed, Mr. Yu!" he announced.

Ill as he was, Dr. Yu consulted with his wife as to which clothes to pawn, then asked Mr. Chi to tip the heralds and see them off. In a few days he recovered, and went to the capital to hand in particulars of his career. On his return, his friends and landlord brought him congratulatory gifts. He set his affairs in order and returned to the capital to take the metropolitan examination, but did not pass.

As luck would have it, Mr. Kang of Changshu County, who had just been appointed provincial governor of Shantung, asked Dr. Yu to accompany him from the capital to his post, to do some secretarial work in his yamen. They were soon on the best of terms. One of the yamen secretaries, Yiu Tzu-shen, struck by Dr. Yu's learning and character offered to become his pupil. He shared a room with him and consulted him on all matters. This was just the time when the emperor was seeking for men of talent, and Governor Kang decided to recommend someone.

"This is a great court ceremony," said Yiu, "I am thinking of asking Governor Kang to recommend you, sir."

"I am not good enough for that," replied Dr. Yu with a smile. "And if Governor Kang wishes to recommend someone, the choice is up to him. To ask such a favour is hardly a sign of high moral character!"

"If you don't want an official career, sir, wait till you receive a summons from the emperor. You may be called for an audience, or you may not; but by refusing to take office and returning home, you will demonstrate your superiority even more clearly."

"You are wrong there," retorted Yu. "You want me to ask for a recommendation, yet refuse to take office if I am summoned into the emperor's presence. That would show lack of sincerity both in requesting a recommendation and in refusing to become an official. What sort of behaviour is that?"

He burst out laughing.

After over two years in Shantung, Dr. Yu went back to the capital to take the examination, only to fail again. Then he took a boat back to the south, and returned to his teaching.

In another three years he was fifty. Asking a steward named Yen from the Yang family to accompany him, he went once more to the capital. This time he passed, was placed in the second rank in the palace examination, and recommended by the authorities for membership of the Han Lin Academy. It so happened that all the other successful candidates over fifty or sixty had represented themselves as much younger than they actually were. He was the only one who had given his true age as fifty.

"This Yu Yu-teh is an elderly man," said the emperor when he saw the record. "Let him be given light duties."

Accordingly, Yu was appointed a doctor of the Imperial College in Nanking.

He was in raptures.

"Nanking is a fine place," he said. "It has mountains and lakes and is close to my home. As soon as I arrive, I shall send for my wife and children, and our family will be reunited. This is better than being a poor academician!"

He bade farewell to his teachers in the capital and to the officials from his own district.

"When you reach Nanking, sir," said Mr. Wang, an old reader of the Han Lin Academy, "you will find that one of your students is a man called Wu Shu, who showed himself a devoted son to his mother and is extremely gifted. I hope you will do what you can for him."

Dr. Yu agreed to this. Then he packed his baggage, travelled to Nanking, and sent a man to Changshu to fetch his family. His son Kan-chi, now eighteen, accompanied his mother to Nanking. After calling on Libationer Li of the Imperial College, Dr. Yu took his seat in the hall, and all the students came to pay their respects. On one of their cards was the name Wu Shu.

"Which of you gentlemen is Wu Shu?" asked Dr. Yu, going out to receive them.

A short man stepped out from the group.

"I am, sir," he said.

"While at the capital I heard of your exemplary filial piety," said Dr. Yu, "and also of your great talent."

He bowed to Wu again, and begged them all to be seated.

"Your scholarship is supreme, sir," said Wu Shu. "We are very lucky to be privileged to learn from you."

"I am a newcomer," replied Dr. Yu. "I shall look to you for guidance in everything. How many years have you been in this college?"

"I will tell you the truth, sir. Since my father died when I was a child, I stayed in the country to look after my mother. With no wife and no brothers, I had to see to our daily food and clothes myself; so while my mother was alive I could not take the examination. When I was unfortunate enough to lose her, Mr. Tu Shao-ching of Tienchang paid all the funeral expenses. Then I studied poetry under Mr. Tu."

"I once saw a collection of his poems on Yiu Tzu-shen's desk," said Dr. Yu. "He shows extraordinary brilliance. Is he here?"

"He lives in one of the riverside houses by Lucky Crossing Bridge."

"There is a Mr. Chuang, too, who was presented with Lotus Lake by the emperor. Does he live by the lake?"

"Yes, he lives there. But he doesn't receive many callers."

"I mean to call on him tomorrow," said Dr. Yu.

"I could not write these *paku* essays," continued Wu Shu. "So when I became desperately poor and looked for a teaching job, I failed to find one. Then I had to buy a few essays to study, until I learned to write them myself after a fashion. After that I sat for the examination and passed; and then my respected teachers saw fit to place me first in the first class, and make me a salaried scholar. Actually my essays are merely second-rate, but I always seem to come first in the poetry tests. Last time one of our teachers tested the students of eight counties together, and I was first of the eight. That is why they sent me to this college. However, I am all too conscious that my essays are unsatisfactory."

"I have no patience with writing *paku* essays either," replied Dr. Yu.

"That is why I have brought no essays today, sir. When I have recopied my poems, I will bring them to you with my *Notes on Old Texts* and other miscellaneous writings for your criticism."

"You must have remarkable gifts. By all means let me see your poems and compositions in the old style, and I will read them carefully. Has your worthy mother received posthumous honours?"

"She is eligible for honours, sir. But because I can't afford the yamen fees, I have kept putting the matter off. This is most remiss of me."

"We must delay no longer," declared Dr. Yu.

He called for his ink-stone.

"Write an account of the matter, Wu Shu," he said.

Then he sent for his clerk.

"Make haste to draw up a statement of Mrs. Wu's fidelity and piety, so that we can send in a written report," he ordered. "I will be responsible for all expenses."

The clerk assented and left.

Wu Shu kowtowed his gratitude, and the others also thanked the doctor on his behalf, then took their leave. Dr. Yu saw them out.

The next day he went to Lotus Lake to pay his respects to Chuang Shao-kuang, but Mr. Chuang did not receive him. He went then to the riverside to call on Tu Shao-ching, and this time he was admitted. When he mentioned that his grandfather had been a pupil of Tu's great-grandfather, Tu addressed him as an uncle. After some conversation about the past, Dr. Yu described how he had just called on Mr. Chuang but unfortunately been denied admittance.

"He doesn't know who you are, uncle," said Tu. "I shall call to tell him."

Dr. Yu then took his leave.

The following day Tu went to Lotus Lake, and found Chuang.

"Why didn't you receive Dr. Yu yesterday?" he asked.

"I am through with all officials," replied Chuang with a smile. "Though his rank is low, I was reluctant to meet him."

"He is quite different from the common run," declared Tu. "There is nothing of the pedant or successful palace graduate about him. For loftiness of character he can be compared with Po Yi[1] and Liu-hsia Huei, or at least with Tao Yuan-ming. You will see this for yourself when you meet him."

Hearing this, Chuang returned Dr. Yu's call. And they immediately became the best of friends. The doctor valued Chuang's air of tranquillity, while Chuang admired the doctor's genial kindliness. They became lifelong friends.

Half a year later, Dr. Yu decided it was time for his son's wedding. The lad was betrothed to one of Mr. Chi's granddaughters who had been Dr. Yu's pupil; for in this way Dr. Yu could ally himself by marriage to the family in which he had been tutor, to show his gratitude to Mr. Chi. The Chi family sent the girl over to the college for the wedding, together with a slave girl. And only then did Dr. Yu's wife have a maid at her beck and call. After the wedding Dr. Yu decided to marry the slave girl to his steward Yen. And the latter brought ten taels to pay for her.

"You'll need to make bedding and clothes," said Dr. Yu. "Let's assume I've made you a gift of ten taels, and take this silver back for your own use."

The steward kowtowed in thanks, then left.

Soon it was the second month, when a plum tree with red blossom which Dr. Yu had planted the previous year after his

---

1 Po Yi lived at the end of the Shang Dynasty (16th to 12th century B.C.), and Liu-hsia Huei during the Spring and Autumn period (770-480 B.C.). Tao Yuan-ming was a great poet of the Tsin Dynasty (317-402). They were men of integrity, who cared nothing for fame and wealth, hence later generations revered them as sages.

arrival began to flower. The doctor was delighted. He bade his family prepare a feast, and invited Tu Shao-ching.

"Spring is already here, Shao-ching," he said, as they were sitting under the plum tree. "I would like to see the plum blossom along the river banks. When shall we go for an outing, taking wine with us?"

"I was thinking the same thing myself," replied Tu. "I would like to invite you and Chuang Shao-kuang for a day's excursion."

As he was speaking, two other guests came in. One was Chu Hsin, the other Yin Chao. They both lived at the entrance to the Imperial College, where they had studied for many years. Dr. Yu greeted them and asked them to sit down, and they declined to take places above Mr. Tu. As soon as they were seated, wine was served and they began to drink.

"At the beginning of spring you ought to celebrate your birthday, sir," said Chu Hsin. "The presents you receive will last you the whole season."

"Yes. Let us send out a notice for you, sir," suggested Yin Chao.

"My birthday falls in the eighth month," replied Dr. Yu. "How can I celebrate it now?"

"That makes no difference," said Yin Chao. "You can have one birthday in the second month, and another in the eighth month."

"What an idea!" cried Dr. Yu. "A fine fool I should look! Drink up, gentlemen."

Tu also smiled.

"I have a favour to ask you, Shao-ching," said Dr. Yu. "I received a request the other day from the Prince of Chung Shan's household to write an epitaph for a virtuous lady who took her own life when her husband died. And I have eighty taels of silver here, which they sent to thank me. I want you to write the epitaph for me, and to take the silver to prepare for our outing to enjoy the blossom."

"Can't you write this epitaph yourself, uncle?" asked Tu. "Why make it over to me?"

"I am not as gifted as you are," replied Dr. Yu with a smile. "Take this, and see what you can write."

He produced from his sleeve an outline of the lady's life, and bade his servant give two packets of silver to Mr. Tu's boy. Returning with the silver, the servant announced:

"Master Tang is here, sir."

"Ask him out here," said Dr. Yu.

The servant handed the silver to Tu's boy, and went in.

"This is a nephew of mine," said Dr. Yu. "When I came to Nanking I left him my house to live in. That must be the reason for his visit."

Master Tang came into the garden, bowed and sat down. After some polite conversation, he said:

"For the last half year I've had no money, uncle. So I've sold your house."

"That's all right," replied Dr. Yu. "If your business was poor, you'd have to sell the house to feed and clothe your family. But why come such a long way just to tell me this?"

"Since selling the house we've nowhere to live, uncle. I come to ask you to lend us some money to rent a few rooms."

Dr. Yu nodded.

"Of course. Since selling it, you've nowhere to live. Well, luckily I have thirty to forty taels left here. You can take that back with you tomorrow to rent some rooms."

Master Tang said no more.

When the feast ended, Tu took his leave. The two other guests stayed behind, and Dr. Yu came back to keep them company.

"Sir, is this Tu Shao-ching an old friend of yours?" asked Yin Chao.

"Yes, an old family friend. He is very gifted."

"I hardly like to say this, sir," said Yin Chao. "But all Nanking knows that Tu was once rich, and is now lying low here because he has squandered his fortune. He tells lies to swindle money out of people, and is a thoroughly disreputable character."

"Why do you call him a thoroughly disreputable character?"

"He is for ever taking his wife to taverns. Everybody laughs at him."

"This simply shows what a romantic he is. Naturally vulgar folk cannot understand him."

"That may be true," said Chu Hsin. "But next time you are commissioned to write something, sir, don't give it to him. He doesn't sit for the examinations, so he couldn't possibly write anything good. I'm afraid he may damage your reputation. There are many students in our college who have passed the examination. If you asked their help, sir, they won't want any money, and they'll produce good compositions."

"I disagree with you," said Dr. Yu gravely. "Mr. Tu is known for his brilliance, and his poems are generally admired. Each time I ask him to write something for me, he reflects credit on me. Besides, I was given a hundred taels for this epitaph; but I have kept twenty for my nephew."

Yin and Chu said no more, but took their leave.

The next morning the local authorities sent over a student accused of gambling, for Dr. Yu to discipline. Leaving the young man in the gate-house, the messenger and runners came in.

"Where shall we lock him up, sir?" they asked.

"Invite him in here," replied Dr. Yu.

The student's name was Tuan, and he was from the country. He came in, tears streaming from his eyes, and knelt on both knees to protest his innocence.

"I understand," said Dr. Yu.

He lodged the youth in the library, ate at the same table with him, and lent him bedding. The next day he went to the yamen to explain that the young man had been falsely accused, and procured his release. The student kowtowed his thanks.

"Though my bones are ground to powder," he declared, "I shall never be able to repay your kindness!"

"This is a trifle," replied Dr. Yu. "Since an injustice was done, it was my duty to clear you."

"Yes, you were good enough to clear me, sir! But that's not all. When they first brought me here, I was afraid. I didn't know what punishment you would give me, how much money the messenger would demand, or in what wretched place I would be shut up. How could I guess you would treat me like an honoured guest? Instead of receiving any punishment here, I have had two of the best days in my life! I don't know how to thank you for such great kindness."

"You have lost several days over this case," said Dr. Yu. "Don't waste time in unnecessary thanks, but hurry home."

The student took his leave.

A few days later the gateman brought in a large red visiting card. On it was written: "Chih Heng-shan, Ma Chun-shang, Chi Wei-hsiao, Chu Hsien-fu, Wu Shu, Yu Ho-sheng and Tu Shao-ching wish to pay their respects."

"What can this mean?" wondered Dr. Yu.

He hurried out to meet his guests.

But to know the reason for this call, you must read the next chapter.

CHAPTER 37

Through sacrifice to an ancient sage,
scholars revive the old ceremony in Nanking.
A filial son is seen off by his friends
to search for his father in Szechuan

Dr. Yu received his guests, and after an exchange of courtesies they sat down.

"We have come in connection with the question of a master of sacrifice for the great ceremony at Tai Po's Temple," said Chih Heng-shan. "Since Tai Po was such a great sage, we all feel it is only fitting that the master of sacrifice should be a man of spotless character. So we are formally requesting you, sir, to perform this part."

"You do me too much honour," replied Dr. Yu. "But of course I shall be glad to take part in such an important ceremony. Has the date been decided yet?"

"The first of the fourth month, sir," said Chih. "And we would like you to go to the temple the day before, in order to spend a night in purification before the ceremony."

When Dr. Yu had consented, tea was served. Then his guests left, to proceed together to Tu's riverside house.

"I'm afraid we are still one or two short," remarked Chih when they had sat down.

"It so happens that a friend from my county has just arrived," said Tu.

He called Tsang Liao-chai in, and introduced him. They bowed to each other.

"We hope you will honour us by taking part in the sacrifice, sir," said Chih.

"I shall be delighted to participate in such an important ceremony," replied Tsang.

Then the guests took their leave.

On the twenty-ninth of the third month Chih Heng-shan assembled his party and left the city through the South Gate. With him were Tu Shao-ching, Ma Chun-shang, Chi Wei-hsiao, Chin Tung-ya, Lu Hua-shih, Hsin Tung-chih, Chu Hsien-fu, Yu Ho-sheng, Lu Hsin-hou, Yu Kan-chi, Chu-ko Tien-shen, Ching Lan-chiang, Kuo Tieh-pi, Hsiao Chin-hsuan, Chu Hsin, Yin Chao, Chi Tien-yi, Chin Yu-liu, Tsung Chi, Wu Shu and Tsang Liao-chai. Soon they were joined by Chuang Shao-kuang. A steep flight of dozens of steps led to the main entrance to Tai Po's Temple, on the left of which was the house where the sacrificial meat was prepared. Just inside the entrance was a large open space, at the far end of which another steep flight of steps led to three gates. These opened into a courtyard flanked by two corridors containing shrines to some minor sages. At the end of the courtyard were five great halls, the largest of which held Tai Po's shrine, with a table before it bearing incense urns and candlesticks. Behind this was a yard with five pavilions, and a library of three rooms on either side. As soon as the scholars passed through the central gate, they saw a placard on high with the inscription in gilt characters: The Temple of Tai Po. Passing through a second door in the east corner and walking down the eastern corridor past the main building, they looked up to see another placard bearing the gilt inscription: The Pavilion for Studying Ceremony. They sat down for a while in the library on the east. Then Chih Heng-shan opened the door of one of the pavilions and went upstairs with Ma Chun-shang, Wu Shu and Chu Hsien-fu to fetch the musical instruments. Some of these they placed in the hall and some in the courtyard. In the hall they also set a prayer board, and beside the incense table a banner for directing the musicians. In the courtyard they set torches, and beside the second door ewers and napkins.

Chin Tzu-fu and Pao Ting-hsi had brought thirty-six boy dancers and musicians to play the jade chime, lyre, cithern, pipe, drum, sonorous wood, bronze tiger, reed organ, big bell, flute, small bells and stone chimes. They came in now to greet the scholars, and Chih Heng-shan gave the boys the vermilion flutes and pheasant feathers for their dance. In the afternoon Dr. Yu arrived, to be ushered in by Chuang, Chih, Ma and Tu. After drinking tea they changed into ceremonial dress, and the same four men led the way to inspect the sacrificial meat. That night they purified themselves in the libraries.

At the fifth watch the next morning the gate of the temple was thrown wide open, and they all got up. Candles and lamps were lit at both ends of the hall and the courtyard, inside and outside each door and along the corridors. The torches were also lit. Chih Heng-shan called upon the master of sacrifice, Dr. Yu, and the second master, Chuang Shao-kuang. But when he asked for a third master of sacrifice, no one would accept the honour.

"It should be Mr. Chih or Mr. Tu," they said.

"We shall be ushers," replied Chih. "Mr. Ma is from Chekiang.[1] Let him be the third."

Ma Chun-shang declined repeatedly, but the others carried him by main force to sit with Dr. Yu and Chuang. When Chih and Tu had taken these three to inspect the preparation of the meat, they came back to ask Chin Tung-ya to act as herald, Wu Shu to signal with the banner, Tsang Liao-chai to recite the prayers, Chi Wei-hsiao, Hsin Tung-chih and Yu Ho-sheng to present wine, Chu Hsien-fu, Lu Hsin-hou and Yu Kan-chi to present jade, Chu-ko Tien-shen, Ching Lan-chiang and Kuo Tieh-pi to present silk, Hsiao Chin-hsuan, Chu Hsin and Yin Chao to present grain, and Chi Tien-yi, Chin Yu-liu and Tsung Chi to present sacrificial viands. Lu Hua-shih was requested to attend the herald. This done, they led all the scholars outside the second gate.

---

[1] After ceding his throne to his brother, Tai Po went south to establish the Kingdom of Wu. Since Wu comprised the modern provinces of Kiangsu and Chekiang, it was fitting that a native of Chekiang should act as master of sacrifice.

Then the drum sounded three times for the sacrifice. Chin Tzu-fu and Pao Ting-hsi led in the players on the jade chime, lyre, cithern, pipe, drum, sonorous wood, bronze tiger, reed organ, big bell, flute, small bells and stone chimes; as well as the thirty-six dancing boys. They took their places at both ends of the hall and the courtyard.

Then Chin Tung-ya, followed by Lu Hua-shih, entered the hall. Coming to a halt, he announced: "Let all taking part attend to their duties!"

The musicians picked up their instruments.

"Take your places!" cried Chin.

Wu Shu with his banner led the men bearing wine, jade and silk to the east of the courtyard. Then he conducted Tsang Liao-chai, who was to read the prayers, to take his place before the prayer tablet on the dais. Next he led the men bearing grain and sacrificial viands to the west of the courtyard, and took his stand below them.

"Music!" cried Chin.

Music sounded from the hall and the courtyard.

"Welcome the spirit!" cried Chin.

With scented candles in both hands, the ushers walked outside, bowing, to welcome the spirit.

"Let the music cease!" cried Chin.

At once it died away in both the hall and courtyard.

"Let the votaries take their places!"

The ushers went out to summon Chuang Shao-kuang and Ma Chun-shang, who took their places to the left of the incense table in the courtyard.

"Let the master of sacrifice take his place!"

The ushers summoned Dr. Yu, who took his place in the middle of the courtyard. Chih and Tu stood one on the right and one on the left of the incense table.

"The ablution!" announced Chih.

He and Tu led the master of sacrifice to wash his hands and return.

"The master of sacrifice approaches the incense table," announced Chih.

There was an aloe-wood urn holding red flags on the incense table, from which Tu now took a flag bearing the word Music. Dr. Yu went up to the incense table.

"Kneel and offer incense!" cried Chih. "Pour a libation on the ground! Prostrate yourself four times! Return to your place!"

Tu took another flag, bearing the word Silence.

"Play 'The Air to Delight the Spirit,'" cried Chin.

Chin Tzu-fu conducted as the musicians in the hall played. Presently the music ceased.

"The first sacrifice!" cried Chin.

Lu Hua-shih carried out from the shrine a placard on which was written First Sacrifice.

With Wu Shu carrying his banner before them, the ushers led the master of sacrifice forward. And as they passed down the east of the courtyard, leading Chi Wei-hsiao bearing wine, Chu Hsien-fu bearing jade, and Chu-ko Tien-shen bearing silk, men came out from the hall to welcome the master of sacrifice. When they came to the west, Hsiao Chin-hsuan bearing grain and Chi Tien-yi bearing viands led the master of sacrifice down the west side, passing in front of the incense table and turning east. When they entered the main hall, the ushers took their places at the right and left of the table. The men bearing wine, jade and silk stood on the left, while those bearing grain and viands stood on the right.

"Take your places!" cried Chih. "Kneel!"

Dr. Yu knelt before the table.

"Offer wine!"

Chi Wei-hsiao knelt to pass the wine to Dr. Yu, who placed it on the table.

"Offer jade!"

Chu Hsien-fu knelt to pass the jade to Dr. Yu, who placed it on the table.

"Offer silk!"

Chu-ko Tien-shen knelt to pass the silk to Dr. Yu, who placed it on the table.

"Offer grain!"

Hsiao Chin-hsuan knelt to pass the grain to Dr. Yu, who placed it on the table.

"Offer viands!"

Chi Tien-yi knelt to pass the viands to Dr. Yu, who placed them on the table.

This sacrifice at an end, the votaries withdrew to their places and Chih bade them prostrate themselves four times.

"The first 'Song and Dance of Supreme Virtue'!" cried Chin.

Clear music sounded from the upper part of the hall, and the thirty-six boys with vermilion flutes and pheasant feathers advanced to dance.

The dance at an end, the herald announced: "Let all kneel below the steps as the prayer is read."

Tsang Liao-chai knelt before the prayer tablet, and read the prayer.

"Return to your places!" cried Chin.

"Rise!" cried Chih.

Wu Shu, the ushers and those who had borne offerings conducted the master of sacrifice off by the west. Dr. Yu returned to his place, and the others to theirs.

"The second sacrifice!" cried Chin.

Lu Hua-shih fetched from the shrine another placard bearing the words Second Sacrifice.

Then the same ceremony was repeated, Chuang Shao-kuang as second master of sacrifice, and different men bearing offerings.

"The last sacrifice!" cried Chin.

Lu Hua-shih fetched from the shrine another placard bearing the words Last Sacrifice.

And again the same ceremony was repeated, with Ma Chun-shang as the third master of sacrifice, and different men presenting offerings.

"Entertain the spirit with a feast and music!" cried Chin.

The ushers led the master of sacrifice in again by the east to kneel before the table

"Music!" cried Chin.

From the hall and the courtyard all the instruments sounded together.

When the music ceased, Chih bade them prostrate themselves four times, then rise.

"Return to your places!" cried Chin.

The ushers led Dr. Yu back by the west to his place as master of sacrifice, then returned to their own positions.

"Remove the offerings!" cried Chin.

Tu took another red flag bearing the words Ring the Bell, and music rang out loudly again. To the strains of this music, the ushers led Dr. Yu from his place by the east to the main hall to kneel before the table. Chih bade him prostrate himself four times, then rise.

"Return to your places!" cried Chin.

The ushers led Dr. Yu back by the west to his place as master of sacrifice, and returned to their own positions. Tu took another flag bearing the word Silence.

"Drink the propitious wine! Receive the sacrificial meat!" cried Chin.

The ushers led the master of sacrifice, the second master of sacrifice, and the last master of sacrifice to kneel before the table, drink the propitious wine and receive the sacrificial meat.

"Return to your places!" cried Chin.

The three masters of sacrifice withdrew.

"Let silk be burnt!" cried Chin.

Then Chu-ko Tien-shen, Ching Lan-chiang and Kuo Tieh-pi burnt the silk.

"The ceremony is ended!" cried Chin.

They cleared away the sacrificial vessels and musical instruments, changed out of their ceremonial costume, and gathered in one of the buildings at the back. Chin Tzu-fu and Pao Ting-hsi also conducted the musicians from the hall and the thirty-six young dancers to the two libraries at the back.

The participants in this great sacrifice included: three masters of sacrifice, one herald, one prayer-reader, one herald's assistant, two ushers, one banner-bearer, and three men each in charge of wine, jade, silk, grain and viands There were also two men to direct the twelve musicians, and thirty-six boy dancers, making a total of seventy-six participants.

Now the cooks dressed an ox and four sheep to serve with the sacrificial viands and some vegetables. Sixteen tables were laid—eight downstairs for the twenty-four scholars, and eight in the two libraries at the sides to entertain the others. After feasting for half a day, Dr. Yu mounted his sedan-chair and returned to the city. Some of the other scholars left by sedan-chair, others on foot. Their path was lined with people who had brought their old folk and children to throng the temple and watch. They were crying out for joy.

"What makes you so pleased?" asked Ma Chun-shang with a smile.

"We are Nanking-born and Nanking-bred," they replied, "and some of us are over seventy or eighty. But we have never seen a ceremony like this, or heard music like this before! The old folk told us the gentleman who was the master of sacrifice is a sage who has come back to the earth; so we all wanted to see him"

Then, with joy in their hearts, the scholars made their way back to the city.

A few days later, Chi Wei-hsiao, Hsiao Po-chuan, Hsin Tung-chih and Chin bade goodbye to Dr. Yu and returned to Yangchow Ma Chun-shang and Chu Hsien-fu called to take their leave of Tu Shao-ching before going back to Chekiang. Upon entering his riverside house, they found Tu and Tsang Liao-chai sitting there with another man. Chu Hsien-fu gave a start.

"This is that Iron-armed Chang, who tricked my uncles with the false head!" he thought. 'What is he doing here?"

They exchanged bows. Iron-armed Chang was also embarrassed by this meeting, and did not know where to look. After drinking tea, Ma and Chu expressed their regret at parting, then took their leave. Tu saw them to the gate.

"What do you know of this fellow Chang?" asked Chu.

"His name is Chang Chun-min, and he comes from Tienchang."

Smiling, Chu described briefly all that Iron-armed Chang had done in Chekiang

"The less you have to do with him the better," he concluded. "So be on your guard, Shao-ching."

"I see," replied Tu.

When his friends had left, Tu went back into the house.

"Were you once known as Iron-armed Chang?" he asked. Iron-armed Chang turned red.

"When I was a youngster," he admitted.

He gave no clear account of himself, and Tu did not press him. But realizing that the game was up now that he had been exposed, Iron-armed Chang left a few days later for Tienchang, taking Tsang Liao-chai with him. Hsiao Chin-hsuan and his two friends had run up bills at the shop and eating house, and could not leave till they paid; so they asked Tu to help them out. After receiving a few taels from him, they went home. Mr. Tsung decided to go back to Hukuang, and brought a portrait for Tu to inscribe. This Tu did in his presence, then saw him off. On his way back he met Wu Shu walking to his house.

"I haven't seen you for a long time," said Tu. "Where have you been?"

"There was an examination the other day for all six classes in our college," replied Wu. "I came first in the first rank again."

"Good for you!" said Tu.

"That is nothing. But it gave me the chance to see something quite extraordinary."

"What was that?"

"The test was ordered by the court to reclassify all the students in the college; therefore all six classes were examined together. And instructions were issued to search everybody from head to foot, just as in the district examinations. We were tested on two passages from the *Four Books* and one from the *Five Classics*, and one fellow who had studied the *Spring and Autumn Annals* took a printed copy in with him. Nothing strange in that, you may say. But when he went out to the latrine, he tucked this crib in his paper by mistake and handed it in to the examiner! Luckily for him, Dr. Yu was examiner that day, with another official to help him invigilate. When the doctor picked up the paper and saw the crib, he stuffed it at once in his boot. The other invigilator asked what it was.

" 'Nothing,' said Dr. Yu.

474

"When the student came in again, the doctor slipped the crib back to him.

" 'Take it,' he said. 'You shouldn't have handed it in just now with your paper. It was lucky for you I saw it, and not someone else.'

"The student sweated to think what might have happened!

"When the results came out, he was in the second rank, so he went to thank Dr. Yu. But the doctor insisted that he didn't know him.

" 'I never spoke to you,' said Dr. Yu. 'You must have mistaken someone else for me.'

"I happened to be there to thank him that day too, and I saw all this. When the student left, I asked: 'Why did you deny helping him, sir? Was it wrong of him to come and thank you?'

" 'All scholars must have self-respect,' said Dr. Yu. 'He felt he had to thank me; but if I'd acknowledged helping him, he would have had no face left.'

"I didn't know the fellow, so I asked his name. But the doctor wouldn't tell me. Don't you agree, sir, that few men would act in such an extraordinary way?"

"The old fellow is always doing things like that," replied Tu.

"He did something even more amusing," said Wu Shu. "You know he married that slave girl who came with his son's bride to his steward, Yen. Well, because that scoundrel realized that this wasn't the sort of yamen where you make money, the day before yesterday he gave notice. Dr. Yu hadn't asked for a cent, but given him the slave girl for nothing. Anybody else would have demanded that he pay for her — and set a high price too — now that he was taking her away. But not Dr. Yu. 'Of course you may leave,' he said. 'But you can't have any money for food and lodging.' He gave him another ten taels. And as soon as he'd let him go, he recommended Yen for a job with a county magistrate. Have you ever heard anything so funny?"

"Scoundrels like that have absolutely no conscience," replied Tu. "But it wasn't because he wanted a reputation for charity that the old man gave him silver twice. *That's* what's so rare."

He kept Wu Shu to a meal.

After leaving Tu, Wu Shu had gone no further than Lucky Crossing Bridge when he met a man in a square cap, old cotton gown, silk girdle and straw sandals. His luggage hung in two bundles from a shoulder pole. His hair was grey, and he was haggard and thin. This man set down his baggage and bowed to Wu.

"Mr. Kuo!" exclaimed Wu. "It is three years since we parted at Chiangning. Where have you been all this time?"

"That is a long story," replied the other.

"Let us sit down in that tea-house," suggested Wu.

They went to the tea-house and sat down.

"I have been travelling the country looking for my father," said Kuo. "Someone told me he was in Chiangnan, so I have been there three times. Now I hear he is not in Chiangnan but Szechuan, where he has shaved his head and become a monk. I am therefore going to Szechuan to look for him."

Wu Shu exclaimed in sympathy.

"This thousand-mile journey will not be easy, sir," he said. "I know one of the magistrates in the Sian Prefecture, a Mr. Yiu, who used to be a colleague of Dr. Yu of the Imperial College. I shall ask Dr. Yu to give you a letter of introduction to him. You will pass that way on your journey, and if you are short of funds he should be able to help you."

"I am a rough country fellow," objected Kuo. "How can I call on an official in the Imperial College?"

"Never mind," said Wu Shu. "A few steps from here is Tu Shao-ching's house. I'll take you there to wait while I get you this letter."

"Tu Shao-ching? Is that the open-handed gentleman from Tienchang who was recommended for office but declined?"

"That's the man."

"I would like to meet him."

They paid the bill, left the tea-house, and walked together to Tu's house. Coming out to greet them, Tu bowed.

"What is this gentleman's honourable name?" he asked.

476

"This is Mr. Kuo Tieh-shan," replied Wu. "For twenty years he has travelled the country in search of his father, so he is known as Filial Kuo."

Upon hearing this, Tu bowed once more and made Kuo take the seat of honour.

"How is it you have not heard from your worthy father for so long?" he asked.

Kuo appeared tongue-tied.

"He was an official in Kiangsi who surrendered to Prince Ning," whispered Wu. "He had to run away."

Tu was amazed, and respected Kuo for his behaviour. He made him put his baggage down.

"You must spend the night here, sir," he said. "You may leave tomorrow."

"The whole empire knows of Tu Shao-ching's liberality," replied Kuo. "I won't stand on ceremony, but will gladly stay."

Tu went to the inner chambers to ask his wife to have Kuo's clothes washed and starched, and a good meal prepared for him. When he returned to his guests, Wu mentioned the letter of introduction for which he wished to ask Dr. Yu.

"That is easy," said Tu. "Please wait here, Mr. Kuo, while Wu Shu and I fetch the letter."

But to know what followed, you must read the next chapter.

CHAPTER 38

Kuo Tieh-shan encounters tigers in the mountain.
A monk from Sweet Dew Temple meets his foe

Tu Shao-ching offered Kuo Tieh-shan a feast in his river-side house, while he and Wu Shu called on Dr. Yu to explain who Kuo was and ask for a letter of introduction for him to take to Sian. Dr. Yu heard them out attentively.

"Of course I will write you a letter," he said. "But more is needed than a mere introduction. Your friend can hardly have money enough for such a long journey, so I shall give you ten taels for him, Shao-ching. Don't tell him, though, it comes from me."

He lost no time in writing a letter and fetching the silver for Tu, who took both introduction and money home with Wu. Tu pawned some clothes for four taels, and Wu raised another two taels at the pawnshop. They insisted on keeping Kuo for another day; and when Chuang Shao-kuang learned of his case he wrote another letter of introduction, and gave it with four taels to Tu. The morning after that, Tu prepared a farewell meal for Kuo, at which Wu accompanied them. After the meal, they roped Kuo's baggage for him and presented him with the twenty taels and two introductory letters. He refused, however, to take the money.

"This silver belongs to a few of us here; it's not stolen!" cried Tu. "You mustn't refuse, sir."

Then Kuo accepted it and left the house, having eaten his fill. Tu and Wu saw him beyond the West Gate.

Travelling by day and resting by night, Kuo Tieh-shan came to the province of Shensi. Since Mr. Yiu was the magistrate of Tungkuan County, Kuo had to go out of his way to call on him. This Mr. Yiu, whose name was Fu-lai, was an old Nanking scholar who had come to this post the previous year and performed a good deed immediately after his arrival. A native of Kwangtung, who was sentenced to exile at the border of Shensi and was travelling there with his wife, had died here. His widow wept and sobbed by the roadside; but when people spoke to her she could not understand their dialect, nor they hers, and they had to take her to the county court. Magistrate Yiu realized that the woman wanted to go back to Kwangtung, and took pity on her. He gave her fifty taels and ordered an old runner to escort her home. Then in his own hand he drew up a moving appeal on white silk, signed it with his own name and sealed it with the Tungkuan County seal.

"Take this lady and this roll of silk," he ordered the runner. "And at each prefectural town or county seat you come to, show this scroll to the local officials. Ask them to set their seals to it. When you have delivered her safely home, bring me back a letter from the authorities there."

The runner promised to do this. And when the woman had kowtowed her thanks they left.

A year or so later the runner returned.

"All the officials on the road who read your appeal were sorry for the woman, Your Honour," he reported. "Some gave her ten taels, some eight, some six. By the time she reached home she had over two hundred. When I saw her back to her family in Kwangtung, over a hundred of her relatives bowed their thanks to Heaven for your goodness. They actually kowtowed to me too, and called me a living Buddha! So, thanks to Your Honour's goodness, even I came in for some praise!"

Magistrate Yiu was delighted, and sent him away with several taels of silver.

Now the gateman brought in a card, announcing that Kuo Tieh-shan had called with a letter from Dr. Yu. When Magistrate Yiu read the letter he was greatly impressed. He invited Kuo in at once, and as soon as they had bowed to

479

each other and sat down a meal was served. While they were talking, the gateman came in.

"Your Honour is asked to go down to the country for the examination," he announced.

"I must leave on public business and shan't be back till the day after tomorrow, sir," said the magistrate to Kuo. "I hope you will be good enough to stay here for three days till I come back, in order that I may profit by your instruction. Indeed, if you are going to Chengtu I would like you to take a letter to an old friend of mine there. Pray don't refuse me!"

"Since you are so kind, how can I refuse?" replied Kuo. "But I am a rough fellow, I can't stay in the yamen. Is there any temple in your honourable district where I can put up for a couple of days?"

"There is a temple, but a very small one," said the magistrate. "However, we have an Ocean Moon Monastery here, whose abbot is a good man. I will send you to him."

He ordered a yamen runner: "Take Mr. Kuo's baggage to Ocean Moon Monastery, and tell the abbot I send him."

The runner assented, and Kuo took his leave. Magistrate Yiu saw him outside the gate.

When Kuo and the runner entered the lodge of Ocean Moon Monastery, an acolyte went in to announce them. The old abbot came out, greeted them, asked them to sit down and offered them tea. The runner left.

"Have you been here long, father?" asked Kuo.

"I used to live in Sweet Dew Temple in Wuhu County," replied the abbot. "Later I was the abbot of the Defender's Temple in Peking. But because I found the capital too noisy, I moved here. So you are Mr. Kuo. May I ask what business takes you to Chengtu?"

The abbot had an ascetic yet kindly face.

"I would not speak of this to others," said Kuo. "But I can confide in you."

He proceeded to give a heart-rending account of his search for his father. The abbot shed tears and sighed, then lodged Kuo in his own quarters and prepared a vegetarian meal for him. When Kuo gave him two pears he had bought on the road, the abbot accepted them with thanks. He bade a scullion carry two vats into the courtyard, put a pear in each, pour several buckets of water over them, and mash the pears with a pole. This done, he beat the clapper and assembled all the monks—over two hundred in all—to drink one bowl apiece. Kuo, looking on, nodded approvingly.

On the third day, Magistrate Yiu came back and invited Kuo to a feast. After the meal, he gave him fifty taels of silver and a letter.

"I would have liked to entertain you for some time, sir, but I must not delay your search for your father," he said. "Take these fifty taels for your expenses on the road. When you reach Chengtu, give this letter to Mr. Hsiao Hao-hsuan. He is a gentleman of the old school who lives at East Mountain, six or seven miles from Chengtu; and if you find yourself in any difficulty, he will help you."

The magistrate was so obviously sincere that Kuo could not refuse. He thanked him, accepted the silver and letter, then went back to Ocean Moon Monastery to take his leave of the abbot.

"When you reach Chengtu and find your worthy father," said the abbot, bringing his palms together, "be sure to send me a letter to end my anxiety."

Kuo promised to do this, and the abbot saw him out.

Shouldering his luggage, Kuo journeyed on for several days along a narrow mountainous track. At every step, his heart was in his mouth. One day dusk fell while he was far from any village; but as he pressed forward he met a man.

"Can you tell me, uncle, how far it is to the nearest inn?" asked Kuo.

"Five or six miles," was the answer. "You must make haste, traveller, for a tiger prowls this path at night. Keep a good lookout!"

When Kuo heard this, he hurried on as fast as his legs would carry him. It was night now, but luckily a full moon climbed up from behind the mountains and sailed high above to illumine the way clearly. As he strode on in the moonlight to the edge of a forest, a high wind sprang up, whirling and rustling the fallen leaves. And, as the wind passed, out leapt a tiger!

"Help!" cried Kuo, falling to the ground.

481

The tiger pounced upon Kuo and squatted over him. After watching him for a time, it decided that since he did not open his eyes he must be dead, and rose to scoop out a pit. Into this pit it lugged Kuo, scattered fallen leaves over him with its paws, then left. From his pit Kuo watched furtively as the tiger loped off to a mountain peak about a mile away, whence it looked back with blazing eyes to see whether he had moved or not. Satisfied that he had not, it loped on. Then Kuo crawled out of the pit.

"Although that brute has gone," he thought, "it's bound to come back to eat me. What shall I do?"

At his wit's end, he noticed a big tree in front, and swarmed up it.

Then it occurred to him: "If the tiger comes back and gives a fearful roar, I shall be so terrified I shall tumble down."

He unwound his puttees, and fastened himself to the tree.

At midnight when the moon was preter-naturally bright, the tiger came back followed by another creature. This second beast was completely white, had a single horn, eyes like huge red lanterns, and held itself erect as it bounded forward. Kuo had no idea what it could be. Upon drawing near, this beast sat down while the tiger hurried to the pit to find the body. But when it discovered that its prey had disappeared, the tiger cringed with fear. The other beast flew into a rage, and thrust out one paw to knock off the tiger's head, felling it to the ground. The strange beast raged up and down, its fur bristling, until raising its head it saw in the moonlight a man perched on the tree; then it hurled itself furiously at Kuo. In its first bound it fell short of its quarry, and slithered to the ground. But leaping again, with all its might, it came within a foot of Kuo.

"This is the end!" thought the wretched man.

As luck would have it, however, there was a dead branch a foot or more long lower down the trunk; and in its furious leap the beast had impaled itself on this branch. The harder it struggled, the deeper the branch drove into its belly. After struggling desperately for half the night, it finally expired on the tree.

With dawn came several hunters carrying fowling-pieces and pronged sticks. At the sight of these two beasts they jumped for fright. When Kuo called out to them from the tree, they helped him down and asked his name.

"I am a traveller," said Kuo. "Heaven took pity on me, and saved my life. But I must hurry on my way now. You may take these two beasts to your local magistrate to ask for a reward."

The hunters gave him some of their dried provisions and venison, and made him eat his fill. Then they carried his load a couple of miles for him before going their own way.

Carrying his baggage, Kuo journeyed on for several more days, and put up one evening in a small temple in a mountain valley. After questioning him on his journey, the monk served a vegetarian meal and sat down by the window to share it with him. While they were eating, there was a blinding red flash outside like some conflagration.

"Help!" cried Kuo dropping his bowl. "Fire!"

"Sit down, sir, and don't be upset," said the monk with a smile. "That is my Snow Brother."

The meal at an end, he cleared the table and opened the window.

"Look, stranger!" he said.

Raising his eyes, Kuo saw an extraordinary creature squatting on the hillside in front. It had a single horn and a single eye behind one ear, and was one of those beasts called *piwans*. No matter how thick a sheet of ice, a *piwan* can shatter it with one roar.

"That is my Snow Brother," said the monk.

That night a tremendous snowstorm started, which lasted for twenty-four hours till the snow lay more than three feet deep. Kuo had no choice but to spend another day there.

The next day, when the snow stopped, Kuo took his leave of the old monk and struggled along the slippery mountain path. There were sheer drops on either side, and icicles as sharp as knives. He made slow headway, and as dusk fell he saw by the glimmer of the snow a red object hanging from a tree in a wood ahead. Another traveller a few hundred yards in front of him toppled straight into the gully when he reached this red object. Kuo froze in his tracks.

"Why should a man fall over at the sight of that red thing?" he wondered.

Straining his eyes, he saw a human being emerge from under the red object, pick up the baggage the dead man had let fall, then vanish once more from sight. With an inkling of what was afoot, Kuo hurried forward to find a woman in red hanging from the tree. Her hair was loose, and from her mouth hung a tongue of crimson felt. In a vat buried at her feet squatted a man, who jumped up at Kuo's approach. When he saw how hefty Kuo looked, however, he dared not attack him, but clasped his hands and stepped forward.

"Go your way, stranger," he said. "This is no business of yours."

"I know what you are up to," said Kuo. "Don't get excited. I can help you. Who is this woman pretending to have hanged herself?"

"My wife."

"Let her down. Where do you live? Suppose we go to your house and have a talk?"

The highwayman undid a rope knotted at the nape of his wife's neck, and let her down. She rolled up her hair, removed the false tongue dangling from her mouth, took off the iron halter round which the rope had been fastened, and divested herself of the red garment. Her husband pointed to a two-roomed thatched cottage by the roadside.

"There's my home," he said.

Husband and wife followed Kuo to their house, invited him to be seated, and brewed a pot of tea.

"Why do such wicked deeds simply for the sake of loot?" asked Kuo. "Frightening people to death is against the will of Heaven. Though I am poor myself, I can't help pitying you when I see how low you have sunk. I have ten taels of silver here which I'll give you and your wife as capital for a small business, so that you can turn over a new leaf. What is your name?"

The highwayman kowtowed.

"Thank you, stranger, for your help," he said. "My name is Mu Nai. My wife and I come of good families, but cold and hunger recently forced us to this. Now, thanks to this money you have given us, we can turn over a new leaf. May I ask your name, sir?"

"My name is Kuo, and I am a native of Hukuang on my way to Chengtu."

Mu's wife came in to thank Kuo too, and prepared him a meal.

"Since you dare hold people up, you must know some of the military arts," said Kuo after eating. "But unless you are expert in them, you will never achieve much. Let me teach you what I know of fencing and boxing."

Mu was overjoyed, and kept him there for two days, during which time Kuo painstakingly taught him fencing and boxing, and Mu acknowledged Kuo as his teacher. On the third day, when Kuo insisted on leaving, they put dried rations and roast meat in his baggage and carried it ten miles for him before bidding him farewell.

Taking over his baggage, Kuo Tieh-shan travelled on for several days. It was bitterly cold, and he was trudging in the teeth of a north-west wind along a mountain path as hard and slippery as wax. He plodded on till evening, when he heard a roar from a cave and another tiger leapt out.

"This is surely the end!" thought Kuo, and fell unconscious to the ground.

Now tigers will devour only those who are afraid of them. Therefore seeing Kuo lie stark and stiff the tiger dared not eat him, but simply sniffed at his face. One of its whiskers tickled Kuo's nose, whereupon he gave such a great sneeze that the tiger jumped for fright, and fled. In a few bounds it reached a mountain top and fell into a chasm, where it was caught on the spear-sharp icicles and frozen to death.

By the time Kuo scrambled to his feet the tiger had disappeared.

"What a narrow escape!"

He sighed with relief, shouldered his baggage and went on.

At last he reached Chengtu, and learned that his father was a monk in a temple a dozen miles away. He made his way straight to the temple and knocked at the gate. The old monk who let him in started at the sight of him. Recognizing his father, Kuo knelt down and sobbed.

"Please get up, sir," said the monk. "I have no son. You must have taken me for someone else."

"I have travelled thousands of miles to find you, father. Why won't you recognize me?"

"I told you just now, I have no son. You must look elsewhere for your father. Why come crying to me?"

"Though I haven't seen you for so many years, father, do you think I don't know you?"

The filial son knelt there, and would not rise.

"I entered orders as a boy," protested the monk. "What son could I have?"

At that Kuo wept bitterly.

"You may not recognize your son, father, but your son insists on recognizing you!"

His persistence made the old monk lose patience.

"You scoundrel!" he shouted. "You've just come to make trouble. Get out now! I'm going to close the temple gate!"

Still Kuo knelt there sobbing, and would not leave.

"If you don't go," threatened the monk, "I'll fetch a knife and kill you!"

"Kill me if you like, father!" cried Kuo, prostrate on the ground. "I cannot leave you!"

In a rage, the old monk pulled Kuo to his feet, seized him by the scruff of his neck and pushed him out, locking the gate behind him. He then went back into the temple, and turned a deaf ear to his son's cries.

Outside the temple, Kuo wept and sobbed, but dared not knock at the gate.

"It is no use," he thought as dusk fell. "It doesn't look as if my father will own me!"

Raising his eyes, he saw that this temple was called Bamboo Hill Temple. He rented a room a few hundred yards away. And the next morning when a priest came out of the temple, he bribed him to take in some fuel and rice every day for his father. In less than a year all his money was spent, and he thought of going to East Mountain to find Hsiao Hao-hsuan, but did not like to leave his father unprovided for. So he hired himself to a nearby family, and by cutting wood and carrying earth for them was able to make a few cents every day with which to support the old man. When he learned that one of the neighbours was going to Shensi, he wrote a detailed account of his search for his father, and asked the neighbour to deliver this to the abbot of Ocean Moon Monastery.

This letter sent the abbot into raptures and increased his admiration for Kuo. A few days later a mendicant monk came to the monastery. This was none other than Chao Ta, the brigand chief, who looked as fierce as ever with his dishevelled hair and wild eyes. The kindly abbot let him stay; but the wicked man drank, brawled and beat the other monks. There was no crime he would not stoop to. The chief monk led a delegation to complain to the abbot.

"If this fellow is allowed to stay, he will lower the tone of the monastery," they declared.

They begged the abbot to drive him out; but when the abbot bade him go, he refused. Later, the chief monk ordered an acolyte to tell Chao: "The abbot says you must leave. If you don't obey him, he will enforce our monastery's rule and have you carried to the back courtyard and burnt!"

When the wicked monk heard this, he was furious. The next day, without taking his leave of the abbot, he put his clothes together and left. Half a year later, the abbot decided to visit Omei Mountain, calling on Kuo Tieh-shan in Chengtu on the way. He bade farewell to the monks, shouldered his baggage and alms bowl and set out for Szechuan.

Thirty or forty miles from Chengtu, the abbot left his inn early one morning to go out and enjoy the scenery, and walked into a tea-house for some tea. There was another monk there who remembered the abbot, though the abbot did not recognize him. He stepped forward and bowed.

"There is no good tea here, brother," he said. "But I live in a small temple not far away. Won't you go there with me to drink tea?"

"With pleasure!" replied the abbot.

The monk led the abbot over two miles by a winding path to a temple. In the front courtyard was a statue of a bodhisattva. There were no images in the building in the back court-yard, but in the middle room was a wicker couch.

"Abbot!" cried the monk once they were in this temple. "Don't you know me?"

The abbot suddenly realized that this was the wicked monk he had driven out. He gave a start.

"For the moment I had forgotten," he said. "Now I know you."

The wicked monk strode over to the couch and sat down, glaring.

"Now you've fallen into my hands, don't think you can escape!" he cried. "There's a wineshop kept by an old woman a few hundred yards up the slope. Take this gourd and have it filled with wine for me. Look sharp!"

Not daring to refuse, the abbot took the gourd, found the old woman on the slope, and handed the gourd to her. She took it, looking the abbot over from head to foot as she did so, and tears welled from her eyes as she poured out the wine. The abbot was most disconcerted.

"What is there about me that distresses you so, granny?" he asked.

"You seem a good man, father. It's too bad you should come to such a cruel end!"

"What cruel end?"

"Did you come from that temple a few hundred yards away, father?"

"Yes. How did you guess?"

"I know this gourd. Whenever he means to eat someone's brains, he sends to my shop for wine. Once you take this wine back, father, you're as good as dead!"

When the abbot heard this, he nearly took leave of his senses.

"What can I do?" he demanded desperately. "I must get away from here!"

"How can you?" she asked. "His bandits are everywhere for a dozen miles around. If anyone escapes from his temple, he has only to sound his clapper, and at once you will be trussed up and carried back!"

The abbot fell, weeping, to the ground.

"Save me, granny!" he begged.

"How can *I* save you?" she retorted. "If they knew I'd told you, they'd kill me too. But you look such a kind man, father, I wouldn't like you to die such a cruel death. I'll tell you how to get to someone who may help you."

"Who is that, granny?"

In her own good time, the old woman told him.

But to know whom she named, you must read the next chapter.

CHAPTER 39

Hsiao Yun-hsien saves a man on Bright Moon Ridge.
Marshal Ping triumphs at Green Maple City

"A few hundred yards from here," the old woman told the
abbot, "is a hill called Bright Moon Ridge. There's a short cut
to it by the steep path behind my house. On the ridge you will
find a young man practising his catapult. Don't say anything;
just kneel before him. And when he asks you, you can tell
him all that's happened. He's the only man who can possibly
save you, so hurry up and beg him for his help! We can't
count on it, though. And if he isn't able to save you, they'll
kill me too for talking!"

Quaking in his shoes, the abbot picked up the gourd which
had been filled with wine, thanked the old woman and climbed
the hill behind her house, pulling himself up by the creepers.
Sure enough, a few hundred yards away he reached a ridge
where a young man was practising his catapult. In the mouth
of a cave he had placed a snow-white pebble no bigger than a
copper coin; and as he took careful aim, each shot from his
catapult found its mark. Drawing near, the abbot saw a fresh-
complexioned, handsome young man in a military cap and
light grey battle dress. This youth was completely absorbed
in his target practice when the abbot came up and fell to
his knees before him. And just as he was about to question
the abbot a flock of sparrows flew up from the valley.

"Wait while I shoot at these sparrows!" cried the youth.

He raised his catapult, and one of the sparrows fell dead. Then he turned to the abbot, who was kneeling with tears in his eyes.

"Please get up, father!" he begged. "I know why you are here. That's why I'm practising· my marksmanship. I'm still not a perfect shot, though, and I haven't dared take action yet for fear something might go wrong. But now that you are here, I mustn't delay any longer. That scoundrel's last day has come! There's no time to be lost. Hurry up and take that wine back to the temple, and on no account show any despair or panic. Do whatever he tells you there, and don't dream of disobeying him. Then I will come and save you."

Carrying the gourd, the abbot took the same path back to the temple. When he reached the inner courtyard he found the wicked monk seated on the couch in the central room, a bright sword in his hand.

"Why have you been so long?" demanded the monk.

"I lost my way, and it took time to find this temple."

"All right. Kneel down!"

The abbot plumped down on both knees.

"Nearer!"

But he dared go no nearer, for fear of the sword.

"If you don't come here," growled the monk, "I'll strike you right away!"

The abbot shuffled forward on his knees.

"Take off your cap!"

With tears running down his cheeks, the abbot took it off.

The wicked monk gripped the abbot's bald head, then poured out the wine from the gourd and took a gulp. The wine in his left hand, he took aim with the sword in his right above the old man's crown. The abbot was fainting with fear! The wicked monk picked out the centre of the skull, where he knew the brains were. When he struck, the brains would spill out— warm and delicious! He raised his sword. But before he could slice the abbot's head, a pellet flew in through the door with a whizz and hit him squarely in the left eye. Dropping his sword in dismay, he put down his wine, clapped a hand to his eye, and rushed out to the front courtyard. On the head of the bodhisattva sat a man; but as the wicked monk looked up, another pellet blinded him completely and he fell to the ground. The young man jumped down and went to the building at the back, where the terrified abbot was grovelling on the floor.

"Get up quickly, father!" cried the young man. "We must leave at once!"

"My bones have turned to water. I can't move."

"Get up! I'll carry you."

He pulled the abbot up, hoisted him on his back, and hurried out of the temple gate. After sprinting a dozen miles without taking breath, he put the old man down.

"Well, father," he said, "you had a narrow escape. In future you should have nothing but good luck!"

Only then did the abbot recover his composure. He knelt down to kowtow his thanks.

"May I ask my benefactor's name?" he said.

"I simply wanted to rid the world of a pest," replied the young man. "I didn't go out of my way to save you, father. Now that you have escaped, you should make up for lost time! Why need you ask my name?"

Although the abbot repeated his question, the young man would not tell him. The old man prostrated himself and kowtowed nine times.

"I will take leave of my benefactor then," he said. "As long as I live I shall try to repay your kindness!"

This said, he rose and went his way.

The young man, who was tired, entered a roadside inn to rest. He found another traveller seated there, with a casket before him. This man was wearing a mourning cap, white hempen gown, and straw sandals. His face was ravaged with grief, and his cheeks were tear-stained. The young man clasped his hands in salute, and sat down facing him.

"The world is quiet and at peace," said the elder man with a smile. "How can you come to this inn and sit down so calmly after blinding a man with your catapult?"

"Where are you from, sir? How did you hear of this?"

"I was merely joking. It is a fine thing to cut off evil-doers and save the good. May I ask your honourable name?"

"My name is Hsiao Yun-hsien. I live at East Mountain, six or seven miles from Chengtu."

The other gave a start.

"There is a Mr. Hsiao Hao-hsuan who lives at East Mountain, six or seven miles from Chengtu. Does he belong to your distinguished family?"

"He is my father. How do you know him, sir?"

"So he is your father!" exclaimed the elder man. Then he told Hsiao his name and reason for coming to Szechuan.

"At Tungkuan county-town I saw Magistrate Yiu, who gave me a letter for your worthy father," he said. "But I was so eager to find my own father that I did not like to break my journey to call at your house. I know the old abbot too, whom you saved just now. This is an unexpected encounter. Just as I am admiring your courage, I find you are Mr. Hsiao's son! Well, friend, I salute you!"

"Since you found your father, why didn't you stay with him, sir? Where are you travelling now alone?"

"Unhappily my father is no more," replied Kuo Tieh-shan, weeping again. "His bones are in this casket. I come from Hukuang, and I am carrying his bones home to bury."

"I am sorry!" said Hsiao, with tears in his eyes. "But now that I have been lucky enough to meet you, sir, may I persuade you to come home with me to see my father?"

"I should have called to pay my respects; but with my father's casket it is not convenient, and I am anxious to reach home for the burial. Give my compliments to your respected father and tell him that in future, if possible, I shall pay him a visit."

From his baggage he took Magistrate Yiu's letter, which he gave to Hsiao Yun-hsien. He also produced a hundred cash and asked the inn-keeper to buy three measures of wine, two catties of meat and some vegetables. When their host had prepared a meal, Kuo and Hsiao fell to.

"You and I are like old friends from the start, brother, and that doesn't happen to many men," said Kuo. "Indeed, the fact that I brought a letter from Shensi for your father sets us apart from the ordinary run of new acquaintances. You have just done a remarkable deed, and one that nobody else today would dream of attempting. But I have a piece of advice to give you, if I may."

"I am young, and was about to ask for your instruction. By all means speak frankly, sir."

"To risk your life for the public good shows courage and gallantry. But this is not the Spring and Autumn period or the age of the Warring States, when you could win fame by such exploits. Now that the whole country is united, a modern Ching Ko or Nieh Cheng[1] would be considered lawless. With your character, looks and talents, brother, to say nothing of your integrity and courage, you ought to serve the state in some capacity. Then with your sword you could win titles for your wife and sons on the battlefield, and make a name to be handed down in history. I tell you, brother, I studied the military arts as a boy to no purpose; for, owing to my father's trouble, these twenty years I have led the hard life of a wanderer. I am old now, and unfit for anything, but you are at the height of your youth and vigour. You mustn't throw away your opportunities. I hope you will remember an old man's words!"

"You have scattered the clouds to let me see the sun, sir. I can't say how grateful I am for your advice."

They went on to speak of other matters. The next morning, after paying the bill, Hsiao saw Kuo six or seven miles to a cross-road, and there with tears they parted.

Hsiao Yun-hsien went home, paid his respects to his father, and handed him Magistrate Yiu's letter.

"My old friend and I have neither met nor corresponded for twenty years," said Hsiao Hao-hsuan. "I am glad to know he is happy in his post. Kuo Tieh-shan and I were equally famous in our young days for our skill in the military arts. Unfortunately we are both old now! When he has carried his father's bones home and buried them, he will have fulfilled the ambition of a lifetime."

Young Hsiao remained at home to wait on his father.

Half a year later, there was trouble between the tribesmen beyond Sungfan and the Han people over some crooked dealings at their common fair. The tribesmen were wild, with no respect for the law. Pouring in with swords and staves,

---

1 Famous assassins of the third century B.C.

they started a fierce fight. Government archers despatched to the rescue were killed or wounded, and Green Maple City was taken by force. When the provincial governor reported this by express courier to the capital, the emperor was very angry. He ordered Marshal Ping Chih to wipe out the rebels and enforce the will of Heaven.

This edict received, Ping swiftly left Peking and set up his headquarters in Sungfan. When Mr. Hsiao knew this, he sent for his son.

"I hear Marshal Ping has come from the capital to Sungfan to suppress the tribesmen," he said. "He and I used to be friends. I want you to join the army; and when you say whose son you are, the marshal may keep you in his camp, in which case you will have a chance to serve the state. This is the time for stout fellows to prove their worth!"

"But you are old, father. I don't like to leave you."

"You shouldn't say that. I may be old, but my health is good. I eat well and sleep well, and don't need you to dance attendance upon me. If you make this an excuse for staying at home in comfort with your wife, then you are not a filial son and I refuse to see you again!"

This speech effectively silenced the young man's scruples. He took his leave of his father, roped his baggage, and set out to join the army. We need not describe his journey in detail.

One day, when he was less than two stages from Sungfan, he left the inn so early that he had covered several miles before dawn. As he strode along, his baggage on his back, he suddenly heard footsteps behind him. Jumping to one side, he whirled round to confront a man with a club; and as this fellow lunged at him, Hsiao shot up a foot to send him sprawling. Then he seized the rascal's club, and prepared to whack him over the head.

"Don't hit me!" cried the man on the ground. "Let me off for my master's sake!"

"Who is your master?" demanded Hsiao, staying his hand.

It was light enough now for him to see this fellow: a man in his thirties with a stubbly growth on his chin, who was wearing a short jacket and hempen shoes.

"My name is Mu Nai. I am a pupil of Kuo Tieh-shan."

Hsiao pulled him up to question him, and Mu Nai explained how he had been a highwayman, till he met Kuo and became his pupil.

"I know your master," said Hsiao. "Where are you going?"

"I heard that Marshal Ping was raising troops at Sungfan to crush the tribesmen, and I was on my way to join the army when I ran out of money. That's why I set on you, brother, just now. Forgive me!"

"I'm going to join the army too," said Hsiao. "Let's go together, shall we?"

Mu Nai was delighted, and offered to act as Hsiao's bodyguard. Upon reaching Sungfan they handed in their applications at the army headquarters. The marshal ordered them to be questioned as to their reasons for coming; and when he knew that this was Hsiao Hao-hsuan's son, he admitted him and appointed him a lieutenant. Mu Nai was alloted a soldier's rations.

Some days later, when all necessary provisions had arrived, Marshal Ping summoned his officers to his headquarters. Hsiao Yun-hsien, arriving early, found two commanders there. He saluted them, and stood to one side.

"When Brigade General Ma led out his troops the other day," said one of the commanders, "he and his horse fell into a pit dug by the tribesmen in Green Maple City. Ma was seriously wounded, and died a couple of days later, but his body hasn't been found yet. Since he was the nephew of a powerful eunuch, the Chamberlain of Ceremony at court, a letter has arrived from the palace insisting that his corpse must be found. Heaven knows what disciplinary action may be taken if it isn't! What's to be done?"

"I've heard there's no water or grass for miles around Green Maple City," said the other. "You have to wait for the snow to melt in spring and run down the mountain before men and beasts can find water. If we led our forces there, we'd start dying off in a few days of thirst. How could we fight?"

Hsiao stepped forward.

"You need have no fears on that score, gentlemen," he said. "Not only are there grass and water at Green Maple City, but the place is unusually rich in rivers and pastures."

"Have you been there, lieutenant?"

"No. I haven't been there."

The two commanders snorted.

"In that case, how do you know?"

"I read in an ancient history that this part abounds in water and vegetation."

The two officers looked disgusted.

"You can't believe all you read in books!" they said.

Hsiao dared say no more.

Presently the clapper sounded, and drums and cymbals were heard at the gate. A council of war was held and orders issued. The two commanders were to head the main force and assist Hsiao Yun-hsien, whose vanguard of five hundred foot soldiers was to lead the way. The marshal himself would command the rearguard. The officers hastened to carry out these orders. Taking Mu Nai with him, Hsiao led his five hundred infantry-men by a forced march to a huge, steep mountain, on which they could faintly discern the flags of the enemy garrison. This was Chair Mountain, the gateway to Green Maple City.

Hsiao gave the order to Mu: "Take two hundred men by small paths to the other side of the mountain, and wait at the entrance to the main approach. As soon as you hear our cannon, shout 'Kill!' and come to our rescue. Mind you don't keep us waiting!"

Mu Nai assented and left.

Hsiao ordered another hundred men to ambush themselves in the valley, and rush out as soon as they heard gunfire, shouting that the main force had arrived. These dispositions made, he led the remaining two hundred men in a wild charge up the mountain. There were several hundred tribesmen at the top, hiding in caves. When they saw men charging up, they swarmed out to give battle. With his catapult at his belt and his sword in his hand, Hsiao charged fearlessly at the head of his men, cutting down all the tribesmen in his path. Daunted by his prowess, the enemy prepared to fly as the two hundred drove forward with all the force of a hurricane. Then a cannon roared, the men in the valley shouted: "The main army's here!" and raced up the slope. At this point also, the two hundred men behind the mountain rushed forward waving their banners and shouting; and the panic-stricken tribesmen fled for their lives, thinking the main army had already taken Green Maple City. They could not escape Hsiao's catapult, however. Smashing their noses and slashing their lips, he cut off their retreat. Then he marshalled his men in one force, and bellowing with rage they mowed down those few hundred tribesmen as easily as you slice melons, capturing innumerable banners and weapons. After this, Hsiao rested his men for a while, then bade them march boldly forward.

Soon they came to a dense forest. After marching for several hours they crossed it and reached a great river, from the bank of which they could see Green Maple City several miles away. As there were no boats in sight, Hsiao ordered his men to chop down bamboos and make rafts. This was quickly done, and they ferried across.

"Our main force is behind," said Hsiao. "For five hundred men to take this city is no joke. Hence the main thing is not to let the enemy know our strength."

He ordered Mu Nai to lead his two hundred men, with a bundle of dry bamboo apiece and rope ladders made out of the captured flags, to a quiet place west of the city. There they were to scale the city wall and set fire to the stores of fodder.

"Then we can storm the East Gate," said Hsiao.

So they made their plans.

Meanwhile the two commanders had reached Chair Mountain with the main force, but did not know whether Hsiao had crossed it or not.

"This is dangerous terrain," they said. "There must be enemy ambushes here. We had better fire our cannon hard so that they dare not come out, and then announce a victory."

Just then, however, up flew a rider with a despatch from the marshal ordering them to press on with all speed to relieve Hsiao Yun-hsien; for Hsiao, being young, was liable to advance too rashly. The commanders dared not disobey, but mustered their men and galloped to the river, where they found ready-made rafts; and as they ferried across, the sky was lit with flames from Green Maple City. Hsiao was even then bombarding the East Gate. The fire in their midst threw the tribesmen into a panic. And when the main troops came up to reinforce the vanguard, our army held the city in a grip of iron. The tribesmen opened the North Gate and fought desperately, but a few dozen horsemen only broke through the encirclement and escaped. By this time the marshal had arrived with the rear-guard, and the remaining citizens, each with incense and flowers on his head, knelt to welcome him into the city. He gave orders to extinguish the flames and pacify the people, forbidding the least unruliness among the troops. Then he wrote a report, and sent an officer to Peking with the news of victory.

Hsiao had welcomed the marshal too, and kowtowed to him. And the marshal in his joy presented him with a sheep and a keg of wine, and praised him warmly. Over ten days later a reply was received from the court. The emperor ordered Ping Chih to return to Peking, the two commanders were to wait at their posts for promotion, and Hsiao's appointment as a lieu-tenant was confirmed. The marshal handed over to Hsiao the administration of the city.

After seeing Marshal Ping off to the capital, Hsiao returned to Green Maple City and wrote a detailed report of the damage to its walls and the destruction of its granaries caused by the fighting. The marshal then granted him permission to repair the city, instructing him to go about the work carefully and to draw up another report after its completion for the emperor.

But to know how Hsiao repaired the city, you must read the next chapter.

CHAPTER 40

Hsiao Yun-hsien enjoys the snow
on Kwangwu Mountain. Shen Chiung-chih sells her poems
at Lucky Crossing Bridge

Acting on the marshal's orders, Hsiao Yun-hsien supervised
the rebuilding of the city, which took between three and four
years. They built a wall over three miles long with six great
gates, and five government offices inside the city. A proclama-
tion was issued inviting vagrants to settle here, and waste
land in the suburbs was reclaimed.

"This is arid land," thought Hsiao. "In a year of drought
the people will lose their harvests. We must irrigate these
fields."

He set aside money and grain for the hire of labourers, and
showed them how to cut channels beside the fields. Between
the channels were trenches, and between the trenches ditches;
until soon there was a complete irrigation system like that in
the Yangtse Valley. When all was completed, Hsiao rode out
with Mu Nai leading his horse to reward the workers. At each
halt, he killed an ox and horse and summoned all the people of
that district. He built an altar, set up a tablet to the God
of Agriculture, and sacrificed cattle. Hsiao in his gauze cap
and official robes stood in front of the altar at the head of the
peasants, with Mu Nai beside him as his herald. After burning incense, pouring a libation, offering three sacrifices and
bowing eight times, he bade the people face north-east and bow
towards the capital to thank the emperor for his favour. Then

he made them sit down in a circle, and sat in their midst to carve meat and pour wine into great bowls. So they drank and made merry for an entire day. And when the feast was ended, Hsiao addressed the people.

"Fate has brought us together to this feast today," he said. "Thanks to the emperor's goodness and your hard work, we have brought all these new fields under cultivation. I, Hsiao, have played my part in this too. Now in memory of this day I am going to plant a willow, and let each of you do the same —if not a willow, then a peach or apricot."

The people gave a great shout of approval, and each planted a fruit tree or willow by the roadside.

In this way Hsiao and Mu feasted for several weeks in one district after another, and tens of thousands of willow trees were planted. To show their appreciation of Hsiao's good-ness, the people built a temple to the God of Agriculture out-side the city, with a shrine to the god in the centre, and next to it a long-life tablet for Hsiao Yun-hsien. An artist was also found to paint Hsiao in his gauze cap and official robes on horseback, with Mu Nai holding his reins and carrying a red banner to encourage the peasants. On the first and fifteenth of every month, all the men and women of the district would come to burn incense, light candles, and do reverence here.

The following year when the willows burst into leaf and the peach and apricot trees blossomed, Hsiao rode out with Mu Nai to enjoy the spring. In the shade of the willows the peasants' children were playing: three or four of them tugging one buffalo, others riding back to front on the buffaloes' backs or sprawling across them sideways. After drinking from the channels by the fields, the cattle plodded slowly past the cot-tages. Hsiao looked on and was glad.

"See that!" he said to Mu Nai. "These folk are able to make a living now. But all these bonny children, who look so bright, ought to have a teacher to teach them reading and writing."

"Didn't you know, sir, that a few days ago a scholar from the Lower Yangtse Valley put up in the Temple to the God of Agriculture? He's probably still there. Why don't you go and talk it over with him?"

501

"What luck!" cried Hsiao.

He galloped to the temple, went in, exchanged greetings with the scholar and sat down.

"I hear you are from the Yangtse Valley, sir," said Hsiao. "What brings you to an outlying region like this? May I ask your honourable name?"

"My name is Shen. I am a native of Changchow. I used to have a relative in business in Green Maple City, and I came to see him. Owing to the disturbances, I have been stranded in these parts for five or six years. Recently I heard that an official named Hsiao had rebuilt the city and irrigated the fields here; so I came to have a look. What is your distinguished name, sir? And where is your honourable yamen?"

"I am the Hsiao Yun-hsien who has been working here on irrigation."

The scholar stood up to bow to him again.

"You are a Pan Chao[1] of modern times, sir," he declared. "I admire you immensely!"

"While you are in this city you must let me be your host, sir. I hope you will move into my office."

Hsiao asked two men to move Mr. Shen's baggage, then bade Mu Nai lead his horse while he walked hand in hand with Mr. Shen to the yamen. He entertained the scholar to a good meal, then told him that they were looking for a teacher. Mr. Shen accepted the post.

"One teacher will not be enough, though," said Hsiao.

He chose ten of the most literate of the two thousand-odd garrison troops under his command, and asked Mr. Shen to give them lessons every day. Then ten schools were opened for the most intelligent children. At the end of two years Mr. Shen began to teach them to write *paku* essays: broaching the subject, following up, enlarging on the theme, and so forth. All the students who mastered this were treated by Hsiao as his equals and granted special privileges. So the people here knew that learning was an honourable thing.

---

[1] In 73 A.D. he was sent by the Han emperor to the Western regions, and spent thirty years in what is now Sinkiang.

When Hsiao's work in the city was done, he wrote a report, and bade Mu Nai deliver it to Marshal Ping. The marshal questioned Mu Nai on certain points, then promoted him to the rank of sergeant; and on the strength of Hsiao's report sent a memorandum to the Ministry of War.

Then the Ministry of Works issued the following statement:

Hsiao Yun-hsien's construction work in Green Maple City has been reported by the officer in charge. On bricks, mortar and workmen he spent 19,360 taels, 12 cents and 15 cash, although where grass and water abound to make bricks and mortar are a simple matter, and where vagrants are newly gathered together there are many men whose labour can be conscripted. Such extravagance must not be condoned. Therefore let 7,525 taels of the construction costs be met by Hsiao Yun-hsien. It appears he is a native of Chengtu in Szechuan. The authorities there should be notified, and requested to see that this sum is paid within a certain time. This order is sanctioned by the emperor.

When Hsiao saw a copy of this statement and received a reimbursement order from his superiors, he wound up his affairs and packed up to return to Chengtu. At home, he found his father ill, unable to leave his bed. Hsiao went to his bedside to ask after his health, and described all that had happened since he joined the army. After that, he kowtowed, and would not rise from the floor.

"You did nothing wrong," said his father. "Why don't you get up?"

Then Hsiao told him how the Ministry of Works insisted that he pay part of the construction expenses.

"A filial son should support his parents," he said. "I have not only failed to save a cent, but now I must ruin you, father. I am less than a man, and feel utterly ashamed!"

"This is a government order," replied his father. "It's not as if you had squandered the money, so don't let it upset you. My property must amount to about seven thousand taels altogether. Make it all over to the state."

To this Hsiao agreed with tears. His father's illness was so grave that for days Hsiao did not undress, but nursed the old man day and night. All his efforts were vain, however. And finally, in tears, he asked:

"Have you any last orders for me, sir?"

"A foolish question!" retorted his father. "As long as I live, I'm the head of the house. The day that I die, you will be master here. The main thing is to be loyal and filial, son. All else takes second place."

This said, he closed his eyes and died.

Hsiao wailed bitterly, and prepared for the burial with full observance of the funeral rites.

"When the old man at the frontier lost his horse, he thought it might be a good thing,"[1] sighed Hsiao. "If I hadn't had to pay that sum, I certainly shouldn't have come home; in which case I couldn't have buried my father myself. So my return can't be called unfortunate!"

By the time his father was buried, all the property was gone; yet Hsiao was still over three hundred taels short, and the local magistrate kept pressing him for the money. Just then, as luck would have it, this magistrate was degraded for his failure to suppress banditry; and the new magistrate was a man who had been recommended by Marshal Ping when the latter was a provincial governor. As soon as this officer reached his post and learned that Hsiao Yun-hsien was one of the marshal's protégés, he drew up a statement that Hsiao had fulfilled his obligation, then advised him to go to Marshal Ping and make up his deficit later.

---

[1] An allusion to a story popular for more than 2,000 years in China. When an old man lost his horse, neighbours condoled with him.

"This may be a good thing," he said.

The horse came back with another horse, and the old man's neighbours congratulated him.

"This may prove unlucky," he said.

When his son, who liked the new horse, rode it and broke his leg, once more the neighbours expressed their sympathy.

"This may turn out for the best," said the old man.

And, indeed, just then the Huns invaded the country and most able-bodied men were conscripted and killed in battle; but thanks to his broken leg the old man's son survived.

The marshal condoled with Hsiao, and wrote a letter on his behalf to the Ministry of War.

"There is no precedent for promoting a man because he reconstructed a city," replied the officials in charge. "Hsiao Yun-hsien will have to remain a lieutenant until he is promoted in the ordinary way to the rank of second captain. Bring him to court again when he is a captain."

Hsiao waited for another five or six months, until he was appointed a second captain at Chianghuai Station in Nanking. He went to the court to receive his appointment, and was ordered to proceed at once to his post. Leaving the capital with his credentials, he set off by the eastern route to Nanking. After Crimson Dragon Bridge he came to Kwangwu Station, and stopped here at an inn because it was late. This was midwinter. At the second watch, the inn-keeper called to his guests:

"Get up, gentlemen! Sergeant Mu is making his rounds!"

They threw jackets over their shoulders and sat on the edge of their beds as four or five soldiers came in with lanterns to light the sergeant's way, and he checked the list of travellers. This sergeant was none other than Mu Nai! He was in raptures at the sight of Hsiao, asked after his health, and insisted on taking him at once to his office to spend the night.

The next morning Hsiao wanted to be on his way.

"Stay for a day, sir," begged Mu Nai. "It looks like snow. We can make a trip to Yuan Chi's Temple on Kwangwu Mountain, and you must let me be host."

To this Hsiao consented.

Mu Nai called for two horses to ride up the mountain. He also ordered one of his men to carry up food and wine to Yuan Chi's Temple. A priest, who welcomed them and asked them to sit down upstairs in a pavilion at the back, did not presume to keep them company but merely brought in tea. Mu Nai opened the six windows which overlooked the mountain. The trees were bare, wind was tossing the stark branches and snowflakes were falling.

"At Green Maple City," said Hsiao, "we saw plenty of snow, but I never found it depressing. Yet these few flakes today make me feel completely frozen!"

505

"Those two commanders must be toasting themselves by the fire now in ermine coats," said Mu Nai. "They're sure to be doing themselves well!"

When they finished drinking, Hsiao stood up and began to stroll about. The walls of a small summer-house to the right of the pavilion were covered with poems by various scholars, and he read them all. The title of one was "Remembering the Past at Kwangwu Mountain." It was a poem in the ancient style with seven characters to each line, and he read it again and again till his tears began to fall. Mu Nai, at his side, could not understand what had upset him. The superscription read: "By Wu Shu of Nanking." And Hsiao made a mental note of this. Then they made ready and went back to Mu Nai's office to spend another night. The next day was fine and Hsiao took his leave of Mu Nai, who saw him past Big Willow Station.

From Pukow Hsiao crossed the Yangtse to Nanking, handed in his credentials, and proceeded to his new post. Having checked the number of porters and boats and gone into various problems, he took over from his predecessor.

One day he asked his transport men: "Do you know a Mr. Wu Shu, who lives in Nanking?"

"Never heard of him, sir," said a runner. "Why do you ask?"

"I saw a poem of his at Kwangwu Station, and would like to meet him."

"If he's a poet," said the runner, "I'll ask at the Imperial College."

"Find out as fast as you can," said Hsiao.

The next day the runner reported: "I've been to the Imperial College, sir. They told me at the gate that there's a residential student named Wu Shu, who lives at Flower Arch."

"Send someone over at once to go with me; I shan't want my full escort," ordered Hsiao. "I'm going to call on him."

He went straight to Flower Arch, to a house facing west, and handed in his card. Wu Shu came out to greet him.

"I'm a military man, newly come to Nanking," said Hsiao. "I admire all worthy scholars and gentlemen. The other day on a wall in Yuan Chi's Temple, I read your masterpiece 'Remembering the Past at Kwangwu Mountain.' That is why I have called today."

"I dashed off that poem in a fit of emotion," Wu answered. "Little did I think you would honour me by reading it."

Tea was brought in.

"Since you come from Kwangwu, sir," said Wu, "am I right in assuming you were posted here from the capital?"

"Well, sir, it's a long story. I joined the expedition against Green Maple City, and, because I spent too much on reconstructing the city, have only just succeeded in making good the deficit. Then I was promoted from a lieutenancy to my present post in Chianghuai Station. Now that I have been lucky enough to meet you, I shall ask your advice in everything. Some other day I have a favour to ask you."

"I shall profit, too, by your instruction," rejoined Wu.

Hsiao rose to go.

As Wu Shu saw him out, one of the college servants came rushing up.

"Dr. Yu is waiting to speak to you, sir!" he announced.

Wu Shu called on Dr. Yu.

"Your mother's ennoblement was rejected three times because the request was sent in too late," said the doctor. "Now at last it has been approved. The money for an archway is in my office; I hope you will collect it as soon as possible."

Wu Shu thanked him and left.

The next day he went with his card to return Captain Hsiao's call. Hsiao invited him into the hall, and they exchanged greetings and sat down.

"Yesterday when you did me the honour of calling, I was very remiss," said Wu. "You praised my poor work so highly, I felt thoroughly ashamed. I have brought some more of my unworthy compositions for your criticism."

With that he produced from his sleeve a volume of poems. Hsiao took it, turned over a few pages, and was full of praise. He invited Wu into the library, and a meal was served. After they had eaten, Hsiao fetched a scroll and handed it to Wu.

"Here are some pictures of my adventures," he said. "I would like to ask you, sir, with your great literary gifts, to write a few words in prose or verse so that my achievements will not be forgotten."

Wu placed the scroll on the table and unrolled it. The title read: "Account of the Western Expedition." There were three illustrations: the first called Routing the Enemy at Chair Mountain, the second The Capture of Green Maple City, the third Encouraging the Peasants in Spring. Each picture was followed by a detailed account. When Wu had read it, he sighed.

"Since ancient times, the Flying General has been unlucky!"[1] he declared. "With such great achievements to your credit, you are still in so humble a position! I will certainly do my best to write something for you. But because your rank is low, your stirring feats on the battlefield will probably not be recorded in official histories. You want several good scholars to write about your adventures, for their works will confer immortality on your loyal deeds and rescue them from oblivion."

"You flatter me," replied Hsiao. "If you will write for me, I shall become immortal."

"No, no," protested Wu. "I will take this scroll with me, though. There are some well-known scholars here who love to extol loyalty and filial piety. If they see this account of your exploits, I am sure they will be glad to write of them. Allow me to show them this manuscript."

"Do you think I should call on your friends first, sir?"

"That is easily done."

Hsiao fetched a red card, and asked Wu to write down their names. Wu gave him the names and addresses of Dr. Yu, Chih Heng-shan, Chuang Shao-kuang and Tu Shao-ching, then picked up the scroll and took his leave.

The next day Hsiao called on these four scholars, and they returned his call. Then he set out with the order from his superiors to take grain to the Huai Valley. The junk on which he travelled to Yangchow moored to the customs wharf. And

---

1 This refers to Li Kuang, a famous general of the Han Dynasty, who lived during the 2nd century B.C. He distinguished himself in the fighting against the Huns, but was never made a noble.

amid the bustle and excitement another boat pushed its way through the shipping towards them.

"Mr. Hsiao!" cried a man standing in the bow. "What are you doing here?"

Hsiao turned round.

"Well!" he exclaimed. "So it's Mr. Shen. When did you come back, sir?"

He bade his junk make fast to the other boat, and Mr. Shen leapt aboard.

"It is several years since we parted at Green Maple City," said Hsiao. "When did you come back to the south, sir?"

"After you helped me, lieutenant, I taught for a couple of years and saved up enough money to come home. I have promised my daughter to Mr. Sung of Yangchow, and am taking her to his home now."

"My congratulations to your daughter!" said Hsiao.

He ordered his man to take the young lady a tael of silver as a congratulatory gift.

"I am delivering official grain to the north, so I dare not delay," continued Hsiao. "When I come back to my office, I shall ask for an interview with you, sir."

He said goodbye, and his junk cast off.

Mr. Shen took his daughter Chiung-chih ashore, hired a small sedan-chair for her, and saw her luggage carried to Great Prosperity Salt Shop near Gaping Gate. The shop assistants welcomed him, and announced his arrival to the merchant, Sung Wei-fu. Sung sent a man out to say:

"The master orders the bride to be carried in. Mr. Shen is invited to stay in our shop, where the manager will prepare a feast for him."

When Mr. Shen heard this, he said to his daughter: "Our original intention was to find temporary lodgings here and wait for him to choose an auspicious day. Why is he so high-handed? It doesn't look as if he's taking you for his principal wife after all. Shall we go through with this match or not? This is up to you, daughter."

"Don't be upset, daddy," said Chiung-chih. "We haven't signed any document selling me to him or received any pay-ment from him, so how can I be his concubine? Since he gives himself such airs, if you quarrel with him it will only lead to talk. Let them carry me in now in this sedan-chair and we'll see how he treats me."

Mr. Shen agreed to this, and looked on while his daughter adorned herself as a bride. When she had put on her chaplet and scarlet tunic, she knelt in farewell to her father, then mounted the chair. One of the servants accompanied the chair to a house with a big gate by the riverside. There were several nursemaids there carrying their master's children and joking with the gateman.

"Is it the bride from the Shen family?" they asked when they saw the chair. "Please get out and go in by the side entrance."

Chiung-chih said nothing, but alighted and walked straight into the hall, where she sat herself down.

"Kindly ask your master to come here!" she said. "The Shens of Changchow are a respectable family! If he wants to marry me, why doesn't he hang lanterns and festoons and choose a lucky day for the wedding, instead of having me carried in on the sly as if I were a concubine? I don't ask anything else — just let him show me the marriage certificate signed by my father, and I'll say no more!"

Quite staggered, the servants hurried to the buildings at the back to report this to their master, who was in the dispensary watching his pharmacist prepare ginseng. And Sung Wei-fu turned red.

"We merchants employed by the state take six or seven concubines a year!" he blustered. "If they were all so pernickety, a fine time I'd have of it! Anyway, now that she's walked in, she can't fly out."

After dithering for some time, he called one of the slave girls.

"Go to the front," he ordered. "Tell the new bride the master isn't at home today, and let her go to her room. If she has anything to say, it can wait till the master comes back."

When the slave girl delivered this message, Chiung-chih thought: "There's no point in sitting here. I may as well go in."

510

She followed the girl out of the hall through a sceptre-shaped door to the left, past three rooms of *nanmu* wood, and a large courtyard filled with boulders from Taihu Lake. Taking a path to the left past these artificial mountains, they came to a garden. Here were clumps of bamboos, summer-houses, and a huge pond for goldfish surrounded by a covered walk with vermilion balustrades. At the far end of this were a small moon gate and a gilt-lacquered double door. Through this door, in a courtyard to itself, was a three-roomed building with a tastefully furnished living room.

"I doubt if this merchant appreciates such seclusion," she thought. "I may as well while away a few days here."

The slave girl went back and told Sung Wei-fu: "This new bride is ever so pretty, but she seems to have a temper. She's not someone you can take liberties with!"

The next day Sung ordered his steward to go to the shop and tell the manager to pay Mr. Shen five hundred taels and send him home. Since his daughter was already in Sung's hands, the merchant thought there was not much the scholar could say.

"This is bad!" exclaimed Mr. Shen. "He's obviously taking my daughter as a concubine. I'm not going to stand for this!"

He went straight to Chiangtu County yamen to lodge a protest.

"As a senior licentiate of Changchow, Shen Ta-nien ranks as one of the gentry," thought the magistrate reading the charge. "He would never willingly let his daughter become a concubine. These salt merchants think they can get away with anything!"

So he accepted the indictment.

As soon as Sung knew of this, he despatched one of his clerks with a charge against Shen, and bribed all the officials. The next day Shen's indictment was endorsed as follows:

"If Shen Ta-nien intended to marry his daughter to Sung Wei-fu as his principal wife, why did he send her secretly to Sung's house? Obviously she was intended all along for a concubine, but he is now misrepresenting the situation. His petition is rejected."

On Sung's charge was written:

"See the decision on Shen Ta-nien."

When Mr. Shen presented another petition, the magistrate was angry and called him a trouble-maker. He ordered two runners to escort him under arrest to Changchow.

Soon Chiung-chih had been several days in Sung's house without news.

"This merchant must be taking steps to silence my father before coming to trouble me," she thought. "I had better run away."

She bundled together all the gold and silver plate, pearls and jewels in the room, put on seven skirts and dressed herself like a maid, then bribed the slave girl to let her out by the back gate before dawn. Early the next morning she passed through the customs house and boarded a boat. There were women of the boatman's family aboard.

"If I go home to my parents in Changchow, our neighbours may laugh at them," thought Chiung-chih. "Nanking is a good place: there are many scholars there. And I can compose verses after a fashion. Why don't I go to Nanking and sell my poems for a living? Perhaps I may meet with good luck."

This decision taken, she changed boats at Yicheng and travelled straight to Nanking.

But to know what followed, you must read the next chapter.

CHAPTER 41

Chuang Cho-chiang talks of old times at Chinhuai River.
Shen Chiung-chih is taken under arrest to Yangchow

After the middle of the fourth month in Nanking, the Chinhuai River becomes quite lovely. Then barges from other
tributaries of the Yangtse dismantle their cabins, set up awnings, and paddle into the river. Each vessel carries a small,
square, gilt-lacquered table, set with an Yihsing stoneware
pot, cups of the finest Cheng Hua or Hsuan Te porcelain, and
the choicest tea brewed with rain water. Boating parties bring
wine, dishes and sweetmeats with them to the canal, and even
people travelling by boat order a few cents worth of good tea
to drink on board as they proceed slowly on their way. At
dusk two bright horn lanterns on each vessel are reflected in
the water as the barges ply to and fro, so that above and below are bright. Fluting and singing are heard all night and
every night from Literary Virtue Bridge to Lucky Crossing
Bridge and East Water Guardhouse. The pleasure-goers buy
water-rat fireworks too, which project from the water and look
like pear trees in blossom when let off. The fun goes on till
the fourth watch each night.

Wu Shu of the Imperial College had his birthday at the
end of the fourth month. He was too poor to give a party,
but Tu Shao-ching prepared refreshments and a few catties
of wine, ordered a sampan with an awning, and invited Wu
Shu to spend the day with him on the river. He asked Wu

513

over early, and after a meal in Tu's riverside house they boarded the boat through the back door which opened on the water.

"Let's first go somewhere quiet, Wu Shu," said Tu.

He ordered the boatman to punt to Pilgrims River and back, while they drank slowly. By the afternoon they were both a little drunk. When they reached Lucky Crossing Bridge and went ashore for a stroll, they noticed a placard on the landing-stage.

"Shen Chiung-chih of Changchow undertakes the finest embroidery, inscribes fans and composes poems," they read. "She lodges in Handkerchief Lane by Palace Pool, where clients will find her signboard."

Wu Shu laughed heartily.

"Look, Mr. Tu!" he cried. "What a freakish place Nanking is! Only prostitutes live in that district. This woman is obviously a prostitute too, yet she hangs up a placard. What a joke!"

"Well, it's no concern of ours," replied Tu. "Let's go back to the boat and brew a pot of tea."

They returned to the sampan and drank no more wine, but brewed some of the best tea and chatted as they sipped it. Presently, looking round, they saw that the bright moon had risen and was bathing their craft in silver as on they punted. At Crescent Moon Pool a number of pleasure boats were letting off fireworks. Among them was a big barge with four horn lanterns and an awning under which a feast was spread. Two guests were sitting in the seat of honour, and the host was wearing a square cap, white gauze gown and slippers. He had a thin, sallow face and a sparse white beard. Next to him sat a fresh-cheeked lad with the beginnings of a moustache, who was shooting glances right and left at the girls.

When their sampan drew near this barge, Tu and Wu recognized the two guests as Lu Hsin-hou and Chuang Shao-kuang, but did not know the other two. Chuang stood up when he saw them.

"Come and sit with us, Shao-ching!" he called.

They boarded the large boat and greeted their host, who asked:

"Who are these gentlemen?"

"This is Tu Shao-ching of Tienchang," replied Chuang. "And this is Wu Shu."

"There used to be a Mr. Tu of Tienchang who was prefect of Kanchow," said the host. "Was he related to you?"

"He was my father," replied Tu, surprised.

"Forty years ago, I spent whole days with your father. In point of relationship, he was my elder cousin."

"Are you my uncle Chuang Cho-chiang?" asked Tu.

"I am, sir."

"I was a child then, so I never met you, uncle. I am delighted to be able to pay my respects to you now."

He bowed once more.

"Is this old gentleman a member of your honourable family?" Wu Shu asked Chuang Shao-kuang.

"He is my nephew," replied Chuang with a smile. "He was my father's pupil. We have not met for forty years, but he arrived recently from Yangchow."

"And *this* gentleman?" asked Wu.

"This is my son," replied Chuang Cho-chiang.

The young man stepped forward to bow, then they all sat down. Their host called for fresh wine, and asked:

"When did you come to Nanking, Shao-ching? Where are you staying?"

"He has been here for eight or nine years now," answered Chuang Shao-kuang. "His house is by this canal."

Chuang Cho-chiang showed surprise.

"Your fine family mansion with its garden, summer-houses and flowers was the best north of the Yangtse," he said. "What induced you to move here?"

In a few sentences Chuang Shao-kuang described Tu's liberality, and how quickly he had run through his fortune. The old man sighed.

"Seventeen or eighteen years ago, as I recall it," he said, "when in Hukuang I received a letter from the fourth Mr. Wei of Wuyi. He told me his passion for wine was growing on him, and for twenty years he had not succeeded in getting really drunk; but in the Tu family's pavilion at Tienchang he had been offered a vat of nine-year-old wine and been gloriously drunk all night. He was so pleased that he wrote me this letter from a thousand miles away to announce the good news. I didn't know at the time which of the Tu family had been his host, but today I feel sure it was Shao-ching."

"Nobody else can play the host with such style," said Wu Shu.

"Is Mr. Wei a friend of yours, uncle?" asked Tu.

"We knew each other as boys," replied Chuang Cho-chiang. "When your father was young, everyone respected him as one of the most famous patrons of his generation. I can see his face and smile today as clearly as if he were standing before us."

When Lu Hsin-hou and Wu Shu spoke of the great sacrifice at Tai Po's Temple, Chuang Cho-chiang clapped a hand on his knee.

"What a pity I came too late to take part in that magnificent ceremony!" he declared. "I must find some great occasion to assemble you all again — that would be worth doing."

They talked freely of past and present, and drank till midnight. By the time they reached Tu's riverside house the lanterns along the canal were fading, and the piping and singing were dying away. Suddenly, close at hand, they heard a jade flute.

"We must be going," they said.

Wu Shu went ashore here too.

Though Chuang Cho-chiang was growing old, he treated Chuang Shao-kuang with great respect. Tu bid farewell when the barge reached his house; but Chuang Cho-chiang took Chuang Shao-kuang by boat to North Gate Bridge, then accompanied him ashore and made his servant light the way with a lantern while he escorted his uncle and Lu all the way home. Chuang Shao-kuang kept Lu for the night, and the next day they spent as usual in his garden in the lake. That day Chuang Cho-chiang wrote a card for himself and his son Fei-hsiung, and called on Tu Shao-ching. Tu went to Lotus Bridge to return the call, and was kept for a day's good talk.

Tu went to Lotus Lake also to see Chuang Shao-kuang.

"This cousin of mine is not an ordinary man," said Chuang. "Forty years ago, he and another merchant opened a pawnshop at Ssuchow. When his partner lost his money, my cousin cheerfully made over to him his own capital of twenty thousand taels and the pawnshop. Then, with his luggage over his shoulder, he rode a jaded ass out of Ssuchow. For the last dozen years he has been travelling on business up and down the Yangtse, and made tens of thousands of taels more. And now that he has a fortune he has come to settle down in Nanking. He's the most friendly, sociable fellow. When his father died he wouldn't let his brothers pay a cent of the funeral expenses, but shouldered the whole cost himself. He buried many old friends, too, who had no one to find them a grave. Acting on my father's advice, he has always shown the greatest respect to scholars, and loves historical monuments. He is spending three or four thousand taels now to build a temple to Prince Tsao Pin on Cockcrow Mountain. When it is finished, Shao-ching, we must ask Chih Heng-shan over and arrange another great sacrifice for him."

Delighted, Tu took his leave.

Soon summer gave way to autumn, when a fresh wind warned of the coming cold, and the face of the Chinhuai River changed once more. The citizens of Nanking hired boats and engaged monks to hang up pictures of Buddha and set up altars for masses to be said. Then, starting from West Water Guardhouse, they scattered food-offerings all the way to Pilgrims River. Incense hung thick in the air for miles around. Drums, cymbals and Buddhist chants could be heard without end. And at dusk, the most beautiful lotus lanterns were lit and floated on the water. There were huge barges also to carry lonely spirits up to heaven, in accordance with the Buddhist legend of the pardoning of offences in the bottommost hell on the fifteenth of the seventh month. So Nanking's Chinhuai River became the land of the Buddhas in the west.

On the twenty-ninth of the seventh month there was a great religious fair at the Earth God's Temple on Chingliang Mountain. Tradition had it that the Earth God kept his eyes closed all the year round, opening them only on this evening. If he saw the whole city filled with incense, flowers and lighted candles, he assumed this was the case the whole year round, and, pleased with the people's piety, afforded them protection.

On this one night, therefore, each household in Nanking set up two tables with incense urns and lit two tapers to burn all night. The road from Central Bridge to Chingliang Mountain was two or three miles long; and it gleamed like a silver dragon, lit up all night by endless censers, which no wind — no matter how strong — could blow out. Men and women from all over the town came out to burn incense and watch the fair.

Shen Chiung-chih, who lived in one of the houses at Palace Pool, went out with her landlord's wife to burn incense too. Since arriving in Nanking and hanging up her signboard, customers had come to her to order poems, calligraphy and embroidery. There were plenty of meddlesome young ruffians too, who brought their friends to stare at this beauty. As Chiung-chih was returning from burning incense, because she was gaudily dressed a great crowd followed her, among it Chuang Fei-hsiung. When he saw her turn into Palace Pool, he wondered who she could be. The next day he called on Tu Shao-ching.

"This Shen Chiung-chih lives at Palace Pool," he told Tu. "But when young toughs take liberties, she lashes them with her tongue. The girl is a mystery. Why don't you go to see her, Shao-ching?"

"I've heard something of the sort too," said Tu. "There are many unfortunate people nowadays, and she may have come here to escape from trouble. I've been meaning to go and find out."

He kept Fei-hsiung there to look at the new moon, and invited Chih Heng-shan and Wu Shu as well. After chatting for a little, Fei-hsiung spoke again of this Shen Chiung-chih who sold poems at Palace Pool.

"Never mind what she is like," said Tu. "If she can write poems, that is quite an accomplishment."

"You forget that we are in Nanking," said Chih Heng-shan. "There are too many scholars here to count, so who would ask a woman to write poems? This is obviously a trick to attract men! We had better leave her alone, whether she can write or not."

"It is very odd though," said Wu Shu, "to find a young woman living all by herself away from home, and supporting herself by selling poems. It can't be. There must be some other reason. But since she is a poetess, why not ask her over to see what her poems are like?"

As they were talking they finished their meal. The new crescent moon, rising from the river, shed its beams on the bridge.

"It's too late today, Wu Shu," said Tu. "You must come and have breakfast with me tomorrow, and we'll call on her together."

Wu Shu agreed to this, then left with Chih Heng-shan and Chuang Fei-hsiung.

The next day Wu Shu came to Tu's house, and after breakfasting they went to Palace Pool. They found a low building, with a score of men clamouring before the gate. Going closer, they saw a girl of eighteen or nineteen, who was scolding in the crowd. She had dressed her hair in the style of low-class women, and was wearing a sapphire-blue gauze cape with a wide collar. After listening for a few minutes, the scholars realized that some of these men had come to buy embroidered incense pouches, and that some local trouble-makers were trying to blackmail them — though they had nothing to go on — but the girl was berating them. When Tu and Wu grasped this, they went in. And at their arrival the others scattered. Seeing that the two newcomers looked different from the ordinary run of customers, Chiung-chih hastened to greet them with a curtsey. They sat down and made polite conversation for a time.

"Mr. Tu Shao-ching is the foremost of our poets here," said Wu Shu. "Because we heard your work praised yesterday, we have come to ask for your instruction."

"In the half year that I have been in Nanking," replied Chiung-chih, "all the men who have come here have taken me either for a prostitute or a member of some brigand's band. How I despise such people! Today you two gentlemen have come neither to take advantage of me, nor because you suspect me. I remember my father saying: 'There are many scholars in Nanking, but Mr. Tu Shao-ching is the only true gallant among them.' How right he was! I don't know whether you are here on a visit, sir, or whether your wife is in Nanking as well?"

"My wife lives with me in one of the riverside houses."

"In that case, may I call to tell her my story?"

Tu consented to this, and left first with Wu Shu.

"She certainly seems a strange case," said Wu Shu. "She doesn't look wanton enough to be a prostitute, nor vulgar enough to be a concubine someone has driven out. And although she's a woman, there is something very gallant about her. That smart costume of hers is quite charming; yet judging by her hands I fancy she is an expert in boxing. Of course, nowadays we are not likely to find swordswomen like the girl in the carriage or Red Thread of the Tang Dynasty. I suspect she is a girl of spirit who has been badly treated and run away. When she comes to your house you must question her, and see if my judgement is correct."

By this time they had reached Tu's threshold, where they found Mrs. Yao with a crate of flowers on her back.

"You've come just at the right time, Mrs. Yao," said Tu. "We are expecting an unusual guest, and you can look on."

He invited Wu Shu inside to sit down, then went in with the flower-seller to tell his wife. Presently Chiung-chih arrived in a sedan-chair and alighted at the gate. Tu ushered her into the inner chambers, where his wife greeted her. They sat down and tea was served. Chiung-chih had the seat of honour, Mrs. Tu the place of hostess, and Mrs. Yao a seat at one side, while Tu sat by the window. After the usual conventional remarks, Mrs. Tu said:

"You are very young, Miss Shen, to be living away from home. Have you no one to keep you company? Do you have parents at home? Are you engaged yet?"

"My father was away for many years as a tutor, and my mother has died. I learned needlework and embroidery as a girl, so I have been trying to make a living by my needle since coming to Nanking. Just now Mr. Tu was kind enough to call and invite me to your house; and now you are so good to me, madam, I feel I am among old friends."

"Miss Shen does the loveliest embroidery!" cried Mrs. Yao. "Yesterday in Ko Lai-kuan's house I saw an embroidered picture of the goddess giving children, which the young mistress there had bought. She said she bought it from Miss Shen. It was prettier than any painting!"

"It was nothing," replied Chiung-chih. "My work is not worth looking at."

Presently Mrs. Yao went out. Then the girl fell on her knees before Mrs. Tu, who, quite taken aback, helped her up. Chiung-chih described how the salt merchant had tried to trick her into becoming his concubine, and how she had then taken some valuables and fled.

"I'm afraid he still wants to get hold of me, and may track me down," she said. "Can you save me, madam?"

"Those rich and powerful salt merchants live in such luxury that scholars often cower before them," said Tu. "You are a weak woman, yet you held them as cheap as dirt. Admirable! This fellow is sure to come after you though; so there is trouble in store for you. Still, there's not much he can do."

As he was speaking, a servant came in.

"Mr. Wu wants to speak to you, sir," he said.

When Tu walked into the room overlooking the river, he saw two men with their arms at their sides by the door. He was disconcerted to see they looked like court runners.

"Where are you from?" he asked. "Who told you to come inside?"

"I told them to come in," said Wu. "This is extraordinary! Our county government has received a warrant from Chiangtu County and sent to arrest that girl, on the grounds that she is the runaway concubine of a salt merchant named Sung. What do you think of my insight?"

"She is in my house now," replied Tu. "If we give her up, it will look as if we put her up to this, and they will think in Yangchow we have been hiding her. I don't care whether she ran away or not; it wouldn't look good to hand her over here."

"That is precisely why I asked the runners in," said Wu Shu. "The best thing, Shao-ching, would be for you to give them a little silver and send them back to Palace Pool. They can arrest her when she goes home."

Tu took Wu Shu's advice and gave the runners forty cents of silver, whereupon they left, not daring to raise a single objection. When Tu went back to his wife's room to tell Chiung-chih what had happened, both Mrs. Tu and Mrs. Yao were shocked.

"Never mind," said Chiung-chih, rising. "Where are the runners? I'm ready to go with them!"

"I sent them away," said Tu. "You must have a simple meal with us; and Mr. Wu is writing a poem for you. Wait till he has finished it!"

He made his wife and Mrs. Yao sit down to a meal with Miss Shen, then went to the room overlooking the river to find a volume of his own poetry. When Wu Shu had finished his poem, Tu weighed out four taels of silver, made a package of it, and bade a servant take this with the poems to his mistress as a parting gift for Miss Shen.

When Chiung-chih had taken her leave, she mounted the chair and went straight back to Handkerchief Lane. The two runners, waiting at the gate, barred her way.

"Will you come with us in the chair or on foot?" they asked. "There's no need to go in."

"Are you from the governor's yamen or the chief censor's yamen?" demanded Chiung-chih. "Have I broken the law, or committed high treason? You've no right to stop me from going in! You can frighten only country folk by your bluster!"

With that she got down from her chair to walk coolly in, and the runners let her pass. Having packed the poems and silver in her jewel box, she came out again.

"Take me to the county yamen!" she ordered the bearers.

The bearers asked for a tip.

"What about us?" put in the runners hastily. "We got up at dawn, waited for hours outside Mr. Tu's house, and to save your face let you come back by chair. Even a woman should know we expect some thanks."

Chiung-chih realized they wanted money, but paid no attention. She promised the chair-bearers an extra twenty-four cash, and they carried her to the yamen. There was nothing the runners could do but report at the magistrate's gate: "We have brought that girl Shen."

The magistrate summoned her to the court for questioning. When she was brought in, he saw that she answered to the description.

"A woman should abide by the conventions," he said. "Why did you run away alone, stealing Mr. Sung's silver, and hide in my district?"

"Sung Wei-fu tried to force a respectable girl to become his concubine," she retorted. "When my father brought a charge against him, he bribed the magistrate so that my father lost his case. I shall never forgive him as long as I live! Besides, though I am not talented, I have had some education. Why should a girl who may later marry Chang Erh be compelled to serve a vulgar slave of Waihuang?[1] So I ran away. This is the truth I'm telling."

"This is not my affair. You'll be questioned in Chiangtu County. You say you have had some education — can you compose a poem for me now?"

"Please set the subject. I shall be glad of your criticism."

The magistrate pointed to the locust tree outside the hall. "Take that as your subject," he said.

Without losing her head in the least, Chiung-chih composed a poem of eight lines with seven characters in each. It was so well done and quickly done that the magistrate was impressed. He ordered the two runners to go back to her lodgings to fetch her luggage and examined it in the court. And when in her jewel box he found a parcel of loose silver, a sealed package inscribed "A gift for the journey," a book and a poem, he knew she was connected with well-known scholars in Nanking. He then wrote an official report.

"Escort Shen Chiung-chih to Chiangtu County," he charged the runners. "Take good care of her on the way, and don't make trouble. I shall want a written report of her safe arrival."

This magistrate had passed the examination in the same year as the magistrate of Chiangtu County and was a good

---

1 During the Warring States period, a woman refused to marry a rich but stupid man in Waihuang; instead she married Chang Erh, who became the Prince of Chao.

friend of his, so he enclosed a confidential letter in his official report, asking his colleague to release Miss Shen and send her back to her father in order that she might marry again.

When Chiung-chih and the runners left the yamen, a chair was hired to carry her outside the West Gate to catch a boat to Yicheng. The runners stowed their baggage in the small hold fore, and rested there while Chiung-chih went into the cabin. She had just sat down when a covered sampan came alongside with two more women, who entered the cabin together. One was twenty-six or seven, the other seventeen or eighteen. They were simply dressed, but played the coquette. The man with them, in a tattered felt hat, had the red face of a toper and short, shaggy eyebrows. He carried their luggage into the cabin, and the two women sat down with Chiung-chih.

"Where are you going to, miss?" they asked.

"To Yangchow. I suppose we shall be travelling together."

"We are not going to Yangchow," said the elder of the two. "We get off at Yicheng."

After a while the boatman came to ask for the fare. The two runners spat and produced the magistrate's note.

"Look!" they cried. "See this? We're on public business, so be thankful we don't ask *you* for money, instead of your demanding fares from us!"

The boatman dared not protest. After he had collected the other passengers' fares they set out, and soon the boat reached Swallow Cliff. There was a south-west wind that night, and first thing the next morning they came to Yellow Mud Bank. The runners asked Chiung-chih for some money.

"I heard quite plainly yesterday," she said. "When you're on public business, you don't pay fares."

"Miss Shen!" protested the runners. "Don't be so sharp! We have our living to make. If everyone was like you and wouldn't give us a cent, we'd have to live on air."

"I'm not going to give you money. Let's see what you dare do about it."

She left the cabin, jumped ashore, and flew off on her two small feet as if she meant to walk all the rest of the way. The runners snatched up their baggage and hurried after her; but when they laid hold of her she knocked them flat with two powerful punches. And when they scrambled up, she started such a scrap that the boatmen and the man in the tattered felt hat had to intervene to call a sedan-chair for her. The two runners followed behind it.

The fellow in the felt hat took the two girls past First Sluice Gate to Feng Family Lane, where they ran into Wang Yi-an.

"Is that Miss Hsi and Miss Shun?" he called. "So you brought them yourself, Old Li! How is business these days at West Water Gate in Nanking?"

"We've been pretty well squeezed out by those boy actors at Huaiching Bridge. That's why I've brought the girls here to you, sir."

"Very good," said Wang. "We're two girls short."

He took the two prostitutes to his house. Upon entering, they saw three thatched rooms divided by matting partitions, with a kitchen behind. A man who was washing his hands in the kitchen went into raptures at the sight of the prostitutes.

But to know what followed, you must read the next chapter.

CHAPTER 42

Young gentlemen discuss the examinations in a brothel.
A servant brings news from the Miao regions

As soon as the two prostitutes went in, Wang Yi-an called
out to the man who was washing his hands:

"Come here, Sixth Master! Look at these two new girls!"

The prostitutes looked up and saw a man with a dark, pock-
marked face and shifty eyes, who was wearing a ragged cap,
greasy black silk gown and old boots with pointed toes. To
wash his hands he had rolled his sleeves right up. But he
looked neither soldier nor scholar.

As he walked out of the kitchen, the girls stepped forward.

"Sixth Master!" they greeted him.

Then, inclining their heads, swaying their hips and lifting
a corner of their jackets with one hand, they dropped him a
curtsey. Sixth Master grabbed them with both hands.

"Fine!" he cried. "You little darlings! What luck for you
to meet me as soon as you get here!"

"What Sixth Master says is right," agreed Wang. "No one
else here can look after you so well, girls. Sit down, sir! Bring
tea for Sixth Master!"

Sixth Master sat down on a bench, pulling both girls with
him — one on each side. He yanked up his trousers, laid a
greasy black leg across Miss Hsi's knee, and made her stroke it
with her soft white hand. After swilling his tea, he produced
a package of betel nuts, stuffed them into his mouth and started

munching away. When the juice trickled out on his moustache and lips, he turned his head from right to left and from left to right, rubbing betel juice on the two girls' cheeks. And when the girls took out handkerchiefs to wipe their cheeks, he grabbed their handkerchiefs to mop his armpits. Wang took his teacup from him, and stood up to ask:

"Have you heard recently from your uncle?"

"I have. Some time ago he sent a man to make twenty huge red brocade flags embroidered with dragons in Nanking, and one big general's pennon of yellow brocade. He's going to the capital this month. In the ninth month at the beginning of the frost they will sacrifice to the flag — the emperor as commander-in-chief and my uncle as his second in command. They will stand side by side on the carpet to kowtow, and after kowtowing my uncle will be a viceroy!"

As he was talking, the pimp called Wang Yi-an out and whispered something to him. Soon Wang came back.

"I beg your pardon, Sixth Master," he said. "But a stranger has called to see Miss Hsi, and knowing you are here he dares not come in."

"What does it matter? Bring him in. I'll drink with him."

Then Wang led in a young merchant.

As soon as the customer had sat down, Wang asked him for a few cents of silver to buy a platter of donkey meat, another of fried fish, and a dozen measures of wine. Since Sixth Master was a Mohammedan, another twenty to thirty eggs were brought and boiled hard, and a lamp was lit. Sixth Master sat in the seat of honour, the customer facing him; but when Sixth Master told Miss Hsi to sit on the customer's bench, she insisted skittishly on sitting with him. When the four of them had sat down, wine was served. Sixth Master made them play the finger game, with the loser drinking and the winner singing. When he won he sang in a husky voice; then Miss Hsi and the customer played, and the prostitute won. Sixth Master called for more wine to drink, while they listened to her singing. When she turned her face away with a laugh and refused, he rapped on the table with his chopsticks to urge her on. Still she just laughed, and would not sing.

"My face is a bamboo blind," Sixth Master warned her. "A blind lets up and down, and I can pull a long face whenever I please. If I want you to sing, my girl, you'll sing!"

Wang Yi-an came in as well to help persuade her, and at last she sang a few lines.

"The sergeant is here," said Wang when she had finished.

In came the sergeant who patrolled the streets; but when he saw Sixth Master he had nothing to say. The prostitutes kowtowed to him, he sat down with them to drink and another half dozen measures of wine were ordered. At the fourth watch Puppy from Sixth Master's uncle's house brought a lantern inscribed with the words "The Brigade General's Household."

"I've come to see you home, Sixth Master," he said.

Sixth Master and Wang Yi-an walked out. The customer went inside, and was asked for tips by the servant who brought him water and by the pimp. After much ado the prostitute combed her hair and washed. So not till cockcrow did they get to bed.

First thing the next morning Sixth Master came to announce that he wanted to give a farewell feast here for his uncle's two sons, who were leaving for Nanking. When Wang heard the brigade general's sons were coming, he could hardly contain himself for joy.

"Are they coming right away, or this evening?" he asked.

Sixth Master pulled a packet of silver from his belt containing fifty-six cents which he gave to Wang, ordering him to prepare seven savoury dishes and two sweet ones.

"If it's not enough then come to me for more."

"I wouldn't think of it," said Wang. "I'll be more than satisfied if you'll choose these two girls for some other parties too. We can't let you pay for this feast — not when you're asking the brigade general's sons."

"That's the spirit! Now you're talking sense," declared Sixth Master. "If your girls are lucky enough to hit it off with these two young gentlemen, their fortunes are made. My uncle's house is crammed with gold, silver, pearls and jewels. If you find a way to the young men's hearts, they'll be shelling out silver in handfuls. Even your pimp and scullion will have their share."

Fourth Li, who was standing by, went into raptures.

After giving his orders, Sixth Master left, and the others worked with a will to prepare the feast. In the afternoon, Sixth Master arrived with his two cousins, who were wearing silk caps and black shoes with white soles. One had a red gown embroidered with gold, the other a pale grey gown embroidered with gold. Though it was broad daylight, the four servants with them were carrying lanterns bearing the inscriptions "The Brigade General's Household" and "The Successful Nanking Candidate." The two young men came in and sat in the seats of honour. The prostitutes kowtowed to them, while Sixth Master stood at one side.

"Here's a bench, Sixth Brother," said Tang Yu, the elder of the two. "Why don't you sit down?"

"Yes, yes. I was just going to ask you — shall we let these girls sit down?"

"Why not?" demanded Tang Shih, the younger brother. "Sit down."

Gingerly and coyly, giggling behind their handkerchiefs, the two prostitutes sat on a bench.

"How old are these girls?" asked Tang Yu.

"One is seventeen," said Sixth Master. "The other's nineteen."

Wang Yi an brought in tea, the prostitutes took the cups, wiped the water from them with their handkerchiefs, then offered them to Tang Yu and Tang Shih. The brothers took the tea and drank it.

"When will you young gentlemen be setting out?" asked Sixth Master.

"Tomorrow," replied Tang Yu. "The chief examiner has already gone to Nanking, so we mustn't delay any longer."

While Sixth Master was talking to his brother, Tang Shih pulled Miss Hsi to his bench and cuddled her.

Presently wine was brought in. They had hired a Mohammedan cook, who served Mohammedan dishes: birds'-nests, duck, chicken and fish. Sixth Master poured out the wine himself, and made his cousins take the seats of honour. He himself sat at the lower end of the table, and the two prostitutes one on each side. One dish was brought in after another. Sixth Master sat there awkwardly, drinking.

"Will you go straight to the examination hall when you reach Nanking?" he asked. "At the fifth watch on the eighth day they start by calling the roll of candidates from Taiping Prefecture. Won't it be late by the time they get round to our Yangchow candidates?"

"Who says they call the roll for Taiping Prefecture?" retorted Tang Yu. "First they fire three salvoes in front of the hall and open the palisade. Then they fire another three salvoes and open the main gate. Then they fire another three salvoes and open the dragon gate. There are nine salvoes altogether."

"Those guns aren't as big as the one at our father's headquarters," put in Tang Shih.

"A little smaller — not much," rejoined his brother. "When the guns have been fired, an incense table is set out in the Hall of Supreme Justice, and the mayor of Nanking in sacrificial head-dress and serpent-embroidered robe bows, stands up and hides his face behind two umbrellas. The secretary of the finance commissioner's office kneels to invite the God of War to the hall to keep order and the God of War's bodyguard to make an inspection. The umbrellas are parted and the mayor bows. Next the finance commissioner's secretary kneels to invite the God of Literature to preside over the hall, and his bodyguard — the star of successful candidates — to come to the hall to shed light."

Sixth Master shot out his tongue in dismay.

"What! You invite all those gods and Buddhas! One can see what a big event it is!"

"How brave you gentlemen are to go into a place with all those Buddhas!" said Miss Shun. "We'd sooner die than go!"

"These gentlemen are stars in heaven," replied Sixth Master gravely. "They can't be compared to girls like you."

"After inviting the God of Literature," continued Tang Yu, "the mayor bows again three times to heaven, and the secretary invites all successful ancestors."

"What do you mean by successful ancestors?" asked Sixth Master.

"Successful ancestors are those who have passed the metropolitan examination and held office," replied Tang Shih. "They're the only ones invited. What would be the use of asking common people or those scholars who grow old taking the district examinations?"

"There's a red flag at the door of each cell, with a black flag beneath it," said Tang Yu. "Under the red flag squat the spirits of those the candidate has helped, under the black flag the spirits of those he has wronged. Now the mayor takes his seat. The secretary calls out: 'Enter the ghosts of all those helped or wronged!' Paper coins are burnt on either side and with a sudden gust of wind — whoosh! — in tumble the spirits and fly with the burnt paper to under the red and black flags!"

"Amida Buddha! It shows you've got to be good!" cried Miss Shun. "At a time like that men appear in their true colours!"

"Your worthy father must have no end of grateful ghosts," said Sixth Master. "Look at all the good deeds he has done at the frontier and the number of lives he has saved. There won't be room for them all under one red flag."

"It's lucky *you* aren't taking the examination, Sixth Brother," said Tang Yu. "If you showed your face there, the ghosts of those you've wronged would carry you off!"

"What do you mean?"

"Look at my friend Yen of Yihsing at the last examination. He's a learned scholar. He had finished seven essays and was reading them at the top of his voice when a sudden draught set the flame of his candle guttering, the curtain was drawn aside and a head thrust in. Yen looked hard, and saw it was a prostitute he had known.

" 'You're dead,' said Yen. 'What are you doing here?'

"The prostitute looked at him and laughed.

"Yen lost his head and banged his fist on the desk, upsetting the ink-stone so that ink poured over his papers, making great black blotches.[1] Then the prostitute disappeared.

---

[1] Candidates were disqualified if there were blots on their papers.

" 'This must be fate!' sighed Yen.

"It was pouring with rain, poor man, as he handed in his papers and left through the downpour. He was laid up for three days with a cold, and when I went to see him he told me what had happened.

" 'You must have abused her,' I said. 'That's why she came to find you.'

"How many people have you abused, Sixth Brother? Are you fit to enter the examination hall?"

The prostitutes clapped their hands and laughed.

"We're the people Sixth Master likes to abuse," they said. "If he goes to the examination hall, we'll be the spirits of those he has wronged!"

After eating for some time, Sixth Master sang a catch in his husky voice; and the Tang brothers sang as well, beating time on their knees. That the girls sang goes without saying. They made merry till midnight, when the brothers left with their lanterns.

The next day they boarded a junk for Nanking, and Sixth Master saw them to the boat. Then the brothers spoke of the excitement that attended entering the examination hall.

"What question d'you think will be set this year?" asked the younger.

"My guess is it's bound to be something connected with our father's suppression of the Miao tribesmen in Kweichow last year."

"That would be set in Kweichow."

"Well, then, it must be either the search for worthy scholars or exemption from taxes, one or the other. There's nothing else it could be."

So they chatted all the way to Nanking. Their steward Whiskers Yiu met them there, and had their baggage carried to lodgings in Fishing Lane. Upon entering, the brothers skirted a two-storey building and went in by a side door to three neat rooms overlooking the river. Sitting down, they saw a row of houses on the opposite bank, with scarlet balustrades, green lattice windows, and speckled bamboo blinds. Successful district graduates from all parts of the province were lodging there and could be heard intoning essays.

The brothers had no sooner sat down than they ordered Whiskers Yiu to buy them two new square caps, as well as baskets, bronze receptacles, awnings, door-curtains, stoves, candlesticks, candle-scissors, and bags for their papers — two of each. Then they hurried to Vulture Peak Temple to hand in their names. They also prepared food for the session: moon cakes, honeyed-orange cakes, lotus seeds, dragons' eyes, ginseng, popped rice, pickled cucumber, ginger and salted duck.

"Take some of that asafoetida from Kweichow," the elder brother advised the younger. "You'll need it to calm your nerves if you write a word wrongly."

It took them a whole day to settle matters to their satisfaction. And they checked everything themselves, remarking:

"We can't afford to take chances when our whole careers are at stake!"

On the morning of the eighth they gave their old square caps to two servants, so that these could attend them to the examination hall. The road from Huaiching Bridge onwards was lined with stalls set up by poor scholars for the sale of gay editions of essays compiled by Hsiao Chin-hsuan, Chu-ko Tien-shen, Chi Tien-yi, Kuang Chao-jen, Ma Chun-shang or Chu Hsien-fu. Their turn did not come till late in the evening after the roll of all the scholars from Yicheng had been called. The servants could go no further than the first gate: now the two brothers had to take their own baskets and shoulder their own bedding. Bonfires on either side lit up the sky as they sat on the ground to unfasten their coats and take off their shoes. From within they could hear someone shouting: "A thorough search must be made!"

They went in with the other candidates, took their papers at the second gate, then passed through the dragon gate and went to their cells. On the tenth they emerged, exhausted, to eat a duck apiece and sleep for a whole day. The three sessions were over. On the sixteenth they bade a servant take a card from the brigade general's yamen to requisition a company of players to thank the gods.

Presently the tea attendant arrived. He was a Mohammedan and had a cook who could prepare feasts, so there was no need to engage another. The players sent over their property chest; after it came a man carrying a dozen lanterns inscribed with the words Three Founts Company. Behind him followed a man with a servant-boy holding a visiting card case. Upon reaching the gate they told their business to the steward, who took in their card, and Tang Yu read:

"Your servant, Pao Ting-hsi, presents two candles and one opera company with his compliments."

Realizing that Pao was a company manager, Tang Yu ordered him to be admitted.

"I am in charge of a small company here," said Ting-hsi after greeting the young gentlemen. "We perform only for scholars and officials. Having heard yesterday that you wanted operas, I have come today to place myself at your service."

Because Pao Ting-hsi seemed a sensible fellow, Tang Yu kept him to a meal. Presently the players arrived, and in the hall overlooking the river they offered paper horses to the God of Literature and the God of War, after which the two brothers kowtowed and sacrificed. Then they sat down at a table with Ting-hsi. Gongs and drums sounded, and four short pieces were played before the soup was served. By this time it was dark, but a dozen horn lanterns lit up the whole hall brightly. At midnight the main opera was finished.

"These boys of mine are quite good at acrobatics," said Ting-hsi. "I'll tell them to put on a horse show to sober you gentlemen up."

Then, dressed in ermine cloaks, pheasant feathers and the brightest costumes, the players raced in, leaping, somersaulting and forming figures. The brothers looked on with delight.

"If you have no objection, gentlemen," said Ting-hsi, "I'll choose two of these boys to stay behind and wait on you."

"What do youngsters like this know about waiting on gentlemen?" asked Tang Yu. "You must find us somewhere amusing."

"That's easy, sir. Just across the river is Ko Lai-kuan's house. He counts as my pupil too, and his name was on the list that year when the seventeenth Mr. Tu of the Tienchang Tu family held the great contest here in the lake, and all the actors were tested and marked. If you go to Water Stocking

534

Lane tomorrow, sir, you'll see the signboard of Surgeon Chou; and across the street, behind a black fence, is Ko's house."

"Does he have women's apartments?" asked Tang Shih. "If so, I'll go with you."

"There's the famous Twelve Pavilions," replied Ting-hsi. "Why not go there, sir, instead of to Ko's house? I'll take you along."

By now the show had ended, and Pao Ting-hsi took his leave.

The next day the elder brother prepared eight pewter jugs from Kweichow, two bottles of goat's blood, four rolls of Miao embroidery, and six baskets of choice tea. He bade his man carry these to Ko Lai-kuan's house. They knocked at the door and were admitted by a woman with big feet. The front building consisted of two rooms which had been partitioned into three. A passage from the door on the left led to rooms overlooking the river at the back. There Ko Lai-kuan in a lined gauze, jade-coloured gown, with a fan of wild goose feathers in his slender tapering fingers, was leaning over the balcony enjoying the breeze. When the two brothers came in, he asked them to be seated.

"Where are you gentlemen from?" he inquired.

"Yesterday Mr. Pao told me you have a fine view of the river from your house," said Tang Yu. "So I came today to call on you. I have brought a few poor presents, which I hope you will accept."

The servant carried in the gifts, and when Lai-kuan saw them he was very happy.

"How can I accept these, sir?" he asked.

He turned to the woman with big feet.

"Take these inside," he ordered. "And tell the mistress to serve a meal."

"I am a Mohammedan," said Tang Yu. "We don't eat meat."

"We have some freshly bought, big Yangchow crabs. Would you care for them, sir?"

"They are from my home town. There is nothing I like better. Our uncle sent a letter home from Kaoyao saying how he missed crabs, but he couldn't get a single one there."

"Is your worthy father a servant of the state?"

"My father is a military governor in Kweichow. I came back to take the examination."

As they spoke, wine was served. The river was wreathed in mist, and households on both banks had lit lamps, while boats glided past unceasingly. When Ko Lai-kuan had drunk a few cups his face turned rosy, and in the flickering candle-light he raised his tapering, jade-like fingers to urge Tang Yu to drink.

"I have had enough wine," said Tang Yu. "I should like some tea."

Lai-kuan told the maid to clear away the crabshells and fruit dishes, wipe the table, fetch a stoneware pot and brew some fragrant tea. They were just enjoying themselves when they heard a commotion outside. Lai-kuan went to the gate and found pot-bellied Surgeon Chou there, red in the face from scolding the big-footed maid for throwing crabshells over his doorstep. As the actor stepped forward to put in a word, the surgeon rounded on him.

"Your house is a house of amphibians!" he shouted. "Why not empty crabshells on your own doorstep, instead of unloading them on us? Are you all arse — no eyes?"

The Tang family steward prevented a brawl by persuading Lai-kuan to go back inside. He had no sooner sat down, however, when a flustered Whiskers Yiu dashed in.

"I have been looking for you everywhere, sir!" he cried. "So you were here all the time!"

"Why are you so hot and bothered?"

"The second master went with that Pao to somebody's house to have tea by Vulture Peak Temple in East Flower Park, but some ruffians there set on him, and tore off his clothes. Pao was so scared he took to his heels. Now the second master is shut up in that house and can't get out. He's frantic! A flower-seller next door called Mrs. Yao, who says she is the girl's aunt, has barred the door and won't let him go!"

The elder brother hastily bade him fetch lanterns from their lodgings to light the way to Vulture Peak Temple.

"We've had no sport like this for a long, long time," the ruffians there were saying. "We mustn't let slip this chance for easy money."

Tang Yu boldly elbowed his way through them, pushed Mrs. Yao aside, and with one blow knocked down the door. When his brother saw who had come, he rushed forward and darted out. The rogues outside would have stopped him; but Tang Yu's martial air and the brigade general's lanterns frightened them off, and they scattered. The brothers returned to their lodgings.

Over twenty days later, when ink and paste were taken into the examination hall to write the blue announcement of those who had failed, they knew the results would soon be out. Two days later the lists were published — neither of them had passed. They sat sulking in their rooms for seven or eight days, then collected the rejected papers — three for Tang Yu, three for Tang Shih. Not a single paper had been read to the end! They fell to inveighing against the stupidity of examiners. And, as they were cursing away, a family servant arrived from Kweichow with a letter from their father, which they read together.

But to know what followed, you must read the next chapter.

CHAPTER 43

The brigade general fights a battle at Wild Goat Pool, and a chieftain raids the camp at the dancing ground

Tang Yu and Tang Shih had taken back their rejected examination papers and were studying them moodily in their lodgings when a family retainer arrived from Chenyuan Prefecture in the province of Kweichow, and handed them a letter. They opened and read it together.

" . . . The wild Miao tribesmen are growing more rebellious," wrote their father. "As soon as the results are published, irrespective of whether you have passed or not, I want you both to come to my headquarters. . . ."

"Father wants us to go to his yamen," said Tang Yu to his brother. "We had better go back to Yicheng and prepare for a long journey."

They told Whiskers Yiu to hire a boat and pay their rent. Then the brothers mounted chairs, and their servants carried their luggage out through the West Gate to the boat. When Ko Lai-kuan heard they were leaving he bought two salted ducks and some refreshments, and went aboard to see them off. Tang Yu slipped him a package containing four taels of silver, after which the actor left. That evening the boat cast off, and the next morning they reached Yicheng, where the brothers landed and went home. They had no sooner washed their faces and sat down to drink tea when the gateman came in.

"Sixth Master is here," he announced.

Sixth Master walked in, followed by a stranger.

"I hear our master is leading troops to suppress the Miaos," he said as soon as he saw them. "When the Miaos are crushed the court will certainly order examinations to be held next year, and both you gentlemen will pass. The master will be made a marquis, and I expect you will look down on hereditary rank of the first degree, so you can give it to me! When I show Miss Hsi my gauze cap, she'll have to pay me a little respect!"

"Do you want a gauze cap just to impress Miss Hsi, Sixth Brother?" asked Tang Yu. "In that case, we might just as well give the cap to Wang Yi-an."

"You two won't stop talking," said Tang Shih. "But where does this fellow come from?"

The stranger stepped forward, kowtowed and greeted them respectfully, then produced a letter and passed it over.

"His name is Tsang Chi and he's from Tienchang County," Sixth Master told them. "The letter is from Tu Shao-ching. He says Tsang Chi is a thoroughly dependable fellow, and recommends him to you gentlemen as a servant."

Tang Shih unfolded the letter and read it with his brother. It opened with inquiries after their father's health, then continued: "Tsang Chi has always worked in Kweichow, and knows every mountain track there. He makes an excellent attendant."

"It's a long time since we saw Tu," said Tang Yu to his brother. "Since he recommends this fellow, let's take him on."

Tsang Chi kowtowed his thanks and withdrew.

The gateman came in again.

"Mr. Wang Han-tse is here," he announced. "He's waiting in the hall."

"Go out and see what he wants," said Tang Yu to Tang Shih, "while Sixth Brother and I start our meal."

Tang Shih went to receive the caller, while his elder brother ordered the meal to be served and sat down to eat with Sixth Master. While they were at table, Tang Shih came back having seen the visitor out.

"What did he have to say?" asked Tang Yu.

"He said his boss, Wan Hsueh-chai, has two boatloads of salt which will be sent off in the next couple of days, and he hopes we will travel with them and keep an eye on them."

Tang Shih joined them at table.

After the meal Sixth Master said: "I must be going now. I'll come back tomorrow to see you off.... If you have time, Second Master, why not go to see Miss Hsi? I'll tell her to wait for you."

"What a pest you are, Sixth Brother!" cried Tang Yu. "Do you want to be the death of us? Who has time to visit that bitch today?"

Sixth Master laughed and left.

The next day they requisitioned a large junk, and Whiskers Yiu, Tsang Chi and some other servants carried the luggage aboard. The banners and placards at their cabin doors made a brave show. Sixth Master saw them to Yellow Mud Bank, then said goodbye and took a sampan home.

Firecrackers were set off as the junk moved upstream. Just before Virgin's Pool a storm sprang up, and Tang Shih ordered the boat to moor at once. The Yangtse was one mass of foaming waves, like fried salt or snowdrifts as far as the eye could see. The two great salt boats were swept aground by the wind. There were two hundred sampans at the shore, and out from the bank sprang two hundred savage-looking men.

"The salt boats have run aground!" they shouted. "Let's help to get them off!"

Paddling over, they swarmed up the salt boats, quick as thought seized all the salt in the holds they could carry, and transferred it packet by packet to their sampans. When their two hundred sampans were filled, they took oars and rowed like mad up a little creek, to vanish without a trace! The helmsman and salt merchant's clerk wrung their hands in dismay, and looked at each other helplessly. Then their glance fell on the boat next to them, which carried the banners of the brigade general's yamen in Kweichow, and they remembered that this was the Tang brothers' boat. They went aboard and threw themselves on their knees.

"We're from two of Mr. Wan's salt boats which have been set on and robbed in broad daylight!" they declared. "You gentlemen saw all that happened. Please think of a way to save us!"

"We come from the same district as your master," said the brothers. "But a case of robbery is the business of the local magistrate. You must go to his yamen and lodge a complaint."

The helmsman and others had to take this advice. They wrote a charge, and took it to Pengtse County yamen. As soon as the magistrate received this charge, he summoned the helmsman, clerks and all the boatmen concerned to the second court.

"Why didn't your salt boats keep going?" he demanded. "What made you stop in my county? Tell me the names of the robbers! Do you know them?"

"Our boats were grounded by the gale, Your Honour," replied one of the helmsmen. "There was a creek there with two hundred sampans and hundreds of scoundrels, who seized and carried off all the salt we had on board."

When the magistrate heard this he was very angry.

"Such a thing couldn't happen in a quiet, law-abiding county like this!" he roared. "Obviously you slaves have been filching your master's salt with the connivance of his clerk, to go whoring and gambling. After stealing and selling it all on the journey, you bring this trumped up charge to clear yourselves! But now you're on trial here — you must speak the truth!"

He hurled down a handful of bamboo slips. At this signal, from both sides rushed fierce attendants, who threw the helmsman to the ground and gave him twenty strokes with the bastinado, till his flesh was torn to shreds. Then the magistrate pointed at the salt merchant's clerk.

"*You* must have been in this plot! Out with the truth now!"

And he reached for another bamboo slip.

This poor clerk had been his master's pampered favourite. But now that his beard was beginning to grow, the salt merchant had sent him out for the first time to escort a cargo. The tender youth had never seen bastinadoes before; so, frightened out of his wits, he said whatever the magistrate wanted to hear, not daring to contradict him. Kowtowing as quickly as a pestle pounding onions, he begged that his life be spared. Then the magistrate swore at the boatmen, threaten-

541

ing to throw them all into gaol and try them the next day. In panic, the salt clerk told one of the boatmen to go to the Tang brothers' boat and beg them to intervene. And Tang Yu sent Tsang Chi with his card to the magistrate.

"Mr. Wan's men were unduly careless," he said. "But not too much salt has been lost, and Your Honour has already punished the helmsman, so that he will be more careful in future. Be good enough to let them off."

The magistrate told Tsang Chi to take back the card with his respects to the two young gentlemen.

"I shall carry out their wishes," he declared.

He took his seat in court, and once more summoned all the men involved.

"You deserve to be sent back to Chiangtu County and forced to make good this loss," he said. "But I shall let you off lightly because this is your first offence."

With that, he drove them all out.

The clerk took the helmsman to the Tang brothers' junk to kowtow and thank them for their help. Then, utterly crestfallen, they returned to their boats.

The next day the wind dropped, and the junk set sail again. After several more stages, the two brothers disembarked and continued by road to Chenyuan Prefecture, where they sent Whiskers Yiu on ahead to announce their arrival, and followed him to their father's yamen.

That day, as it happened, Brigade General Tang was entertaining the prefect of Chenyuan, Lei Kang-hsi. Prefect Lei was a metropolitan graduate in his sixties, who had passed the examinations long ago. A native of Tahsing County, he had been promoted to this post from a ministry; and after five or six years in office here, he had an excellent knowledge of the Miaos. After a meal in the brigade general's western hall, tea was served, and they began to speak of the tribesmen.

"We have two types of Miaos — the wild and the tame," said the prefect. "The tame Miaos are a law-abiding lot, who never dare make mischief; but the wild Miaos are always stirring up trouble. The tribesmen of Big Rock Cliff, Golden Dog Cave and all that region are the worst of the lot! The other day Tien Te the local officer reported: 'The scholar Feng

Chun-jui has been carried off by Pieh Chuang-yen, the Miao chieftain of Golden Dog Cave, who won't let him go except for a ransom of five hundred taels. How do you think we should deal with this matter, general?"

"Since Feng Chun-jui is a Chinese scholar, the prestige of the court is at stake," replied Tang. "How dare Pieh carry him off and demand a ransom? What utter contempt for the law! The only way to deal with this is to lead troops to their valley, wipe out all the rebellious tribesmen there, bring Feng Chun-jui back and hand him over to the local authorities to find out the cause of the trouble, before having him duly punished. What other solution is there?"

"Your proposal is undoubtedly correct, general," replied the prefect. "But it seems a pity to mobilize our forces for the sake of one man. In my humble opinion, it would be better to send Tien to their valley to reason with the Miao chieftain and persuade him to hand Feng back, so that no more need be said."

"You're wrong there, Your Honour," said Tang. "Suppose when Tien goes to their valley the Miao rebels should kidnap him too and demand a thousand taels for his ransom, then if you were to go in person to reason with them, they would hold you for ransom for ten thousand taels. In that case what could we do? Besides, why does the government spend millions in grain and money every year on maintaining soldiers, generals and captains? If we're afraid of mobilizing our forces, we shouldn't feed so many idle men!"

The two officials were at loggerheads.

"Very well," said the prefect, "I shall send a brief report to the provincial governor to see what his decision is. Then we'll carry out his instructions."

He thanked his host, and went back to his own yamen.

In the brigade general's headquarters, cannon were fired and the office closed. When Tang went back after seeing off his guest, his sons greeted him and paid their respects. Tsang Chi kowtowed as well. After some talk about home affairs, they went to bed.

A few days later an order arrived from the military governor:

"Let the brigade general lead his local force to wipe out the Miao rebels and establish law and order. These instructions should be obeyed without delay."

As soon as Tang received this order, he summoned the clerk of the prefectural garrison, and had him shut up in the library. The clerk was terrified, not knowing the reason for this. Not till nearly midnight did the brigade general go to the library to see the clerk, having ordered his attendants to withdraw. He produced a fifty-tael bar of silver and put it on the table.

"Take this, sir," he said. "I have asked you here simply to buy one word from you."

The clerk was shaking with fear.

"Just tell me what you want, Your Honour, and I will do it," he stammered. "I would sooner die than accept such a gift from you!"

"Don't say that. I won't get you into any trouble. Tomorrow an order will come from above for the despatch of troops. When the notification of this reaches you from the prefecture, just change the four words 'lead his local force' to 'lead a strong force.' This silver is your fee as scribe. I'm not asking for anything else."

The clerk agreed, accepted the silver and was allowed to leave.

A few days later, the prefecture passed on the government's decree ordering Brigade General Tang to lead out his troops without delay. "Lead a strong force," said the notice from the prefecture. Tang called out his three battalions, as well as his two auxiliary forces. Provisions for the troops were already prepared.

It was New Year's Eve. The lieutenant colonel of Chingchiang and the second captain of Tungjen reported: "To fight when the moon is on the wane runs counter to military tactics."

"Never mind that," said Tang. "Tactics depend on how they are used. Today the Miaos are celebrating New Year. We can take them by surprise, and catch them off their guard."

He ordered the lieutenant colonel of Chingchiang to lead his force from Small Rock Cliff to Drum Tower Slope to cut off the enemy's retreat, and commanded the second captain of

Tungjen to advance from Stone Screen Hill to Nine Twists Mount to attack the enemy vanguard. He himself would lead the main force to Wild Goat Pool. These orders given, the advance began.

"These rebels have their headquarters at Wild Goat Pool," said Tang. "If we approach by the highway, they will man their defences and have the advantage of us. It will take some time to overcome their resistance."

So he asked Tsang Chi: "Do you know of any path that will take us to their rear?"

"I do," said Tsang Chi. "You can save six miles by climbing the mountain from Tripod Cliff, and wading up Iron Stream to their rear. But that stream is bitterly cold, for there's ice in it now. It's hard going."

"Never mind that," said Tang.

He ordered his cavalry to wear waterproof boots and his infantry light climbing shoes. Then the whole main force set out along this path.

Now the Miao chieftain had assembled all the men and women of his tribe in the valley to celebrate the New Year with wine and music. The scoundrel Feng Chun-jui had married the chieftain's daughter, and he and his father-in-law were watching the Miao women in red and green as they beat gongs, sounded drums and performed Miao plays. Suddenly a sentry flew in.

"Alas!" he cried. "The great emperor has sent troops to wipe us out. They're already at Nine Twists Mount!"

The chieftain's soul nearly flew from his body in fear. He hastily ordered two hundred spearmen to hold the enemy at bay. Then another sentry rushed in.

"A great force of infantry and cavalry has reached Drum Tower Slope!" he reported. "Too many of them to count!"

While the chieftain and Feng Chun-jui were wringing their hands, a cannon roared, torches blazed out on the hill behind, and with shouts of "Kill!" which reached the sky the enemy poured down on them out of the blue! The chieftain led out his men and they put up a desperate fight. But they were no match for Tang's troops, who with lances and halberds swept all before them till they came to Wild Goat Pool. Over half the Miao forces were killed or wounded. The chieftain and Feng Chun-jui escaped by a small track to another Miao settlement.

The second captain with his vanguard and the lieutenant colonel with his rearguard now gathered at Wild Goat Pool. They ransacked the caves, killing all the tribesmen left and taking the women as slaves. The brigade general ordered his three forces to encamp at Wild Goat Pool. Then the lieutenant colonel and second captain came to his tent to congratulate him on the victory.

"We must not relax our vigilance," said Tang. "Though the rebels have been defeated, they have fled to another valley and are certain to ask for reinforcements to attack our camp tonight. We must take defensive measures."

He asked Tsang Chi: "Which is the closest settlement to this?"

"It is less than ten miles to Straight Eye Cave," said Tsang.

"I see," said Tang.

"Gentlemen!" He turned to his subordinates. "Ambush your forces to the left and the right of Stone Pillar Bridge, for the rebels are bound to go back that way. Wait till they're retreating and you hear the cannon; then let all your men spring up and mow them down."

His officers went to carry out these orders.

Then Tang chose the best singers among the women captives, made them comb up their hair, put on their embroidered clothes, and sing and dance barefoot in the main tent, while all the soldiers, horses and officers hid themselves in the gully. Sure enough, at the fifth watch, the Miao chieftain led forth a force armed with swords and spears from Straight Eye Cave to slip silently over Stone Pillar Bridge. When they saw lanterns and candles burning brightly in the big tent, and heard singing and music there, they charged with a great battle cry. But they drew a blank. There were only Miao women there. Once they knew they had been tricked, they darted wildly out. Then the troops concealed in the gully rose up together, their shouts reaching the skies. The Miao chieftain was making a desperate dash with his men for Stone Pillar Bridge, when a cannon shot rang out, and the ambush leapt out from under the bridge to close round the tribesmen. Luckily for them, the Miaos have thick soles, impervious alike to steep cliffs or sharp thorns: they scattered and fled up the mountains like startled monkeys or hares.

The brigade general had won a great victory. And when he called the roll of his three battalions and two auxiliary forces, it appeared the losses were slight. They returned triumphantly to Chenyuan, where Prefect Lei met them and offered congratulations. Then he asked what had become of Pieh Chuang-yen, the Miao chieftain, and Feng Chun-jui.

"We defeated them several times, till they had to flee for their lives," replied Tang. "I expect they have killed themselves."

"No doubt," said Prefect Lei. "But when our superiors ask about this, it won't be easy to answer them. Such a reply sounds too specious."

Tang had no retort to make to this. He went back to his yamen, where his two sons greeted him and inquired after his health. But he could not set his heart at rest, and he had no sleep that night. The next day he sent in a detailed report of his expedition and victory. The viceroy's comment was like Prefect Lei's — he asked only about the chief culprits, Pieh Chuang-yen and Feng Chun-jui.

"They must be captured at once and taken to the yamen," he wrote. "Then only can we send a report to the government."

Tang was desperate, but did not know what to do. Then Tsang Chi, who was beside him, knelt down to make a request.

"I know all the paths in the wild Miao settlements," he said. "Let me go and find out where Pieh Chuang-yen is now; then you can think of a way to capture him."

Brigade General Tang was delighted. He gave Tsang fifty taels of silver, bidding him go and make a careful search.

Eight or nine days later Tsang Chi came back.

"I went all the way to Straight Eye Cave," he reported. "I found out that because Pieh Chuang-yen borrowed troops to attack your camp and was defeated, the chief of that settlement quarrelled with him, and now Pieh is living in White Worm Cave. When I went on to White Worm Cave, I learned that Feng Chun-jui is there as well. Only a dozen or so of Pieh's clan are left, and he hasn't a single soldier or horse. I also heard of a plot they've made. On the eighteenth of the first month, they say, the spirit of Iron Stream comes out, and everybody in Chenyuan stays indoors. They mean to dress up as ghosts that day and break into your yamen, sir, to take their revenge. I hope you will take due precautions."

"I see," said Tang.

He gave Tsang Chi a sheep and wine, and told him to go and rest.

This was, in fact, the tradition in Chenyuan Prefecture. On the eighteenth of the first month, the local people said, the dragon king of Iron Stream gave his younger sister in marriage. But because she was so ugly that she wanted no one to see her, he sent an escort of shrimp soldiers and crab generals to conduct her to her wedding. All households had to close their doors, and it was forbidden to go out to watch. If the dragon king's sister caught anyone spying, she would send such violent wind and rain that water would lie three feet deep on the level ground, and many people would be drowned. This was an old belief here.

On the seventeenth, Tang summoned his bodyguard.

"Do any of you know Feng Chun-jui?" he asked.

A tall fellow stepped forward and knelt down.

"I know him, sir," he announced.

"Very good," said Tang.

He ordered this man to put on a long white gown and a tall black paper hat, and to smear his face with lime, for this was how the local devil was supposed to look. He also made his servants dress up in oxheads and horses' masks, like the King of Hell and his devils or other savage ogres.

"When you see Feng Chun-jui, you must seize him," he told the tall man. "I will see you are well rewarded."

When all was ready, he ordered the porter of the North Gate to open the city gate before dawn.

Disguised as country folk going to the fair, but each with a hidden dagger, Pieh Chuang-yen and Feng Chun-jui came to the North Gate at midnight. When they found the city gate open, they rushed to the stable wall of the brigade general's yamen. A dozen of them, with weapons in their hands, climbed the wall and dropped into the courtyard. Pale moonlight lit up the great deserted court, and they were wondering which way to turn when they saw a monster crouched at one end of the far wall. It had a small gong in its hand, which it now struck twice. Then the whole wall toppled down, as if in an earthquake. Scores of torches were lit, and scores of devils leapt forward with iron prongs and spears.

Pieh and Feng were so terrified that their feet seemed nailed to the ground. Then the local devil strode forward and hooked Feng with his spear.

"I've caught Feng Chun-jui!" he shouted.

All the others went into action, and seized the dozen tribesmen. Not one was allowed to escape. They marched them to the second hall, where the brigade general counted them, and the next day they were taken to the prefect's yamen. Prefect Lei was delighted too that the rebel chief and Feng Chun-jui had been captured. After saluting the emperor, he brought out the imperial decree and imperial sword, had the rebels' heads cut off to display to the public and the other tribesmen killed. This done, he sent a report to the capital.

The official reply was as follows:

"To suppress the Miao bandits of Golden Dog Cave, Tang Chou advanced recklessly and wasted both money and provisions. Let him be degraded three ranks and transferred to another post, as a warning to other ambitious officers."

When Tang received a copy of this he sighed. Soon afterwards, a despatch came from the ministry, and his successor arrived. After handing over his seals, Tang took counsel with his sons, and they packed up to go home.

But to know what followed, you must read the next chapter.

CHAPTER 44

His work accomplished,
Brigade General Tang goes home. Senior Licentiate Yu
discusses burial customs at a feast

After taking counsel with his sons, Brigade General Tang
packed up to go home. Prefect Lei sent over four taels instead
of a feast, asking the cooks in Tang's yamen to prepare a farewell feast for him in his own office. When Tang left, he was
seen off by all the officials in the city. He travelled by boat
to Changteh, crossed Tungting Lake, then proceeded down the
Yangtse to Yicheng. It was an uneventful trip, during which
he questioned his sons about their studies and they enjoyed
the river scenery. In less than twenty days they reached Gauze
Cap Island, and sent a servant on ahead to prepare the household for their return. As soon as Sixth Master knew they were
coming he went to Yellow Mud Bank to meet them, paid his
respects to his uncle and greeted his cousins, then gave them
some local news. Tang was disgusted by his glib tongue.

"In the thirty years I've been away, you have grown up,"
said Tang. "But where did you learn these low-class ways?"

Then he noticed how each time his nephew opened his mouth
it was "Your Worship this," and "Your Worship that."

"What gibberish is this, you ill-bred boor?" The general
was really angry. "I'm your uncle, aren't I? Why don't you
call me uncle instead of Your Worship?"

Sixth Master also invariably referred to his cousins as First Master and Second Master. This enraged their father even more.

"You brigand!" he cried. "You deserve to be killed for this! Instead of advising and keeping an eye on your cousins, you call them First Master and Second Master!"

He berated him till Sixth Master hung his head.

Upon reaching home, the general bowed to his ancestors and had his luggage unpacked. His brother, the former magistrate of Kaoyao County, had retired now; and glad to meet again, these two middle-aged men feasted for several days. Tang went neither to the city nor to call on other officials, but had a villa built beside the river, installed his books and lute there, and taught his sons. After three or four months, however, he was still dissatisfied with their *paku* essays.

"They will never pass if they write like this!" he thought. "Now that I'm at home, I must find a tutor for them."

This was constantly on his mind.

One day the gateman came in.

"Second Master Hsiao of Yangchow has called," he announced.

"His father was my colleague," said Tang, "but I shan't recognize this young man when I see him."

He ordered him to be admitted at once, whereupon Hsiao Po-chuan came in and greeted him. He was handsome and dressed with taste and distinction. The general greeted him, and they sat down.

"Congratulations on your return home, uncle," said Hsiao. "I should have come earlier to pay my respects. But recently Mr. Kao, the Hanlin reader in Nanking, came home on leave; and since he passed Yangchow, I kept him company for some time. That is what delayed me."

"May I ask if you have passed the examination?"

"The last examiner was good enough to rank me as one of the pupils of the Imperial Doctors. The rank is common enough, but I am glad to say everybody in town was reading my essays three days ago, for this shows the examiner's judgement was not at fault."

He spoke so well that the general kept him to lunch in the library, summoning his sons to keep him company. And that afternoon, Tang told him that he hoped to find a tutor to coach his sons.

"I know of a tutor, sir," said Hsiao. "He's a man named Yu Yu-ta from Wuho County, a senior licentiate who is well up in the examination subjects. He is tutoring now in a salt merchant's house, but is not too happy there. If you want to engage a tutor, uncle, you'll not find anyone better. If you write him an invitation and send one of your sons with me to call on him, Mr. Yu can come back with your son. He won't want more than sixty taels a year."

Tang was most pleased to hear this. He kept Hsiao Po-chuan for two days while he drew up a contract, then ordered his elder son to hire a fast boat and accompany Hsiao to Yang-chow to call on Mr. Yu in the riverside house of a salt merchant named Wu.

Hsiao told Tang Yu to write a card with the form of address used by a junior to his senior, which he could change after Mr. Yu became his tutor for the form used by a pupil to his teacher.

"He will be half teacher, half friend," objected Tang Yu. "I'll sign myself 'your colleague and younger brother.'"

Since Hsiao could not convince him, they took this card and called on Mr. Yu. The gateman handed in Hsiao's card, then asked them into the library. Mr. Yu was wearing a square cap, an old sapphire-blue gown, and crimson slippers. He had a clear complexion and a beard, was near-sighted and looked about fifty. After entering the library, he greeted them and sat down.

"You were going to Yicheng a few days ago, Po-chuan," said Yu. "When did you come back?"

"I went to Yicheng to see my uncle, Brigade General Tang, who kept me for a few days. This is his son, Tang Yu."

Then he took Tang Yu's card from his sleeve. After looking at it, Yu put it on the table.

"This is too much of an honour," he said.

Hsiao told him the general hoped he would be their tutor.

"That is why we have called today, sir," he explained. "If you condescend to accept, I shall send you the contract and salary."

Yu Yu-ta smiled.

"The general's rank is so high and his sons are both so talented, an old dunce like myself can hardly set up as their tutor! Please let me consider the matter before I reply."

The young men took their leave.

The next day Yu returned Hsiao's call.

"Po-chuan," he said, "I can't accept yesterday's offer."

"Why is that?" asked Hsiao.

"If he wants me to be his tutor," said Yu with a smile, "why should he write a younger brother's card? He obviously doesn't really intend to learn from me. That's how it is. I have an old friend who's the prefect of Wuwei, and the other day I received a letter from him inviting me there, and I mean to call on him. If he can help me a little, I'll do better than after a year's teaching. I shall resign in a couple of days and leave here. Please recommend someone else to Brigade General Tang."

Unable to prevail on him, Hsiao gave this answer to Tang Yu, who found another tutor.

A few days later, Yu Yu-ta did indeed resign, pack up his belongings and go back to Wuho. His house was in Yu Family Lane. As he entered the gate, his brother came out to meet him. This brother, Yu Yu-chung, was also one of the most learned licentiates in that county.

At this time the Peng family was on the upgrade in Wuho, having produced several metropolitan graduates, two of whom had been made Hanlins. Since the people of Wuho were a provincial lot, the whole county started making up to these Pengs. There was also a family from Hueichow named Fang, who had opened a pawnshop in Wuho and gone into the salt business, then declared themselves natives here and begun marrying the local people.

Now it happened that the Yus of Yu Family Lane had always married members of an old family of local gentry — the Yoos. To begin with, neither the Yus nor the Yoos were willing to marry the Fangs. But then some men in these

553

families became so thick-skinned and thick-headed that, tempted by the Fangs' rich wedding gifts, they began to marry their daughters. So their families became related by marriage. After several such weddings, however, not only did the Fangs stop giving rich wedding portions, they declared that the Yus and the Yoos were so impressed by their wealth that they were eager to be allied with them.

Thus in these two families were two types of men who cared nothing for their ancestors' good name. The first were fools, of whom it was said: "They marry only Fangs, make friends only with Pengs." The second were clever rascals, and of them it was said: "They think only of the Fangs, talk only of the Pengs." In other words, had no Fangs claimed citizenship in Wuho, those shameless dolts could have done without wives; and had there been no successful scholars named Peng, they could have done without friends. These men thought themselves remarkably shrewd, whereas in fact they were thoroughgoing fools. As for the cunning ones, they wanted to marry Fangs, but the Fangs would not have them. Instead of admitting this frankly, though, they lied to try to impress people.

"Old Mr. Peng is my teacher," one would say. "The third Mr. Peng invited me into his study, and we had a long, heart-to-heart talk."

Or: "The fourth Mr. Peng has written me a letter from Peking."

Thanks to such talk, they were often invited out to feasts in the hope that they would hold forth in this way to impress the other guests. Such was the depth to which the people of Wuho had sunk.

But the brothers Yu Yu-ta and Yu Yu-chung obeyed their forbears' precepts and studied behind closed doors, not speaking of mundane matters which did not concern them. The elder brother had made friends with not a few magistrates during his journeys through different prefectures and counties, but he never dared mention officials on his return. The reason for this was the fixed belief of the citizens of Wuho that a successful metropolitan or provincial graduate was the same as a district or county magistrate, and that when such scholars went to the yamen to ask a favour the magistrate had to grant it. If anyone had told them that a magistrate might respect a man for his character or make friends with him because he was a good scholar, the people of that county would have laughed their mouths crooked. As for unsuccessful candidates, if they sent in a card to the magistrate he could have them thrown out—this was how the local people saw it. As regards both character and learning, the Yu brothers had rarely been equalled. But because the local magistrate never called on them and they had neither married into the Fang family nor made friends with the Peng family, although those who knew them dared not look down on them, they were not looked up to either.

Now Yu Yu-chung ushered his elder brother in, greeted him and prepared a feast to welcome him home, during which they spoke of all that had happened during the last year or more. The feast at an end, Yu Yu-ta did not go to his room but shared a bed in the study with his brother. During the night he mentioned his intention of going to Wuwei to see a friend.

"I hope you'll stay at home for a while, brother," said Yu Yu-chung. "I want to go to take the prefectural examination. Wait for me to come back before you go."

"You don't realize that I've spent all the money I made in Yangchow. I must hurry to Wuwei to raise funds for the summer. But you can go and take the examination; my wife and yours can look after the house between them. We always live quietly behind closed doors—why do you need me at home?"

"If you're given a few scores of taels on this trip, brother, we can bury our father and mother when you come back. Their coffins have been in the house for more than ten years, and I can't help feeling remiss about it."

"I agree with you. We must do that when I come back."

A few days later, Yu Yu-ta set out for Wuwei. About a dozen days after that, when the chief examiner reached Fengyang, Yu Yu-chung packed up and went there, renting a room to stay in. That was the eighth of the fourth month. On the ninth, the examiner offered incense. On the tenth, a notice was issued that reports would be received. On the eleventh, it was announced that the students of the eight counties in that prefecture would be tested. On the fifteenth, the results came out: three students had passed from each county, Yu Yu-chung among them. On the sixteenth, he sat for the next examination; and on the seventeenth, the result was published—he was second in the first rank. He stayed in Fengyang till the twenty-fourth when, having seen the examiner off, he went back himself to Wuho.

When Yu Yu-ta reached Wuwei, the district magistrate, truly mindful of old friendship, entertained him for several days.

"I have not been in office long, sir," said the magistrate. "I cannot give you much silver. But a case has come up in which you can intercede, and I shall accept your plea. Then the defendant will pay four hundred taels, to be divided among three people. Your share will be over a hundred and thirty taels, sir, with which you can bury your parents when you reach home. I will do something more for you later."

Yu was more than satisfied. He thanked the magistrate and went to see the defendant, a man named Feng Ying, who was involved in a murder. Yu Yu-ta interceded for him, and the district yamen cleared him. Upon his release he weighed out the silver, and Yu took his leave of the magistrate and packed up to go home.

Since he travelled by way of Nanking, it occurred to him: "Tu Shao-ching of Tienchang lives in one of the Nanking riverside houses, at Lucky Crossing Bridge. He is my cousin, so I may as well call on him."

He entered the city and went to Tu Shao-ching's house. Tu came out to meet him, and was pleased to see him. After greeting each other they sat down, and spoke of all that had happened in the dozen years since they last met.

"What a pity, cousin," remarked Yu with a sigh, "that you gave up your fine property. You, who were once a patron, are reduced to making a living by your pen. You must find it hard to grow used to such a come-down!"

"I enjoy the scenery here and the company of good friends," replied Tu. "I am used to it. As a matter of fact, cousin, I'm an ignorant fellow with simple tastes. I live quite con-

tentedly with my wife and sons, though we can't afford meat
and our clothing is all of cotton. What's past is gone and
done with."

As he said this, he offered Yu tea.

When they had finished the tea, Tu went in to ask his wife
if they could give Yu a feast of welcome. By now Tu was too
poor to invite guests, so he started considering what he could
send to the pawnshop. Luckily, it was the third of the fifth
month, and just at this moment Chuang Shao-kuang sent over
a load of presents for the Double Fifth Festival. A servant
with a box came with the porter carrying gifts: a shad, a brace
of duck, a hundred sticky rice dumplings, and two catties of
white sugar, as well as four taels in the box. Tu accepted
these gifts and wrote a card of thanks. Then the servant
left.

"Now I can play host!" said Tu to his wife.

He bought a few more dishes, which his wife prepared herself. And since Chih Heng-shan and Wu Shu were close
neighbours, he sent them notes inviting them over to meet
his cousin. When they arrived, after the usual polite conversation they sat down to a feast in the room overlooking the
river.

While feasting, Yu mentioned his intention to look for a
burial ground for his parents.

"Sir," said Chih Heng-shan, "if the ground is dry and
warm and free from wind and ants, you can bury your parents
safely. All that talk about wealth and fame is nonsense."

"Exactly," replied Yu. "Yet where I come from they take
it very seriously. And people are often so hard to satisfy that
they delay their parents' burial. I have never made a study
of geomancy. Can you gentlemen tell me the origin of Kuo
Pu's teachings?"

"Since the ancient practice of appointing an officer in
charge of graves was abolished," replied Chih with a sigh, "and
the rule of burial by clans no longer observed, many cultured
men have been taken in by all that talk about dragons' lairs,
mountains and water. Men want their families to prosper; but
in their attempts to achieve this, they actually prove most
unfilial."

"What do you mean?" asked Yu, much shocked.

"Let me recite you a verse, sir.

> *Can spirits live where cold winds blow?*
> *What logic can your science show?*
> *A bloody death you had to die;*
> *Yet on your book men still rely!*

"This was written by an earlier poet at Kuo's grave. Nothing enrages me more than the way geomancers nowadays, who quote Kuo as an authority, say: 'This plot will ensure that your descendants come first in the palace examination and are Number One Palace Graduates.' I ask you, sir: Since the rank of Number One Palace Graduate was instituted in the Tang Dynasty, how could Kuo Pu, who lived in the Tsin Dynasty, know of this Tang title and decree that a certain type of ground would produce this rank? This is absolutely ridiculous! If the ancients could foretell honours and rank from the soil, how is it that Han Hsin, who chose a high and spacious burial ground for his mother, first became a noble and then had three branches of his clan wiped out? Was that site good or bad? It is even more ridiculous when these charlatans claim that the site for the first Ming emperor's sepulchre was chosen by Liu Chi of our dynasty. Liu Chi was the most talented man of his time, but he was so busy studying military science, agriculture, ceremony and music that he had not a single day's leisure. What time did he have to choose a burial site? No, when the First Emperor ascended the throne, he merely relied on the geomancers to choose an auspicious burial ground for his line. Liu Chi had nothing to do with it!"

"Your arguments, sir," said Yu, "would make a deaf man hear and a blind man see."

"Mr. Chih is entirely right," remarked Wu Shu. "A curious thing happened here the year before last, which you might care to hear."

"I should be most interested," replied Yu.

"This happened to the household of Censor Shih, who lives in Shih Family Lane by Lower Floating Bridge."

"I heard some talk of that," put in Chih, "but never knew the details."

"Censor Shih has a younger brother," continued Wu Shu, "who maintained that the reason his elder brother had passed the metropolitan examination and he had not was because their mother's burial ground was no good—it aided the first son only, not the second. He kept one of these wind-and-water men in his house, and spent his whole time discussing where to move her grave.

" 'She's been buried some time,' said the censor. 'Better not move her.'

"He wept, bowed and pleaded with his younger brother, but the latter insisted that the grave must be moved. And the geomancer frightened him by saying: 'If the grave is not moved, not only will the Second Master never become an official — he will grow blind!'

"The second son became more and more frantic, and sent this geomancer all over the place in search of a site. Now if you keep one wind-and-water man in your house, you get to know a lot of others outside. When his private geomancer found a site, the second brother called in others to check on it. And, oddly enough, the way of these wind-and-water men is for son to scoff at father and father to scoff at son. No two of them can agree. Whenever this geomancer found a site, the others who checked on it would prove it was no good.

"At last the home-kept geomancer grew desperate. He produced another plot; and this time he bribed a man living to the left of it to say that one night he had dreamed that old Mrs. Shih in ceremonial dress had pointed out this plot to him and signified that she wanted her grave moved here. Since the old lady had chosen this plot herself, the other geomancers couldn't oppose it; and the younger brother insisted on moving the coffin.

"On the day of the removal, Censor Shih and his brother knelt by their mother's grave. As soon as the grave was opened and they saw the coffin, a puff of hot air from the tomb rose straight into the younger brother's eyes. He was blinded on the spot! But that only convinced him more than ever that this wind-and-water man was a living immortal, who knew both past and future; and later he paid him several hundred taels."

"People in our parts have a passion for moving graves too," said Yu. "Is this right or not, Shao-ching?"

"I'll tell you what I think," said Tu. "The government should enact a law requiring anyone who wants to move a grave to hand in a petition at the yamen, and the geomancer to put down in black and white just how many inches of water there are on the coffin, and how many pints of ants. If they prove right when the grave is opened, good. If not, then the executioner, who must stand by when the grave is opened, shall cut off that dog of a geomancer's head. And the man who wanted to move the grave shall be executed like a parricide, by being sliced into pieces. Then this craze might die out by degrees."

Yu, Chih and Wu clapped their hands.

"Well said!" they cried. "Well said! Let's have big cups to drink to that!"

Presently Yu told them how Brigade General Tang had invited him to tutor his two sons.

"That's what rough soldiers are like!" he concluded with a laugh.

"Some rough soldiers are most cultured people," countered Wu Shu.

Then he told them Hsiao Yun-hsien's story.

"Won't you fetch that scroll, Shao-ching," he said, "for Mr. Yu to see."

Tu brought it in, and after looking at the paintings Yu read the poems by Dr. Yu and the rest. Then, under the influence of wine, he composed a new poem in the rhyme scheme of each. The three others applauded him heartily. They drank till midnight, and Yu stayed with Tu for three days.

On the third day, a duck-seller from Wuho arrived with a letter from Yu's house, which he said was from Yu's brother. When Yu Yu-ta opened and read it, his face turned pale.

But to know what was in the letter, you must read the following chapter.

CHAPTER 45

In which Yu Yu-chung takes the blame for his brother.
They bury their parents and speak of geomancy

Yu Yu-ta showed Tu Shao-ching his letter from home, which read: "Some trouble has just cropped up here. Don't come home on any account! I hear you are with our cousin, Tu Shao-ching; so just set your mind at rest and stay on with him. When I've cleared up this business, I'll come to fetch you home."

"What can have happened?" said Yu Yu-ta.

"Since your brother wouldn't say, you've no way of finding out at present," replied Tu. "Just stay here, and you'll know all in good time."

Yu wrote to his younger brother: "What is this trouble? Write me a full account at once, and I promise not to worry. But if you won't tell me, you'll only make me more anxious."

The duck-seller took this letter back to Wuho and gave it to Yu Yu-chung, who was talking to a runner from the yamen. Yu took the letter, and sent the duck-seller off.

"This warrant," said Yu to the runner, "is for the arrest of the criminal Yu Yu-chung. I've never been to Wuwei. Why should I go to the yamen?"

"Who knows if you've been there or not?" retorted the runner. "All we yamen officials can do is find the man who answers to this description. When we take thieves to our

yamen, they won't confess though we clap them in ankle-
presses. Who'll tell the truth straight off?"

Then Yu had to go with him. He knelt before the magistrate, who was holding court.

"I have never been to Wuwei, Your Honour," he announced. "I know nothing of this affair."

"I don't know whether you were there or not," said
the magistrate. "But I've a warrant here from Wuwei. Since
you say you were never there, take a look at this."

He picked up a despatch with a red seal on it, and ordered a runner to pass it to Yu Yu-chung.

Yu read: "This concerns the acceptance of briber by
the magistrate of Wuwei. Yu Yu-chung, a senior licentiate
who accepted a bribe, is a native of Wuho...."

"I can clear myself, Your Honour," said Yu. "This despatch asks for the senior licentiate, Yu Yu-chung. It'll take
me at least ten years to become a senior licentiate."

This said, he returned the despatch and turned to go.

"Just a minute, Mr. Yu," said the magistrate. "I see
your point." And he asked his clerks: "Is there another
Yu Yu-chung in this county who is a senior licentiate?"

"There's a senior licentiate in his family," replied the
clerk on duty. "But his name isn't Yu Yu-chung."

"This is obviously a mare's-nest," put in Yu.

He stood up again to leave.

"Go home, Mr. Yu," directed the magistrate, "and write
me a plea protesting your innocence. Then I shall refute
the charge for you."

Assenting to this, Yu left.

He went out of the yamen with the runner, and they sat
down in a tea-house to drink a pot of tea. Then Yu stood
up to go.

"Where are you off to, Mr. Yu?" The runner laid hold
of him. "I got up bright and early, but I've tasted neither
rice nor water and had to walk all the way from your house
to the yamen. Even if this were an affair of the Imperial
Court, I deserve some consideration. I'll be darned if I
go any farther with you!"

"The magistrate told me to come out and write a plea."

"You said in court you're a licentiate. Licentiates write for people all the year round, but you want someone else to write for you! Across the street behind this tea-house is the place where you licentiates write your plaints. You can go in there to write."

Yu had to go to a building behind the tea-house with the runner, who called to a man inside:

"The second Mr. Yu wants to write a plea. You write it for him. He'll draft it himself, then you copy it out and put a chop on it. If he doesn't pay you, so much the worse for me! The fellow in that business yesterday is still shut up in the inn. I'll come back when I've seen him."

Yu clasped his hands to greet the clerk, then saw a man sitting on a bench by the table. He was wearing a ragged head-cloth, a tattered gown, and shoes with the soles flapping loose. Yu recognized him as Tang San-tan, a pettifogging lawyer.

"So it's you, Mr. Yu," said Tang. "Have a seat."

"You're early, Third Brother Tang," said Yu sitting down.

"Not really," answered Tang. "I got up early to have noodles with the sixth Mr. Fang, and came on here after seeing him out of town. I know all about your business."

He pulled Yu to one side and whispered:

"Although this is not a case of treason, Mr. Yu, it's bound to come to that. Who doesn't know your good brother is at Nanking? But in cases like this, the established procedure has always been to consider the local verdict as cast-iron evidence. The thing is to get the local magistrate on your side. And the magistrate will do whatever the Pengs tell him. You'd better lose no time in calling on the third Mr. Peng to discuss it with him. All the rest of his family are as fierce as dragons and tigers; he's the only good man of the lot. And if you ask his help now that you're in a fix, he may not bear you a grudge for not paying your respects before. He's a kind, open-hearted man. You needn't be afraid. Or, if you like, I'll go with you. Strictly speaking, you ought to have kept on better terms with the local gentry; but your brother was always too proud. Now that you're in trouble, you've no one you can turn to."

"Thank you for showing such concern," said Yu. "But just now the magistrate told me to write a reply. I'll consider again what to do after I've written my plea and he's sent it in."

"All right," said Tang. "I'll watch you write your plea."

Yu wrote it straight away, and handed it in at the yamen. On the basis of this, the magistrate told his clerk to draft a reply to Wuwei. And the clerk, it goes without saying, demanded money from Yu for paper and brushes.

Half a month later another despatch arrived, this time with a clear description:

"The malefactor Yu Yu-chung is a senior licentiate of Wuho, of medium height, with a white face and thin beard, in his fifties. On the eighth of the fourth month he was in Wuwei, and met Feng Ying in the Guardian Deity's Temple to hush up a murder case. On the eleventh he went to the prefectural yamen to intercede. After sentence was passed on the sixteenth, Feng Ying sent a feast to the Guardian Deity's Temple, and divided four hundred taels between three people. Yu Yu-chung received one hundred and thirty-three taels as his share. On the twentieth he left the yamen, to travel back to Wuho by way of Nanking. Since we have proof that he received this bribe, how can you claim there is no such man? This is a murder case, and the law has been flouted. We must trouble your district to look into this, and immediately send the criminal here to us under arrest, so that the case can be closed. This matter is urgent!"

The magistrate sent for Yu Yu-chung again.

"This is even easier to answer," said Yu. "Let me write a more detailed plea. I beg Your Honour to be my judge."

Having said this he went home and wrote another plea.

"You're not going about this the right way," said his wife's brother, Chao Lin-shu. "It's obvious your elder brother did this, and now writs are falling right and left like snowflakes—why take the blame on yourself? You'd much better tell the truth and say that your brother is in Nanking now, so that they can send a writ there and you will be cleared. If the baby doesn't cry, the milk doesn't flow. Why lug someone else's coffin to your door and cry over it?"

"I know how to deal with this business of my brother's," replied Yu. "Don't worry about me."

"I wouldn't mention this otherwise," said Chao, "but your brother's temper is so bad he's always offending people. Take the third Mr. Fang of Benevolent Fortune Shop or the sixth Mr. Fang of Benevolent Greatness Shop, two of the biggest men in Wuho. They're on the same footing as Magistrate Wang, yet your brother will insult them. A day or two ago, the second Mr. Fang became engaged to one of the daughters of the fifth Mr. Peng, who's just passed the metropolitan examination. They say Magistrate Wang was their go-between, and the wedding has been fixed for the third of next month. This business is sure to be mentioned at the feast. The fifth Mr. Peng won't have to describe your brother's faults straight out—one hint will be enough for the magistrate. And if Magistrate Wang cuts up rough, he'll say you've been sheltering your brother, and that'll be awkward for you! You'd better take my advice."

"I'll send in another plea first. If they press me hard, I can tell them the truth."

"Surely you can ask the fifth Mr. Peng to help?"

"Let's wait a little," answered Yu with a smile.

When Chao could not convince him, he went away. Yu sent another plea to the yamen; and, with this to go on, the yamen wrote in reply:

"The despatch from your honourable prefecture read: 'The malefactor Yu Yu-chung is a senior licentiate of Wuho, of medium height, with a white face and thin beard, in his fifties. On the eighth of the fourth month he was in Wuwei, and met Feng Ying in the Guardian Deity's Temple, to hush up a murder case. On the eleventh he went to the prefectural yamen to intercede. After sentence was passed on the sixteenth, Feng Ying sent a feast to the Guardian Deity's Temple, and divided four hundred taels between three people. Yu Yu-chung received one hundred and thirty-three taels as his share. Since we have proof that he received this bribe, how

565

can you claim there is no such man? This is a murder case, and the law has been flouted. We must trouble your district to look into this, and send the criminal here to us under arrest, so that the case can be closed. This matter is urgent.' As soon as our county received this, we sent for this licentiate. According to his plea, Yu Yu-chung is of medium height, has a pock-marked face and slight beard, and is forty-four. He is still a stipendiary, not a senior licentiate. On the eighth of the fourth month this year, the examiner went to Fengyang; on the ninth he offered incense, on the tenth he issued a notice, on the eleventh he examined the licentiates of eight counties. This licentiate Yu Yu-chung took the examination. On the fifteenth the results were announced and he had passed. The next day Yu Yu-chung took the second examination, and passed second in the second class. On the twenty-fourth he saw the examiner off, then came back home to study. How could he be taking a bribe in Wuwei when he was taking the examination at Fengyang? We checked his evidence with our school records, and it is a fact that he took the examination at Fengyang, therefore could not have gone to Wuwei to receive a bribe. Thus we cannot arrest him. We suspect some scoundrel has been using Yu Yu-chung's name, and are reporting this to you so that you can look elsewhere for the culprit and close your case."

After this despatch was sent off, no more was heard from Wuwei. Yu Yu-chung felt relieved of a crushing load, and wrote to recall his brother. When Yu Yu-ta reached home, he wanted to know exactly what had happened.

"I owe a great deal to you, brother!" he cried. "How much silver did you have to spend at the yamen?"

"Never mind about that," replied Yu Yu-chung. "We can use that silver you've brought to prepare for the burial."

A few days later the brothers agreed to call on Chang Yun-feng the geomancer. It so happened, however, that a relative invited them to a feast. Therefore having paid their respects to Chang Yun-feng, they went to their relative's house. There were no outsiders invited, only two cousins of theirs, Yu Fu and Yu Yin, who made haste to bow when the two Yu brothers came in. They sat down and exchanged news.

"Magistrate Wang is feasting today with the second Mr. Peng," said Yu Fu.

"He hasn't arrived there yet," said their host from the lower end of the table. "He has only just sent the necromancer there with his card."

"The fourth Mr. Peng is going to be the chief examiner," said Yu Yin. "I hear that the other day, when he left court, the emperor cuffed him for making a slip in his speech."

"I doubt if he made any slip," said Yu Yu-ta with a laugh. "Even if he did, the emperor would be too far away to hit him."

"No, no!" Yu Yin turned red. "He's a high official now, the chief academician of the Han Lin Academy, in charge of the crown prince's household. He stands in the inner pavilion of the great assembly hall to give advice every day. If he said something wrong, of course the emperor would cuff him. Do you think the emperor's afraid of him?"

"When you were in Nanking," said their host to Yu Yu-ta, "did you hear that the mayor of Nanking had gone to Peking?"

Before Yu Yu-ta could answer, Yu Fu said:

"The fourth Mr. Peng was responsible for that too. One day the emperor asked whether it wasn't time for the mayor of Nanking to be changed. Since Mr. Peng wanted to recommend his fellow student Tang Tsou, he said yes. But he didn't want to offend the mayor, so he wrote him a letter at once, inviting him to court for an audience. That's why he's gone to Peking."

"Hanlins can't decide the appointment of high officials," said Yu Yu-chung. "I doubt the truth of this tale."

"That's what Magistrate Wang himself said the day before yesterday when he was feasting at Benevolent Greatness Shop," retorted Yu Yin. "It must be true."

Just then the feast was served. There were nine dishes: cauliflower with meat, fried carp, chicken with rice, omelette, prawns with onion, preserved ginseng, melon seeds, pomegranates and dried beancurd. A sealed jar of wine was also brought in piping hot. When they had drunk for some time, their host went inside to fetch a red cloth bag tied with a red cord containing clods of earth.

"I asked you here today," he said to Yu Fu and Yu Yin, "to judge the soil on this hill. I don't know whether it will do or not."

"When was this soil taken?" asked Yu Yu-chung.

"The day before yesterday," replied their host.

Before Yu Fu could open the bag, Yu Yin snatched at it. "Let me look first," he said.

He grabbed it, took out a clod of earth, put it in front of him, cocked his head to the right to look at it, then cocked his head to the left to look at it. Finally he broke off a piece, put it in his mouth and started chewing hard. After chewing for some time, he passed a clod to Yu Fu.

"What do you think of this earth, Fourth Brother?" he asked.

Yu Fu took the clod and turned it over under the light. He examined first the top side, after that the bottom side; then broke some off and put it in his mouth. Shutting his mouth and closing his eyes, he munched slowly. After munching for some time, he opened his eyes and sniffed hard at the clod. He sniffed for quite a while.

"This soil is no good!" he announced.

"Can it be used for a grave?" their host asked eagerly.

"No, it can't," replied Yu Yin. "If you bury someone in this, you'll bankrupt your family."

"I've been away for over ten years," said Yu Yu-ta. "I didn't realize you two were such experts on soil."

"I can speak frankly to you," said Yu Fu. "There's no arguing about the soil my brother and I have tested."

"Which hill is this from?" asked Yu Yu-ta.

"From his fourth uncle's grave." Yu Yu-chung indicated their host. "They're thinking of moving the grave."

"*We* didn't find this site," replied Yu Yin. "The plot we've found is at Three Point Peak. Let me show you what it's like."

He moved aside two of the dishes, dipped his finger in the wine jar and traced a circle on the table.

"See there! That's Three Point Peak. The vein starts a long way away. It begins in the mountain at Pukow: a peak, a ridge; a peak, a ridge; a peak, a ridge. It twists and turns, and rolls right along to Chou Family Hill in our district, for all the world like a dragon sprawling across the valley. Then another peak, another ridge, and it rolls through dozens of ridges to form a figure. That figure is called 'The lotus emerging from water.'"

The servant brought in five bowls of noodles, and their host offered them vinegar, then heaped their bowls with cauliflower and meat. They picked up their chopsticks and ate. When Yu Yin had had about enough, he took two noodles and twisted them on the table into the shape of a dragon. Then he opened wide his eyes.

"This plot of ours will produce a Number One Graduate!" he declared. "If you make a grave there and you come second only in the examination, you can pluck out both my eyes!"

"Are you sure this place will bring good luck?" asked their host.

"It certainly will. Right away!" replied Yu Fu. "You won't have to wait many years."

"Just touch it and you'll prosper," declared Yu Yin. "You'll find that out as soon as you've moved the grave there."

"Not long ago in Nanking," said Yu Yu-ta, "some friends were saying the only criterion in choosing a burial site is one's parents' comfort. All that talk about prosperity for the descendants can't be relied on."

"No, no!" exclaimed Yu Fu. "If the parents are snug, of course their sons will prosper."

"No, indeed!" cried Yu Yin. "Look at the Pengs' graveyard. A dragon's paw is resting on their father's left arm: that's why the fourth Mr. Peng was given that slap the other day. Do you deny that it was a dragon's paw? If you don't believe me, First Brother, I'll take you there tomorrow to see for yourself."

After a few more cups, they got up and thanked their host. Then a servant with a lantern lighted them back to Yu Family Lane, and each went home to sleep.

The next day Yu Yu-ta asked his brother: "What did you think of what our cousins said yesterday?"

"It sounded all very fine, but they didn't study under proper masters   We'd better consult Chang Yun-feng."

"You're quite right," agreed Yu Yu-ta.

The day after that, they invited Chang to a meal.

"You gentlemen have always been good to me," said the geomancer. "Of course I will do my best, now that you have consulted me about your parents' burial."

"We are poor scholars," replied Yu Yu-ta. "We hope you will be kind enough to overlook any lack of respect."

"All we want is to bury the old couple decently," said Yu Yu-chung. "That is why we are asking your help. We aren't interested in becoming rich or noble. So long as the ground is dry and warm, and there are no ants or wind, we shall be most grateful to you."

Chang promised to do as they asked. A few days later he found a site beside their ancestral graveyard. The Yu brothers went with him to the hill to inspect the ground, then bought it from the owner for twenty taels, and asked the geomancer to choose a date.

One day, before Chang had chosen a date and when they had nothing to do, Yu Yu-ta bought two catties of wine and six or seven dishes, intending to have a good talk with his brother. That afternoon, however, they received a note from the fourth Mr. Yoo, who lived on the main street.

"I have prepared a simple meal for this evening," wrote Yoo Liang. "Please come over for a chat. Don't refuse now."

"Very well," said Yu Yu-ta to the servant. "Give our respects to your master. We shall come."

As soon as the servant had left, a native of Soochow who was a brewer here sent a messenger to invite them both to his brewery for a bath.

"This fellow Ling must be asking us to a meal too," said Yu Yu-ta. "Let's go to Ling Feng first and then to Yoo."

When they reached Ling's gate, they heard shouting and cursing inside. Because the brewer's family was not here, he had hired two big-footed country-women, and was carrying on with both of them. All the men in Wuho are accustomed to sleeping with these big-footed maids. Even at feasts in respectable families, when this custom is mentioned people laugh till their eyes are slits, thinking it a great sport and nothing to be in the least ashamed of. But the two maids in Ling's house had grown jealous. Each suspected the other of getting more of their master's money, and through jealousy started scrapping. They made a clean breast of things, both admitting to sleeping with the assistant, and the assistant joined in the quarrel too. After smashing all the bowls, plates and dishes in the kitchen, the maids with their big feet kicked over all the tubs. Instead of the feast and bath they had expected, the Yu brothers spent a long time as mediators, then took their leave of their host. Ling, much embarrassed, poured out a thousand apologies, and promised to invite them another day. Then the two brothers went to Yoo's house, only to find the feast there at an end and the gate closed.

"Let's go home," said Yu Yu-ta with a laugh. "We shall have to eat our own feast."

Yu Yu-chung laughed too, and going home together they called for the wine. But the two catties of wine and six dishes had been finished by their wives — there were only an empty pot and some empty dishes left.

"We had three feasts today but weren't able to eat one," said Yu Yu-ta. "This proves that every bite and sup is predestined!"

Laughing, they made their supper off pickled vegetables and rice, and after a few cups of tea each went to his room.

At the fourth watch there was a great shouting outside. Startled from their beds, the brothers saw that all outside the windows was red. A fire had broken out across the street! They bundled on their clothes and hurried out to ask neighbours to help them carry their parents' coffins to the street. Two houses were burnt, but by dawn the fire was extinguished. Now the coffins were in the street, and tradition in Wuho had it that if a coffin had been carried into the street and you took it back into the house, your family would be ruined. So all their friends and relatives urged them to carry the coffins to the hill, and choose a day for the burial.

"When we bury our parents," said Yu Yu-ta to his brother, "we must naturally do the thing properly: announce it in the temple, sacrifice to bid farewell to their spirits, and invite all our kinsmen and friends. How can we take it so lightly? I propose that we carry the coffins back into the main hall, and choose a day for the interment later."

"Of course," replied Yu Yu-chung. "If anyone is ruined, it will be us."

They turned a deaf ear to all arguments, and called men to carry the coffins back into the hall, until Chang Yun-feng should select a day for their burial. They were careful to conform with all etiquette. On the day of the interment, relatives came from all over the district, and several of the Tu family from Tienchang arrived too. In Wuho, however, this was the talk of the town.

"The Yu brothers are growing dafter and dafter," they said. "To do something like this is simply asking for trouble!"

But to know what followed, you must read the next chapter.

CHAPTER 46

Talented men bid farewell
at Three Mountains Gate. The people of Wuho
are blinded by profit and power

When Yu Yu-ta had buried his parents, he told his younger
brother he meant to go back to Nanking. to thank Tu Shao-
ching and look for a teaching post since his money was finished.
He packed his things, said goodbye to Yu Yu-chung, crossed the
Yangtse, and came to Tu's riverside house. When questioned
about the lawsuit, he described all that had happened, and Tu
was much impressed by Yu Yu-chung's conduct. As they were
chatting, it was announced that Mr. Tang of Yicheng had called.
Yu inquired who he was.

"He's the man who asked you to tutor his sons," said Tu.
"You may as well meet him."

In came Brigade General Tang, greeted them and sat down.

"When I was privileged to meet you in Dr. Yu's house the
day before yesterday, Shao-ching," said Tang, "I felt all base
sentiments vanish in your presence. I called on you yesterday
but found you out, so I have been waiting eagerly for a whole
day to see you again. What is this gentleman's honourable
name?"

"This is my cousin Yu Yu-ta," said Tu. "Last year you
invited him to be your tutor."

"I did not expect to meet another eminent scholar today."
The general was delighted. "This is a real pleasure."

He bowed again, then sat down.

"Sir," said Yu Yu-ta, "after achieving great deeds for your country, you now live in retirement and remain silent about your exploits. This is the way of great generals of old!"

"I have no choice in the matter," replied Tang. "Thinking back, I realize I was somewhat too impulsive and achieved nothing for the state, simply offending my colleague. It's no use regretting it now."

"The world knows what to think," responded Yu. "You must not be over-modest, sir."

"May I ask what brings you here, uncle?" inquired Tu. "Where are you staying?"

"I had nothing to do at home, so I decided to come to Nanking to meet some talented men. I am staying at the Temple of Imperial Favour. I intend to pay my respects to Dr. Yu, Chuang Shao-kuang and his nephew."

When the tea was drunk, the general took his leave, and the other two escorted him to his chair. Then Yu stayed for a time with Tu.

When Brigade General Tang called at the Imperial College and handed in his card, he was told the doctor was out. He went on to North Gate Bridge to see Chuang Cho-chiang, who invited him in as soon as his card was presented. Tang alighted and entered the hall. And when his host came in, they bowed and sat down, each saying how happy he was to meet the other. Then Tang mentioned his intention of calling on Chuang Shao-kuang at Lotus Lake.

"He happens to be here," said Chuang. "Would you like to meet him?"

"Nothing could please me better," responded Tang.

Chuang ordered a servant to invite his uncle in. Presently Chuang Shao-kuang came in, greeted Tang, and sat down. Then tea was served again.

"Fortunately you have come just before Dr. Yu's departure," said Chuang Shao-kuang to Tang. "The Double Ninth Festival is near. Why don't we make up a party to celebrate the festival and bid farewell to Dr. Yu? We can spend an enjoyable day together."

574

"An excellent idea," said Chuang Cho-chiang. "On that date we can all meet here."

Soon Tang got up to go.

"I shall see you again before long at this gathering," he said. "Then we can talk all day."

The other two saw him out. The general also called on Chih Heng-shan and Wu Shu. Chuang Cho-chiang's servant took five taels to Tang's lodging in lieu of a feast, and three days later Chuang's steward arrived with an invitation requesting the guests to be there early. Chuang Cho-chiang was waiting for them, and Chuang Shao-kuang was already there. Soon Chih Heng-shan, Wu Shu and Tu Shao-ching arrived. Chuang Cho-chiang had cleared out a roomy pavilion, which was planted on all sides with chrysanthemums. It was the fifth of the ninth month, and the weather was dry and clear. Wearing lined gowns, they chatted as they sipped tea, and presently Brigade General Tang, Second Captain Hsiao and Dr. Yu arrived. The others welcomed them in, and after making their bows they all sat down.

"We come from many different parts of the country," said Tang, "and are fortunate to attend a gathering of such distinguished men. This meeting was surely predestined! I am only sorry Dr. Yu will be leaving so soon, and wonder when we shall have the pleasure of meeting again."

"My humble house is honoured by the presence of so many eminent citizens," said Chuang Cho-chiang. "The stars in heaven must reflect that the worthies for hundreds of miles around are here."

Once they were seated, a servant brought in tea. When the bowls were uncovered the tea looked as pale as water; but it gave off a rare fragrance, and the leaves were floating on the surface. Following this, some Tientu tea was served. And although the leaves had been kept for over a year, this brew was even more fragrant than the first.

"When you two gentlemen were in the army," said Dr. Yu with a smile, "I doubt if you ever set eyes on tea like this."

"Not to speak of the army," replied Hsiao Yun-hsien, "during my six years' stay at Green Maple City, I thought myself

575

lucky to be drinking fresh water — it was so much better than horse dung!"

"So it was true that the water and grass at Green Maple City were enough for several years," said Tang.

"Captain Hsiao is even a match for Tsui Hao[1] of Northern Wei," said Chuang Shao-kuang.

"Conditions may change from one generation to another," remarked Chih.

"Prime ministers and generals should be scholars," said Tu. "If not for his learning, how could Captain Hsiao have achieved so much?"

"What I find most amusing," said Wu Shu, "is the fact that the commanders at the frontier didn't know there was grass or water, but the clerks in the capital knew all right when they estimated costs. Now was it the ministers in the capital who knew all that, or was it their clerks? If the ministers are so learned, no wonder the court thinks more highly of civil than military officers; on the other hand, if it is the clerks who do the checking, that shows how essential the filing system is."

At this there was general laughter.

The music stopped now, and they took their seats at table. As the players came in to pay their respects, Chuang Fei-hsiung stood up and said:

"Since you gentlemen are our guests today, I have engaged the nineteen famous actors on the Pear Garden List, and hope each of you will name a scene to be played."

"What is the Pear Garden List?" asked Dr. Yu.

Yu Yu-ta described the romantic contest which Tu Shen-ching had held here, and they all laughed heartily.

"Has your worthy cousin joined the ministry yet?" Tang asked Tu.

Tu answered that he had.

"Shen-ching's judgement was most fair and discriminating," said Wu Shu. "I'm only afraid after he's joined the government and become chief examiner, he will miss genuine talent when he marks the candidates' papers."

---

[1] A famous scholar and military strategist of the fifth century.

The others laughed again. They feasted till dusk, when the operas were over and they went home. Chuang Cho-chiang found a skilful artist to paint this farewell feast, and all the guests wrote poems. Then each sent a feast to Dr. Yu to bid him farewell.

Over a thousand families in Nanking bade farewell to Dr. Yu, who became so tired of this that he would not let anyone see him to his boat. He hired a small boat, and boarded it at West Water Gate, letting Tu Shao-ching alone come to see him off.

"When you have gone, uncle," said Tu, "I shall have no one to whom to turn."

Dr. Yu could not help being sad. He invited Tu into the cabin.

"I can speak frankly to you, Shao-ching," he said. "I used to be a poor scholar, but during the six or seven years that I've been in Nanking I've saved enough to buy a paddy field producing thirty bushels a year. Now I may be appointed to a ministry, or I may be made a prefect or magistrate. I shall stay at my post two years, or three at the most, and save up enough to buy another plot of land worth twenty bushels of rice a year. Then my wife and I needn't starve, and that's good enough for me. I am not concerned for my son and grandchildren, because in addition to teaching my son the classics I have taught him medicine so that he can make his own living. Why should I be an official? I'll be writing to you constantly."

Then, shedding tears, they parted. Tu went ashore, and did not turn back till the doctor's boat was out of sight. Yu Yu-ta was staying with him, and Tu told him what Dr. Yu had said.

" 'Reluctant to advance, glad to retire,' the doctor is one of Nature's true gentlemen," declared Yu admiringly. "If we become officials, we should take him as our model."

They marvelled together at Dr. Yu.

That evening a letter arrived from Yu Yu-chung, asking his brother to come home.

"The tutor whom our cousin Yoo Liang invited has left," he wrote. "Yoo wants you to teach his son, and would like

577

you to take up your duties soon. Come back as fast as you can."

Yu Yu-ta explained this to Tu, and said he must leave. The next day he packed up and crossed the Yangtse. Tu saw him across the river, then went home.

When Yu Yu-ta reached home, his brother met him and showed him this note:

"Yoo Liang respectfully invites his cousin Yu Yu-ta to be his son's tutor at a salary of forty taels a year, with additional gifts at festivals."

The next day Yu went to return Yoo's call. The latter greeted him and was pleased to see him. When they had bowed and sat down a servant brought in tea.

"My son is a stupid boy," said Yoo, "who has had no schooling since he was a child. I have wanted for years to ask you to teach him, cousin; but you were always away. It is my son's good fortune now that you are home. Your family and mine have produced successful provincial and metropolitan graduates by the cartload — that means little to us. Above all, under your tuition, I want my son to learn your moral character. This is the most important thing."

"I am old and foolish," answered Yu. "Our families are closely related, but you are the only one I find congenial. Since I look on your son as my own, I shall certainly teach him to the best of my ability. As for passing the provincial or metropolitan examinations, since I have never passed myself I may not be the best teacher. And as for moral character, your son has your family tradition to guide him: there is nothing I can add."

They both chuckled at this. Then a lucky day was chosen for the new tutor to take up his duties. Yu turned up early that morning, and Young Master Yoo came in to pay his respects. He was a very intelligent boy. Yoo escorted Yu to the classroom, and the tutor took his seat there. Yoo then left him, and went to his study.

Almost at once the gateman brought in a guest. This was Tang San's brother, Tang Erh, who had passed the last provincial examination for civil officers and entered the college in the same year as Yoo Liang. He had come today to keep the new tutor company. Yoo made him sit down, and offered him tea.

"So your son starts his studies today!" said Tang.

"Yes."

"This tutor is excellent, but he lacks patience and goes in for miscellaneous subjects to the detriment of his orthodox studies. Although Mr. Yu is not guilty of the worst practices of modern scholars, he likes to imitate the scholars of the early years of our dynasty, and this is rather radical."

"My son is still too young to take examinations. I have invited my cousin to teach him some moral principles, so that he won't turn out a low, obsequious character."

A little later Tang Erh said: "I have something to ask a man of your erudition."

"What erudition have I? Don't make fun of me!"

"No, indeed. 1 want your advice. During the last examination, which I was lucky enough to pass, a nephew of mine passed at the same time in Fengyang Prefecture; so besides being my fellow-candidate he was passed by the same examiner. He's not been here since then, but now he's come to sacrifice to his ancestors. He called on me yesterday, with a card inscribed 'Your fellow-candidate and nephew.' When I return his call, should I style myself 'Your fellow-candidate and uncle.'?"

"What do you mean?" asked Yoo.

"You heard what I said. My nephew passed the same time that I did, under the same examiner. He inscribes his card 'Your fellow-candidate and nephew.' Should I call on him with a similar card?"

"Of course I know that two men who pass under one examiner are called fellow-candidates. But he must be out of his mind to write 'Your fellow-candidate and nephew.' "

"Why is he out of his mind?"

Yoo leant back and laughed.

"I never heard anything so absurd!" he declared.

Tang Erh's face fell.

"Don't take offence, friend," he said. "Although yours is a distinguished family, it hasn't produced officials for some time, and you've never passed yourself. Perhaps you don't know the official etiquette! My nephew has met no end of high officials in Peking, and he must have a reason for writing his card this way. He can't have got it out of his own head."

"If you think this way correct, brother, why consult me?"

"I see you don't know. Wait till Mr. Yu comes out for a meal, and I'll ask him."

Just then a servant came in.

"The fifth Mr. Yao is here," he said.

Yoo and Tang stood up as Mr. Yao came in. They bowed to each other and sat down.

"Fifth cousin," said Yoo, "why did you disappear after lunch yesterday? We had wine ready in the evening, but you didn't come."

"Did you have lunch here yesterday, Mr. Yao?" asked Tang. "I met you in the afternoon, and you said you'd just had lunch with the sixth Mr. Fang in Benevolent Fortune Shop. Why tell a lie like that?"

The servant brought in food, and they asked Mr. Yu in. The tutor sat in the highest seat, with Tang Erh opposite him, Mr. Yao in the place of a guest, and Yoo as host. After the meal, Yoo told Yu Yu-ta with a chuckle about the card. Yu's face turned purple, and the veins on his neck swelled with anger.

"Who could say such a thing?" he exploded. "Tell me, which is more important in life, ancestors or success in examinations?"

"Ancestors, of course," said Yoo. "That goes without saying."

"In that case," said Yu, "how can a man who's only just passed the provincial examination abandon family relationships and consider himself his uncle's fellow-candidate? May I never again hear of such a flouting of Confucian morality! This nephew of yours was lucky to pass, Mr. Tang! He must be a complete moron! If he were my nephew, I'd take him to the ancestral hall and give him a few dozen strokes before the ancestors' shrines!"

When Tang and Yao saw Yu was red with rage, and knew he was in one of his tempers again, they changed the conversation.

Soon the tea was finished, and Yu went back to his class-room.

"I'll take a stroll and then come back," said Yao standing up.

"I suppose today when you go out, you'll say you've been dining with the second Mr. Peng!" sneered Tang.

Yao gave a guffaw.

"Today everybody knows I was here with the new tutor. I can't pretend to have been anywhere else."

He went out grinning. Before long he was back.

"There's a guest in the hall to see you," he said to Yoo. "He says he's from the prefect's yamen, and he's sitting in the hall. Hurry up and receive him."

"I know no such man," said Yoo. "Where can he be from?"

While he was wondering, the stranger's card was brought in.

"Your fellow-student and relative, Chi Wei-hsiao, pays his respects."

Yoo went to the hall to meet him. When they had bowed and sat down, Chi Wei-hsiao produced a letter and handed it to Yoo.

"I have been in Peking," said Chi. "But because I was going to accompany the prefect to your honourable district, your worthy cousin Tu Shen-ching asked me to bring you a letter. I am happy to have the honour of meeting you."

Yoo opened the letter and read it through.

"Are you a friend sir, of Prefect Li?" he asked.

"Prefect Li was a student of my uncle's, Governor Hsun. So he has invited me to work in his yamen."

"What business brings you here, sir?"

"Since there are no outsiders here, I can tell you. The exorbitant interest in the pawnshops here is more than the people can stand; therefore the prefect has sent me to make an investigation. If the charge proves true, we must do away with this evil."

Yoo moved his chair closer to Chi Wei-hsiao.

"This shows the prefect's benevolence," he whispered. "No pawnshops dare charge high interest, but the two Fang pawnshops, Benevolent Fortune and Benevolent Greatness. The

Fangs are local gentry in the salt business, who are on the best of terms with the county and prefectural officials; so they do just as they please, and the people dare not protest. If you want to do away with this abuse, you need only close these two shops. Since the prefect is a high official, why should he have any dealings with such men? Please bear in mind what I've said, sir, but don't disclose that I told you!"

"I am grateful for your information," said Chi.

"I ought to invite you to a meal to express my gratitude and profit from your conversation," said Yoo. "But I am afraid I could not prepare anything good enough, and this little place is all ears and eyes. I shall send a poor meal to your lodging tomorrow. Please don't take this amiss!"

"You do me too much honour," protested Chi.

Then he took his leave, and Yoo went back to the study.

"Did he come from the prefect?" demanded the fifth Mr. Yao.

"Certainly."

"I don't believe it!" Yao shook his head and laughed.

Tang Erh thought hard, then said: "Yao's probably right. How could he be from the prefect's yamen? The prefect is not a friend of yours. He's friends with the third Mr. Peng and the sixth Mr. Fang. When I heard this man had come, that set me thinking. If he were sent here from the prefect's yamen, wouldn't he call on Mr. Peng and Mr. Fang instead of on you, brother? It all sounds too unlikely. I suspect the fellow is passing himself off as from the prefect's yamen to go round cheating people out of money. You'd better be on your guard!"

"He may have called on them first," said Yoo.

"He certainly hasn't!" Mr. Yao laughed. "If he'd called on them, why should he call on you?"

"It wasn't the prefect who told him to call," replied Yoo. "My cousin Tu Shen-ching of Tienchang, who's in the capital, gave him a letter for me. He's the well-known Chi Wei-hsiao."

'That's even more impossible!" Tang Erh waved this explanation aside. "Chi Wei-hsiao is a famous scholar who judged that Pear Garden Contest. Since he's such a celebrity he must know all the Hanlins and officials in the capital. Besides, Tu Shen-ching of Tienchang is very thick with the fourth Mr. Peng. If Chi brought a letter from Peking for you from Mr. Tu, wouldn't he bring one for Mr. Peng? It can't be Chi Wei-hsiao!"

"Well, never mind whether it is or it isn't," said Yoo. "It's time to change the subject." He called sharply to a servant: "Why isn't the meal ready yet?"

One servant came in and announced: "The meal is served, sir."

Another servant came in with a pack on his back.

"Old Mr. Cheng is here from the country," he said.

In came a grizzled man in a square cap, blue cotton gown and thin-soled cloth shoes, who had a toper's complexion. He bowed and sat down.

"This is fine!" he declared. "I happen to come on the day you've engaged a tutor. I can join in the feast to celebrate!"

Yoo ordered a servant to fetch water for Mr. Cheng to wash in, and to brush off the mud on his clothes and legs. Then he asked them all into the hall, where the feast was served. Yu sat in the highest place, with the others below him. And since it was dusk, they lit two glass lanterns in the hall. These lanterns had been a gift from the emperor to Yoo's great-grandfather when he was secretary of state over sixty years before, but they looked as new as ever.

"Old houses have tall trees," quoted Yu Yu-ta. "That saying is perfectly true. No other family here has lanterns like these."

"Mr. Yu," said Cheng, "for thirty years people east of the river prosper, then for thirty years those on the west. Thirty years ago, how powerful your two families were! I saw it with my own eyes. But now the Pengs and the Fangs are doing better each year. Not to mention anything else, see how thick the prefect and Magistrate Wang are with them! They're always sending yamen secretaries with important messages to their houses. Of course, common folk are afraid of them! These secretaries never call on anyone else."

"Have any secretaries come recently from the yamen?" asked Tang.

"A man called Chi has come down on some business. He's staying with the abbot in Precious Wood Temple. He called first thing this morning on the sixth Mr. Fang in Benevolent Fortune Shop. And Mr. Fang asked the second Mr. Peng over as well. The three of them went into the library, and had a long, long talk. I don't know who's in the prefect's bad books now that he should send this fellow Chi here."

Tang looked at Yao, and gave a sarcastic laugh.

"What did I say?" he cried.

Yu Yu-ta was disgusted by the way they talked.

"Were you granted the clothes and cap of a licentiate last year, sir?" he asked Mr. Cheng.

"I was," said Cheng. "Luckily the examiner was a colleague of the fourth Mr. Peng's. So I got Mr. Peng to write a letter, and that's how it was granted."

Yu laughed. "When the examiner saw your ruddy face and youthful appearance, uncle, I'm surprised he granted your request."

"I told him my face was swollen," said Mr. Cheng.

They laughed at that, and went on drinking.

"You and I are old, Mr. Yu," said Cheng. "We're no good for anything now. Only young men can prove their worth. I hope our brother Yoo here will pass the next examination with honours, and become a metropolitan graduate at the same time as Tang Erh. Even if they don't go as far as the fourth Mr. Peng, they may be appointed magistrates elect like the second and third Mr. Peng, to bring glory on their ancestors and reflect credit on us!"

Such talk disgusted Yu Yu-ta even more.

"Let's not talk about such things," he said. "Let's play a drinking game."

At once they played the game called Happy Drinking. And they drank for half a night, till they all were tipsy. Then Mr. Cheng was helped to a room to sleep, and lanterns were lit to light Yu, Tang and Yao to their homes.

In the middle of the night Cheng woke up retching. And before it was light he called a servant-boy, and secretly bade him send in two of the stewards in charge of rents. After a stealthy consultation with them, he told them to ask their master in.

But to know what followed, you must read the next chapter.

CHAPTER 47

Licentiate Yoo repairs Yuanwu Pavilion.
Salt Merchant Fang shocks scholars at the enshrining
of virtuous women

Yoo Liang was not an ordinary man. At seven or eight,
he was a precocious boy. Later he read, studied and thoroughly
digested all the Confucian canons, histories, philosophical and
miscellaneous works, so that by his twenties he was an accomplished scholar. He could immediately grasp any reference
to military science, husbandry, ceremony, music, engineering,
hunting, water conservancy or fire-watching. His compositions
and poems were excellent too. In fact, because his great-
grandfather had served as a minister, his grandfather as a
Hanlin, and his father as a prefect, his family had acquired
true distinction. But in spite of his learning, the inhabitants
of Wuho had no respect for him. If a man was praised in
Wuho for moral character, the local people would simply scoff,
at mention of ancient families, they would snort, while if a
scholar was commended for writing in the classical style, the
citizens' very eyebrows would twitch with laughter. If you
asked what there was of note in Wuho, they would tell you, "Mr.
Peng." If you asked what Wuho was remarkable for, they
would tell you, "Mr. Peng." If you asked what men of learning there were, they would answer, "Mr. Peng." If you asked
after talent or moral character, the reply was still, "Mr. Peng."
What impressed local people most was marriage into the
Fang family of Hueichow, and what they enjoyed most was

producing ingots of silver to purchase land. Yoo Liang owned several *mou* of land in this vulgar district, which prevented his moving elsewhere; hence he became quite a misanthropist. His father was a man of probity who had lived frugally while a prefect, and Yoo Liang's family ate and dressed simply, and had saved a little silver. Now the prefect had retired and given up the management of the household. Each year by strict economy Yoo saved a few more taels, then summoned brokers to ask the price of a plot of land or a house. But when agreement was nearly reached, he would vent his indignation by cursing these fellows, and refuse to buy after all. The whole district thought him mad. Still, envying his wealth, they made up to him.

Old Mr. Cheng was the head of the brokers' guild. He bade the stewards invite their master out, and sat down with Yoo in the library.

"There's a plot of land to my left," said Cheng. "You needn't worry about flood or drought, and you'll get six hundred bushels of rice from it every year. The fellow wants two thousand taels. The day before yesterday the sixth Mr. Fang made a bid for it, and the owner would have sold it if the tenants hadn't protested."

"Why did the tenants protest?" inquired Yoo.

"Because when Fang's bailiffs go down to his farms they expect the tenants to burn incense to welcome them, and if the rent's in arrears the tenants are beaten. That's why they didn't want the land sold to him."

"But why choose to sell it to me?" demanded Yoo. "Will they raise a stink when I go down to the country? If I don't beat them, will they beat me instead?"

"That's not how it is at all. They know you're a kind-hearted, liberal master, who won't ill-treat them like some other people. That's why I've come to offer you this bargain. Do you have any ready money?"

"Naturally, I have. I'll tell my man to fetch it out to show you."

He ordered a servant to bring in thirty great ingots of silver, which he tossed upon the table, and Cheng's eyes followed the ingots as they rolled. Then Yoo had the silver carried inside again.

"I wasn't lying about my money, was I?" he said. "Go back to the country and fix up the business. When you come back, I'll buy the land."

"I can't go back just yet."

"What business have you here?"

"Tomorrow I must call on Magistrate Wang to collect silver for an arch for a dead aunt of mine who was chaste; and I mean to pay my taxes at the same time. The day after that, the second Mr. Peng's daughter will be ten, and I must call to wish her a long life. The day after that, the sixth Mr. Fang has asked me to lunch. I can't go back till I've accepted his invitation."

Yoo suppressed a snort of laughter, and kept old Cheng to lunch. When the old man went to the yamen, Yoo sent a servant to find Tang San. Because the Fangs invited Tang Erh alone to their feasts, Tang San kept a close watch on their movements. He knew in advance when the Fangs were having guests and whom they were inviting, and his information was always accurate. Knowing this foible of his, Yoo asked him over.

"May I trouble you," said Yoo, "to find out if the sixth Mr. Fang of Benevolent Fortune Shop is inviting old Cheng three days from now? If you bring me reliable information, I'll invite you to a meal that day."

Tang San agreed to this. After quite a time he came back.

"No," he said. "Three days from now the sixth Mr. Fang is not inviting anyone."

"Capital!" cried Yoo. "Come here early three days from now, and we'll feast all day."

When Tang had agreed and left, Yoo told his servant to go to the chandler's and ask the clerk in confidence to write on a red invitation card:

Will you honour me at lunch on the eighteenth?

Fang Cho

This was put in an envelope and sealed, then left on the desk in the room where old Cheng slept. When Cheng came back that evening from paying his taxes, he was thrown into raptures by this invitation.

"I'm in luck at last!" he thought. "My fib has come true, and on the same day too!"

He went cheerfully to sleep.

On the eighteenth, Tang San turned up very early. Yoo invited Cheng to join them in the hall, and the old man saw servant after servant passing the door to the kitchen. One carried wine, one chicken and duck, one turtle and trotters, one four packages of sweetmeats, and one a large plate of meat dumplings. He knew these were for a feast, but asked no questions.

"Have you spoken to the carpenters and masons about repairing Yuanwu Pavilion?" Yoo asked Tang.

"I have," replied Tang. "You'll need plenty of materials. The outer wall has crumbled and will have to be rebuilt and a new stairway will have to be made as well. It'll take the masons three months. The beams and pillars inside need replacing, and the rafters nailing. A great many carpenters will be required. But all the repair men, carpenters and masons will work half time only. You reckoned on three hundred taels, but I'm afraid it will cost you five hundred to finish the job."

"Your worthy ancestors built Yuanwu Pavilion," said Cheng, "and it has brought such luck to our district that many scholars have passed the examinations. But nowadays only the Pengs are passing, so they ought to pay for repairs. It's nothing to do with you. Why spend so much on it?"

"That's right." Yoo bowed with clasped hands. "Will you be so good as to mention it to them, and ask them to contribute a few taels? I shall find some way of thanking you."

"I'll mention it when I see them," said Cheng. "Although there are so many officials in their family and they look so high and mighty, they pay a good deal of attention to what I say."

Now Yoo's servant privately hailed a hay-vendor at the back gate, and gave him four coppers to go in through the front gate and say: "Mr. Cheng, I've come from the sixth Mr. Fang. He's waiting for you to go over."

"Give my respects to your master," said Cheng. "I'll be there right away."

Then the hay-vendor left.

Old Cheng took leave of his host, and went straight to Benevolent Fortune Shop. The gateman showed him in, and the sixth Mr. Fang came out to see him. They bowed and sat down.

"When did you come to town?" asked Mr. Fang.

"The day before yesterday." Cheng was taken aback.

"Where are you staying?"

"With Yoo Liang." Cheng was even more bewildered.

A servant brought in tea.

"It's a fine day," ventured Cheng.

"Yes, isn't it?" rejoined Fang.

"Have you seen much of Magistrate Wang recently?"

"I saw him the day before yesterday."

They sat there with nothing to say, and sipped some more tea.

"The prefect hasn't been here for some time," said Cheng. "If he comes to our district he's bound to call on you before anyone else, sir. He thinks more highly of you than anyone else. In fact, you're the only man he looks up to in all this district. Who else of the local gentry can compare with you?"

"The new judicial commissioner has arrived. I expect the prefect will pay us a visit soon."

"Very true."

They went on sitting there while tea was served again, but no other guests arrived and no feast was spread. Filled with misgivings, Cheng began to be hungry. He decided to take his leave and see what Fang said.

"I will bid you goodbye, sir, now." He stood up to go.

"Won't you stay a little longer?" Fang stood up too.

"No, I really must be going."

Cheng took his leave and was seen to the door. He was a puzzled man as he left the gate.

"Did I come too early?" he wondered. "Have I offended him in any way? Or did I read the invitation wrongly?"

He could not understand what had happened.

"Yoo Liang is giving a feast," he thought. "I'll go back to eat before trying to get to the bottom of this."

He went straight to Yoo's house.

Yoo had had a table set in the library, and there he was with Tang San, the fifth Mr. Yao and two relatives, enjoying half a dozen piping-hot dishes. They stood up when Cheng came in.

"Mr. Cheng deserted us to enjoy Mr. Fang's richer fare," said Yoo. "He must have had a good time. Hurry up and give Mr. Cheng a seat over there, and brew him some good strong tea to help his digestion."

A servant placed a seat some way from the table, and invited Cheng to be seated. Then bowls of strong tea were brought him one after another. The more he drank, the hungrier he grew—the poor man suffered torments. As he watched them stuffing themselves with meat, duck and turtle, he was so enraged he nearly went up in smoke. They ate till dusk, and Cheng went hungry till dusk. But as soon as Yoo saw off the guests, Cheng went on the sly to one of the stewards' rooms, and asked for a bowl of fried rice, which he ate with hot water. Then he went to bed, but could not sleep for anger. The next day he told Yoo he must go back to the country.

"When shall we see you again?" asked Yoo.

"As soon as I've settled about that land. If that question can't be settled, I'll wait for the day when my aunt is enshrined with the other chaste women."

This said, he left.

Tang San called one day when Yoo had nothing to do.

"Friend Yoo," he said, "that Mr. Chi who stayed in Precious Wood Temple did come from the prefect. The sixth Mr. Fang and the second Mr. Peng both saw him. So it was true after all!"

"Last time you said it couldn't be true, today you say it is. Never mind whether it's true or not. It's not worth talking about."

"I've never met the prefect, brother. You'll have to go to the prefecture to return this Mr. Chi's call. Will you take me with you to see the prefect?"

"I can do that," said Yoo.

A few days later, they hired two sedan-chairs and went to Fengyang. They handed their cards in at the yamen. Yoo had brought another card for Chi Wei-hsiao, and that was taken too. Presently a man came out to announce:

"Mr. Chi has gone to Yangchow, but His Honour will see you now."

They went in and the prefect received them in his study. Upon coming out, they found lodgings in the east of the town. The prefect had invited them to a meal.

"The prefect is inviting us tomorrow," said Tang. "But it wouldn't be right for us to stay here and wait while he sends a man all that way to fetch us. Let's wait in Rising Dragon Temple just outside the yamen, so that we can go in as soon as he sends for us."

"All right," said Yoo with a laugh.

The next day after lunch, they went to wait in a monk's house at Rising Dragon Temple. They could hear delightful music and singing from another monk's house next door.

"That's a good performance," remarked Tang San. "I'm going to have a look."

He came back presently, quite crest-fallen.

"You've done me a bad turn!" he said to Yoo. "Who do you think is having a party there? It's the sixth Mr. Fang of Benevolent Fortune Shop, and the son of Prefect Li. The table is splendidly set out, and each of them is cuddling a young actor. They're having the time of their lives! If I'd known they were on such friendly terms, I'd have come the day before yesterday with Mr. Fang. If I'd come with him, I'd be with the prefect's son now. Coming with you, I've seen the prefect, but we're not on a familiar footing like that. This isn't half so much fun."

"You were the one to suggest it," countered Yoo. "I didn't force you to come. If Mr. Fang is there, why don't you join him?"

"Colleagues must stand by each other. I shall have to go with you to dine with the prefect."

Just then a messenger arrived to fetch them, and they went into the yamen. The prefect greeted them and declared himself glad to see them.

"When are your chaste women to be enshrined?" he asked. "I want to go down for the sacrifice."

"When we go back we will fix a date," they told him. "Your Honour will naturally be invited."

After the meal they left. The next day they sent in cards to take their leave, and went back to their district.

The day after Yoo reached home, Yu Yu-ta came to him.

"The third of next month has been settled on," said Yu, "to celebrate womanly virtue. There are several great-aunts and aunts in our two families who ought to be enshrined. We should prepare a sacrifice and gather together all our clansmen to escort their shrines to the ancestral temple. I suggest we go and pass the word around."

"Most certainly," agreed Yoo. "My family has one to be enshrined, your family has two. Our two clans must have nearly a hundred and fifty members. We should all assemble in official dress to welcome the retinue, as befits two distinguished families."

"I'll go to tell my kinsmen. You tell yours."

Yoo made the round of his relatives, and was absolutely enraged. He was much too angry to sleep that night. Early the next day Yu arrived, rolling his eyes in fury.

"What did your clan say, cousin?" asked Yu.

"Well! What did *your* clan say? Why are you so angry?"

"Don't remind me of it! I went to tell my kinsmen, and if they'd refused to come it wouldn't have mattered. But they said since old Mrs. Fang is being enshrined, they must join in her procession! They urged me to join it too! And when I took exception to this, they jeered at me for being old-fashioned. Have you ever heard anything so infuriating?"

"My family was the same," said Yoo with a smile. "I couldn't sleep for rage! Tomorrow I shall prepare a sacrifice, and escort my own great-aunt's shrine without them."

"I shall have to do the same."

So the matter was settled.

On the third, Yoo put on new clothes and a new cap, and ordered a servant to carry a table of offerings to his eighth cousin's house. He found the place deserted, without a soul to be seen. His eighth cousin, who was a poor licentiate, came out in a ragged cap and gown to greet him. Yoo Liang went in to bow before his great-aunt's shrine, then carried it to the stand. They had hired an old, sedan-like stand and two shoulder poles. And four country fellows carried this lopsidedly along, without any retinue. Four musicians blew a ragged fanfare in front as they carried the shrine to the street, while Yoo and his cousin followed behind. From the door of the ancestral temple they could make out two other derelict stands in the distance, escorted by no musicians but followed by Yu Yu-ta and Yu Yu-chung. When the Yu brothers reached the temple, the four scholars greeted each other. Honouring the Classics Pavilion before the temple was hung with lanterns and streamers, and there a feast had been laid. This was a high pavilion in the middle of the road, commanding a fine view on every side, and actors were carrying up their properties.

"Mr. Fang's actors have come!" the stand-bearers said.

They stood there for a little, till they heard three cannon shots.

"Old Mrs. Fang has started!" said the bearers.

Presently gonging and drumming filled the street. Two yellow umbrellas and eight flags appeared, as well as four groups of horsemen bearing placards inscribed: "The Minister of Ceremony," "The Hanlin," "The Provincial Director of Education," and "The Number One Graduate." These had been lent by the Yu and Yoo families. As the procession drew near, gongs and trumpets sounded, incense was burnt, and the crowd thronged round Mrs. Fang's shrine, which was carried by eight big-footed maids. The sixth Mr. Fang in a gauze cap and round collar followed respectfully behind. After him came two groups: the gentry and the scholars. The gentry included the second, third, fifth and seventh Peng brothers. Then came the metropolitan and provincial graduates, senior licentiates and college scholars of the Yu and Yoo families—sixty to seventy in all. In gauze caps and round collars, they followed respectfully behind the Pengs. In their wake came another sixty to seventy licentiates from the Yu and Yoo families, in scholars' caps and gowns, who scuttled hastily after them. The last of the local gentry, Tang Erh, held a notebook in which he was writing down a record. The last of the licentiates, Tang San, also carried a notebook in which he was writing a record. Because the Yu and Yoo families had a scholarly tradition and some proper feeling, when they reached the ancestral temple and saw their own aunts' shrines there, seven or eight of them came over to bow. Then they all surged after Mrs. Fang's shrine into the temple. Behind them were the magistrate, local teacher, district police warden and sergeant, who came with the retinue to play music and set up the shrine. The magistrate, teacher, police warden and sergeant each sacrificed in turn. Then the local gentry and scholars sacrificed, and last of all the Fang family sacrificed. When this was over, they all rushed noisily out and mounted Honouring the Classics Pavilion for the feast.

When the crowd had left, Yu and Yoo carried their shrines inside and set them in the proper places. Yoo had prepared a table of sacrificial objects, Yu Yu-ta three offerings. The sacrifice at an end, the table was carried out; but since there was nowhere to enjoy the food, they decided to go to a college attendant's house. Yu Yu-ta looked up at the richly dressed men on Honouring the Classics Pavilion, who were toasting each other. The sixth Mr. Fang seemed uncomfortable after such a long ceremony. He replaced his gauze cap and round collar with a head-cloth and ordinary gown, then wandered up and down the balconies. Soon a flower-seller named Chuang came along, and with her big feet climbed the pavilion stairway.

"I came to see the old lady enshrined!" she chuckled.

The sixth Mr. Fang fairly beamed. He stood beside her, leaning against the railing, watching the flags and musicians, pointing out this and that and explaining things to her. The flower woman kept one hand on the railing, and with the other undid her clothes to search for lice, which she popped in her mouth as she caught them. Yu Yu-ta was completely disgusted.

"Let's not feast here," he suggested. "Have the table carried home, cousin, and my brother and I will come to your house. We'd better not look at such maddening sights!"

The table was carried off, and the four of them followed it home.

"Cousin," said Yu Yu-ta on the way, "this district of ours has no sense of morality left! Nor is there a single good teacher in the college! Such things could never be done before Dr. Yu in Nanking!"

"Dr. Yu doesn't lay down restrictions," said Yu Yu-chung. "But people are so influenced by his virtue that they naturally refrain from improper conduct."

They sighed, returned home and feasted, then went their ways.

By now work had started on Yuanwu Pavilion, and Yoo went over every day to supervise the repairs. One evening when he came home, he found old Cheng sitting in the library. Yoo bowed to him and tea was served.

"Why didn't you come the other day, uncle," asked Yoo, "when the chaste wives and widows were enshrined?"

"I meant to come, but I was too ill," replied Cheng. "When my brother came to the country, he said it was a splendid sight. The Fangs' procession filled half the street, with Magistrate Wang as well as the Peng family escorting the shrine. There was a feast and opera performance at Honouring the Classics Pavilion, and people flocked in from all the country around. 'None but the Fangs could put on such a show!' they said. You must have been drinking without me at the pavilion."

"Didn't you know I escorted my eighth great-aunt that day?"

"Your eighth cousin is too poor to buy himself trousers," sneered Cheng. "Not one of your relatives will call on him. You must be joking. Of course you escorted Mrs. Fang!"

"Well, let's not talk of what is past," replied Yoo.

After dinner Cheng said: "The owner of that land and the middleman have both come to town and are staying in Precious Wood Temple. If you want the land, the thing can be settled tomorrow."

"Let's assume I want it," said Yoo.

"There's another thing. I was the one to tell you about this land, and I want a fifty-tael fee out of this transaction.

I'd like *you* to pay me that. I'll get the middleman's money out of him."

"Of course! You shall have a whole ingot, uncle."

Cheng gave him an account of the taxes, land cost, balance to be used, the quality of the silver, the price of the fowl and fodder, the fee for the witnesses and the deed, and so forth. He brought the landlord and middleman to Yoo's house first thing the next morning. But when he went into the study to ask Yoo to sign the contract, he saw a crowd of carpenters and masons drawing their pay. Yoo was handing out fifty-tael ingots right and left, and had soon disposed of several hundred taels. When he had finished, Cheng asked him to sign the contract.

"The land's too dear! I don't want it!" Yoo glared at him.

Old Cheng was frightened nearly out of his wits.

"I mean it, uncle," said Yoo. "I don't want the land." And he ordered his servants: "Go and turn those muddy-legged bumpkins out of the hall."

Between anger and dismay, Cheng's face was a study. But he had to go out to send the countrymen away.

To know what followed, you must read the next chapter.

CHAPTER 48

A virtuous widow of Huichow
follows her husband to the grave. Later scholars
admire the old ways at Tai Po's Temple

As tutor in Yoo's household, Yu Yu-ta came each day to teach. One morning he rose, washed, drank tea, and set out as usual for his classroom. He had barely left the gate, though, when three horsemen rode up, alighted, and offered him their congratulations.

"What is the meaning of this?" asked Yu.

The messengers showed him a notice announcing that he had been appointed tutor to the prefectural college at Huichow. In joy, Yu treated them to a meal, then sent them off with a tip. Yoo Liang came to congratulate him, and so did his kinsmen and friends. He was busy for several days entertaining guests, then set his affairs in order and went to Anching for credentials. On his return he took his family to his new post, having invited his brother to accompany them.

"You are a poorly-paid tutor, brother," objected Yu Yu-chung. "While you are settling down there, you may not have even enough for yourselves. I'd better stay here."

"Each extra day we can be together is to the good," replied Yu Yu-ta. "We used to teach in different places, and often didn't see each other for two years at a time. Now we're old, and as long as we can be together what does it matter if we sometimes go hungry? We can always find some way out.

I imagine being a college tutor is better than tutoring in a private family. Come with me, brother!"

Then Yu Yu-chung consented. They packed up together and went to Huichow. Since Yu Yu-ta's scholarship was well-known, the people of Huichow had heard of him and rejoiced upon learning that he was to be posted here. After his arrival, when they found how frank and open he was and how genial his conversation, licentiates who had not intended to come called on him after all. They realized they had an enlightened tutor. Moreover, when they met Yu Yu-chung and discovered how learned he was, they felt even more respectful. So several licentiates called on them every day.

One day Yu Yu-ta was sitting in the hall when in walked a licentiate in a square cap and old blue gown, with a swarthy face and grey beard, who looked over sixty. He had a card in his hand, which he handed to Yu Yu-ta. On it was written: "Your student, Wang Yun."

After presenting his card the licentiate bowed, and Yu returned his bow.

"Is your other name Yu-huei, by any chance?" he asked.

"It is, sir."

"I have been wanting to meet you for twenty years, and today at last I have my wish! You and I should be like brothers: we need not observe the usual vulgar conventions."

He invited Wang into the study, and bade a servant fetch his younger brother. Yu Yu-chung came in and was introduced, and after the usual courtesies they sat down.

"I have been a licentiate in this college for over thirty years," said Wang. "I am nothing but a pedant. In the past, I never saw my tutor except officially; but now that I have such a famous teacher and uncle here, I shall call on you frequently to ask for your instruction. I must beg you not to look on me as one of the many college students but to accept me as your disciple."

"We are old friends, brother," protested Yu Yu-ta. "Why should you talk like this?"

"I have heard of your straitened circumstances," said Yu Yu-chung. "Are you doing any tutoring at present? How have you supported yourself all these years?"

"Speaking frankly, uncle, all my life I have had but one aim: to compile three books to help young people."

"What three books?" asked Yu Yu-ta.

"One book on ceremony, one on etymology, and one on country etiquette."

"With what does the book on ceremony deal?" asked Yu Yu-chung.

"It divides up the three classics of ceremony into such categories as The Ceremony of Serving Parents, and The Ceremony of Respecting Elders. The main text from the classics will be in large type, with quotations beneath from the classics and histories by way of illustration. Students can study this from their childhood."

"Such a book should be recommended by the government for general study and circulated throughout the country," said Yu Yu-ta. "What will your book on etymology be like?"

"It is a manual of etymology that takes seven years to study. This book is already completed. I will bring it you, sir, for your opinion."

"The science of etymology has long been neglected," said Yu Yu-chung. "A book like this should prove very valuable. May I ask what type of book that on country etiquette is?"

"It simply supplies some additional ceremonies to help civilize the people. These three books have kept me so busy, I have had no time to teach."

"How many sons do you have?" asked Yu Yu-ta.

"Just one son, and four daughters. My eldest daughter is a widow at home. The others have not been married more than a year."

Yu Yu-ta kept Wang to a meal, and refused to accept his card inscribed as from a pupil to a teacher.

"My brother and I shall often be imposing on you by asking you over to chat," he said. "Please don't be offended by our poor country fare."

The Yu brothers saw him out, and Wang went slowly home. He lived five miles from the city.

Upon reaching home, Wang told his wife and son how good Yu Yu-ta had been to him. The next day, Yu Yu-ta came down to the village by chair to call on him, and sat for some time in Wang's hall. The following day Yu Yu-chung came on foot, with a porter carrying a bushel of rice. He came in, greeted Wang, and they sat down.

"This is a bushel of my brother's rice allowance," said Yu Yu-chung. "And this"—he produced an ingot of silver —"is one tael of his salary. He sends them to you, brother, as a stipend."

"I have shown no respect to my teacher and uncle," said Wang as he took the silver. "How can I accept such kindness?"

"This is not worth speaking of," replied Yu Yu-chung with a smile. "But the college salary is low, and my brother has only just come to this post. Dr. Yu used to present scores of taels to deserving scholars in Nanking, and my brother would like to learn from him."

"I dare not refuse a superior's gift," quoted Wang. "I accept this, then, with thanks."

He kept Yu Yu-chung to a meal, and showed him the manuscripts of his three books. Yu read them carefully, and expressed his admiration. During the afternoon a man came in.

"Mr. Wang," he said, "our young master is very ill, and the young mistress asked me to invite you over. Can you set out at once?"

"This man comes from my third daughter," said Wang to Yu. "My son-in-law is ill, and they want me to go there."

"In that case, I'll leave you now," said Yu Yu-chung. "I will take your manuscripts to show my brother, and return them when he's read them."

So saying, he took his leave. The porter, who had eaten too, put the manuscripts in his empty basket and shouldered this load back to town.

Mr. Wang walked six or seven miles to his son-in-law's house, and found the young man seriously ill. A doctor was there, but no drugs were of any avail. A few days later his son-in-law died, and Wang mourned bitterly for him; while his daughter's tears must have moved both heaven and earth. When her husband was in his coffin, she paid her respects to his parents and her father.

"Father," she said, "since my elder sister's husband died, you have had to support her at home. Now my husband has died, will you have to support me too? A poor scholar like you can't afford to feed so many daughters!"

"What do you want to do?" her father asked.

"I want to bid farewell to you and my husband's parents, and follow my husband to the grave."

When the dead man's parents heard this, their tears fell like rain.

"Child!" they cried. "You must be out of your mind! Even ants and insects want to live—how can you suggest such a thing? In life you're one of our household, in death you'll be one of our ghosts. Of course we'll look after you, and not expect your father to support you! You mustn't talk like that!"

"You are old," said the girl. "Instead of helping you, I should just be a burden to you, and that would make me unhappy. Please let me have my own way. But it will be a few days before I die. I'd like you, father, to go home and tell my mother, and ask her to come so that I can say goodbye to her. This means a lot to me."

"Kinsmen," said Wang Yu-huei to his son-in-law's parents, "now that I think this over, I believe, since my daughter sincerely wants to die for her husband, we should let her have her way. You can't stop someone whose mind is made up. As for you, daughter, since this is the case, your name will be recorded in history. Why should I try to dissuade you? You know what you must do. I'll go home now and send your mother over to say goodbye to you."

Her parents-in-law would not hear of this, but Wang Yu-huei insisted. He went straight home, and told his wife what had happened.

"You must be in your dotage!" she protested. "If our daughter wants to die, you should talk her out of it, instead of egging her on. I never heard such a thing!"

"Matters like these are beyond you," retorted Wang.

When his wife heard this, the tears streamed down her cheeks. She immediately hired a chair and went to reason with her daughter, while her husband went on reading and writing at home as he waited for news of his child. In vain did Mrs. Wang argue with her daughter. Each day the girl washed and combed her hair, and sat there keeping her mother company; but no bite or sup passed her lips. Though the old folk begged and implored her, and used all the wiles they could think of, she simply refused to eat. And after fasting for six days she had no strength to get up. The sight of this nearly broke her mother's heart. She fell ill herself, and had to be carried home and put to bed.

When three more days had passed, torches appeared at the second watch, and some men came to knock at their door.

"Your daughter fasted for eight days," they announced. "At midday today she died."

When the mother heard this, she screamed and fainted away. And when they brought her round, she would not stop sobbing. Her husband walked up to her bed.

"You're a silly old woman!" he said. "Our third daughter is now an immortal. What are you crying for? She made a good death. I only wish I could die for such a good cause myself."

He threw back his head and laughed.

"She died well!" he cried. "She died well!"

Then, laughing, he left the room.

Yu Yu-ta was amazed when he heard of this the next day, and could not help but be sad. Buying incense and three sacrificial offerings, he went to pay his respects before her coffin. This done, he returned to the yamen, and ordered his clerk to draw up a petition requesting the authorities to honour this devoted widow. His younger brother helped to draft the petition, which was despatched that same night. Then Yu Yu-chung took offerings and sacrificed before the coffin. When the college students saw their tutor show the dead woman such respect, a great many of them also went to sacrifice. And two months later the authorities decreed that a shrine should be made and placed in the temple, and an archway erected before her home. On the day that she was enshrined, Mr. Yu invited the magistrate to accompany the retinue which escorted the virtuous widow into the temple. All the local gentry, in official robes, joined the procession

on foot. Having entered the temple and set the shrine in its place, the magistrate, college tutors and Yu each sacrificed. Then the gentry, scholars and relatives sacrificed; and last of all the two families sacrificed. The ceremony lasted all day, and they feasted afterwards in the Hall of Manifest Propriety. The other scholars urged Wang to join the feast, declaring that by bringing up such a virtuous daughter he had reflected glory on his clan. But by now Wang was beginning to feel quite sick at heart, so he declined to join them. After feasting in the Hall of Manifest Propriety, the others went home.

The next day Wang went to the college to thank Mr. Yu. The two brothers received him, and kept him to a meal.

"I can't stand it at home, with my wife grieving all the time," said Wang. "I would like to go on a trip, and I think the best place to visit is Nanking. That's a large printing centre. I may find someone to print these three books of mine."

"What a pity Dr. Yu isn't there," said Yu Yu-ta, "since you're going to Nanking! If he were there and saw these books, his praise would make all the printers rush to have them."

"If you are going to Nanking, sir," said Yu Yu-chung, "my brother can write you letters of introduction to our cousin Tu Shao-ching and Mr. Chuang Shao-kuang. Their words carry weight."

Yu Yu-ta gladly wrote introductions to Chuang Shao-kuang, Tu Shao-ching, Chih Heng-shan and ⋅Wu Shu.

Too old to travel by road, Wang Yu-huei took a boat to Yenchow and the West Lake. The beautiful scenery on the way made him grieve all the more for his daughter, and he travelled gloomily all the way to Soochow, where he had to change boats.

"I've an old friend at Tengwei Hill," he remembered, "who always liked my writings. Why don't I call on him?"

He left his luggage in an inn at Mountain Lake, and booked a passage to Tengwei Hill. It was still the morning then, and his boat would not leave till evening.

"What places of interest are there near here?" he asked the waiter.

"A couple of miles from here, you'll come to Huchiu Mount. That's a lively spot all right!"

Wang locked his door and went out. The street was narrow at first, but after about a mile it widened out. He sat in a tea-house beside the road to drink a bowl of tea as he watched the boats going past. Some were large craft with carved beams and painted pillars, and the passengers burnt incense and feasted all the way to Huchiu Mount. After a number of barges came several boatloads of women. They had hung no bamboo curtains, but were sitting there drinking, dressed in the brightest costumes.

"This Soochow custom is not a good one," thought Wang. "Women should stay in the inner chambers. Who ever heard of them cruising up and down in pleasure boats!"

Soon he noticed a girl in white on one of the barges, who reminded him of his daughter. Then his heart ached, and hot tears rolled down his cheeks. Drying his eyes, he left the tea-house and started up Huchiu Mount. Along the roadside were vendors selling soya-bean cheese, mats, toys and flowers of every season: all was bustle and animation. There were restaurants too, and other shops selling sweetmeats. Since Wang was not a good walker, it took him a long time to reach the gate of Huchiu Temple. Climbing the steps and rounding a corner, he came to Thousand Men Boulder, where tables were also set out for tea. He sat down and drank a bowl, while he gazed at the magnificent view all around him. The sky was overcast, though, as if it were going to rain; so instead of sitting there longer he went out through the temple gate. Half way back he felt hungry, and stopped at a shop to eat pork dumplings costing six coppers each, then paid the bill and left. By the time he had walked slowly back to the inn, it was dusk and the boatmen were clamouring to be off. He carried his luggage back to the boat; and, since it was only drizzling, the junk was able to travel all that night. Arrived at Tengwei Hill, Wang went to look for his friend. He found a low house, with willows shading the entrance; but the double gate was closed and pasted with white. He gave a start, and knocked. Then his friend's son came out in mourning to open the door.

"Why have you come so late, uncle?" asked the youth. "My father longed to see you every day! Right up to the last he was sorry he couldn't meet you once more, and regretted that he'd never read all your books."

When Wang knew his friend was dead, the warm tears gushed from his eyes.

"How long ago did your father die?" he asked.

"Less than a week ago."

"Is his coffin still in the house?"

"Yes, uncle, it is."

"Take me there."

"First wash your face and have some tea, uncle. Then I'll take you to it."

He offered Wang a seat in the hall, and brought him some water to wash in. But when Wang declined tea and asked to be taken straight to his old friend's coffin, the young man led him to the central room. The coffin was in the middle, with incense burners, candles, and the dead man's portrait, as well as a spirit flag. Wang wept, then knelt and bowed four times; and his friend's son offered him thanks. After that he drank tea, and used part of his travelling money to buy incense, paper coins, sacrificial meat and wine, placing his manuscripts before the coffin as he sacrificed. And then he wailed again. He spent the night there, but said he must leave the next morning. His young host could not keep him. Sobbing, Wang bade farewell to his old friend, then returned to the boat with tears in his eyes, escorted by his old friend's son.

At Soochow Wang changed boats again, then went ashore at West Water Gate in Nanking. Entering the city, he found a lodging at Niu Kung's Temple. He spent the whole of the next day looking for the men to whom he had introductions. But Dr. Yu had been transferred to Chekiang, and Tu Shaoching had gone to pay him a visit, while Chuang Shao-kuang had gone home to repair his ancestral tombs, and both Chih Heng-shan and Wu Shu had left for official posts in distant parts. Not one of them did he meet. Wang was not unduly disappointed, however, but let it go at that, and spent each day in the temple reading.

605

Over a month later, when his money was finished, during one of his strolls he ran into a man at the end of his lane who bowed to him.

"What brings you here, uncle?" asked this man.

It was a fellow-villager named Teng Chih-fu. His father had passed the examination in the same year as Wang, who had acted as Teng Chih-fu's guarantor when he entered college. Hence the young man addressed him as his uncle.

"It is years since we met," said Wang. "Where have you been?"

"Where are you staying, uncle?" asked Teng.

"In Niu Kung's Temple in front. It's not far."

"I'll go with you to your lodging."

When they entered the room, Teng bowed to Wang.

"Since I left you, I've been in Yangchow for four or five years," he said. "Recently my employer sent me here to sell up-river salt, and I'm staying in the Temple for Worshipping Heaven. I have often thought of you, uncle. Have you kept well? Why did you come to Nanking?"

Wang asked him to be seated.

"Nephew," he said, "when your mother was widowed and a neighbour's house caught fire, because she prayed to Heaven a wind sprang up which blew out the flames. Everyone knows that story proving her chastity. Now my third daughter, too, is renowned as a virtuous widow."

He described how his daughter had starved herself after her husband's death.

"My wife's constant crying was more than I could bear," he said. "Mr. Yu of the prefectural college wrote me some letters of introduction to friends in Nanking, but I haven't succeeded in meeting any of them."

"Who are they?"

Wang told him their names, and Teng sighed.

"I'm sorry I couldn't come here before," he said. "When Dr. Yu was in Nanking, there were many famous scholars here. The whole country knows of that sacrifice at Tai Po's Temple. But since Dr. Yu went away, these worthies have scattered like clouds before the wind. I came last year and met Mr. Tu Shao-ching, and thanks to him I met Mr. Chuang at Lotus

Lake as well. But none of them are at home now. These lodgings of yours are not too comfortable, uncle. Won't you move for the time being to the temple where I'm staying?"

This Wang agreed to do. He said goodbye to the monk and paid his rent, then called a man to carry his baggage to the Temple for Worshipping Heaven. That evening Teng prepared a feast, and they spoke again of the Temple of Tai Po.

"Where is the temple?" asked Wang. "I'd like to go and look at it tomorrow."

"I'll go with you, uncle," said Teng.

The next day they went out through the South Gate. Teng Chih-fu gave a few cents of silver to the care-taker, who opened the door and showed them into the hall. After paying their respects here, they went to the buildings at the back. On the ground floor they found the programme of ceremony and order of the processions which Chih Heng-shan had pasted on the wall, and dusted these off with their sleeves to read them. Then they went upstairs, where they saw eight large cupboards in which the musical instruments and sacrificial implements were locked. Wang wanted to look at these.

"The key is in Mr. Chih's house," said the care-taker.

There was nothing for it but to come downstairs. They walked along both corridors, and looked at the two libraries and at the building where the meat offerings were inspected. Then they took their leave of the care-taker, and went on to the Temple of Kindness Repaid. They had a bowl of tea under Glazed Pagoda; then dined in a tavern near the temple gate.

"I am tired of living outside," said Wang. "I would like to go home. But I can't afford the journey."

"How can you say that, uncle!" protested Teng. "I'll provide your fare and see you off."

He prepared a farewell feast, and produced over a dozen taels of silver, then hired a sedan-chair and saw Wang off to Huichow.

"Although you're leaving, uncle," he said, "you might give me Mr. Yu's letters of introduction. When those scholars return, I'll send them in, and they'll know that you called on them."

"Very well," said Wang.

He handed the letters to Teng, then left.

Wang Yu-huei had been gone for some time when Teng heard that Wu Shu was back, and took the letter to call on him. It happened that Wu Shu was out that day paying a call; so Teng did not see him, but left the letter there.

"My name is Teng, and I live in the Temple for Worshipping Heaven," he told Wu's servant, "I would like to explain this letter to your master."

When Wu Shu came back and saw the letter, he decided to go to the temple to return Teng's call. Just then, however, he received an invitation from Mr. Kao, a Hanlin.

But to know what followed, you must read the next chapter.

CHAPTER 49

A Hanlin discourses on the examinations.
An impostor masquerades as an official

Wu Shu was about to return Teng Chih-fu's call when an invitation card was brought in.

"Mr. Kao of the Han Lin Academy invites you to be his guest today."

"I'll come as soon as I've returned a call," Wu told the messenger. "Go back and tell your master that."

"My master sends you his warmest regards, sir," said the man. "The chief guest is a Mr. Wan of Chekiang, who is an old sworn brother of our master's. You and Mr. Chih are the only ones invited to meet him, apart from our master's relative, Mr. Chin."

Hearing that Chih Heng-shan would be there, Wu reluctantly consented to go.

He returned Teng's call, but found him out. After noon one of Mr. Kao's servants came twice to fetch him. Then Wu Shu went to the Hanlin's house. After Mr. Kao had greeted him, Censor Shih walked out of the library; then Chin, a secretary of the Imperial Patent Office, arrived and was introduced. They were sipping tea when Chih Heng-shan was announced, and Mr. Kao ordered his steward to urge Mr. Wan to come over.

"My friend Wan is one of the most capable men of Chekiang," said Kao to Shih. "He writes an excellent hand. I met him at Yangchow twenty years ago, when he was also a licentiate; but the way he carried himself already marked him off from ordinary men. None of the Salt Gabelle officers dared treat him disrespectfully, and he managed even better than I did there. After I went to Peking, though, we lost touch. The day before yesterday he arrived here from the capital. He tells me he has been appointed a secretary of the Patent Office; so he will be a colleague of my kinsman Chin."

"Why should you act as host for a colleague of mine?" Chin laughed. "You must come to my house tomorrow."

By now Wan had reached the gate and handed in his card. The Hanlin stood with clasped hands under the eaves of the hall to greet him, ordering the steward to open the gate and let the sedan-chair in. But Wan alighted outside and hurried in. They bowed and took seats in the hall.

"You honour me too much with this invitation," said Wan. "After parting with you twenty years ago, I am eager to talk with you over wine. Have you asked any other guests?"

"There are no outsiders today," replied Kao. "Only Censor Shih, my relative Mr. Chin, and two friends from the college here: Wu and Chih. They are now in the western hall."

"Pray ask them to join us," said Wan.

The steward invited the four other guests into the main hall.

"Mr. Kao was good enough to ask me over to keep you company," remarked Censor Shih.

"I met Mr. Kao twenty years ago in Yangchow before he rose to eminence," said Wan. "But I knew from his distinguished air he was bound to become a pillar of the state. After he passed the higher examinations, I travelled all over the country but never went to the capital to see him. And when I reached Peking last year, I found to my regret he was on leave. Yesterday I had some business with a few old Yangchow acquaintances, which meant I could not call here before today. I am lucky to have this chance of seeking your instruction."

"When will you be appointed to a post, sir?" asked Secretary Chin. "What business brings you here from the capital?"

"Both metropolitan graduates and students of the Imperial College may be appointed to our office," said Wan. "Since I was promoted through administrative channels, I shall never be able to leave the administrative side. I'm afraid I shall never join the Han Lin Academy. It has recently been hard to find any post."

"This type of appointment is worse than none at all," rejoined Chin.

Wan did not follow this up, but turned to Wu Shu and Chih Heng-shan.

"I have long known you gentlemen by reputation," he said. "Great instruments are never quickly forged. This post of mine is nothing. Scholars should base their careers on success in the examinations."

"How can insignificant students like ourselves compare with someone of your great talent?" asked Chih.

"Mr. Kao was your sworn brother," said Wu Shu. "You will equal each other in achievement."

Just then a servant came in.

"A meal is ready in the western hall," he announced.

"After a simple meal we can have a good talk," said Kao.

When they had finished feasting in the western hall, Kao ordered his steward to open the door to the garden and invited his guests to have a look round. Through a moon gate to the right they reached a long, whitewashed wall, and passed through a small door at one end of it to a covered walk. Then, turning east, they descended some pebble-paved steps to a plot of orchids. The day was warm and the orchids were in bloom. In front were an artificial mountain and screen, both skilfully carved of stone. A small pavilion on the mountain could seat three or four people. Beside the screen were two porcelain stools, and behind it about a hundred bamboos. Low vermilion railings beyond the bamboo grove surrounded a bed of peonies still in bud. Kao took Wan's hand and spoke softly to him as he led him to the pavilion, while Shih and Chin sat down by the stone screen, and Chih and Wu strolled through the bamboos to the peony plot.

"It's a neat little garden," said Chih. "But there aren't enough trees."

"Remember what the men of old said," remarked Wu. "Pavilions and lakes are like official rank, which a stroke of luck may bring within your grasp. But trees are like the noblest character, which can only be attained through long cultivation."

Kao and Wan came down from the pavilion and walked up to them.

"Last year in Chuang Cho-chiang's house," said Kao, "I read Mr. Wu's poem to the Red Peony. It will soon be peony time again."

The host and his five guests strolled up and down for some time, then went back to sit in the western hall. The steward ordered fruit-tea after the usual tea.

"I have a friend in your honourable province, sir," said Chih Heng-shan to Wan. "He is a native of Chuchow. I wonder if you know him?"

"The most well-known Chuchow scholar is Ma Chun-shang," replied Wan. "I have a few other college friends, but I don't know which you mean."

"I was speaking of Mr. Ma."

"Ma Chun-shang is my sworn brother: of course I know him. He has gone to Peking now. Once in the capital, he is sure to go far."

"Why has he gone to Peking?" asked Wu Shu quickly. "He has not yet passed the provincial examination."

"When the last provincial director of education completed his three years in office, he recommended Ma for his excellent conduct. He has gone to the capital now to take a short cut to officialdom. That's why I say he will go far."

"When all's said and done," remarked Censor Shih, "these unorthodox careers won't take one very far. A man of character should stick to the examinations."

"During his visit last year," said Chih Heng-shan, "I was struck by Ma's genuine knowledge of his subject. It is strange that after all these years he is still a licentiate. It looks as if the examination system is not infallible after all."

"You are wrong there, Mr. Chih," protested Kao. "This is the only matter in which there has been not the slightest change for the last two hundred years. Scholars who deserve to come first will always come first. Ma Chun-shang's writings on this subject are merely superficial: of the finer points he knows absolutely nothing. If he were a licentiate for three hundred years and came first in two hundred prefectural tests, he would still fail every time in the prefectural examinations!"

"Do you mean to say," asked Wu, "that the examiners and the provincial director of education don't see eye to eye?"

"Certainly!" answered Kao. "All the students that rank high on the provincial list will fail in the real examinations. That's why before I passed I gave all my attention to the examinations. The provincial director often placed me in the third rank!"

"That essay of yours, sir, which won the first place," said Wan, "has been carefully studied by everyone in our province."

"Careful study," responded Kao, "is the golden key to success. In my three essays for the district examination, not a single phrase was written at random: each was culled from the classics. That is how I succeeded in passing. Without careful study, even a sage cannot pass. Mr. Ma has been expounding essays all these years; but what he teaches simply cannot pass muster. If he understood the meaning of 'careful study,' he would be a high official!"

"Your words are a guide to the young, sir," answered Wan. "But I still consider my friend Ma Chun-shang a fine scholar. I saw his edition of *The Spring and Autumn Annals* in a friend's house in Yangchow, and I thought he had made a very good job of it."

"How can you say such a thing!" protested Kao. "There is a Mr. Chuang here, who was summoned by the court for a special appointment and who works at home on a commentary of *The Book of Change.*[1] Not long ago, a friend of mine met him at a feast and heard him say: 'Mr. Ma knows how to advance but not to withdraw, like the dragon in *The Book of Change.*' Of course, Ma Chun-shang can't be compared to a dragon; but how ridiculous, also, to use a living licentiate to illustrate a point in the sage's works!"

_____

[1] An ancient book on divination, edited by Confucius.

"Mr. Chuang was simply joking, sir," observed Wu. "If you say living men can't be used as illustrations, why did King Wen and the Duke of Chou refer to Wei Tzu and Chi Tzu? And why did Confucius later refer to Yen Tze? These men were all contemporaries."

"Your comment displays your erudition," said Kao. "My field is *The Book of Songs* not *The Book of Change*; hence there are points on which I am not too clear."

"Your mention of *The Book of Songs* reminds me of another ridiculous thing," continued Wu. "Those who take the examinations nowadays cling blindly to Chu Hsi's interpretations, growing more confused the more they try to explain them. Four or five years ago, when Tu Shao-ching compiled a commentary on *The Book of Songs* and made use of certain Han commentators, his friends were quite amazed. There is obviously no true scholarship today!"

"That is only partly true," put in Chih Heng-shan. "As I see it, scholars should stick to scholarship without trying to become officials, and officials should stick to officialdom without trying to be scholars too. A man who wants to be both will succeed in neither!"

Just then the steward came in.

"Please take your seats at table, gentlemen," he said.

Kao ushered Wan to the highest place and sat Censor Shih in the second, Chih in the third, Wu in the fourth, and his relative Chin in the fifth, taking the place of host himself. The feast was served at three tables in the western hall, and the food was excellent though there was no opera to watch. During the meal they spoke of state affairs.

"Since Dr. Yu left," said Chih to Wu, "there have been fewer gatherings than before."

Soon another feast was laid and candles were lit. After the meal Wan stood up to go, but Chin laid hold of him.

"My kinsman's sworn brother is my kinsman too!" he cried. "Besides, we are colleagues, and after the next appointment we shall no doubt be working together. I must insist that you come to my house tomorrow. I'll go home now to write invitations."

He turned to look at the others.

"Tomorrow we'll have not one guest more and not one less," he said. "Just the same six as today."

Chih and Wu said nothing.

"Very well," said Censor Shih. "I had meant to invite Mr. Wan myself: now I shall have to wait till the day after."

"I only arrived here yesterday," said Wan, "and didn't expect to be Mr. Kao's guest today. Before I have called at your honourable houses, how can I presume on you all like this?"

"Never mind that!" said Kao. "My kinsman belongs to your yamen: you must make an exception for him. Be sure to go in good time tomorrow."

Wan muttered a vague assent. Then they took their leave and went their different ways. Chin, upon reaching home, wrote five invitation cards and sent a servant to deliver them. He also sent out to requisition a company of players for the following morning. In addition, he ordered his staff to warn the tea attendants and cooks that this feast must be outstanding.

When Wan got up the next day, he thought: "If I call first on Mr. Chin, he'll probably keep me. Then I shan't be able to call on the rest and they'll take offence, saying I go only to the houses which feast me. I'll call on the others first and Mr. Chin last."

He wrote four cards and went first to Censor Shih. The censor received him but did not press him to stay, knowing he was going on to feast with Chin. Next he called on Chih Heng-shan.

"He had to leave town last night," Chih's servant told him. "He went to Chujung to see to the college repairs."

Wan went on to see Wu Shu.

"Our master didn't come home last night," said Wu's servant. "He'll return your call when he comes back."

By the time for the morning meal Wan reached Chin's house. In front of the gate was a dark wall, the length of a bowshot, with an alcove in the centre. There was a large archway too, with ornamentation in relief. As his chair stopped at the gate, he saw pasted on the whitewashed screen a red paper inscribed in vermilion: "The Secretary of the Imperial Patent Office." On either side stood a smart row of stewards, and behind them were hat-stands bearing official announcements.

When Wan's card was sent in, Chin came out to greet him and the middle door was opened. Wan alighted from his chair and took Chin's hand to enter the hall. They bowed and sat down; then tea was served.

"I am honoured to be your colleague," said Wan. "I shall seek your advice on all matters in future. I sent in my card today as a sign of respect. I shall call again later to thank you for your hospitality."

"My kinsman has told me how brilliant you are," replied Chin. "When I become an official, I shall always rely on you."

"Has your relative arrived yet?"

"He sent to say he would certainly come. He should be here any time now."

At that point Kao and Shih arrived, alighted from their chairs and walked in. They sat down and drank tea.

"Shouldn't Chih and Wu be here by now?" Kao asked his kinsman.

"I have sent a man to fetch them," answered Chin.

"Mr. Wu may be coming," said Wan, "but not Mr. Chih."

"How do you know?" asked Kao.

"I went to call on them both," replied Wan. "At Mr. Wu's house they told me he didn't go home last night. And Mr. Chih has gone to Chujung to see to the repairs of the college; so I know he won't be coming."

"They're a strange pair," commented Censor Shih. "Nine times out of ten they ignore our invitations. Licentiates can't be as busy as all that! And why should a mere licentiate put on airs?"

"Well, since you and my kinsman are here, sir," said Chin, "I don't care whether they come or not."

"I suppose they are very good scholars," said Wan.

"Scholars!" scoffed Kao. "If they had any scholarship they wouldn't still be licentiates! Because Dr. Yu of the Imperial College showed them favour we condescended to take them up. But recently we've been seeing less of them."

616

Suddenly, they were all surprised to hear a man in the room on the left shout: "Wonderful!"

Chin told his steward to go to the back of the study and see who was shouting.

"It's the second master's friend, the fourth Mr. Feng," reported the steward.

"So Mr. Feng is back there," said Chin. "Why didn't you ask him in?"

The steward went through the study to invite him.

In came a tall man in his forties, with prominent eyes, straight eyebrows, and a long black beard which swept his chest. He was wearing an athlete's cap, a tight-sleeved black silk gown, boots with pointed toes, and a silken girdle. He also carried a dagger. Walking in, he bowed to the company.

"I didn't realize back there that all you gentlemen were here," he said. "Please excuse me."

Chin made him be seated. Then pointing to Feng he said to Wan:

"Mr. Feng is one of our most gallant men. He has great skill in boxing, and knows *The Manual of Physical Fitness* by heart. When he flexes his muscles he doesn't feel it even if a stone weighing thousands of catties falls on him. My younger brother has been keeping him here as an instructor, in order to learn his art."

"I can see from Mr. Feng's features," said Wan, "that he is a remarkable man. He looks no weakling either."

"What made you shout 'Wonderful' just now?" asked Chin.

"It wasn't I but your brother," answered Feng. "He was saying that a man is either born strong or he isn't. So I told him to take a deep breath, then made a man hit him with a club, and he didn't feel anything. He was so pleased he shouted 'Wonderful!'"

"If your brother is at home," said Wan to Chin, "why don't you invite him in?"

Chin told the steward to do so. But his brother had ridden out through the back gate to watch the soldiers practise archery in their camp. The guests were now asked inside to sit down to a meal, after which the servants opened a door at the left and invited them through. They found two chambers, smaller than the main hall but most tastefully furnished. There they sat down as they pleased and twelve varieties of fruit-tea were served while a twelve-year-old boy added incense to the censer.

"This place has style," thought Wan. "When I get home, I'll fix things up like this. I can't put up such a splendid show, though, because I can't get officials to come to my house and I haven't all these people to wait on me."

A small-role actor in bright clothes came in with a list of plays. He walked forward and knelt on one knee.

"Please choose a few scenes, sir," he said.

Wan tried ineffectively to persuade Mr. Kao and Censor Shih to choose first, then selected "An Invitation to a Feast" and "The Farewell." Shih chose "Brothers Meet on Mount Wu Tai," and Kao "The Pursuit of Han Hsin." The actor wrote these titles on his tablet, then went back to where the other actors were preparing. Mr. Chin called for another round of green tea.

"Please take seats outside, gentlemen," said the steward.

They followed Wan out from the main to the second hall, where a stage had been neatly erected, with five arm-chairs before it covered in scarlet and gold. When they had taken their places the head of the company led in the actors, dressed for their parts, to pay their respects. Musicians took their stand in front of the stage and softly sounded their clappers. The actor in Hung Niang's role came swaying in. The head of the company entered again, and knelt down on one knee.

"You may take seats," he announced.

The musicians sat down.

Hung Niang had just begun singing, when gongs were heard at the gate and guards in red and black caps marched shouting into the hall.

The guests were puzzled.

"This is a new way of performing this scene!" they thought.

Then a steward came rushing over, speechless with horror. And in came an official in gauze cap, jade-coloured gown, and black shoes with white soles. He was followed by

two dozen constables. The two foremost strode up to Wan and arrested him, then fastened an iron chain round his neck and proceeded to lead him away. The officer also left without a word. The scholars gazed at each other in consternation.

But to know what happened next, you must read the following chapter.

CHAPTER 50

A bogus official is put to shame. A champion procures official rank for a friend

As Wan was watching the opera in Chin's house, the magistrate burst in with constables and carried him off in chains. Censor Shih, Kao the Hanlin and Secretary Chin gazed at each other in horror and did not know what to do. The opera came to a stop. Censor Shih was the first to break the silence.

"No doubt, sir," he said to Kao, "you can guess at the reason for your friend's arrest?"

"I haven't the slightest idea. But I do think Magistrate Fang was ridiculous to put on an act like that."

"You've made me lose face very badly by having one of my guests arrested," said Chin.

"You are wrong there, kinsman," protested Kao. "At home on leave, how could I know he was in trouble! In any case, he was the one arrested, not I. So what are you afraid of?"

At this point the steward came in.

"Sir," he said, "the players want to know if you would like them to go on or to leave?"

"My guest is in trouble, not I. Let them go on!"

As they sat down once more to watch the opera, they noticed the fourth Mr. Feng sitting watching them from a distance with a sarcastic smile.

"Fourth Brother Feng," said Chin, "do you know anything about this?"

"How could I?"

"In that case, why are you smiling?"

"I am smiling at you gentlemen. Your friend has already been hauled off: worrying won't help matters. In my humble opinion, you should send an intelligent man to the county yamen to find out what has happened. In the first place, you'll learn what's become of Mr. Wan; in the second, you'll learn whether you are involved or not."

"He's quite right!" agreed the censor hastily.

"Quite right! Quite right!" responded Chin at once.

He immediately sent a steward to the yamen to find out what had happened.

The four of them sat down again, and the players came on once more to perform "An Invitation to a Feast" and "Farewell."

"His choice of scenes was unlucky," remarked Censor Shih to Kao. "No sooner had he invited someone to a feast than he had to say farewell. In fact, the invitation fell through and he had just the farewell!"

Next, "Brothers Meet on Mount Wu Tai" was performed. The players were about to give "The Pursuit of Han Hsin," when the steward came back and walked up to his master.

"Even in the yamen they don't know," he reported. "I saw the clerk in charge of the files, and asked him to make a copy of the circular."

He handed it to Chin, and the others came round to read it. Scrawled on a thin piece of paper were these words:

Prefect Chi of Taichow on a case involving an important coastal area. We have received from Provincial Governor Tsou of Chekiang an indictment against Wan Li (alias Wan Ching-yun), one of the ringleaders in the case of Brigade General Miao Erh-hsiu of Taichow. Wan has been struck off the list of licentiates in this prefecture. Forty-nine years old, of medium height with a sallow complexion and a sparse beard, he has fled from our prefecture. Since the provincial governor has issued an order

for his arrest, we have sent out constables to apprehend
him, and all the counties are to be notified. When he has
been arrested, kindly send him here without delay to stand
trial. This matter is urgent!

An additional sentence read: Let all county officials take
notice of this.

A runner had brought this circular to the county yamen.
The magistrate happened to be from Chekiang himself, and
when he saw that this criminal was wanted by the governor
of his own province he led the constables to arrest him. But
even the magistrate did not know the details of the charge.

"Not only was the arrest a muddled affair," said Kao,
"the language of the circular is muddled too. Wan says he
is a secretary, yet here he is described as a licentiate struck
off the list. Even if that were true, how could he be involved
with this brigade general?"

"You were laughing at us not long ago," Chin told Feng.
"Do you understand what has happened now?"

"What can stewards discover?" retorted Feng. "Let me
find out for you."

He stood up to go.

"Do you mean it?" demanded Chin.

"Why should I lie?"

And with these words he left.

The fourth Mr. Feng went to the yamen gate, and found
two police sergeants there. These sergeants were willing to
do whatever he wanted. If he said east it was east, if west
it was west. When Feng asked to see the runners from
Chekiang, they took him straight to Three Officials Hall to
find them.

"Are you from the Taichow yamen?" Feng asked.

"We are."

"What trouble is this Mr. Wan in exactly?"

"We don't know. Our prefect issued a circular saying
he is a dangerous criminal, so summonses have been sent to
the different provinces. But if you have any orders, sir, we
shall do what we can for you."

"Where is he now?"

"Magistrate Fang has just finished questioning him, but Wan can't explain the charge. He's now in the outer gaol. Tomorrow when we're given the official report, we shall probably have to start back. Do you want to see him, sir?"

"If he's in the outer gaol I know how to reach him. After you're given the official report tomorrow, be sure to wait for me here before you leave."

The runners agreed to do so.

Feng went with the sergeants to the gaol to see Wan.

"A great injustice has been done me," said Wan. "Please give my regards to Mr. Kao and Mr. Chin when you go back. I don't know if we shall ever meet again."

Feng questioned him closely, but Wan could not explain clearly what had happened.

"I shall have to go to Chekiang," thought Feng, "if I want to get to the bottom of this case."

He did not say this, however, to Wan, but promised to return the next day. Then he hurried back to Chin's house. The players had left, and so had Censor Shih, but Kao was still waiting for news.

"What actually happened?" he asked the moment Feng came in.

"It is certainly very strange," replied Feng. "Not only don't they know in the yamen, but the runners from Chekiang don't know either. Even Wan himself doesn't know. This business is so confused, I shall have to go with him to Chekiang to clear it up."

"There's no need for that," protested Chin. "We're not responsible for his troubles."

"I've decided to leave with him tomorrow," said Feng. "If the charge is a serious one, I'll help him in court. I owe this to him as a friend."

Since Kao was afraid of being involved, he encouraged Feng to go. And that evening he took ten silver taels to his house.

"This is for your journey, Fourth Brother," he explained.

Feng accepted the silver.

The next day, as soon as he got up he went to Three Officials Hall to see the runners.

623

"You're early, sir!" they said.

He went round the corner with them to the yamen and called at the file clerk's office to see Mr. Hsiao, to ask him to hurry up with his report of this case. When the documents were ready, four runners went to ask the magistrate to assign them duties. The magistrate put his seal on the documents, then told the runners on duty to fetch Wan to the hall. The runners from Taichow waited outside the gate. Wan was still dressed in a gauze cap and official robes of the seventh rank.

"The circular said a licentiate struck off the list," thought the magistrate suddenly. "Why is he dressed like this?"

He checked the name and description again, but there was no mistake.

"Are you a licentiate or an official?" he asked.

"I used to be a licentiate of the Taichow prefectural college," answered Wan. "This year in the capital, because of my good calligraphy, I was promoted to the post of secretary in the Imperial Patent Office. I have never been struck off the list."

"No doubt your letter of appointment never reached Taichow," said the magistrate. "And because of this charge the provincial governor struck your name off the list. We have no means of knowing. But you are a Chekiang man and so am I: I don't want to make things hard for you. Go back and clear yourself."

He thought to himself: "When he goes back, the local authorities can call him a licentiate struck off the list and punish him as an ordinary citizen. But as a fellow provincial I must do what I can for him."

With his vermilion brush he endorsed the circular as follows:

The age and appearance of the felon Wan Li tally with the description given. But he is wearing a gauze cap and official dress of the seventh rank, and claims that this year in Peking he was appointed a secretary of the Imperial Patent Office. I am sending him as he is. The runners are not to extort any money from him, nor must they let him escape.

Having written this, he sent for the runner Chao Sheng and called the Taichow runners in as well.

"This man is not a bandit," he told them. "Two of you, with one more man from our district, will be quite enough to escort him. You must take great care on the road."

The three runners took the official report and escorted Wan out. They found Feng waiting for them.

"Are you the escort?" he asked the local runner. "Have you checked your man?"

"He's checked," said the Taichow runners. "This is the escort."

When a man in a gauze cap and official robes left the yamen in chains, two hundred people crowded round to stare. The runners could not get past.

"Where do you live, Mr. Chao?" asked Feng.

"Just round the corner," said Chao.

"Let's go to your house first."

When they had reached Chao's house and sat down in the hall, Feng asked Chao to unfasten the chains on Wan's neck. Then he took off his outer gown and told Wan to change his official robes for civilian dress. He also told the runners from Taichow to go to Mr. Wan's lodgings to fetch his steward. The runners came back and reported:

"None of the stewards are there. They must have run away. His baggage is there, but the monk wouldn't let us take it."

When Feng heard this he took off his own hat for Wan to put on. He had only a skull cap and jacket now himself.

"These rooms are small; let's go to my house," he suggested.

Wan and the runners followed Feng to Hung Wu Street. They went into the inner hall, where Wan kowtowed.

"This is no time for ceremony," said Feng as he helped him up. "Sit down, sir."

Then he turned to the runners.

"You are all men of sense. I don't have to waste words on you. I want you all to stay here. Mr. Wan is a friend of mine, and I mean to go with him to see him through this lawsuit. I shan't give you any trouble."

"What do you say?" Chao asked the other runners.

"Of course we shall do whatever Mr. Feng says. But we hope you won't be long, sir."

"Certainly not," said Feng.

He showed the three runners into an empty room opposite the hall.

"Stay here for a couple of days," he said. "You can move your baggage here."

Leaving Wan in Feng's hands, the runners went off quite confidently to fetch their baggage. Then Feng took Wan into the left-hand study, and offered him a seat.

"Now, Mr. Wan," he said, "you must tell me the truth about this trouble you're in. However serious it is, I shall try to help you. But if you prevaricate, I can't do anything."

"You are behaving like a true gallant, sir," responded Wan. "I won't deceive you. I shan't lose my case in Taichow, but here in Chiangning County."

"What do you mean by that? Magistrate Fang of our county has treated you very well."

"The truth is, sir, I am a licentiate, not a secretary of the Patent Office. Because I couldn't make a living at home I started drifting from place to place. If I'd said I was a licentiate, I should have had to go hungry; but when I said I was in the Patent Office, the merchants and local gentry were willing to help me. Little did I think the magistrate today would record my official robes and rank on that despatch. I don't mind facing a serious charge when I get back to Taichow, but the charge of passing myself off as an official is more than I can face."

"Mr. Wan," said Feng after thinking hard, "if you were in fact an official, would you win your case?"

"I met Brigade General Miao only once, and I've never taken bribes or broken the law—I can't be involved very deeply. So long as they don't know of this imposture, I ought to be all right."

"Wait here," said Feng. "I have a plan."

Having ensconced Wan in the study and the runners in the empty room opposite the hall, Feng ordered his servants to prepare a feast while he called on Chin.

When Chin heard that Feng has come, he hurried out without stopping to put on his outer gown.

"What's happened now, Fourth Brother Feng?" he asked.

"You may well ask! Here you are sitting at home while disaster descends upon you! Haven't you heard?"

"Heard what? Heard what?" Chin was thrown into a panic.

"Nothing much—just a charge that will take you half a lifetime to disprove!"

Chin's face turned the colour of earth. He was much too frightened to speak.

"What is his rank really?" asked Feng.

"He says he's a secretary of the Imperial Patent Office."

"He may become one in hell—he isn't one here."

"Do you mean to say he's bogus?"

"Of course he is. A man who is charged with a serious crime has been arrested in your house as an impostor. The Governor of Chekiang doesn't need any special indictment against you, sir. He has merely to mention the matter and, if you'll pardon me for saying so, you'll find yourself like a rat in scalding water!"

Chin stared at Feng in horror.

"Fourth Brother Feng, you're an able man!" he cried. "Tell me—what can I do?"

"There's no good way out, I'm afraid. But if you can stop him losing his case, you'll be all right."

"How can we stop him losing?"

"If he's a bogus official he'll lose; if he's a true one he'll win."

"But we know he's bogus—how can we make him true?"

"Is your rank bogus too?"

"I was properly recommended."

"If you can be recommended, why can't he?"

"Even if he is, it won't be in time."

"Why not? With money you can become an official. You have Censor Shih right here to help arrange it."

"In that case, tell Wan to go ahead at once."

"If he could afford to do this, he wouldn't be posing."

"Then what's to be done?"

"My view is this: if you're not afraid of being involved, then let him go through with it. But if you want to play safe, then get him this post. He can pay you back later, after he's won his case and is an official. It doesn't matter if you take a little discount."

When Chin heard this he sighed.

"I owe all this to my good kinsman!" he said. "Well, there's nothing else to be done, Fourth Brother. I'll provide the silver; you make the arrangements."

"You want me to pluck the moon from the lake—it simply can't be done. Mr. Kao must make the arrangements."

"Why Kao?"

"Censor Shih is a good friend of his. Mr. Kao can ask him to send in a request to the cabinet at once. We need to have such a request on record."

"Fourth Brother Feng, you're a man of experience!"

Chin immediately wrote a card asking Mr. Kao to come over to discuss some urgent business. Soon the Hanlin arrived. Chin received him and told him all that Feng had said.

"I'll see to it," said Kao at once.

"This is very urgent," put in Feng, who was with them. "Mr. Chin, you must give Mr. Kao the wherewithal to take with him."

Chin went hastily to his bedroom, and presently had his stewards carry out twelve packets of silver each worth a hundred taels, which he gave to Kao.

"We must count half on friendship, half on money," he said. "I've provided this for the expenses in the Inner Chancery. Please ask Censor Shih to arrange this business, kinsman."

Embarrassed as he was, Kao had to agree. He took the money, called on Censor Shih, and persuaded him to send a man that same day to Peking.

628

Feng went home and hurried straight to the study. He found Wan sitting there looking dazed.

"Congratulations!" said Feng. "Now your rank is real."

He told him all that had happened.

Wan threw himself on the ground and kowtowed to Feng a good two dozen times. Feng had the greatest difficulty in pulling him to his feet.

"Tomorrow," said Feng, "you must put on your official robes again and go to those two scholars' houses to thank them."

"I certainly should. But it's going to be very awkward."

The runners came in to ask Feng when they could leave.

"We can't go tomorrow. Let it be the day after."

The next day Feng reminded Wan to go and thank Kao and Chin. The two scholars accepted Wan's card, but declared themselves not at home. When Wan came back, Feng sent him to the Temple of Imperial Favour for his baggage. The following day Feng packed his own baggage too, and set out with the three runners to escort Wan to Taichow Prefecture for his trial.

To know what happened next, you must read the chapter which follows.

CHAPTER 51

A young woman tricks a man into losing his money.
A hero undergoes torture willingly

When the fourth Mr. Feng had arranged for Wan to become an authentic secretary of the Patent Office, he packed up his baggage and set out with the three runners to escort Wan to Taichow for his trial. Since it was the beginning of the fourth month and the weather was warm, all five of them were wearing unlined clothes. Leaving Nanking by the West Gate, they searched for a long time for a boat to Chekiang; but they could not find a single boat to Hangchow, and had to board one bound for Soochow instead. At Soochow Feng paid the fare, and they changed for a junk to Hangchow which was half as large again as the Nanking boat.

"We don't need such a large junk," said Feng. "We'll simply take two cabins."

He paid one tael and eight cents at the dock to reserve the middle and back cabins. Then the five of them went aboard, and after a whole day's wait the boatmen found a buyer of raw silk to take the front cabin. He was a handsome young fellow in his twenties, with only one load of baggage, but that very heavy. That evening, the boatmen cast off, and punted over a mile to a little village.

"Make fast the hawser and lower the second anchor," ordered the helmsman. "See to the passengers while I go home and have a look round."

"So you're going to ask for a fair wind," chuckled the Taichow runners.

The helmsman grinned and left.

Wan and Feng went ashore to stretch their legs, and watched the evening mist scatter as the moon cast its bright reflection in the water. After strolling for a time they went back to the boat to turn in. They heard the creak of oars as a sampan rowed upstream to moor beside their junk. The boatmen were sleeping with their quilts wrapped round them, while the runners had lit a lamp and were playing cards. Only Wan, Feng and the young silk buyer were in the cabins; and they opened the windows to enjoy the moon. The sampan drew alongside, punted by a thin man in his forties who was standing in the bow. A young woman of eighteen or nineteen was steering from the stern; but when she saw the three men on the junk watching the moon she hid herself in the back cabin. Presently Feng and Wan went to sleep, leaving only the silk buyer up.

Before sunrise the next day the helmsman returned with a bundle on his back, and immediately they cast off. They travelled about ten miles before breakfast. At noon Feng was sitting idly in the cabin talking to Wan.

"I don't suppose you'll come to serious harm, sir, in this lawsuit," he said. "Still, a charge brought by the governor is always troublesome. I suggest that when you're questioned, no matter what you're accused of, you say it was done by a guest of yours named Feng Ming-chi. I know what to do when I'm sent for."

Just then the silk buyer came in from the front cabin. His eyes were red with weeping.

"What's the matter?" asked Feng and the rest.

The young man did not answer.

Suddenly it dawned on Feng, who pointed at him.

"I know!" he cried. "You're young and green, so you fell into a trap."

Tears poured down the shamefaced buyer's cheeks. Feng questioned him closely and learned that the night before, when everyone else was sleeping, he had leaned out of the cabin to watch the girl in the sampan. When she saw the two others had left, she came out of the cabin and smiled at him. The two vessels were lying alongside, and although on different boats they were very close, so the young man petted her till she smiled and climbed into his cabin, and they had a night of love. Once the buyer was asleep, the woman stole four packages of silver worth two hundred taels from his baggage. When the junk cast off at dawn, the young man was still half-asleep. He had only just realized that his bag had been opened and he had been robbed. Now, like a dumb man dreaming of his mother, he could not express his despair!

Feng thought for a moment, then asked the boatmen:

"Would you know that sampan again?"

"We'd know it, but that's no proof in a court of law. We can't bring a charge against them. What's to be done?"

"As long as you know it, that's all right," said Feng. "Since they robbed us yesterday they must have taken the opposite direction. Unfurl the sail and fit up your oars to row back. When you see the boat, we'll moor some distance off. If we recover the money, you'll be rewarded."

The boatmen rowed back. Not till dusk did they reach the village where they had stopped the night before. But the sampan had disappeared.

"Row on," said Feng.

They rowed for nearly another mile, then sighted the sampan moored beneath an old willow. There seemed to be no one aboard. Feng told the boatmen to anchor a little closer, under another old willow, then asked them to lie down and not make a sound while he himself went ashore. He walked up to the sampan, and it was indeed the same. The woman was talking with the thin man in the cabin. Feng strolled up and down for a while, and by the time he went back to the junk the sampan had moored beside it and the thin man had vanished. The moon was brighter than on the previous night. It lit up the girl, who was combing her hair, and showed she was dressed in a white cotton jacket and black silk skirt. She was all alone in her cabin enjoying the moon.

"There's no one about," called Feng softly. "Aren't you afraid, little girl, all alone on that boat?"

"What business is it of yours? I'm used to being alone on board. What's there to be afraid of?"

She threw him a sidelong glance.

Feng jumped aboard and took her in his arms. Though she made a show of resisting, she kept quiet. He picked her up and set her on his right knee. She did not budge, but cuddled up to his chest.

"There's no one on your boat. Won't you keep me company for one night?" asked Feng. "Our meeting was predestined."

"We boat people are a respectable lot," said the girl. "But there's nobody here tonight, and there's nothing I can do now you've come along. Stay here though. I don't want to go to your junk."

"I've money in my baggage. I don't like to leave it."

He picked her gently up, and carried her over. All those on the junk seemed to be fast asleep; but one lamp was lit in the middle cabin and there was a single quilt there. As soon as Feng set her down, the girl took off her clothes and snuggled inside the quilt. To her surprise Feng did not undress, but she heard the sound of oars. When she tried to raise her head, he held her down with one knee so that she could not budge. By listening closely, though, she could tell the boat was moving!

"Why has the boat cast off?" she asked frantically.

"Let them do what they like with the boat, while we have a good time!"

"Let me go!" She grew more desperate.

"Little fool! You trick men out of their money, I trick them out of their wives! Since you're a cheat yourself, why get so upset?"

Then the girl knew she was trapped.

"Let me go!" she begged. "I'll return you whatever I took."

"I can only let you go when the silver is brought back. But I promise not to make trouble."

By the time he let her up, even her trousers had disappeared. And when Wan and the buyer came in from the other cabin, they could not help laughing to see her in such a state. Feng found out where she lived and her husband's name, then asked the boatmen to wait in some quiet place. As soon as it was light he told the buyer to wrap up every stitch of the young woman's clothing and walk several miles back to find her husband. This rascal, having discovered his boat gone and his wife missing, was standing anxiously beneath the willow. The buyer recognized and accosted him.

"You've lost the campaign and your wife into the bargain!" The young man clapped his shoulder. "Even so, you should count yourself lucky!"

He opened the bundle and took out the girl's clothes: trousers, underwear and shoes. Then the husband knelt down in desperation, and kowtowed as fast as a knife chops onions.

"I'm not going to arrest you," said the buyer. "Hurry up and return me the four packages of silver you stole from me yesterday. Then I'll give you back your wife."

Covered with confusion, the husband boarded his boat, and from under the lower cabin deck at the bow took out a sack.

"The silver hasn't been touched," he said. "Be generous, sir, and give me back my wife!"

The buyer slung the silver over his back. The husband walked back beside him with the girl's clothes, but dared not board the junk till he heard his wife calling. He found her wrapped in a quilt in the middle cabin, stepped forward and gave her the clothes. When she had dressed she kowtowed twice, then left the boat with the cuckold looking thoroughly ashamed. The buyer gave Feng one packet of silver containing fifty taels to thank him, and after a moment's thought Feng accepted it. He divided it into three, and gave it to the runners.

"Yours is a hard job," he said. "Here is something for your pains."

They thanked him.

Soon they arrived at Hangchow and changed boats for Taichow. The five of them approached the town together.

"Word of this may have leaked out, Mr. Feng," said the runners. "If the prefect learns what we've done, how can we answer for it?"

"Leave that to me," said Feng.

634

He hired four chairs outside the town, let down the curtains, and made the runners and Wan go by chair while he followed on foot to Wan's house. Inside the gate were two wings built next to the road, and in the inner courtyard were two rooms partitioned into three. As they entered they heard crying inside the house, but soon this stopped and a meal was served.

"Don't go just yet," said Feng when they had eaten. "Wait till the lamps are lit, then ask the clerk in charge of this case to come here. I know what to say to him."

The runners agreed. As soon as the lamps were lit, they went secretly to the Taichow yamen to find the clerk Chao Chin. Chao was amazed to learn that the fourth Mr. Feng of Nanking was with them.

"Feng is a champion of justice," he said. "How did Mr. Wan meet him? Well, Mr. Wan is in luck!"

He went with them to Wan's house, and as soon as he and Feng met they seemed like old friends.

"I ask one thing only of you, Mr. Chao," said Feng. "Make things as easy for us as you can before the prefect calls for a confession."

The clerk agreed to this.

The next day Wan took a small sedan-chair to the Tutelary God's Temple in front of the yamen. He was still wearing official dress of the seventh rank, gauze cap, and boots; but inside his collar was a chain. The Taichow runners handed in his warrant, and Prefect Chi took his seat in court at once. The escort from Nanking presented the official reply for the prefect to endorse, and Wan was brought into court. The prefect gave a start when he saw Wan's gauze cap and round collar. And he gave another start when he read that Wan was a secretary of the Patent Office. He raised his eyes to Wan, who, sure enough, had not knelt down but was standing.

"When did you receive this appointment?" asked the prefect.

"In the first month this year."

"Why have I had no notice of it?"

"It has to go from the cabinet to the ministry, and from the ministry to the provincial governor. All that takes time. Still, it should be here soon."

"Well, you'll soon lose this secretaryship."

"I went up to Peking last year, and this year came back to Nanking. I have done nothing wrong all this time. May I ask why Your Honour sent runners to arrest me in a different province? I assume there must be some reason."

"Because Brigade General Miao neglected the defence of the coast, he was arrested by the governor. In his office they found a poem you had written for him, with a dedication couched in most flattering terms. You were bribed by him to write, and we know the amount of the bribe. Do you still pretend to be innocent?"

"This is a libel!" protested Wan. "When at home I never set eyes on Brigade General Miao. How could I send him a poem?"

"I have seen the poem myself. It is quite a length. It is signed with your literary name and sealed with your seal. His Excellency the governor is inspecting the coastal regions, and is putting up in our prefecture until this case is settled. How dare you deny your guilt?"

"Although I belong to the college, I have never been able to write poems. I have never used a seal with my literary name. I have a guest staying with me, though, who last year cut several seals of different sizes for me. I left them in the library, and never put them away. He must have written this poem and used my name. I beg Your Honour to make further investigations."

"What is this man's name? Where is he now?"

"His name is Feng Ming-chi. He is staying in my house."

The prefect picked up a bamboo slip, and ordered the same runners to fetch Feng at once for questioning. Soon the runners came back with Feng. The prefect resumed his seat in court, and the runners came up to announce:

"Feng Ming-chi is here, Your Honour."

The prefect called him forward.

"Are you Feng Ming-chi? How long have you been a friend of Brigade General Miao?"

636

"I have never met him, Your Honour."

"Wan Li wrote a poem for him. Today, when questioned, Wan said you had written this poem and cut the seal with his name on it as well. Why did you act in such a lawless manner?"

"I have never written a poem in my life. And even if I had, that's not a crime."

"How dare you answer back, you scoundrel!"

The prefect ordered Feng to be tortured. The runners above and below the dais raised a shout, brought in the ankle-screws, and tossed them down at the entrance to the court. Two of them then threw Feng to the ground and fitted the ankle-screws on him.

"Put some strength into it!" said the prefect.

The runner holding the ropes gave a great tug. Crack! the ankle-screws broke into six pieces.

"Is this scoundrel using magic?" demanded the prefect.

He ordered them to bring a new pair of screws, which were sealed with vermilion writing. He examined these and added his official seal, then the runners started again. But before the ropes could be pulled another crack was heard, and the ankle-screws broke once more. Three pairs of screws were brought; but all that remained of them was eighteen fragments scattered all over the floor. And all Feng did was smile: he would not confess.

Prefect Chi was alarmed. He left the court, sending the prisoners to gaol while he went by chair to the official hostel to report this to the military governor. When the governor heard what had happened, because he knew Feng's fame as a champion of the wronged, he suspected that some injustice had been done. By this time, moreover, Brigade General Miao had died in gaol, and the announcement of Wan's appointment to the Patent Office had arrived. Wan's offence was not a great one in any case. So the governor ordered the prefect to pass a lenient sentence and close the case. Then Wan and Feng were released, and the governor went back to Hangchow. Feng had dealt successfully with this dangerous charge!

When the case was dismissed and Wan had seen off the runners, he went home with Feng and poured out his gratitude

"You are father and mother to me!" he declared. "How shall I ever repay you?"

"We are not old friends, my dear sir," said Feng with a laugh. "And I was under no obligation to you. It was merely a whim of mine to help you like this. If you really insist on thanking me, I shall think it rather bad taste. I must go to Hangchow now to look for a friend, and I mean to set out tomorrow."

In vain did Wan beg him to stay: Feng insisted on going. The next day he took his leave of Wan, without taking so much as a cup of water in thanks, and set out alone for Hangchow.

But to know who Feng went to look for, you will have to read the next chapter.

CHAPTER 52

**A young man is wounded in an athletic contest.
A hero tears down a house to collect a debt**

The fourth Mr. Feng said goodbye to Secretary Wan and travelled alone to Hangchow, where he had a friend named Chen Cheng-kung to whom he had lent several dozen taels of silver.

"I may as well look him up," he thought, "and collect the debt for my journey home."

Chen lived outside Chientang Gate, and Feng set out to find him. He had not gone far when he saw a group of men gathered round two riders who were practising their horsemanship under the willows on Su Dyke. One of the riders recognized Feng from a distance.

"Fourth Brother Feng!" he shouted. "Where have you come from?"

As Feng drew nearer, this rider dismounted and seized his hand.

"So it's the second Mr. Chin!" exclaimed Feng. "When did you arrive? And what are you doing here?"

"Fancy your being away so long!" declared Chin. "What had Wan's troubles to do with you? Aren't you a fool, when your own slate is clean, to interfere in other people's business? Well, I'm very glad that you're back. Eighth Brother Hu here and I have been thinking of you."

"What is this gentleman's name?"

"This is Mr. Hu, the eighth son of Minister Hu of Hangchow. He's very good company, and one of my closest friends."

When Hu learned who this was, he and Feng exchanged compliments.

"Since Fourth Brother Feng has come, let's stop riding and go to my rooms for a drink," suggested Chin.

"I've another friend to look up," objected Feng.

"Look for your friend tomorrow," said Hu. "This chance is too good to miss. Let's go now to Chin's rooms."

They would not take no for an answer, but laid hold of Feng and ordered the groom to bring another horse for him. Upon reaching Wu Tzu-hsu's Temple, they dismounted and went in.

Chin lived on the ground floor of a house at the back. Feng went in, bowed and sat down. Chin ordered a meal at once, saying they would drink with their rice.

"Fourth Brother Feng's return is a great occasion," said Chin to Hu. "Tomorrow you'll see a fine athletic display. Another day we shall call on you to pay our respects. We'll be troubling you all the time."

"You must certainly come," said Hu.

Feng pointed at a scroll he saw on the wall.

"I used to know this Hung Kan-hsien," he remarked. "There was a time when he studied the military arts. But later, I don't know why, he started dabbling in the occult and persuading people to practise alchemy. Is he still alive, I wonder?"

"That was quite a joke," said Hu. "My third brother was nearly swindled by him. That year Hung had made friends with Ma Chun-shang of Chuchow, and they talked my brother into making the philosopher's stone. The silver was all ready done up in packages when luckily for my brother Hung suddenly fell ill, and a few days later he died. My brother would have lost all his money otherwise."

"Is your brother's name Hu Chen?"

"It is. He and I are totally unlike. He makes friends with a pack of nondescript fellows who write verses and call themselves scholars. He hasn't drunk a single catty of good wine or eaten a single catty of good meat; yet he lets himself be cheated of hundreds and thousands of taels without so much as blinking. I've always liked to keep a stable, but he used to find fault with my horses, claiming they messed up his yard. Not long ago, when I'd had enough of this, I made over the old house to him and moved out. I've made a clean break with him."

"Eighth Brother's new place is very clean," said Chin. "When we call on him, Fourth Brother, you'll see for yourself."

The wine was brought in and they started toasting each other.

"Fourth Brother," said Chin when they were slightly tipsy, "who is the friend you said you were looking for?"

"A local man called Chen Cheng-kung. He owes me a little silver, and I thought of collecting the debt."

"Used he to live in Bamboo Road?" asked Hu. "Has he moved to near Chientang Gate?"

"That's the man."

"He's not at home just now. He's gone with Whiskers Mao to Nanking to sell silk. Whiskers was one of my brother's protégés. You needn't go to look for him, Fourth Brother. I'll send a servant with a message for you, asking him to call on you when he comes back."

When the meal was finished the party broke up. Hu said goodbye and went home, but Chin kept Feng as his guest. The next day he took Feng to call on Hu, who later returned the call. Then Hu sent a servant to say: "My master invites both you gentlemen to come early tomorrow for a simple meal. He says he won't send invitation cards to close friends."

The next day after breakfast Chin called for two horses. Accompanied by a servant, he and Feng rode to Hu's house. Their host welcomed them and they sat down in the hall.

"Why don't we sit in the library?" asked Chin.

"Wait till we've had some tea," said Hu.

After tea he took them to the back by a path which was covered with horse dung. In the library they found some other guests—the horsemen and swordsmen with whom Hu spent most of his time. These sportsmen had come today to see what Feng could do. Everyone bowed, then sat down.

"These friends are all kindred spirits," said Hu. "When they heard that you would be here today, Fourth Brother, they came to learn from you."

"You flatter me," said Feng.

After another cup of tea they went outside to stroll. The two-storeyed building with three rooms in which Hu lived was not very large. There were covered walks all round it, cluttered up with saddles and quivers of arrows leaning against the wall. Having passed through a moon gate they came to a big courtyard and stable.

"Second Brother Chin," said Hu, "the other day I bought a new horse—quite a likely nag—I'd like to know how much you think it's worth."

He ordered a groom to lead the roan horse over, and the guests crowded round to look. The horse was a spirited one. Because they were not on their guard, it lashed out with one hind leg and kicked one young guest in the thigh. He crumpled up on the ground, doubled up with pain. Hu flew into a rage. Striding forward, with a well-aimed kick he broke the horse's leg. The others gasped.

"Some kick that!" Chin exclaimed. "All this time that I haven't seen you, you must have been improving it."

They sent the young guest home. Then a feast was spread and they sat down to eat. The host and his seven guests played the finger game. With big bowls and big dishes, they all made a hearty meal.

"Now, Fourth Brother," said Chin when they rose from the table, "you must show us what you can do."

The others chimed in to second this request.

"I shall only disgrace myself," said Feng. "What would you like me to do?"

He pointed to a raised flower-bed in the yard.

"Let's have a few of those square bricks carried over."

Chin ordered a servant to carry eight bricks to the side of the steps. They watched as Feng rolled up his right sleeve. The eight bricks were piled up neatly, over four feet high, on the steps. Then Feng clapped his hand on the top brick, and all eight were smashed into fragments right to the bottom of the pile. The other men applauded.

"Fourth Brother is a past master in this," observed Chin. "That boxing manual of his says: 'His clenched fist can shatter a tiger's head, and with the side of his palm he can fell an ox.' But this is not his most remarkable skill. Here, Eighth Brother Hu! You must have powerful muscles in the leg with which you kicked that horse just now. If you dare kick Feng in the groin, you'll deserve your reputation."

"No, no! You can't do that!" The others laughed.

"If you care to try, Mr. Hu," said Feng, "you're welcome. If I'm hurt I won't blame you but Mr. Chin."

"If Mr. Feng is willing," said the others, "he must be fairly confident."

They urged Hu to go ahead.

"This Feng is no titan or giant," thought Hu. "Why should I be afraid?"

"Very well, Fourth Brother," he said. "I'll make so bold as to kick you."

Feng raised the front of his gown. Then Hu's right foot flew up, and with all his might he kicked Feng in the groin. But—most extraordinary—it did not feel like flesh that Hu was kicking, but like a piece of iron. His toes were nearly broken, and he almost fainted with pain. For some time he could not move that leg at all.

"Forgive me," said Feng walking up to him.

All the spectators were amazed and diverted. After a little more horseplay they thanked their host and left. Hu limped to the door to see them off, but on his return could not pull off his boot however hard he tried. His foot was swollen and painful for a week.

Feng stayed with Chin and boxed or rode each day, so he was never bored. One day he was practising boxing when in walked a thin, short fellow of about twenty, who asked for the fourth Mr. Feng of Nanking. Feng saw it was Chen Cheng-kung's nephew, Chen the Shrimp. He asked him why he had come.

"The other day Mr. Hu sent to say you had arrived," said the Shrimp. "My uncle has gone to Nanking to sell silk, and I'm going there now to accompany him back. I can take him a message for you."

"I wanted to meet him, that's all. He borrowed fifty taels from me, and I'd like it returned as soon as convenient. I shall be staying here for some time; so I'll wait for him to come back. Please give your uncle my best regards. I shan't be writing now."

The Shrimp assented, went home and packed, then took a boat to Nanking. He went to Fu's silk shop in front of Chiangning County yamen to find his uncle. Chen Cheng-kung was eating at one table with Whiskers Mao. He bade his nephew join them and asked for news of home. The Shrimp gave him the fourth Mr. Feng's message, then unpacked his luggage upstairs.

This Whiskers Mao, who had a thread shop in Hangchow, had started with two thousand taels capital, then ingratiated himself with the third Mr. Hu and made another two thousand out of him. With this he moved to Chiahsing and opened a small pawnshop. He was miserly to an inordinate degree, prizing one copper as highly as his life. Recently he had joined forces with Chen to sell silk. And since Chen was another man who prized one copper as highly as his life, the two of them hit it off well together.

Now the buyers for Nanking's silk guild fared better than buyers elsewhere.

"The guild head gives us meat at every meal," said Whiskers Mao to Chen. "This is not his meat but ours—he'll be making us pay for it. We'd better just eat his vegetables and buy our own meat in future. Won't that work out much cheaper?"

"You're quite right," agreed Chen Cheng-kung.

When meal-time came he told the Shrimp to buy fourteen coppers' worth of sausage at the cooked meat stall for the three of them. Very little of this was the Shrimp himself able to eat; but he had to suffer in silence.

One day Whiskers said to Chen: "I heard from a friend yesterday that Secretary Chin in Rouge Lane wants to go to Peking to be given a post; but he can't raise the money all at once. He wants to borrow a thousand taels at a seventy per cent discount. He's a very safe customer, and is bound to pay you back within three months. You've over two hundred taels, brother, left from that sum for buying silk. Why not weigh out two hundred and ten taels to lend him? In three months you'll get three hundred back. You'll make more out of this than out of selling silk. If you don't believe me, I'll write you a guarantee. I know his middlemen. Nothing can go wrong."

Chen took his advice, and three months later Whiskers returned his capital with interest. The silver was of the finest, the weight was fair, and Chen was simply delighted.

Another time Whiskers said: "I met a friend yesterday, a man who sells ginseng. He told me that the ninth Mr. Hsu in the palace has a cousin, the fourth Mr. Chen, who bought over a catty of ginseng from him. Now this merchant wants to go back to Soochow, and Mr. Chen can't lay hands on so much silver, so he's willing to borrow at a fifty per cent discount to repay him. If you lend him a hundred taels, he'll repay you two hundred at the end of two months. This deal is completely safe too."

Chen produced another hundred taels for Whiskers to lend. At the end of two months he received a good two hundred taels—there was thirty cents over, in fact. Chen was in raptures.

The Shrimp was so shabbily treated by Whiskers Mao that he had no wine or meat, and he felt as bitter as the sourest vinegar. One day he said to Chen:

"Uncle, you're here to sell silk. When you've extra money, you should give it to the guild head to buy silk. If you buy the best silk and pawn it, you can make a pretty profit. With that profit you can buy more silk and get more from the pawnshop. The interest asked by the pawnshop is very small. In that way, buying and pawning, with a thousand taels capital you can make two thousand taels. Wouldn't that be better? Why do you always listen to Whiskers Mao, and act as a moneylender? Lending money is always a risky business. And if you keep hanging on here, when shall we go home?"

"Never mind," said Chen. "In a few more days we'll pack up and go back."

One day Whiskers Mao received a letter from home. When he read it he smacked his lips, and sat there lost in thought.

"What's the news from your home?" asked Chen. "Why are you thinking so hard?"

"It's nothing," said Whiskers Mao. "I don't like to mention it."

Chen asked him again and again.

"Here's a letter from my son," said Whiskers. "The Tan family pawnshop in the east street has gone bankrupt and is to be mortgaged. They've a roomful of goods worth one thousand six hundred taels. Now they're desperate, they'll let them go for one thousand. I was thinking that if I could get those goods for my pawnshop, it would be a good stroke of business. But it can't be done—I haven't the ready money."

"Why don't you bring someone else in?"

"I thought of that. If I raised a loan from someone willing to take one point eight per cent interest, I could still make a little profit. But if he wanted two per cent or more, I'd miss the goat flesh and just get the smell of the goat! That wouldn't be worth my while."

"Don't be such a fool!" cried Chen. "Why couldn't you ask my help? I've still a little silver I can lend you for this deal. I'm not afraid you'll cheat me!"

"No, no! There's always a risk in business. If I were to lose and find I couldn't repay you, I would never be able to face you again."

Impressed by his sincerity, Chen insisted on lending him the silver.

"Let's work it out together properly," he said. "You can take this silver of mine to buy up his goods. I won't ask you for a high interest: just two per cent a month. The bulk of the profit will be yours, and you can repay me in instalments later. Even if you don't repay me in full, we're such old friends that I shan't hold it against you."

"That is very good of you, brother. But we need a middleman to write a detailed promissory note for you to keep as evidence. Then you needn't worry. We can't just arrange this between the two of us."

"I know you're reliable: I'm not worrying. We not only don't need a middleman, there's no need for a written agreement. We'll rely on mutual trust."

Thereupon, without telling the Shrimp, Chen took all the silver left in his bag as well as the debts he had collected, and made a package of a thousand taels which he gave to Whiskers Mao.

"I'm waiting for the guild head to fix a price for my silk," he said. "I meant to use this silver to buy some more silk in Huchow; but now I'll give it to you, brother, to go back and put through that deal. After a few more days I'll be leaving too."

Whiskers thanked him and took the silver. The next day he boarded a boat and went back to Chiahsing.

Some days later Chen Cheng-kung finished collecting payment for his silk, took his leave of the guild head and boarded a boat with the Shrimp for Hangchow. Since their boat had to pass Chiahsing, they went ashore there to call on Whiskers Mao. His small pawnshop was in the west street. Having been directed there, they found a three-roomed building overlooking the street, and a spirit screen. They went in and looked round the spirit screen, and in the courtyard saw another building in which counters had been built. A few assistants were doing business there.

"Is this the second Mr. Mao's pawnshop?" asked Chen.

"What is your name, sir?" asked an assistant behind the counter.

"I am Chen Cheng-kung. I've come from Nanking to see Mr. Mao."

"Please take a seat inside," said the assistant.

Behind there was a two-storeyed storehouse. They went in and sat down, and an assistant brought them tea.

"Is Mr. Mao at home?" asked Chen as he sipped his tea.

"This shop used to belong to Mr. Mao," was the reply. "But he turned it over to our master, Mr. Wang."

"Did he come here the other day?" Chen was taken aback.

"This isn't his shop; why should he come here?"

"Where is he now?"

"He wanders all over the place. He may have gone to Nanking or even Peking."

The horse's mouth didn't fit the donkey's head—this story didn't tally with Whiskers Mao's! Chen broke into a cold sweat. He went back to the boat with the Shrimp and they travelled straight home.

The next morning someone knocked at the gate, and when they opened it there was the fourth Mr. Feng. They invited him into the hall and greetings were exchanged.

"I should have returned your silver long ago," said Chen. "Unfortunately a few days ago I was cheated; so I've no way of paying you at present."

Feng asked what had happened, and Chen told him the whole story.

"Never mind," said Feng. "Just leave it to me. Tomorrow I'm setting off for Nanking with Mr. Chin. Wait for me in Chiahsing. I promise to get you back your money, not a cent short. How about that?"

"If you will do that, I can never thank you enough, sir!"

"Don't say any more about thanks."

Feng went back to Chin's rooms and told him this.

"So you've found another job," said Chin. "How you enjoy such missions!"

He ordered his servant to pay the rent and pack, then they boarded a boat at Broken Bay.

"I'll come with you to watch the fun," said Chin as they neared Chiahsing.

He went ashore with Feng and they walked to Whiskers Mao's pawnshop. They found Chen Cheng-kung making a scene inside. Taking two steps in one, Feng strode past the spirit screen.

"Is that fellow Mao in?" he shouted. "Is he going to repay the silver he owes Chen or not?"

Before the assistants could come out to answer him, Feng grasped the gate with both hands, bent back a little, then brought half the wall down with a crash. Chin, who was coming in to watch, was nearly knocked on the head. The customers and assistants simply gaped. Feng swung around and strode to the second building, where he stood with his back to one of the counter pillars.

"If you value your lives, then hurry up and clear out!"

648

He put his hands behind him and wrenched, uprooting the pillar and twisting it crooked. Half the ceiling collapsed, while bricks and tiles came hurtling down and a cloud of dust sprang up. Luckily for them, the assistants had taken quickly to their heels; so none of them lost their lives. By this time the passers-by had heard the crash, and a crowd gathered round to watch.

Whiskers Mao saw the game was up, and had to come out. Feng, his face streaked with dust, looked more energetic than ever. He walked into the storehouse, and stood with his back to the main pillar there. The others rushed forward to plead with him; and Whiskers admitted his fault and promised to pay Chen back in full if Mr. Feng would stop pulling down his property.

Feng roared with laughter.

"However large a nest you had," he cried, "in the time it takes for a meal I could raze it to the ground!"

By now Chin and Chen were sitting there.

"You were in the wrong, Brother Mao," said Chin. "You thought, because there was no middleman, Chen couldn't take the case to court or sue you; so you tried to trick him. But you know the saying: 'Never mind how poor the debtor is, it's the courage of the one who duns that matters!' Now you've met your match here in Fourth Brother Feng!"

There was nothing Whiskers Mao could do but return the loan with interest; and so this trouble was settled. When Chen had the silver he saw Chin and Feng to their boat. And when they had washed their faces, he gave Feng a hundred taels in two packets to show his appreciation.

"It was my whim to help you," chuckled Feng. "I don't want any thanks. I'll keep the fifty taels you owed me; but you must take the other fifty back."

Chen thanked him again and again as he pocketed the silver; then he said goodbye, hired a small boat and left.

Laughing and talking all the way, Chin and Feng soon reached Nanking and went to their homes. Two days later Feng went to Rouge Lane to call on Secretary Chin.

"Our master is never at home now," said the gateman. "He's been spending all his time recently with the fourth Mr. Chen from Taiping Prefecture, amusing himself in the Chang house at Welcome Pavilion."

When Feng saw the secretary later, he warned him against such behaviour. Just then, as luck would have it, a letter came from the capital announcing that Chin's appointment would soon be published; so he packed and set out for Peking. Only the fourth Mr. Chen was left at Welcome Pavilion.

But to know what this Welcome Pavilion was like, you must read the chapter which follows.

CHAPTER 53

A guest is entertained one snowy night at the palace.
A girl has an unlucky dream at Welcome Pavilion

The front gate of the courtesans' quarter in Nanking was
at Military Pacification Bridge, the back gate at Long Plank
Bridge at the south end of Treasury Street in East Park.
When the first emperor pacified the country, he made pimps and
prostitutes of all the families of high Yuan Dynasty officials,
and set an officer in charge of them. This man, who had runners to do his bidding, also held court and beat people. Yet
when young men of noble families came, he dared not treat
them as equals but stood to attention like a subordinate.

During the second and third months of spring the girls
here painted and powdered themselves and stood beneath the
willows and flowering trees beside their gates, inviting friends
to join them. There was also an arcade where the girls liked
to gather, for there the choicest food and drinks were served,
and all the cooks tried to outshine each other. The prostitutes
with any claims to beauty would not receive just anyone and
everyone. There were plenty of old toadies too, who came
here to burn the incense, polish the censers, move the flower
pots, dust the tables and chairs, and teach the girls lyre-playing
and chess or calligraphy and painting. Though the prostitutes
had many lovers, they liked to receive a few scholars to raise
the tone of their house.

651

There was a girl called Pin-niang in Welcome Pavilion. Her father-in-law, who had played women's parts in the Advent of Spring Company, had been extremely popular in his time. After his beard grew, however, he had to give up this business. He married a wife in the hope that she might take over his customers; but she was so fat and swarthy that not a ghost crossed their threshold. At last there was nothing for it but to adopt a son and find a child bride for him. By the age of sixteen this girl had become a beauty, and clients kept thronging their door. But although Pin-niang was a prostitute, she preferred officials to all other men. Her uncle Chin Hsiu-yi, the son of Chin Tzu-fu, often brought one or two officials to her house.

One day Chin said to her: "A gentleman is coming tomorrow to see you. He's the cousin of the ninth Mr. Hsu of the duke's palace. His name is Chen, and since he's the fourth of his family everyone calls him the fourth Mr. Chen. We gave a performance yesterday in the palace, and this Mr. Chen told me he'd heard a great deal about you and wanted to come to see you. Once you know him, you'll be able to meet Mr. Hsu. This is a fine thing for you!"

Pin-niang was overjoyed, Chin Hsiu-yi drank his tea and left.

The next day Chin went back to see Mr. Chen. Chen was a native of Taiping Prefecture who lived in Mr. Tung's riverside house at East Water Guardhouse. When Chin reached his door he was shown in by two attendants in brand-new clothes. Chen came out dressed in a square cap, jade-coloured gown of brocade over a fox fur jacket, and black shoes with white soles. He had a fair complexion and was twenty-eight or nine.

"Did you deliver my message yesterday?" he asked. "When had I better go?"

"I went there yesterday, sir. She's expecting you today."

"Very well, I'll go with you now."

He went inside to change into new clothes, then came out again and ordered his attendants to call the chair-bearers. Just then a boy came in with a note. Chen knew the lad worked for the ninth Mr. Hsu. He opened the note and read it.

To my cousin Mu-nan, from Hsu Yung.

It is clearing up now after all that snow, and the red plum in our garden is beginning to blossom. I hope you'll come over, cousin, to chat with me all day beside the brazier. You simply mustn't refuse!

"I have to go to the palace," Chen told Chin. "Come back again tomorrow."

As Chin left, Chen mounted his chair and went to Great Achievement Arch with his two attendants. His chair stopped at the palace gate, and the attendants announced him. After some time he was invited in. He alighted from his chair and walked through the great gate, then down a passage at the side of the Silver Court. The ninth Mr. Hsu was standing at the entrance to Vista Garden.

"Fourth Brother!" he cried, stepping forward to meet him. "Why are you wearing so much?"

Chen saw that Hsu was dressed in a black sable cap, a lined brocade gown embroidered with clouds in golden thread, a silken sash, and vermilion shoes. The two of them took hands. The garden was filled with artificial mountains of different sizes made of the rock from Taihu Lake, and the snow on these boulders had not melted yet. Hsu led Chen down a winding, balustraded path till they came to a pavilion. This pavilion was the highest thing in the garden: from it you could see several hundred plum trees, all of them breaking into crimson blossom.

"The weather turns warm so early now in Nanking," observed Hsu, "the plum blossom comes out before the tenth month is over."

"Your palace is not like elsewhere, cousin. Though this pavilion is open on all sides, one doesn't feel the least bit chilly here. As the Tang poet said: 'No one could guess how cold it is outside.' Without coming here, I couldn't have appreciated the old poet's way of putting it!"

As they were speaking, wine was brought in. The service, of beaten silver, was fitted into a stand; and lighted alcohol in the lowest receptacle was burning merrily, keeping the dishes warm without any fumes.

"They make all these things in new-fangled shapes nowadays," remarked Hsu as they started drinking. "I don't know what the ancients used. I doubt if they had anything as ingenious as this."

"I'm sorry I came to Nanking so late," said Chen. "When Dr. Yu was in the Imperial College, Chih Heng-shan asked him to preside over a sacrifice at Tai Po's Temple, and all their music and ceremony were ancient. The sacrificial vessels were all antiques. If I had been in Nanking I should certainly have gone to that sacrifice, and then I could have seen what the ancient's system was like."

"For the last dozen years I have been in Peking," said Hsu. "I had no idea there were such worthies here in my home. I am very sorry I missed them."

After drinking for some time, Chen Mu-nan became uncomfortably hot and stood up to take off his outer gown. A steward hastily took it, folded it up and put it on a stand.

"They say," remarked Hsu, "that a Mr. Tu of Tienchang held a contest for actors at Carefree Lake. There were still some famous actors then. How is it that nowadays we can't find a single personable actor to play young men or women's parts? Aren't such people born any more?"

"As a matter of fact, Mr. Tu created a dangerous precedent," said Chen. "Women have never been noble or base of themselves. Even a prostitute may become a concubine, while if she has a son who becomes an official, she as his mother will be granted a noble title. But players, however good, have always been looked down on. Since Mr. Tu's contest, though, whenever the local gentry or scholars give a feast they invite a few actors to sit among the officials and talk with them as equals. What a scandal it is! Mr. Tu should be held responsible for this!"

"It's also the fault of those newly rich. In my household no actor would dare take such liberties!"

Presently Chen felt too hot again, and removed another garment.

"I know your palace is not like elsewhere," he said. "But what makes it so very warm?"

"Do you see how the snow has melted for ten feet around this pavilion? This was built in the time of the duke—my father. It is made entirely of pewter, and heated by means of charcoal burnt inside. You won't find another like it anywhere else."

Then Chen Mu-nan understood. The two of them drank till dusk, when sheep-horn lanterns were hung from the hundreds of trees, some high some low. And these, when lit, looked like a thousand bright pearls, shedding light across the branches to make the plum blossom seem more lovely than ever. After the wine they drank tea; then Chen took his leave and went home.

The next day Chen Mu-nan ordered his attendant to take a note to Mr. Hsu in the palace to borrow two hundred taels. With this he bought lengths of brocade and had several costumes made, then set out with his attendants to take these to Pin-niang as his gifts on meeting. As they reached the entrance to Welcome Pavilion, a lap-dog yapped once or twice, and the fat, swarthy procuress came out to meet them. When she saw how distinguished Chen looked, she hastily asked him in. There were two bedrooms in her house and a small dressing-room upstairs which was furnished in excellent taste with vases and incense stands. Pin-niang was playing Chinese draughts. As Chen came in she hastily cleared the board and greeted him.

"I didn't know you had come, sir. Please excuse me," she said.

"This is the fourth Mr. Chen of Taiping," explained the bawd. "You are always reading his poems and saying you would like to meet him. He's just come from the palace."

"Here are two costumes, ma'am," said Chen, "if you'll condescend to accept them."

"The idea! You are doing us too much honour!"

"What is this gentleman's name?"

"This is Mr. Tsou Tai-lai of North Gate Bridge," said Pin-niang. "He's the best draughts player in Nanking, and is teaching me."

"Delighted to meet you," said Chen.

"Is this the fourth Mr. Chen!" inquired Tsou. "I hear you are a cousin of the ninth Mr. Hsu, and a true gentleman. Pin-niang is lucky to have such a visitor."

"You must be a good player too, sir," said Pin-niang. "Won't you have a game with Mr. Tsou? I've been learning from him for two years, but never yet learned his skill."

"Yes, have a game with Mr. Tsou," urged the bawd, "while I get you a meal."

"How can I trouble you to instruct me!" protested Chen.

"Never mind that," said Pin-niang. "Mr. Tsou likes nothing better than playing draughts."

She sorted out the black from the white, and invited the men to be seated.

"Of course we will play as equals," said Mr. Tsou.

"You are a champion, sir," objected Chen. "I am no match for you! You must allow me a few draughtsmen."

Pin-niang, who was sitting beside him, needed no further prompting but set out seven black pieces for Mr. Chen.

"Why so many!" expostulated Tsou. "Do you want me to look a fool!"

"I know you don't play for nothing, sir. Here is a stake," said Chen.

He handed an ingot of silver to Pin-niang, who urged her teacher to start; and Tsou reluctantly forced himself to play. At first Chen did not realize what was happening, but halfway through the game he found himself hemmed in on every side. When he tried to take the offensive, Tsou occupied all the corners; but when Chen stopped attacking, he found his own men were finished. In the end, though he had two pieces more than Tsou, he was worn out with the effort!

"You're a good player, Mr. Chen," said Tsou. "You'll be just the opponent for Pin-niang."

"Mr. Tsou never lets himself be beaten," observed the girl. "But today he's lost a game!"

"Mr. Tsou was obviously being polite," said Chen. "I am no match for him. Give me another two men, sir, and let's have another game."

Because they were playing for a stake and Chen was such a poor player, Tsou allowed him nine pieces without any fear of offending him, and beat him by over thirty. Inwardly fuming with rage, Chen insisted on playing on. Yet though Tsou allowed him as much as thirteen pieces, the young man still could not win.

"You play too well, sir," said Chen. "You must let me have a few more."

"There's nowhere to put any more," objected Tsou.

"Let's play a different way," suggested Pin-niang. "To start with we won't let you move, Mr. Tsou. I'll drop your first piece and let it lie where it falls. This is called Letting Heaven Decide."

"What sort of game is that!" said Tsou with a smile. "I never heard such a thing!"

But since Chen insisted on playing, Tsou had to let Pin-niang drop a white piece on the board and take up the game from there. In this game four or five of Tsou's positions were taken by Chen. And Chen was secretly gloating, when Tsou created a diversion which complicated matters. Chen was going to lose again. Just then, however, the black cat with white feet which Pin-niang was holding gave a sudden leap in the air and upset the board. The two men laughed and stood up. And at the same moment the bawd came in to announce that their meal was ready.

When the wine was brought in, Pin-niang raised high her sapphire-blue sleeve and drank the first cup to Mr. Chen. She raised her cup next to toast Mr. Tsou. He would not let her drain it, however, but took it from her and put it on the table. The bawd came, too, and sat down beside them. When Chen had drained one cup, she drank to him.

"You have tasted good wine and food in the palace, sir," she said. "How can you eat in a humble house like ours?"

"What a chatterbox my mother is!" cried Pin-niang. "Do you suppose Mr. Chen doesn't eat well in his own home? Does he have to go to the palace to have a good meal?"

"The girl is right," replied the bawd with a chuckle. "Since I was wrong, I'll drink a cup as a forfeit!"

She poured herself a big cup of wine and drained it.

"The dishes and wine are the same," rejoined Chen with a smile.

657

"I've lived over fifty years in Nanking," continued the bawd. "And every day I hear talk about the duke's palace; but I've never set foot inside. It must be just like heaven! I hear tell they don't burn candles in the palace."

"What old woman's gossip is this!" scoffed Mr. Tsou. "They don't burn candles because they burn oil lamps!"

"Go on with you, Mr. Tsou!" The bawd snapped her fingers at him. "They don't burn candles because they burn oil lamps, indeed! I tell you, they don't burn candles because all the ladies there have great big pearls hanging from the rafters to light the whole room up! Isn't that so, Mr. Chen?"

"There *are* pearls in the palace," said Chen, "but I don't think they're used as candles. My cousin's wife is a very sweet-tempered lady. When I take Pin-niang to see her, it'll be quite easy for you to dress up as her maid and carry a bundle of clothes. Then you can look at her room."

The bawd clasped her hands together.

"Amida Buddha! If I see such a sight I shan't have lived in vain! I burn incense and pray to Buddha every day, and now a noble star in the person of Mr. Chen has come to my house and promised to take me to heaven. If I have such luck as this, I shall become a human being in my next life instead of an ass or horse!"

"When the first emperor took Mother Wang and Father Chi to the palace," observed Mr. Tsou, "they thought it was some old temple. When you go to the palace, ma'am, you may make the same mistake."

They burst out laughing at that.

After two more cups of wine the bawd was tipsy.

"Those palace ladies must all be as lovely as pictures," she said with a leer. "If you take Pin-niang there, sir, how can she compare with them?"

Pin-niang gave her a cold look.

"It's not being nobly born that makes you pretty," she said. "Do you mean to say all the daughters of officials and rich men are beautiful? I once went to offer incense at the Stone Kuanyin Temple, where a dozen ladies from the palace had just got down from their chairs. They all had plump round faces — there was nothing special about them!"

"My mistake again!" cried the bawd. "The girl is right. I'll drink another big cup as forfeit."

After several more big cups she was reeling right and left. She cleared the table and told the pimp to light Mr. Tsou home, while she showed Mr. Chen his room.

When Chen went downstairs and into Pin-niang's room, he was met by a waft of fragrance. There was a mirror-stand on the rosewood table by the window, a painting by Chen Mei-kung on the wall, and a jade Kuanyin on the side table which was flanked by eight polished *nanmu* chairs. In the middle of the room was a bed inlaid with mother-of-pearl, hung with curtains of scarlet silk. The mattresses and quilts were piled over three feet high. At the head of the bed was a warming pan, and in front of the bed a stand bearing dozens of citrons arranged in the form of a love knot. There was also a copper brazier in which glowing charcoal was burning; and over this, in a copper pot, rain water was being heated.

With her slender hands Pin-niang took the finest tea from a pewter canister, and dropped it in an Yihsing pot. When the tea was infused she offered it to Chen, then sat down beside him and told her slave girl to bring more hot water.

Pin-niang spread her scarlet handkerchief on Chen's knee.

"Mr. Chen!" she said. "Since you're related to the duke's family, when will you become an official?"

"I wouldn't tell this to anyone else but you. My elder cousin has already recommended me in Peking, and in another year I shall be a prefect. If you like, I'll speak to your mistress and spend a few hundred taels to buy you from her, then take you with me to my post."

Pin-niang took his hand and fell into his arms.

"Listen, Lamp God, to what he's just said!" she cried. "If you abandon me, Mr. Chen, I warn you this Kuanyin of mine is very powerful! I have only to turn her face to the wall, and whenever you sleep with another girl your head will start to ache. As soon as you get up your headache will stop! I come from a respectable family, and I'm not just anxious to be an official's wife, but I've fallen in love with you! You mustn't let me down!"

The slave girl pushed open the door to bring in the water. Pin-niang sprang up and opened a drawer from which she took a packet of powdered sandalwood and poured it into the basin. Then she added water, asked Chen to be seated, and washed his feet for him.

At this point in came another slave with a lantern, followed by four or five other prostitutes, all wearing sable ear-muffs and ermine or squirrel furs. They sat down giggling on the *nanmu* seats.

"You've a distinguished visitor today, Pin-niang," they said. "We must have a party in your house tomorrow, and you must pay for us all!"

"Of course I will," said Pin-niang.

After joking for some time the other girls left. Pin-niang undressed herself, and when Chen saw how plump and soft she was, he went into ecstasies. Later Pin-niang fell asleep, to be wakened suddenly by the sputtering of the lamp wick. She turned to look at Chen, who was sleeping soundly, as the third watch sounded outside. Having tucked the quilt around Mr. Chen, she snuggled up to him to sleep again.

She had slept for some time when she heard a gonging outside.

"It is after midnight," she thought. "What are gongs doing at this hour outside our door?"

The gongs came closer and closer, and someone outside announced:

"Your Ladyship, will you please proceed to your post?"

Throwing an embroidered jacket over her shoulders, with her slippers only half on, Pin-niang hurried out. Four maids who were waiting knelt down upon both knees.

"The fourth Mr. Chen has gone to his post as prefect of Hangchow," they said. "He sent us to escort Your Ladyship there to share his wealth and splendour."

Pin-niang hastened back to her room to comb her hair and put on her outer garments. The maids handed her a chaplet and official robes to put on, too. A large sedan-chair was waiting outside the hall, and into this she stepped. Once carried out of the gate, she saw a whole procession of gongs, flags, umbrellas, musicians and attendants.

"Carry her first to the palace," she heard someone say.

They were proceeding in style when a sallow-faced abbess with a shaven head stepped forward and dragged Pin-niang out of the chair.

"This is my disciple!" The abbess cursed the attendants. "Where are you taking her?"

"I am the wife of the prefect of Hangchow," protested Pin-niang. "How dare you pull me about, you bald-headed nun!"

She was going to order the attendants to seize the abbess, when she saw they had disappeared! In her dismay she gave a cry and bumped into Chen Mu-nan, then woke to discover that it had all been a dream.

But to know what happened after, you must read the chapter which follows.

CHAPTER 54

A beautiful invalid has her fortune told in a bawdy house.
A foolish scholar offers poems to a courtesan

When Pin-niang slept with Chen Mu-nan, she dreamed that
he went to Hangchow to take up his prefectship, then woke
with a start to find the windows bright. She washed and
combed her hair, and Chen got up as well. The bawd came in
to wish him good morning, and they had just breakfasted when
Chin Hsiu-yi arrived and insisted jokingly that Chen should invite him to a wedding feast.

"I am going to the palace today," said Chen. "I'll come
back and treat you tomorrow."

Chin went into Pin-niang's room, and found she had not
yet finished combing her hair. Her long, black tresses reached
halfway to the ground.

"Congratulations, Pin-niang!" he cried. "What a distinguished guest you've entertained! Just look at you — not yet
fit to be seen at this hour—I'm afraid you're growing spoilt!"

"What time will you come tomorrow?" he asked Chen. "I'll
play the flute and Pin-niang can sing to you. There's not
another girl in this quarter who sings Li Pai's songs to the
peony as well as she does."

As he was speaking, Pin-niang flicked the dust from Chen's
cap with her handkerchief.

"Be sure now to come this evening!" she implored him.
"Don't keep me waiting too long!"

Having promised to come, Chen walked out and went home with his two attendants. Since he had no money left, he sent an attendant to the palace with another note asking the ninth Mr. Hsu to lend him another two hundred taels so that he would have enough to spend.

After some time his man came back and reported: "Mr. Hsu sends you his greetings, sir. The third master has just arrived from Peking. He has been appointed prefect of Chang-chow in Fukien, and will be setting out for his new post in a day or two. The ninth Mr. Hsu will go to Fukien with him to help him. He says he will call tomorrow to say goodbye, and bring the silver then."

"If the third master is here," said Chen, "I'd better call on him."

He mounted his chair and was carried to the palace, followed by his attendants. When he was announced, a steward came out to say: "The third and ninth masters have gone to a feast with Prince Mu. If you have any message, sir, I can pass it on."

"I have no special business," answered Chen. "I came simply to pay my respects to the third master."

He went back to his lodgings.

The next day the third and ninth Hsu brothers came to his riverside house to say goodbye. They alighted from their chairs at his door, and Chen asked them into his hall and offered them seats.

"We have not met for a long time," said the third Mr. Hsu. "You are looking more handsome than ever. When your mother died I was far away in Peking, and could not come back to mourn for her in person. I am sure you have become a fine scholar during my absence."

"My mother has been dead now for more than three years. Because I admired my ninth cousin's scholarship, I came to Nanking to profit by his instruction morning and evening. If he accompanies you to your post in Fukien, I shall miss you both very much."

"Why not come with us, cousin?" suggested the ninth Mr. Hsu. "You will be good company during the long journey."

663

"I would like to, but there are one or two small matters I must first attend to here. In two or three months I shall join you at your post, cousin."

The ninth Mr. Hsu told a servant to bring in a gift box containing two hundred taels and give it to Mr. Chen.

"I am looking forward to your visit," said the third brother. "I shall want your help in my new post."

"I shall certainly come and try to be of service."

By now they had drunk their tea, and the brothers rose to go. Chen escorted them back to the palace in his chair. He saw them all the way to their boat, then said goodbye and went home.

Chin Hsiu-yi was waiting there to take him to Welcome Pavilion. They walked through the gate and into Pin-niang's bedroom, but found her looking very pale and unwell.

"Not seeing Mr. Chen for several days has brought that old heartburn of yours back again," said Chin.

"She's been spoilt since she was a child," declared the bawd. "And she has this heart disease which comes on whenever she's vexed. Because you didn't come back for two days, sir, she said she must have annoyed you, and fell ill."

With tears in her eyes Pin-niang gazed at Chen in silence.

"Where does it hurt?" he asked. "What do you need to get better? When you had this trouble before, how did you cure it?"

"When she had this trouble before," replied the bawd, "she wouldn't swallow so much as a drop of water. The doctor came and prescribed some medicine for her, but she wouldn't take it because it tasted so bitter, and I had to boil ginseng and give it her little by little. That's how I pulled her through."

"I've silver here," said Chen. "I'll leave you fifty taels to buy ginseng for her. I shall buy some of the best ginseng, too, and bring it here myself."

Pin-niang leant against her embroidered pillow to listen, sitting up inside her quilt. She was wearing a scarlet bodice.

"Whenever I have this illness," she said with a sigh, "I don't know why, but I always feel so frightened! The doctors say if you eat nothing but ginseng it brings out all the hot

664

humours; so I used to mix it with gentian, and brew them together. That was the only way I could get any sleep at night. If not for that, I'd lie wide-awake till dawn!"

"That's easy," said Chen. "I'll bring you some gentian to-morrow too."

"They set no store by ginseng and gentian in the palace," said Chin. "Pin-niang won't be able to finish all Mr. Chen brings her!"

"I don't know why it is," went on Pin-niang, "but my heart feels all of a flutter. If I close my eyes I have such ridiculous dreams that even in the daytime I'm rather afraid!"

"You're too delicate," said Chin. "You can't stand any hardship or disappointment."

"Do you think you've offended some spirit?" inquired the bawd. "I can ask the abbess in to exorcize you."

That same moment a clapper was heard outside. The bawd went out and saw it was Pen Huei, abbess of Long Life Nunnery, who had come to collect the monthly offerings.

"Aiya!" cried the bawd. "So it's Abbess Pen! I've not seen you for two months. Have you been very busy at the nunnery?"

"The truth is, ma'am, I've had bad luck this year. One of my nuns, who was twenty, died the month before last. I couldn't even hold the mass to Kuanyin. How is your daughter-in-law?"

"She's well one day, ill the next," replied the bawd. "I'm glad to say the fourth Mr. Chen of Taiping is looking after her. He's a cousin of the ninth Mr. Hsu in the palace, and often comes to my house. But Pin-niang was born unlucky — her old trouble has started again. Go in and have a look at her."

The abbess followed her into Pin-niang's room.

"This is the fourth Mr. Chen of the palace," said the bawd.

Abbess Pen stepped forward and greeted him.

"This is Abbess Pen, Mr. Chen," said Chin Hsiu-yi. "She's well versed in religious matters."

After greeting Chen, the abbess went up to the bed to look at Pin-niang.

"We were speaking just now of driving out the evil spirit," said Chin. "Why not ask Abbess Pen to perform the ceremony for us?"

"I can't exorcize evil spirits," replied the abbess. "I'll just have a look at her colour."

She sat down on the edge of the bed.

Pin-niang knew this woman, of course. But when she looked up and saw the sallow face and shaved head, she seemed to see the abbess of her dream. It gave her a great shock.

"Excuse me!" she cried, and covered her head with the quilt.

"Your daughter-in-law is upset," said Abbess Pen. "I'd better leave you now."

She said goodbye to them all and left the room. When the bawd had paid her monthly offerings, the abbess went off with her clapper in her left hand and her wallet in her right.

Chen went home too, and gave his attendants some silver to buy ginseng and gentian. His landlady, Mrs. Tung, came out leaning on a stick.

"There's nothing wrong with you, Mr. Chen," she said. "Why are you buying all that ginseng and gentian? I hear you've been amusing yourself outside. I'm your landlady and an old woman, so I haven't liked to say anything. But don't you know the proverb? A whole boatload of gold and silver won't be enough for a courtesan. Women like that don't have any heart, I tell you. When your money is spent, they'll turn their backs on you. I'm over seventy now, and I read the Buddhist scriptures. As Kuanyin is my witness, how can I watch and say nothing when I see you cheated like this?"

"You are right, ma'am, I know," said Chen. "They asked me in the palace to buy this ginseng and gentian." To escape a further scolding, he went on: "I doubt if my men know what to buy. I must see to it myself."

He went to the medicine shop to find his attendants, and bought half a catty each of ginseng and gentian, then carried this like a treasure to Welcome Pavilion. As soon as he entered the gate he heard a three-stringed fiddle being played inside. The bawd had hired a blind man to tell Pin-niang's fortune. Having given the medicine to the bawd, the young man sat down to listen.

"The girl is seventeen this year and is going to have great good fortune," said the blind man. "A noble star is coming into her life. Not all her influences are so auspicious, though. An evil spirit is making trouble for her, and causing her anxiety. Still, this will not prove too serious. Excuse me for speaking frankly, but the girl has offended another wicked spirit. She must dedicate herself to one of the bodhisattvas if she wants to counteract this evil influence. Then she will marry an official, wear a chaplet and splendid robes and be a great lady."

He raised his fiddle and sang again, then stood up to take his leave. The bawd made him stay for some tea, and brought out a dish of walnut wafers and another of black dates, which she put on a little table. She made him sit down again. A slave girl poured out the tea and offered him some.

"Is your business good in Nanking?" asked Chen.

"Don't speak of it!" said the blind man. "It's nothing like in the old days. In the past we blind folk were the only ones to tell fortunes; but nowadays people who can see have taken to fortune-telling too and squeezed us out of business. Twenty years ago there was a Chen Ho-fu in Nanking — not a local man. As soon as he arrived, he grabbed all the business with official families. He's dead now, but he left a scoundrelly son who married into my neighbour's family and quarrels every day with his father-in-law. They don't give us any peace. When I go home I shall hear them squabbling again."

He stood up, thanked them and left. When he reached a lane in East Garden, sure enough, he heard Chen Ho-fu's son, Chen Ssu-yuan, quarrelling with his wife's father.

"You tell fortunes outside every day," said the father-in-law. "You must make a few dozen cash. But you spend it all gorging yourself on pig's head and flaky cakes, and don't bring a copper home. Do you expect me to feed your wife for you? All right, you may say, she's my daughter. But why don't you pay for the pork *you* eat? Instead, you ask *me* for the money and make such a scene about it. What did I do to deserve such bad luck?"

"If you'd eaten the pig's head yourself, dad, you'd have to pay up."

"You fool! If I ate it myself, of course I'd pay. But *you* ate it!"

"Let's suppose I've already paid you the money, dad, but you've spent it on something else. You have to make it up now."

The old man swore.

"You're the one in debt," he fumed. "How can you accuse me of spending your money?"

"If the pig hadn't had a head, do you think they'd ask me for money?"

Enraged by such foolish talk, the father-in-law picked up a forked stick and belaboured his son-in-law with it. The blind man groped his way over to make peace.

"Sir!" cried the old man, quivering with rage. "He simply isn't human! When I give him a piece of my mind, he answers me back like an idiot. It's enough to make anyone wild!"

"I didn't talk like an idiot, dad," protested Chen Ssu-yuan. "I don't drink, gamble or go whoring, do I? I read a volume of poems every day between my fortune-telling. What's wrong with that?"

"We can leave everything else out of it; but you're wrong to neglect your wife and expect me to look after her. I can't afford it!"

"If you're sorry your daughter's my wife, dad, take her back."

"Curse you! Why should I take my daughter back?"

"To let her marry again."

"A plague on you!" The father-in-law was furious. "Unless you die or become a monk, how can she marry again?"

"I shan't be dying just yet, but I'll become a monk tomorrow."

"Go and become a monk then!" The old man was in a towering rage.

After hearing all the nonsense they were talking, the blind man gave up trying to reason with them and groped his way back to his room.

The next day Chen Ssu-yuan shaved his head, sold his tile-shaped hat and bought a monk's cap. Then he presented himself before his father-in-law and placed his palms together in a monk's greeting.

"The monk has come to say goodbye, dad," he said.

The old man gave a start, and tears ran down his cheeks. He reproached his son-in-law again; but when he found that Chen was already a monk, he told him to write a divorce certificate and took his daughter away.

After this, as a bachelor, Chen Ssu-yuan had plenty of meat. He bought pork each day with the proceeds from his fortune-telling, and when he had eaten his fill he would sit at his table by Literary Virtue Bridge reading poetry. He had not a care in the world.

One day about half a year later, he was reading there when a colleague named Ting Yen-chih strolled over to see him.

"When did you buy that book?" asked Ting.

"Three or four days ago."

"Those poems were written at Oriole-Throat Lake," remarked Ting. "That year the third Mr. Hu invited those famous scholars Chao Hsueh-chai, Ching Lan-chiang, Yang Chih-chung, Kuang Chao-jen and Ma Chun-shang to a party at Oriole-Throat Lake. They distributed rhymes and wrote these poems. I remember Chao Hsueh-chai drew the rhyme *chi*. Look at this first line: 'The lake is like an oriole's throat, and the sun is sinking low!' In a single line the subject is set forth; and each succeeding line is so apt, it couldn't apply to any other party."

"You don't know what you're talking about, you ought to ask me!" scoffed Chen. "The third Mr. Hu was not the host at Oriole-Throat Lake. That party was given by the third and fourth Lou brothers of the minister's family. My father was on a most friendly footing with the Lou gentlemen. He was one of the party at Oriole-Throat Lake, with Mr. Yang Chih-chung, Mr. Chuan Wu-yung, Mr. Niu Pu-yi, Mr. Chu Hsien-fu, Iron-armed Chang and the two Lou brothers. Mr. Yang's son was also there, making nine of them altogether. My father told me this. As if I didn't know and *you* did!"

"Do you mean to say," retorted Ting, "that these poems by Chao Hsueh-chai and Ching Lan-chiang are really by other people? Just think: could *you* write them?"

"What you're saying now makes even less sense," jeered Chen. "Chao Hsueh-chai and the others wrote their poems at the West Lake, not at Oriole-Throat Lake."

"It's written quite clearly, 'The lake is like an oriole's throat.' How can you say it refers to a different party?"

"This is an anthology of poems by many different scholars. Look at Ma Chun-shang, for example. He doesn't write poems usually: then why is there one here by him?"

"You're talking absolute rubbish! Ma Chun-shang and Chu Hsien-fu have written no end of poems; but of course you've never seen them!"

"I've not seen them, but *you* have, I suppose! Apparently you are unaware of the fact that at the Oriole-Throat Lake party no poems were written. You get hold of some crazy idea, and come here to argue with me like a madman!"

"I don't believe it! How could so many famous scholars get together without writing poems? Just wait and see. It may turn out that your father never went to that Oriole-Throat Lake party. If he did, that means he was a true scholar, and I doubt if you can really be his son!"

"You're raving!" shouted Chen furiously. "Who ever heard of a man falsely claiming a father?"

"Chen Ssu-yuan! Go ahead and write poems if you like; but why do you have to pose as Chen Ho-fu's son?"

"Who do you think you are, Ting Yen-chih? You thrust yourself forward, when all you've done is learn to recite a few poems by Chao Hsueh-chai. Yet you hold forth like an authority on scholars!"

Ting leapt in his rage.

"So I shouldn't talk about scholars, eh? Well, you're not a scholar anyway."

The two flared up, seized each other by the collar, and started fighting. Ting punched the monk on his shaved head till it nearly split with pain, and together they dragged each other up the bridge. Chen narrowed his eyes to a baleful slit, intending to pull Ting into the river with him. But Ting shoved him over first, and he rolled to the foot of the bridge where he started howling and cursing.

Just then Chen Mu-nan came by and saw the monk flat on the ground in a shocking state. He hastily helped him up.

"What's the meaning of this?" he asked.

The monk, who knew who Chen was, pointed up the bridge.

"Look at that ignoramus, Ting!" he cried. "He walks up to me and claims the party at Oriole-Throat Lake was given by the third Mr. Hu! When I tell him the real facts, he refuses to believe me. And he says Chen Ho-fu is not my father! How can he say such a thing?"

"Why quarrel over a little thing like that? Ting shouldn't have said that about your father, though. That was wrong of him."

"You don't understand, Mr. Chen," protested Ting. "Of course I know he's Chen Ho-fu's son. But he puts on airs like a scholar — it's too ridiculous."

"You're colleagues," said Chen with a laugh. "Why act like this? If Chen puts on scholarly airs, how could Dr. Yu and Chuang Shao-kuang have behaved? I'll have a bowl of tea with you both while you make it up. You mustn't quarrel any more."

He took them to a small tea-house by the bridge, where they drank some tea.

"I hear your cousins asked you to go to Fukien, Mr. Chen," said the monk. "Why haven't you started yet?"

"That's why I came to see you," said Chen: "I wanted my fortune told. When shall I be able to go?"

"Our fortune-telling is nothing but a trick, sir," said Ting. "Just choose a good day and start. You don't need to have your fortune told."

"Half a year ago, sir," said the monk, "we were never able to see you. The day after I became a monk I wrote a poem on shaving my head and joining holy orders, then took it to your house for your criticism. But Mrs. Tung said you were out again. Where were you all the time? Why are you out today without your stewards?"

671

"Pin-niang of Welcome Pavilion here appreciates my poems, so I often call to see her."

'She must be a cultured prostitute if she admires talent! You see!" Ting turned to the monk. "She's only a woman, yet she reads poetry. How could they do without poems at Oriole-Throat Lake?"

"Chen is right all the same," said Chen Mu-nan. "The third Mr. Lou was one of my father's classmates. He used to be very friendly with Yang Chih-chung and Chuan Wu-yung, but neither of them was famous for his poems."

"I heard that Mr. Chuan Wu-yung got into trouble later," said the monk. "What happened in the end?"

"He was slandered by some licentiates in his college. Later he was cleared of that charge."

After chatting for a time the monk and Ting took their leave.

Chen Mu-nan paid for the tea, then walked to Welcome Pavilion. He found the bawd just inside the gate, threading cassia into balls with a flower-seller.

"Have a seat, Mr. Chen," she said casually.

"I'll go upstairs to see Pin-niang," said he.

"She's not at home today. She's gone to a party at Light Smoke Pavilion."

"I've come to say goodbye to her. I'm leaving soon for Fukien."

"Are you starting at once, Mr. Chen. Will you come back?"

The slave girl brought out a cup of tea and handed it to Chen. But after one sip he put it down—the tea was cold.

"Why don't you brew some fresh tea?" demanded the bawd.

She put down the cassia balls, and went into the gate-house to curse the pimp.

When Chen saw that he was being given the cold shoulder, he marched off. He had not gone far when he knocked into a man.

"Mr. Chen!" cried this fellow. "You ought to keep your word! Why do you make us run after you all the time?"

"Yours is such a large ginseng shop," protested Chen, "why worry about a few dozen taels of silver? You know I'll .a\ you eventually."

"I can't find your two attendants now," said the other. "When I go to your house the old landlady comes to the door. You can't expect me to argue with a woman."

"Don't get so excited," said Chen. "The runaway monk can't run away with the temple. Of course I shall settle my bills. Come to my house tomorrow."

"You must pay us tomorrow morning, and not keep us running around!"

Saying this, the shop-keeper left, and Chen went back to his lodgings.

"I'm in a fix," he thought. "My attendants have gone, and the bawd won't let me in. I've finished my silver and piled up all these debts. I'd better go to Fukien."

Without a word to Mrs. Tung, he was off like a streak of smoke.

Early the next morning the ginseng-seller came to his house. He sat there for a long time, but not even a ghost appeared. Then with a creak the gate opened and another man came in. He was holding a fan inscribed with a poem, and had a scholarly air. The ginseng-seller stood up.

"What is your name, sir?" he asked.

"I am Ting Yen-chih. I have come to ask the fourth Mr. Chen's opinion of a new poem I have written."

"I'm looking for him too," said the ginseng-seller.

They sat there a good deal longer, but still no one came out. Then the ginseng-seller rapped on the spirit screen. Mrs. Tung came out then, leaning on a stick.

"Who do you want?" she asked.

"I've come to collect a debt from the fourth Mr. Chen."

"Mr. Chen? By this time he must be at Kuanyin Gate."

"In that case, did he leave my money with you, ma'am?" asked the shop-keeper in dismay.

"What a question! He's even done me out of my rent! Ever since he lost his head over that witch at Welcome Pavilion, he's swindled everyone and got up to his neck in debt. You expect him to pay you your few taels of silver!"

When the ginseng-seller heard this, he was like a dumb man dreaming of his mother — he couldn't voice his distress. He stamped frantically in anger.

"Don't be so angry," Ting advised him. "It's no use losing your temper. You had better go back to your shop. The fourth Mr. Chen is a scholar; I'm sure he won't really cheat you. When he comes back, he is bound to clear his debts."

After stamping helplessly up and down, the ginseng-seller left. Ting strolled away flaunting his fan.

"So women can read poems too," he thought. "I've never been to the courtesans' quarter. I'll take the few silver pieces I've saved, and go there to have some fun."

His mind made up, he fetched a scroll of poetry from his home, changed into the newest gown he had — which was half worn — and put on a square scholar's cap. Then he went to Welcome Pavilion. When the pimp saw what a simpleton he looked, he asked him what he wanted.

"I've come to discuss a poem with your young lady."

"Please pay the admission fee then."

He took up a yellow balance. Ting fumblingly produced a wallet from his belt, with just over two taels and forty-five cents in loose silver.

"That's fifty-five cents short," said the pimp.

"I'll bring you the rest when I've seen her."

Upstairs he found Pin-niang studying chess moves. He stepped forward and made a deep bow. Wanting to laugh, she offered him a seat and asked him his business.

"I have long heard of your fondness for poetry, madam, and have brought one of my unworthy compositions to ask your opinion of it."

"The rule of our house is not to read poems without first receiving a fee. I'll read your poem, sir, when I've seen your money."

Ting fumbled for a long time in his belt; but all he fished out was twenty coppers which he placed on the rosewood table. Pin-niang gave a peal of laughter.

"You'd better give your money to the pimp at Feng Family Lane in Yicheng!" she said. "Don't dirty my table with it! Take it back at once to buy a few mouthfuls of food!"

Turning red and white by turns in his confusion, Ting hung his head, rolled up the scroll and put it in his gown, then crept downstairs and slunk home.

The pimp had heard her ask this simple customer for a tip; so now he climbed the stairs.

"How many taels did you get from that fool?" he asked. "Give them to me. I want to buy some brocade."

"The poor fool had no silver," said Pin-niang. "He offered me twenty coppers, but of course I wouldn't take it! When I laughed at him, he left."

"You clever hussy! You get a fool as a client, but instead of making a handsome sum out of him, you let him get away! Do you think I believe you? You've been getting a lot of fat tips from your customers, but have I ever seen a cent of them?"

"Are you blaming me for making so much money for you? Why make such a scene over a trifle like this? I shall marry and be a lady. How can you let a fool like that come upstairs? You should be glad I don't scold you; but instead you come here to nag at me!"

The pimp lost his temper and strode forward. With a cuff, he knocked Pin-niang over. The girl rolled on the floor, tearing her hair and sobbing.

"What have I done to be so hardly used! You've plenty of silver!" she screamed. "You can get another girl. Let me go before I die!"

After sobbing and cursing the pimp, she screamed for a knife to cut her own throat or a rope to hang herself. Soon all her hair had come down. The pimp took fright, and called his wife up. She reasoned and pleaded with the girl, but Pin-niang would not listen. She flew into such a temper that they had to give in to her. They let her go to Abbess Pen Huei in Long Life Nunnery, where she shaved her head and became a nun.

But to know what happened next, you must read the chapter which follows.

CHAPTER 55

**In which four new characters
are introduced to link the past with the present,
and the story ends with an epilogue**

By the twenty-third year of the Wan Li period,[1] all the well-known scholars had disappeared from Nanking. Of Dr. Yu's generation, some were old, some had died, some had gone far away, and some had closed their doors and paid no attention to affairs outside. Pleasure haunts and taverns were no longer frequented by men of talent, and honest men no longer occupied themselves with ceremony or letters. As far as scholarship was concerned, all who passed the examinations were considered brilliant and all who failed fools. And as for liberality, the rich indulged in ostentatious gestures while the poor were forced to seem shabby. You might have the genius of Li Pai or Tu Fu and the moral worth of Yen Hui or Tseng Shen,[2] but no one would ask your advice. So at coming of age ceremonies, marriages, funerals or sacrifices in big families and in the halls of the local gentry, nothing was discussed but promotions, transfers and recalls in the official world. And all impecunious scholars did was to try by various tricks to find favour with the examiners. Among the townsfolk, however, some outstanding figures emerged.

---

[1] 1595.

[2] Disciples of Confucius.

One was a calligrapher named Chi Hsia-nien. Having no home and no means of support from his childhood, he had to put up in temples. When the monks beat the clapper in the hall, he would pick up an earthenware bowl and stand there to eat with them, and the monks did not object to him. His calligraphy was superb. He would not study ancient writing, though, but created a style of his own and wrote as his brush dictated. Three days before he was to write he would fast for a day, then grind ink for a day — no one else could do this for him — and even for a couplet of fourteen characters he prepared half a bowl of ink. He would use only brushes other folk had discarded, and would not start writing till he had three or four people to hold his paper. Moreover, if they did not hold it properly, he would swear at them and beat them. He wrote only if he happened to be in the mood. If he was not in the mood, then no matter whether you were prince, duke, general or minister, or what silver you heaped on him, he would not even look at you. He did not care for appearances either, but wore a tattered gown and a pair of straw sandals which barely held together. When he received his fee, he would buy what he needed to eat and give what was left to any poor man he happened to meet, not keeping a cent himself.

One day he walked through a snowstorm to visit a friend, and his sodden sandals trailed slush all over the study floor. Knowing Chi's temper, the host tried to hide his annoyance. He simply said:

"Your shoes are worn out, Mr. Chi. Why don't you buy a new pair?"

"I can't afford to," said Chi.

"If you'll write me a couplet, I'll buy you a pair of shoes."

"Haven't I shoes of my own? I don't want yours!"

Disgusted by his slovenly ways, his host went inside to fetch a pair of slippers.

"Please change into these," he said. "Your feet must be cold."

Chi lost his temper at that, and marched out without saying goodbye.

"Who do you think you are?" he shouted. "Aren't my shoes good enough for your study? I honour you by sitting in your house! What do I care for your shoes!"

He walked straight back to the Heavenly Kingdom Monastery, and angrily ate with the monks. Then he saw a case of the finest, most fragrant ink in the chief monk's room.

"Are you going to write something with this ink?" he asked.

"Censor Shih's grandson sent me this yesterday," replied the monk. "I'm keeping it to give to one of our patrons. I don't intend to use it."

"Let me write a scroll," said Chi.

He would not take no for an answer, but went to his room to fetch a large ink-stone, selected a stick of ink, poured out some water, and sat on the monk's bed to grind the ink. The monk, who knew quite well what he was like, had deliberately provoked him in order to make him write. As Chi was grinding happily away, a servant came up to the monk.

"Mr. Shih from Lower Floating Bridge is here," he announced.

The monk went out to greet the censor's grandson, who had already reached the hall. Shih saw Chi Hsia-nien, but they did not greet each other. Instead, the visitor walked to one side to chat with the monk, while Chi finished grinding his ink and fetched a sheet of paper. He spread this on the table and ordered four acolytes to hold it for him. Then, taking up an old brush and dipping it well in the ink, he stared at the paper for some time, and wrote a line all in one breath. Then the acolyte at the far right-hand corner moved, and Chi jabbed him with his brush so that he shrank to half his height and shouted as if he were being murdered. The monk, running over to see what was happening, found Chi still bellowing with rage. He urged him to calm down, and held the paper himself while Chi finished writing. Censor Shih's grandson came over to look as well, then took his leave of the monk.

The next day a servant from the Shih family came to Heavenly Kingdom Monastery, and happened to meet Chi Hsia-nien.

"Is there a calligrapher here named Chi?" he asked.

"Why do you want to know?"

"My master wants him to come to our house tomorrow to write."

"All right," said Chi. "He isn't here today. I'll tell him to go tomorrow."

The next day he went to Shih's house at Lower Floating Bridge. But when he tried to go in, the gateman stopped him.

"Who are you?" called the gateman. "Trying to sneak in like that!"

"I've come here to write," said Chi.

Just then the servant came out of the gate-house and saw him.

"So it's you!" he said. "Can *you* write?"

He took him to the hall and went in to announce him. As soon as Censor Shih's grandson rounded the screen, Chi turned on him and cursed him.

"Who do you think you are to order me to write for you! I don't want your money, I'm not impressed by your position, and I don't expect any favours from you! How dare you order me to write!"

He shouted and swore till Mr. Shih, quite speechless, hung his head and went back inside. After a few more oaths, Chi returned to the monastery.

Another was a seller of spills named Wang Tai. He came from a family of market-gardeners at the Three Arches, but his father lost so much money that they had to sell all their land. As a child, Wang liked nothing better than Chinese draughts. After his father died and he had nothing to live on, he went every day to Couching Tiger Pass to sell spills. One day there was a fair at Subtle Conception Nunnery near Black Dragon Pool. It was early summer and fresh, newly-opened lotus were floating on the water. In the nunnery were winding paths and pavilions; so passers-by often went in to enjoy themselves. Wang Tai wandered round the grounds till he came to a stone table under a willow with four stone stools at each side, where three or four high officials had gathered to watch two men play draughts.

"Our Mr. Ma," said a man in sapphire blue, "played for a stake of a hundred and ten taels with the salt merchants in Yangchow. He won more than two thousand taels."

"Mr. Ma has no equal in the whole country," declared a young man in a jade-coloured gown. "Mr. Pien's the only one who's a match for him, and even then he has to be given two pieces. It'll be very hard for us, though, to reach Mr. Pien's standard."

Wang Tai squeezed his way forward to have a look. When the servants saw how shabbily he was dressed, they tried to push him back.

"Can a fellow like you enjoy watching draughts?" asked the man in the place of host.

"I've studied the game a little," answered Wang.

He stood there watching for a time, then laughed.

"The fellow is laughing!" said the man called Ma. "Do you think you play better than I do?"

"I think I might."

"Who are *you*," protested the host, "to play with Mr. Ma!"

"As he's so bold why not teach him a lesson," said Pien. "Then he'll know better than to laugh next time he sees gentlemen playing!"

Wang did not decline but made ready his draughtsmen and offered Mr. Ma the first move, to the great amusement of the onlookers. After a few moves, Ma realized that this was no common player. And halfway through the game he stood up.

"I've lost by half a piece!" he said.

The others were quite bewildered.

"Yes, Mr. Ma has a little the worse of it," confirmed Pien.

Amazed, they invited Wang Tai to a feast.

"There is nothing more pleasant than beating a second-rate player," Wang replied. "After beating a second-rate player, I'm so happy I don't need wine!"

He burst into hearty laughter, and walked away without a backward glance.

Another was Kai Kuan who kept a tea-house. Once he had owned a pawnshop, for when he was in his twenties his family

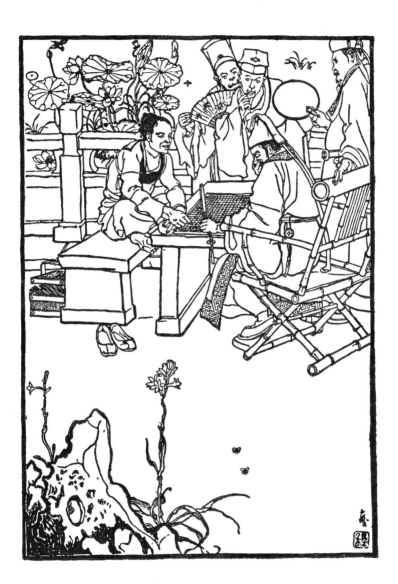

was rich. Besides a pawnshop they had fields and marshlands. All his relatives were wealthy, but he despised their vulgarity, and would sit every day in his library reading or writing poems. He was fond of painting too, and began to paint so well that other poets and artists came to see him. Though their poems and paintings were not as good as his, Kai Kuan prized talent so much that when such visitors called he would feast them, and there would be talk and laughter. And when these friends were short of silver to pay for a wedding or funeral, they had only to ask for a loan and he would give them dozens or hundreds of taels. Once the pawnshop assistants knew this, they said their master must be a fool, and cheated him right and left till his capital melted away. For several years running, too, his fields were flooded, and he had to make good the loss in seeds and grain. Then some shady characters advised him to sell, and the purchasers, claiming that the land was poor, would pay no more than five or six hundred taels for land well worth a thousand. Yet Kai had no choice but to sell. Instead of making good use of the proceeds, however, he kept the silver at home to use as he needed. So it did not last very long. When this was gone, he had nothing but the income from his marshlands with which to pay his debts. But his assistants were a bad lot who set fire to his fuel stacks; and luck was against Kai Kuan, for after several fires all his thousands of bundles of fuel were burnt to ashes. The reeds fused when they burnt, and twisted into odd shapes like the stones from Taihu Lake. The assistants brought some of these stumps to show him, and finding them amusing he kept them in his house.

"These will bring you bad luck," warned his servants. "You mustn't keep them."

He turned a deaf ear, though, and kept the stumps in his study. Now that the marshlands were done for, his assistants deserted him. Within half a year he had nothing left to live on, and sold his big house to move to a smaller one. In another half year his wife died, and to bury her he sold the small house too.

Then, with his son and daughter, the poor man moved to a two-roomed cottage in a quiet lane and started a tea-house there. He made over the inside room to his son and daughter.

In the outer room he put several tables for tea, and under the back eaves set up a stove. On the right he had a counter, with two earthenware vats behind it filled with rain water. He would get up early to light the fire, and when he had fanned it into a blaze would put on a kettle to heat, then sit behind his counter to read or paint. In a vase on the counter he kept a few blooms of whichever flowers were in season, and next to this was a pile of old books. He had sold all his other possessions, but could not bear to part with these precious volumes. When customers came in, he would put down his book to bring them a teapot and cups. There was not much money in this. He made one copper on each pot of tea, and since he sold no more than fifty or sixty a day, he made no more than fifty or sixty coppers, which barely sufficed to keep them in fuel and rice!

He was sitting at his counter one day when an old neighbour dropped in for a chat, and saw that though it was the tenth month Kai was still in a linen gown.

"My friend," he said, "I can see you are very hard up. You helped a great many people in the past, but none of them come here now. All your relatives are quite comfortably off; why don't you go to talk things over with them and borrow enough to set up a proper business, so that you can make a living?"

"Why, uncle," replied Kai Kuan, "don't you know the proverb? Warm feelings may turn to coldness. Men are drawn to prosperity but not to adversity. When I had money I dressed respectably and had smart attendants to wait on me. I didn't disgrace my relatives when I saw them. But if I called on them as I am today, even if they didn't take offence, I should feel out of place myself. As for the people you say I helped in the past, they are all of them too poor to pay me back. They have gone to look for other rich men now; why should they call on me? If I go to look them up, I shall only annoy them for nothing. That would be pointless."

When the neighbour heard how bitterly he spoke, he said: "Your tea-house is very quiet. I doubt if you'll have many customers today. Since the weather's fine, let's take a walk outside the South Gate."

"That would be very pleasant," responded Kai Kuan. "I have no money though."

"I've a little loose silver. Enough for a simple meal."

"Well, this is very good of you."

Kai called his son out to mind the shop, then walked off with the old man through the South Gate. For five silver cents they had a vegetarian meal in a Mohammedan eating-house. When the neighbour had paid the bill and left a tip, they walked on into the Temple of Kindness Repaid. They looked at the hall and south corridor, at Tripitaka's burial place and the great frying pan, then went back to the entrance to buy a packet of sweetmeats, and sat down in a tea-house behind the pagoda to drink a pot of tea.

"The world has changed," said Kai's neighbour. "There are fewer visitors now to the Temple of Kindness Repaid. And they buy less sweetmeats than twenty years ago."

"You must have seen a good deal, uncle, in the seventy years of your life. But things are not what they were. If I'd lived in the time of Dr. Yu and the others, with my slight gift for painting I needn't have worried about each bowl of rice! Who could have thought things would come to such a pass!"

"You've reminded me of something," said his neighbour. "To the left of Rain Flower Mount is Tai Po's Temple, built by a Mr. Chih of Chujung. That was a fine sight the year when he asked Dr. Yu to sacrifice here! I was little more than twenty then, and I squeezed through the crowd to watch, losing my cap in the crush! But today there is nobody to look after the temple, and the buildings are falling down. When we've finished our tea, let's go there to have a look."

They ate a dish of dried beancurd, paid for the tea and left. Having climbed the left side of Rain Flower Mount, they saw the main hall of Tai Po's Temple with the front half of the roof caving in. Five or six children were playing football beside the double gate, one half of which had fallen to the ground. Going in, they came upon three or four old women, who were picking shepherd's purse in the temple courtyard. All the lattice-work in the hall had disappeared, and the five buildings at the back were completely stripped—not even a floor plank was left. After walking around, Kai sighed.

"To think that so famous a place should have fallen into such ruins!" he said. "And no one will repair an ancient sage's temple!"

"In those days," said his neighbour, "Mr. Chih bought many utensils, all of the antique kind, and kept them in large cupboards on the ground floor of this building. Now even those cupboards have gone!"

"It makes you sad to speak of old times," said Kai. "We had better go back."

They slowly retraced their steps.

"Shall we go to the top of Rain Flower Mount?" suggested Kai's neighbour.

They gazed at the green, fresh mountains across the river, and the boats plying to and fro—they could see each sail quite clearly. The red sun was gradually sinking behind the mountains when the two of them paced down the hill and back to the city. For another half year Kai Kuan went on selling tea. In the third month of the following year he accepted a post as tutor at a salary of eight taels.

Another was a man over fifty named Ching Yuan, who kept a tailor's shop in Three Mountains Street. After finishing work each day he would play the lyre and practise calligraphy. He also liked to write poems.

"Since you want to be so refined," said his friends and acquaintances, "why do you stick to your honourable profession? Why not mix with some college scholars?"

"I'm not trying to be refined," replied Ching Yuan. "I just happen to like these things: that's why I take them up from time to time. As for my humble trade, it was handed down to me by my ancestors, and I'm not disgracing my studies by tailoring. Those college scholars don't look at things the way we do. They would never be friends with us. As it is, I make six or seven silver cents a day; and when I've eaten my fill, if I want to strum my lyre or do some writing, there's nobody to stop me. I don't want to be rich or noble, or to make up to any man. Isn't it pleasant to be one's own master like this?"

When his friends heard him talk this way, they began to treat him coldly.

One day when Ching Yuan had finished his meal and was free, he walked to Chingliang Mountain, the quietest spot in the west of Nanking city. He had an old friend there named Yu, who lived at the back of the mountain. Yu did not study or trade, but had brought up five sons, the oldest of whom was now over forty and the youngest over twenty. Old Yu supervised his sons' work on their vegetable farm. They had two or three hundred *mou* of land, and in an empty plot in the middle had planted flowers and trees and piled up artificial mountains. The old man had built a thatched cottage here, and the plane trees he had planted had grown to a great size. When he had seen his sons tend the vegetables, he would go to his cottage and light the fire to brew tea, feasting his eyes on the fresh green as he drank.

When Ching Yuan arrived, Old Yu said: "I haven't seen you, brother, for some time. Have you been very busy?"

"Yes," replied Ching. "Today was the first time I could get away to see you, uncle."

"I've just made a pot of tea. Please have a cup."

He poured out a cup and passed it to Ching, who sat down.

"This tea looks, smells and tastes delicious, uncle," said Ching. "Where do you get such good water?"

"We're better off than you folk in the south city. We can drink from all the wells here in the west."

"The ancients longed for a Peach Blossom Stream where they could escape from the world. I don't think any Peach Blossom Stream is needed. To live quietly and contentedly in a green plot in the city as you do, uncle, is as good as being an immortal!"

"Yes, but there's nothing I can turn my hand to. I wish I could play the lyre as you do, brother. That would help to pass the time. You must be playing better than ever now. When will you let me hear you?"

"That's easy," said Ching. "I'll bring my lyre tomorrow."

After some more conversation he went home.

The next day Ching Yuan carried his lyre over. Old Yu had lit a censer of fine incense, and was waiting for him. After they had greeted each other and chatted a little, Old Yu put Ching's lyre on a stone bench for him. Ching sat on the ground, and Old Yu sat beside him. Ching slowly tuned his strings and began to play. The clear notes woke the echoes all around, and the birds alighted in the boughs to listen. Soon he turned to a tragic air, expressing grief and longing, and as Old Yu heard the most moving passages the tears ran down his cheeks.

After this, the two friends were constantly together. But now Ching took his leave.

> *For love of the Chinhuai River, in the old days I left*
>   *home;*
> *I wandered up and down behind Plum Root Forge,*
> *And strolled about in Apricot Blossom Village;*
> *Like a phoenix that rests on a plane*
> *Or a cricket that chirps in the yard,*
> *I used to compete with the scholars of the day;*
> *But now I have cast off my official robes*
> *As cicadas shed their skin;*
> *I wash my feet in the limpid stream,*
> *And in idle moments fill my cup with wine,*
> *And call in a few new friends to drink with me.*
> *A hundred years are soon gone, so why despair?*
> *Yet immortal fame is not easy to attain!*
> *Writing of men I knew in the Yangtse Valley*
> *Has made me sick at heart.*
> *In days to come,*
> *I shall stay by my medicine stove and Buddhist sutras,*
> *And practise religion alone.*

THE EXAMINATION SYSTEM AND OFFICIAL RANKS REFERRED TO IN THIS NOVEL

Since many references are made in this book to examinations and official posts, some brief explanations of these terms may be useful.

The author represents all the incidents in this novel as taking place in the Ming Dynasty (1368-1644), whereas the examination system and official titles he describes really belong to the Ching Dynasty (1644-1911). In the main, the civil service examinations and the official hierarchy were the same in both dynasties, with some minor differences only.

The imperial examinations were the narrow path by which the sons of landowners entered politics. At one end of this path were the scholars studying the art of writing *paku* essays, at the other end the official posts for different grades of graduates.

The examination system can be divided into three main stages: the prefectural examination 院試 ; the provincial examination 乡試; and the highest examinations comprising the metropolitan examination 会試, the test examination 复試 and the palace examination 殿試, as well as a final test at the imperial court.

The prefectural examination was preceded by two preliminary tests, the first being the county test 县試, presided over by the local magistrate. After passing this, candidates took another test at the prefecture 府試, presided over by the prefect; and those who reached the required standard were called pupils 童生. The prefect then sent the list of students to the prefectural college where the prefectural examination was held, and students who passed this were called licentiates 秀才 The commissioner of studies 学道 who was in charge of this examination held office for three years, during which he had to go to each prefecture under his jurisdiction in turn to hold two examinations.

The purpose of the prefectural examination was to select licentiates from the students and to grade the various licentiates. Those who did well were commended, and those who did badly were punished. The number of licentiates varied in different prefectures according to the number of students, ranging from eight or nine to as many as twenty.

A limited number of licentiates each year were made stipendiaries or salaried licentiates 廩生, so called because they received a stipend from the government.

Special examinations held as an act of imperial favour enabled some licentiates to attain the rank of senior licentiate 貢生 . These men were eligible for official posts after passing a further examination.

Licentiates, in general, did not need to be very learned. Provided a man could write *paku* essays, he had a chance of success. There were, indeed, licentiates who could not even write essays but prevailed on other people to take the examination for them. It was also possible to obtain the licentiate's rank by bribing the examiner.

A licentiate's status was not very high, yet none the less he was higher than the common people. This was because he could approach officials directly. A licentiate need not kneel to a magistrate, and might even treat the latter as his equal. With access to officials and their support, he could oppress ordinary citizens. More important was the fact that after a man became a licentiate his livelihood was assured, for if all else failed he could teach. There were a few exceptions to this, however, and some unfortunate licentiates became so poor that they even had to sell their children.

The provincial examination, which came next, was held every three years in the various provincial capitals as well as in

Peking and Nanking. The scholars eligible for this examination were licentiates, senior licentiates, and those who had failed in the prefectural examination but had by some other means procured the rank of imperial college student 监生. Success in this examination entitled scholars to the title of provincial graduate 举人.

The Imperial College 国子监 at Peking, with a branch in Nanking, was the highest institution of learning during the Ming and Ching Dynasties, and according to regulations only senior licentiates or young nobles could study there; but by the Ching Dynasty a man could enter the college upon payment of a fee. Obviously, this system of hereditary privilege and the purchase of ranks were a short cut to wealth and prestige for rich and powerful families.

The chief examiner 主考 presided over the provincial examination, assisted by vice-examiners. These men were appointed by the emperor after a test. There were also associate examiners who helped to look through the essays, and some of the chief local officials served as invigilators.

The number of graduates varied, according to the size of the provinces, from fifty to more than a hundred. To become a provincial graduate was an important event. It qualified a man to take the metropolitan examination, and, even if he failed in this, he could still become an official.

The metropolitan examination was held by the Ministry of Rites, the test examination by an official appointed by the emperor, and the palace examination by the emperor himself.

Of these three higher examinations, the metropolitan examination was of decisive importance. It took place every three years in Peking, the year after the provincial examination. Provincial graduates from all over the country could sit for this, and the two or three hundred who passed were known as selected scholars 贡士. Only selected scholars took the test examination, in which there were seldom any failures.

The test examination was followed by the palace examination, the scholars who passed this becoming palace graduates 进士 of one of three grades. There were three men in the first grade, the highest being called the Number One Scholar 状元. The second grade comprised sixty to seventy men.

Soon after this, the palace graduates were given official posts. The three in the first grade received appointments before the final examination, the Number One Scholar being made chief compiler of the Han Lin Academy while the other two also were appointed compilers. All palace graduates could become officials, and even if a man declined an official post his social position was still very high.

The official hierarchy, based on the Ming system, consisted of the central administration and the provincial or local administration.

The central administration was made up of two main sections: the chief government offices such as the Inner Chancery 內閣, the Six Ministries 六部, the Censorate 都察院, the Office of Transmission 通政使司, the Han Lin Academy 翰林院, the Imperial College 国子監; and offices to serve the imperial house, such as the Imperial Physicians' Office 太医院.

The highest official in the central administration was the grand secretary 大学士 whose function was like that of a prime minister. Under him were associate secretaries 侍讀学士 and readers 侍讀, who were responsible for checking documents, as well as secretaries of the Imperial Patent Office 中書 who drafted and copied documents. The post of secretary of the Patent Office could be purchased.

The Six Ministries were the Ministry of Civil Office 吏部, of Rites 礼部, of Revenue 戶部, of War 兵部, of Punishments 刑部 and of Works 工部. These were the chief administrative organs.

The Censorate was responsible for checking up on government officials. Its functionaries included the left and right chief censors 左右都御史, the left and right vice-censors, and a number of subordinate censors who might either remain in the capital or be sent out to different provinces.

The head of the Office of Transmission was the chief commissioner of transmission 通政使, who was aided by the left and right commissioners. Their function was to open, record and transmit to the Inner Chancery all memorials received from the provinces.

The Han Lin Academy was an assembly of scholars under a director 掌院学士. Other members of the academy were readers 侍讀学士 and expositors 侍講学士, whose function it was to draft imperial decrees, and editors 修撰 and compilers 編修 who compiled histories.

From the middle of the Ming Dynasty onwards, almost all members of the Inner Chancery were drawn from the academy; thus a man who became an academician might later become the chief minister of the state. After the eighteenth century all the provincial examiners were selected from among Han Lin Academy compilers or vice-ministers promoted from the Han Lin Academy. And all members of the academy had to be palace graduates. Thus we see the close relationship between the examination system and the official hierarchy.

The Imperial College 国子监 was the highest government institute of learning. Its principal was known as the libationer 祭酒, the vice-principal as the tutor 司業. There were also assistant tutors and doctors.

Certain honorary titles such as Grand Guardian 太保 and Junior Guardian 少保 were conferred on the highest ministers of state. Knighthood of the fourth rank 中宪大夫, mentioned in chapter twenty-six, was also an honorary title.

The local administration of the Ching Dynasty dealt with four types of administrative area: provinces 省, circuits 道, prefectures 府 (and sub-prefectures 州), and counties 县.

The military governor 总督 and provincial governor 巡撫 were the highest administrative officers in the local administration. Subordinate to them were the finance commissioner 布政使 and the judicial commissioner 按察使.

During the Ming and early Ching Dynasties, military governors were appointed only to strategic areas. Not till the eighteenth century did this post become fully established, with one military governor for two or three provinces. By this time it was also decreed that each province should have one governor. In certain provinces, like Szechuan and Chihli where there were no provincial governors, their work was done by the military governors.

The finance commissioner was the head of the civil service in each province and treasurer of the provincial exchequer, in charge of the revenue and the census. The judicial commissioner, of equal status, was the provincial judge and supervised the postal service.

The intendant of a circuit 道台 was a functionary with administrative control over two or more prefectures. The head of a prefecture was the prefect 知府, the head of a county the magistrate 知县. There were two kinds of sub-prefecture, some directly under the jurisdiction of the provincial finance commissioner, and others under the jurisdiction of the prefect.

In the villages there were village wardens 保甲.

In the various prefectures, sub-prefectures and counties were tutors 学官 who kept the lists of students, and other officers in charge of Buddhist monks and Taoist priests.

During the Ming and Ching Dynasties, the central government controlled the minority peoples through their chieftains, who were granted various official ranks.

In provinces where salt was produced, there were salt comptrollers 鹽运使 who handled the revenue derived from the provincial gabelle or salt monopoly. Since the salt was transported by private merchants under government control, the big salt merchants often wielded considerable authority.

As for the army, a brigade general 提督 was the chief officer of one or more military posts. Under him were lieutenant colonels 参将, second captains 守备, lieutenants 千总, sergeants 把总 and other officers.

p. 130
p135